THE

NEW MYSTERIES

OF

LONDON.

𝕴llustrated

BY

HABLOT K. BROWNE, ESQ., (PHIZ.)

LONDON:

J. A. BERGER, 13, CATHERINE STREET, STRAND.

CONTENTS.

ILLUSTRATIONS.

THE NEW
MYSTERIES OF LONDON.

THE RESURRECTIONIST. IS TERRIFIED AT THE MOVEMENT OF THE CORPSE.

CHAPTER I.

THE RESURRECTIONISTS.

UPON the night of the tenth of November, 1830, a strange and horrible scene was enacting in an old churchyard in the city of London.

The night was wild and stormy. The streets were deserted; none but the most wretched of homeless outcasts were abroad, and these were only to be found crouching in dark doorways, shivering in their rags and misery.

Very little was to be seen of such of the police force whose ill luck it was to be on duty. Here and there only, at rare intervals, might one's presence have been detected, when the light of a street lamp flickered faintly upon his oilskin cape.

All that was honest and respectable had long since gone to bed. Only the lonely watcher by the sick bedside; only the wretched needlewoman, plying her blinding trade; only the poor and struggling, who have no time for rest; or the depraved and debauched, who turn night into day, were yet awake.

The City slept. The eye of the law was drowsy. It was an hour well chosen for the perpetration of a crime.

Down a winding City lane, where high, dark, and silent warehouses, craning forwards across the roadway, blocked out air and light, a man, muffled in a great coat and comforter, drove a cart. He peeped out from beneath the slouched brim of his battered hat, as he slowly progressed towards his journey's end, and suspiciously eyed every dark hole and corner he passed by, as though in search of spies. Very cautiously proceeding, in this fashion, he came to a halt at last, by a churchyard wall, under the deep shadow of which he stopped his horse. Then, descending to the ground, he peeped about, as he had done before ; and satisfied, as it seemed, that the coast was clear, whistled softly twice.

The signal was not long in calling forth a response. After a few moments pause, a low, soft whistle replied from within the churchyard.

Then the man who had brought the cart whistled again, and then a head appeared above the churchyard wall.

"Is it you, Jaggers ?" asked the man from the wall, in a low tone, scarce above a whisper.

"Yes."

"Is all quiet ?"

"Not a soul to be seen. Have you nearly finished ?"

"We have only just come. We have been delayed by one thing and another. We shan't be long though."

"Shall I drive away and come again ?"

"No, the cart wheels sound like thunder down the lane. You've made noise enough, as it is. Besides, I can't work single-handed. Gouge has been keeping watch. You had better take his place, and he can help me in the grave."

"Very well," replied the other man, in a somewhat discontented tone, "don't be longer than you can help."

"We shan't do that, for our own sakes."

"Blogg !"

The man inside the wall was creeping away, when the other called him back.

"Hush ! What is it ?"

"If I whistle, it will be for you to take care."

"Very well. Don't frighten us if there's no occasion, and don't go to sleep."

It was so wet and windy a night, and withal so bitterly cold, that it was difficult to imagine sleep to be practicable under such disadvantageous circumstances ; but the last speaker was evidently familiar with his associate's weakness. He had not been gone many minutes before the latter began to nod.

Jaggers had first of all solaced himself by a deep draught from a pocket-pistol ; then climbing back into the cart, which he had drawn up as close as possible to the wall-side, thereby avoiding much wind and rain, he wrapped himself round and about with sacking, tugged at his coat collar, shrank down into his coat, and closed his eyes.

He opened them again at the first faint sound in the lane, and listened attentively. Then, satisfied that all was right, closed them again, and rocked softly to and fro. So violent a tilt forwards did he make, however, before long, that he deemed it advisable to get out of the cart, and walk about, to keep himself awake.

All was quiet up the lane : the warehouses on either side were black and silent as ever. Down the other way he could detect a faint rushing, whispering sound, from time to time, which was made by the river washing against the green and slimy stonework of a quay, some twenty yards from where he stood.

It was awfully still. All at once, too, it struck him that it was awfully lonely, and he thought it would be livelier to go round to the churchyard-gate, at a few yards distance, and peep in at his friends at work.

It was a quaint, old-fashioned iron gate, very heavy and rusty, the bars of which were so close together that it was only here and there that a good view of the churchyard could be obtained through it. The watcher, to get

a sight of the workers, stooped down, and placing his face close to the bars, peered eagerly into the deep gloom within. While thus occupied, a faint rustle behind him caused him suddenly to turn round ; and he turned to confront a tall woman in deep mourning, whose face shone deadly white in the light of the lamp overhead.

The apparition was so sudden, its approach so noiseless, that the man was for a moment totally bereft of breath and reason, and stood with glaring eyes and chattering teeth, clinging to the gate for support, and trembling like a leaf.

But the figure before him was not, as he at first imagined, a visitor from the other world. It was that of a lady, in some respects richly dressed, though wearing over her rustling silk a thick black cloak, of coarse material.

She laid a delicate white hand upon his arm ; and his eyes, following the movement, detected the glitter of some jewel upon her wrist. As she touched him, she spoke—

"Are you the sexton ?" she asked, in a low tone, which, though scarce above a whisper, was strangely deep and thrilling. "I think I recollect your face."

"Ye-es," stammered the man, uncertain what reply to make.

"Can you let me into the church-yard ?"

"N-no, not to-night."

"Do you remember me ? You buried my husband to-day. I want to see his grave."

The man started slightly, and tightened his clutch upon the gate. Then, seeming to recollect that his only chance of safety lay in his perfect coolness and self-possession, he overcame his agitation with a desperate struggle, and replied—

"You cannot go into the yard to-night, madam. It is against my orders to allow it."

"But I must. Have you the keys ?"

"I cannot allow you."

"Have you the keys ?"

"You can't go in."

The lady's eyes lighted up, as he thought, with anger, and she appeared with difficulty to suppress an outburst of passion. Mastering her feelings, however, she drew from her pocket a small purse, which, as she opened it, emitted a jingle deliciously melodious to the listener's ears.

"Here," she said, offering him a couple of sovereigns. "Let me go in."

It was a sore struggle for him to resist the impulse to clutch the proffered coin ; but necessity compelled him so to do.

The gate was locked, and he possessed no means of opening it ; and even if he had possessed those means he would have hesitated, when he knew that it was the grave which this lady wished to see that his companions were at that moment rifling of its corpse.

"No," he said, pushing back the money, "I cannot let you in. There, you have got all you can out of me. Please take no for an answer."

"You mean it ?"

"Yes."

The woman, with a sigh, turned away ; then, turning again as quickly, said—

"You have just left the churchyard?"

"Yes."

"All was safe there ?"

"Safe—yes."

"Was his grave safe ?"

"Perfectly safe."

"That is well. If you are sure of that, I have no wish to see it. You will think it strange I should come here ; but I had a dreadful dream, and I thought that the grave had been robbed. Here, take the money, and be sure and watch the churchyard well. How lonely it is," she added, with a shudder. "How dark and lonely. Is it haunted ?"

Without waiting for a reply, she drew her cloak

about her, and moved away as noiselessly as she had come.

He stood for a moment, still holding the gate. When he stepped out into the road to look after her—the darkness had swallowed her up. She must have gone towards the river, for her footsteps were no longer audible.

"I hope she is gone," muttered the man, beneath his breath, when he had stood silently listening for a few moments; "I hope she wont come back till the job is over."

As he was speaking thus to himself, dropping his eyes on the ground, he fancied he saw something glitter at his feet, and, stooping, picked up a bracelet.

"That must be hers," he thought; "pretty stones too! I wonder what it's worth! What a strange affair altogether! I wonder what I can make out of this bracelet."

While, however, he was yet turning the matter over in his mind, a low whistle from within the churchyard recalled him to his post.

When he reached the cart, he found Jaggers and his companion looking over the churchyard wall.

"Well?"

"Are you ready?"

"Quite."

"Look out, then, below."

He climbed into the cart, and prepared to receive a heavy sack, which the two men lowered gently into his arms. Together, they laid it out carefully at the bottom of the vehicle, and by its side, a bag containing tools. Then they climbed in themselves; the horse's head was turned round, and the cart drove away, the three men sitting silently upon the seat in front; while the contents of the sack, to the shape of which its covering clung horribly close, as clings always the updrawn sheet upon a bed of death, lay cold and stiff and motionless, save when the jolting of the vehicle imparted to it a spasmodic motion, ghastly in the extreme.

CHAPTER II.

THE THIEVES' DEN IN GUNN STREET, BOROUGH.

HAD Jaggers, the resurrection man, had the time and opportunity allowed him to follow the mysterious lady upon her night ramble, he would in all probability have been somewhat astonished at the locality which she selected for that purpose.

Leaving the City lane, she threaded a string of alleys, with the topography of which she seemed to be perfectly familiar; then, at length, ascending the stairs at the foot of London Bridge, crossed to the Surrey side, and plunged into the labyrinth of villanous streets in which the Borough to this day abounds.

Here, in a dark turning, called Gunn-street, she paused before the door of a low, beetle-browed public-house; and, after a momentary hesitation, which was evidently more attributable to uncertainty respecting the locality than fear at entering what was without doubt a haunt of thieves and ruffians, she pushed open the swinging door, and walked boldly in.

It was a queer place, and the customers had certainly a rather suspicious exterior. Some were splendidly attired, and wore what seemed to be hundreds of pounds worth of costly jewellery, while others were covered by the filthiest rags; but they all appeared to be on the most familiar terms with one another, and the well-dressed gentlemen were as affable as may be, while some of the raggedest stood upon their dignity, and were apparently treated with no little consideration.

A few of the men hanging round the bar turned to stare at the lady as she came in; but she managed to escape with but little notice, for there was some general topic of conversation which occupied all the persons composing the crowd.

She had certainly been in the place before, and knew her way, after the first momentary uncertainty.

She passed by the bar and up a short passage; then opened a door upon the right hand side, which led into the parlour behind the bar.

Here she found a careworn, middle-aged woman—the landlady—who came forward to meet her.

"It is so late, I thought you wouldn't have come, my la——"

"Hush!" said the other, raising her hand to her lips. "Mind what you're saying. Of course, I have come, as I promised to do so. Has he come?"

"He's behind, in the club-room."

"Is the meeting over?"

"No; only just begun. Shall I fetch him out?"

"Not yet. If I could get a glimpse of him first, I should like to. Can you manage it?"

"Yes, my la——; yes, ma'am."

The speaker motioned to the lady in black to follow her; and, leading the way down the passage and out into the back yard, pointed to a small window, about four feet from the ground, through which shone a bright light—the light of the club-room the landlady had spoken of.

Through this window a sight could be obtained of the company within, with little fear of detection; and the lady, raising her veil, looked in for some moments, silent and deeply attentive.

It was a strange scene to any one unfamiliar with the mysteries of thief life in London—or to one whose knowledge of the dangerous classes had been derived only from the perusal of exaggerated romances.

A long table occupied the centre of the apartment upon either side of which sat a motley collection of men and women, such as filled the space before the bar—some gorgeously attired, and some the pictures of misery.

They were all thieves. There were cracksmen, magsmen, smashers, cadgers, and common sneaks; every branch of the profession had its representative.

Some of the women were pretty, and well-dressed; the generality, however, looked somewhat careworn and shabby; the men, too, were rather quiet and subdued.

They were all drinking and smoking; but, as the night was young, perhaps, the fun, such as it was, had yet to come. Upon the walls of the room, here and there, had been stuck up a small handbill, or card, which may explain the object of the meeting. It ran thus:—

RALLY ROUND!

On Monday Night, the 10th November,

AT THE OLD DRUM IN GUNN STREET,

JACK CHINNERY,

LATELY OUT OF TROUBLE, WILL TAKE A BEN.,

When will be Raffled for,

A SILK POCKETHANDKERCHIEF.

Admission, One Shilling.

At the moment that the lady took her place of observation at the window, a very solemn-looking young man, with a very closely cropped head of light hair, was walking round the table, handing to each person in turn a dice-box, with which each threw a number somewhat carelessly, returning him to hand to the next. When he had come round again to the place from which he had started, he took from a nail, where it hung over the mantelpiece, a blue and red silk handkerchief, and handed it to the highest thrower, who, having folded it with great precision, and as though about to perform a conjuring trick, rose from his seat, and presented it very solemnly to another closely cropped young man, sitting at the end of the table; whereupon, the remainder of the company expressed mild approbation with their knuckles and the heels of their boots—where they had any.

"That is Chinnery," whispered the landlady, indicating the recipient of the handkerchief; and she was going to add something else, when the man alluded to rose to his feet to address the meeting, and the applause drowned his words.

The recently liberated convict was about twenty-seven years of age, well built, and handsome, in spite of his closely shaven face and his closely cropped head. He wore a velvet coat; and his clothes, though shabby, were fashionably cut.

He might have been a gentleman if he had not been quite so slangy. He was smoking a cigar; and wore, on the little finger of a somewhat dirty hand, a massive gilt ring, in which a large piece of glass glittered brightly, doing its best to look like a diamond.

When he rose to speak, he stood in a lounging attitude, with one hand in his trousers pocket. With the other he held his cigar, and puffed at it carelessly, from time to time, between the sentences.

He had an astonishingly free and easy style, and an easy flow of language, such as it was; and a bold, clear voice.

He had a good-humoured smile, too, and twinkling eyes, full of devilry. He was, in short, as fascinating a scoundrel as ever swore a false oath to a trustful maid-servant, and emptied the plate-basket upon the luckless night she imprudently admitted him to the kitchen when master was out.

"Will he do?" whispered the landlady.

"I think he is the very man for the work. What was he convicted of, did you say?"

"Burglary. A beautiful crack it was; did not you read of it in the newspaper?"

"No, I forget. Hush, let us listen to him."

"Very well; I must leave you for a short time."

"I'm very much obliged to you, ladies and gentlemen," said Jack Chinnery; "and I'm not surprised either that you've done the handsome thing. I always said I'd slip my darbies when they lagged me; and I've given the dubsman a holiday before my time is up, by an average spell; for, by rights, I'd fourteen years of it. Yes, friends, I've come back, as you see; but I can't say things look very flash this side the herring pond. I'm down on my luck myself, and don't see much chance out of it. My driz kemesa's* up the spout, and my fawnied famms,† and thimble of ridge,‡ and all the biling; and I should like to have a tip as to how I am to work the rig to get 'em out again. I don't want to go back to the old lay; but what's there open to me? The beaks wont let me be on the square; and on the cross, curse me if there's a living!—I don't want to stand here pattering about what you know quite as well as me; but I will say that it's precious hard to come back and find the doors shut in one's face, and nothing open for you but the quod you've give leg bail to."

He sat down after delivering himself of this jargon, and the company hammered approval with the feet of their rummers and the bottoms of their pewters, whilst a murmur of assent ran round the table.

"It's no lie, neither," one old man broke in with; "the police wont let you alone if you would be quiet; and there's nothing to be done in the trade if you stick to it. There's nothing left for one but to work on, living hand to mouth, till the little game's played out."

"It's nobody but the fences make anything at it," grumbled one of the women; "them as has no risk, and no trouble."§

"Smashing don't pay for the boot leather now-a-days," said another.

---

* Dress shirt.   † Rings.   ‡ Watch.
§ By the recent statistics of the metropolitan police, it appears that there are upwards of 2800 houses where stolen property may be disposed of, but the prices given for the goods are most contemptible—viz., silk handkerchiefs, the best quality, 1s.; good broadcloth, worth a guinea, 4s. or 5s. a yard; best kid gloves, 6d.; women's boots, worth 10s. 6d., about 1s. 6d.; and so on.

"There's not one crib out of a score where there's any swag to pay one for the job."

"What's the road worth, too?"

"Look here, friends," cried Jack Chinnery, with some difficulty making his voice heard above the rest; "things are about as bad as they can be, and if we don't cut out a fresh line, the profession will go to smash. Winter's coming on, and the dark nights have come. If we are to do anything, now's the time."

"What are we to do?" asked a chorus of discontented voices.

"You must chuck up the old game you've been on up to now, that's certain; and try something more profitable."

"Give it a name, then."

"We can't do anything without we work in a body; that's what it is. A fellow all alone has nothing to keep his pluck up. We ought to unite into a society; and we want a leader, so——We're all friends here, aren't we?"

"Yes, yes!" murmured the listeners.

But, as he spoke, each member of the comunity glanced suspiciously at his neighbour; for it was evident that treachery was not uncommon among them. Each, therefore, eyed the others askance, and seemed half doubtful whether or not the speech which Chinnery was making was not some artful plot to effect the ruin of them all.

Chinnery, however, it was easy to see, spoke in all good faith.

"There's no spies amongst us, I suppose," said he; "but there may be eavesdroppers close at hand. Is that window shut?"

One of the men rose from his seat, and went up to it, cautiously. The lady in the veil drew back, trembling, as he approached; and so sheltered herself behind the projecting wood work as to be invisible.

Apparently satisfied that all was safe in this quarter, the man next peeped out into the passage, closed the door again, locked it, and—*unlocked it again*, with such dexterity that the double turn was almost inaudible.

"All square," he muttered, as he came back to his seat; "you can speak out now."

He was not a very straightforward looking person this, who had taken the office upon himself of providing against eavesdropping. He wore an even more hang-dog and low cunning look about his sallow face and restless grey eyes than any of his unprepossessing comrades. He did not appear to be known to the others present; but, perhaps, each thought him to be a friend of some one else, and he thus passed comparatively unnoticed.

"If I can speak out safely," said Chinnery, in continuation, "I will tell you the plan I've got in my head. I haven't been so idle since I've been out as you might suppose. I've done as pretty a crack in a gentleman's crib, at Hampstead, as ever I had a hand in; and I and my pal, here, Jim, are willing to share the swag among them as will join us in the new lay; and, in lieu of a better man, I'll propose myself as captain——"

But when he had got thus far he suddenly paused; for the man who had been to the door had, at the mention of Hampstead, risen to his feet, and, under pretence of getting a light for his pipe, crept close up to Chinnery's side. And now, seizing the speaker by the collar, and pinning him, with lightning speed, against the wall, he, at the same moment, gave a shrill whistle; at the sound of which, the door flew wide open, and half a dozen policemen, in plain clothes, came pouring into the room.

"It's no good struggling, Jack," said his assailant, quickly. "It will only make it worse for you. My name is Trail, and I'm a detective officer, and I swore I'd be the first to nab you."

But the speaker had reckoned without his host. If it had been one of the half-scared, sneaking rascals with whom he had in general to deal, the arrest would have been easily enough effected ; but Chinnery was not one of their sort.

With a suddenness and an exertion of physical strength which, to the beholders, seemed almost super-human, the robber seized the detective in his arms, and wrenching loose his hold upon his coat, flung him with fearful violence backwards upon the table, where, falling among the glass with a deafening crash, he scattered the fragments far and wide.

Next moment, dragging from his breast-pocket a heavy life-preserver, Chinnery rushed towards the door, striking out right and left, indiscriminately among friends and foes, for both police and thieves were strangers to him.

Amidst the shrieks and groans and smashing of furniture, which ensued in the general pell-mell fight, the gas was suddenly extinguished, and above the hellish din could at times be heard the voice of Trail, the detective, calling loudly for lights.

The lady in black, who until then had remained an astonished and horrified spectator of the violent scene occurring within the room, now turned to fly ; but as she dragged open the door leading into the passage, a rough hand clutched her by the wrist, and looking up she found herself in the grasp of a policeman.

"Let me go !" she cried, in terror. "Let me get out of this dreadful place."

"Not so fast, if you please," retorted her captor. "Nobody goes out of here except it's to the station-house. We mean to have the whole gang of you, and break up the society."

"Gang ! Society ! You don't suppose——"

"I don't suppose anything," said the policeman, enclosing her wrists in handcuffs as he spoke ; "you need not criminate yourself."

"Oh ! let me go, I say !" the woman cried, bursting into passionate tears and trembling violently. "You have made a mistake. I do not belong to these people. I can easily prove what I say ; but I shall be utterly ruined if my name transpires. Let me go, and I will give you whatever you choose."

"I'm not to be bribed," said the policeman ; "and, besides, it wont wash. If you've got anything to prove, you'd better prove it at the police-station."

CHAPTER III.

ALONE WITH THE DEAD.

MEANWHILE the body snatchers, in their cart, had also crossed to the Surrey side of the water, and driven down a narrow turning, leading to the back door of a doctor's house in Blackman-street, Southwark-bridge-road. Then, unloading the cart of its contents, the man who had previously kept watch alighted, and approaching the door gently, rang the bell.

He had not many seconds to wait before his summons was responded to, and the doctor, standing in the passage, which was perfectly dark, asked who was there.

"It's only us, sir."

"Have you brought it ?"

"Yes."

"Bring it in."

Jaggers returned to the cart ; and presently he and Gouge, bearing between them the sack and its contents, entered the house, the doctor closing the door behind them.

"I did not expect you to-night at all, from what you said," observed the latter, as he did so. "I suppose you must have your money ?"

"Ours is a ready-money business," replied Gouge.

"Very well. You can have it, of course ; but you must wait a short time. Stop here."

"We've got another job on, and time is pressing," Gouge interrupted. "Suppose my mate here waits for it, while Blogg and me gets on to the yard."

"Very well."

"We'll take the cart then, Jaggers, and you follow as quick as you can. It's not much more than a stone's throw."

The men mumbled together for a minute, and then Gouge departed.

Presently the doctor heard the sound of the retreating wheels.

"Suppose we take the body upstairs," said the doctor. "Shall I help you ?"

"No ; I can do very well myself. If you would shine a light, though."

"I will fetch one."

The doctor went upstairs as he said this, and presently returned, bearing a lighted candle.

He was a thin, cadaverous young man, with scanty hair turned prematurely grey, and deep-set eyes, black and lustrous.

His name was Caul. He was very clever, but very poor. He struggled manfully with his poverty, and studied night and day, and won at length a name and fame which lives now that he is dead.

At the period of this history, and when he became mixed up in the strange and mysterious events with which this history has to deal, he lived here, and kept a small blue bottle shop, gave advice gratis, sold drugs when he got an opportunity, and practised surgery when he had the chance.

Those who have read Du Chaillu's book, and deem his pictures of the human beasts he found in Gorilla land improbable, should visit some of the haunts of the London savage. His lairs are to be found even to this day, at this present writing, in the wilds of Westminster, and among the filthy labyrinths lying in the neighbourhood of the Southwark-bridge-road.

At the time of which I write, however, they were even worse. Down the squalid courts and loathsome alleys were congregated the lowest and vilest.

These ill-lighted and foul-smelling courts and alleys, were the hotbeds of crime in its most revolting shapes ; and from thence were vomitted forth upon society every horrible form of human deformity, mental and physical.

The male population were, with but few exceptions, the most hardened ruffians and blackguards ; the women, shrill-tongued, slatternly, draggle-tailed ; the boys, slouching, hang-dog, thievish ; the girls, leering and shameless ; the children, cellar-born and gutter-bred, wallowed in the filth, and passed a pig-like infancy, preparing to walk in the footsteps of their parents down that crooked lane which leads, with many twists and windings, gallowswards.

Here, in this vile neighbourhood, the young doctor worked early and late, and though making but a poor living of it for the present, laying up a store of knowledge, which in the end brought him wealth, and left him famous when he died.

He was a single man, and lived in a crazy old house with only his assistant and a wholly deaf and half-childish old woman, his housekeeper, to keep him company. But he was an uncommunicative man, and lived only in his own thoughts, his books, and studies.

In the latter, and in the scientific experiments he made, he refused all assistance, and his laboratory was free from intrusion. For that matter he pursued his operations chiefly at a late hour of the night when the other two members of the household had retired to bed.

The grimy denizens of the adjacent courts, some-times seeing strange fitful glares of light, and hearing unaccountable noises issue from the room, which was the scene of his labours, set him down as a necromancer or a mad searcher for the philosopher's stone ; and it got about among the street savages that he had sold himself to the devil, upon which account they occasionally hooted him when he appeared abroad.

His labours, however, did not attract much attention: for his neighbours had enough to do to fight their hard battle of life, to keep famine from the door step, to skulk and hide, and give the double to Jack Ketch.

The young doctor, then, could do strange things unnoticed, try strange experiments, receive strange visitors, and experimentalize upon strange substances. Such, for instance, as that brought to him in a sack by these resurrectionists, upon the 10th of November, 1830.

"Come up stairs," said the doctor, "and walk as gently as you can."

The resurrectionist, bearing the body upon his back, stumbled heavily upon the stairs, clinging to the handrail as he went.

When they reached the second-floor, after several halts by the way, together they laid out the corpse upon a table, and covered it with a sheet.

"The money is at the other end of the house," said the doctor, "I must leave you here while I fetch it. I shall not be long—you wont be afraid, I suppose, to be left in the dark?"

"Not I!"

"I shall not be long."

So saying, the doctor quitted the room, closing the door after him.

He locked it.

"He needn't have done that," muttered Jaggers to himself. "Did he think I wanted to make off with the stiff 'un?"

The ruffian sniggered at his joke. He was not at all timid about being left alone. He was not particularly fond of the dark, when he had too much of it. He was not afraid of dead bodies, of course, for they were his stock-in-trade.

He, therefore, leant carelessly against the table, with his back to the body, and, to pass the time away, hummed a tune.

When he had hummed it out though, and hummed it over for the second time, he began to think that the doctor was a long time coming.

After this thought, came the one that it was very dark; and then that there was not a breath of air—that the room was as still and stifling as a tomb.

What a long while the doctor was coming.

He had left off humming; and though he tried to begin again, the first bar of the tune stuck like a fish bone in his throat.

He was not afraid of anything, because what was there to be afraid of? Yet he determined, if he possibly could, not to think of that lonely churchyard and the mysterious lady in black, and the corpse stretched out in the pitchy darkness behind him.

He was quite determined not to think about it, and yet for the life of him——

How horribly sudden that white-faced woman crept upon him with a rustle—rustle——

He started rigidly upright, and every muscle in his body seemed for the moment strained to the utmost, as he listened with intense eagerness.

The cold sweat burst out, in big drops, upon his ashy face.

His knees knocked together, and bent beneath his weight.

He would have torn himself away from the spot had he but had the power to do so; for his strength had left him, and he felt as one in a nightmare, and as weak and helpless as an infant.

He would have shrieked, but his tongue clove to the roof of his mouth.

Presently his horror reached its climax. The rustling had crept nearer and nearer towards him. The cold, deathlike touch which had fallen on his hand, crept upwards towards his throat.

He was in the arms of the corpse. Then overtaxed nature gave way at last, and he uttered a piercing shriek, and fell in a swoon upon the floor.

CHAPTER IV.

THE DOCTOR AND HIS SUBJECT.

THE body-snatcher's shrieks of terror brought the doctor running to the scene of action, his hair streaming, the candle he carried flaring and guttering in the wind. When he unlocked and flung wide open the door of the laboratory, where he had left Jaggers and the body, he found the former standing in the middle of the room, his face as white as death, his knees knocking together, and his teeth chatting like the castanets of a fandango dancer. But the body lay still and silent, much in the same position as that in which it was lying when the doctor left the room.

"What on earth is the matter?" asked Caul, in amazement.

The resurrectionist, however, was perfectly speechless with fright. For some time he could not find his tongue. He made a rush at the door, but the doctor barred his passage. "What is the matter?" he asked again. "What has happened? What have you been doing?"

"Let me pass, will you?"

"What has frightened you?"

"Don't you see? It—it has had hold of me. It is coming."

"What has had hold of you? What is coming? Are you mad, man, or drunk?" The doctor still maintained a tight grip of the other's collar, clinging to him tenaciously, in spite of the efforts which Jaggers made to shake loose his hold. In their struggle the resurrectionist swung round a little, so as to get his face towards the table on which the body lay. Turning his eyes in that direction, he stood transfixed.

"Why, it isn't! But it was!"

"Was what?"

"The body! the body!"

He could not give any coherent account of what had taken place, for as yet his terror had not subsided. The doctor, however, understood that the body was the cause of his alarm, and together they advanced towards the table. It lay there, still enough, and there was apparently no change in its attitude. Caul cast only a careless glance towards the face; and then, placing the candle upon the table's edge, he drew his purse from his pocket, with the intention of paying Jaggers for the "subject;" as he did so, half turning his back upon it, while Jaggers, bewildered beyond all power of reason, and with momentarily increasing dread of something indescribably horrible taking place, retreated to a few yards distance, and propping himself up with his back to the wall, rolled his eyes slowly round the room, ever and anon reverting to the body, and travelling off again upon another voyage of discovery among skeletons, mummies, and hideous anatomical preparations which decorated the ghastly apartment.

"Is this right?" asked the doctor, when he had selected from his purse certain pieces of gold which it had contained.

"Yes; quite right, master."

"Well?"

"Well, master?"

The man stood glaring idiotically around, without making any movement towards the door.

"Is there anything more you want?" asked Caul.

"No, master; only——"

"Only what?"

"My hat."

"I haven't got it. Where is it?"

"There—under the table."

"Pick it up then, and I'll light you out."

But Jaggers, with a violent shudder, and something like a sickly smile, said :—

"I'd rather not, master, if you wouldn't mind."

The doctor looked at him in surprise, then stooped, picked up the hat, and handed it to him.

"Anything else?" he said, interrogatively.

"No; I'll say good night."

"Certainly. Take care of the stairs. Don't go so fast; you'll tumble."

The warning, however, came rather late; for the body-snatcher had already missed his footing, rolled down the stairs, and lay sprawling upon the mat. The doctor called to him, to ask if he were hurt, and came hastily forward with the light; but Jaggers did not wait for his arrival—picking himself up, and thrusting on the side of his head a hat which he had knocked into a shapeless mass by the tumble, he tore open the door and rushed out into the street, leaving Mr. Caul aghast at the strangeness of his conduct.

"He's mad!" the doctor said to himself, "or drunk. What could have frightened the fool, upstairs? Being left in the dark, I suppose. I couldn't have believed it."

He walked downstairs, and before closing the street door, peered out into the night.

"A fool!" he muttered betwixt his teeth. "He made noise enough to waken the whole parish. If any of the people in the court are playing the spy to-night, they'll have something to talk about to-morrow. What a noise he made."

The doctor paused to listen as he said this, for he fancied that he heard a slight movement upstairs.

He listened for a moment or two, but all was still.

Then he turned to close the door.

"I hope Farquarson has not been disturbed, or the old woman. They might think somebody was breaking into the house. That idiot made noise enough to waken the dead."

He had his back to the stairs now, and was engaged in fastening the door. It was rather a tedious process, for the bolts were rusty and hard to draw; and he was anxious to avoid any more noise, fearing, as he did, that already his assistant or his old housekeeper might have been aroused by Jaggers' heavy fall upon the old creaking staircase. It was a large, rambling house though; and the doctor, for reasons of his own, had so contrived its inner arrangements that the sleeping apartments and the domestic offices were all far removed from the back staircase and laboratory which formed the scene of the events just described. He carefully bolted and barred the door, and then turned to ascend the stairs; but as he made the first step forward, casting his eyes accidentally upon the ground, he saw lying there one of the guineas which he had given to Jaggers. It had no doubt fallen from the resurrectionist's pocket, and he had gone away unconscious of his loss. The doctor bit his lip with vexation as he stooped to pick it up; for the thought very naturally occurred to him—would not the man, when he discovered that he had dropped the money, at once conclude that it had slipped out of his pocket when he fell, and return to demand its restitution?

"Then there will be more noise," the doctor muttered. "This is intolerable!"

He had some idea of opening the door again and waiting; but, upon reflection, thought he would go up-stairs, and if the man did come back, he would of course hear the bell. But he stooped again, to look whether anything else might not have been left lying upon the floor. To see the better, he waved the candle which he held. It was badly set up in the candlestick; and in tilting it slightly on one side, it overbalanced and fell to the ground.

The light was extinguished.

In no very amiable frame of mind, the doctor went down on his hands and knees, and groped about upon the floor for the candle, which had perversely enough rolled into a distant corner.

While thus engaged, for a second time he fancied that he heard a movement upstairs, and again listened.

But, as before, all was still.

He had some lucifer matches in his laboratory, and he carried the candle and candlestick upstairs with him.

He groped his way cautiously when he got into the room, for there were so many articles spread about that he was fearful lest at every step he took he should overturn or break something standing in his way.

When he found the matches, he struck one, and having relighted the candle, involuntarily glanced across the room towards the table where he had left the body lying.

It was gone!

Gone! He could not believe his eyes. He stared for a moment in blank astonishment at the empty table, and the colour died from his face. Then, all in a tremble, and with a sick terror at his heart, he looked round the room to see whether he could in any way account for so strange a phenomenon.

The room was lumbered up with a variety of glass cases; there were roomy cupboards, and deep recesses, into which a person might easily creep.

It would have been the best and wisest course upon the spur of the moment to have made a sudden rush, and explored all these probable hiding-places, in which, if the dead man had returned to life, he had perhaps hidden himself.

But a moment's hesitation rendered such a course almost impossible.

The bravest are often enough daunted by the dread of an *unknown* danger. The resurrection man, who could have slept comfortably enough in a dead house, with a candle burning, grew timid in the dark; and the dead body, which, while dead, had no terrors for him, was something awfully horrible when coming to life. So it was with the doctor. Had he returned to the room and found that suspended animation was returning, he might at first have been very much startled, but the fear would rapidly have subsided; but it was the fact of its having gone—gone, he knew not where—which, in spite of his reason, threw him into a deadly fright.

It was the dreadful dread of its springing out upon him suddenly from some unexpected place, peeping out at him stealthily from some dark corner, creeping down upon him before he was aware of its approach, and encircling him in its corpse-like clutch.

He stood motionless, and as though of a sudden he had been changed to stone by the sight of the bare table.

He stood and listened and waited, starting and trembling at the faintest sound which met his ear. At last, with a violent effort, he shook off the lethargy which was gradually overcoming him, and rushed towards the door. Upon the threshold of the room, however, with a stifled shriek, he staggered back; for there stood that of which he was in search.

There, in his grave-clothes, grim and ghastly, stood the man whose body he had purchased not half an hour ago, believing him to be a corpse.

There he stood, facing the doctor—with a staring terror in his pallid face, almost as great as that with which the other regarded him.

A momentary agonizing pause, in which Caul's heart seemed to cease to beat, and then the appalling horror of the sight gave way before reason, and the doctor understood the other's state, and mastered his own fears.

* * * *

When the daylight was breaking over the squalid misery of the court below, a light still burnt in the doctor's laboratory; and had any one been desirous and capable of playing the spy, a strange sight would then have presented itself to his astonished eyes.

Two men sat there over a small table, on which a candle, with a long wick, burning dimly, shed a faint and fluttering light upon their faces. One of these men was the doctor, Caul; the other, the man whose body the resurrectionist had brought thither on the preceding evening. They were conversing together in a low tone, and their conversation appeared to be of the most vital importance and thrilling interest. Before the doctor lay an open book, printed in black letter; and respecting a passage in this work he was now speaking to his companion.

"I can easily understand how it has been done," said he, "if we are to place belief in what we are told in this volume and others, among the works of now almost forgotten writers."

"But how could such drugs have been obtained, except through the agency of a medical man?"

"I do not think they could have been; and I believe that whoever administered the drug to you must have had such an accomplice."

"I cannot understand how that could have been; The person whom I suspect of having attempted my murder, I believe to be far too crafty to place herself in another's power."

"Of course you are the best judge of that, and know whom to suspect."

"Will you once more read that passage from your medical book?"

The doctor, turning over one of the leaves of the volume before him, and speaking in a low, perfectly distinct tone of voice, read as follows:—

"The drug specified in these proportions, having been compounded in the way I have herein set down, will, without causing death, produce an appearance which will so exactly counterfeit it that the most cunning shall be deceived. The administration of this drug will cause for a time the body of the patient to become icy cold; the eyes will glaze and fix, the breathing and beating of the heart will become so faint as not to be discoverable. The spark of life, however, will not have died out, although, during the trance, the person may have been buried; of course, should the exclusion of the air endure for too long a period, he must inevitably perish. The power of this drug will be exhausted at the end of five days; although during that time the faculties of the sufferer will not be entirely dimmed, and he will be, to some extent, sensible of what is happening around him."

There was a pause of some seconds when the doctor closed his book.

The other man sat silent and thoughtful.

"Such a drug may have been used," he said at last; "but if so, it was only administered in a mistake for poison. I tell you I am certain that my murder was intended, and I can at any moment lay my hand upon the murderess."

"Murderess!"

"Yes—upon my wife!"

"But are you certain? Let me beg of you before making an accusation——"

"Stay. I intend to make no accusation until the proofs have been established without the faintest chance of her escape. You have promised to aid me, and to keep what you know of this night's work a perfect secret."

"Yes; I have sworn to do all that you desire; and, in return——"

"The price of your services shall be paid to you."

"And your motive for desiring your recovery from the grave to remain a secret is——"

"Exactly what I have already told you. In the first place, to obtain the amount of insurance I have effected upon my life; in the second——"

"In the second," repeated the doctor, seeing that he hesitated.

"In the second, to be revenged upon the fair, false fiend who would have murdered me. On her do I swear now, in the face of heaven, to wreak a vengeance so bloody and terrible, that——"

"Hush, hush; not so loud; the walls may have ears, for what we know. We will talk it all over presently. In the meantime you require rest. I will show you into a room where you can sleep in perfect security and without fear of intrusion. I, while you are there——"

"Will find the man who is to help us. Have you any idea where to look for one?"

"Oh, yes; I have, visiting professionally in the slums of this neighbourhood, necessarily formed the acquaintance of a vast number of scoundrels of every shade; I fancy, that as luck will have it, the very man for our business returned from transportation two days ago."

"What is he?"

"A burglar he was. There is no knowing what he may turn his hand to—a plausible, good-looking scoundrel, with much low cunning and devilish ingenuity, and with talents too of a higher order had they not been neglected."

"What is the fellow's name?"

"He has a score of aliases. He has been called among other things, 'The Snake'—he is so wily, and sleek, and venomous. His real name, if he has a real one—though he has the credit of being the unacknowledged offspring of a great court lady, a model of piety, and the most charitable of living countesses—is Jack Chinnery."

"This very night, then, if we can find him, we will put this vagabond upon the scent, and track the murderess down.

CHAPTER V.

THE VEILED LADY.

WHILST, however, this strange scene was enacting in the doctor's house, and the first link of that chain of crime, of which this is the chronicle, was being forged by two cunning brains, their would-be tool, Jack Chinnery, the Snake, was doing his best to escape out of the clutches of the police, who had so unexpectedly interrupted his little schemes for the future.

When the light was extinguished in the room where the thieves' meeting had been held, one of the policemen had slammed to the door, leaning his back against it, to keep it shut. But he was not able very long to hold his position; for Chinnery, who had broken away through the struggling crowd of thieves and police officers, fell upon him with the ferocity of a tiger, and rained down upon his devoted head a shower of savage blows which covered his face with blood.

Then, tearing open the door, the bolt of which snapped like a straw before his giant's strength, the desperate robber plunged out headlong into the passage without, where two more policemen awaited him.

Without a moment's hesitation, and before the man, unprepared for so ferocious an onslaught, could make an effort to defend himself, Chinnery dealt him a violent blow in the face, which felled him to the ground as a bullock falls beneath the butcher's poleaxe.

Free so far, the robber, without attempting to molest the other officer, made an effort to get out through the door leading into the back yard, in which the veiled lady had been discovered.

But in this endeavour he was opposed by the second policeman, who, making a spring upon him from the back, strove to drag him down.

Snakelike, though, he wriggled in his would-be captor's clutches, and again the deadly weapon which he grasped showered down its crushing blows, and the policeman lay bleeding at his feet.

Then with a spring, clearing his body, Chinnery rushed through the doorway into the yard.

His escape now was almost a certainty. Only a low wall, easily scaled by the aid of some rabbit-hutches standing against it, divided him from a narrow lane by which he could easily reach the open street.

JACK CHINNERY FINDS THE PRISONER IN THE DUNGEON.

He pulled the door to behind him, and stepped forward; but something lying upon the ground and against which his feet brushed as he passed, caused him to twist suddenly round and throw himself into a defensive attitude, expecting another enemy.

But the object which had excited his fears was the prostrate form of a woman apparently dead or in a swoon.

The robber was not at first inclined to take any further notice of her, but while the coast was still clear, to lose no time in making good his escape; but the light, which some one inside the room had succeeded in igniting, falling full upon the handcuffs which encircled a pair of delicate white wrists caused him to pause for a moment and hesitate whether he should not help her if it lay in his power.

The thought flashed through his mind at once—" If she is pretty I will."

Then, for a moment dropping down upon his knees by the side of the prostrate and motionless form, he raised the head and looked eagerly into a face which, though as pale as death, had something in its delicate beauty that was strangely fascinating, something in its dark sad eyes full of a shrinking terror that thrilled through his frame, and held him for a moment powerless of action.

Only a moment, however.

In the next he had raised the woman in his arms, and striding across the yard, scaled the wall in the way that I have already indicated, and slipped with his fair burden gently to the ground.

The coast was clear. Not a soul was to be seen at either extremity of the narrow lane in which he found himself. He turned to the left, and still carrying his half-fainting companion in his arms, hurried onwards at as rapid a pace as possible, determined not to pause for breath until he had placed a very respectable distance between him and his enemies.

He came out, after walking for about a couple of hundred yards, through a series of winding alleys, all alike dark and deserted, to an archway which led out into the main road.

Here he came to a full stop, and was looking round for some convenient place to rest his interesting burthen, when the sound of footsteps, running towards him from the direction in which he had come, caused him to start on again at an increased speed.

A few yards from the archway in the street stood a hackney coach, the driver of which, hearing his approaching footsteps, turned round and raised his whip in token of his being for hire. Chinnery eyed him distrustfully, keeping as much as possible in the shadow of the arch.

The footsteps behind were coming nearer and nearer. By the coach there was a chance of escape—in no other direction could he fly.

The driver's face was sufficiently ill-looking and sinister in its expression to indicate that its owner would not be over-scrupulous with regard to the respectability of his fare. The vehicle itself appeared to be almost in the last stage of decay—a broken-down, crazy machine, such as might be used to convey dead bodies from the workhouses to the hospitals at dead of night.

Jack Chinnery then resolved to delay no longer. Coming forward, he deposited his burthen in the coach, jumped in himself, and mentioning at random the name of a street upon the Middlesex side of the water, bade the driver make as much haste as possible to arrive there.

It was truly a most diabolical machine into which he had ventured, and the bumping and jolting to which he was subjected in the course of the first half-mile's journey was of a sufficiently painful description to call forth his deep-muttered curses.

The violent shaking of the crazy vehicle presently caused his companion to open her eyes, and, with a deep-drawn sigh, she gazed about, at a loss to account for the place in which she found herself.

But a glance down at the handcuffs upon her wrists instantly brought back to her mind the recollection of what had occurred. She remembered the thieves' den which she had so imprudently visited—the deadly fray of which she had been an unwilling witness—the police-officer into whose hands she had fallen. With the horror of her situation upon her, the certainty of discovery and exposure staring her in the face, she must have fainted; and she returned to consciousness to find herself—where? Probably upon the way to the police-office.

At the horrible thought her senses returned. The terror of this dread alternative lent her a desperate strength which completely overcame her woman's weakness.

She raised her hands in supplication, and sinking upon her knees before her astonished companion, piteously entreated him to set her free.

"Don't be afraid, my dear," replied Jack Chinnery, stooping to raise her from the posture into which she had fallen. "Don't be afraid; we're safe enough now."

"Safe! safe!" she murmured, wildly. "Where are you taking me?"

"I'll take you wherever you want to go, if you'll tell me where that is."

"What! you will agree to my terms, then?"

"Eh?"

"You will not expose me—you will not drag me to shame and disgrace?"

"Not if I can help it."

"Oh, thank you! thank you! But you shall not go unrewarded. You have trusted me. Trust me only a short time longer, and you will see that this will be one of the best night's work you ever did."

"I hope so," said Chinnery, who was thoroughly convinced by this time that he had to deal with a mad woman.

They rode on silently for a short time; he earnestly regarding the pale face before him, over which a stray lock of golden hair was hanging, having escaped from the white widow's cap which confined the rest securely; she, the while, her eyes bent thoughtfully upon the ground, doubtless searching for the best method of escaping from the dilemma into which her imprudence had caused her to fall.

All at once she raised her handcuffs, and said, looking him full in the face—

"Please take these off."

Chinnery looked down at the small white hands and the slender fingers, glittering with rings, and at the cruel fetters which confined her delicate wrists.

The sight of the small hands and the jewels puzzled him.

For the first time a faint suspicion crept into his mind that, after all, this might not be a swell-mobsman's mistress, or a ladylike shoplifter.

Under the pretence of looking at the handcuffs, he took the tiny white hands in his, and stooping down over them, closely examined the glittering rings which had so excited his curiosity.

There could be no doubt about the matter, the jewels were genuine. The hands, too, so slim and taper, had never done an hour's hard work in all their owner's life.

What was she? What had she been doing in the house in which he had found her? What could her business be in such a den of infamy? Why was she in custody?

In rapid succession he asked himself these questions, but could find no answer for any one of them.

His companion interrupted the course of his thoughts by saying—

"Will you unlock these handcuffs?"

"That's not so easily done as said," the man replied; "but I think I can manage it."

"You must be able to take them off, as you put them on."

"I put them on?"

"Yes; did not—ah! I took you for the policeman."

She looked steadfastly into his face as she spoke, and a passing lamp at the moment, for the first time, plainly revealed his features.

In an instant she had recognised him; and almost as instantaneous was the change in her manner.

Her fears were at once dissipated; the wild look of shrinking dread left her eyes. She faced him boldly, and said—

"I was mistaken in you; but I was so frightened for the moment. Can you undo these things, do you think? They hurt me horribly."

Jack Chinnery took out of his pocket a large clasp knife, which contained, besides some half-dozen blades of various sorts and sizes, a collection of oddly-shaped instruments; some of them of a character which, in the eyes of a police-officer, would have seriously affected their owner's character as an honest man.

With one of these he very ingeniously unfastened the fetters, and having looked at them with some admiration, placed them in his pocket, saying that if the lady had no objection he should like to add them to the contents of his museum.

"Where are we going?" asked his companion, looking wistfully out into the dark streets through which they were rapidly passing. "Tell him where I want to go."

"If you tell me first."

"Yes."

She named a square in that gloomy respectable quarter of the town which lies at the back of the Foundling Hospital, west of the Gray's-inn-road.

The burglar gave the direction to the driver, and they proceeded for some time in silence. Then the mysterious lady, looking suddenly up, said—

"You wonder why I came to be in such a place as that you found me in, don't you?"

"I confess I do."

"I came there to look for you."

"For me!" he exclaimed, with a start back, and half afraid that he had fallen into some trap set by the police. "What do you mean?"

"As you told me just now," replied the lady, "you need not be afraid. I came here, Mr. Jack Chinnery, because I wished for your services, for which I am willing to pay you."

"I—I shall be very glad to serve you."

"It was very strange that you should have rescued me from the hands of the police, as I presume was the case by my being here with you. Did the landlady tell you to do so?"

"No; it was quite an accident I happened to find you."

"That was very strange; but evidently it was to be."

"And how can I serve you?"

"I came to that house to-night to see you, and decide whether you were a person likely to answer my purpose."

"And am I?"

"Yes; but I cannot now tell you the exact nature of the service I require. If you will meet me to-morrow night, or rather I should say to-night, for it is very nearly daybreak, at a place that I will name, I will tell you what you are to do; and as I have already said, I will pay you well."

"I am sure of that. And may I know who you are?"

"No; that is one of the conditions of our bargain. You do your work—you are paid for it—and there is an end to all communication between us. On no account must you seek to follow me, or endeavour to find out anything concerning me—for if you do, you shall as surely die, John Chinnery, as surely as you are listening and I am talking, and there is a God above us who sees and hears all that is done or said."

There was something in the tone with which the last words were uttered—something in the expression of the face of the woman who uttered them which surprised the man she addressed into a scared silence.

Was it possible so pretty a hand could clutch a murderous knife, that such gentle eyes could glare up with deadly hate, and that those red pouting lips, now drawn so tightly over the white gleaming teeth, could smile falsely whilst the poisoned cup was prepared? Could such a woman commit a murder? Would she? Had she already committed some crime, to conceal which she required his assistance? Or did she want to hire him as an assassin?

"None of that," thought Chinnery to himself; and as the idea passed through his brain he wiped away the big beads of perspiration which burst out upon his brow.

"But it can't be anything of that kind," he thought presently; "she's nothing half as horrible. It isn't possible."

Not possible! What is not possible in these days of undiscovered crime, of secret poisoning, of midnight murder, stealthy, sure, and trackless?

"You must meet me to-morrow night in the Birdcage Walk," she said, after a pause, during which she appeared to have been endeavouring to fix upon a convenient spot for the proposed rendezvous. "I will be in waiting in a coach at ten o'clock precisely. You will be exact."

"To the moment."

"Very good; and now please to stop the driver; I want to get out."

They had arrived at the square by this time, and the driver, of his own accord, had pulled up to inquire which house they wanted.

The lady drew from her pocket a tiny purse.

"I will pay the man," said Chinnery, stretching out his hand to prevent her doing so. "I am going on further."

"I am going to pay you," she answered, coldly. "Here are five guineas on account for the work which I require at your hands."

"But—— but——"

"Well?"

"I was going to say, if the work was——"

"Was not to your taste?"

"Exactly."

"I am not afraid of that," she said, with a grim smile. "Keep the money."

And as she spoke she leapt lightly out upon the pavement. "Good night."

"Good night," said Chinnery, and stretched out his hand.

But she drew back with a contemptuous expression upon her face which there was no mistaking. She did not admit a burglar into her friendship. He was to be her tool only.

And when he had served her end?

Chinnery felt a little bit uneasy as he peered into the future. But what was there to be afraid of, he asked himself.

Was this woman, with her golden hair, and blue eyes, and her white, delicate face, so very terrible already?

Was he already under the spell?

Absurd! He was ashamed of himself. Why should he allow himself to be hood-winked by her now? Why should not he follow her?

She had walked rapidly away down a narrow turning, which appeared to be the entrance of a mews.

Where was she going? Through the back door into one of the houses in the square. If he could but catch her in the act of opening the door!

Should he follow? Why not? Was he to be afraid of a woman?

He sprang from the coach, slipped some silver into the driver's hand, and bid him wait.

"If she catches sight of me before I see her, and asks what I want, I can pretend that I had forgotten what hour she said I was to meet her."

With this reflection he hurried forward, feeling that no time was to be lost if he hoped to overtake her, for she had already had a pretty good start.

But the mews, down which his mysterious companion had disappeared, was pitch dark.

He staggered onwards for a few yards.

Then came to a standstill and listened.

As he did so there was a faint rustle behind him.

With a quick suspicion of treachery he turned suddenly in the direction from which the sound proceeded.

But scarcely had he faced round when he received a violent blow upon the right temple, which felled him to the ground.

He lay there perfectly stunned for some time, unconscious of all that happened around him. When at length he struggled on to his feet he was so weak and giddy that he could scarcely stand.

He managed, however, to stagger out to the entrance of the mews, and looked about for the coach.

It had disappeared.

He stared about him, wondering where it could have gone; and as he stood there swaying unsteadily to and fro, as though he had been drunk, he dreamily felt in his pocket for the five guineas.

He had put them into his trousers pocket with some other gold, part of the produce of the late robbery at Hampstead.

There was nothing in his pocket now.

He fumbled about among his other pockets. All his money had gone.

Where?

Steadying himself by the wall he staggered round again to the spot where he had fallen.

He knelt down and groped about upon the ground, hoping to find the money which he supposed he had let fall out of his pocket.

But he could find nothing.

He searched round about, and yet could not find a halfpenny.

He could not have dropped it all, though: it was impossible. He must have been robbed.

But he yet felt so weak and giddy that he was not able to continue the search any longer at present.

He reeled a few yards distance, and sank down upon a door step, beneath a quaint old portico, and closing his eyes lapsed into unconsciousness.

When he again aroused himself day was breaking. He felt very cold, and his head ached slightly, but he had in a great measure recovered from the effects of the blow he had received.

It was, as well as he could judge, six o'clock; but there were as yet no signs of life in the mews. It appeared to be a ruined and deserted spot. He listened in vain for the trampling of horses' hoofs, and the snorting and rattling of chains, sounds which are so common in such places. Here there was nothing of the sort.

There were certainly a number of stable doors; but the stables they belonged to seemed to be empty. In a corner, at a little distance from the spot where he was sitting, there were the ruins of an old post-chaise, and one melancholy barn-door fowl, with at most half a handful of feathers upon its meagre body, was pecking on a dust heap, and hungrily attacking a rotten cabbage stalk.

He rose, and returned again to the search, but not a sign could be found of the money he had lost, in all, some twelve or thirteen pounds.

"I've made a nice night's work of it," he said, moodily, as he retraced his steps to the door-step he had just left, and reseated himself. "I've made a very nice night's work of it. I've lost every halfpenny I've got in the world, for I'll wager a crown that Jim has fallen into the hands of the police, and they have searched his lodgings and laid hands on every pennyworth of the swag. I don't feel as though I was able to walk home, and I've nothing to pay for a coach. For that matter, though, I've no home to go to. I'd hardly like to show my nose where I expect the bobbies are waiting for me half a dozen deep. Curse them!"

He leant back and closed his eyes wearily for a few moments. Then opening them again prepared to rise.

"It wont do to sit here for ever and a day, though God knows where I'm to go to when I move on. My prospects are rather blooming, certainly. The profession is no go, that's certain—a pack of dirty sneaks! There isn't a a faker in London that has the pluck of a mouse. No, hang me; I've a good mind to turn policeman myself, if they'd only let me."

He shook his head, however, at this idea, thinking, very truly, that his hope of propitiating the authorities at Bow-street was but a very poor one.

"My mysterious lady friend, too," he continued, after a long silence. "What's her particular little game, I wonder? Shall I go to Birdcage-walk at ten? It strikes me I'd better drop her acquaintance. What a devil she looked when she talked about making away with me. She is a devil too, that's sure enough. It must have been her who lay in wait for me round that dark corner, and hit me on the head. That was a pretty little trick to begin with, and then—no, I can't believe she robbed me. It's altogether awfully mysterious! I can't make head or tail out of it. But what am I to do? I wish to the Lord something would turn up!"

"Something would turn up!" Perhaps something very singular was turning up at the very moment that he spoke.

He was sitting in the corner of a doorway, meditating after the above fashion, and nursing his head in his hands, when all at once he became aware of a very peculiar sound close by his side.

He raised his head and listened, and after a little hesitation decided that it was the voice of a woman sobbing.

When once he had arrived at this conclusion he very naturally looked about him, to try and ascertain from whence the sound proceeded. He looked up, and he looked down. He looked inquiringly upon every side of him without being able to discover anybody.

And yet, as certainly as he sat there, a woman, close at hand, was sobbing piteously—sobbing as though in the direst grief and anguish—heartsick, hopeless.

"Where the deuce is she?" said Chinnery to himself. "She's not six yards off, but I can't see her, unless—— By Jove! she's there, down the grating."

CHAPTER VI.

THE SECRETS OF A NUNNERY.

THE interior of the old house, upon the door-step of which the burglar had been reposing, was one which, upon examination, was certainly calculated to arouse a stranger's curiosity.

It had evidently in its time been an edifice of some pretensions; but it had now fallen into ruin and decay, and, at first sight, bore all the appearance of being uninhabited. The paint had peeled off the door. The door-step was green and grass-grown. Some of the lower windows had been broken, and patched with rags and paper.

All around, what had been a mews, was in a like ruined and forlorn state; and, if it were possible to suppose that a motive could exist for such a strange course of conduct, it would appear, upon inquiry, that this state of things was not altogether unintentional, for had you asked for information of those in whose power it lay to give it you, you would have heard that this old house, and the mews itself, belonged to the same person, and that, although there had been from time to time numerous applications for the hire of the stables which the mews contained, all offers made for them, although in some cases at an exorbitantly high price, had been invariably refused.

It was a very large rambling-house, with, as I have said, a quaintly carved portico, and attached to it was a somewhat extensive garden surrounded by a very high red brick wall, the summit of which presented a most formidable array of spikes to the contemplation of the burglariously inclined.

In like fashion were the windows secured from attack by thick iron bars so closely placed that the rooms within must at mid-day have been dark and gloomy.

The whole appearance of the place now at this quiet hour, when it stood silently in the dull leaden light of breaking day, was sinister and threatening.

It looked like a haunted house, if such things are.

Or a house where a murder had been committed, or on which lay a heavy curse.

A house that had been damned.

While Jack Chinnery gazed upwards at its frowning front, he wondered whether the sound that he had heard could proceed from some one who had been accidentally locked in the cellar, and who, unable to attract any one's notice, was dying by inches of starvation.

"I'm doomed to be the rescuer of females in distress," said Jack to himself, with a chuckle. "Here goes for number two—but it's to be hoped I shan't get into quite such a mess as I did over my last little bit of chivalry. I feel now that I had a precious sight better leave this young woman alone—but I'm a soft-hearted fool, and—here goes!"

He went down on his knees by the side of a small grating close to the door and peered down into the darkness beneath.

But he could see nothing, and the sobbing still continued.

"Hallo!" said Jack, in a loud whisper.

The sound suddenly ceased.

"Hallo!" said he again; "what's the matter?"

He listened for a reply, and presently heard something which sounded to him like the rattling of a chain—he knew the sound perfectly from long experience—and then another sound, for which at first he could not account.

But presently he knew that it was the sound of bare feet being dragged over the stone-floor of a cell.

In increasing wonder Chinnery peered down eagerly through the grating, and strained his eyes to see what was down below.

"Who's there?" he asked.

But at the moment that he spoke a white face appeared so suddenly upon the other side of the grating, and so close to his, that he jumped backwards almost half a yard.

Recovering his equanimity, however, with an effort, he approached the grating once more, and once more peered in.

The white face was there still.

"What is the matter?" asked Chinnery.

"Who are you?" asked a low faint voice within—the voice of some one evidently in the last stage of exhaustion and suffering.

"A friend, if you want one," replied Chinnery.

"Are you speaking the truth?"

"Yes."

"Will you assist me?"

"If I can."

"You can, if you will, rescue me from this awful place."

"Where are you?"

"In a cellar that I have broken into out of a dungeon where I have been kept for days in the dark."

"Who has kept you there?"

"The Sisters."

"Who?"

"The Sisters."

"What sort of place is it? I don't understand."

"Don't you know this is a convent?"

"No. How should I? Are you a nun, then?"

"Yes—that is, they want to make me take the veil."

"And you want to escape?"

"Oh, yes!—yes! God grant that I may, before I am murdered! I have been trying to do so, but cannot. When they find I have broken out of my dungeon, they will kill me. They have already tortured me almost to madness. Oh! for mercy's sake, do not desert me in my misery!"

And the woman burst into passionate sobs and tears.

"I will help you if I can," said Chinnery. "Don't fear that I shall leave you. But how, to begin? I must get into the house first, but I don't exactly know how."

And drawing from his pocket the wonderful knife already mentioned, he approached the door and commenced operations upon the lock.

To open an ordinary lock was not a matter of much difficulty to the expert cracksman. He was reckoned one of the neatest hands in the profession. The police, previous to his transportation, had, upon being shown the traces of a burglary, professed to be able at once to say whether or not it was Jack Chinnery's handiwork.

With that pretty little pocket instrument which he carried, he very easily undid the lock of the door, but he was not able, when this was effected, to gain admission into the house.

"I didn't suppose," said he to himself, in an apologetic tone, "that they would trust to a lock only in a place where they bar the windows as they do here. But it was just as well to try that chance first."

The question was, what should he try next.

It would almost have been as easy a job for a thief to have broken in or out of Newgate as to gain admission into this strongly-fortified edifice.

But the Snake was not a man to be very easily daunted. He came out into the road and availed himself of such light as there was in scrutinizing the exterior of the building.

"There's nothing to be done in front," he said. "The only chance lies the other side of the wall."

But what a wall! How was he to get up? How was he to get over?

Not being able to do one or the other, he did the next best thing, which was to walk round.

By the side of the archway which led into the mews there was a weaker place in the fortifications than any which he had yet seen. Here he managed, with some considerable difficulty to climb up. But, arrived at the top, he found that the height upon the inside was even greater than on the outside, and that if he jumped down he would have to fall upon some flag-stones. He was in a great fix. At the place where he had climbed up, the top of the wall was so fortified by sharp glass and spikes that it was impossible for him to sit or kneel.

The only way was to jump, and to this alternative he certainly did not look forward with any large amount of confidence.

"It's more than probable that I shall break my leg," said he to himself. "I certainly am having a night of it."

Just then the heavy boots of a policeman were heard approaching.

He had not time to get back again into the mews. If he were caught standing on the wall, he would be taken into custody—that would lead to his recognition, and, then, who could say what would be the result? Transportation, perhaps, or death.

If he had not been forced to do it in this way, he would, probably, have hesitated longer before taking the leap. But, now, there was not a moment to lose.

He screwed up his courage and his eyes, and jumped with his feet together, falling upon them, and then forward upon his hands and knees.

The shock was a most terrific one, and, for some time, he was not quite sure that all his limbs were not broken. As he lay, too, upon the ground, he heard the policeman, outside, pause in his walk, and supposing, of course, that he was listening to try and find out what had occasioned the noise, Chinnery kept perfectly still until he went on again.

Then, rising to his feet, he looked around him.

He was in a dark, paved yard, in which grew three yew trees, throwing a deep shadow on the flag-stones around them, green, and moss-grown. A quantity of ivy clung about the old walls, and, half-hidden by it, here and there, he was astonished to see tomb-stones.

He crossed the yard, and approached the back-door. This, he supposed, would, in all probability, be locked and bolted as the front one was. He looked round, therefore, to see whether there might be a window somewhere which was not so strongly protected.

Just over the door there was one; a small square loop-hole, through which he could probably force his way in.

There was a water-pipe against the wall, running up to it, and by its aid, with the assistance of the ivy stem, he contrived to reach the window.

Being, as we have seen, an adept in his art, he was not now very long in effecting an entrance. The room within was dark as pitch, and he let himself cautiously down, fearful of making the least noise, lest he might disturb some sleeper in the apartment.

He groped his way along with the greatest caution, and felt all round and round in search of the door.

He put his hand upon a bare table, then upon a chair back, and then upon the curtain of a bed. It seemed to him that he found everything but the means of egress. In groping about he got round to the other side of the bed, and stumbling, lost his balance, and fell forward upon it.

For the moment he was terrified out of his wits, for he made sure that, at the very least, he must have got into the bedroom of the lady abbess.

But the bed was empty, and he rose into an upright posture with a deep sigh of relief.

As no one was in the room, he need not use quite so much tedious caution in making his movements; but, at the same time, any noise might prove fatal.

It seemed to him, in the pitchy darkness, to be a room of enormous size. Presently, he came to a very curious piece of furniture, standing in the middle of the apartment, which puzzled him considerably.

It was a long box standing upon tressels.

"What have they got here?" he thought; and placed his hand inside the box.

But he withdrew it with a shudder when the truth was revealed to him.

He had laid his hand upon the face of a corpse.

He groped his way tremblingly in the darkness until, at length, he reached the wall, and with a feeling of intense delight at length grasped the door handle.

"This is a very good beginning," he thought, as he carefully opened the door; "it seems to be a sort of whole-sale slaughter-house. I only hope they wont do as much by me. It would be awfully unsatisfactory to be murdered here without anybody knowing anything about it, and to be buried out in that back yard with the rest of them."

He found himself on the landing of a broad stone staircase, and before going any further, he drew from his pocket a pair of thick list slippers, which he put on over his boots.

Then taking out his clasp-knife, he opened the dagger-blade, and replaced it open in his pocket.

"I'm ready for them now," he said, with a chuckle; "as long as they don't come more than two or three at a time."

It was not a matter of great difficulty to descend the stone stairs noiselessly, but, as may be supposed, the journey was not without its dangers, for how could he tell but that any moment he might be surprised by somebody popping suddenly out upon him from one of the doors.

He wanted to make his way down to the cellar, in which the woman was confined, whose rescue he was bent upon effecting.

But it was pitch dark upon the ground floor, and he had no idea where to find the stairs leading down to the lower regions. He groped about in the dark, and tried the handles of all the doors.

Most of them, however, were locked. Those which were open led into rooms that were cold and damp—perhaps unfurnished.

Feeling his way along, however, he came to a small recess in the wall, where stood a candle and a box of matches.

"Ha!" he thought, "I shall do better now."

He struck a light at once, and renewed his voyage of discovery.

The first door he opened led into a chapel—a gloomy place, with a quantity of black hangings and sombre woodwork; and facing him a great black crucifix of wood, upon which was nailed a life-sized figure, that gleamed ghastly in the yellow candle-light.

By the side of an altar stood some large candlesticks, which appeared to be of massive silver, and the robber could not refrain from taking one up to weigh it in his hand, and calculate its probable worth.

"If I had the time," thought he, "I should like to come here with a sack; there must be some fine pickings. I'd give a trifle to go over the place quietly and take an inventory."

He left the chapel and returned to the passage, to search for the staircase. He found, at last, at the extreme end of a long arched corridor, a heavy portal, strongly barred; and, drawing back the rusty bolts with care, he found himself at the head of a flight of steep stone steps.

He thought it best to close the door gently behind him, and then he commenced the descent.

Gradually, as he got lower down, the air grew colder and damper. Moisture hung heavily upon the walls, which were slimy, as though with the exhalations of a sewer.

When he had almost reached the bottom of the steps, a sudden scuttering sound caused him to halt.

A large rat rushed past him precipitately, and plunged into the dark recesses of a cellar, where it fell with a splash.

Looking down at his feet he found that the floor was quite wet, and, in some places, where the brickwork had sunk into hollows, pools of water stood.

Chinnery could not repress a shudder when he thought of the prisoner, whose white face he had seen peeping up through the grating. In what horrible dungeon was she confined?

There were a row of doors all fastened by strong padlocks, and he knocked at each in succession, hoping that she would reply to the summons.

Then he thought that perhaps she might not understand what was meant, and that it was he who had come to rescue her.

He therefore whispered softly at each door in succession, hoping to attract her attention, but without success.

It was only a small scrap of candle, and would not last long. In the dark he could do nothing. In fact he dare not think of such an alternative, for he could not hope to find his way back again without the candle's aid.

"I can't open all the locks, one after another, to find out where she is," he muttered, discontentedly. "If she wont let me help her, she must stay."

Just then, however, a weak voice upon the other side of the door at which he was standing, called to him to make haste.

"It has just struck half-past six," the woman said. "They will come to visit me in less than half an hour. We shall not have time to escape."

"Time, indeed!" muttered Chinnery. "They must be stirring in the house above now. I shall never be able to get back the same way. I shall be caught to a certainty." He pulled out that useful knife of his, closed the blade, produced the picklock, and began his work.

It was no easy matter now that he was pressed for time, and his hand was not perhaps the steadiest.

Within the cellar, in feverish anxiety, the terrified woman entreated him, in agonized accents, to make haste.

At length the work was done. He pulled off the lock and opened the door.

Then holding high the light, looked into the cellar.

A fearful sight met his eyes. A sickening stench pervaded the horrible dungeon into which he had penetrated. A greater part of the floor was several inches deep in water. Upon a few rough planks, loosely nailed together, in one corner, was stretched some filthy straw.

There was no window or opening of any kind except the door he had come in at, and another door, leading through into an inner cellar, which the prisoner had contrived to break open.

The prisoner herself, a girl of, at the oldest, nineteen, but whose face was so terribly altered by the sufferings through which she had passed that she appeared to be at least forty, was clothed only in some miserable rags, which hung about her form, wasted almost to a skeleton, leaving bare her long, thin arms, and her feet red and swollen with cold and wet.

Her hair was one tangled mass, and hung over her face, half hiding her deep sunken eyes, which, large and bloodshot, peered out at him from beneath the shade of her thin hand, held up to protect them from the light, too powerful for their weak sight, dim as it was.

To one of her ankles was fastened a chain, which had cruelly chafed the skin, although she had striven to dull the iron's edge by wrapping it round with morsels of rag.

So pitiful an object was she, that for a few moments the burglar could find no words to express the feelings which the sight of her caused him.

"Good God!" he said. "Who could have brought you to this miserable plight? Do they wish to murder you?"

"I think so," replied the girl, in a faint voice. "They will murder me if you leave me here. Oh! come, let us lose no more time, but fly at once."

"How are you to go through the streets in this plight, I wonder?" Chinnery said, hesitating.

"I do not know; but let us get out of this dreadful house."

"Yes, we must wait no longer. If we can only reach the streets we shall be all right. I can get a vehicle and take you to some place of safety. How about that chain?"

He found, however, that he could not very easily remove it, and it was best not to delay their departure.

They therefore ascended the stairs, and Chinnery gently turned the handle of the door, and pressed forward. But it did not yield an inch.

With a muttered oath, he now threw himself against the pannel with all his might.

But he only shook the door, without being able to force it open.

"What shall we do?" the girl asked, in a terrified whisper.

"Curse it!" the robber answered; "the door must have stuck fast somehow—what could have happened?"

"Try again!—Do try again!"

Chinnery used every effort, but in vain.

"We are in a trap," he said; "we can do nothing now, but wait until some one comes to open it."

"Heaven help me!" cried the girl, sick at heart with the awful disappointment; "there is nothing left for me now but death."

"Hush!" whispered Chinnery, suddenly; "do you hear anything?"

"I hear footsteps approaching."

"So I thought! What is to be done?"

"Let us go back; perhaps we can hide ourselves."

"There is no time for that now; they are here!"

A heavy footfall was heard in the passage, and a hand was laid upon the door.

The two listeners waited with blanched faces and suspended breath.

At that moment the candle which had burnt down to the last gasp went suddenly out.

CHAPTER VII.

THE SHADOW OF GUILT.

BUT the progress of our story demands that we should leave Jack Chinnery for a time, even although we leave him in rather an awkward fix, while we follow the fortunes of the veiled lady who had so mysteriously disappeared down the dark mews.

If the Snake had only persevered in his search, it is probable that he would have discovered, about fifty yards further on than the door of the nunnery, a small green gate, at the end of a long narrow strip of weed-grown garden ground, behind a smoky red-brick house, the front door of which was in the adjacent square, mentioned by the lady in her instructions for the cabman.

Through this gate the lady passed when she had satisfied herself that she was not followed; and, crossing the garden, let herself noiselessly into the house by a small door, which was so hidden by the ivy and creeping plants, covering a summer-house in its close vicinity, as to be almost invisible, and only to be discovered by dragging away the shrubs and branches which concealed it.

It was evidently a door long kept in disuse, and the outside was covered with dirt and cobwebs, and green with damp; but at the same time a somewhat closer inspection would have shown that it had recently been opened—that the mud encrusted upon other parts had been broken all round the edges—that the lock, too,

had evidently been very carefully cleared from dust and oiled.

The lady, when she reached this sly portal, took from her pocket a small key, and very easily effected an entrance. Then, closing the door behind her, she stole cautiously up a flight of thirty carpeted stairs, which led into a spacious, but gloomy hall, wherein a swinging lamp of stained glass, burning dimly, cast a subdued light around upon the richly-carved oak panelling, and the heavy gilt frames of the quaint oil paintings lining the walls.

It was evidently a grand house into which the veiled lady had thus secretly admitted herself, and she appeared to be perfectly well-acquainted with its interior, though, at the same time, her visit was evidently an unlicensed one, or she was for some secret reason very fearful of her night journey being discovered by the other inmates.

Walking with the greatest caution, and pausing almost at every other step to listen, she at length reached the hall, and glanced fearfully around.

All was still, and she proceeded onwards; but not for far. A few steps further she suddenly came upon the form of a man stretched sleeping on the mat, at the foot of the stairs. She had not time to draw back or check her progress.

Before she was aware of his close proximity she had trodden upon his outstretched hand.

The man, with a loud curse, started into an upright posture.

The lady, quick as thought, darted towards the wall, and touching a small handle, the whereabouts of which she was well acquainted with, instantly extinguished the lamp; then stood perfectly still.

"Hallo!" said the man, rubbing his eyes, and staring about him hopelessly in the darkness, "who was that?"

There was a movement in a room, the door of which opened into the passage,—the sound of a heavy body rolling upon a sofa.

Then a hoarse voice called out—

"What is it, Bill?"

"Blest if I know," responded Bill, surlily.

"What were you bawling out about?"

"Something as woke me up."

"A noise, was it?"

"No; something jumped on to my hand, I think."

"The cat, I dare say?"

"I dare say it was. Better not let me get hold of it, that's all, or I'll precious soon wring its neck round."

"Wasn't any of them moving the sticks away, was it?"

"No, no fear of that; they wont be able to move them over my body very well without wakening me, I fancy!"

"I should think not, Bill. Try and hold your row, though, if you can manage it convenient. Blest if I wasn't having the sweetest nap when you squawked out."

"So would you a-squawked out, I guess, if you had a tom-cat, as black as your hat and as big as a haystack, bounce down upon——"

"There, shut up, then. Good night to you."

"Good night," grumbled the other, rolling over again, and making himself as comfortable as the hardness of his bed would permit.

He yawned loudly as he did so; and it was not long before his regular breathing assured the anxious listener that he was sleeping soundly.

Then gathering together her skirts, and raising them several inches above the tops of a tiny pair of exquisitely-shaped kid boots, she stepped over the man's prostrate form, and crept up the broad staircase.

The thickness of the rich carpet covering them, most completely smothered the sound of her light footsteps, and the obscurity, even had the man been awake, would have effectually concealed her, save when, for a moment, she paused on the broad landing, before the richly stained glass of the staircase window, through which the first faint streaks of daylight cast a ruddy hue upon her white statuelike face, and the thick mass of soft golden hair that formed a kind of glory round her small delicate features.

She paused to listen again here, and to peer down inquiringly into the deep darkness below, and then she noiselessly resumed her upward progress until she reached the door of a bedroom upon the second floor.

The handle of this door she carefully turned, and closing it behind her with the same caution, walked forward into the apartment.

It was, in the first place, an ante-room in which she found herself, communicating with a bedroom, both sumptuously furnished, with every contrivance that could minister to the most luxurious indolence.

The rooms were divided by a heavy damask curtain, richly embroidered with gold, which now hung down, darkening the outer apartment : the lady raised one end of it and looked in.

A bright fire was burning, which threw a warm and rosy glow upon the delicate white drapery of the dressing-table ; the elaborate gilding of an arm-chair, with full soft cushions of crimson velvet, and the thick piled carpet—a snowy ground, with roses strewed here and there with exquisite taste.

She looked in for a moment at this room, the bed-curtains of which hid the fireplace from her, although its rays penetrated to the most distant corners. But she was quite satisfied, it appeared, to find that the fire was still burning, and, letting fall the curtain, groped about upon a side table for a match-box and candle.

When she had found the desired articles, and struck a light, she took off her black cloak and the bonnet and veil which had hitherto hidden her face, and stood before a pier-glass, wistfully contemplating her pale face, and the golden ringlets which, escaping from their confinement, fell in a hundred wavy curls upon her shoulders bare and white. She wore a low dress of black silk, upon which jewels sparkled brightly in the candlelight. She pushed back her light hair from her pale face, and gazed at herself earnestly in the glass before her ; then heaved a deep sigh.

"How old and haggard I look !" she muttered to herself ; "how old and haggard. The misery of these few days past has added ten years to my age. Oh God ! how I have suffered, and how I shall yet have to suffer before I can rest in safety. Rest !—I shall never rest any more !"

She turned wearily away with an expression of intense anguish upon her deathlike face, which the passing agony so distorted from its beauty as to render it scarcely recognisable.

The tears rose up into her eyes, and bitter sobs vibrated through her frame ; but she subdued her emotion with a violent effort, and passionately wiped away the traces of her weakness from her soft peachy cheeks.

"Heaven lend me strength !" she murmured, softly ; "Heaven lend me courage to meet my enemies ! I must be calm and cautious, for this night will not see the last of the dangers which encompass me. So far I have triumphed, in spite of the lynx eyes set to spy upon me. I have been out to-night, and returned, without my absence being for a moment suspected. Ah ! courage ! courage ! I shall be equal with them yet."

A gleam of triumph lit up her eyes and imparted to her pale cheeks a faint flush of colour which heightened the beauty of her delicate face, as she drew aside the heavy drapery, and entered the bed-chamber.

She walked boldly forward, dreaming not of impending danger. She approached the fire with the smile still flickering in her eyes and about the corners of her mouth, and reached the hearth, before she became conscious of the presence of a second person in the room.

But arriving here, in a spot where the firelight fell full upon the graceful outlines of her form, she started back with a half-suppressed scream at the sight of a dark, swarthy face, and two cold grey eyes, overshadowed by shaggy grey eyebrows, which glared at her menacingly.

It was a woman who was seated there by the fireside, bolt upright in the most uncomfortable—if any could be uncomfortable—chair in the room.

The clothes she wore, and the hideous frilled night-cap upon her head denoted her sex, but otherwise there was nothing feminine about the face, with its harsh features, high cheek bones, and cruel, thin lipped mouth.

A woman of about sixty years of age, thin and angular, with great bony hands, and big, red knuckles, looking swollen and shiny. When she opened her thin lips she showed great, fang-like teeth, which stood so far out of her shrivelled gums, that they appeared to be upon the point of dropping out ; and when, at times, she laughed, in a spiteful, apish fashion, she seemed to open her great jaws like a horse.

She did not laugh now, however, but sat with her eyes immovably fixed upon the shrinking woman, who had thus unexpectedly come upon her.

The other was so completely thrown off her guard by the suddenness of the meeting, and was so utterly unprepared for such an event, that for some moments she stood transfixed, as though the old woman's eyes had petrified her into stone.

The old woman seemed to notice this, and there flickered upon her ugly mouth something like a grim leer of triumph.

"Well, my lady," she said, in a harsh, grating voice, "what frightens you so ?"

"Nothing frightens me," answered the other, recovering to some extent the courage and composure which had just deserted her.

"Oh !"

"Nothing frightens me," repeated the younger woman ; "except that your sitting there so silent like —like a ghost, startled me a little at first, as—as it might have startled any—anybody."

"I didn't know there was anything so very horrible about me."

"There's nothing very horrible about you, perhaps ; but that nightcap does not improve you."

"You did not think to find me sitting up waiting for you," said the old woman, with significant emphasis.

"No. Tell me what brings you here at all, Mrs. Worwold, in my room ?"

"No harm, I trust, my lady."

"I do not say it is ; but at the same time I must remind you that I have several times already expressed a wish that my room should be kept private."

Mrs. Worwold affected not to hear these words, but pretended to be fully occupied in stirring the fire, and raking out the ashes from between the lower bars.

Her companion watched her with fast gathering impatience ; her fingers clutching nervously at the back of a chair, against which she stood.

At last the old woman looked up again, and fixed her cold fish eyes upon her face.

"Where have you been all night, my lady ?"

The other changed colour, and shrank timidly back as this question was addressed to her.

"Down stairs," she replied, "in the library."

"Oh ! I went down there to look for you, but could not see you."

"I suppose I was somewhere else at the time—in the drawing-room."

"I looked in the drawing-room."

There was a silence of some minutes.

"WELL, MY LADY, WHAT FRIGHTENS YOU SO?" ASKED MRS. WORWOLD.

"How muddy your dress is," said the old woman, looking down at the hem of her companion's gown; "and," she added, applying her long, lean fingers to it before the other was aware of her motive, and could interfere to prevent it, "how wet!"

"Yes," answered the other, with gathering confusion. "Yes, I went into the garden after my lap dog; I thought—that is—— You wont think it rude of me, I hope, if I say I want to go to bed."

"No, my dear; why should I? You must be tired, for it's dreadfully late."

"But if you still remain here I can't——"

"Do I hinder you, my lady?"

"Yes; to tell the truth, you do."

"Why?"

"Because I always sleep with the door locked, and I shall have to get out of bed again to lock it."

"I'll go, then. I shouldn't like to be thought a hindrance or a trouble to any one. But I am that. Old women always are. I was a hindrance to my poor dead-and-gone son, and to his beautiful wife—oh! yes, my dear, I was—I was. But I can't come between you any more now. That's all over. That's all past and gone!"

She smeared her face with a coloured handkerchief she carried as she moved towards the door. Then turn-ing on the threshold to face the other woman, whose eyes were fixed upon her with an ill-disguised expression of dread, loathing, and abhorrence, she said—

"Don't be vexed, my dear. Good night. I didn't think there was any harm in sitting a while by your fire, and I came up to warm myself; and finding you weren't here I got uneasy, and looked for you everywhere, and so I thought I'd wait till you came in, and—— I can't think wherever you could have hidden yourself all this time. And how ill you look."

"I am ill. For God's sake, woman, leave me! I want to rest."

"I wouldn't be a hindrance for all the world;—good-night, again. I hope you'll sleep and have no ugly dreams such as I dreamt just now while I was waiting for you—ugly dreams about the dead. Good-night, my dear. I hope you wont think me a hindrance."

She was gone at last, and the lady left by herself.

Left at length to commune with her own thoughts.

To kneel by the bed-side, to weep passionate tears of sorrow and regret.

To ask God's pardon on a guilty soul—to pray for help—to shudderingly hide her face among the bed-clothes, and lie sobbing and trembling in the cold, grey light of morning.

A pale, shrinking, terror-stricken woman, with wild violet eyes, and streaming hair, a dead gold lustrous colour, which, hanging in tangled masses round her pallid face, gave her the appearance of a drowned sea nymph lying cold and stark upon the shore, washed up, and left there by the fickle waves.

CHAPTER VIII.

THE FALSE CERTIFICATE OF DEATH.

THAT there was some dark shadow of mystery and crime which overhung the gloomy residence of Lady Fane it seemed no sleight of fancy to suppose. It was a very grand mansion, but very dark and sombre, and the dust lay thick in unvisited corners and upon sideboards covered with costly ornaments. In the front of the house the blinds were all drawn down as though it contained a dead body, but such was not the case, for the remains of Mr. Jabez Worwold had, upon the previous day, been carried to their last resting place, in the church-yard of Saint Evresmond, in Willow Hithe, city of London. The window-blinds, however, contrary to the custom in such cases, still remained closely drawn.

No air or light had yet been let into the house; and its dreary entrance-hall was well nigh as dark and close as a vault.

Upon the morning which succeeded the strange events already recorded, the table in the breakfast-room was spread for three persons, and the clock was just upon the stroke of eight when the first of these three who composed the family made her appearance.

This was Mrs. Worwold.

Soon after, an old man, thin and careworn, with something that was *aristocratic* and noble, and yet weak and childish, in his thin, kindred features, came half creeping into the room, and, with a timid glance at the woman, took his seat by the fire, and, while he rubbed one hand slowly over the other, eyed his companion with evident fear and mistrust.

She was dressed in rusty black, without the least attempt at ornament to relieve the sombre monotony of her attire.

He affected something of a feeble juvenility which was rather distressing to look at. He had quite a childish head of hair, although it is true it was only a wig—a light, curly auburn.

He wore a thin pair of trousers, which fell into his shape and exposed the sharp bony outline of his legs. He wore a flower in in his button hole, and had a light and jaunty style of walk. He carried a gold-headed cane, and wore a very bright, new hat when he walked abroad, which he cocked a good deal on one side in a rollicking sort of fashion, as he strutted along upon the sunny side of the street, ogling the passing girls through an antiquated gold eye-glass, and screwing up his miserable old countenance into some apish contortions which he weakly supposed to be full of fascination for the susceptible heart of weak womankind, and most potent in their seductive powers.

This was Mr. Balfour Fenwick, Lady Fane's father.

The third person was Lady Fane, a pale and delicately beautiful woman; the deep black of whose attire showed off the bright transparent pallor of her skin, which again contrasted strongly, and lent deep brilliancy to her large dreamy eyes of liquid blue.

This was Lady Fane—the mysterious veiled lady of last night.

These three composed the family now that Mr. Jabez Worwold was dead. Lady Fane, when she married him, was the widow of Sir Leonard Fane, and the daughter of Mr. Balfour Fenwick, partner in the firm of Fenwick and Edwards, solicitors, of Lincoln's-inn-fields.

Mr. Balfour was the eldest son of the Fenwick who had originally been head partner in the legal firm above named. He had not been a business man, however, and had chiefly distinguished himself by spending instead of earning money. The consequence was, that, when his father died, and the other partner, Edwards, shortly afterwards followed him to the grave, the business seemed to be very surely on the way to the dogs.

But it was then that Mr. Jabez Worwold stepped in to the rescue. He was at that time only a clerk in the office. He had begun as an errand boy, and slowly but surely worked his way upwards to be head clerk, and now was made partner.

In his hands things went on better, apparently—outwardly, at any rate. He was a perfect genius at figures, and his legal knowledge was most extensive.

It was only natural that Mr. Balfour should be deeply grateful to him, and willing to reward him to the utmost that lay in his power.

Mr. Jabez Worwold named his reward.

It was the hand of his partner's daughter—Lady Fane—the young and beautiful widow of a wealthy baronet.

Mr. Fenwick was puzzled, and discontented at the choice. He was in the man's power—a mere tool in his hands.

He was willing that his daughter should be sacrificed. But would she consent?

Mr. Jabez smiled and chuckled, and said he should like to be allowed to ask her.

In the meantime, however, the father broke the news himself. He had supposed that it was not over palatable; but he had never anticipated the violent outburst of passion with which the wild, headstrong woman—the spoilt child of fortune—received it.

The shamefaced old man retreated in confusion, and begged his partner to think no more of the match, for it was quite hopeless.

"Hopeless!" cried Jabez, showing his dog's teeth with an angry snarl. "We shall see!"

He begged for, and obtained an interview with the scornful beauty, who had always treated him with ill-concealed aversion and contempt.

When he had closed the door behind him he took out his pocket-book, and showed her something which it contained.

Presently the bell was heard to ring violently, and the terrified servants coming flocking into the room, in answer to Jabez Worwold's loud cries for help, found their young mistress in a swoon.

She had, however, given her consent to the union, and they were shortly afterwards man and wife.

Upon this morning, with which we have to do, the three persons described met together and breakfast, and silently took their seats after a tender greeting between the father and the daughter, and a mumbled something from the old woman, which might or might not have been intended for "good morning."

None of the three appeared to have much appetite, and the food remained upon the table as it had been placed there—scarcely tasted.

They were not either in any humour for conversation. The old woman sat sipping her tea, her cold, fish-like eyes from time to time, when she thought herself to be unobserved, wandering furtively across the table towards the faces of her companions.

The juvenile old gentleman, with the aid of his eye-glass, was struggling with the Court News. Lady Fane had half turned her chair round towards the fire, and was gazing with a deep, anxious look upon her pale face into the bright red embers, which glowed there beneath a covering of grey ash, and anon fell with a faint, tinkling sound down upon the stone beneath.

At last Mr. Fenwick was the first to break the silence.

"When is the sale to take place?" he asked.

"On Friday next," replied his daughter.

"Heigho! I wonder what it will realize."

"I have no idea, father. Nor can it much signify to you or me."

"No, my dear; no. That's true enough. Every penny will go to his creditors, and then, I'm told, that if they realize twice the amount they're worth, it wont pay half his debts. He treated me very badly, my dear; but he was—yes, he certainly was a very remarkable man!"

The old woman looked up and scowled at the speaker, then dropped her eyes again into her teacup.

"It's most extraordinary how he ever got so into debt," Mr. Fenwick presently resumed. "What a speculator he was; but what bubbles he must have chosen to invest in! Though certainly if I'd gone the same way I should have no doubt done a great deal worse. But then it is very sad, now he's gone, for us all to be left in such a plight, and the money gone, and the bailiffs in the house, and—and—how very bad this tea is!"

He went rambling on in quite a childish sort of way, until at length, finding that nobody answered him, or seemed to take any interest in the subject which he was discussing, he subsided into his newspaper.

A rap came at the door at this juncture, and a servant entering the room, handed Lady Fane a card.

Upon it was written, in small capitals, "Mr. Gerard Wilde."

A faint flush suffused her ladyship's pallid cheek as she read the name, and a slight tremor shook her voice as she said—

"I will come presently."

Her father had looked up from his newspaper, and inquired, when the servant had left the room, who it was. But Lady Fane saw that the old woman's eyes were eagerly fixed upon her; and, instead of replying, handed him the card.

He, however, did not use the same caution, but read the name aloud.

"The doctor, isn't it?" he asked.

"Yes, father."

"Ah, you need not have left your breakfast."

"I have finished."

"He has called very early. Hasn't he?"

"It is early."

"By-the-way, my dear, what is your opinion about him? Do you think him a clever man?

"I think him very clever."

"He has no reputation to speak of, though; has he?"

"I believe not much."

"No—I think not; and yet, somehow, do you know, I fancy I have heard his name before."

"Indeed!"

"Yes, I have, certainly; but my memory is so bad, and I've had so much to trouble me lately, and—and I really can't recollect where I have heard it."

"I cannot help you, father."

"No—no, my dear. I daresay not. And so you think him clever. Now do you know I should like to ask him a question?"

"What is that?"

"Well, I hardly like to tell you. But, still, I do not know why I shouldn't.—Oh! it's such a dreadful idea! —but, you see—oh! it is a ridiculous idea!"

"What is it, father?"

"Well, then, we know now what a fix poor Worwold was in about his money affairs, though, when he was alive, he kept it all so quiet; and don't you think it possible—has it not occurred to you——"

"What—what?"

"That—that he might have attempted his own life?"

"Father!"

"It was very sudden you know—and—and——"

"Father!" said her ladyship, in a waning voice, "Father! for heaven's sake, silence!"

She spoke with passionate energy.

She stretched out her hands imploringly, as though she would entreat the old man to beware what he said; and as he sank back into his chair, looking scared and bewildered, the old woman clutching the edge of the table, contemplated the two, with her stony eyes full of an expression which it was impossible to understand, but which lent a look to her sallow wrinkled face that was positively horrible.

Lady Fane, without waiting for a reply from her father, quitted the apartment, and went straight to the room where the doctor awaited her coming.

He was a young man of about eight-and-twenty, straight and handsome, with a dark complexion, and black curly hair.

There was something, though, about his face which was not altogether pleasing—a sly look about the eyes, perhaps, which wandered restlessly to and fro, without ever fairly meeting those of the person to whom he spoke.

He rose as her ladyship entered the room, and stood silently waiting for her to speak.

She did not, however, utter a word until she had carefully closed the door behind her.

Then advancing rapidly towards him, she said, in a low tone, which, had there been listeners in the hall without, it would have been almost impossible for them to have heard—

"I am glad you are here so soon, Gerard; I have passed a sleepless night, but, thank God, all hitherto goes well. I have something here to reward you for what you have done. Here it is."

"Is this ——"

"It is the forged bill!"

He started violently at the word, and caught at her dress, as though to warn her to be cautious.

The colour faded from his face, and a sickly pallor overspread it.

He did not look as handsome in his terror, and there was something not a little contemptible in the celerity with which he ran to the door, and leaped out upon the landing, and finding no one there, tried another door at the opposite side of the room, which, however, only opened into a dark cupboard, where a tray-stand and a wine-cooler reposed in a grim obscurity.

Lady Fane had not moved from the spot where she was standing when last she spoke.

She still remained there in the same attitude, holding the paper in her hand; and there was upon her face just the faintest possible indication of a scornful smile of pity for her companion's weakness.

When he returned to her side, she stretched out her hand and held the paper towards him.

"Here is the bill," she said.

He eagerly snatched at it.

"Is that the one?"

"Ye—es, yes; this is it. There only was one. This is it sure enough."

He examined the long narrow strip of paper which she had given to him, with a rapid glance. It was yellow, as though with age, and it had been folded and refolded, so that it had become very limp and flimsy, and in the creases was almost torn apart.

When he had looked at it back and front, and had read his own name scribbled in the corner, he folded it again, and was about to thrust it back into his pocket, when she stayed his hand.

He looked up at her inquiringly.

"What is the matter?"

"What are you going to do?"

"Take it away."

"Take it away?"

"Yes."

"Is that the safest course?"

"Safe enough; it shall never leave my possession again, now that I have got it back."

"Would it not be best to destroy it?"

As she spoke, she turned and fetched from a sideboard an inlaid inkstand, in which there was a wax taper; lighting this, she placed it before him.

"Burn it," she said.

"Yes, that will be best."

CHAPTER IX.

THE OMEN.

HE drew the paper forth, and screwing it up, lighted it at the taper.

As he did so, his hand trembled visibly.

The lady watched him, and the same faint smile of scorn flitted across her face.

Her eyes were fixed steadfastly upon his face; but, as she gazed upon him their expression grew more and more dim and unmeaning.

She was not thinking of him, it would seem, or of the matter in hand, but her thoughts had strayed far away over the boundaries of the irrevocable past—a past, of who knows how much bitter sorrow and suffering—a past, which had perchance left its impress of deadly crime upon her soul.

Without heeding her, her companion had burnt the paper to ashes, turning it round and round in his fingers, and unfolding it by degrees, so that the flame could reach every portion; and, at length, allowing the last smouldering embers to fall into the candlestick, where they lay a blue shapeless mass.

Having thus made sure of the destruction of the bill, he blew out the taper, and replaced the inkstand upon the sideboard, and as he again approached Lady Fane's side, it was evident that no small weight had been taken off his mind by the little arrangement which he had just effected.

"There is an end of that," he said, with a smile.

She awoke from her reverie at the sound of his voice, and turned towards him.

"An end of what?" she asked.

"Of my anxiety!"

She opened her eyes slightly, as though in surprise; then fixed them upon him with a frown.

"An end of your anxiety?" she repeated. "So soon?"

"Not very soon!" he answered; "it has hung over me a weary while, blighting my life; but it is destroyed now, and with it my fears for the future. Thank God! I am a free man again!"

She laid her hand upon his arm.

"Have you nothing else to fear?"

"Eh?—no—what do you mean?"

"Have you forgotten the certificate which you signed four days ago?"

Again the colour faded from his face, and he looked uneasily towards his companion.

"There need be no fear on that account," he said.

Still no reply.

"Who could prove anything?"

She made no answer.

"Only you and I know that the certificate of death was false, and——"

"Well?"

"I am not likely to betray myself."

"You may rest assured that I shall keep your secret," she said, turning away.

The doctor pondered silently for a few moments. Some half-formed suspicion agitated his mind.

Presently he spoke, as though with an effort, and in a hesitating tone, as though he were half afraid of giving offence.

"It is to your advantage also that—that——"

"That what?"

"That no one—that the secret——"

"Should not be betrayed?"

"Yes—it was for your sake I did it!"

"I am well aware that I prompted the lie, and I paid you the price you desired. Yes, the accommodation was upon both sides alike. Do not think either that I wish to escape from my share of the danger; for if you think fit to betray me——"

"Betray you? I——"

"And yourself at the same time; for, of course, I could not fall without dragging you down too——"

"But there is no occasion for that. I never hinted at such a thing. I—I would rather die."

"To be sure. I believe you. I mistook your words. Think no more about it."

"No," said the doctor, wiping the perspiration off his face. "I don't see why we should alarm ourselves at all."

"Not on that account. As far as we are concerned there is no fear. I only thought—but no matter—no matter."

The doctor regarded her with increasing uneasiness and mistrust.

"What do you fear?" he asked. "For God's sake tell me if there is any danger, that I may be prepared."

"I have nothing to tell you. I should only alarm you without cause."

"But I should like to hear it. There might be reason for fear. And yet I cannot imagine how. Nothing but a post-mortem examination of the body could prove that he was murdered—that it was a false certificate of death which I wrote. No, no. There is no danger. The grave hides our secret. Dead men tell no tales."

She seemed to be upon the point of making some suggestion, but checked herself with the words upon her lips. Then, after a brief pause, said—

"I will delay you no longer, Mr. Wilde. In future the less we see of one another, perhaps the better."

She moved towards the door as she spoke, and turned the handle.

She stood there for a moment, drawn up to her full height, with an air of inexpressible grace, dignity, and beauty.

The sunlight shone in her golden hair and upon her fair face—its skin, so clearly transparent, so deadly pale, with a kind of delicate and exalted loveliness upon it, which one sees sometimes in pictures of angels.

She was not the sort of woman you could have believed capable of petty meanness and deceit. There was something in her countenance which appeared like truth itself—open—fearless—uncompromising; and yet from sunrise to sunrise her life was one awful acted lie.

As she stood thus upon the threshold of the door, her proud eyes fixed upon the doctor's face, he shrank back beneath her gaze, and dropped his own eyes beneath the stern look fixed upon him.

But as she turned to go his warning courage revived, and, catching at her sleeve, he cried, in a pleading tone—

"You—you will not leave me so, Ethel—after all our vows—after all that has passed between us——"

"Silence!" she cried, and turned upon him fiercely, with eyes that glared like those of an angry tigress. "Silence! How dare you! All that has passed between us passed long ago, when I was a girl—a child—a fool to be gulled by your soft phrases. All that is past, is past—is ended. I should have thought you need not have been told as much by me—that your own sense would have taught you the width of the gulf between us. Never dare to speak so again. Rather never let us meet. If I loved you—and I own I did love you once—it is over now. My love has died out in my heart with the other delusions of my youth. Good-bye, Gerard Wilde. Let this be our last meeting."

She passed through the door as she spoke, dragging from his grasp the heavy skirt of brocaded silk, which rustled as it swept the ground, as dead leaves rattle in the fall of the year, in the dull dreariness of autumn time.

He would have recalled her.

The half-uttered words were on his lips when his eyes met those of Mrs. Worwold, who, coming unseen and unheard up the passage, now confronted the speakers.

Wilde shrank back abashed—a conscious flush upon his face.

But her ladyship coldly returned the old woman's look full of inquisitive speculation ; and, bowing to the doctor, ascended the stairs towards her own room.

Gerard Wilde, on his side, lost no time in effecting his escape out into the street, and hurried away as fast as a Hansom cab could take him.

But when he had in some measure recovered from the confusion into which the interruption had thrown him, he sat ruminating, with knit brows, and biting his teeth to assist him in his meditations.

"I acted like a fool," he muttered to himself. "I began too precipitately. I should not have alluded to the past. I might have known, if I had not been an idiot, that that was the worst course in the world ; and now—now, perhaps, I have ruined my chance for ever. Yet that cannot be. She would never dare to quarrel with me altogether when I know so much. No! I must somehow make up for my mistake, and—and I must get some money somehow. I *must* have money ; and she is my only hope!"

He rode away to the city, and spent the remainder of the day in visiting the offices of certain well-to-do children of Israel who discounted bills upon good personal security. It would have appeared, though, from the unsatisfactory result of his day's work, that his own personal security was not quite as good as it might have been, for he returned to his home penniless in the course of the evening, and solaced himself for his disappointment by sundry tumblers of steaming punch and half-a-dozen full-flavoured Havannahs.

It would also have appeared that Mr. Gerard Wilde's practice, as a medical man, was extremely limited ; for during the course of the day he had been to call upon no patients, neither had any patients been to call upon him.

When he arrived at home, he found several letters awaiting his arrival ; a glance at the superscriptions of which was sufficient to convince him that they were from duns.

Some of them he flung, unopened, into the fire. Others he read through and thrust into his pocket with a curse.

He sat until a late hour, with one foot upon either hob, his chin resting on his hand, puffing at his cigars, and swallowing his grog by huge gulps.

The fire burnt low in the grate before he thought of mending it. The two candles upon the table behind him had flaming wicks, which fell at last, and spluttered in the fat for want of snuffing.

"I must have money," he muttered between his teeth. "I must have money from somewhere, if I have to murder somebody to get it."

Something flew out of the fire, and lay smoking upon the hearth. He stooped to raise it.

"It's a purse, I hope," said he ; "if it is, that's a good omen!"

But it was not. *It was a coffin.*

CHAPTER X.

THE PIT-HOLE.

A MORE horrible predicament than that in which Jack Chinnery found himself, when, having penetrated into the nunnery and released the miserable captive from her loathsome cell, he would have effected his escape, and discovered that he also was a prisoner, it would be difficult to imagine.

In the pitchy darkness which enveloped him it was impossible for him to use any efforts to open the door which were likely to prove at all successful. Again, if he made any noise, he would arouse the inmates of the house ; in which case, should he be overpowered by superior numbers, there was no knowing what dreadful fate might await him ; for he felt convinced, from what little he had already seen of the secrets of this mysterious establishment, that he was in the hands of persons at once as vindictive, cruel, and unscrupulous as they were powerful.

So his only hope lay in a sudden rush.

If the door was opened, and he could spring out upon those who opened it, before they were aware of his presence, and fight his way into the street—that was the sole chance of escape open to him.

He supposed, too, at first, that this event was not far distant, for he certainly had heard footsteps approaching.

But just at the moment that he supposed the door would fly open, and when he was preparing himself for a rush, the sound without suddenly ceased.

He had heard, he fancied, a hand laid upon the door. It had been withdrawn again.

He exerted his sense of hearing to the utmost. He listened intently, but could hear nothing.

Was any one outside? Had any one been there? What had become of them? Had they gone on? Were they still standing there?

The perplexity of the position was maddening.

He was fearful of making the slightest movement lest the sound should reach the ears of the listener without—if a listener were there.

He tightly grasped the wrist of his companion, to compel her also to maintain silence and remain motionless, for she was shivering like an aspen leaf and quaking with fear.

They waited thus a long while, the time appearing to them ten times greater than it really was, listening for a noise without, and every moment expecting an attack from some unseen enemy.

But when at length, after long waiting, they found that no one came to interfere with them, they began whispering together in the lowest and most cautious tone.

"Are they gone?"

"I think so."

"They must have heard you moving, and have come down to look round the bottom of the house."

"They are looking, then, in some of the rooms!"

"Did you think that the steps passed the door?"

"Yes."

"They are gone, then, into the chapel."

"And will return?"

"No doubt."

"They must not find me here, or else your chance of escape is gone. I might, perhaps, get away ; but there would be no chance for you!"

"Oh! for God's sake, do not desert me! Say you will not leave me in this dreadful place!"

"No, no ; make your mind easy on that score. I will help you if I can."

"What shall we do?—what shall we do?"

"That is for you to suggest."

"I can think of nothing."

"Is there no chance of getting out down below?"

"Shall we try! I think there is a way ; but—but——"

"But what?"

"We shall never be able to use it—you would never dare."

"I would dare a good deal if there was any occasion ; but—hush!"

Again there was a sound of footsteps above.

Of the footsteps of several persons, accompanied by a low murmur of voices, passing the door.

Again Chinnery clenched his teeth, and made ready for a spring ; but the persons, whoever they were, passed by the door, and all was again silent.

"There's not a ghost of a hope for us up this way,"

muttered Chinnery. "Creep down as gently as you can, and show me how we can break out from below stairs."

They silently descended, and wit such a slight noise as to be almost inaudible.

As they reached the floor of the cellars there was again a rushing and splashing in the distance.

Chinnery shuddered slightly at the sound.

"Curse the rats!" he muttered. "There's nothing in the world I have such a horror of as that sort of vermin."

"There are hundreds down here," his companion whispered. "I have been half frightened out of my life by them. I have been afraid to go to sleep for fear they should attack me."

"Let's get out of the horrid hole as soon as we can, for the love of heaven! Nobody in their senses would believe there could be such things in London."

"Nobody would believe that such atrocities could be perpetrated as daily occur in this house," replied the woman, in a hollow tone. "But come, let us begin at once."

"What am I to do?"

She led him along a narrow passage, groping her way and guiding herself by the walls, moist and slimy to her touch.

At last she paused, and appeared to be feeling out in vain for some object.

"I cannot find it," she said.

"Find what?"

"The door. There should be a door somewhere here."

"I can feel one, but it is stuck fast. Ah! that's it! Curse it, what a noise it has made!"

The door, yielding to his strength, had given way with a prolonged screech, which echoed plaintively through the cellars.

"We shall be heard!" said Chinnery, after a pause, during which they had both been listening, and holding their breath. "We haven't a moment to lose! Which way now?"

He was stepping forward into the gaping aperture which yawned beyond the open door, when the woman clung to his arm, and drew him back.

"Stay—stay, for God's sake! There is a well!"

"A what?"

A sickly feeling crept over him at the words, and he retreated a few steps with a shudder.

In another moment he would have fallen into the yawning pit at his feet!

"What are we to do?" he asked. "What was your plan?"

"I thought—I thought—but no, it is impossible!"

"Nothing is impossible if you make your mind up. Speak out at once. What is it?"

"There is a deep well here, and it is about four feet wide."

"Yes."

"Upon the other side there is a space about a yard wide."

"Yes, yes."

"There is a door beyond, which leads into another cellar—the cellar of the next house—by which we might escape."

"Is it an uninhabited house?"

"No; it belongs to Mr. Worwold, a solicitor, and Lady Fane his wife."

"Then the door on the other side is probably locked?"

"No; the cellar is not used, and the door is not fastened."

"Are you sure of it?"

"Certain. I have seen through—when first I was brought into the nunnery."

"But is there any way out of their cellar except through the house?"

"Yes, a way out into the back garden, from which we can get out into the mews."

"But—but the next question is——"

"Is what?"

"Is, how are we to get over the well?"

"Dare you jump?"

"Jump! Good Lord! what do you mean?"

"Can you jump as far as four feet?"

"Yes—yes, I could jump eight feet easily enough if I was put to it—on straight ground, not in the dark! No, it is impossible!"

"Then there is no hope for me. Go and do what you will, and leave me to my fate."

"Don't talk like that," retorted Chinnery, rather angrily; "I didn't say I was going to desert you. I said I wouldn't, and damn me if I do!"

"But you say it is impossible to jump over the well."

"Well, yes. That is, I meant it would be rather a tight job; but nothing is impossible, as I said before, and, of course, it must be as easy to jump four feet in the dark as the broad daylight, if one was only used to it; only the worst of it is—the worst of it is I'm not used to it, you see."

He paused, while he was speaking, to listen again, for he fancied that he heard the sound of voices at the top of the stairs, and some one trying the door.

The woman heard it also, and her terror increased.

"There is no time left," she cried. "We're lost! we're lost!"

"Not yet," said Chinnery. "I'll try my luck, if I die for it. How broad did you say the space was on the other side?"

"About a yard."

"Is it less?"

"More, I think."

"Well, I must try. If I could only have a run, though!"

"Only make haste."

"You don't think there's a plank or anything we might put across?"

"No, no! I'm certain that there is not. I have already tried to find one."

"But when I am across, how can I help you?"

"You can easily do that, I'm sure. There is a quantity of timber and old pieces of wood in the other cellar. Only make haste."

"It's very well talking about making haste," thought Chinnery to himself, rather discontentedly. "Make haste for what? To get into the next world. That's about the size of it."

But again he heard voices upon the top of the stairs.

For a moment he thought they had opened the door. They were consulting together, close to the outside.

There was no more time to be lost.

If he meant to jump at all, he must jump at once.

But the very thought of so desperate an alternative, was surely enough to make the stoutest heart quail with fear.

To jump over a well four feet broad, in the pitchy darkness—to be even uncertain of the exact width—uncertain of the landing-place on the other side.

"Good God!" he thought. "Suppose there should be no landing-place, and the door should be close up to the well side!"

The flag-stones were moist and slippery round the edge of the pit.

It was with the greatest difficulty, at times, that he could keep his footing.

How could he hope to spring with any certainty?

But if it was to be done at all, it must be done at once; and he screwed up his courage to the sticking point.

Perhaps at this critical moment, Mr. Jack Chinnery very much regretted having intruded himself into the nunnery.

Perhaps he might have registered something like a

vow, that if he only got out of this scrape with his life, he would never more get into another by the performance of any acts of chivalry.

He might have done either of these things. It was more or less uncertain.

One thing is certain, though, that he felt quite convinced that his last hour had arrived, and rummaged about in his dim recollection for such small scraps of prayer and pious sentiment which he thought suited to the occasion.

Then having prepared himself for etenity in this rough fashion, he commenced preparations for his awful leap.

First of all, steadying himself by the doorpost, he felt cautiously about with his foot for the edge of the pit.

Having found it, he requested his companion to stand upon one side, so that he might not knock her in when he jumped.

Then he placed himself exactly in the middle of the door, so that when he took the run which he intended, he might not strike against either side, and so fling himself to a dead certainty into the pit.

Then he took three long steps back, and got ready for his run.

But it took much longer getting ready, than those who read this sitting on their own hearthrugs might suppose.

His run must be exactly three steps forward. If two of the steps were longer than all the three had been going backwards, there was a certain end of him.

How could he be certain of the exact distance in the pitchy darkness?

But he must try.

He was half inclined to spring, without a run, from the extreme edge of the pit. But the flagstones were slippery as glass.

At last he felt that he could delay no longer. The sound of the voices was now distinctly audible.

He heard the sound of the bolts being withdrawn in the door at the top of the stairs.

Again he measured the distance between him and the mouth of the pit. Again stepped back.

Clenched his teeth.

Ran!

Jumped!

He was upon the other side, scarcely conscious of having passed the yawning chasm! He was clutching at the woodwork of the door.

It seemed to him, though, that the space was scarcely broad enough for him to find a resting-place for his feet. He could not stand upright.

He was clutching at the woodwork round the panel to save himself from falling back again into the pit.

It seemed to him that the door was not straight, but leant over towards the pit's mouth.

He struggled frantically to gain an upright posture—to keep his footing upon the slippery stones.

But the door seemed pressing him down.

The space appeared to get less and less.

At first he could not comprehend his horrible position. He could not understand the meaning of a creaking noise he heard around him, of which he was scarcely conscious.

But all at once the fearful truth flashed upon him.

The door was giving way!

It would press him down into the pit.

Next moment, scarcely had he realized the frightful fate in store for him, than the door fell.

He uttered a shriek as he slipped back from his landing place.

The door came down with a fearful crash and hurled him into the yawning abyss beneath.

He had a vague, indistinct notion of the flashing of lights, and a sound of several voices on the other side of the pit's mouth.

Of the despairing shriek of the wretched creature, whose rescue he had endeavoured to effect, and who again had fallen into the hands of her pitiless tormentors.

Then he fell, dashed senseless into the black gulf; and all the world became a blank to him.

CHAPTER XI.

THE SISTERS' MERCY.

CHINNERY lay for a long time stunned, bruised, and senseless.

He lay powerless, passive, and cold, yet not quite dead. Yet there existed a faint spark of existing life, torpid and flickering.

How long this state of insensibility lasted he had no means of judging. It might have been only for a few moments. It might have been days, weeks, months, years for all he knew!

When at last he slowly opened his eyes he was yet in pitchy darkness.

But he could form no notion of his whereabouts. He tried, in a hazy way, to recall the events of the last few hours.

He was still in the nunnery, he supposed. Was he still in the pit?

Had he been rescued thence and placed in one of the cells?

If in the pit, how long was his captivity likely to last? Would he ever escape with life?

He strained his eyes to pierce the dense obscurity of his prison. But in vain!

Not the faintest spark of light could he perceive in any direction.

It was not possible that any cell or dungeon could be as dark as this.

He must yet be down in the well.

He felt about upon the ground—it was wet and slimy, and one of his feet he fancied was half covered by water.

But if he was still in the well there would surely be more water than this. And yet again the well might be dry.

He could not unravel the mystery, only as he passed his hand over his clothes he found that they were saturated with moisture. He found that his hair, too, was wringing wet.

And for a moment he drew back his hand in horror, fancying that it was wet with his blood!

It was a strange sensation which had possession of him, and held him as it were enthralled!

A strange lethargy which he could not shake off.

He lay there, not caring much what became of him; but at last he felt that there was a necessity for immediate action—that he must at once make an effort to escape, if he was ever to escape again, from his horrible prison-house.

He endeavoured to rise, but he found his limbs cramped and useless.

He thought at first that his legs were broken, and after a struggle to get upon his feet, fell back again with a groan.

But after a while he renewed his endeavours, and finding the wall, crawled towards it upon his hands and knees, and got at last, by many painful efforts, into an upright posture.

But he could not maintain this position for very long. He soon found, by the pain which he suffered, that in his fall he had cut his head very badly, and had lost a large quantity of blood!

The effect of his wound was to render him sick and giddy and helpless, and presently he was obliged to lie down again upon his hard bed, uninviting as it was.

So great was the pain he suffered that for a long while he did not venture any fresh efforts.

While lying thus, he either fell asleep, or, a faintness coming over him, lapsed into a state of insensibility; for all outward objects became a blank, and he could form no idea of how long he again remained in this condition.

He opened his eyes at last to the same impenetrable darkness, but he felt to some extent refreshed, and that his strength was slowly returning.

He thought that he would try to get up again, and with great labour rolled on to his hands and knees, but he found that he could not stand.

At the first movement he fancied he heard a strange rushing noise round about him, the meaning of which he could not comprehend!

But he was still giddy, and there was a curious singing in his head, which confused him.

He rested for some time, sitting upon the ground, with his hands spread out upon either side, and while in this position something ran over one of them.

It was a rat!

In another moment he was upon his feet! He had risen with one spring, although a moment before he had felt so weak that he could not struggle into an upright posture.

His sudden movement caused apparently a panic among his fellow prisoners, of which, by the riot they made, there appeared to be a goodly company.

Chinnery staggered back against the wall, and his flesh crept with horror.

There was hardly any other foe he would not have more willingly encountered.

His terror and disgust for these loathsome animals was great.

How long was he to be left thus? How many of the wretches were there? Would they attack him?

He had little doubt of this last!

As yet they were frightened, but presently they would grow bolder. When his power to defend himself was gone they would come upon him in large numbers. He would be torn to pieces by these horrid beasts!—The flesh torn from his face—his bones picked in this hideous charnel-house!

Had he any means of defending himself?

He felt in his pocket for the knife he had placed there, but it was gone!

He felt hurriedly all over his other pockets, and found that they were all empty. He had been searched then! After all he could not be down the well, as he had supposed.

He groped his way round, keeping his hand upon the wall, and presently reached a door!

Upon feeling over it he found that it was massive and impregnable; but yet the knowledge that he had been removed from the pit gave him hope.

It would appear that it was not the intention of his captors, whoever they might be, to allow him to lie there and die.

When, however, would they come to visit him?

While he was asking himself this question he fancied he heard a noise in the passage without.

He listened! Yes, footsteps were approaching!

Next moment a small grating, in the upper part of the door, was opened, and a lantern held up to it.

Then a voice upon the outside called, "Hallo!"

Chinnery did not at first reply, but rubbing his eyes so as to be able to meet the light which, faint as it was, appeared to him after the dense obscurity of his prison-house as glaring as the sun at noon-day, peered out through the trap at the person who had spoken, and who was holding up the lantern.

Scarcely ever had it been his lot to look upon so horrible a countenance as that which presented itself to his view. It was a matter of impossibility to guess at its owner's age, though it was probably that of an old man, with a few straggling locks surrounding it, which were grey and grizzled.

The skin of the face was swollen and distended, and covered with horrible blotches. The nose appeared to have been broken and was very much on one side. The mouth, a great gash, full of ill-shaped teeth, all at sixes and sevens, to which the fact of it being lipless added a hideousness which was positively ghastly.

Chinnery could not repress a slight shudder at sight of this horrible object.

Was this his jailer?

"Hallo!" said the man without. "Are you awake yet?"

"Yes! yes! How long are you going to keep me a prisoner here?"

"I don't know how long you will be kept. I have brought you some food."

"I don't want any food; I want to come out!"

"You'd better have it; you may be hungry before you get your liberty."

"What do you mean?"

"Only what I say!"

"But you can't intend to keep me in this frightful place much longer?"

"I tell you, it is nothing to do with me!"

"Then let me out."

"I can't do that."

"I'll make it worth your while."

"It's better worth my while to keep you where you are."

And the man began to close up the trap again.

"Stop! stop!" cried Chinnery; "for God's sake do not leave me!"

"What do you want?"

"I want to get out, I tell you. It's impossible that any one could want to keep me here unless they wanted to kill me. Why should they want to do that?"

"What made you come here?"

"Because I was a fool," said Chinnery, with a groan.

"You were!" replied the other, with a horrible chuckle. "A great fool to come here of your own accord!"

"If ever I get out——"

"If ever you do, keep clear of us for the future. But the Sisters do not allow strangers to learn their secrets with impunity."

The man closed the wicket as he said this; and through another trap at the bottom of the door pushed in a stone pitcher and a loaf of bread.

As, after this, the trap was closed to, and the man was retreating, Chinnery began to shake the door violently, and to battle at it with his fist, calling with all his might upon his jailer to come back.

The man returned and opened the upper trap.

"It's no good making that noise," he said. "Not a soul can hear you or help you. I shall not come back again if you call ever so loud."

"For mercy's sake don't leave me here then unarmed, to be devoured by rats!"

"Rats?"

"Yes; the place is swarming with the vermin."

"They wont hurt you."

"They'll only eat me alive."

"Not they! They'll be afraid to touch you if you leave them alone!"

"Stop! stop! I say; for Heaven's sake do not take away the light. Do not leave me in the dark."

"You can see as well without a light as I can with one," replied the jailer, grinning.

The horrified prisoner looking towards him, saw that the man's eyes were sightless. He was evidently stone-blind!

"Leave me the lantern, then! It can be no use to you."

"I don't know whether I ought to do so. In fact I am sure the Sisters would not allow it. But I'll do so if you think you'll be more comfortable."

He closed the top trap again, and thrust the lantern through at the lower one.

JACK CHINNERY IS STABBED BY THE JAILER IN THE DARK DUNGEON.

The prisoner eagerly clutched it.

Then the door was closed, and the jailor without another word retired.

Chinnery listened until his footsteps were no longer audible, and then looked around him and endeavoured to obtain a more comprehensive notion of his dungeon than he had hitherto had the opportunity of doing.

It was truly a horrible place in which he found himself. The floor wet and filthy, with small pools of stagnant water standing here and there.

There was no window, loophole, or opening of any kind, except the door, which was of such a massive nature that without tools it was an impossibility to force his way out in that direction.

No ! escape seemed to be perfectly hopeless. He was in the power of some merciless wretches, and had nought to look forward to but death to release him from his dreadful captivity.

And yet it was perfectly incredible that such should be his fate in the heart of London, the most civilized city in the world, but a few hundred yards removed from a leading thoroughfare teeming with busy life.

How could such horrors be perpetrated ? How could such a place exist as this nunnery into which he had penetrated ?

And yet it did exist as surely as there was a sky shining unseen above him.

Without an effort he recalled many strange stories of outrage and assassination which had been perpetrated, and the guilty parties never discovered.

Well did he know that in this great city Death walked hand in hand with Life ; and there were all kinds of horrible mysteries yet to be unravelled.

But never in all his experience of the dark side of existence, thief and convict as he was, had he come across anything at all to equal the inner mysteries and horrors of this dark abode of secret crime, where he now found himself a helpless captive.

If ever he gained his liberty again—an event of which he had but very little hope—he determined he would leave no stone unturned until he rooted out this nest of horrors—until he had succeeded in liberating such wretched victims as might still be languishing at the mercy of the Sisters.

Before he could do this, however, he must obtain his own liberty.

And when he reflected upon the difficulties which lay in his path, the hopelessness of the case almost crushed him.

He felt so weak and ill from loss of blood and want of food that he was not at all in the right sort of condition to make the attempt.

The food which had been provided for him, when he came to inspect it, was of such a character as would not have been ventured upon by any one in any state short of absolute starvation.

The bread was as hard as a stone, the water dirty and foul smelling.

Chinnery turned away in disgust, and as he suspected that the candle given to him by the blind jailor would not last a very long while, he thought it best to make good use of his time, and go a tour of inspection round the cell.

The result, however, was most unsatisfactory. He found that it was quite impossible to open the door, or to open the two small traps in it, which latter if he could have done he might have hoped to have been able to have passed out his arm and pulled back the bolts.

No, nothing could be done in that way. But an artful scheme suggested itself to him.

He would wait until the jailor came, and pretend to be dead. The jailor might then come into the cell, and he would then be able to spring up and rush suddenly out.

In the meantime, however, he could do nothing but wait as patiently as might be.

There was no seat of any kind in the dungeon, no straw for him to lie upon, and the floor was revoltingly dirty. But yet he was so fatigued and weary that he felt that he must rest.

He stood up a long while, leaning against the wall. Then he sat upon the floor, nursing his knees, and still leaning. Finding this position, however, in the end to become very irksome, he eventually laid down at full length.

He had not been thus very long, when the rats begun to come out.

CHAPTER XII.

THE BATTLE WITH THE RATS.

At the first appearance of his disgusting companions, Jack Chinnery shouted out loudly to scare them away.

His cries had the desired effect. They all scuttled back into their holes.

But not to remain very long.

They came out in larger numbers than ever.

Several times he shouted loudly; but when they found no great harm came to them, they lost all fear, and approaching closer, began to nibble at his hair and his boots.

Up he jumped, and performed a kind of war-dance, screaming at the top of his voice.

In a moment the enemy had retired to their entrenchments, and he was master of the situation.

But presently, when he was lying down again, they began to peep out of their holes, and to crawl towards him, and to nibble away as before.

They took a great fancy to the lantern—surrounded it, scrambled on the top of it, and knocked it over.

Again Chinnery shouted, and waved his arms, and kicked in all directions; but as he did not get upon his feet, and chase his enemy round the cell, they would not retreat altogether, but defied him from distant corners.

He was so dreadfully sleepy, he could not for the life of him keep his eyes open very long at a time. He began to doze again. But a great crash awoke him.

The lantern had been overthrown, and a rat was making off with the lighted candle.

He gave chase, but was too late. The robber escaped, carrying the booty with him.

What was he to do now? Would it be safe for him to go to sleep, surrounded by these savage and dangerous beasts?

But could he possibly keep awake, without the aid of a light?

He weakly persuaded himself that he could do so, lying upon his back; but he had not been in this position very long, before he had closed his eyes and was slumbering.

He awoke suddenly, with an indescribable sensation of pain and suffocation.

A sharp pang at his throat aroused him; and as he opened his eyes, he felt some cold, heavy object sprawling over his face.

He sprang up, and screamed, and struggled.

He had been set upon and half worried by the horrible vermin with which the cell was swarming.

He rushed up and down, shaking the brutes from him as he went. He trampled upon and smashed them beneath his feet.

The whole floor seemed alive with the revolting monsters; and again and again they flew upwards, aiming at his face.

He came in the course of the struggle to the spot where he had left the stone pitcher, and seizing this in both hands, he waved it wildly round him, and dashed it here and there, until it was broken to pieces.

Nothing could well exceed the horror of the scene. The terrified prisoner, bruised and bleeding, rushing frantically from side to side of his cell, warding off the expected attacks of his unseen enemies. The hideous foe—some dead—some dying—some crouching, wounded and vindictive, with glittering eyes and snarling teeth.

How long this strange and awful contest continued, it would be impossible to say. Utterly worn out and exhausted, he fell at length upon the ground, unable any longer to prolong the fight.

It was now that, having him at their mercy, the rats might have swarmed upon him, and worried him, and torn the flesh from his face, and hands, and throat; but the jailor, hearing some of the disturbance probably, came back to ascertain the cause.

He groped his way to the door, drew back the bolts, and called out, as before—

"Hallo!"

At the sound of his voice, Jack Chinnery, exerting all the strength which yet remained, rose as noiselessly as possible to his feet.

But he made no answer.

"Don't you hear me?" the blind man said. "Where have you got to?"

Chinnery crouched close to the wall, and kept perfectly still.

"Hallo! hallo!" cried the blind man again. "Are you gone to sleep?"

No answer.

The jailor paused, and appeared to listen.

"What's up with him, I wonder?" Chinnery heard him mutter.

Then he came groping his way cautiously into the cell. Before he had gone very far, he kicked his foot against something, and stooped to pick it up.

It was a dead rat.

"Hallo!" said the jailor. "There's been a battle. Here's one of the slain."

A step or so further on he found something else.

This was a wounded rat, which, when he picked it up, turned upon and bit him.

This put a stop to further investigation, as far as the rats were concerned. Indeed, coming accidentally on to the loaf, he jumped nearly half a yard high, fancying that he had knocked against some patriarch of the rat-tribe, which next moment would fasten on his throat.

"Hallo! hallo!" the jailor cried, now pausing in the middle of the cell, and calling out at the top of his voice, "Where are you? What's become of you? What's the matter?"

He, however, received no reply, and went on, after a pause, groping his way into a remote corner.

He passed by Chinnery, with his outstretched fingers scarcely six inches from the prisoner's breast.

Jack kept as close as possible to the wall. He would have screwed himself into the stones if he had been able.

He held his breath, and noiselessly felt his way towards the door.

Never in his life before had he felt such an awful desire to get over so short a space of ground in so short a space of time. He still wore his list slippers, but his feet appeared to him to drag heavily upon the ground, with a noise which he fancied must be audible to the jailor.

He took his steps with the greatest possible caution; but yet he could not help kicking his foot against one of the objects lying in his path. It was a piece of the broken pitcher.

Driven before his foot, it skimmed the flags of the cell after the manner known to stone-throwers as a "duck-and-drake," and clattered against the opposite wall.

The blind man immediately made a dart at the spot where it fell, and thumped his head tremendously against the wall.

He was perfectly silent and motionless after this, listening, perhaps; though Chinnery, in spite of the terror of the situation, could not help chuckling a little as he thought how his companion must have punished that ugly head of his.

"He was no beauty to begin with," thought Chinnery. "But if he goes on that way, he'll make his head as big as two."

But he had no time for joking, and he crept on, cautiously making for the door.

But when he reached the spot where he supposed he would find it, he discovered that he had made a miscalculation. He was against the wall.

Now he must grope his way round, and feel for it.

The question was, which way?

Having once made a mistake, he could now form no notion whereabouts he was likely to find it. Of course, under ordinary circumstances, it would have been easy enough; but with the fear of running into the arms of the blind man, the matter became fearfully perplexing.

But it must either be to the right or to the left. He chose the right, and chose the wrong.

At the point from which he started he was, at the most, twelve inches from the door. He consequently set off to make the whole tour of the room.

Scarcely had he made three steps forward, however, before the death-like silence reigning in the cell warned him that the blind man was listening. Chinnery stood perfectly still, listening also.

So complete was the stillness, that the captive fancied that the violent throbbing of his heart must have been audible.

He clenched his teeth, and strove to hold his breath, straining his sense of hearing with painful intensity.

But so long did the silence endure, that he almost fancied the jailor must have fallen in a swoon upon the ground.

But then a horrible suspicion flashed across his mind!

The blind man was also muffling his footsteps, and crawling silently in the dark.

It was the case. The jailor suspecting treachery, had unsheathed a dagger-knife he carried with him, and was cautiously feeling his way back to the door, prepared for an attack.

Scarcely a step did either man take without pausing to listen before creeping on again through the pitchy darkness.

The jailor had also lost his calculation respecting the situation of the outlet, and as the darkness was as great without as within, had he, like Chinnery, had his power of sight, it would have been no service to him.

Onward they stole, and so cautiously did they pick their steps that not the faintest sound of their movements was audible.

On and on they worked their way, feeling gently for the obstacles which they anticipated might lie in their path, and noiselessly removing them; but at last the jailor stumbled over a piece of the pitcher and staggered against the wall. At the same time catching at it to save himself, he let fall his knife.

Chinnery heard the rattle of the steel upon the flags, and the knowledge that his antagonist was armed added fresh terror to the situation.

His only hope was that he might not be able to find the weapon again.

"If I could only get to the door now," thought Chinnery. "If the pitcher was not broken, and I had it in my hand, I would wager a hundred pounds I could hit him, though it's in the dark."

As it was, however, he thought a better opportunity could hardly occur of making up for lost time. He would make a rush.

He had already gone round two sides of the room. Luck must indeed be against him if the door was in the fourth instead of the third side. He would run for it.

He wasted no more time in considering. While the jailor was groping for the fallen knife, he made a rush.

He ran straight into the blind man's arms. They came together with a stunning shock, which threw them both to the ground.

In an instant they had scrambled to their feet again.

The jailor, clutching his knife, struck out at random in the darkness. The blow took effect. It pierced the prisoner's left hand, and pinned it quivering to the wall.

For the moment the agony was so intense that Chinnery could scarce forbear from shrieking aloud as he writhed with the blade still fixed and deeply imbedded in his flesh.

But with an awful effort he stifled the cry that rose up to his lips, and kept perfectly still.

The jailor drew out the knife, little thinking how near his enemy was; and stood listening for the sound of his footsteps.

Next moment, Chinnery, who with the other hand had stood grasping the door-post, bounded out into the passage and slammed to the door.

Frantically he scrambled after the bolts—shot one to, and flung himself against the panels.

Scarce had he done it, though, before the jailor was hammering furiously at the other side.

Struggling and wrenching, and heaving against the woodwork, which, however, placed all his efforts at defiance.

"Not if I know it," said Chinnery, with something like the ghost of a chuckle, as he bound his handkerchief around his bleeding hand. "Damn you—you're there, and there you'll stick!"

"Let me out," yelled the blind man, still drubbing with his fists upon the panel.

"Not if I know it," retorted Chinnery.

"Let me out! Let me out!"

"Take your turn with the rats!"

"I shall be eaten alive!"

"I hope so."

A savage howl followed these words, and the blind man began wildly to stab at the door with his knife.

But the result of this mad freak was to break off the point. He was fairly caught in his own trap, and Chinnery held all the trump cards in his hand. He was determined also to play the remainder of the game out to the best advantage.

"If I only had a light," he thought, "I would soon make my way out of this infernal place; or if I had that blind villain's keys they might be some use to me."

He thought he would negotiate.

To begin with, he kicked at the door, calling to the jailor to hold his noise.

"You're in a fix, you see," said Chinnery, "and you can't get out of it without my help."

The blind man howled.

In about a couple of hours' time you will probably be eaten. I should have been if you had not kindly come to my assistance."

Another howl from the inside.

"As your only hope lies with me, you must agree to my terms."

"I wont agree to anything."

"Very well, then—die your own way. Good night!"

"Stay! stay! Don't go like that. What do you want me to do?"

"I want your keys!"

"I haven't got any."

"Very well. Good night, then."

"Stop a minute."

"What is it?"

"If you open the door I'll give them to you."

"Not if I know it!"

"Well, what do you want me to do?"

"Put them through the top trap."

"Very well. If you come close to it on your side, I'll hand them to you."

"Hand them, then."

Chinnery heard the keys rattling.

"Are you close to the trap?" said the blind man.

"Yes."

"Don't let them fall, then. Where's your hand?"

"At the trap."

Next moment thud went the blind man's knife into the woodwork.

Chinnery, whose hand was not there at the time, felt considerably relieved by the thought that he had once more outwitted his antagonist; but he at the same time, as may be supposed, felt wonderfully savage.

He heard the old wretch chuckling, but pretended not to have detected his treachery.

"Why don't you hand the keys?" he said.

The blind man reluctantly thrust them forward, but snatched them back again very quickly, saying—

"If I give 'em you, you'll leave me here!"

"You'll have to trust in me in any case. If you don't give them to me you stand no chance of getting out. If you do give them without any more of your tricks, perhaps I shall take mercy on you."

The jailer considered for a few moments, and then growled out—

"Here they are."

But again he made a feint; for he only thrust out his hand, intending to grasp his companion's hand and drag it through the trap. This time, however, the biter was bitten.

Chinnery feeling his hand there, suddenly slammed to the trap.

The most awful howl proved that the blind man was suffering almost as much as the other had done awhile ago.

"That's 'tit for tat,'" said Chinnery. "I owed you one, my fine fellow."

The blind man struggled with all his might and main, but Chinnery remorselessly held tight the trap, and kept him prisoner.

His desperate efforts, however, availed him nought, and at last, when his strength was entirely exhausted, he sobbed and whined, and in the end came to terms.

"If you let me loose, I'll give you the keys."

"Give me them without, if you please."

"How can I?"

"Put them through the bottom trap."

"I can't."

"Yes you can."

"I can't, I tell you."

"Try."

"Oh dear! Oh dear!"

"If you don't, I sha'n't let go."

"Oh, you hard man! Oh, what torture! Oh! I can't."

"Take your own time, only you'll have to do it before I let go of you."

"Oh, Lord! Oh, Lord! Oh, what agony!"

"Shall I pinch a little tighter?"

The blind man howled frightfully.

"Be quick!" said Chinnery; "or I shall get a little out of patience."

And as a reminder, he squeezed the trap to slightly, and wrung from the blind man a yell more terrific than any which preceded it.

"Come, now, will you give me the keys?"

"Ye-es."

"Do so, then."

"Let me loose first."

"No."

"Only a little."

"No."

"Oh Lord! Oh Lord!"

"Give me the keys."

"Oh! oh!"

"The keys."

"Oh! oh! oh!"

"The keys, I say."

The keys at length were flung through the lower trap, accompanied by a bitter curse, when the blind man could no longer endure the agony which the pinching of his hand occasioned him. Then Chinnery picked them up, fastened both traps, and groped his way cautiously along the passage.

Very cautiously indeed, for he was fearful lest at any moment he should again tumble into the pit-hole from which he had been raised before he was thrown into the dungeon he had just escaped from.

After he had crawled along for a time, he found himself at the bottom of a flight of stone steps—probably the steps he had originally descended. He mounted to the top, and found a door the lock of which one of the keys opened.

The sound of the blind man's cries had gradually grown fainter and fainter. He was shaking the door now, trying to force it open.

Chinnery chose this moment for passing out into the passage above.

As he did so, and closed the door behind him, the house was silent as the grave.

The passage was dark, too, as upon the occasion when he passed through it before.

What time was it? A day must have passed. It was again night.

The inmates of the convent slept, and he could now, if he chose, very easily effect his escape.

But still he hesitated.

"I would give the world," he said to himself, "to know a little more of the mysteries of this place. Why shouldn't I now?"

CHAPTER XIII.

THE ARREST.

It was noon before the servant at Gerald Wilde's lodgings came to tidy the sitting-room, light the fire, and lay the breakfast things. It was a somewhat irregular household, that in which the young medical man resided, and as a rule he was not a very early riser, so that his rooms were not set to rights very often until the afternoon.

The servant-girl entering upon this particular occasion, found the lodger stretched upon the sofa, with his head hanging down upon one side, looking very black and swollen, and horrible in the yellow light of a foggy November morning.

She thought at first that he was dead—such a ghastly appearance did his face and figure present—and she raised a woful howl at the sight of him, letting fall her dust-pan and brush.

He struggled into an upright posture, however, aroused by the noise, and asked with an oath what she was bawling about.

"Lor'! sir, how you frightened me!"

"I frightened you?"

"Yes, sir; I thought sir, that you was—"

"Was what?"

"Nothing sir; only you frightened me, seeing you lying like that."

"I suppose I can lie as I choose in my own lodgings," growled the young doctor, turning over with his face towards the wall.

"Haven't you been to-bed, sir?"

"No!"

"Oh! lor'! Why it's past twelve o'clock. Shall I get you any breakfast?"

"No. I can't eat anything. Get me some tea and a quartern of brandy, and don't make a noise with that fireplace. I don't want any fire lit. I'm going out."

The servant-girl went away rather scared by Wilde's manner, and carefully closed the door after her. She returned presently with the refreshment he had ordered, to which, upon her own responsibility, she had added a red-herring.

Wilde rose from his uneasy couch, and with a number of oaths directed against all things animate and inanimate which the house contained, swallowed a few mouthfuls of food, took a saucerful of tea, drank up the brandy, and lit a cigar.

He opened the window of his sitting-room, and resting his head upon his hand, stared out at the smoky square which lay in front of the house, unutterably dismal and woe begone, with its lank, leafless trees, stunted bushes, grass-grown paths, and rusty iron railings.

"A pretty thing to cheer one's spirits, that is!" he said, as he gloomily contemplated this dreary scene.

An organ-man catching sight of him, stopped in front of the house, and commenced a selection of popular tunes, but Wilde roared to him, with a curse, to go about his business. Then a beggar came up and solicited alms, and was in like fashion anathematized.

Then the surly sot cursed the day for being so dark, and the sun for shining so dimly, and the window-sill for being so hard to lean upon, and the cigar for going out; but, above all, he cursed his own fate for having been born so poor.

"There's not a fellow I used to know at the university that hasn't got on better than I have," he muttered savagely. "But I have no luck. They've all had a chance, but I never had—I never shall have. Nobody in the world will give me a helping hand if I ask 'em. Nobody ever did. And as for that pale-faced fiend, with the golden hair, what have I to expect from her? Nothing but a knife in my heart in the dark! She'd like to see me dead—I know that well enough; and if she sets her mind on killing me, ecod! my life's not worth a week's purchase. Bah! I'm not afraid of her,

though. She sha'n't cow me with her frowns and her flashing snake's eyes. I'll go to her this very day, and ask her for some money. I will, by Heaven!"

He set about making his toilet, which he had not completed, until nearly three o'clock. Then he wandered out into the streets. He felt so out of sorts that before making the call which he contemplated, he thought he would go and have a chop and a pint of wine at the Cock in Fleet-street.

Although so poor, it must not be supposed that he walked, although the distance was not very great In the same way, while complaining of his poverty, he was smoking expensive cigars, and he now selected an expensive tavern instead of one of those cheap eating-houses with which London abounds, and where one would have thought a needy person would have been more likely to have gone.

He stopped the hackney carriage just before he arrived at the narrow passage leading up to the famous hostelry, and tossing the jarvey his fare, flung away the stump of his cigar as he stepped down upon the pavement.

Just before him was a waggon, blocking up the road, and a coach for the last twenty yards after passing through Temple Bar, had been proceeding only at a walking pace; therefore, two men who had been standing under an archway at the opening of a court leading towards Lincoln's-inn Fields, and who had caught sight of Wilde's face, and whispered together eagerly, had been able to follow in the rear of the coach, and now stood waiting for the fare to alight.

Almost at the same moment that Wilde stepped upon the pavement, one of these men laid his hand upon his shoulder.

"Mr. Wilde, sir, I think?" said the man, and Wilde turning, saw before his eyes an ominous slip of parchment, upon which he traced the words—

"By the grace of God greeting"—"that you take the body of Gerard Wilde and him safely keep"—"and for so doing this shall be your warrant."

There were other words as well, but though Wilde read only these, and a sum of money, amounting to something more than fifty pounds sterling, he required no elaborate explanation to understand that he had been arrested for debt.

"All right," he said; "I'm going in here to have something to eat—you had better come too. But stay—p'rhaps we had better go into Peele's."

He had some doubts whether his companion would pass muster at the place where he was at first thinking of getting his lunch.

"I don't mind taking a little something, Mr. Wilde; in course, and many thanks to yer! But of course my time ain't exactly my own, nor more is my mate's here—asking your pardon for alludin' to him."

The gentleman alluded to, whose chief peculiarities were a large red nose and a very greasy white hat, made a low bow, and wiped his nose on the sleeve of his coat.

"The gennelman 'll give you 'arf a crown to go an' amuse yerself with, Sam'ls," said the man, who had hitherto spoken, "he don't want to be seen along o' the likes o' you out in a public thoro'fare."

The gentleman with the nose, who seemed to think it a great joke that anyone should be ashamed to be seen with him, expressed his willingness to make himself scarce, and pocketing the half-crown which was given to him, said in a stage-whisper to the sheriff's officer—

"I shall be handy if wanted."

Then taking off his hat, with another low bow, he bonneted himself and shuffled off.

The person left with Gerard Wilde, who was no other than the famous Mr. Moses McKnab, of the Middlesex bailiwick, with whom many in difficulties must have had the pleasure some time or other of making the acquaintance, was a tall and rather dashing, though a trifle too dirty and greasy a gentleman, dressed in a fashionable style, with what seemed to be a small fortune in watch-guards, rings, and neck-pins, all of which he wore double.

When they arrived at Peele's coffee-house, Wilde ordered a pint of wine for his companion, and the recent capture having somehow or other deprived him of his appetite, he himself called for writing materials, and sat down to pen a letter to those among his acquaintance who he thought most likely to accommodate with a temporary loan ; for it is perhaps unnecessary to state that in spite of his complaints of want of assistance, he had all his life through been helped over and over again by every one he had come in contact with.

"I've had a deal of trouble catching you, Mr. Wilde," said Mr. McKnab, as he sipped his wine. "Dear heart, what a dance you have led us. This is about the sixth time I've had the pleasure I think—"

"I dare say," replied Wilde surlily.

"I suppose it can be arranged?"

"I hope so."

"That's right !" said Mr. McKnab. "If you can get the money it's much better to pay at once, tho' I think there's some pals o' yours up at the hold drum, and you might get thro' a Sunday very comfortable."

Wilde groaned in reply, and went on writing. Mr. McKnab, however, launched into a somewhat lengthy lament upon the folly of gentlemen letting things go too far. He ran through the particulars of the case in hand for Mr. Wilde's especial benefit, saying, "That's how things is done." The sheriff of Middlesex had had, he said, a writ of *fi-fa*, or *fieri facias* against Mr. Wilde's goods, but the lodgings having been visited, and the scanty supply of luggage inspected, a return of *nulla bona*, or no goods, had been made ; when a *ca-sa* or *capias ad satisfaciendum* was taken out against Mr. Wilde's body, or, as Mr. McKnab termed it, though without any intention of disrespect, "carcase," by the aid of which awful instrument Mr. Wilde had been effectually "nobbled."

"As soon as you've done talking," said the doctor, angrily, "and will do me the favour of holding your tongue, I will write my letters."

Mr. McKnab begged a thousand pardons, sipped his wine, and subsided into silence.

Four or five letters did the doctor write to as many of his friends, determined that he would leave no stone unturned ; in case help failed him at one quarter it might come from another.

"Hang them ! they're just as likely all to refuse," he said, as he sealed the last epistle. "But it's worth trying—and it's better than parting with my watch, at any rate, because I shall have to get that out again."

"We'll send the notes by Sam'ls, if you like, sir ?"

"Yes."

Mr. McKnab stepped to the door, and raising his finger mysteriously in the air, beckoned forth, as it were from the bowels of the earth, the attendant sprite with the nose. To him the letters were confided ; and then Mr. McKnab came back to ask where Gerard Wilde would like to go.

"Can't I stop here?"

"Till the answers comes?"

"To be sure !"

"That might be some time, mightn't it ?"

"Perhaps. Let us go, then."

"I think it would be better, sir, if you don't mind."

"Where to ?"

"To where you choose, sir, of course. To Choker's, shall we say? Or to the hold drum at once?"

"I'll go to Cursitor-street for an hour or two."

They called a coach, for Wilde did not fancy walking through the street with his friend who was so well known in that part of the town ; and they proceeded at once to the house of the before-named Choker, officer to the Sheriff of Middlesex.

Here they found the windows very strongly barred, and the doors very tightly locked and bolted ; but at Mr. McKnab's knock admission was soon obtained, and Choker with open arms came forth to meet them.

Wilde refused an offer of a private room, but went up-stairs into the coffee-room—a dreary apartment, smelling strongly of tobacco-smoke—where a rakish-looking young gentleman, of about eighteen years of age, was playing at cards with a bald-headed and benevolent divine, who smoked a long clay pipe.

Here, seating himself by the fireside, Wilde plunged his hands deeply into his trousers pockets, and gave himself up to his reflections, which were not of the most agreeable character. In a while Mr. Sam'ls returned with the answers to the notes Wilde had written. They were very unsatisfactory.

One of his friends had gone out of town ; another might be back in five minutes, but might not be back all night, and Mr. Sam'ls had been advised not to wait. Another would have been "very happy to oblige you, old boy," but he was unfortunately at this moment, as he expressed it, "awfully hard up." The last hope replied in a few words, to the effect that he would see Mr. Gerard Wilde hanged before he would lend him another penny ; but he would be glad to have some of the money back again with which, like a fool, he upon previous occasions had parted

Wilde crumpled up the last letter in his hand, and flung it from him with a curse.

"I ought to have written to her !" he muttered. "She would have sent it. I must have it But, no ! It would be foolish to spoil my chance for such a trifle. I will go to Whitecross-street, and write to the vagabond who locked me up. I shall get out for paying something down, I suppose, and giving a new bill. That will be the way to manage it."

He determined not to remain any longer than he could help at Choker's, as a sojourn in that gentleman's hospitable abode was extremely expensive. As it was, he had about fifteen shillings to pay for the use of the coffee-room, and a glass of brandy-and-water ; and having made a small present to a number of dirty-looking Jews, who turned up at unexpected junctures, pulling their forelocks and bowing low as he passed down-stairs, he got out into the street, and into a cab, and he and Mr. McKnab were shortly afterwards on their way to the debtors' prison.

As they rode along, Wilde's companion entertained him with stories of remarkable captures he had effected in times gone by.

"I once potted a live bishop," said he. "He was part proprietor of a music-hall, that didn't answer, over on the Surrey side, and an awful show-up there would have been about it, if he couldn't have got out on Sunday morning in time for service at the Cathedral. It was me that took Charley Flathers, the actor, and a hard job that was, I can tell you, when we waited for him at all the wings, five or six of us, and he gave us the double by going down a trap. Bless you ! they used to say he came to the house of a night in a double-bass case, and was carried away in a tin box that was supposed to contain Madame's dresses. Howsomedever, I did nobble him in the end, though he pulled me on to the stage, and rigged me finely before the audience. I took him up in the flies, where he had gone to in Jupiter's car at the end of the extravaganza ; and a devil of a fight I had up in the celestial regions with him and Jupiter and a couple of cherry-bims, as was in private life the sons of the stage-carpenter, and let me have it scandalous with their Blucher-boots while my back was turned to 'm."

Wilde had been by this time several hours in custody, and it was quite dark.

They stopped before the prison-door, walked up a steep flight of steps, and the prisoner having been delivered over to the safe keeping of the jail authorities, Mr. McKnab bade him good night.

Then the door banged to behind him with a sullen clang, and Gerard walked forward into the prison.

CHAPTER XIV.

"BURDON'S HOTEL," WHITECROSS-STREET.

THE first night Wilde was in Whitecross-street Prison, he spent it alone in a dreary place called the Reception Ward. He slept upon an iron bedstead, in a room with a cold stone floor. He went to-bed at a very early hour—several hours before his usual retiring time, and was alone and remarkably miserable, lying awake for hours listening to the sound of voices without the prison walls. Next morning a turnkey woke him up unreasonably early, and conducted him to what he called the Middle-sex side, which was a long, dirty-looking yard, upon each side of which were several doors leading into coffee-rooms and wards, and conducting by staircases to bed-rooms above.

None ot the prisoners were about, and the morning was remarkably cold, and bleak, and miserable.

Wilde was taken into one of the wards, and left there.

It was a large room, with cross tables and benches, and windows secured by many bars. There was a large fire burning at one end, and at this several persons were sitting—prisoners, as Wilde supposed. Some were smoking pipes and drinking beer, early as it was. They were mostly unshorn, seedy, and slipshod; and there was about all of them a jail-bird look impossible to mis-take.

The turnkey took Wilde up to a stout, jovial, and rather red-faced man, in a suit of very dirty check-tweed, whom he introduced to him as the steward of the ward; and this person at once allotted to him a seat at one of the tables, in consideration of an entrance-fee of one guinea, entitling him to have his boots cleaned, his meals cooked, and his bed made.

The steward receiving the money smiled, and explained that in case Wilde had not been able to have paid it, he would have been allowed three days' grace, and would, at the expiration of that time, had the money not been forthcoming, have been obliged to remove to the poor side of the prison, when Government would kindly have provided for him the sum of three and six-pence a week to purchase his food.

The steward then informed him that if he chose he could purchase anything at a shop in the yard, and the cook would prepare it for him if he liked, or if he did not like the trouble he might dine at his—the steward's—table.

Wilde had some breakfast, and then lounged out into the yard, and stared dreamily about him upon his seedy fellow-prisoners. Such seedy ones they all were. Such poor, spiritless, shuffling, white-faced fellows. The only man with anything like a complexion, or with anything brisk and hearty about him that Wilde could see, was one of the turnkeys upon the "lock," who was nursing a chubby baby, and whistling to a bullfinch in a cage.

Wilde lounged wearily about, staring at the other seedy prisoners, and wondering who they were, and what they were in for; until, all at once, while he was basking in half a foot's breadth of sunshine, which some-how or other had crept between the bars into the yard, a shrill, broken voice called to him by name.

Wilde glanced upwards, and saw at a short distance from him a rather remarkable-looking young man in a magnificently flowered dressing-gown, splendidly em-broidered Turkish smoking-cap, and a pair of velvet slippers, covered with gold thread, but rather dusty and soiled with beer-stains.

The individual thus attired was certainly a remark-ably silly-looking, fat-faced youth, with a great mouth, rather on one side. His hair was parted down the middle, he had great goggle eyes, inclined to be weak, and about twenty hairs in a line on his upper lip.

"Hallo, Wilde!" he called out; "hallo, old fellow! —demme! if I'm not glad to see you! I am, upon my soul—demme!"

"Mr. Winder," said Wilde, "the pleasure's mutual, I can assure you. I found it awfully slow in here the little while I have been, and it's a great bore, you know; but I was taken quite unexpectedly, and those infernal lawyers of mine, who have some thousands in their hands, made some fuss about—and so, in fact—"

"You were nabbed!" screamed Mr. Winder, bursting into a shrill laugh, digging his friend in the ribs, and staggering back a pace or two to look at him, while he gasped. "How do you like it, old fellow? Were you ever in Burdon's Hotel before? It doesn't quite come up to the Burlington, does it? although there's capital accommodation for man and beast—particularly beast. That's not bad, Wilde, is it? I made it, demme!"

Mr. Wilde laughed as heartily as if the joke had con-tained the concentrated wit of twenty volumes of *Punch*. It was not difficult to see that he had his reasons for being polite to this very gorgeously attired, goggle-eyed young gentleman.

"I've been here ever so many times before, demme!" continued Mr. Winder; "and I don't mind it a bit. I'm always paid out, you know. I'm like an eight-day clock, that runs down and is pulled up again. Some of the Jews heard I was going to be married to-morrow, and they came down on me. Dooced awkward, isn't it? demme!"

"I hope it wont cause your wedding to be post-poned," said Wilde.

"Bless you! no. Why should it? I shall be paid out, I tell you, the same as usual, this afternoon. Only a fellow likes to do what he chooses with the two or three days before he gets married. That's the bore, you know. I expect the lawyer-fellow here with the tin in an hour's time, or a couple of hours at the most; and I tell you what—he shall pay you out, too, demme!"

"My dear fellow!" cried Wilde, "I couldn't think of it. I should never forgive myself."

"What for? It's all right, You can pay me back again to-morrow, or any time, demme! The money's yours if I have it. What are you in for? Is it over a hundred?"

"My dear Winder, I'm ashamed to tell you what it is. It's the most measly sum. But, as I told you last night, I was taken all by surprise."

"Well, I don't care, demme! what it is. My lawyer fellow will look to all that. Let's stash it, and talk of something else. How are you, for instance?"

"Pretty well, thank you," said Wilde, taking his cheerful friend's arm. "You can't have been keeping it up here, surely?"

"Gad! haven't we, though. The whole ward was blind drunk at my expense last night. An old chap here, who's a broken-kneed rector, or something of that sort, is supposed to have a private still somewhere up the chimney. Though I say I think he makes it square with the governor, who stands in to share the plunder, demme! And it's the finest gin you ever tasted in all your life, and only a shilling a quartern, demme!"

"Who have you got here in the way of notorieties?"

"We're rather slack just at present; for anybody who's in for any time gets the *habeas* and is moved on to Belvedere Place. But there are one or two celebri-ties. The short, stout man over there is the Lord Chief Baron. He's capital company. That's Charley Flathers, the actor. That queer-looking old gent in the gig-lamps is always here for contempt of court; but he don't look very cheeky, does he? The party in the wonder-ful waistcoat is in for the costs of a breach of promise of marriage case. He's as rich as Crœsus, but wont shell out, to spite the lady."

They walked about, pacing the yard from end to end

very wearily, and Mr. Winder repeatedly consulted his watch, to see whether the time had not almost arrived which had been fixed for the visit of his "lawyer fellow."

"I shall really take it as a great favour," he said, "if you will allow me, Wilde, to pay you out; because I want you to do me a good turn, and I know I can count upon you."

"You know there's nothing you could ask me that I would not do," said Wilde, wringing his hand.

"I'll tell you all about it to-night after my supper-party. You must be there, of course. We shall have roaring fun, for it's the last spread that I can give while I'm a free man. So mind, now, you do not sell me, demme!"

"You may depend on me," said Wilde, wringing his hand again. "I would come if it was from the other end of the world."

"You were always a trump," said Mr. Winder. "So have another cigar, and let's make our miserable minds happy till they come to take us out."

But still they walked wearily to and fro from one end to the other of the paved yard, waiting for the release, which was a long while coming.

"You'd better come as a visitor to my table," said Winder. "We've got roast pork. Have you ever tasted it? I've had it every day since I've been here; and it's the jolliest lark I know, demme!"

Wilde went away with his friend in the direction indicated, and they endeavoured to wile away a portion of the weary time yet to wait, by partaking of the culinary delicacies prepared for them by the broken-kneed rector before alluded to.

It was late in the afternoon, however, before the long-looked-for money arrived. Then there was another delay in procuring the release of Mr. Gerard Wilde.

"Hang it! old fellow," said Winder, when he heard the amount of the detainer against his medical friend. "How was it you did not pay yourself out?"

"Because I couldn't," replied Wilde, with a roar of laughter.

"Why not?" asked Winder, looking rather blank.

"Those infernal lawyer fellows of mine," said Wilde, "they were keeping me in to spite me."

CHAPTER XV.

A GAY SUPPER-PARTY.

"Hurrah! hurrah! hurrah!"

"One cheer more," cried Tommy Watkins, the wit of the party. And another cheer was accorded.

"A little one in," screamed Tommy. And a deafening yell rent the air.

Mr. Winder's supper-party was upon its last legs. So were his guests. Some, indeed, had no legs to stand upon. Nor had they had for some time past. One had gone to sleep on the sofa, and one was sitting outside in the passage among the dirty plates, with a morose and melancholy expression of countenance of a somewhat greenish hue.

The fun had been fast and furious, but it had died out an hour or so ago, and the affair by this time was getting not a little disorderly and very slow. Some of the gayest men about town were present, and the choicest sprigs of fashion. The Honourable Jemmy Mac's grey hair might have been seen looming through the tobacco-smoke. There were also Lord Alfred and Lord William, Mademoiselle Château-Renard, from the King's Theatre, magnificently attired, and very tipsy.

Two ladies who had come in their own equipages, and had been as mincing as might be in the early part of the evening, had just had a dreadful row about some cause unknown, and would have settled their difference in the pugilistic fashion, had not the Honourable Jemmy thrown himself gallantly between them, and received the wrath of both about his head and shoulders.

Mr. Winder getting upon his legs to return thanks for the hearty, not to say uproarous fashion in which his health had been proposed and responded to, said that, dem him! it was the happiest moment in his life; when recollecting that he would soon have to say the same thing on a somewhat dissimilar occasion, he burst into a fit of laughter, and wandering away from the point proposed a song and began it, and broke down, and presently would have fallen asleep, had not a resumption of the hostilities between the two carriage ladies aroused him.

Then he rose up and expostulated.

"Look here, demme! you know, don't break the things, you know. Hadn't some of you better go home? Not that I want to hurry you, demme! Only I've got to go out somewhere myself, and—I say Wilde—why Wilde, where are you?"

He looked round the room in search of his friend, but could see him nowhere.

Presently, however, he was discovered to be the morose and melancholy gentleman before alluded to.

"I say, Wilde," cried Mr. Winder, swaying to and fro uneasily as he addressed his friend. "Don't you recollect you promised to aid me?"

"Don't bother," replied Mr. Wilde from among the dishes.

"I say, Gerard, I don't think this is friendly."

"Hold your jaw!"

"Wilde!"

"Can't you see I'm not well? What are you bawling about?"

"Don't you remember your promise?"

"Well, it isn't to-morrow, is it? If you want your money back—"

"Suppose I did," said Mr. Winder indignantly.

"You'd better prove your debt then, and lock me up again."

Mr. Winder hurried away disgusted with his friend's ingratitude.

Mr. Wilde laid his head down among the dirty dishes, and no persuasion or threat could induce him to enter again into conversation.

Winder walked back into his drawing-room and looked round somewhat contemptuously upon the "jolly companions—every one," who had been imbibing so largely at his expense.

"How long are they going to stop here, I wonder, hang them!" he muttered aloud. "I don't believe there's one among the lot would do a friendly action in my favour."

"Don't say that, Mr. Winder," said a hearty voice just behind him; and the host turned quickly round to see who had spoken. It was a jovial, rollicking, handsome, though scarcely gentlemanly young man, with a ragged head of hair and a great tawny moustache and beard. He was dressed in a negligent, somewhat slommicking fashion, and his clothes were evidently of a foreign origin.

His name was Frank Harley, and he was an artist. He had been brought to Mr. Winder's supper-party by a mutual friend, but it was the first time that he and his host had ever met.

"What were you pleased to say," asked Mr. Winder, staring at him somewhat rudely, and in a way which would probably have called forth the resentment of most persons under like circumstances. But this Harley, who seemed to be a very free-and-easy, reckless young fellow, not particularly thin-skinned, either, could not, or would not, perceive the other's rudeness.

"You said you wanted a friend, I think?" observed the artist. "If I can be of any service to you I shall be most happy. Our friends here seem a little maudlin—begging the ladies' pardon. Is there anything that I can do?"

"I don't know why not, after all," replied Winder, "if you'll be so good."

JANE ROYDON IS CARRIED TO THE TORTURE-ROOM OF THE NUNNERY.

"You may command my services."

"Well, it's rather a confidential affair," said Winder, "and requires a good deal of delicacy in managing it. Not that you—but you understand, of course."

"To be sure. Nothing will come much out of the way to me, though, I think, either in love or war."

"Have you any time to spare?"

"Years of it."

"Are you afraid of danger?"

"Not a rap."

"Aren't you afraid to meet a—a she-devil?"

"A woman, do you mean?"

"Yes—but something terrific!"

"An old one?"

"No."

"Young?"

"Of course."

"Ugly as sin, I suppose?"

"Beautiful as an angel, on the contrary."

"I'm on then—lead the way."

"Stop, though!" cried Winter, clutching his impetuous friend by the arm. "I must warn you beforehand."

"Warn me of what?"

"Of this woman."

"What more is there about her? Is she a wehrwolr or a vampire?"

"Neither of those, but—she has reason to be in a great rage with me, and when she is in a rage—"

"What then?"

"She would be quite capable of sticking a knife into either or both of us."

"Is that all? I'll take my chance of that."

"You seem a plucky sort of fellow, demme!"

"I ought to be something. I'm as poor as a chapel mouse, which is worse, if anything, than one in a church. I've no talents and no friends, and as little luck as ever fell to the share of mortal. If I'm not plucky, I'm nothing."

"Pluck is all that's wanted now," said Winder; "but, by Jove! you'll want a good deal of that. Yes, you will, demme!"

"All right."

"Shall we be off?"

"Certainly. As soon as you like."

"You must take something first."

"Not a drop, thank you."

"Not some brandy?—neat?"

"No thank you. If a fellow can't get his courage up without alcohol it is rather a case with him."

"Come along then!" said Winder, looking at his watch. "I'm in hopes that the coast may be clear. But mind, in any case, you promise to stand by me."

"You may rely upon me."

"I've warned you, mind, of what you may expect."

"What—the knife?"

"Yes."

"Well, one can't die twice; and I'd rather be killed by a pretty woman than by an ugly one, perhaps."

"I will tell you all about it as we go along. It is a most awful affair, though; and I expect you'll want to back out."

"I'll stick by you, sir, to the death."

Thus saying the young artist knocked his hat on to his head, buttoned up his coat, and followed Mr. Winder downstairs.

The night without was black and lowering, and a neighbouring clock struck the hour of one as they set forth on their strange and perilous adventure.

CHAPTER XVI.

A DELICATE ADVENTURE.

For some time they walked along in silence.

Winder appeared to be seeking for the proper words to begin his story, and was evidently unable to find any suitable for the purpose.

At last, however, in desperation he broke the ice.

"Demme!" said he, "there's no good mincing the matter. I've acted rather like a blackguard in this matter."

"Behaved badly to the ferocious one?"

"Yes. The fact is, I used to live with her, and promised to marry her, and you see, demme—"

"She's not the lady you're going to marry to-morrow, I suppose?"

"Well, to tell the truth, she isn't. Now look here, I'm not what you may call a very wise sort of fellow. Perhaps you've noticed it?"

"I thought I observed a little something."

"That's right—be candid with me. The first moment you saw me didn't you think I was a fool?"

"Not the first moment."

"Didn't you? But I am—upon my soul—demme! Perhaps you wouldn't find it out directly, but most people do, and they cheat me at every turn. That Wilde, and all the rest of them. Chateau Renard has had pounds and pounds out of me, and has stuck me in for duffing bills, with a lot of her friends that she's got me to ask to dinner."

"That's rather hard."

"But it isn't the worst. All my relations try to cheat me out of everything they can. They'd try to make me out mad if they could, and lock me up in a lunatic asylum. If I was to marry the Baby—"

"The Baby? You don't want to marry a baby, do you? You might as well want to marry your great-grandmother."

"You don't understand—Baby Bell is the name of the one I want to break off with. It's a sort of name she has among her friends."

"Oh! I see—go on."

"Well, if I was to marry her, all my sisters, who were awfully riled at my being born just in time to cut them

out of the money, would have an inquiry in *de lunatico* before the honeymoon was over. They always do that; you know, in rich families, when a fellow marries—"

"To be sure—it's supposed that the swell has been dragged into it. Besides, it's pretty safe generally—particularly if the swell dies. Then the girl is easily bounced out of the money."

"And there are no lies that my sisters wouldn't tell, mind you, to get the money back and get the best of poor Baby."

"If you care for her, why don't you marry her like a man, and run the risk? I don't think you're more mad than most people."

"I don't know. I am a fool, you know, and there's no disguising it. They used to say so at school, and they called me 'Mad Tom.'"

"Well, what do you propose to do?"

"To break it off—I must break it off—there's no help for it. And—and I am in such an awful fright, demme!"

"What are we to do now?"

"We are going to her place."

"Are you going to tell her that you are going to break it off?"

"Me! good heavens, no! I wouldn't for a thousand pounds!"

"Am I to do it for you?"

"If I'd have only known of you before, you should have done—"

"Humph!"

"I don't want you for that, though."

"What for, then?"

"She has got a lot of letters and things of mine, and I want to get them back."

"Do you want me to break into the house like a burglar?"

"No, bless you!—I've got a latch-key."

"Am I to go in and steal them?"

"No, I shall take them."

"What am I to do?"

"To go with me."

"What, to keep her quiet?"

"Bless you, no.—You don't think I'm such a fool as that?"

"As what?"

"As to allow her to be in the place at all."

"What do *you* mean?"

"Why, I've got rid of her in the most artful style."

"How?"

"I've got her out of the house, I mean. I wrote her an anonymous letter, and made an appointment—at least it wasn't exactly an anonymous letter.—It was a letter supposed to be from a fellow she used to be rather sweet on; and—wasn't it a fine idea?"

"I suppose you're sure she's kept the appointment?"

"I haven't a doubt of it."

"It would seem, then, that she didn't care much for you?"

"Oh! yes she does, in her way; but, then, you know what women are."

"Some, you mean?"

"Bless you, no!—all of 'em. I'm not such a fool as that, demme!"

Frank Harley laughed rather bitterly, but made no comment.

They walked on for some time without any further conversation passing between them.

At last the artist said—

"I don't exactly see, though, as yet, what I have got to do in this affair."

"Oh! you will have," cried Winder, eagerly; "you'll have lots to do if she happens to come home. You'll have to take care that she doesn't murder me, or get back the letters."

"I'm to go in, then, for the bully line. Well, one

never knows what one may come to. I dare say I shall find it to pay better than the fine arts."

"My dear fellow, I'll give—I mean to say—lend you anything, if you'll only help me through this mess, and don't desert me."

"There! there! I say, don't insult me any more than you can help, although I am rather shabby!" said Harley, with a laugh. "Leave it to me to ask when I want to be paid."

"Hang him!" thought Winder, "he'll open his mouth wide enough, I'll be bound. I was a great fool to ask him. I expect he's like all the rest."

By this time they had arrived in front of a house in Halfmoon-street, Piccadilly, near to which locality the supper-party which has just been described had taken place.

The exterior of the residence before which they paused betokened at once the wealth and taste of its owner. There were flowers upon the balcony tastefully arranged, and a creeping-plant with copper-coloured leaves ran up the house-side.

In the arrangement of the plants and flowers a woman's hand was plainly visible—a woman's care was evident in all.

The front of the house was dark—the blinds drawn down, and no one visible.

Winder, however, approached upon tiptoe, motioning to his friend to be alike circumspect in his movements.

The former took from his pocket a latch-key, and very cautiously opened the door. Then peeped in, for all the world as though he were poking his head into a lion's den.

He pulled it back presently, and held up his forefinger as a sign to his friend that the greatest caution was necessary.

"What's the matter?" asked Harley.

"Nothing!"

"All right, then."

"All right so far. I hope it's all right upstairs."

"We'd better try."

"Come along then. Keep close to me."

"How you're shaking!"

"It's so infernally cold. Don't you think so?"

"I think it's rather hot."

"It will be, perhaps," said Winder, with a groan. "I say—"

"What now?"

"Suppose she was to fly out at us?"

"You jump behind me, if she does."

"I shall, I can tell you."

"Go on, then."

"I say—"

"What on earth do you want now?"

"I wish I'd brought some brandy with me."

"Hang the brandy! Haven't you got any spirit of your own?"

"Don't do that, please, at such a moment. I am—I am, demme! all in a quake."

"You might be going to face a regiment of amazons, instead of one woman! Is she a very big one?"

"No—not particularly. Only under the circumstances. Besides, you've never seen her in a passion, as I have."

"I swear I shall leave you if you don't screw up your courage a little."

This threat was such a terrific one, that the poor coward felt that it was dangerous to provoke his friend any more, and that he must at once face the enemy.

Very cautiously then they crept up the stairs.

All was dark above.

They paused and listened more than once upon the way.

But all was perfectly still.

They entered a room in the front of the house, Winder leading the way, and from the softness of the carpet beneath his feet the artist judged that they must be in a drawing-room.

Presently, as he groped his way forward, Harley knocked his foot against some article of furniture which emitted a sharp, clear sound. It was a piano.

"Hush! hush!" whispered his companion, grasping his arm; "for God's sake don't make a noise."

Winder left him, felt his way across the room in the dark, found a match-box in a spot where he knew it to be, and struck a light.

When he had ignited a candle which he found ready to his hand, Frank Harley looked round the room and took a wondering glance at the objects which it contained. It was luxuriously furnished, and countless articles of great value filled up every available nook and corner. Cabinet paintings of great cost, Sèvres vases and rich specimens of Bohemian coloured glass were strewed on Marqueterie tables.

A pretty hat lay upon the sky-blue Utrecht velvet couch. On the table were some handsomely bound books and some music.

But the peculiarity of the room was the quantity of flowers, evidently costly hot-house plants, for this was November, and from the great profusion it would seem that the purchaser spared no money in ministering to the expensive taste of the reigning goddess.

And who was the owner of this little paradise Harley asked himself as he cast his eyes inquiringly around. Upon the walls hung several oil-paintings and water-colour sketches exquisitely finished, and his artist's eye naturally led him to inspect these works of art with interest.

There was one picture—a portrait, which specially attracted his attention—a beautiful woman's face it was, with liquid grey eyes and soft brown hair, and an expression about the features that was extraordinarily mild and gentle.

Harley looked at this portrait for some time, silently wondering whether or not it could be the owner of the room. "A lovely face," he thought, "but by no means the expression of countenance I should have expected in the termigant my strong-minded friend has described her to me."

He sat astride of a chair, with chin resting upon his hands, watching the picture with a curious interest which he could scarce define to himself. Never in his life, he thought, had he seen anything half as beautiful, and with the suspicion fast growing in his mind that it might really be the woman of whom Winder had spoken, grew up a strong desire to act to her the part of champion, and watch her welfare.

"If it is she," he thought, "this selfish scamp is behaving badly to her. However, I shall see. If he has seduced me into coming here to do any shabby trick, he'll find himself very much mistaken. Confound the fellow! how could I for a moment suppose that what he said was true, and that what he said was right, when I had once heard him talk? A paltry, cowardly—"

He was interrupted when he had reached thus far in his soliloquy, by a sharp sound behind him.

It was Winder, who had opened a secretary, and unexpectedly let fall the lid.

When the artist turned round, he found his companion with an alarmed expression of countenance, rolling his eyes and trembling visibly.

"Peep out at the door," he whispered in terrified accents. "Do you see anybody on the stairs?"

Harley curled his lip contemptuously, but made no movement in the direction indicated.

"This horrible desk made such a row," Winder said, "I expect we shall be discovered."

"Do what you've got to do," replied the other coldly, "and don't cry 'wolf' before there's any occasion. Am I not here to protect you?"

"It's all very well for you to talk big," said Winder. "You only just have anything to say to Alice when she's in her tantrums."

"Haven't you nearly finished then ?" asked Harley, with his eyes still fixed upon the portrait.

There was no reply ; and on turning round to ascertain the cause, he saw that Winder was lost in a letter —with the contents of which he seemed to be highly delighted.

"Hang it ! Winder, I can't stand that. Take the trash with you, and let's be off."

"You'll excuse my saying it—" said Winder, "you know I'm not a conceited man—but I do know how to write letters to a gal—demme !"

"Let's try a specimen," said Frank Harley, snatching the letter from Winder's hand.

"Oh ! I say—here don't get reading a fellow's letters —'tisn't the thing, demme !"

But the artist, without heeding his friend, read the following epistle aloud :—

" ' My own sweet Popps'——"

"Oh ! come I say—no, demme !"

But the remorseless artist continued—

" ' Unless you consent to see me at once, the pistol or the poison-cup must be my doom ! Why are you so hard-hearted ? Your Winder adores you ! Your Felbridge dies for you—for unless you answer at once, the pistol or the poison-cup must be my doom !'

"You got hold of a flowery bit there, Winder," said Harley.

"Yes, not so bad, demme ! Now some fellows' *billets-doux* are such infernal rot !"

"Here's another," said Harley, snatching one up.

"No—demme ! I say—"

"They're quite a treat, Winder," said the artist gravely ; and opening the letter he read aloud—

"My darling Ally." "Ally ?" said Harley.

"Yes ; short for Alice."

"Oh ! I see. ' My darling Ally, in two hours I shall be with you. To accomplish this, I shall have to drag myself away from the fascination of a lady who lives on my smile.' I can't stand that," said Harley, throwing it down in disgust.

"What do you say ?" demanded Winder, looking up from a letter on which he was engaged.

"Deuced good ! You'd make your fortune in Spain."

"This one isn't so bad either," said the gratified Winder, half holding out a letter towards Harley, but remonstrating, as before, when Harley took it.

" ' Winder's love ! Felbridge's life ! Forgive me this once, and your own will offend no more. I give in—you are right—you are always right. I was wrong. I am always wrong. I admit it. There are two n's in "bonnet." I'm at the lamp-post opposite. Look out at once in forgiveness, or the pistol or the poison-cup shall blow out the brains——' "

"Hang it !" interrupted the artist laughing. "The poison-cup's a very good thing in its way, but you'd be puzzled to blow out your brains with it."

"No, no—demme ! No—pistol—don't you see ?"

"I see—but what are you going to do with this pack of letters ?"

"Burn them. Just light a match."

And the next minute Winder's poetic effusions were blazing on the hearth. One he seemed very disinclined to part with.

"I was two days knocking that up, Harley," he said ; "sad pity to burn it, demme !"

"Is it at all different from the others ?"

"Rather—*it's in poetry.*"

The words had barely escaped him when Harley made a dart at the letter, and after a slight struggle secured it ; remarking—

"I wouldn't miss this one for a pony."

"Oh ! I say, though—"

"You shall have it back this week. And now, is that all ?"

"All the letters—but now there's the portrait."

"What—your miniature ?"

"No—that painting there."

"But you're never going to cart away that thing ?"

"Ain't I, though. I had on a favourite waistcoat when that was taken. A waistcoat the Marchioness of Crutchingford admired. My dem'd valet stole it, so I'm very particular about the portrait,—besides, I'm told it's a deuced good likeness—good expression."

"Then it can't be like—"

"What do you mean ?"

"Never mind. Do you really mean to take the picture ?"

"Yes ; but we can leave the frame."

Winder got on a chair and took down the portrait, and, aided by Harley, removed it from the frame, which he carefully hung up, remarking—

"How deuced odd it looks with nothing in it !"

"In that respect," said his friend, " I don't see much change."

At length Winder shouldered the portrait and led the way. He paused on the threshold to call his friend, who had returned to the portrait of the girl, in which he seemed lost with rapture ; and on turning round to resume his walk, Winder found himself face to face with the original.

Yes, the woman he was cruelly tricking stood in the life before him.

CHAPTER XVII.

THE TORTURE-ROOM IN THE NUNNERY.

ANY person in the full possession of his senses must certainly have come to the conclusion that when Jack Chinnery had made his escape from the underground cellar and found himself so near to the street-door, the best and wisest course open to him to pursue was most undoubtedly to make his escape.

What then could have induced him, once having got out of the lion's clutches, to insanely venture his head again within the gaping jaws of the savage beast ?

He had his hand upon the lock of the door. In another moment he could have been out in the street, when his evil genius prompted him to retrace his steps.

Was he acting rightly, he asked himself, in thus abandoning to her fate the unfortunate girl whom he had come there to rescue ?

What had become of her ? Ought he not to make an effort to save her before he saved himself ?

He was not quite certain, though, upon this point. He thought if he could obtain some additional assistance from without, that he might be able very easily to effect this purpose.

But then when he came to reflect, how was he to get any help ? To whom was he to appeal ? Dare he show his face in a public police-office ? Who would listen to him ?

No. If he meant to help this woman he must do it single-handed. He could rely upon no one but himself.

The blind man's knife-thrust had cruelly crippled him, as we have seen, and he felt weak from loss of blood ; but so intense was his curiosity respecting the fate of the miserable creature whose champion he had elected himself, that he determined to venture all and run all risks to learn something more respecting her fate.

He relinquished his hold of the door, and after a moment's reflection, retraced his steps up the passage.

Which way should he go ? All within the house was dark and silent. He was uncertain in which direction he should bend his steps.

At length, feeling that delays were dangerous, he decided upon exploring the lower part of the premises, and he thought he would begin with the chapel.

This he remembered well was at the end of the passage, and having placed the light which he carried in a niche in the wall, while he used his one practicable hand, he gently unfastened the door, and entered the gloomy and vault-like apartment into which he had penetrated upon his former voyage of discovery.

It was as before—dark, silent, and sepulchral ; and as before, the naked life-size figure upon the crucifix gleamed ghastly in the yellow light which the candle he carried threw upon it.

Jack Chinnery gazed curiously around upon the altar, with its array of silver candlesticks set forth in the same way that they had been when last he visited the chapel, and again he made up his mind to appropriate them when the proper time should come. His eyes fell upon the rough wooden pews and a pulpit of the most primitive description. The chapel looked very cold and bare, and the black heavy drapery with which the walls were in some places hung, gave it more than aught else the appearance of a receptacle for the dead.

No living soul was to be seen, and nothing presenting itself to call for any lengthened scrutiny, Chinnery was turning to leave, when the sound of low voices murmuring at a short distance from the spot where he stood caught his ear, and caused him to start violently, as the thought struck him that, perhaps, he had unthinkingly overlooked some inmates of the nunnery kneeling in one of the pews.

But nobody was there. He looked anxiously round, and could see no outlet save the door through which he had himself entered a few moments previously.

He listened again, this time with more attention.

The voices were close at hand, and the sound he fancied must come from behind the drapery.

He walked upon tiptoe, listening as he went, and reached at length the spot from which the sound emanated. Then with the greatest care he raised the curtains, and discovered a faint light streaming through the crevice of a half-closed door.

To this opening he eagerly applied his eye, having first extinguished his light, lest its rays might betray his presence to those within.

It was a vault-like apartment into which he looked, the roof, of solid masonry, rising into a semicircular arch, the walls of brick, black with age. In one corner stood an oaken cupboard, the door of which was ajar. On the floor lay some curious wood-work, and iron bars, and chains lying in a confused mass, the nature or use of which it was impossible to imagine.

Three persons occupied this room ; and streaming in a wavering line from a lamp hanging from the ceiling a sickly flame of a candle fell upon their faces and figures, throwing them into the darkest relief, and casting their opaque and fantastical shadows opaquely across the damp flagstones of the floor.

Two of these persons were women, the third a man.

One was a female of about forty years of age, in whose countenance time had not obliterated its striking beauty of expression, or driven the roses from its peachy cheeks.

It was a face at once majestical and severe. Its contour was formed in the purest Grecian mould, and might have served as a model for a deity, so admirable was the gloomy grandeur of the brow, the severe chiselling of the lip, the rounded beauty of the throat, and the faultless symmetry of her full form.

Shaded by the nun's headdress which she wore, her lofty forehead would have been displayed to the greatest advantage, had it not been at this moment knit and deformed by angry passion.

It was truly a beautiful face when seen in its serenity, and not disfigured by either the vices of rage, avarice, or lust, which so often leant to it an expression almost demoniacal in its intense fiendishness.

Then it was the face of a beautiful devil ; and so thought Chinnery, as he gazed upon it now.

The other woman, who was also habited in a nun's apparel, presented a striking contrast to her handsome companion.

She was very old, and very ugly. Her skin was as sallow and unwholesome in its hue as the skin of a toad, and hideously wrinkled. Her cheeks were withered, and her mouth puckered.

There scarcely seemed to be any flesh upon her bones, and what there was was so bloodless, so corpselike, one could liken it only to leather. Her long, lank fingers, with their brown and wrinkled skin, and great fleshless joints, looked like a coil of lizards, as she rubbed them one over another with a creeping kind of motion horrible to look at.

She was more like an animated mummy than aught else; and one might almost have been led to imagine that she had existed for centuries in the same state, and would probably continue to exist for as long a period still ; only that in the heavy bloodshot eyes it was evident that the vital spark was waning, and save when at rare intervals they were lighted up by a savage glitter called forth by her yet unsubdued passions, they were sinister and sunken.

The third of this remarkable trio was an aged negro, with a figure almost as lean and lank as a skeleton, and whose perfectly bald head looked like some smoke-dried skull, allowing for the overhanging and hoary eyebrows, and the deep-seated and sunken green, cat-like orbs, which gleamed with feverish lustre.

Chinnery looked in at this strange company with intense curiosity, and greedily listened to their low-muttered conversation. When he found he was the subject of it, as may be supposed, his interest did not subside.

"Have you been down to see him lately?" the handsome woman asked of the negro.

"Lazarus is down there with him now."

"I hope Lazarus is taking proper care of him. He was very much shaken by his fall, and we must mind that he does not die before we learn who sent him here to play the spy upon us."

"We'll wring the truth out of him, if he has a gasp of life left in his body," cried the old woman, in a shrill tone, which sounded like the snarl of a dog.

Chinnery winced as he heard it.

"She'd pinch pieces out of me, with red-hot pincers, if she had her way!" he thought ; and his eyes instinctively wandered to the curious instruments lying in a corner of the vault, which before had puzzled him.

Could it be possible that they were instruments of torture ?

"We must not let him die," the handsome lady continued, after a pause, "without first having ascertained whether it was through the connivance of this Jane Roydon that he entered the house."

"It must have been," said the old woman. "Was not he helping her to escape?"

"We have one question to settle, at any rate," replied the other. "Is he some friend, or connexion, of hers? or did she attract his attention from the street?"

"The latter is next to impossible. Is it likely that any man would enter the house to help a stranger? Nobody but a madman either would have believed her tale."

"No. Any stranger must have believed her to be mad herself."

"In any case, no one but a madman would have ventured into the house in the way that he did, with such an absurd idea of rescuing the woman single-handed."

Chinnery was of the same opinion. He would go about it in a different way now, he thought, if he had his time to come over again.

As it was, was he not still acting a madman's part to remain? Ought he not rather to make good his escape while he yet had the chance ?

They were evidently the heads of the establishment, consulting together in this strange vault-like chamber. He had secured the blind man downstairs. Most likely there was nobody else in the house to interfere with him.

Suppose he were to slam-to the door, and secure it on the outside? There were bolts.

Or, suppose he were to steal away upon tiptoe, and make his escape unheard? That was the best plan, perhaps.

Certainly, any one in his senses would have adopted the latter course, and have made good his retreat while he had the opportunity of so doing; but this was not Jack Chinnery's idea.

He was determined to see a little more of the inner mysteries of this strange establishment into which he had forced an entrance.

What would this terrible trio say next? What villanies were they concocting?

What was the nature of this vault-like chamber, in which they hatched their plots?

Above all, what was the meaning of those curious contrivances in wood and iron lying in the corner, which had puzzled Chinnery more and more every time his attention had wandered to the spot?

Presently, the conversation within the room was continued.

"Jane Roydon still appears to be as obstinate as ever, I suppose?" said the youngest and handsomest of the women, who appeared to be the one most in authority.

"She would agree to nothing, when last I was with her. We can do nothing with her unless we use the instruments."

"We will use them, then, if she does not yield very soon."

"Why delay any longer?" asked the old woman, looking up eagerly, her spiteful eyes glittering like those of a venomous snake.

"Why delay any longer? It is only giving her an opportunity to recover her strength."

"She is in a weakly state now."

"She is rapidly sinking; and I have frightened her almost to death with the descriptions of what we shall do to her if she does not yield to our wishes."

"She shall yield," cried the handsome woman, in an imperious tone. "Poor fool! does she suppose we are going to be thwarted by her, after our other victories? No. She shall sign the documents, and will her property to us. Every farthing she possesses in the world shall be ours; and then—"

"And then the sooner she dies the better."

"Yes. We care little what becomes of her when our end is served; but she shall do exactly as we wish."

The old woman made no answer for some time, but mumbled discontentedly to herself.

"I should have voted for doing as we have done before," she broke in, at last. "Why should we take all this trouble? Why should we not make sure of her at once, and then will away her property, as we have done with the others?"

"Because," answered her companion, angrily, "it is not safe to do so, as I have told you before. Suspicions have arisen out of doors respecting the validity of our claims. Soon, if we had gone on in the old way, some questions would have been asked. We might have got into a court of law, and then nothing but ruin could have followed."

"No—no; we must not risk that. We must have no public inquiry."

"Certainly not. We must have none *afterwards*—but before we should admit her relations, and in their presence she shall sign away her property. Then there can be no question—then there can be no public scandal."

"But how can we trust her in their presence?"

"Before we try the experiment we must gain such dominion over her that we can trust her with them in safety."

"It will be a hazardous experiment."

"It will be a dangerous one; but it is worth the risk."

"Yes—yes. I think so, if we only dare—"

"We must try. She shall only see them, too, when on the point of death; so that she will be weak, and easily terrified."

"Yes;—but I have been thinking, to insure her silence—"

"Well—"

"I know one plan by which we could silence her; and then we might be quite sure she would not betray us; because she would only be likely to do it by a few words whispered suddenly. Don't you think so?"

"Yes; if we gave her the chance. But what is your plan?"

The old woman glanced round at the negro, as though she were fearful that her atrocious suggestion might even prove too revolting for this vile instrument of their inhuman cruelties.

Then she sank her voice to a low whisper, which was scarcely audible to the attentive listener without.

"Suppose," she said, fixing her eyes upon her companion, who, cool as she was, shrank back with a shudder when she heard the dreadful words—"Suppose, to make quite sure of her, *we cut out her tongue?*"

There was a pause of some moments after this hideous suggestion had been made by the savage old hag, and her two companions sat looking at each other with a sort of stealthy guilt, which lent to their faces an expression of fiendish vindictiveness truly horrible.

Before either of the three had time to speak again, a church clock without began to strike the hour of twelve.

The youngest of the women listened to the strokes, glanced at a watch she carried, and then said—

"What can detain Lazarus so long? Go and look for him, Joel," she continued, addressing the negro. "It is growing late, and I am determined that this night shall not pass without our bringing this woman to reason."

"No," said the old hag, eagerly; "there is no time to lose. No time like time present."

The negro moved towards the door, and Chinnery, seeing him coming, crept hastily behind the heavy drapery hanging upon the chapel wall, which afforded him ample shelter.

He crept close to the wall, and stood perfectly motionless, while the black, carrying a lantern in his hand, passed through the gloomy chapel, opening and closing behind him the chapel door, and then he was about to steal cautiously back to his place of observation, when the thought occurred to him that such a course would not be the wisest, and that while he had a few moments to spare, he could not do better than seek for some place of concealment, because it was very certain that when the negro found the blind man had changed places with the prisoner, and the prisoner was free, a rigorous search would be instituted for the fugitive.

Behind this drapery was a capital place for concealment, and if he could only find some recess into which he could creep, he thought he would not be very likely to be discovered.

"They will think, too, I got out the way I got in, perhaps; or else, as I have the keys, I might have opened some door or other and locked it after me. Of course they will think I am not such a fool as to remain in their murderous den when I get a chance of escape. And I shouldn't, if it was not that I want to see what the wretches mean to do to that poor girl, and to prevent them if it is possible."

It would be rather difficult to explain what were Jack Chinnery's precise plans upon the subject, or to satisfactorily account for the rather wild notion of his being able, single-handed, to contend with the girl's torturers.

But then Jack was one of those reckless fellows, whose courage at times verged into foolhardiness.

He hardly knew what it was to be afraid, and though he now had a wounded hand, and was half dead with loss of blood, he felt himself equal to a struggle with any half-dozen assailants.

While he was groping his way, however, behind the drapery, he came to a low door, which was secured by bolts, but not locked.

He could not help thinking that it would be the wisest plan to have this exit at his service in case he should require it, and he with great care, avoiding all noise, drew the bolts.

Fortunately the door was not locked, so that he had no further difficulty upon that score, and had only to turn a handle to open it.

Then he peeped out into the darkness without, and found himself at the back of the house, looking on to the grass-grown garden, where at the moment the pale moon shone upon the white tombstones he had before noticed, and which bore a horrible significance now that he was somewhat better acquainted with the fearful mysteries of the house to which they belonged.

"How many have they murdered?" he thought, with a shudder. "How many more are doomed? Shall I leave the place before I know all? No. It was intended that I should come here to discover these horrors, and bring them to light. There is a new destiny opening before me. I will not turn my back upon it yet, come what may."

He drew back, and very gently closed the door again, but did not bolt it.

A little distance further on, he found a kind of recess behind an altar, where he could very easily conceal himself, and into this he crept, waiting for what might happen next.

He had not to wait very long before he heard the sound of footsteps approaching.

The negro was returning, bringing the blind man, Lazarus, with him.

They were talking eagerly about his flight as they passed by, and Chinnery heard the negro suggest that he must have unlocked the street-door and effected his escape.

When they got back into the vault where they had left the two women, a loud and angry discussion took place between the four; but what they said was not audible to Chinnery in his place of concealment, and he deemed it unsafe to venture out just yet.

They all came out presently, and crossed the chapel, talking as they went of searching the house.

Chinnery kept close in his hiding-place, and held his breath. He listened to their retreating steps, and then to the banging of doors in the lower part of the house, and presently to a great outcry when it was discovered that the street-door was bolted upon the inside.

Almost the moment afterwards the chapel-door was flung open, and the two men came running in. They crossed the floor straight in the direction of the door which Chinnery had just unbolted—the black leading the way, and pulling his companion after him.

They tore on one side the drapery, and uttered a howl of disappointment when they found the door unfastened.

"He has gone this way," cried the black. "But perhaps he has not got over the wall."

"Oh! yes, he has. There's no doubt of that."

"Why?"

"Because there's nothing could stop such a ramping devil as he is."

"He's as weak as a cat from loss of blood."

"But he can climb like one in spite of that."

"He must be a good climber to get over the wall."

"Unless he used the ladder."

"Is it out there still?"

"It's lying in the corner by the trees."

"Curse you! that's like your carelessness. Didn't I tell you to bring it in?"

They went out talking thus; and Chinnery listened to their voices as long as they were audible, with an inward chuckle.

"I'll look after that ladder when the time comes," he thought to himself, "if they don't move it away."

After a brief interval, the men returned to the house, and closed and bolted the door again. Then they silently returned across the chapel floor, shutting the door at the end, leading into the passage.

Chinnery remained for some time perfectly silent and motionless in his place of concealment, for he could form no notion how soon they might return.

It was very provoking that they had said nothing as they retired which might lead him to understand whether or not they had come to the conclusion that he had escaped over the wall.

There was little doubt, however, that such must be the case, for they could not have thought otherwise after finding the door unbolted.

"It was awfully lucky I did it," said Jack Chinnery to himself, "but it was a great chance too. If I had only been a few moments later it would, ten to one, have been all over with me."

He waited a long while very silently, but with fast gathering impatience for their return.

"What are they doing now, I wonder?" he thought; "Are they torturing that wretched girl? No, I should hear her shrieking if they were. What are they doing? I wonder if they are coming back any more?"

He determined after a time—so long a delay having ensued—that they were not likely to return, and he conceived the idea of venturing out to have a peep at the curious vault-like chamber in which the conference had been held that he had heard some portion of.

He felt his way very cautiously along, fearful of making a noise, until he reached the door he had previously unbolted, the bolts of which he now drew back for the second time.

"They'll never look at that again," he thought, shrewdly, "and I can beat a retreat that way easily enough if there is any occasion."

When he had settled this matter, and made quite sure that there was no other impediment in the way of a rapid exit in this direction, he crept from out the drapery, and feeling for the door of the vault, cautiously turned the handle.

He started back though, for there was a light within.

Was some one there?

But a moment's reflection assured him that this could not be the case, because he had heard the voices of all four as they passed through the chapel.

He peeped in.

No—no one was there, and he entered the vault.

The light which at first had startled him came from the candle hanging in the lamp which has been described. By its aid he could now look round upon the objects which the mysterious apartment contained.

There was a rough wooden table and four chairs, all of black, unpainted wood.

There was the closet in one corner of the room, which, when he opened it, he found with some disappointment to be full of shelves, for he had fancied that it might prove to be a good place of concealment.

But there was something upon one of the shelves which he thought well repaid him for the trouble of looking into it.

There were two black masks.

He looked at these with some wonder, and his mind involuntarily wandered to the horrible stories he had heard of the mysteries of the Inquisition, and the brutalities to this day even perpetrated at home and abroad among the strongholds of Jesuitism.

His eyes now wandered inquiringly round the bare walls of the vault-like apartment, and settled at length upon the confused mass of iron and wood-work lying in the corner, which had before so excited his curiosity.

Now that he was nearer to it, he could see that it had a shape.

It looked something like the frame of a bed, and there were screws which appeared to be so fashioned that it could be either shortened or lengthened at the operator's pleasure, and there were places which might have been intended to fit wrists and ankles.

What was it in the name of all that was mysterious and horrible?

Jack Chinnery asked himself the question in wondering amazement, but for some time could find no solution to the puzzling enigma.

It was a machine of some kind to do something, but what?

Not a machine to print with, or to manufacture any article. Could it be possible that it was an instrument of torture?

The idea seemed so wild a one—the fact so improbable—he could not believe that such could possibly be the case.

And yet it must be. When he came more carefully to scrutinize the diabolical contrivance, he was sure of it.

It was a rack!

It was one of those hellish engines of cruelty by which in the dark ages monsters in human shape had practised their fiendish arts upon their poor, shrinking, shrieking victims.

By which they had torn and lacerated their tortured flesh—wrenched out their arms—dragged from their sockets every agonized joint.

Was it possible that such deeds of horror could be perpetrated now in this age of enlightenment?—in this, the most civilized city in the world?

Chinnery remained for some time as it were dumbfounded by the horror of the discovery that he had made. But the sound of some one opening the further door into the chapel recalled him to himself, and urged upon him the necessity for action.

He looked round in the hope that he might be able to find some hiding-place he could creep into.

But there was nowhere in the room where he could hope to conceal himself, and he had not a moment to spare.

He heard the sound of many voices and footsteps in the passage without the chapel door, and had not something occurred to detain them there for a moment or two and distract their attention, he must certainly have been discovered.

As it was, however, he very fortunately contrived to slip through the doorway and dive behind the drapery.

Scarcely had he disappeared into his hiding-place when the door of the chapel was flung open and the negro and Lazarus made their appearance, carrying some object between them.

Chinnery eagerly peeped forth through a rent in the black funereal hangings which concealed him from their gaze, and with some difficulty at first, made out that it was the body of a woman which the men were conveying towards him.

For some time he could distinguish nothing, though, save the dim outline of her form as they bore her onwards; but arriving at last at the door of the vault, they paused while the Lady Superior, for such Chinnery guessed to be the handsomer of the two women he had heard consulting together, stepped forward to open the door wide enough to admit of their passage into the room.

Then was it that the old hag, waving high a lighted candle she carried in her hand, threw the reflection of the flame full upon the face of the victim.

Chinnery could not, strong man as he was, refrain from a terrific shudder at the appalling sight that met his eyes.

It was the face of the poor creature whom he had endeavoured to rescue from the noisome cellar below.

He had no doubt of that; indeed, he had been pre-

pared to expect that she would be the victim, but he was unprepared for the great and awful change which only a few hours had wrought in her emaciated and shrunken features.

Nothing so ghastly had he ever before looked upon.

He could not have believed, had not his own eyes been witness of the truth, that such a face could belong to any one endowed with life.

A death-like pallor overspread the pinched features; the thin blue lips were parted with an expression of pain.

The lower jaw had fallen, and the head lolled back as though there were not strength enough to support it.

There was no sign of life visible in the poor victim's face, except that the half glazed eyes rolled feebly from time to time, as the rough jolting of her supporters caused her an extra pang of agony.

She appeared to be so weak as hardly to be capable of making any movement herself, or of uttering any sound.

But from time to time a weak, wailing kind of cry, scarcely loud enough to be audible to the sympathizing listener, burst from her suffering breast.

They carried her onwards, the old hag waving to and fro the light she carried, and her illuminated features looking indescribably horrible and fiendish.

The two men conveyed their intended victim within the doorway, and then the women followed, and as Chinnery thrust his head outside the dark drapery behind which he had been hiding, the heavy door of the torture-chamber was closed with an ominous bang, that thrilled painfully through his heart and chilled his very blood with horror.

But he could not endure to remain passive any longer, and involuntarily sprang forward towards the heavy portal which hid from his view the dread horrors his excited mind pictured vividly.

Reckless of his unarmed state and of the momentarily increasing weakness, which was occasioned by the want of food and rest, and by the fatigue and excitement he had lately passed through, he caught hold of the door-handle and strove to wrench it round, but it was fast bolted within.

He listened, trembling with horror; but a death-like silence reigned within.

An awful sickness crept over him, and his brain reeled giddily. He clung to the door-post to steady himself, for he felt upon the point of fainting.

While in this state he might have remained unconscious of the lapse of time for almost ten minutes.

A sound from the interior of the torture-room, however, aroused him suddenly.

It was the sound of a piercing shriek, wrung in the intensity of her agony from the very soul of the poor suffering wretch upon whom these fiends in human form were exercising their devilish arts.

A long, shrill, shivering cry, fraught with unutterable horror to the throbbing heart of the listener without, whose ignorance as to its cause doubled the terror of the incident, fearful as it was in sheer reality.

What were the monsters doing to the poor helpless creature they had locked in within their impenetrable vault like chamber?

He dare not ask himself: he dare not think.

The sound had died away, or rather given place to another, if possible, more fearful than the last. An awful choking, gurgling noise followed, which curdled his blood in his veins as he thought of the hideous suggestion of the brutal old hag.

Were they cutting out her tongue?

CHAPTER XVIII.

THE END OF A "LIAISON."

WE left Mr. Winder and his friend face to face with Alice Willoughby.

"GIVE HER A SHAKING, SCRUNCHER!" CRIED THE RESURRECTIONIST.

It was rather an awkward meeting, and for a moment they had neither a word to say. Then the girl exclaimed :—

"Felbridge !"

"Alice !"

"The devil !" put in the artist.

There was a fearful pause for some moments, during which the chattering of Winder's teeth was very audible. The silence was ultimately broken by Frank Harley.

"Madam, ——" said he.

"Sir !" said the new comer, sharply.

"Ahem ! You'll excuse me, but my friend Winder——"

"Your friend Winder, sir," interrupted the girl, "can surely explain for himself."

"Doubtless, madam ; but——"

"But, sir," she said, passionately, "if you are a gentleman, you must surely see that it is very bad taste on your part thus to intrude your presence."

"True," said the artist, colouring with mortification. "Madam, your most——"

"Stop," said Winder. "Do you remember your promise ?"

"I—No. But it was given under a false understanding. I thought you were coming across some termagant, whose violence threatened your personal safety. Had I known whom I was to see, you should have made no cat's-paw of me. Although I am fain to confess I should have had a hard struggle to keep myself from the pleasure of an interview with this lady, whatever might be the nature of it."

And having delivered himself of this somewhat windy oration, Mr. Frank Harley proceeded slowly towards the door—very slowly, for he hoped to be called back, and he was not disappointed.

"I say, old fellow, don't you know ?" said Winder, beginning to be alarmed at the prospect of a *tête-à-tête* with the fair Alice Willoughby.

to "What, pray, is the meaning of all this, Fel bridge? Why do you come like a thief, in my absence, ——"

"Your absence," said Winder, rallying a little. "That's it! Your absence. And where were you absent?"

"Where?"

"Yes, where! Shall I tell you?"

"Tell me?" repeated the girl, in astonishment.

"Tell you," blustered Winder, endeavouring to persuade himself that he was not afraid. "It's no use, madam, you're discovered."

"What do you mean by all this nonsense?" demanded Alice.

"How about the rendezvous you've been keeping?"

"Rendezvous?" repeated the girl.

"Yes—that letter."

"Then you know about that letter?"

"Hah!" exclaimed Winder, in mock triumph, "then you admit it, madam?"

"I admit I received a letter—that you will admit was no fault of mine."

"No I shall not. In our relations to each other it was decidedly a fault."

"Which letter," continued the girl, "contained an assignation to which I was not party."

"That is more easily said than—than believed!"

"Sir," said the girl, with dignity, "do you wish to insult me!"

"Come, stop that, Winder," said Frank Harley, "I can't stand it!"

"What do you mean by interfering?" said Winder, turning upon him savagely.

"My meaning is obvious," retorted the artist.

Winder was rather alarmed at this. He made a variety of winks and masonic signs to Harley, which he, to Winder's discomfiture, totally refused to acknowledge.

"Ha! Felbridge, I see how it is," said the poor girl, sadly; "you are determined to quarrel."

"Madam," said Winder, in what he intended to be a look of injured innocence, "you are unjust. I come here to find that you have gone to keep an appointment, and when I venture to remonstrate, you, in the most unblushing manner—I say, in the most unblushing manner——" here he bungled and stammered dreadfully. This for Winder was a very long speech, and the result of the previous day's study. But although he had been letter-perfect in the rehearsal, he now forgot his part, and stuck hopelessly.

"But, Felbridge," said Alice, appealingly, "when I assure you that I have not kept this appointment—that I love you too dearly to be led away by——"

"That's enough," interrupted Winder, brutally. "If it is as you say, why did you not tell me of this letter, eh?"

"I feared to create a difference between you and——"

"And my fortunate rival!" said Winder, with stagy bitterness.

"But how came you to know of this letter, Felbridge?"

This was a question he was quite unprepared for, and he blushed and stammered something which was perfectly unintelligible. The girl immediately perceived his confusion, and attributing it to a wrong cause, her face cleared up, and she said to him, with a smile, as she placed her hand affectionately upon his arm—

"Now I see it all. You've sent me this letter yourself."

"I—I——" stammered Winder, blushing more than ever.

"Yes," continued Alice, "merely to try me."

This must have been a cue that he was awaiting by his ready reply.

"No madam," he said, waiving her off majestically; "the lady that I honour—ahem! that is, the lady who possesses my heart—ahem!—in short, my affections."

Here he floundered about from the point and was hopelessly lost. Harley, who had been silently enjoying the ludicrous affectation and pomposity of Winder, in spite of his mute appeal, refused to come to his assistance.

"I never heard you speak thus before," said Alice, in mournful surprise.

"Because I never had the occasion," said Winder, slightly recovering himself.

"Then you deny that this letter was merely sent by you to try me?"

"Of course I do!"

"Then now I am convinced that my first idea was correct. That this is merely a base subterfuge."

"A subterfuge, madam! demme!"

"A paltry pretext for quarrelling,—for what end I am unable to tell."

"Since, madam," said Winder, returning to his lesson; "since you can think so meanly of one you have professed to love—there remains but one thing—namely, to part."

"Winder, do you wish to kill me?"

"Certainly!—that is—I mean——" here he lost himself again. He had expected her to repeat his cruel sentence in blank dismay, and had prepared his answer accordingly.

"Indeed, I almost begin to believe that possible," said the girl, weeping.

"No," said Winder, extricating himself with some difficulty: "what I meant to say was, that where there is no respect there can be no love, and that—that——"

Poor Winder's memory was dreadfully bad, and he quite forgot the tag of this cruel drama which he had spent hours in preparing while in the debtor's prison, so he happily thought of his last speech, and wound up with—

"There remains but one thing, and that is—namely, to part."

As he said this he made a rush to the door, followed by Frank Harley, who began to feel heartily ashamed of the whole affair, and was glad to escape. His contempt for the unworthy object of Alice Willoughby's love was only equalled by the extraordinary interest he felt in the lady herself.

"Felbridge, if you ever loved me," said Alice, entreatingly, "I conjure you to give some explanation of your strange conduct."

But the heartless fellow went on hurriedly, followed by his friend the artist. A scream reached them, and the sound of a fall, from which they judged that Alice had fainted. Harley would have returned to her aid, but he was prevented by Winder, who hurried him on into the street.

"Pheugh! Deuced awkward, Harley, demme!"

"Awkward!" echoed the artist. "Well, Winder, I knew you were a fool——"

"A what?"

"A fool—you told me so yourself. But, hang me! if I thought you were such an infernal scoundrel."

"That's rather strong, Mr. Harley, demme!"

"Not more strong than true!"

"I tell you what it is; don't you know; I don't like your bullying style."

"Then you can easily seek the remedy."

Which settled the harangue, for Winder's courage was of the Bob Acres kind. This brought them half-way down the street, where Harley suddenly pulled up short.

"What's the matter?" asked Winder.

"If you're such a d—d cold-hearted villain, I'm not, and I'm going back to see if I can be of any assistance."

"Come, I say," said Winder; but Harley went on. They had left the door open on going out, and Harley quickly ran upstairs into the room where they had left the unhappy girl. At first he could not see her, and was about to leave the room, when he perceived that she had fallen fainting behind the door.

He quickly raised her in his arms and administered such restoratives as were at hand. She slowly returned to consciousness with a deep sigh, and murmured the name of her worthless lover.

"Hang him for a cold-blooded villain!" said Harley, between his clenched teeth. "He is no more worthy of this fair creature than I am to hold her in my arms thus. By heavens! How beautiful!"

"Has he really gone?" she asked.

"I grieve for your sake to say he has."

This was scarcely true. He was rather pleased than not at Winder's departure.

"Then why do you remain?"

"To offer any assistance that lies in my power."

"You really wish to serve me?" demanded Alice, with a look that sent the blood rushing to his heart.

"Tell me how I can do so, that I may prove my devotion."

"Devotion!"

"Devotion to my friend."

"And are you his friend?"

"I was until his harshness towards you caused me to despise him."

"Then can you restore him to me?"

"Nay, believe me, Miss Willoughby, he is not worthy your consideration."

"Not worthy my consideration? Ah! sir, I fear your friendship is like his love."

"Why, surely, Miss Willoughby, you couldn't expect me to esteem a man who has so wronged you?"

"Then why are you here, if not to take his part?"

"Why—ah! In fact, Miss Willoughby, my desire to serve you is greater even than my dislike to him. For your sake, much as it goes against me, I would willingly do my utmost to reclaim the man who can afford to repay your devotion by such baseness; but alas! he is to be married to-morrow."

"Married to-morrow?"

"Ay, Miss Willoughby, or rather to-day. I hear by that clock that it doesn't want many hours of daybreak."

"This, then, explains all."

"That is the whole truth, Miss Willoughby."

"And, as I surmised, this letter was a forgery—a mere pretext to break with me?"

"Yes."

"To which you were a party?"

"By heavens! no, Miss Willoughby. He so put the case to me that I was totally deceived. Had I known all, I should never have been here to-night, and thus have saved my future peace of mind."

As he said this he endeavoured to take her hand.

"Sir," said Alice, drawing back, "your motives appear so interested that you make me doubt your veracity."

"I swear by all that's good I have spoken the truth. We have just come from his farewell bachelor supper, at which he announced to all his friends that his marriage is to take place to-day at noon."

"Where?" demanded Alice, eagerly.

"St. George's, Hanover-square."

"I'll be there."

"You, Miss Willoughby?"

"Yes—I; and so test the truth of your *disinterested* assertion."

"Miss Willoughby, your doubts are torture."

"I can offer no apology for them, sir."

"But when you have seen for yourself that I speak the truth, may I then—" here he stammered and looked confused.

"What, sir?"

"May I hope that you will forget this faithless Winder; and that the devotion of a life—"

At this he fell on one knee and seized her hand.

"Rise, sir!" she exclaimed, affrightedly.

"Nay," said Harley, passionately; "not until you promise me that when you have witnessed the heartlessness of Winder you will see me again."

"To what end?"

"To what end! Miss Willoughby, I love you."

"Sir!" she exclaimed, coldly; "this attachment is too sudden."

"Nay, I swear."

"Moreover, there is no reciprocity of feeling. I do not love you. I cannot form attachments on half an hour's acquaintance."

"Ah, Miss Willoughby! I loved you before I saw you."

"How, sir?"

"From your portrait. I read in it the soul—the truth of the original."

"Sir, if it were not for the unhappy occurrences of this night, I could laugh. Alas! I feel as if I should never laugh more." And the unhappy Alice Willoughby burst into tears.

"I'll call the villain out!" exclaimed Harley, passionately. "I'll shoot him before his honeymoon's over, or my name's not Frank Harley!"

"And thus, sir, cause me to hate you."

"Miss Willoughby, your cruel words cut me to the quick. Is there no hope?"

"None!"

"Would not a life of devotion—"

"Nay, sir!" interrupted Alice, impatiently. "Think you I can change my affection as I would a glove? What would such love be worth?"

"Sadly true! Tell me, at least, how I can serve you."

"By departing at once."

"Madam, I'm gone." He walked to the door, but paused on the threshold.

"Miss Willoughby," he said, "here is my card. If you should ever want my aid, I need not say that I am devoted to your interest. Farewell!"

"Farewell."

Before he left the apartment, he turned to her again, with an entreating gesture.

"You'll not see me again, Miss Willoughby?"

"I shall be at the church at noon," answered Alice, somewhat moved. "And now, good-night."

"Farewell—au revoir!" exclaimed the artist, joyfully; and he skipped lightly downstairs and into the street. He walked along in ecstacies, never heeding the curses of the policemen and the stray passengers whom he jostled in his eagerness, or whose corns he mercilessly crushed.

Very different were the feelings of the broken-hearted Alice Willoughby. Immediately upon the departure of the happy Frank Harley, she had given way to her bitter grief, and with a mingled sensation of despair and impatience, wearily passed the few hours that must elapse before the wedding was to take place,—the wedding that was to crown her misery.

But to return to the faithless Adonis, Felbridge Winder.

He stood gazing after Harley as he ran back to the house, unable to comprehend his meaning. He waited some few minutes at the corner of Half-Moon-street; but seeing no signs of his friend, he shouldered his portrait, and trudged on down Piccadilly, considerably relieved now that his disagreeable business was over.

Carriages were rattling along, and more than once their occupants saluted Winder.

"What's all this dem'd hubbub, I wonder?" he said, as he raised his hat in acknowledgment of a bow from a brougham. "By Jove! Lady Simper's little Sunday evening tea-fights. I'm in for it, demme! And I promised Amatoria faithfully to be there. Hallo! bless me, if this isn't her trap!"

As he spoke, a magnificent brougham, drawn by a superb pair of chesnuts, came up. Winder, having advanced to the edge of the kerb, made a very elaborate bow, which was returned by the only occupant of the carriage—a lady in evening dress—and at the same instant the carriage was stopped.

"Jump in, Mr. Winder," she said.

"Beg pardon, Lady Crutchingford," replied Winder; "but I'm hurrying home to—"

"Nonsense," said her ladyship, in a low voice, only intended for his ear. "Jump in!"

And muttering some remonstrances, he got in the carriage. This exactly suited his inclinations, although he had many preparations to make for the important event which was to take place at noon, for the fickle-hearted Winder had been desperately in love with the fair Lady Amatoria Crutchingford for the last week, and he had reason to believe that his passion was returned.

The object of his attachment was very beautiful and extremely rich. She had splendid houses in town and country; splendid carriages and horses. Splendid is but weak praise to use when speaking of the dazzling magnificence of the symmetrical creatures who waited behind her ladyship's chair, or smiled compassionately upon the shabby outer world from the portals of the May-fair mansion. She had a box on the grand tier at the Opera, and tickets for all the fashionable fêtes. Her jewels were justly the envy of all her female friends. She had, in short, all that wealth could purchase, or caprice could suggest. Last and least, a solemn, stately, unobtrusive old man for a husband, who never contradicted or bothered her in the least.

Felbridge Winder was therefore not a little vain of the Platonic attachment which existed between them. It was not every day that ladies of rank were smitten with him; although, notwithstanding that beyond his family connexions he had nothing to recommend him, he counted his *liasons* amongst the untitled of the "upper ten" by dozens.

"What ever have you got there, Winder?" asked Lady Crutchingford, as soon as they were fairly seated.

"A portrait."

"Lady?"

"No—myself; and a deuced good one, I think," answered Winder, holding it up.

"Yes—not bad; but I can't see it very well here. Rather an elaborate waistcoat, it strikes me."

"Ah!" said Winder; "I knew you would like it. You have such taste, demme!"

"But why were you not at Lady Simper's to-night!"

"Most important business. Is his lordship at home?"

"I believe so—I haven't seen him to-day. Do you want to see him?"

"No. I—"

"Because, if you do, you may as well come in and take a cup of coffee. His lordship is an early riser, and you will not have to wait long. I don't intend to go to-bed now."

"Indeed!" said Winder, catching at the suggestion. "Well, I did rather wish to see him, and if I do not disturb you—"

"Not at all," answered her ladyship. "I can never sleep if I pass five o'clock."

The carriage stopped, and they alighted.

"Show Mr. Winder into the library," said Lady Amatoria to the servant who admitted them. And then turning to Winder, she continued, "If you will excuse me for a moment, Mr. Winder, I will see if his lordship has retired."

"Certainly, Lady Crutchingford," said Winder, who took it as it was intended—for the servant's ear. "I hope she won't carry her dem'd prudence so far, though," he thought to himself as he was shown into the library. "I can't endure that horrid old bore."

The room into which Winder was shown by the servant resembled a library, inasmuch as it had book-cases ranged all round the room, filled with elegantly-bound novels. But here the likeness ceased. The sumptuousness and luxury of the general arrangements gave it far more the appearance of a lady's boudoir than aught else.

Winder languidly flung himself on to an ottoman, and ordered the servant to bring him coffee and brandy. This killed the few minutes that Lady Amatoria took to complete her toilet, and she entered the room.

"I think of going to Richmond this morning, Felbridge," she said.

"I should be delighted to accompany you, but—"

"But!—My dear Winder, I haven't asked you yet. No; a friend of his lordship's is to accompany me—Major Beele; do you know him?"

"Long fellow—sandy whiskers—swivel eye?"

"Yes, that's his portrait," said Lady Amatoria, laughing. "But you had better not give it out publicly; he's a dreadful fire-eater."

"I'd give a hundred pounds to cut him out to-day."

"You could do it for less than that."

"Then name the price."

"Simply start before he arrives. He's always late."

"Amatoria, I'm yours for ever." This was a regular set phrase of Winder's.

"The major was to have escorted me to-night to the masquerade, but I suppose that he will be rather offended at not finding me here when he arrives."

"Then you will allow me—"

"Unless you are otherwise engaged," said her ladyship, with a seductive smile.

Oh, my lady! Oh, Mr. Winder!

Oh! poor Mr. Winder's intended wife!

CHAPTER XIX.

"THE SHAMBLES."

WITH the reader's kind permission, I will introduce him to the private residence of John Jaggers, the Resurrectionist.

This worthy and industrious tradesman resided in a rather dreary suburb lying upon the east of London, beyond Spitalfields.

It was but a very straggling, life-forsaken spot, which did not quite belong to the town, but was yet a great deal too smoky and sooty, and grimly unfertile, to pass itself off as anything rustic.

It abounded in low, mean, one-storied houses, with narrow strips of garden, where abortive horticulture was practised upon an extremely limited scale, and where weeds flourished mightily, and reached surprising lengths.

Some of these hovels were built of the wood of broken-up vessels, pitched over to make them weather-proof, and looking in the pale winter's sunshine very black and sticky.

Such as were inhabited by nautical parties—retired skippers, partially decayed officers of the merchant service, with a slight smuggling cut about their figure-heads, or by small dealers in marine stores—who instinctively clung to the waterside in their declining years—had imparted to their residences as much as they possibly could of a maritime air.

Some of them had raised a mast over their roofs, and some had added cross-trees and stays and a vane, so that they might upon occasions of festivity hoist a Union-Jack.

Other parts of their dwelling-houses, though, bore evident signs of their origin. There were traces of ship-paint here and there, iron cramps and ring-bolts stuck out from the shrived and warped planks, which composed in some cases the little arbour, stuck in one corner among the rotten cabbages, and half-choked by rank vegetation, while strewed about were fragments of broken gun-carriages, staved in water-barrels, and rusty scraps of superannuated cabin-stoves.

Some of these persons who had settled here in this

dreary quarter were, as I have said, nautical, but for the most part the profession of the greater part of the population could only properly be described as "shy."

There was a good deal of doubt as to what some of them were, or how they got their living. They had a nasty habit of lounging through the entire day, occupied only by the consumption of coarse and unsavoury tobacco, or in the contemplation of a lean and remarkably foul-smelling pig, which generally formed a prominent part of their belongings.

When, however, the shades of evening closed in, signs of preparation were visible in these gentlemen's residences. Mysteriously-shaped tools were brought forth from dark corners;—they had an odd knack of keeping them stowed away between the mattresses of the bed, thrust up the kitchen-chimney, or in some cases even buried among the coals in the cellar;—and a great deal of inspecting, polishing, cleaning and oiling went on, after which their owner would get himself up for going out, and retire to business in a somewhat stealthy and sneaking fashion; not unfrequently carrying with him a bag in which to place his stock-in-trade, whatever that might be.

Visitors at the dwellings of these worthy artizans were few and far between; but occasionally a member of the police-force honoured them by a flying visit, coming in a gig or a hackney coach, and bringing with him a most pressing invitation from the sitting magistrate at Bow-street.

Now and then a doctor would make a call at one of the cottages, and talk business with the proprietor for an hour or so, with carefully closed doors, and upon the same evening it was customary for the industrious operative who had been consulted with, to go abroad, accompanied by a pick and spade among the other eccentric implements of his peculiar craft, though for what purpose it was difficult to say; for even supposing his profession had been that of a gardener, it is not customary to do gardening work after dark.

Mr. Jaggers was one of those mysterious tradesmen, and he lived in one of the tumble-down tenements just described. At the back of his house there was a yard surrounded by a very high wall, which was surmounted by sharp fragments of broken bottles, and otherwise carefully protected from the invasion of any one of an inquiring mind and climbing capabilities; although it certainly was rather difficult to imagine what motive could prompt a burglarious visit to Mr. Jagger's abode.

The only way in which this extreme care could be accounted for, was that Mr. Jaggers was the proprietor of bull-dogs; and as these animals are, though ferocious, sometimes rather valuable, Mr. Jaggers must have been afraid that without the protection of the high wall some one might come and steal them. Though certainly after seeing their wide gaping, savage jaws, and hearing their ferocious snarlings and snappings, it was difficult to suppose that there existed any one hardy enough to endeavour to grapple with them and bear them away.

But what else could the high wall have been intended to protect?

If nothing, perhaps it might have been to conceal something going on within.

If so, what? There are many strange and horrible mysteries of London life with which the writer of this history will have to deal. This among others :—

One night when dusky, swarming London lay stretched out supine in the bleary November fog, a certain antiquated, though still sprightly sprig of fashion, picked his way through the noise and bustle of the East-end streets, which reeked with exhalations of vile cookshops and low taverns, upon his way to Mr. Jaggers's abode. This gentleman was Mr. Balfour Fenwick, Lady Fane's venerable papa.

Eleven o'clock had just struck from the steeple of some obscure church, when the old man of fashion extricated himself from a labyrinth of shabby, dirty, and crowded streets, and entered the mournful district where Jaggers's house was situated.

Here all was solitary and mournful. Long lanes formed by high brickwalls, some of the former so narrow as to be obviously intended for foot passengers only, intersected each other, and down these he plunged, cursing loudly when at intervals he came upon and plunged into, unawares, some muddy puddle, which penetrated through the soles of his thin polished boots.

Leaving these walls behind, at last he reached a dreary expanse of brick-fields; and then, in time, came to the patches of garden-ground, and the curious maritime residences already described.

He appeared to know the locality pretty well, and made straight for Mr. Jaggers's house, at the door of which he rapped sharply with his knuckles.

Let us peep inside the house. Mr. Jaggers was there enjoying his pipe. He had no business appointment that evening, and as he fancied the weather seemed rather inclined to be stormy, he had determined to stop at home and enjoy himself.

He had rather a curious idea of enjoyment, though, as enjoyment goes, and it mostly consisted in bullying Mrs. Jaggers, who remained at home to keep him company.

Mrs. J. was a weak-looking creature, with drab-coloured hair, and eyes which blinked like those of a sleepy owl in a strong light.

She was a poor, thin, wisp of a woman, unsteady on her legs, spare, bony, and big jointed.

She was very tall and narrow, with the symmetry of a deal board, and it mattering but little which side was front.

She was much taller than her lord and master, upon whom she could look down very easily, but her superior height did not add to her courage, and she truckled to and trembled before the undersized, but sturdy ruffian in a way that was pitiful to behold.

Mr. Jaggers was, as has been said, smoking his pipe. He was also partaking of a glass of grog, which he made nice and strong, according to his somewhat eccentric fancy—adding no water, but heating the spirit in a pipkin, which stood ready to his hand upon the hob.

Mr. Jaggers sat right in front of the fire, with one foot upon either hob, and this attitude effectually blocked out all warmth for poor Mrs. J., who sat chattering with cold in a dark corner behind him.

Seated upon the boiler, with his head just visible in the dim obscurity of the chimney, was an impish boy, with a head of fiery red hair as coarse as hay. A horrible young wretch was this, with an unwholesome face, and an awful squint; and as he sat perched up there in a wonderfully uncouth and uncomfortable attitude, he looked like a goblin elf.

He did not appear to be altogether fire-proof, though, in spite of the warm place he had chosen, for every now and then he kicked his legs about wildly, and roared out lustily when his amiable parent, Mr. Jaggers, having heated the poker in the fire, amused himself by lunging at him with it.

"Leave me alone, curse you, will you?" cried the young gentleman in loud accents of rage, when Mr. Jaggers had repeated the assault for about the twentieth time, upon each succeeding occasion increasing the poker's heat.

"Does it hurt you?" asked Mr. Jaggers, with a grin of much enjoyment. "I hope it does, for cursing your father, you unnatural young warmint. Where do you expect to go to, I wonder?"

"Much you cares where I goes," retorted the ill-looking lad, making, if possible, a more horrible face than usual at his kind parent.

"There's your mother, too," said Mr. Jaggers, looking over his shoulder, with a sneer. "She's a pretty picture of what a woman ought to be, she is. I wonder she can sleep comfortable o'nights, when she thinks how she's neglected her duty by you. Blowed if I don't."

"You've neither on you done wery much, you hevn't," said the imp.

"Now, none of your sarce, young gent," said Mr. Jaggers, sternly; "else I shall bore a hole through you with this here bit of iron. I don't see why I shouldn't. You're no particular good as it is, and I might make a something by exhibiting you in a show, if you was only the least bit uglier nor you are."

The imp made no reply to this taunt; and Mr. Jaggers, after lunging out at his offspring with the hot poker two or three times, went on with his pipe in silence.

When the time presently arrived that his glass required replenishing, the resurrection man looked about for the spirit-bottle, and discovered, with a loud curse, that it had been upset by the imp's struggles during their last little bout with the hot poker.

"You infernal young thief!" cried the doting father. "I'll strangle you. I'll brob your eye out—I'll wrench your ear off—I'll draw all your teeth with the tongs—I'll—I'll—take that, you tarnation warmint!"

And, suiting the action to the word, he showered down a perfect volley of ferocious blows upon the thin legs of his hopeful progeny, who dodged frantically to avoid the punishment, screeching at the same time like an owl.

When Mr. Jaggers, however, had somewhat tired himself by this playful exercise, he went back to his pipe, and feeling rather warm, drew back from the fire.

It was then that his eyes lighted upon the bony wife of his bosom, sitting, crouching and shivering, in the corner in a strong draught.

"Wake up!" roared Mr. Jaggers.

But as the unfortunate woman was in the habit of sleeping through the most awful dins, she did not open her eyes very readily.

Mr. Jaggers was impatient, and could not wait. So he picked a nice lump of coal out of the skuttle standing by his side and flung it at her.

His aim was very good, and it rattled upon the crown of her head.

Mrs. Jaggers woke up with a snort, and rubbed the place; at which Mr. Jaggers, junior, who was not, perhaps, the most affectionate child in the world, burst into a loud scream of laughter.

"Curse your sleepy head!" cried the resurrectionist; "haven't you rest enough when I'm not at home, that you must go snoring in company? If I catch you at it again, I'll raise a lump on your ear as big as a hostrich's egg,"

"What do you want?" the woman asked, getting up, and shivering.

"What do you expect I want, except it's to be waited on in my own house?"

"Do you want me to get you anything?"

"Yes; you'll have to pack off for some more gin."

"What, more to-night?" asked the woman, in a tone of mingled astonishment and reproach; for she did not know, of course, that the bottle had been overturned, and its contents spilt.

"Don't stand there argyfying," roared Jaggers, in a terrible tone; "what do you mean by it?"

"I—I—I meant nothing, Jaggers."

"Look sharp, then; and don't try to jaw me, or I'll teach you."

The poor victim knew to her sorrow what his "teaching" meant, and began to tremble in anticipation of his ill treatment.

"Stir your stumps, will you?" roared Jaggers, in a tone of thunder; but his voice only frightened her, and made her look more scared than before.

Mr. Jaggers, then, thinking that she required, as he termed it, "stirring up a trifle," picked out another lump of coal, and threw it at her.

It hit her a sharp blow upon one of her long, lean hands, and brought blood; at which act of cruelty the poor creature burst out crying.

"Oh! that's the game, now, is it?" cried Jaggers, in a fury. "I'll give you something to squeak about, my beauty."

He looked about, uncertain for a time what barbarity he should practise.

A surly-looking bull-dog lay in the corner, which, at intervals snapped and snarled when the voice of his master's playful occupations disturbed his slumbers.

"Here, Scruncher!" cried the resurrectionist. "Give her a shaking, my lad."

The dog did not wait to be told twice, but started up and ran at the unfortunate woman.

She saw him coming, and fled, screaming, round the room; the dog following, snapping at her heels.

It was not the first time that this brutal and unmanly pastime had been practised by the vagabond who now was urging on the dog by oaths and cries; and he was well up to his work.

The poor woman, scared out of her wits, shrieked loudly, and ran to and fro, panting for breath between her cries.

Every moment the dog seemed upon the point of making his fangs meet in her flesh.

To save herself then, she wildly plunged and dodged the brute from behind a chair, getting, in her terror, into attitudes which were outrageously grotesque and laughable, had not the brutality of the exhibition, and the sufferings of the poor, terrified creature been taken into account.

At last her frantic terror reached the climax. She could struggle no longer, could bear no more, and she fell half fainting to the ground.

Then only did the ruffian husband think fit to call off the dog and the impish lad to cease from the savage laughter with which he had hitherto greeted his poor mother's despairing efforts to escape the laceration of her flesh from the teeth of the snarling brute pursuing her.

The hubbub having at length terminated thus, Jaggers became suddenly aware that there was a knock at the outer door.

He started to his feet, hit his hopeful son a sharp slap in the mouth to make him hold his tongue, kicked the bull-dog into a corner, pulled his wife off the ground and thrust her into a chair with a violent shake and a recommendation not to make a fool of herself, then went towards the door.

He was rather doubtful about opening it, having some slight misgiving that it might be some one in the police-force paying him a visit.

A loud summons coming again in another moment, however, he made up his mind to face the visitor whoever he was, and shoving back the bolt which secured the door, raised the latch, and faced the applicant for admission.

It was Mr. Balfour Fenwick, who wore a short cloak with the collar turned up, and a comforter tied round the lower part of his face, as though he wished to conceal his features as much as possible.

Jaggers stood staring at him for a moment without being able to recognise his visitor. Mr. Fenwick meanwhile peeped in over his shoulder, desirous of ascertaining the cause of the awful din he had heard as he approached the resurrectionist's abode.

"Wh-what the dickens are you about, my friend?" asked the antiquated Buck, looking in very pale and frightened. "Wh-what a noise you're making!"

"What the devil is it to you what we're doing?" retorted Jaggers, fiercely. "Who are you, and— Lor', Mr. Fenwick, sir, I hope I see you nicely."

"Yes— yes, thank you, quite well; only a little tired by the walk, and a little—a little put out by this ugly neighbourhood of yours."

"It is a cursed ugly bit of country, and that's no lie," replied Jaggers, "and hardly a safe one for a spicy old bloke like you to be walking about in by yourself. There's parties about here, bless you, as wouldn't—as wouldn't—"

"Wouldn't what?" asked Mr. Fenwick, nervously.

"Mind slitting your weazen, if you know what that is," answered Jaggers, with a brutal laugh.

"I don't," said Mr. Fenwick; "I haven't the remotest notion, but it sounds very horrible, for all that."

Jaggers meanwhile had closed the door and handed his visitor a chair. Then he picked up the overturned bottle from where it lay, and handed it to his wife.

"Come, bundle out and get some more gin," said he, "and don't let me have to wake you up again this evening, there's a dear."

He accompanied the last words by a wrench of the woman's wrist, which made her wince and groan. She made no remonstrance or resistance though, but set off upon her errand.

"Jaggers," said Mr. Fenwick, when she was gone and the door was closed behind her, "I want to speak to you."

"I'm your servant, sir."

"Are we alone?"

"Not quite. Here, Satan's own, go to blazes."

He flung a handful of coal at his youthful progeny as he spoke, and sent him roaring out of the room.

"Don't get a listening," said Jaggers, in a warning voice, "or I'll have out one of your eye-teeth, so you know what you've got to expect."

Mr. Jaggers had not very much faith, however, in his son's trustworthiness, but presently peeped out into the passage, jerking open the door suddenly, and kicking furiously out into space.

The imp, though, fortunately for himself, was either not there at all or was out of harm's way, for the only result of this manœuvre was that the fond parent almost disjointed his leg, and came back to his seat limping and cursing horribly.

"Curse him," muttered Jaggers, rubbing his leg; "he's not at his tricks; lucky for him. Now, sir, what have you got to talk to me about?"

"I'm in a deuce of a mess, Jaggers, and I want your assistance."

"What am I to do?"

"There's no one listening, you think?"

"No—no; it's right enough now."

"If what I am going to tell you were overheard it would be— as much as my life's worth."

"Is it a hanging matter?"

"Yes."

"Speak low, then, for fear of accidents. Or stay; come with me to the shambles, and we'll talk it over quietly."

So speaking, Jaggers rose, and carrying the candle in his hand, led the way down a dark passage out into the enclosed yard beyond, which was, as has been described, surrounded by a high wall, and to which its proprietor had given a name horribly suggestive of blood and violence.

CHAPTER XX.

THE FIRST LINK IN THE CHAIN OF GUILT.

IT was a very gloomy and uninviting spot this, to which Jaggers had conducted Mr. Balfour Fenwick, and the latter peered round with increasing uneasiness into the dark shadows which blocked up the distant corners and hid from him he knew not what unknown horrors.

Scarcely had he taken half-a-dozen steps forward, when a savage bull-dog flew out at him and ground its shining teeth within a foot of his leg.

The old fop, shaking like a leaf, sheltered himself behind his companion, and cried out wildly for protection, but Jaggers had only to roar out an oath at the brute to cause it to slink back into its kennel, and they proceeded onwards in safety.

A few yards further on they came to some object upon the ground, which again caused Mr. Fenwick to start and stop.

A horrible mass of torn and mangled flesh, from which gleamed forth white naked bones, lay directly in his pathway.

"Wh-what's that, in God's name?" cried the ancient fop, shaking so violently that he could scarcely keep his false teeth in his head.

"It's all right," replied the other, with a grin. "Come on."

"But—but—"

"It wont bite you, man."

"What is it, I say?"

"It's only the carcase of a horse the dogs have been worrying. Come on, will you?"

The old man followed trembling, and inwardly wishing himself anywhere else on the wide face of the earth than where he chanced to find himself.

But he had gone too far now to retract, and so put the best face he could find upon the matter. He kept his eyes, however, warily fixed upon his companion, whose air was horribly wild and fierce, for he was far gone under the influence of the liquor he had been imbibing, and at such times was little better than a madman.

Indeed, Mr. Fenwick had serious doubts cross his mind more than once as to whether his accomplice was in a fit state to receive the communication he was about to make to him, and it is probable that nothing but the extreme urgency of the case, and the danger of losing any more time than was absolutely necessary, compelled him finally to make the revelation.

He did so at last, when Jaggers having led the way to a small outhouse or shed he stuck the candle down upon a rough wooden table, and taking a seat beside it, said:—

"It's all right here. Now we can talk."

"I told you I was in a mess," said Mr. Fenwick, speaking with some hesitation, "didn't I?"

"Yes—yes; I ain't a bit surprised at it."

"What do you mean?"

"That you've been in one so often before, that's all."

"Never in such a horrible fix as the one I am in now, Mr. Jaggers. Never in half such a fix."

"Oh, this is something very bad, is it?"

"I shall be ruined if you don't help me. It is a matter of life and death."

Jaggers glanced up at his companion's eager, terrified face, which was quivering with emotion.

"You—you haven't been murdering anyone, have you?" he asked.

"No—no; nothing of that sort. It's only appropriating some—some money."

"Collaring some one else's kelter, in other words."

"I borrowed it, thinking I should be able to return it before the loss was discovered."

"Humph! ah! exactly!" said Jaggers, rubbing his chin. "That's the case with all you swells that does a bit of faking. Us common blokes drops our ogle on to a thing, and grabs it without no humbug one way nor t'other; but there's so much blarney about you genteel 'uns."

"I should have been able to have paid back the money if I had not been come upon unexpectedly—if I had only a few days' warning—"

"To be sure."

"It was some plate I had intrusted to my care, and —and—"

"You melted it down?"

"No—no; not as bad as that."

"What then?"

"I—I got some money advanced upon them."

"Took them to your uncle's?"

"No—no; not exactly that. To a private person who lends money on all kinds of property."

"Same sort of thing in the end. I suppose an unlicensed pawnbroker—that's all. Bit of the tally business it sounds like. However, you pawned the swag, and can't get the money to redeem it. Ain't that the ticket ?"

"Yes; that is the state of the case."

"Do you want me to help you to prig it back again, then ?"

"No; there's no chance of that. That is impossible."

"What am I to do ?"

"I do not want you to commit a robbery. Only—only to pretend—"

"Pretend ? Why, what the blazes—"

"I will explain, if you are not so violent. I want you to bring your instruments—housebreaking tools, I mean, and operate on my office-door, and my desk, and strong box, so as to make it look, you know, as if there had been thieves."

"Oh ! you sly old fox. I understand, exactly. When the party comes to ask you for the swag, it's been prigged. Only my fine friend—"

"Only what ?"

"How about the party as lent you the money ?"

"What of him ?"

"Wont he blow on you ?"

"Not he; he had the jewels at half their value."

"Well ?"

"And he has agreed, if I let him keep them, to say nothing."

"Obliging individual !"

"Can you help me, do you think ?"

"Of course I can, my dear sir. I'm your man for anything that's daring or delicate, only give it a name, as long as you pay well, for I'm cursedly hard up. Body-snatching ain't what it used to be, and—and somehow"—here the ruffian gave a horrible shudder—"I don't take to it kindly since I had a bit of a start the other night with one of the subjects."

"What was that ?" asked Mr. Fenwick, looking at his companion in alarm, and glancing timidly round.

"Oh ! nothing worth speaking of," replied Jaggers, after a moment's silence. "Nothing worth speaking of. By the way, talking of jewels, I have a trifle in that line to dispose of, if you could find me a customer."

He drew a small parcel from his breast as he spoke, and unfolding the paper in which it was wrapped, exhibited to his companion a beautiful little bracelet, sparkling with gems; the same which the mysterious lady had let fall at the gate of the city churchyard.

"A sweet thing, ain't it ?" said Jaggers; "and to be had dirt cheap."

Mr. Fenwick took it in his hand, turned it over in astonishment, and exclaimed—

"Where did you get it ? Good heavens ! It is my daughter's !"

CHAPTER XXI.

THE MISSING BRIDEGROOM.

IT was near twelve o'clock, and St. George's, Hanover-square, was a scene of grand confusion. A string of carriages blocked up all the surrounding thoroughfares, and the elegance of the ladies' dresses, the superabundance of orange-blossom, clematis, lilies of the valley, and the gigantic bouquets and favours of the coachmen and footmen, announced that a fashionable wedding of importance was taking, or about to take place.

A motley crowd surrounded the steps of the church, which the zealous and excited policemen were doing their best to keep back. Whilst the pompous fat functionary in a cocked hat and a large quantity of gold lace, yclept the beadle, was striking attitudes as he received the company and marshalled them down the centre aisle of the church, at the same time keeping a very large weather-eye open for the stray half-crowns.

The bridesmaids, groomsmen, father, and every one, were assembled in the vestry—the bride arrived, but the man of all others—he who was to be made the happiest fellow in existence—was late !

Various were the unpleasant speeches with regard to this extraordinary conduct; and many were the cruel things said at the expense of Felbridge Winder.

"Such an insult to the bride !" said one.

"It's abominable !" said a second.

"The conceited ape," said a third. This was an incipient swell, and a rival of Winder's in the affections of an enormously rich widow.

"And what an insult to us all !" chorused two or three dowagers.

"If he doesn't show up soon," said a long guardsman who "went in" for ferocity, "I shall take it as a personal affront !"

The bride and her relations were now showing signs of uneasiness, and every one offered a surmise as to the cause of his absence, thus creating no small confusion in the sacred edifice.

The Bishop of Narrow Bands, assisted by two reverend gentlemen, were ready robed, and growing impatient at the delay. But still no signs of the bridegroom.

Beyond one or two dear lady friends of the bride, no one, perhaps, seemed more pleased at the non-arrival of the volatile Winder than a veiled lady, who stood in a pew near the altar, and glanced round toward the door from time to time, as if in anxious expectation.

As the time went on, and surprise and consternation was on every face, she seemed to grow reassured, and whispered continually to an artistic-looking gentleman who stood by her side, and who alone, of all present, seemed the only person not interested in the proceedings for which they were assembled. He appeared to have no eyes but for the veiled lady at his side, and drank in every word she uttered with an eagerness that spoke volumes.

"He's not arrived yet," whispered the lady, trembling visibly.

"No," replied her companion, "there must be some accident."

"Accident !" repeated the lady, apparently alarmed.

"I don't mean anything serious. Perhaps his tailor has disappointed him—or he may have overslept himself. You know he was up until very late."

"Or he may have repented—may even have returned to Half-moon-street." As she said this, she looked up into her companion's face, evidently hoping to read there the confirmation of her surmise. But his expression was simply one of sadness, as she recurred to what appeared to be to him a painful subject.

Half-past twelve—a quarter to one—one o'clock, and no bridegroom ! The lookers-on were gradually dropping off; and now some of the party prepared to depart. The Right Reverend Bishop and the reverend gentlemen were beginning to disrobe—but no bridegroom ! The expression on the faces of the sisters and parents of the bride had now changed from anxiety to dismay, and the bride was led in a half-fainting condition from the church. And as they embarked in Maddox-street, to spare the feelings of the unhappy girl that Winder was to have made miserable for life, the retreating carriages were greeted with the yells and hootings of the disappointed mob, who were awaiting the return of the party in the front.

The last persons to leave the church were the veiled lady and the artistic-looking gentleman. The bearing of the former was very different to what it had been on entering the church. She now walked with an elastic step, and her face had assumed a tranquil and hopeful expression; whilst her companion, on the contrary, appeared somewhat saddened by the unexpected termination of the wedding they had come to witness.

MR. FENWICK TRIES TO ESCAPE FROM THE HOUSE OF THE RESURRECTIONIST.

They walked slowly down Bond-street — the lady forcing the pace as much as the apparent disinclination to do so on the part of her companion would permit. Half-way down the street the gentleman paused before a music-seller's, and called the lady's attention to the illustrated title-page of the latest waltz.

She looked up carelessly, as a matter of politeness, her thoughts being, it was very evident, elsewhere, when her attention was arrested by seeing a gentleman in the shop who was purchasing some tickets.

"Good heavens!" she exclaimed; "there's Winder!"

"Winder! Egad! it is. What can the truant bride-groom be doing there?"

"See—he's coming out. Shall we step aside and watch his movements?"

"As you please, Miss Willoughby."

Accordingly, they walked a few paces down the street, and, surely enough, Mr. Felbridge Winder—whom everybody had been awaiting an hour and more at the church—stepped forth from the music-seller's shop, looking as unconcerned as possible.

A carriage was standing before the shop-door, into which Mr. Winder, after calling out directions to the coachman, jumped, and was whirled rapidly down Bond-street towards Piccadilly.

As they passed the spot where the watchers stood, they caught a glimpse of Winder, with his face expressing as much animation as he had in him, laughing and chatting to a beautiful and elegantly-dressed lady who sat beside him, and perfectly oblivious of the amount of food for scandal he had provided for the fashionable world by his extraordinary absence on his wedding-day.

The lady alluded to, it need scarely be said, was the Lady Amatoria Crutchingford.

"That woman, too !" exclaimed Alice Willoughby.

"Who is she ?" demanded her companion.

"Lady Amatoria Crutchingford. It is for her that Felbridge has deserted me, Mr. Harley."

"What !" said the artist ; "the wife of old Lord Crutchingford ?"

"The same," said Alice, bitterly. "The woman is a perfect scandal. But where can they be going to now ?"

"I don't know—unless to May-fair with her ladyship. But Winder must be surely mad to go about openly with this woman, after the events of the morning."

"If I only knew where they were going to. Stay—he was buying tickets at the music-seller's. You could easily ascertain what they were for, by inquiring in the shop under some pretext."

"A good idea," said the artist. And they walked back towards the shop. As he was about to enter, he caught sight of a bill in the window of a masquerade for that evening.

"Here it is," he said. "Masquerade to-night."

"Yes, that is it, no doubt," said Alice Willoughby. "And I shall be there to meet them."

"But surely, Miss Willoughby, you'll never go to the ball alone."

"Unless you will accompany me."

"Accompany you, Alice—that is, Miss Willoughby," exclaimed the artist, with rapture. "You make me the happiest of men !"

But here Alice put a stop to his ecstasies by observing—"And then we must make one more effort to reclaim him."

"Ah ! of course," said Harley, grimly.

They walked on in silence until they came to the corner of Half-moon-street, where Alice Willoughby withdrew her arm from his.

"And now, Mr. Harley," she said, "I will not trouble you to come any farther."

"Trouble, Miss Willoughby !"

"And if I might again trespass so far on your kindness as to beg you to bring tickets for the masquerade to-night, and early—for I shall be eager to get there——"

"Miss Willoughby, the thought is intoxication !"

"Then at seven I shall expect you."

"At six, if you please—but would you do me an enormous favour, Miss Willoughby ?"

"Anything that lies in my power, Mr. Harley. I should, indeed, be ungrateful else for your kindness. But this favour is ——?"

"That you would call me Frank."

"It would sound strange, I think ; but as you wish it I will. Good bye."

"Good bye till six," said Frank Harley.

"No," said Alice, laughing. "At seven I shall expect you, Frank."

The artist stood gazing after her until she entered the house, in a state of ecstatic oblivion to all around. She had called him "Frank," and it had taken his breath away. How beautiful his name had sounded from her lips ! And he turned, with a last fond look in the direction of her house, and proceeded homewards, to pass a miserable time until he should be with her again.

As he passed the Quadrant his attention was attracted by a row of men bearing advertising-boards announcing the grand masquerade as taking place "to-night," which reminded him that he had to purchase the tickets, and he let his hands drop into his pockets—but, alas ! no welcome chink greeted their entrance.

"Not a stiver, by all that's unfortunate !" he muttered. "What's to be done ?" As he spoke he instinctively drew out his watch—an unpretending silver Geneva.

"Thirty shillings, at the very least," he exclaimed, examining it with the air of a connoisseur ; and he proceeded to look about for the emblem of riches—the three golden balls—working out small problems in mental arithmetic as he went.

"Fifteen shillings ticket—cab there and back, three shillings — one ice for Alice, a shilling — nineteen shillings, leaving me a balance in hand of eleven shillings. Couldn't do better if I was worth a thousand a year."

He looked about him in every direction, and the street being tolerably clear made a sudden rush up a narrow court by the side of a pawnbroker's, and dived into one of the gloomy little boxes, to find himself in company with two or three females of the lower class who were raising the funds upon the security of some flat-irons and various articles of domestic utility.

With an exclamation of disgust he rushed out and into the next one, where he was greeted by a gruff voice, demanding "What the devil d'you want here ?"

Harley muttered out some indistinct apology to the uncivil personage, who was a young man muffled up and his hat drawn over his eyes, so that his face was perfectly invisible, and who spoke in an assumed voice, as if everybody who entered had a peculiar motive in piercing his incognito, and beat a hasty retreat.

Next door he was more fortunate. He had the satisfaction to find himself alone, and seeing, to his great comfort, that the door possessed a bolt, he was enabled to secure himself against intrusion.

He walked up to the counter to wait until the shopman was disengaged ; but seeing the ladies, who were disposing of the cooking utensils and the flat-irons a few boxes off, had an ugly knack of lolling their arms over the counter, and exchanging salutes with acquaintances in the other boxes, he retreated as far back into the compartment as possible, and silently divested himself of his watch.

"What can I do for you, sir ?" demanded mine uncle.

"What can you advance me upon the security of this," said Harley, in a whisper.

"That's not the question," said his relation. "What do you want on it ?"

"Well, I wanted the utmost ; but I could do with thirty shillings."

"Thirteen shillings," said the man. "No, couldn't do more than twelve."

"Twelve !" gasped Frank Harley. "I said thirty !"

"Thirty—impossible ! Might at a pinch make it fourteen, but then we shall be four or five shillings out of pocket if you don't redeem it."

"That's no use. I must go elsewhere," said Harley, picking up his watch.

"Stay," said mine uncle. "What have you had on it before ?"

"Sir !" said the artist, indignantly.

"I mean to say the last time," said the man, who mistook the artist's exclamation of offence for an interrogation.

Without a word Harley stalked to the door and was going out, when the shopman stopped him with—

"If you'll say what you want, sir, we could come to terms, perhaps."

"A pound is the lowest I could take."

"Then you'll never get it on that. I can spring another shilling or two—say sixteen shillings."

Harley paused. "No," he said. "Eighteen I might do with."

"Then we'll meet half-way," said the shopman. "Say seventeen."

"Harley ran up an addition before replying. "Ticket fifteen shillings ; cab there two shillings, seventeen shillings ; ice for Alice—oh ! she'll never be able to think of ices." Then he added aloud to the close-fisted shopman, "Very well, then—seventeen."

"What name, please ?"

"Personne."

"What address ?"

"Nimporte-street."

"What's this ? You have only given me sixteen and elevenpence."

"Penny for the ticket, sir."

"Confound it!" muttered the artist between his clenched teeth. "What an infernal swindle!"

He carefully looked up and down the court before making his exit, and seeing the coast clear he darted into the main street with a rush that brought down upon the unfortunate artist the very result he had taken such pains to avoid. Two or three urchins were playing at pitch and toss in the court,—probably residents, used to the sort of thing,—and one of them shouted out after him some unpleasant familiarities, insinuating that he had been disposing of his linen under-garment by the process vulgarly known as "spouting."

Harley mentally consigned the urchins to—well, anywhere but their present play-ground, and resumed his arithmetical problem.

"Ticket fifteen shillings. Cab there two shillings. No, it's only an eighteen-penny ride. Sixteen and sixpence, leaving a clear balance in hand of fivepence. Couldn't do better if I was worth ten thousand a year!"

And with this very excellent philosophy Frank Harley struggled to convince himself that he was perfectly at ease in his mind with regard to his financial position. He had some very serious doubts in his heart of hearts, but he soon quieted these with the thought that he would go with *her* under any circumstances, however unpleasant.

He ran along with a hop, skim, and a jump, and in a few minutes was at home. Frank Harley's studio was situated on the second floor of a gloomy-looking old house in an inn, which I shall take the liberty of christening, for obvious reasons, and shall call it—"Hobson's," and which is situated not a hundred miles from High Holborn.

He took his key from the man at the porter's lodge in an abstracted manner, without so much as thanking him.

"There's a letter for you, Mr. Harley," said the porter.

"Yes, Podge, it is, very fine," said the artist, passing on without having heard what the man had said.

"I said there was a letter for you, sir," said Mr. Podge.

"Letter—oh! thank you."

"I put it into your letter-box, sir."

Harley again nodded his thanks to the porter and ran up the stairs, smiling to himself. "From Dawber, no doubt," he said; "deuced fortunate! I shouldn't have managed the masquerade very well, after all, upon sixteen and elevenpence."

He took the letter out of the box, but before opening it he ran up another addition. "Ticket fifteen shillings—cabs four shillings—refreshments, say a pound; and as I've got this five pounds I may as well hire a costume instead of putting myself under the obligation of borrowing Whiffler's seedy cavalier's dress. Dress, say another pound—a clear balance in hand of two pounds seventeen and elevenpence."

As he spoke he tore off the envelope and read aloud—

"Dear Harley." "Good heavens!" he exclaimed, changing colour, "it isn't from Dawber," and he continued, "Dear Harley, you are the only friend I have who is really a trump. I am in a devil of a hobble, and for a paltry fiver. Knowing you too well, old fellow, to insult you by even asking your assistance, I merely mention that you will learn full particulars at "The Gridiron," where you are anxiously awaited by Mark Dashleigh!"

"Sponge," "cadger," "fool," and "idiot," were the least opprobrious epithets applied by the disappointed and chagrined artist to the writer of this unfortunate epistle.

However, there was no help for it, and the easy-going Harley's philosophy soon supplanted his temporary disappointment; and not five minutes after he had been venting his spleen in such violent language against his unexpected correspondent, he had returned to the mental arithmetic, and again wound up the problem by solemnly assuring himself that he could not do it better on a thousand a year.

CHAPTER XXII.

THE ACCUSATION.

WHEN Mr. Balfour Fenwick claimed acquaintance with the bracelet, Jaggers's first idea was that it was a trick upon the old gentleman's part to obtain possession of the ornament upon very moderate terms; and as such a proceeding did not quite agree with his views upon the subject, he wrathfully snatched it out of his companion's hands, and demanded in an indignant tone what he meant.

Mr. Fenwick stared at him in astonishment.

"What do *you* mean?" he ventured to ask, after a pause. "I don't quite understand you."

"Oh, you know well enough," grumbled the other. "Don't try it on again, that's all."

"Try what on?"

"Try to lay a claim to that little bit of ornament."

"I have no wish to lay a claim to it or to take it from you without sufficient compensation."

"What do *you* mean, then?"

"I only mean that I recognise that bracelet as belonging to my daughter."

"How?"

"By certain peculiarities in the workmanship."

"Oh!"

"And by the initials."

"What initials?"

"Worked into the scroll upon the clasp."

Jaggers reproduced the bracelet from his pocket, into which he had thrust it precipitately after having snatched it out of Mr. Fenwick's hands; then, holding it close to the candle, scrutinized it earnestly.

"I don't see none," he said, presently. "Where is it?"

"There, on the clasp."

"Oh, ah! I didn't see it before. What's the letters?"

"E. F."

Mr. Jaggers sat upon the table, holding the bracelet in his hand, and slowly looking from it to his companion and back again. He was trying to bring his mind to bear upon a certain suspicion that was buzzing through his head, but the potations he had imbibed in the earlier part of the evening had so muddled his intellect that it was only with the greatest difficulty he could grasp the difficulties of the case.

In the meantime, Mr. Fenwick, who had been gazing upon the resurrectionist with gathering wonder, broke a long silence by inquiring how he had obtained possession of the article in question.

"I found it," replied Jaggers, at last.

Mr. Fenwick smiled rather incredulously.

"You came by it in the regular routine of business, I suppose," said he, attempting a small joke. "Is that what you mean?"

"I mean what I say; I found it."

"Where?"

"In—in the street."

"Long ago?"

"A week."

"That's curious."

"Why is it?"

"Because I should have supposed that my daughter would have mentioned her loss before now."

"Why?"

"Because it was a favourite ornament of hers. I gave it her years ago, in happier times—before she was married."

"I don't see why she should tell you about it," said Jaggers, after a moment's reflection; "most likely she was afraid to."

" Afraid of annoying me—to be sure. I did not think of that at the moment; and still, when I think of it again, I hardly believe that was the reason. She would have been sure to mention it, and ask my advice —she always does upon any matter of business."

Mr. Jaggers smiled rather insultingly upon the man of business who was speaking, and who probably looked as unlike what he represented as one well could who had been all his life a man of fashion, and had grown grey and wrinkled, spindle-legged and shrunken in the service of the fickle goddess.

Presently the resurrectionist volunteered another suggestion.

" Suppose it has been stolen out of her boxes without her knowing it."

" But you said——"

" Said *I* hadn't stole it—I didn't answer for any one else."

" No, no—certainly."

" There's other thieves in the world, aint there ?"

" Yes, yes—to be sure."

" Without going a thousand miles."

" I'm sure I beg your pardon, Mr. Jaggers, and hope you wont take offence where none——"

" I aint taking offence, but I can't say a word without your putting in your blessed spoke. Praps I may help you to find out something about this 'ere bracelet, and about them as took it, if so be as you'll keep your spoke out for half a minute."

" Certainly, certainly, Mr. Jaggers; if you can throw any light upon the affair I shall be very much obliged to you."

" Perhaps it may be to your benefit that I do, and perhaps it mayn't," said Jaggers, sententiously, and wagging his head at the candle while he talked. " Perhaps I may have my reasons for wanting to know something about this bracelet, and perhaps I mayn't. It all depends. There's no answering for nobody nor nothing in this world, and there's no saying——"

He paused here, and looking up from the candle to Mr. Fenwick's face, blinked at it with intense and somewhat ludicrous seriousness.

" No," said Mr. Fenwick, thinking he was called upon to say something.

Jaggers leant back and frowned ominously.

" Why no ?" he asked, sternly. " Why not yes ?" If you know all about it, and so much better than me, find it out yourself."

" I don't know anything about it," replied Mr. Fenwick, growing very weary of this lengthy consultation; and observing that his companion's inebriety had steadily increased for some time past, he began to ask himself how Jaggers could perform the burglarious feats that he required at his hands before next morning.

" I don't suppose you do know much," said Jaggers, contemptuously; " but let me ask you a question or two."

" What are they ?"

" Has your daughter a lady's-maid ?"

" Yes."

" Is she tall or short ?"

" Rather short."

" Oh ! it wasn't her, then."

" What wasn't ?"

" Never you mind just yet. But tell me who there is in your house that's tall and slight, and has yellow-coloured hair."

" That is my daughter's description."

" So I thought; she's in mourning, too, isn't she ?"

" Yes; in mourning for her husband."

" Ah, to be sure. A City gentleman, wasn't he ?"

" He was my partner."

" In Lincoln's-inn-fields ?"

" Yes."

" And he had nothing to do with the City, hadn't he ? How was it, then ?"

But Mr. Jaggers caught himself up abruptly when upon the point of asking a question, and stroked his chin slowly as he reflected.

" I always thought he was in the City," he said, after a brief pause, " but I don't know how I came to get it into my head."

" He was my partner, and, consequently, a solicitor."

" To be sure. And he was precious rich, according to all accounts, and you, too; but I suppose it's all a sham. Your daughter, though, I suppose she's well provided for ?"

" On the contrary; she has only a small income left her, which is derived from other sources."

" That's a bad job."

" Mr. Worwold was mixed up in a hundred and one speculations, as perhaps you are aware. Very luckily I was never led into them myself. As to the office business, I'm afraid some ugly little things will turn up, and I also have been rather imprudent in this case of the jewels, so that it's just probable that—that——"

" That you'll have to make yourself scarce, I am not surprised," mumbled Jaggers to himself.

" I never should have imagined that Worwold would have gone the lengths he did, as I can't make out what could have become of the money, because he hadn't the expensive tastes that have been the ruin of me. He must have put his capital into very rotten speculations. I was very much astonished, though, when I came to know the whole truth at his death. But I am not the only one who was deceived. Why, some people thought him to be a model of piety; and the minister of the old church where he was buried, in the City——"

" Ah !"

" What's the matter ?"

" Nothing—nothing; I was listening to what you were saying. You don't bear him any particular goodwill, I should suppose, from what you say; and your daughter—she was very fond of him, I suppose ?"

He uttered these words in a tone which immediately arrested the old man's attention, who looked at him in silent alarm.

Jaggers fixed his eyes upon the old man's face, then stretched forth his hand and grasped him by the wrist.

" Did she benefit by his death," asked the resurrection man, in a hissing whisper, " or did she hate him ?"

But the old man made no answer. A ghastly pallor had crept over his pinched features, which seemed to age him suddenly by a score of years.

He trembled violently in every limb, and his false teeth chattered like castanets.

For awhile the power of speech seemed to have entirely diserted him, but at length, grasping the resurrectionist's arm with his thin wasted hands, he fell upon his knees before him, and, clinging frantically to him, cried in a tone of shuddering entreaty—

" No, no, Jaggers, don't say that. Don't accuse her. For God's sake don't accuse her. You don't know what a villain he was—what a cold-blooded, cruel tyrant. He deserved twice his death; but she—no—no. In Mercy's name do not bring my poor child to the gallows."

CHAPTER XXIII.

CIVILIZED SAVAGES.

IT is impossible to guess what would have been Jaggers's reply to the old man's wild prayer for mercy had not an event at this particular moment occurred to bring the strange scene to an abrupt termination.

The interruption was caused by that poor whisp of a woman, Mrs. Jaggers, coming running out into the back-yard, with a flaring candle in her hand, to say that some gentlemen had come to look at the dogs.

" All right, you fool," responded her amiable husband. " Where are they ?"

"I didn't know whether you could see the gentlemen."

"You haven't been idiot enough to send 'em away, surely ?"

"No, I said I would go and see if you were at the back. I thought you might be engaged."

"So I am," said Jaggers, with a nod of his head towards the old man, who had by this time risen to his feet. "Particular engaged here along of my friend Mr. Fenwick."

"Hush !" cried the other, making a warning gesture with his hand, which caution, however, Mr. Jaggers thought fit totally to disregard.

"Along of my friend Mr. Fenwick," he repeated, in an offensively familiar tone, though the old man made no attempt to resent it. "But Mr. Fenwick wont mind putting off his business for a bit until I have seen these here other gents ; and, indeed, he'll be glad to see 'em, too."

Fenwick caught the speaker eagerly by the arm—

"No, no !" he said. "Not for worlds !"

"What's the matter now ?"

"I cannot meet those people here."

"Why not ? Aint they good enough company for you. It's the parties that were here yesterday, aint it ?" he asked his wife.

"Yes."

"A live lord one of 'em is, then, and a honourable, and another one or two tip-top swells, with handles to their names as long as Aldgate pump."

"But—but—I did not wish my visit to be——"

"Is there any 'arm in a gent dropping in at my place to pick out a dawg from my stock, as is the finest in all London, or is there any 'arm in his stopping an hour in the shambles to see a real right down bit of sport."

"No, no, there can be no harm in that, but——"

"But you'll stop, Mr. Fenwick, if you please. I can't take no for a answer ; and when I set my mind on a thing——"

"If I choose to leave, Jaggers——"

"Exactly ; and if I choose to let you——"

"Do you threaten me ?"

"Not I. I'm not that sort at all, you know. I like to take things easy and comfortable. Come, now, make your miserable mind happy, will you ? I want to have a long talk with you presently about you know what, and I don't want us to part company in the meanwhile."

The foregoing conversation had been carried on in a low tone of voice, for Mrs. Jaggers was only standing at a short distance from the spot where it took place, waiting until it should be her liege lord's pleasure to give her further orders.

The old man seemed to be utterly cowed by his ruffianly associate, and subsided into silence, without making any further attempt to assert his right to have a will of his own. Then Jaggers gave directions that the gentlemen should be admitted.

"I shall be ruined !" groaned Mr. Fenwick, when the woman was gone.

"Stuff and nonsense !" replied the other, with a loud laugh ; "us two must see more of one another for the future. I don't see why not, myself, so don't begin getting ashamed of me so soon, that'll never do."

The old man made no answer, but something escaped his lips very like a groan.

He felt himself to be entirely in the ruffian's power.

Had he possessed any strength, moral or physical, it is probable that he would at once have shaken off this irksome thraldom, but all his life he had been a poor, weak creature, incapable of decisive action, and had been led on by minds stronger and more vicious than his to a career of wickedness, profligacy and extravagance that in the end had caused him to commit the criminal breach of trust to avoid the consequences of which he now was obliged to seek the aid of the scoundrel at whose mercy he found himself.

It would have been easy enough to have freed himself now if he only had the pluck.

But he had not.

If he could have summoned up a little courage to his aid at this moment he might have shaken off the hold that the ruffian had got upon him.

At best it was only a suspicion which the other entertained respecting the death of Jabez Worwold.

Suppose he defied him ?

But, then, the breach of trust—the felonious appropriation of the jewels ?

Well, as yet, Jaggers knew none of the particulars.

The plot of the sham burglary was only in its infancy.

Why not abandon it, and escape from the scoundrel's dominion ?

At one time he was almost on the point of asserting his rights, and had drawn himself up and pursed his lips as though for the utterance of the first word, when Jaggers, turning round towards him, attracted by the sound of the movement that he made, fixed his eyes upon the unfortunate old man, and fairly scowled him again into subjection.

No, no. It was no good struggling.

The miserably weak old profligate subsided again into the state of helplessness which he had endeavoured to shake off, and was as docile as a child in the hands of the burly vagabond whose abject slave he had become.

"Make yourself at home," said Jaggers, with a grin. "You'll find these 'ere gents the most agreeable company, and you'll see some first-class sport."

"They are young men of fashion, you said ?" the old gentleman plucked up courage to inquire, for he was not a little desirous of ascertaining whom he was about to be brought in contact with.

"Yes, they're top sawyers, everyone," responded Jaggers. "Sprigs of nobility, and flowers of fashion."

"One is a lord, you said ?"

"The fastest-going young blade upon town."

"And he is——"

"Young Lord Vultureville. You've heard of him, haven't you ?"

"Yes, yes, I know him slightly."

"Devil doubt you. If there's a rapscallion to be found within a circuit of a hundred miles that's got a title to his back you're pals with him."

"I always liked to mix in good society."

"Ha ! ha ! that's rich, that is," cried Jaggers, with a hoarse scream, which he intended to represent laughter. "You call it good society, do you ? A lot of young nobs that tries their hardest to make themselves out worse blackguards than them as is blackguards born. If that's good society, I'm done."

He roared with laughter at what he was pleased to look upon as wit ; and the old man was fain to wait until his mirth had quite subsided before he could venture to make any more inquiries.

"Oh, you're a ornament to the upper circles, you are," cried Jaggers, derisively. "You're a sweet blossom, and al'ays was. Why, you're every bit as bad as the young uns, now, I do believe, although you're nothing better nor a animated skeleting. He ! he ! blowed if you are."

It was so very soothing for the poor antiquated old beau's feelings to be thus jibed and jeered at by the coarse ruffian who was pleased to select him as a butt for his delicate pleasantries ; but there was no hope for it, and he was obliged to smile, as though he thought the fun rather pleasant than otherwise.

When Jaggers had had his laugh out, he ventured to resume the questions which had been interrupted.

"Who is there besides Vultureville ?" he asked.

"There was the young Marquis of Springheels the other evening, besides a lot of young swells I didn't know the names of ; but as they're all hangers on of them two young bloods as finds the tin for the company's amusement,—and tin they do find, too,—I dont know what I should do without their patronage."

"Yes, they spend their money like water, I know that ; but they have lots of it, that's one thing."

"Lots, they've buckets full. You know they call young Vulturevile Champagne Charley in at the "Finish." You've seen him there, old gent, I bet a penny, or at Jessop's, standing dozen after dozen of champagne to the young ladies. He's quite at home among 'em, he is ; and so he ought to be, for his great great grandmother was very much in the same line as they are, only on a rather flasher style, for everybody knows she was made a peeress only because she sold herself to Charles the Second."

"Yes, yes, that's true enough."

"It's not the only one as has got on in life through their female relations," said Mr. Jaggers, with a grin. "It ain't a bad thing sometimes to have a few good looks kicking about in the family."

"Is that your case ?" asked the old gentleman, with a feeble effort at retalliation.

"Well, no," replied Jaggers very seriously, for he did not think that his companion was laughing at him ; "no such luck."

There was a pause, during which the old man curiously scanned his companion's face, almost as ugly as a baboon, and wondered whether it was possible that at any time there could have existed anything at all approaching to beauty for many past generations of Jaggerses.

But the resurrectionist by this time had begun to grow impatient at the delay in his young patron's arrival.

He sat listening for the footfalls, and wondering what on earth could detain them.

"It's that idiot of a woman," he muttered ; "she's been bungling again, as usual."

"Why don't they come in ?" asked the old man.

"Who can tell ?" said Jaggers, savagely. "Am I keeping 'em back ?"

"Your wife must have told them to go away again in a mistake," said Mr. Fenwick, who could not refrain from something very like a chuckle of satisfaction as he spoke, when he reflected that after all he might escape from Jaggers's house unseen.

Unfortunately for him, however, the ruffian caught sight of the faint smile upon his face, and his rage was immense.

"She'd better not have made any blunder," he cried, "or, by the Lord, I'll half-flay her."

Mr. Fenwick eyed him in alarm.

"And you too."

Mr. Fenwick became preternaturally serious.

"You'd like me to lose the little bit of money I've got to live upon."

"No, Jaggers, I'm certain——"

"That's what you'd like, curse you !"

"No, Jaggers, I assure you I didn't mean——"

"I don't want to hear what you meant. I suppose nothing else than that it's that infernal idiot ; but I'll dress her."

And so saying, the ruffian rose to his feet, and, taking the light in his hand, staggered across the yard in the direction of the back-door, into which he presently disappeared.

No sooner was he gone than Mr. Fenwick got up and looked round for the means of escape.

Here was a chance which would not offer again very soon. Should he not avail himself of it ?

But he was in an awful fright lest the ruffian should return with his patrons before he could get clear off.

"How long will he be, I wonder ?" the old gentleman asked himself. "Should I have time ?"

He came out from the shed very cautiously and peeped about.

But he had not taken three steps forward when he fancied he heard Jaggers's voice approaching.

He turned in a moment, and retreated precipitately.

With such random haste, indeed, that he caught his foot against a projecting piece of woodwork at the entrance of the shed, and sprawled full length upon the ground.

He was a very feeble old gentleman, in spite of his attempts at sprightliness, and the violence of the fall shook him well-nigh to pieces.

It knocked his hat off, which ran away as though for a wager to a distant part of the shed.

It dislodged his teeth, and almost choked him with them.

It unfastened his wig, which flew off after his hat.

The poor old gentleman lay upon his nose for some moments more dead than alive, and groaned piteously.

It was some time before he could pick himself up and shake himself together ; but when at length he recovered the use of his limbs he crawled about upon all-fours in search of his fallen property.

He first of all arranged his teeth, which had got somehow crosswise in his mouth, and were sticking into the roof, and gagging him painfully.

Then he crawled along, groping as he went, for his hat and wig.

Almost the first thing that he did, as may be supposed, was to knock his head violently against the table.

The second thing was, very naturally, to rub it.

The third was to swear a good round dozen of oaths.

When he had done this he went on groping in the darkness, though with much more caution than before, for he did not fancy stoving in the crown of his head against some sharp angle.

He was in a great fright, though, for fear the young noblemen might return before he could cover his poor bare poll.

It is questionable whether at the moment he most desired to effect his escape or cover his silly old noddle.

The hope of getting away had somewhat subsided at the alarm of Jaggers's return, and his only object now was to put in a respectable appearance when the young noblemen and their escort should arrive.

But, as some time had elapsed, and Jaggers and his aristocratic friends did not make their appearance, the hope of escape revived in his breast, and he determined to make a struggle for liberty.

How to do it, though, was the question.

One great drawback was, that for the life of him, he could not lay his hands upon his wig.

He groped his way all over the floor of the shed.

There was not, to the best of his judgment, half a foot of floor that he did not feel over in his search, but without success.

Exasperated beyond measure at the delay, which he feared would be his ruin, he groped about wildly, describing circles on the floor, going unconsciously over and over the same place, but still being as far off the desired object as ever.

Wildly he groped his way, but could find nothing ; and, maddened at length by his frequent disappointments, and exasperated beyond measure by the continual bumps upon the head which he met with by the way, he resolved at length to leave the wig to its fate, and slapping on his hat, which being of course a mile too large for him now that his light-brown curly hair was gone, bonneted him most effectually, he felt his way out into the yard.

All was quiet, and he looked round again for the means of escape.

The coast seemed clear, but it was as dark as pitch.

Mr. Fenwick crept out upon tip-toe, and peeped cautiously from beneath the brim of his hat.

"It's an awful place, this," he thought, "and I shall be tumbling down again if I don't mind."

He, however, managed a few yards in safety.

"I hope there's no hole anywhere."

A few more steps.

"There's a well, I'm certain, but I forget where it is."

A little further.

"If I had only begun at once I should have got clear off by this time."

He was in the middle of the yard now.

"I hear nothing of that scoundrel. The young noblemen must have gone away, and he has gone after them. Curse him, I wish he would never come back. How awfully dark it is."

It was certainly as dark as it well could be. He strained his eyes in vain to pierce the dense obscurity, and cautiously proceeded, feeling his way as he went.

"I expect I've come in the wrong direction. I want to find the wall. There's a weak place somewhere, I fancy, and I might manage to scramble up."

By dint of staring hard into the pitchy darkness he by this time had grown sufficiently accustomed to it to be able to make out something of a high black mass, blacker by some degrees than the darkness beyond.

"That's the wall," he muttered; "I'm all right now."

He proceeded with greater boldness after he had made this discovery, and gradually he could discern the position of the house, and make a sort of calculation respecting the spot where the weak place in the wall, of which he had spoken, was to be found.

His movements hitherto had been almost noiseless, but now, proceeding with less caution, he contrived to kick his foot against a loose stone, which he sent flying over the gravel with a great clatter.

Scarcely had he done so than half-a-dozen dogs burst out, barking furiously.

At the same time the fierce rattling of a chain just behind him apprised him of the terrible fact of his close proximity to one of the savage beasts Mr. Jaggers kept fastened up in his yard.

"I shall be torn to pieces," the old man cried aloud in his terror.

And he rushed forward half-a-dozen yards to escape from the danger threatening him.

But he was only flying out of the frying-pan into the fire.

Where he flew for shelter was worse than the place he had fled from.

As he approached, a terrific growl saluted him, and a loud jangling of a chain.

Another of the ferocious dogs rushed at him, open-mouthed, out of the darkness.

He bounded back again, and a third snapped and snarled at his heels.

Forward, in frantic terror, but only to come upon another of the brutes, gnashing its teeth, eager for a bite at him.

The old man, in an agony of fear, drew himself bolt upright.

He was afraid to move a step in any direction. Indeed it was so awfully dark that he could form no notion where the most danger lay.

He had no idea whether he ought to run to the right or the left, to run back or straightforward.

He seemed to be safe where he was, but for how long would he be so?

The terrible growling and snarling, and jingling of chains around him, well-nigh scared him out of his wits.

He expected every moment he would be worried, and wished with all his heart that he had never left the shed, where, anyhow, his life was safe.

What surprised him though, not a little, was that the hellish din which the dogs made did not bring out Jaggers to see what was the cause of the disturbance.

He could not be in the house the old man thought, or else it was very certain that he would have heard the noise, and come running out before this.

Now, then, was the time to escape, if he could only manage it. But how could he?

He knew very well that he had come safe enough to the spot where he found himself, consequently there must be a way back.

But oh! the terrible risk he would run in endeavouring to find it.

"I shall be eaten alive among them," groaned the old man; "I know that well enough. One of the beasts will break his chain in another moment, and I shall literally be torn to bits."

But the intolerable suspense attendant upon the dangerous position in which he found himself placed sharpened the old gentleman's wits.

A great idea occurred to him. He carried some cigar-lights in his pocket—a wonderful new invention at the time of which we write, for this was yet the days of flint and steel.

He took one out, and, after several ineffectual efforts, struck a light and looked around.

The tiny firework only blazed for a moment, but that short time was sufficient for him to glance round, and take in the particulars of the situation.

He saw where there was an opening by which he might escape from his difficulties.

He also got a vague idea of the plan of the yard.

One thing he saw, and that was a short ladder leaning against a shed, which occupied one corner of the wall.

As soon as the flame died out, he dropped the match and made for the spot indicated.

The dogs snarled and snapped madly at his heels.

They strove desperately to tear themselves away from their chains, or their chains from the fastenings which held them.

The old gentleman, with almost superhuman agility, skipped past them.

He reached the shed in a couple of wild, fawnlike bounds.

He sprang up the ladder and clutched at the roof of the shed, when—something seized him by the coat-tail.

He could not doubt what it was.

The smothered snarling in his rear convinced him of the dreadful truth.

One of the brutes had got hold of him.

Had snapped and caught at the strong broadcloth which formed the skirts of his fashionable paletôt.

He was hanging on to it with the gripe of grim death, and poor Mr. Fenwick's frantic efforts to disengage himself were utterly thrown away.

The old man not being very strong, the weight of the dog dragged him backwards, and all but tore him from his hold upon the roof.

But he struggled with all his might and main, and climbed up another round, thinking to drag the dog with him.

He could not manage that though, and the harder he dragged the heavier did the weight appear to become.

The reason of this was that the dog which had got hold of his coat-tail had not broken its chain, but had snapped at him as he came within its reach.

It was therefore suspended in mid-air.

The chain holding it back.

The old gentleman dragging it forward.

He could not drag very much longer, though, he was sure of that.

He felt his strength was giving way.

"Would to God my coat-tail would do so!" he thought to himself.

There was an old burlesque by Albert Smith, a burlesque of "Esmeralda," where the Hunchback threw the old priest from the tower of Notre Dame, and the priest, hanging by his cassock, heard its stitches slowly cracking, and cursed his fate for ever having given ear to the allurements of a cheap Jew clothier.

"If I had only bought my gowns of a respectable tradesman, and given a respectable price for them," he thought, "they might have saved my life now."

Quite the contrary, however, were poor Mr. Fenwick's opinions upon this occasion.

He cursed the durability of broadcloth.

He would have preferred his tail to have been composed of a material no stronger than tissue-paper.

He wished he wore rags.

He wished he had had on a sailor's jacket.

He wished he had been naked.

"No, no, good Lord! not that, either," thought the old gentleman. "He might have set his teeth into ——. Perhaps my coat-tail protected me."

But how was he to escape? Was he to be thwarted thus upon the very threshold of liberty?

Above him was the wall, only a matter of two or three yards off.

He could very easily climb along the roof, he thought, if he could only shake off this awful incubus behind.

But that seemed to be impossible.

He shook and dragged.

He clung like a leech to the roof, and sprained every muscle in his body.

But in spite of that he could not free himself.

No; there was only one way, and that was a most hazardous one.

He must let the dog pull his coat off.

In these days of loose habits such a proceeding might not have been so very difficult, but in the time of which we write peg-top sleeves had not come into fashion; sleeves, on the contrary, were worn very tight, and buttoned at the wrist.

It was a matter of no small difficulty for the poor old gentleman at any time to struggle out of his coat, for his old joints were very stiff, and worked very rustily in their sockets.

He must make an effort, though, or he was lost.

He clung frantically with one hand, and let the dog drag the coat backwards; but he soon found that he had not strength enough in one hand to hold himself up.

He was obliged to cling hold again with the other, or he must inevitably have fallen down into the dog's mouth.

Just, however, when he was giving himself up to despair, and had arrived at the conclusion that it was only a question of time, and that sooner or later his strength would give way—his hold upon the roof would relax, and then down he must come with a run ;—just, however, when this fate seemed to be most threatening, his coat-tail gave way with a sudden rent.

Oh, joyful sound! Surely music was never sweeter.

The dog tore furiously at the cloth.

The old man scrambled upwards.

He was saved!

That is to say, for the present.

But hardly had he reached the roof than Jaggers and his noble patrons made their appearance in the yard.

The old gentleman looked hopelessly up at the wall above him.

He could not hope to reach it without the aid of the ladder; but the ladder was not to be had.

In climbing up and struggling on to the roof, he had kicked it wildly away from him.

He was now in a worse fix than ever. He could not get up and over the wall without being seen.

Suppose he was discovered in the ridiculous position in which he found himself. That would never do.

It was too far for him to jump down again upon the hard gravel beneath.

Such a fall would have shaken his poor old body to pieces, if it did not break some of his limbs.

What could he do?

There was only one thing left for him. It was a flat roof upon which he had scrambled, and there was a brick parapet about half-a-yard high upon one side—the side on which he had scrambled up.

He would lie down behind this and hide himself.

If he escaped observation there was yet a chance that he might get away.

At any rate he would not be seen by the young gentlemen, which was his main object.

There was no time to lose if he carried this determination into effect, though, for already Jaggers had discovered that he had left the other shed, and was loudly shouting to him to show himself.

"Fenwick! Fenwick!" he roared out.

The old gentleman gnashed his teeth in shame and annoyance.

What was now the use of further concealment? His name had been revealed by the ruffian to his noble patrons.

It was probable that some sport was intended at his expense, for the young men began talking among themselves, and regretting that he had gone.

"What's become of the old pimp?" one asked.

"Where have you hidden him, Jaggers?"

"I hope you haven't let your dogs eat him up."

"There wouldn't be much picking on his old carcase," said Jaggers, with a brutal laugh. "He's a regular old scarecrow."

"He can't have got far, though."

"Well, I should think not."

"The walls are too high to climb over."

"He must have got through the house."

"I'll take my oath he hasn't done that," said the imp, putting in his spoke, for he had accompanied the gentlemen out into the yard.

"Let's rout him out, then; he's hiding somewhere," cried one, of a shrill voice, which Mr. Fenwick knew to be Lord Vultureville's.

"Let's let all the dogs loose, and chivey him," cried the Marquis of Springheels.

"One of the bloodhounds will find him."

"Set on one of the bull-dogs."

"Curse the old beggar!" growled Jaggers. "He's managed to make his escape somehow or other. If he's got over the wall, all the harm I wish him is that he's broke his neck, that's all. What the blazes made him sneak off that way?"

"I hope he hasn't done that, though," said one of the gentlemen, who had not hitherto spoken.

Mr. Fenwick nervously popped up his head, at the risk of being detected.

He fancied he had heard this gentleman's voice before, and that he was a person who was the last in the world he would have liked to have met in this place.

"Why are you so interested in him?" asked one of the others.

"For a very good reason, indeed," answered the young man, with a smile.

"Is it a secret?"

"Not at all."

"Out with it, then."

"It is simply because he has some property belonging to me, which I want to have back again with as little delay as possible."

"If it's those jewels you spoke of," said the other speaker, "and you want to take them with you to-morrow, you ought to see him to-night."

"I have tried all I could. I have been twice to his house to-day, and have left word where he is to send them, if he can do so, this evening."

"The old boy is thinking of something else besides your jewels," said the other. "He's a larky old chap, you see. He has a taste for dog-fighting, and such like."

"Look here, you fellows," cried Vultureville, who was getting a little out of patience at the delay. "Are we going to see sport to-night, or are we not?"

"As soon as you like," said Jaggers.

"What's it to be, then?"

"What you choose. A bit of ratting?"

"Hang that. That's too slow."

THE MASQUERADE.

"I can show you a little dust up between two game birds, gentlemen, that will entertain you."

"No, it wont. Don't think it."

"Dogs, then?"

"No, no. Let's have the bloodhounds out, and see a bit of worrying."

"That comes rather expensive, you see, my lord."

"Damn you. I can pay, can't I?"

"If you don't mind a fiver, of course."

"Let's see a good bit of fun, and we wont grumble at the price."

"This way, then, my lords and gentlemen. This is the way to the shambles."

And so speaking, he let these civilized young savages into the shed upon the roof of which Mr. Fenwick lay quaking with fear, and, closing the doors, prepared for a scene of brutal cruelty scarcely credible in a land of enlightenment, the details of which must be reserved for another chapter.

CHAPTER XXIV.

THE MASQUERADE.

THE night was growing old, and the theatre was blazing with all the splendour and gloriously-exciting confusion of the bal masque, the dense crowd of plea-sure-seekers that thronged the house illustrating what a misnomer was the word bal for the masquerade.

Dancing was, as usual on such occasions, a mere idea. The M.C.s were struggling through the motley throng, and making commendable efforts to make the fête worthy of its name; but every attempt to organize a quadrille proved abortive.

Some few of the female portion of the company persevered for a minute or two in the hopeless cause—for women will dance under any circumstances,—but even they soon gave it up as a bad job. The majority of the visitors seemed perfectly contented to promenade about —but this was a matter of some difficulty.

A Brigand and a Fairy, a Jack Tar and a Débardeur, a Pierrot and a Spanish Dancer, a Cardinal with a plump Milk-maid, a kilted Highlander with suspiciously-smart legs and Lady Bountiful, Jupiter with a Buy-a-broom Girl, Julius Cæsar and Columbine, Dusty Bob and Lady Macbeth, Blue Beard and Venus, Othello and Mother Shipton, the Emperor of the Celestials and a fascinating Soubrette, Corinthian Tom and Diana, Mephistophiles and Minerva, Britannia and Guy Fawkes, a fat Monk and a bewitching Juno, Ajax and Proserpine, having formed themselves into a regular procession, were elbowing their way through myriads of fairies, gipsies, soldiers, sailors, &c., &c., followed by the Graces, represented by three gigantic guardsmen with enormous beards, with their arms entwined round each other's waists, and Macbeth's Witches personated by three lovely damsels; and immediately in the rear of these were a couple to which we must call the reader's immediate attention.

A tall and stately Cavalier of the Charles-the-Martyr epoch, bore on his arm a lady habited after the fashion of Lady Castlemaine of the next reign, and the portraits of whom she was not at all unlike. The lady was looking about in every direction, and peering into every mask with an earnestness that showed she was anxiously expecting some one; whilst the coxcombs, who attributed her interest to the captivating influence of their persons, which their disguises but imperfectly hid, blew her kisses from the tips of their fingers and otherwise saluted her, much to the annoyance of her companion; we say her companion, for the lady herself was too much occupied in her search to heed their impertinences.

They made the tour of the promenade twice without meeting the object of my Lady Castlemaine's scrutiny.

"He's not come," she said to her Cavalier. "We were mistaken, perhaps."

"Possibly, but I don't think it very likely," was the reply.

"Do you think he would come later, perhaps?"

"I can't say," replied her companion. And then he endeavoured to change the topic, as if it were distasteful to him. "That's very good! Do you see her Majesty the good Queen Bess?"

"Ha, yes! Let us go close up; he's probably attracted there, and we shall see him in the crowd."

She put this interrogatively to her Cavalier, and looked up into his face for a reply; but he only heaved a sigh and let her arm fall from his. "Don't you think so?" she continued, not noticing his neglect in her eagerness to obtain an answer.

"I can't say," was the abrupt reply.

"Shall we go and see?"

The Cavalier turned half round from her and bit his lip in silent vexation. Lady Castlemaine looked into his face, or rather his mask, with such a graceful and bewitching air of entreaty, and again taking his arm, pressed it gently as she spoke.

"You'll go with me, Frank?"

The enthralled Cavalier started at her touch as if it had been an electric shock, and, blushing like a girl of fifteen, moved slowly along towards the direction indicated.

There stood her most virgin Majesty, of glorious memory, surrounded by her regiment of lovers and courtiers. Prominent in the group stood Sir Walter Raleigh, wearing a long pipe as a sword, and a necklace of small potatoes threaded like beads on a string.

Next him stood Sir Christopher Hatton, borrowed from Sheridan's "Critic," who was fraternizing with a lank, lean man in armour, who would have passed muster as our old friend Don Quixote, but who was such a miserable failure for Essex that not even his appearance in company with the Elizabethan world gave the bystanders, who were not of their party, the least idea for whom he was intended.

Philip of Spain was engaged in a confidential chat with a gigantic Beefeater, and their conversation was apparently about their very gay Leicester, who was holding an animated flirtation with a tantalizingly light-robed Euphrosyne, that lady having deserted her sisters twain upon recognising a friend in the Elizabethan dandy.

The party was tolerably complete, and proved the centre of attraction of the masquerade. Our Cavalier and lady couple had, therefore, some considerable difficulty in making their way to the spot; but, by dint of a great deal of energetic pushing on the part of my Lady Castlemaine, and the exertions of her Cavalier to prevent her being crushed, they managed to reach the front of the circle formed round the Queen and her Court.

The lady eagerly scanned every mask in rapid succession; but still not finding the object of her search.

"No, no," she whispered to her companion; "he's not here."

"If he is not," returned the Cavalier, "he has more prudence than I gave him credit for."

At this moment a roar of laughter caused them to look round. The maiden Queen (who, par parenthèse, was represented by a fat, red-whiskered man) had been toying with the Duke of Sussex, and from patting his cheek playfully, had suddenly administered him a smart slap for the amusement of the spectators, when his Grace replied to this pleasantry by giving his Sovereign a dig in the ribs, which doubled her up in a manner perfectly inconsistent with Majesty.

The frolic, although not exactly refined, took with the spectators, and a roar of delight, that shook the building, rewarded them for their buffooneries.

"Bravo!" shouted an enthusiastic harlequin, with a lady in a maroon domino and mask on his arm. "Deuced good, demme!"

Our Cavalier, pricking up his ears, looked round in the direction of the speaker, and then down to his companion, to witness, it seemed, the effect of the harlequin's voice on her. Apparently she had not noticed it, and, with a sigh of relief, he endeavoured to lead her from the spot.

"What makes you so anxious to go away from here?" she asked, looking up into his face as if she divined his motive.

"No—I'm not anxious to go way, I assure you," he replied, confusedly.

"You have seen him!" exclaimed the girl, staring into his face, while her eyes, like two live coals, appeared to be almost protruding through her mask. "He's near here, and you wish to hurry me away. Ah! I see I'm right!"

"No; believe me—I——"

But here a repetition of the laughter cut short his protestations; and, as if to give him the lie, the harlequin's laugh rang out above all the others.

"There!" exclaimed the lady, convulsively clutching her Cavalier's arm. "Did you hear that?"

"What?" demanded the Cavalier.

"Did you not distinguish Winder's laugh?"

"No. You must mistake."

"No, no; you know too well that I am right. See there—that's he."

"Where?"

"In the harlequin's dress. Let us follow him."

"No, no."

"And who is that woman in the plum-coloured domino?—Lady Crutchingford again?"

"Never!" exclaimed the Cavalier. "He must be surely mad."

The Harlequin and his lady threaded their way through the many-coated crowds, followed at a short distance by the Cavalier and his lady—the latter, as before, almost dragging on her companion in her eagerness.

The Maroon Domino pulled the Harlequin by the sleeve when under the dress-circle, and drew him into the shadow of one of the columns that served as a support.

"See, they have stopped there," said my Lady Castlemaine to her companion. "Come to the other side of the pillar, and—and——"

She paused.

"And listen?" suggested the Cavalier, somewhat severely.

The lady hung her head, and was silent. They had now drawn so close to the column that they were within hearing—and almost by accident.

"Winder," said the Domino, placing her hand on her companion's spangled sleeves to invite caution, "be careful. Don't speak out much."

"Why?" demanded the Harlequin.

"Peel is here."

"What then?"

"Simply, that he more than half suspects that I have deserted him for you."

"And then?"

"And then! How dull you are! Hearing your voice he will never rest until he has discovered me here; and you've no idea of the extent of a disappointed suitor's revenge."

"Revenge?"

"Yes. I know the major well. He's quite capable of unmasking me before the whole room."

"Not while I am here to look after you, Amatoria," said Winder, with a mixture of tenderness and bombast.

As he spoke, he placed his arm around the Domino's waist, and squeezed her gently. At this the Cavalier felt his lady trembling violently at his side, and he endeavoured to lead her from the spot; but she would not stir.

"But be cautious, Winder, I beg."

"All right, my dear."

"For even your protection," continued the Domino, gazing tenderly into his face, "would avail me little, if he should discover me."

"Is he, then, really so terrible?" demanded Winder, in whose tones might be discovered the slightest tinge of apprehension mixed with his bantering strain.

"He is remorseless!"

This was said with a shiver that seemed to impart itself to Winder; and the pair strolled on.

The lady, clasping the Cavalier's arm, endeavoured to drag him on to follow; but he resolutely refused to move.

"Let us follow them, I implore," she said.

"Nay, Miss Willoughby—Alice. You place me in a most disagreeable position. Believe me, the part of eavesdropper is equally unworthy of us both."

"Oh, Mr. Harley!" and she hid her face in her hands.

"Forgive me. I wouldn't wound your feelings for anything. You should show some spirit. The man who can slight a love like yours, believe me, is unworthy of a second thought."

"And this is your reasoning, Mr. Harley?"

"Why not?"

"And you, who profess to love——"

"Profess!—Alice, you are cruel."

"Well, then, you who really do love——"

"Ah!"

"You, who proffer your love to me—I, who am so unworthy of your esteem, much less your love——"

"Nay——"

"And persist, in spite of my objection—in spite of my slighting—no, I can never slight you—but, although I still avow my love for Winder—to press your suit."

"The case is not the same."

"That I deny. It is exactly the same. But let us follow them."

"But I don't know where they have gone to now."

"To the refreshment-saloon. Come!"

"Nay—I beg——"

"Then must I go alone, Frank?"

This was too much for the love-sick artist, and, with a deep sigh, he allowed her to take his arm and lead him slowly in pursuit of the fickle Harlequin and the Maroon Domino.

They entered the refreshment-saloon, and there, at the farther end, at a table, by themselves, sat the faithless pair, discussing a bottle of Moselle.

"Call for something, and take the next table to them," whispered Alice Willoughby.

The slight, familiar squeeze which accompanied this request, sent Harley's heart into his mouth, and he silently obeyed.

"What will you have, Alice?"

"Anything—an ice," replied Miss Willoughby, with her eyes fixed on the couple at the next table.

"Waiter!"

"Yes, sir."

"Ices."

"Ices, sir; yes, sir."

The waiter had barely skipped off to execute the order, when a most unpleasant thought caused the artist to soliloquize in the following brief but expressive manner:—

"The devil!"

Alice after all had had time to think of an ice. In vain he ran up mental additions—figures are dreadful realities.

"Tickets, fifteen shillings," he muttered, half aloud; "cab, eighteen-pence; clear balance in hand—fourpence." And he gave vent to something closely resembling a groan.

"Two ices, two shillings—waiter, sixpence—two-and-sixpence; fourpence in hand. Bankrupt for two-and-twopence, by the living Jingo!"

"Did you speak, Frank?" demanded Alice.

"Oh, no! I merely——ahem!"

But Alice, intent upon watching her faithless lover and her rival, had not noticed either his confusion or his excuse.

"What's to be done?" he groaned; "I shall be walked off for a cheat, for two-and-twopence. Something must be done." And he sprang up from his seat.

"Where are you going to, Mr. Harley?" asked Alice.

"To death!—no, I don't mean that; I shall return directly."

And with this he walked hurriedly from the saloon. He had no plan of action; his only thought was to avoid the waiter and the ices.

"There's only one thing, and that is to go out—jump into a cab, and run round to Dawker—offer to knock off twenty per cent.—that's it!"

With this he dashed into the sea of maskers, and boldly buffeted his way through to gain the exit, which was on the opposite side of the building.

Never heeding the imprecations of such as he upset, or the opposition of those who obstinately refused to give way, he was making good progress when he had the misfortune to come in contact with a Demon with such violence as made him perform a fair pirouette.

Now, as the infernal deity was at this moment holding a conversation with an enchanting Fatima, in pink satin Turkish continuations, he was not over-pleased at being so unceremoniously handled.

"Hang you for a clumsy idiot!" he said, fiercely.

The artist, however, instead of resenting this rough speech, seemed highly delighted at the meeting.

"Gerard Wilde!" he exclaimed, holding out his hand.

"What, Frank Harley?"

"Yes;" and they shook hands cordially.

"Where were you going in such a deuce of a hurry, Harley?"

"I was just off to——, but p'rhaps you can assist me."

"Most willingly—what is it?"

Harley bent close to Gerald, and whispered in his ear—

"Deuced awkward predicament, Wilde. Got such a thing as a sovereign about you?"

Wilde's only reply was to press a coin into his hand, which coin the artist endeavoured to transfer to the pocket of his pantaloons without being observed. Then, giving him a cordial grasp, he again plunged into the crowd, and hastily retraced his steps to the refreshment-saloon.

She was gone! Yes, Alice Willoughby had disappeared, and with her Harlequin Winder and the Maroon Domino.

There on the table were the two untouched ices which had been the source of Frank Harley's temporary uneasiness.

"She will be back directly," he said to himself, and endeavoured to believe it. He seated himself at the table, and began eating the ice.

As he was taking the last spoonful, the waiter who had attended to him came up, and smilingly observed that he had been almost afeared as the gent had sloped when he see the table vacated.

The artist smiled grimly as he thought what he might have done had he not so opportunely met with Gerald Wilde. He then drew out the coin which the latter had lent him, and tossed it to the waiter with easy *non-chalance.*

"What's this, sir?"

"For the ice."

"But the lady was with you, sir."

"Certainly."

"Well, then, aint you goin' to pay the lot, sir?"

"Of course. Take for both."

"What out of this?"

And he held up the coin, showing, to Harley's surprise and discomfiture, that it was *a shilling!*

"A shilling!" gasped the artist.

"Pre-cisely."

"And there is two shillings to pay?"

"That's the sum total, sir."

The artist hastily breathed another small calculation—

"Bankrupt, after all my struggles, for eightpence!"

Then he continued aloud to the waiter, as easily as he could, "A most singular mistake, waiter, I thought it was a sovereign."

"Dare say, sir. These things will happen, sir."

"But the most unfortunate thing is that I—I—ahem! in short, I haven't any more money with me."

It was now the waiter's turn to look blank.

"You see," continued Harley, "having changed my clothes——"

"And do you think I'm a goin' to stand this?"

"There's no need to speak so loud, my good man."

"Oh! there aint."

"No; it's only a temporary difficulty, and——"

"Walker!"

"I have friends in the ball-room."

"So have I," said the waiter, with terrible significance; "some friends in blue!"

"But I assure you——"

"It don't do."

"I can give you my card, and——"

"No use, my swell."

"Do, for Heaven's sake, speak lower, my man. We can settle it without so much noise."

"I'll just show you how to do the heavy with your ices. Hi! Jim!"—this was to a waiter who was passing at the moment—"just fetch in the p'lice."

"What's up?" from the individual thus addressed.

"Only a fellow been doin' his ices on the bounce."

"How dare you insult me thus?" indignantly demanded the artist.

"All right. That's very good in its way. Just send 'em in, Jim."

Frank Harley was now getting thoroughly alarmed. He greatly dreaded a scene for many reasons. But, above all, he feared to appear ridiculous in the eyes of Alice Willoughby; he knew how that would destroy every hope of obtaining her love—such an enemy is ridicule to the tender passion.

The loud and insulting tones of the waiter had attracted the attention of many persons about, and he felt that some decisive step alone could avert the much-dreaded climax.

His resolution was taken in a moment, and he quietly rose from his seat and walked towards the door. The dapper little waiter perceived his intention, and stepped before him to bar his exit.

"Stand out of the way," muttered Harley between his teeth.

"No, you don't," said the man.

But he *did,* for the words had barely passed his lips, when the artist seized him by the collar—gave him one vigorous push, which sent him sprawling on the floor some half-dozen paces off, and darted into the crowd of maskers.

By the time that the waiter had regained his feet, Frank Harley had disappeared.

Harley pushed his way through as quickly as he could, making for the door, when his attention was arrested by a loud cry of "Shame! shame!" by several voices. This was followed by an angry speech in a loud, man's voice, the purport of which he did not catch, and feminine tones in supplication.

Something familiar in the latter voice drew him to the spot from whence it proceeded, and there he saw the Maroon Domino struggling with a tall man in a brigand's costume; the latter evidently trying to remove her mask.

The bystanders were crying out shame, but no one attempted to interfere. Winder was not at hand to aid her, and the Domino must have lost the day, had not the artist, like the *preux chevalier* of old, darted forward to the rescue.

"Unhand that lady instantly!" he exclaimed.

"Be off!" growled the Brigand, without quitting his hold. "You wont interfere if you're wise."

"Unhand that lady, unmanly ruffian!"

"Bah!"

"I warn you to desist. You will not? Then, cur! take that!"

Harley, as he spoke, dashed his clenched fist into the Brigand's face with a force that sent him reeling back, and he himself recoiled from the strength of the blow.

"Sir," said the Domino, in a low voice, to the artist, "you have saved me. Farewell!"

She silently pressed his hand, and was lost in the crowd.

CHAPTER XXV.

COMING TO GRIEF.

THE place called by Mr. Jaggers the Shambles was a large shed, more than twenty feet square, the centre of which was occupied by a deep pit, almost as broad as the shed, and surrounded only by a narrow ledge, where there were benches arranged in a line and protected from the pit by a strong wooden rail.

It would have appeared that there was seldom a large audience to see the brutalities that Mr. Jaggers provided for his patrons' amusement, for there was not accommodation for more than twenty at the outside.

At one end of the shed there was a large door, through

which a high horse might very easily have passed, and when the gentlemen were seated, Mr. Jaggers told his son to bring out the quadruped.

The imp immediately opened the door, and, entering another shed to which this was the entrance, was heard shouting to and belabouring some unfortunate animal.

A brief pause ensued, and then he returned dragging after him one of the most miserable old hacks which it was possible for human imagination to picture up.

It was so awfully thin that its poor bones seemed bursting from its skin.

Its hide had been rubbed off here and there in patches, which were red and raw.

The knees had been broken by unfortunate stumbles.

It appeared to be totally blind of one eye, and the sight was injured of the other, or else it looked very dim and watery. In any case, the miserable animal wagged its head helplessly to and fro, and occasionally knocked it against the pit-side.

It was such a melancholy object—this poor bony brute —that the sight of it was surely enough to have moved any human heart to pity.

Such, however, was not the case with these young sprigs of fashion here assembled. On the contrary, they burst into loud shouts of laughter, and cracked their jokes upon the poor victim's mangy condition.

" There's blood for you," some said.

" There's an action."

" He knows you, Charley. You must belong to him."

" It's one of his stud he's always talking about, you may take your oath of that."

" What's your price a pound, old man ?"

" Now, then, Trussels, let's see you prance a bit. Put him through his paces, Mr. Jaggers."

The brute addressed, in obedience to this suggestion, prodded the unfortunate animal with a driver's dog that he kept hard by for that purpose, and caused it to lay back its ears and kick out behind with all the vigour of which it was capable.

The gentlemen screamed with laughter at the melancholy exhibition, and were, if possible, even more witty than before at the victim's expense.

" He's as good as dead now," said Lord Vultureville, rather discontentedly. " He'll kick the bucket the moment the hound has got hold of him."

" I wish you would see the dogs instead, then," observed Jaggers. " I have a splendid pup, too, to dispose of ; let me show him to you, my lord."

" I don't want to look at it."

" It wont delay you a moment. Fetch the pup here, will you !"

And the boy addressed disappeared, and returned almost immediately, carrying in his arms the animal in question.

" A perfect beauty, he is," said Jaggers. " I had him from a Sheffield butcher, who chopped his mother up to show what stuff she was made of."

" Did what ?" asked his lordship.

" He said she would be game to hold on while there was a gasp of life left in her body."

" Well ?"

" She'd got hold of another dog, then, by the throttle, and they'd been twisting her tail and the deuce knows what to show how hard she'd stick, when the butcher says, ' Catch hold of the other dog and let her swing to his throat by her teeth.' "

" Well ?"

" So they did, and then he takes his chopper and hacks off her hind quarters—she sticking to it till she dropped off stone dead."

" What made him waste a good dog that way ?" asked Lord Vultureville, when the horrible anecdote was concluded, though without exhibiting any of the disgust which such a recital merited.

" Don't you see," answered Jaggers, " she'd got a litter of pups, and when the swells saw what a plucky one the mother was, they dropped willingly a tidy sum for the pups. This pup is one, and I'll take ten pounds for it, neither more nor less."

" You can take it back to where you took it from, when you've done prating," observed the Marquis of Springheels, drily.

And Mr. Jaggers, thus rebuked, seeing that there was not a chance of doing a stroke of business, thought he had better do as suggested.

A lengthy pause ensued, during which the noble patrons began to grow rather impatient.

But Jaggers returned at length dragging in, or rather dragging back, a lank and savage bloodhound with a wide gaping mouth, garnished with glistening teeth, out of which lolled a great swollen tongue.

" Now for it," cried Vultureville ; " we're going to see a little sport at last."

He had not to wait very long, now.

Jaggers opened a small door, just large enough to admit the dog, and stood there holding the savage beast between his knees.

The dog seemed, though, already to understand the reason for which he had been brought there.

No sooner were his bloodshot eyes fixed upon the miserable horse than he began to lash his tail furiously, to lick his lips, and to struggle desperately to free himself from Jaggers's hold.

But the ruffian retained his grasp upon the dog's collar with a violent exertion, and at the same time did his best to taunt the dog into a state of savage frenzy.

Very little taunting did the furious brute require to make it ready for the work.

He raged and snarled.

He snorted and choked and strangled.

At last he wrenched himself away with a violent jerk, which almost flung Jaggers upon his face, and rushed forward.

The poor victim appeared to have a vague instinct of danger.

He pricked up his ears and sniffed the air.

When he heard the dog's low, savage growl he shivered violently, and burst out into a sweat of terror which was a heartrending spectacle to look upon.

When the bloodhound at length made a rush upon him, the poor victim made a frantic but feeble attempt to escape.

But the dog flew upon him and brought him sprawling to the ground, setting his hideous fangs deep in the poor beast's flank.

There was no chance for him.

He struggled desperately to get upon his legs, but the bloodhound charged him down.

His miserable hide was ripped open as easily as though it had been as thin as the skin of a fish.

The poor brute's entrails were laid bare, the monster assaulting it positively eating its way into the victim's body.

The scene became at length so sickingly horrible that one or two of the noble patrons turned away disgusted.

Lord Vultureville, however, remained until the last— until the poor beast had bleated out its dying breath, and then turned away with a brutal laugh.

" How he did worry it !" he said. " Fancy, Springheels, if you had the bad luck to be a runaway nigger, and that infernal dog was after you."

" Rather a beastly sight," said the Marquis, with something very like a shudder. " I should like a drop of brandy, if there's any handy."

Some one else besides the Marquis was horrified and disgusted by the scene which had just occurred.

This was none other than Mr. Fenwick, who had remained until the end, peeping through a crevice in the roof, and so entranced by the fearful horror of the sight that he was unable, in spite of all his efforts, to tear himself away.

When at length, however, the spectators below made

a movement towards the door, the old gentleman contrived to drag his white face from the peephole, and to scramble on to his hand and knees.

But he felt sick and giddy, and stumbled forward at the first movement.

Unfortunately, he fell with all his weight upon the tiles, which were supported only by slender laths.

The roof was not strong enough to hold him, and in another moment his feet shot through, and he sat outside upon a beam, which, chancing to be there, probably saved his life.

The men below, hearing the crash, and feeling the weight of some fragments of tiles, laths and plaster rattling down upon the crowns of their hats, thought that the whole roof was coming down about their ears, and rushed pellmell out of the doors, each striving to be first and mercilessly jostling his neighbour.

But when they had waited a moment, and found that nothing very terrible took place, Lord Vultureville peeped in at the door again, and caught sight of Mr. Fenwick's thin legs sticking through the roof.

"Hallo !" cried his lordship.

"What is it ?" asked the rest, trying to peep over his shoulder.

"Just look here."

"Where ?"

"Up at the ceiling."

"Why, what the deuce are those ?"

"Legs they are meant for."

"Are they ?"

"They're something of the shape."

"Whose are they, in the name of wonder ?"

"Where's the rest of him ?"

The rest of him was outside, hopelessly stuck fast ; and it was only with the greatest difficulty, and with the united strength of the entire company, that the old gentleman was at length dragged up from the holes he had broken with his long thin legs.

When they got him out at last, and helped him down into the yard, there were loud shouts of laughter at his expense.

He certainly did look a most mournful object.

His hat being too large for him looked like an extinguisher, and would have covered him up most completely, had not his ears propped it up at the sides, and so prevented its falling down upon the bridge of his nose.

His coat-tail the bulldog had torn off, taking with it a large three-cornered slice out of the back.

His trousers were rent and ragged, in consequence of the scraping of the sharp-edged tiles as he slipped through, and one of his poor thin shanks was visible, bare and bruised.

If there had been any possible chance of making a bolt of it and getting clean away, it is rather probable that he would have made the attempt now.   But there was not a ghost of a chance.

He must brazen it out the best way he could, and give the best and most probable explanation of his very extraordinary conduct in the shortest possible time.

When they had done laughing, which was not for several minutes, Jaggers, in a tone which was anything but respectful, demanded the reason for Mr. Fenwick's extraordinary behaviour.

He mumbled out something about having been charged by one of the dogs, and having got upon the roof for safety—a story which the rest of the company, not knowing that any other motive could exist to account for the old gentleman's rather singular position, accepted as the truth.

Jaggers, mumbling out something about his not coming when he was called, scowled at him threateningly, as he walked away.

The old gentleman then began to congratulate himself about having got out of the mess so easily ; and somebody having picked up and restored to him his curly brown wig, he clapped it on to his bald pate, set his hat jauntily upon the top of it, and tried to make the best of his dilapidated wardrobe by the aid of pins, with which Mrs. Jaggers supplied him.

Jaggers having conducted his patrons into a remarkably-evil smelling room, ornamented with stuffed bulldog pups, dried fish, and dusty-looking birds, with here and there some feeble oil-painting, representing bygone wonders in the rat-killing way, he sent out the imp for a bottle of brandy, and producing a very unique collection of odd glasses, all of them cracked or broken in some place or other, provided what he was pleased to term, a little refreshment.

The old gentleman did not feel inclined to join in these festivities, and remained in the kitchen with Mrs. Jaggers, consoling himself as well as he could with a glass of hot grog. Presently, the young noblemen and party departed, though not without a passing joke at Mr. Fenwick's expense, as they passed through the kitchen.

The old gentleman watched them out, looking as pleasant as he could, and making a ghastly smile at their facetiousness ; and when they were gone, inwardly thanked Heaven for his deliverance from their persecution.

But his prayer proved to be rather premature, for the worst had to come.

The gentleman who had spoken about the jewels returned, and asked to be allowed to have a few moments' private conversation.

The heart of the unfortunate old beau sank within him.

He knew what was coming.

He knew that the thunderbolt was about to descend upon his unfortunate head.

However, he must put the best face upon the matter, and make the best tale he could.

He was in such a dreadful fright that he trembled visibly. The gentleman, noticing his agitation, asked if he were ill.

"No, no, I am very well, thank you," cried the old man, becoming absurdly sprightly all at once.

The other looked at him in some surprise, and then said—

"I trust you will excuse me if I have chosen an inopportune moment for speaking to you, Mr. Fenwick, for I must allow that this is hardly the time or place to speak of business. I should not trouble you now, sir, if it were not a matter of some importance."

"No, no, certainly," stammered the old gentleman, who had not the remotest notion what he was talking about.

"I came home unexpectedly yesterday, and I called at your office and at your private residence in the hope of seeing you."

The speaker paused, and looked towards him, supposing that he would make some explanation.

But the old man looked up feebly, and looked down again, and up again, and at last said "Oh !"

This reply not being very satisfactory, or, indeed, explanatory, the speaker waited a little longer, and then continued—

"I could hear nothing of you, and was obliged to wait till to-day."

"Oh !" said Mr. Fenwick again.

"To-day I have been several times both to your house and to your private residence, but have not been able to obtain any information respecting to your whereabouts. I was told yesterday at your office that you had not come yet, and then that you were out of town ; but at your private residence they said that you had left in the morning to go to your office, and would be home again at five. When I went at five, I was told that you had gone out for the evening. In fact, there have been all kinds of mistakes and misunderstandings ; and I really thought this afternoon when I called at your office that I should never be able to see you any more."

Again he paused for some explanation.

The old gentleman fidgeted about, and looked very uncomfortable.

He had gone through so much lately that what little sense he had remaining seemed quite knocked out of him.

He stood there, with his eyes fixed upon the floor, and volunteered no remark. The other stood silently waiting for his reply, and watching him with gathering distrust.

"I should never have thought of speaking to you about this matter at such a place as this had I supposed you to be the severe man of business I at first imagined; but finding you here, and, apparently, upon friendly terms with this man Jaggers, I cannot suppose that you will think my conduct contains an unpardonable breach of etiquette."

The old man looked up again, and then once more averted his gaze, but still offered no remark.

"Well, sir," said the other, somewhat sternly; "I am awaiting your pleasure."

"What do you want?" cried Fenwick suddenly, in a peevish tone. "What are you hunting me about for all over London? Do you suppose I am a thief?"

The other regarded him in blank astonishment.

"Suppose what?" he said.

"Suppose that I—that I want to rob—suppose—what do you want, sir, now you have found me, that's what I wish to know? That's what I wish to know, sir?"

"I can tell you in two words, Mr. Fenwick, what it is that I require."

"Tell me, then," cried the old man, in the same state of extraordinary excitement. "Let's hear it, sir. Out with it, sir. I should very much like to have an explanation."

"I will not beat about the bush, then, since you've put it in this way," replied the other, angrily. "I gave some valuable jewels into your custody before I went abroad. I only require them to be restored to me with as little delay as possible, I being on the point of leaving England again for some years."

"Certainly," said Mr. Fenwick, a thought occurring to him. "Certainly, my dear sir; if that is all, nothing could be easier. Certainly you shall have them."

"If I could only have seen you yesterday there would have been no trouble about the matter; but now it must put you to some inconvenience to give them to me at this late hour, and I start the first thing in the morning."

"What time?"

"Four or five o'clock."

"Very well, I will send them to you. Give me your address."

"I will not put you to that trouble," said the other, quickly. "If you will allow me, I will accompany you and wait."

"No, no, don't do that. You can't do that. It is impossible."

"Impossible?"

"Yes, quite impossible."

"May I ask the reason?"

"I have not got them at home."

"They are at your office, I suppose?"

Fenwick hesitated.

He had some idea of saying no, and pretending that he had put them into the hands of his bankers.

But this was rather dangerous, for the banker would be consulted, and then there would be an awkward exposure. No, it would be the best plan to say that the jewels were at the office.

Then, if he could only have contrived the sham burglary he would have been all right. But there was no time for that.

Well, what should he say? How could he get out of the scrape?

Surely, never was anyone in a more awful fix than was this unfortunate old gentleman.

The other could not avoid noticing his confusion, and his suspicions, which had before been aroused, pointed more and more certainly at some act of roguery upon Fenwick's part.

"Are the jewels at your office?" he asked, impatiently.

"Yes."

"Let us go there, then, at once."

"That is no good."

"Why?"

"Because the key is at my private residence."

"Very well, then, we must go to your home first."

"Yes—no—that is to say——"

"To say what? What fresh difficulty is there?"

"Oh, no difficulty. Of course, I would be the last to throw any in your way; but—but——"

"But—what?" cried the other, losing all patience.

"Nothing; only that it is rather late to knock them up, and it would alarm my family."

"But you need not alarm them, I should think. Haven't you a latch-key?"

"No, no, I never carry one."

"What do you do, then, pray, when you return from your dog-fighting friends?" asked the other, with a slight smile of contempt.

"I sleep at an hotel."

"Oh, I am very sorry, but I am afraid I must oblige you to get the key at once, even at the risk of disturbing your family, Mr. Fenwick, for, as I have said already, I have no time to spare."

"But could not I send the jewels after you?"

"No, I must take them now."

Mr. Fenwick felt that his doom was rapidly approaching.

He could not hope much longer to ward off exposure. But he would make one last attempt. He would try bluster.

"Upon my word, Mr. Harcourt, I don't quite understand this sort of behaviour. It's—it's extremely unprofessional. It's extremely unjust to expect that I should be put to all this inconvenience. I—I really can't submit to it, sir. No, sir; as I said before, it's—it's extremely unprofessional——"

He was going on in the same strain to any length, when Harcourt interrupted him, and there was that now in his tone which very clearly indicated his determination to be no longer trifled with.

"Let us understand one another, Mr. Fenwick," said he, taking the old man's arm within the grasp of his strong fingers. "Don't talk nonsense—that is only wasting time. I had no idea when I left those jewels in your care what a very unprofessional person I was trusting."

"D-do you mean to say, sir, that—that I'm—that ——"

"That what, sir?"

"That—that the jewels——"

"Well?"

"That I want to cheat you of them, in point of fact?"

"I am glad that you have come to that point yourself, Mr. Fenwick, for I should have felt some delicacy in doing so. But since you ask me, allow me to ask you in return, what possible conclusion can I come to when you make so many objections to acting in a straightforward way, and throw so many obstacles in the path?"

"Look here, Mr. Harcourt," said the old man, with the courage of despair. "I wont be bullied or browbeaten by any man. If you like to send to my office during office hours to-morrow you shall have your property, but not now; and I shall not put myself out of the way to oblige you any further in the matter after—after your unjust and—and actionable language."

"Very well, sir," said the other," after a brief pause

of astonishment. "I will call upon you at your office to-morrow. At what time will be most convenient?"

"Any time between ten and four."

"At eleven, then."

"I will have the jewels ready for you."

Mr. Harcourt said no more, but, turning on his heel, walked straight out of the house, without even looking behind him; and the old man, with a sigh of relief, sank down upon a chair, and wiped his clammy face with his pocket-handkerchief.

"Thank God I have got rid of him for the present," Fenwick muttered to himself. "I shall have a little time now to consider what I ought to do next."

Mrs. Jaggers had left the room, the imp was also absent, and Jaggers himself had not yet returned.

He had plenty of time and opportunity for reflection if he had been capable of bringing his poor wandering and bewildered senses to bear upon the subject.

But he could see no way out of the scrape he had fallen into. Nothing but disgrace and ruin awaited him. There was no escape.

"I'll wait for Jaggers," he said at last, aloud; but the woman, who had entered the room at the moment, and who overheard the words, ventured to address him.

"Do you want to see my husband again to-night?" she asked.

"Yes," he replied, quickly; "of course I do. I want him particularly to talk about some business of importance."

"But, sir, I am afraid you cannot."

"Why?"

"I am afraid he could not have understood rightly."

"Why?"

"Because he will not be back for some hours—not all night, I should say."

"Not back all night?" cried the old man, wildly. "Where is he? Good heavens! you must be wrong."

"No, sir; he's gone away with the gentlemen, and they said they were going to make a night of it. They have taken my husband with them."

"But where?"

"There's no saying, sir, I am sure. They'll take him from one place to another. You'd never find him."

Fenwick clasped his head in his hands and groaned aloud. Then rising to his feet after a few moments' silence, he rushed out of the house.

Unseen, a dark figure followed him, dogging his steps.

CHAPTER XXVI.

BARRABAS THE JEW.

FENWICK BALFOUR, all ragged and mud-bespattered, ran wildly from Jaggers's house, and, heeding not what puddles he stepped into, and how many times he brought his poor toes in contact with the stray brickbats, broken bottles, and discarded saucepans and kettles which lay scattered in his path, pursued his mad career, and soon made his escape from the neighbourhood where he had suffered so much misery.

Arriving in good time upon the limits of civilization, he found a hackney-coach stand, called a coach, and bade the man drive to the west end of the town.

Scarcely, however, had his vehicle started, than a man, who had followed him, unseen, from Jaggers's house, called another coach, and bade the driver keep in the wake of the first—but at a respectful distance, for fear Mr. Fenwick might look behind.

The journey thus commenced proved to be a long one; for the occupant of the first coach, after proceeding a considerable distance upon the way to the place he had first mentioned as his destination, altered his mind, and caused the horse's head to be turned towards the north.

Such a long way off was the place to which the coach was proceeding that the man following had begun to despair of its ever coming to a halt, when, suddenly, it drew up short at a street corner, and the old gentleman, alighting, paid the fare and walked away.

In another moment the other coach stopped, the spy sprang to the ground, and, discharging the Jarvey, followed in Fenwick's steps, the two coachmen driving off together.

The old man walked some little distance down the street, and then turned round a corner, and, walking about twenty yards, stood still to look up at the window of a house upon the opposite side of the way.

A light in the first-floor window caused his face to brighten up with a faint gleam of satisfaction.

"Thank heaven, he is in; that's good, so far. I must put it to him the best way that I can, and I think he must hear reason."

So saying, Fenwick crossed the road, and stopping before the house upon the door of which was a small brass plate, with the name "Barrabas" upon it, he timidly pulled the bell.

It was a miserable, poverty-stricken street to which Mr. Fenwick had come, but the house of which he had rung the bell was of a much more pretentious character than any of its neighbours. It was, indeed, one of those old red-brick edifices with a quaintly-carved portico, which we find now and then in a small back street, elbowed up and put upon by the mean, paltry tenements which have risen around it since the days of its youth and grandeur, and the days when perriwigs were fashionable.

Although a fine old house, however, and evidently one that had seen better days, it was in a ruined and neglected state, the paint peeled from the door, the railings rusty and bent, the window-panes broken and patched with paper, while the shutters, fastened in all the lower rooms, seemed to indicate that a large portion of the building was unused by its proprietor.

Mr. Fenwick, having rung the bell, waited very patiently for a long time, but, receiving no answer, he ventured at last upon a somewhat stronger and longer pull, which had the effect, after a considerable delay, of bringing some one downstairs.

Mr. Fenwick listened to a shambling footfall upon the stairs and along the passage, and presently to the screeching of the rusty bolts as they were slowly drawn back in their sockets by the person upon the other side of the door.

Then a harsh voice called out—

"Who's there?"

"I want to speak to you a moment, Mr. Barrabas," said the other.

"Who are you?" asked the voice within. "I can't see you, whoever you are. You'd better come again to-morrow."

"No, no; I must speak to you for a minute."

"Is it you, Fenwick? I think I know your voice."

"Yes, sir," replied the old man, humbly; "I want most particularly to see you."

"What about? Go away. I can't talk to you to-night."

"I wont detain you a moment; but you must let me in."

"I can't—I shan't, I tell you. Come to-morrow."

And the old man heard the bolts being pushed back into their places.

But he was desperate, and would not take "no" for an answer.

He hammered loudly with his fists upon the panels, and called loudly upon the proprietor of the house by name, entreating him to grant an audience of only a few moments, for the love of heaven.

He was not a very sharp person, this old scampish profligate, as we know already, nor had he his wits about him as a general rule; but upon this occasion he certainly could not have adopted any course so likely to gain the end in view as the one he had chosen.

MR. FENWICK IS DETECTED TRYNIG TO PLAN A SHAM BURGLARY.

Mr. Barrabas, it would seem, was by no means desirous of attracting public attention to himself or his visitors, and, therefore, after several times indignantly desiring Fenwick to hold his noise and go about his business, and finding that he would do nothing of the kind, he suddenly opened the door, and seizing the old man by the collar, dragged him into the passage.

While Fenwick was gasping in astonishment, he bolted and chained the door again; and then, turning upon him sharply, said:—

"What now, pray? What do you mean by kicking up that idiotic row on my doorstep? Are you mad?"

"Pretty nearly," replied the other, with a weary sigh. "I shall be soon."

"What about?"

But Fenwick, passing his hand over his forehead, replied only with a groan.

The other looked at him silently for awhile, then leading the way upstairs, said:—

"Come up, will you? We'll talk in my room."

Fenwick followed him to the first-floor front, which was fitted up as a kind of office, with a couple of rickety desks, and two or three mangy-looking chairs, some old deed boxes, a few ragged books and fly-blown maps, and a huge quantity of dusty papers, tied up in bundles with scraps of red tape, out of which the colour had faded through old age and exposure to the air.

Arrived here, Mr. Barrabas motioned to his visitor to take a seat, while he himself went back to the chair from which, it would appear, he had risen awhile ago, when he went to open the door.

Here were spread out his writing materials, and a mass of creasy, crumpled letters, which he appeared to be sorting; and dipping a melancholy stump of a pen into some muddy ink, he went on with his work for some minutes, as though he were unconscious of the other's presence.

He was a small, wiry-looking man, between fifty and sixty, with a skin like some smoke-dried old parchment, scanty red hair fringing his bare crown, long teeth, which looked like a dog's when he grinned, and foxy eyebrows overhanging cunning little eyes. He had, besides, large blubbering lips, and a nose that was unmistakeably a Jew's.

Mr. Barrabas collected rents. He also dabbled a little in the law. He called himself a commission-agent and an accountant.

He, at various times, described himself as pursuing a variety of callings, none of which, however, were of a very lucrative character; for the fact was, he made his living by lending money upon good security, at ever so many hundred per cent.,—a trade, which, though troublesome, is, in some cases, a paying one.

Not that it appeared that Mr. Barrabas had flourished, for a more miserable object than he was it would be rather difficult to imagine.

At once bloated and emaciated, he appeared never in all his life to have had a good meal.

He certainly kept no servant, and all the food he ate he purchased out of doors, and cooked for himself after his own fashion.

There were, indeed, all kinds of extraordinary stories current in the neighbourhood, respecting him and his ways of life.

He was supposed to be a miser, and enormously rich; and great sums of money were believed to be secreted upon the premises—only, upon one or two occasions, when his house had been broken into, nothing had been discovered.

It was his habit to dodge about among the butchers' shops in the lowest neighbourhoods, to purchase the scraps of meat usually thrown away or given to the dogs. There was a story told of his having been seen to steal a bone from a hungry canine, and put it in his pocket. He kept his eye, it is said, upon all the cheapest markets, and bargained for decayed fruit, stale pastry, fly-blown meat, and other abominations, which, to judge by appearances, he did not find to be very nourishing.

Mr. Fenwick sat watching this melancholy object working away with his stumpy pen and muddy ink, making illegible notes upon the creasy documents before him, and carefully tying them up with scraps of dingy tape, used for the hundredth time, and carefully preserved in a drawer.

He remained for a long time silently observant of the other's movements—supposing, perhaps, that presently, when he had finished his work, he would enter into conversation.

It appeared, however, that he was doomed to wait a long while if he waited for Barrabas to speak first; and therefore, plucking up courage at length he ventured upon a " Hem !"

Barrabas took no notice of him, working on as before.

" Ahem !" said Mr. Fenwick, again. " I beg your pardon——."

" What about ?" snapped the Jew, suddenly twisting round to face him.

" No—nothing," stammered the old gentleman, " only for interrupting you."

" Oh ! is that all ?" And the Jew went back to his work.

" Could you spare me a few moments ?" the old gentleman presently ventured to ask.

" What for ?"

" While I talk to you."

" Talk away. I don't hinder you, do I ?"

" No. Only I thought you were engaged."

" So I am ; but I can listen. Go on."

" It's—it's about those jewels, then."

" What about them ?"

" I've come here to ask you to let me have them back."

" Certainly. Have you brought the money with you ?"

" No."

" No !"

" I haven't brought the money now, but——"

" Fetch it, then ; the jewels are ready for you whenever you choose to redeem them."

" It's no good fencing about," said Fenwick, desperately, " or beating about the bush, or talking nonsense."

" Not if you can help it," snarled the Jew.

" I must have those diamonds back, Barrabas, or I shall be ruined."

" Indeed !"

" Yes ; the owner has come back."

" You told me so yesterday."

" Yes, yes, I know ; and I thought I could have deceived him ; but it is impossible. I must give up the jewels."

" Why so ?"

" Oh ! don't drive me mad, with questions. I am almost beside myself as it is. I tell you I am in such a fix now, that I must give up the jewels."

" How about the sham burglary you were so full of ?"

" It wont do. It cannot be managed."

" Ah, I thought the scheme was rather a wild one."

" It was the only way, I thought."

" Why not try it now, then ?"

" Because I have seen the owner of the diamonds, and he has asked me for them."

" What did you say ?"

" That they were at my office."

" Well ?"

" He is to call to-morrow at eleven."

" Well ?"

" When he does it will all come out. I shall be ruined and disgraced—given into custody as a common felon."

" Nonsense ; he can't do that."

" But I shall be disgraced. You can't point out any way in which I can avoid disgrace."

" Why not try the burglary dodge now ?"

" Oh, no—no, I cannot do that. He would suspect that it was a trick. Besides—oh, no. It would be simple madness."

" What do you propose, then ?" asked the Jew, with a cold stare. And the unfortunate old gentleman shuffled uneasily on his chair, uncertain what to say next.

But he gulped it out at last in desperation—feeling that the ground was gradually slipping away from under his feet, and that this was the last chance left.

" Look here, Barrabas ; you know well enough that nothing will save me unless I have those diamonds back, that I may show him they are safe in my possession."

" Doesn't he want to take them away ?"

" Oh, no ; only to look at them."

" Look here, Balfour Fenwick, Esquire, Gentleman," said the Jew. " You're what in vulgar life would be called a thief, and you know it. He has asked you for the diamonds back again, and you think you're going to cheat me out of them—not if I know it, though."

" What do you mean ?—I—I——"

" Hold your tongue. It wont do, I tell you. Give me the money, and I'll give you back the things ; if not, I'll keep them, or give you into custody—which you like."

" No, no, Barrabas," cried the old man, seeing that there was no other course open to him but entreaty. " Don't use me so. For God's sake, don't be so cruel. I that have dealt with you so well for years and years, and brought you so much business. Don't be so cruel to me, pray."

" I don't understand you," growled the other. " What do you want ? what do you mean ?"

"I want you to let me have the diamonds back."

"But you have no money to pay me."

"Wont you take my note of hand for five hundred—for—for a thousand? Come, come—for what you like?"

"Bother your notes of hand, I've enough of 'em as it is. They're not worth the paper they're written on, you know that well enough."

"I know nothing of the kind. Haven't I always renewed regularly?"

"Oh, you've renewed fast enough, but you've never paid. No—no, Mr. Fenwick; it wont do, I say. You must try some other shop. Besides——"

"Besides what?"

"What are you worth, I should like to know? Didn't your vagabond partner rig every one he came across? Oh, the pair of you have carried on a pretty game, you have—carried on, the pair of you, playing into one another's hands!"

"It's false, I say. I never knew what he had done. He never let me into any of the secrets of the business."

"More fool you, then; that's all I've got to say."

"But you will help me."

"I shan't, and so I don't deceive you. No, you've had quite enough out of me already. I wont be bled of another blessed sixpence."

The poor old gentleman wrung his hands and fairly blubbered aloud.

"For God's sake trust me," he cried. "I'll do anything you like—pay anything—sign anything——"

"Devil doubt you," retorted the other. "You were always uncommonly ready with that autograph of yours; but what is it worth? you're half-way into the Bankruptcy Court now, you know that well enough."

"It is not true. You wrong me, you know."

"If you are so well off, why don't you find the money to redeem these diamonds?"

This last question was certainly to the point. The man could find no answer, but continued to wring his hands and weep and wail.

Barrabas presently lost all patience, and having by this time packed up his papers, put away his writing materials and concluded his work for the night, intimated that he wanted to go to bed, and that his visitor could say good night as soon as he was ready.

Then the old man, finding that his case was growing desperate, begged and implored the Jew to help him.

Barrabas buttoned up his breeches pocket, and hummed a tune.

Fenwick at last fell upon his knees and sobbed, and clung to the money-lender's skirts. There was no self-abasement and humiliation too great for him if he could only have softened the heart of the obdurate wretch at whose mercy he was.

But the Jew was not to be coaxed out of his determination.

"It wont do," he said. "You're not going to have the jewels without you pay me the money, and so it's no good wasting any more time."

"Oh, pray listen to me!"

"I've listened quite long enough."

"Don't send me away."

"I can't sit up all night listening to your folly."

"Oh dear, oh dear! I shall be ruined."

"I can't help that."

"But—but, wont you help me?"

"How can I?"

"Oh dear, oh dear! you know well enough."

"Come," said the Jew, "take yourself off, if you please, or I must call in some one that will make you."

He spoke in so determined a tone there was no gainsaying him, and the miserable old gentleman at length sneaked downstairs and allowed himself to be hustled into the street, when the door of the Jew's house was violently slammed to upon his heels, and he was left to take himself off where he chose.

Where? That was the question.

What could he do! There seemed no way open for him now but to carry out that mad scheme of a sham burglary which he had proposed to the resurrectionist.

He hesitated only for a moment, gazing wildly around as though uncertain whither to bend his steps. Then set off at a rapid pace, something between a run and a walk.

Again the figure which had dogged his footsteps followed stealthily at a distance—near enough, however, to keep him in view.

Before he had proceeded any great distance, the old man came across a hackney-coach, into which he scrambled, giving a direction to the jarvey.

As before, the spy obtained another vehicle, and following, was seen in the rear.

This time Mr. Fenwick was conveyed to Lincoln's-inn-fields, at the north-west corner of which he stopped the driver and alighted.

Then, loitering about until the man had driven away, he turned to the right, and proceeding for some distance down, in the direction of the Strand, stopped before a house standing further back than the rest, with a covered way leading up to the door.

He paused, and looked round anxiously.

Another coach had driven into the square, and drove slowly past the door where the old man stood, some one the while peering out from the window.

But Fenwick hid himself as much as possible from view, and trembled like a leaf.

The cab having driven past, he hastily took from his pocket a small latch-key that he carried, and let himself into the house.

Scarcely a minute after the door had closed upon his retreating form, the person who had passed the outer gate in the cab, and who was, of course, the same who throughout the evening had been dodging the lawyer's footsteps, stealthily approached.

He stole up the stone passage leading to the house door, against which he pushed.

But the door was fastened.

There was a low window easily reached. He clambered over the railings on to the window-sill, and endeavoured to raise the sash.

It was fastened.

This did not, however, appear to offer any very material obstacle in the path of this somewhat unscrupulous personage.

He drew from his pocket a small dark lantern—such as burglars carry when plying their nefarious trade.

Then he took from another pocket a small parcel, which turned out to contain putty. This he heated at the lantern, and applied to the glass of the window.

Having pressed it closely, so as to cause it to stick, he drew forth a glazier's diamond, and neatly cut round the putty in a circle, holding it as he did so.

Next moment the piece of glass was in his hand, and there was a round hole in the window about twelve inches in circumference.

Through this aperture he deftly introduced his hand, and turned and unfastened the window.

He pushed up the sash, and stepped down into the room.

In doing so the light of the lantern that he carried flashed upon his face, and revealed the features of the man to whom belonged the jewels of which Fenwick had fraudulently disposed.

It was Stephen Harcourt.

CHAPTER XXVII.

JANE ROYDON'S AGONY.

IT is, always has been, and always will be, the custom to accuse the romancist of exaggeration should he venture to describe scenes and characters with the particulars of which the reader may not be acquainted, and that he meets with, for the first time, in the pages of fiction.

To venture, then, upon a recital of the horrors perpetrated in the mysterious house, dubbed by its inmates a nunnery, into which Jack Chinnery had effected an entrance, is a hazardous proceeding, as we want to keep up our character for veracity, as it must naturally strike any one unacquainted with the secret mysteries and dark and terrible crimes which lie hidden beneath the smooth surface of this humdrum city's life that what is here written is nothing but a wild creation of the writer's brain.

If such is the reader's verdict we must abide by it, and are content to allow him to believe accordingly that " 'tis but fancy's sketch." Would that the murdered victims of fiendish cruelty could be recalled to life to tell their own stories and give their own testimony in corroboration of the writer's unvarnished tale!

We left Jack Chinnery horrified by the sound of a piercing shriek, wrung, he supposed, in her bitter agony, from the suffering breast of the tortured girl whom the monsters had conveyed into the vaulted chamber. He struggled violently with the door, and flung himself with all the strength which yet remained in his enfeebled and exhausted frame against the portal that shut him out, as he thought, from the scene of horror.

Suddenly, however, the door gave way, and he staggered forward into the room.

With difficulty he saved himself from falling.

Then, next moment, he threw himself into an attitude of defence, expecting that an attack would be instantly made upon him.

But, much to his astonishment, no one interfered with his violent entrance.

He stared round, but his gaze only encountered the bare walls.

What did it mean?

He rubbed his eyes in blank astonishment. He could not believe that he had seen aright.

But yet it was so. There could be no doubt of the fact.

The room was empty.

The furniture, certainly, was the same as when he had last seen it, for at the first glance he fancied that he had got into a wrong room; but where were the people?

He had seen the negro Joel, Lazarus the blind man, the old woman, the proud cruel woman, and the unhappy victim who had fallen into their power, all enter the apartment. But what had become of them?

It was altogether such a perplexing business that he could not, for the life of him, find any solution to the enigma.

He left the room again, and dragging upon one side the tapestry which hid the walls, sought for some door which might lead to another apartment.

But no, there was none.

They had entered this vault-like chamber, and must be —where?

His reason told him that these persons could not have melted away into thin air. What, then, had become of them?

He searched eagerly round the room in the hope of finding some secret door which at first he had not perceived.

But nothing of the kind met his eye.

The walls looked perfectly solid.

There was no sign of a trap-door in the floor. The ceiling was out of the question.

And yet they must have gone somewhere.

He listened intently, fancying that, perhaps, he might hear some sound that would serve as a guide to the direction in which the wretches had taken their unhappy captive.

But now all was perfectly still.

Not a sound broke the death-like silence, and this awful stillness was, if anything, more horrible than would have been the sound of piercing shrieks.

They were torturing the unhappy girl, he thought, in some place where her cries were smothered by walls and double doors.

They might have murdered her by this time.

And then the harrowing thought rushed through his brain : Would he be in time to save her?

*   *   *   *   *   *

Had Jack Chinnery been acquainted with the mysteries of the nunnery he would have known that by pressing a tiny spring, half hidden by one of the shelves in the cupboard where he had found the black marks, he could have opened a secret door and disclosed a dark cavernous opening, from which ran down a precipitate flight of stone steps.

It was by this way that the two sisters and their myrmidons had borne their unfortunate captive to a subterranean chamber, where they could, without fear of interruption, practise their fiendish cruelties.

It was a vaulted room, somewhat similar to those above, but rather larger.

The feeble and flickering rays of the light which they brought with them was scarcely powerful enough to shadow forth the grim horrors.

The grim obscurity enhanced the terror of the dreadful place.

But when in time these were revealed to the affrighted sight of the helpless victim brought to them, they were enough to make the stoutest heart quail.

All round the walls were hung the most diabolical instruments of cruelty, such as the fell ingenuity of incarnate demons could alone contrive.

Instruments of torture, such as flourished years ago in the dark ages of intolerant ignorance, as flourish now even in the vile dungeons of the Inquisition, where priestly power holds its cruel sway.

When some years after the period of this story these establishments were broken into, and these horrible contrivances for wringing agony from the human frame were discovered, those who found them were at first at a loss to conceive what could be the use of these incomprehensible instruments.

When at length, however, the fearful truth dawned upon them, the most intense wonder succeeded, respecting the way in which the nuns could have obtained possession of them.

It was utterly unreasonable to suppose that they could have been manufactured expressly for their use, and it was supposed that they must, on the contrary, have been handed down from generation to generation, and preserved by this so-called religious community which, from its first institution, had battened upon the innocent blood of its tortured victims.

Ostentatiously displayed upon the walls were cruel whips, to the pig's-hide lashes of which were attached small jagged pieces of iron to tear the naked flesh, until even the palpitating tendons were laid bare and quivering.

Horrible pincers, too, were to be seen, which the monsters made red-hot in braziers provided for the purpose.

Horrible knives, jagged like saws.

Twisted scissors, rough and purposely blunt.

Dreadful instruments, shaped like fish-hooks, to be forced into, and wrenched backwards out of the victim's flesh.

There was one awful instrument, simple enough to look at, with which unutterable agony was caused to the sufferer.

The victim's wrists were tied with waxed string behind her. One end of a rope was fastened to a strong iron ring attached to the thinner cord, and by the aid of a pulley she was drawn up from the ground to the ceiling, and then let down with a run to within *a few feet of the ground.*

The result of this premeditated shock was, to wrench round the wrong way the unhappy victim's arms, dislocating the joints, and in the end, if the torture were persevered in, tearing the arms out of their sockets, with an intensity of suffering which it would be impossible to conceive.

Again, there was a thumb-screw, a frightful machine, of which the name is probably familiar to most readers, although the nature of the torture is more dreadful than is generally supposed, for by means of a vice enclosing the thumb, gradually pressed tighter and tighter, the blood at length was forced out beneath the victim's nail.

Other fiendish contrivances were there to be found in this stronghold of demoniacal cruelty; but the soul sickens at the idea of all these accumulated horrors, increasing instead of decreasing in brutality as their details reached the spectator's terrified eyes.

There was the iron boot, into which, by the introduction of long wedges, driven by a mallet between the iron and the limb, the bones of the foot were crushed.

There was the mask with steel bands, to screw upon the victim's face and scour off the skin.

There was the iron collar to gripe the throat, so that all the agonies of strangulation would ensue, without actual death.

Upon the floor were two racks, one of which was for administering the question by water. This process was arrived at by stretching the sufferer on the machinery, bound tight by the ankles and wrists, and placing a piece of linen over the mouth—then pouring water on to the linen, and allowing it to run through drop by drop, giving dreadful agony to the tortured.

The other rack was one intended to dislocate all the limbs by means of a complex mechanism of fiendish ingenuity.

To this last did Joel, the Black, and Lazarus, the blind man, carry the inanimate form of the wretched girl.

The aspect of the torture-room, when she slowly opened her eyes, drew from her lips a piercing shriek, and with all the strength of which she was capable she endeavoured to struggle out of their grasp.

It was this cry of terror that had reached the ears of Chinnery in the chapel above.

But soon a great weakness overpowering her, she sank helplessly back, and lay motionless in the position in which they placed her on the cold, moist flags of the noisome dungeon.

Finding her thus unresisting, the two male demons then took the opportunity of assuming their black crape masks.

After she had lain there for a short time, they raised her again, and placed her in a high-backed, wooden chair.

A table was then placed in front of her, on which were paper, pens, and ink.

The handsome woman—the younger of the two sisters—then approached the victim and said—

"Do you intend to continue in this obstinate state?"

The girl made no answer.

"I have before warned you what you will have to suffer. Understand now, for the last time, that you shall yield to our wishes—or die! Will you sign the paper?"

The girl slowly rolled her head from side to side, and looked up helplessly at the speaker.

She appeared scarcely to understand the meaning of the words addressed to her.

She gazed at the woman with a vacant stare, and her dull eyes looked as though the sight had left them.

"Unless you do as I bid you, we will torture you to death. We will break your stubborn, obdurate heart."

An expression of wild terror passed over the victim's face as she heard these words. The blood froze in her veins, and her limbs were rigid as though in death.

The sister fiercely pinched her fleshless arm, and pointed to the hideous machinery lying upon the ground.

The unhappy victim closed her eyes, as though to shut out the dreadful object, and groaned aloud. But yet she was firm in her resolve.

Perhaps she could not believe that they would carry out their fiendish threat. Perhaps she thought that the instruments of torture that met her eye at every turn were only intended as objects of terror, not for use.

"For the last time I ask you, will you consent?"

"No, no!"

The sister turned away, grinding her teeth with rage.

"Take her to the rack," she said, fiercely. And Lazarus and the negro came forward to do her bidding.

They carried her to the dreadful instrument, and fastened her wrists and ankles with coarse, strong rope to the rings attached to the head and foot of the machine.

A low wail of terror escaped her lips when she found herself tied fast and helpless, and the dread reality of her situation flashed across her affrighted mind.

But the torture had not yet commenced. They allowed her to lie there bound and helpless, and the old woman in her turn approaching, bade her not to be a fool, but to agree to what they proposed.

The girl, however, although she had scarcely strength to speak, still managed to murmur a negative.

The old hag then fiercely shrieked out to the negro to begin his horrible work.

The awful mechanism of the rack was set in motion.

The unhappy victim's entire frame experienced a terribly jerking shock, which appeared to loosen every limb in its socket.

She moaned in agony.

Horribly she writhed and struggled, and her groans broke into plaintive wails.

Again was the machinery set in motion. Again did the woodwork creak, and the wheels grind round.

This time, however, the shock was much more terrible.

Every bone appeared to be wrenched loose.

Every muscle, tendon, and fibre to crack and tear.

Her sufferings were harrowing. Her anguish indescribable.

Large drops of perspiration streamed down her ghastly face.

Her writhings grew more intense, and her groans fainter, as though with exhaustion.

Again the cruel wretch demanded of her whether she would yield.

But, again summoning what little strength remained to her, and collecting her scattered senses, which, in the terrific throes of agony had well nigh deserted her, she refused.

But once more came the terrible torture.

This time, however, it was more than she could bear.

The torments were utterly unendurable — excruciating, maddening.

She uttered a piercing shriek, and her head fell backwards. Her mouth opened, and her jaw dropped.

The negro, rapidly loosening the screws, bent down over her, and raised her in his arms.

There was a death-like silence in the place, which so lately had echoed with the wild shrieks of the tortured victim.

The women crowded round, and looked eagerly down into the girl's face.

"Is she dead?" the youngest asked, in a low, half-stifled tone.

"I think you've gone a little too far this time," replied the Black. "I thought myself she wouldn't be able to stand it."

Then they raised the victim in their arms, and prepared to carry her out of the dreadful chamber.

For some time none of them spoke. The old woman was the first to break the silence.

"If this gets wind," she said, "we must hide all the instruments."

"There is no fear of its being discovered," said the younger woman.

"The doctor can arrange all that."

"The first thing to do, in any case, though, is to communicate with Jane Roydon's friends."

As they thus spoke, they came out into the small vaulted room above, through the secret door behind the cupboard.

Chinnery, however, had not sufficient notice of their approach to get well out of the other door before they entered.

He was passing through when they made their appearance, and the Black caught sight of his retreating form.

Relinquishing his hold of the burden they were carrying, the negro sprang towards the chapel, into which Chinnery ran for safety.

The robber had not a moment allowed him for hesitation.

Luckily, however, he ran towards the door which he had previously unbolted.

He sprang through, and banged it to behind him.

Everything at this moment luckily favoured his escape. The ladder, about which the men had spoken, stood reared up against the wall, and was plainly visibly in the moonlight.

He climbed up with the agility of a cat, and clambered over, reckless of the broken bottles.

In another moment he was in the street.

"Jane Roydon," he muttered to himself, "that's the woman's name, is it ? Her friends shall hear of it ; but in a different way to that those wretches would like if they had their way."

He ran along with all the speed he could exert, and paused only at last for want of breath to find that he had no pursuers.

"I thought I should never have got away with my life," said Jack to himself, wiping his moist face. "But they haven't done with me yet. I'll pay them another visit before very long, I hope."

And it can be no serious breach of confidence to say that Jack Chinnery, at no distant period, obtained his wish, though under what circumstances it would not at this place be fair to state.

CHAPTER XXVIII.

THE QUARREL AND ITS RESULT.

But we must now return to our friends at the masquerade.

There is little doubt but that the defeated brigand would have taken summary vengeance upon the courageous artist, had he not been withheld by the crowd, who, now that Harley had broken the ice, did not mind taking an active part in the mêlée.

Frank Harley stood there, calm and erect, awaiting the other's attack ; but, the first burst of passion over, the brigand grew quiet enough, although when he addressed his opponent it was in a voice of ill-concealed hate.

"You shall suffer for this, fellow," he said.

"*You have* suffered for it," retorted Harley, with a grim smile.

But the brigand here made a hasty movement, as though he would have rushed upon him, had not some of the bystanders interposed themselves.

"If you have the courage to back your cavaliership's conduct, you will follow me at once," he hissed betwixt his set teeth.

"Go on, Sir Brigand. Your character is well chosen."

With these and similar taunts exchanged by the way, the two would-be combatants made for the door, regardless of the shrieks of the ladies and expostulations of the gentlemen.

"What's all this, Harley ?" asked Gerard Wilde, who came up as they reached the ball-room.

"Just the very man !" exclaimed the artist, taking his arm. "It is only a little difference of opinion between this gentleman and I. You'll be my friend, I know."

"I shall be delighted," answered Wilde ; and he only spoke the truth, for he possessed to a large degree the thoroughly English *penchant* for a row.

*　　　　*　　　　*　　　　*

But what had become of Alice Willoughby all this time ?

She was so occupied by the doing of the masquers at the next table—Mr. Winder and his fair domino—that she scarcely noticed the absence of her devoted artist.

With the eagerness of jealousy her eyes were fixed upon the mask of the marone domino as though she would have pierced through the black satin screen and discovered what features lay concealed beneath. But suddenly she noticed that her supposed rival's attention was drawn to the entrance of the refreshment saloon, and, following the direction of her eyes, beheld a tall brigand, big and fierce-looking enough to combine in him the terrors of " Fra Diavolo" and " Mazzaroni."

The new comer entered gazing about him in every direction, and peering almost impertinently into every face, apparently seeking eagerly for an acquaintance among the masquers, his two jet black eyes glistening like lustres through his mask.

"See, that is he."

Alice heard the downward whisper to Winder.

"Who, Beele ?"

"Yes."

"The devil !"

"He has somehow pierced my disguise. See, he has already caught sight of me. Don't speak. Look another way. Now saunter into the ball-room."

Here Winder made a very faint remonstrance, but his objections were very easily overruled, and he accordingly did as she bade him.

He rose leisurely from his seat, and, endeavouring to appear perfectly at his ease, lounged out into the ball-room. But once there he dashed into the thick of it, and in a trice was far removed from the scene of danger.

He rapidly crossed the ball-room, and making his way to the dress-circle, found a snug corner from which he could watch his late companion's movements.

Immediately that Winder had quitted her, the lady arose and walked slowly up towards the brigand, who had apparently excited her fears.

As she drew closer, he made her a stiff bow, and said in very stiff tones, " So, my Lady Crutchingford."

But the lady walked straight on, seeming not to notice him, although she almost brushed him with her domino and passed on into the ball-room.

The brigand stared after her in astonishment, and then would the lady's fears have ended, had she not imprudently looked round and quickened her pace.

The brigand, however, perceived from this that it was only a bold *ruse*, and started in pursuit.

The lady glanced nervously over her shoulder, and found the man was in pursuit of her, and though she pushed on her way as quickly as possible, he was another moment at her side.

At first she pretended not to understand him, but, as she had predicted to Winder, he was unmanly enough to attempt to remove her mask.

It was then that Frank Harley had so opportunely arrived on the scene.

Mr. Winder had witnessed the whole affair from the first circle, and upon recognising the artist's voice, hastily descended to the scene of action.

"It's all very well," muttered Winder to himself ; " but what the deuce would all the world say when it came out that he had to take care of Amatoria when I got her into the scrape ! Gad, I've an idea—demme. I'll ask him. He's an easy-going sort of a fellow, and he wants to borrow my money."

Saying this, he quickened his steps and overtook the party outside the theatre.

"Harley!"

"Hollo, Mr. Harlequin!"

"Hush! It's me, Winder."

"I know. What do you want then, my lion heart?"

"Hush! They're looking round. Where are you going? I want to speak to you in private."

"You can't; those gentlemen are waiting."

"Let us follow them in another cab; I want you to do me a favour."

"So I thought."

"But will you oblige me?"

"I must first know the nature of the service you require."

"I hardly like to ask you."

"Why do you keep me here, then?"

"In short, would you change dresses with me?"

"What!"

"Not with the motive you may think. I merely want to—to——."

"A singular request; and I have not time to grant it, even if I would."

"Stop, stop!"

"What now?"

"If you would oblige me, we could change as you go along."

"But what would be the benefit to me?"

This was a poser that was almost too much for the selfish Winder.

Luckily, however, a thought occurred to him.

"Do you mean to fight that man?" he asked.

"Of course I do."

"Swords?"

"Can't say."

"The choice is with you. Choose swords if you can do anything in that way, and then my dress would serve you well."

"How so?"

"It's much thicker than yours, and covered with spangles."

"Pooh, pooh! Why, do you suppose that anything made to fit your diminutive anatomy would do for me?"

And thus saying, Harley turned upon his heel with a jeering laugh, and followed Gerald Wilde into the coach provided for them.

They rode along, Harley describing to his companion by the way the circumstances of the quarrel.

They paused, after about a quarter of an hour's ride, at the door of an hotel in May-fair—where they had called, Harley's adversary's second explained, for the purpose of obtaining the weapons.

They were very soon upon their way again, and travelled rapidly towards the north.

Arrived at Hampstead, a spot favourable for the encounter was very soon found; and now Harley, for the first time, as he stood opposite to his antagonist with a sword in his hand, could believe the reality of the whole affair, which had hitherto seemed more like a dream than aught else.

The daylight was breaking coldly over the valley, and the trees around looked grey and grim.

It was very cold, too, and it was with difficulty that the artist could prevent his teeth from chattering a little—an event which, lest it might be attributed to cowardice, he was most anxious to avoid.

He was no coward, though, and he took his place bravely before the other's sword.

He fell, and his blood dyed the fresh green sward, from which the dew-drops had been trampled out by the movements of the duellist's feet.

They carried him away—cold, and white, and bloody; and the brigand and his party scrambled into their cab,

and made the best of their way to town, only too happy at avoiding a meeting with the rustic police.

CHAPTER XXIX.

THE GHOST IN THE BACK YARD.

MR. BELFOUR FENWICK, all unconscious that he was the object of so much scouting, having let himself into the house in Lincoln's-inn, without loss of time set about putting into immediate execution the project which had brought him thither.

This was, of course, the getting up of the evidence of a sham burglary.

It was a matter of no small difficulty, as may be supposed, to the old man, who was not only unacquainted with the way in which burglaries were usually conducted, but was also so weak and feeble that any manual labour requiring more strength than a child was capable of exerting, was, in his case, almost impossible of achievement.

But he must do something. If he had had Jaggers to help him it would not have been such a very difficult matter, because he would have brought with him his house-breaking tools, and very easily have picked the locks.

As it was, Mr. Fenwick's ideas respecting the manner in which the locks should be forced were of the very vaguest and most unsatisfactory character.

In the first place, he was well aware of one thing most necessary for the proper carrying out of the scheme. That was, that he should make no noise.

He cautiously opened the door and crept along the passage upon tip-toe.

The boards of the floor creaked in the fashion that he had never heard them to do before.

When he laid his hand upon the lock it went off with a great click, almost as loud, he fancied, as the report of a pocket pistol.

Trying to save it from going to with a noise, he closed it with a great bang.

Then he stood perspiring with fright, expecting every moment that the grim night-cap of the laundress would be poked up from the lower storey round the opening leading to the kitchen stairs.

But he was somewhat reassured when he presently found that nothing had happened, and that his movements appeared not to have disturbed the old woman.

Mr. Fenwick's offices were on the ground floor, front and back. The front room was the clerk's office. The middle room was Mr. Fenwick's when he attended to business. The small room at the end, the window of which looked out upon a leaky waterbutt in the back yard, had been the late Mr. Worwold's.

The old man carried a key in his pocket, with which he let himself through the outer door; and this, with great caution, he contrived to close noiselessly behind him.

He started back, however, when he had gone but a few steps into the middle room, at finding that the office fire had not yet gone out.

At first, he thought that one of the clerks might still be at work, and inwardly he cursed them for their over-industry.

"What do the fools stop here for after time?" he muttered; "that wont get what wages are due to them as it is. They need not try to make the debt any larger. However, they're gone, that's one blessing. How long ago, I wonder? They must have left a large fire burning, if it was long ago."

As this thought passed through his brain, the old man, looking at his watch, saw that it was very nearly three o'clock.

"There is no time to waste," he said, half aloud; "I must get to work directly."

He found, and lit a small oil-lamp, used for sealing letters, and opened the door leading into Worwold's room.

All here was cold and dismal as the grave.

Through the window the moonlight flickered faintly upon the shutters ; and a leafless tree, standing at a short distance from the house, cast a goblin-like shadow upon the room-floor.

When Fenwick peeped out through the window, he fancied he had never in his life beheld so dreary and cheerless a scene as that which the stived-up little yard, with its background of gloomy brick buildings, presented.

The shutters were not made to close, and there was no blind ; so that he could not shut out the objectionable view. But he made up his mind to be no longer than possible over the work he had in hand.

As he turned round, something gave him a dreadful start. It was nothing more than an office coat which had fallen into a somewhat fantastic attitude upon the seat of the arm-chair that Worwold used to occupy.

At the first glance this garment had assumed something awfully like the form and attitude of Fenwick's late partner.

There were the thin arms squared out, and the high shoulders ; and a patch of moonlight just above might have been the white, death-like face turned towards him.

The old man almost dropped the lamp, and it was a long time before he could recover his equanimity ; and his thoughts having once fallen into this unpleasant channel, he could not drive the subject from his mind.

No—everywhere something met his eye, and reminded him of the dead man.

In life he had always had an awful way of creeping in upon his partner, without giving any notice of his approach.

If he should creep in now ?

The fraudulent trustee shook like an aspen leaf as he approached the door of the safe where the jewels ought to have been.

He unlocked it, and dragged the papers out upon the floor.

Properly to give the idea of a burglary having been committed he ought to have smashed the lock ; but with his puny strength this feat was impossible.

He contented himself, therefore, by prising and wrenching at some of the drawers of the office-table, the contents of which he also scattered upon the ground.

He threw the whole room into confusion, and, to the best of his ability, gave the place the appearance of having been ransacked by some robber. But it was, as may be supposed after all, but a very clumsy affair, and if the old man had not been half-crazy at the time, he must have known that the most bungling of London detectives would have discovered the fraud at a glance.

When he had nearly finished, he looked round upon the confusion he had created, he could not, for the life of him, help thinking what ever would Worwold, who was such a particular and exact sort of person when alive, have said to such a scene in the room about which he was so particular !

As he thought so, a slight noise at the back window caused him to raise his eyes.

He uttered a wild shriek, and let fall his lamp ; for then, to his unutterable horror, he saw the white face of Worwold peeping in.

For a moment he was so terror-stricken that he had not the power to tear himself from the spot.

But at last, with a violent effort, he shook off the spell which seemed to hold him prisoner, and rushed towards the door.

He had not time to pass the threshold ere an iron grip encircled his throat.

He reeled back, gasping and breathless ; and his captor flung him heavily to the ground, and set his knee upon the old man's breast.

CHAPTER XXX.

TERROR.

FOR some few moments Balfour Fenwick lay quaking with fear, and unable to utter a word.

He made sure that it was his late partner's ghost that had got hold of him.

But then, when he began to reflect that he had seen his partner's ghost in front, and this, whatever it was, had got hold of him behind, a horrible suspicion of his having tumbled right into the middle of a party of ghosts, almost effectually deprived him of what scanty stock of brains he ordinarily possessed.

The gripe upon his throat was, however, of two substantial a nature to be ghostly, and Mr. Fenwick was gradually choked into the belief that somebody of flesh and blood had got hold of him.

Got hold very tight, too, it seemed ; and, wrenching him round, in spite of the old man's struggles to free himself, forced him down upon the floor and held him tight.

Then presently a bull's-eye lantern was produced, and began to dance to and fro before Mr. Fenwick's eyes.

"What the deuce are you about, old gentleman ?" asked the new-comer, who had thus so unceremoniously treated him.

The old gentleman's mouth opened and shut like that of a fish, but from it issued no sound.

"What are you about ?" replied the other. "Why are you so frightened ? Stand up, will you ?"

Mr. Fenwick was only too glad to avail himself of the offer, and to scramble to his feet.

When the other had seated him in a chair, and he had got his breath a little, he recognised who it was into whose hands he had fallen, and great was his terror when he saw that it was the proprietor of the diamonds that he had made away with.

The gentleman, opening his lantern, looked round upon the scene of confusion which the office presented.

"What have you been doing here ?" he asked ; "everything seems upside down."

"I—I've been looking——"

"Looking for what ?"

"For—for your jewels."

"What do you mean ? Are not they here ?"

"They were here just now—that is to say to-day.—I mean yesterday."

"I don't think you know what you mean," said the younger man, sternly ; "but tell me, without any further prevarication, what you have done with my property."

"Without any pre—pre—vary——"

"When were these jewels last in your possession ?"

A wild idea entered the old man's head.

"Four days ago," he said ; "and then I missed them—I can't think where I could have put them. I've been so much worried by my private misfortunes, I haven't known what I've been about."

"Do you mean to say that you've mislaid them ?"

"Yes—I think so. Unless they have been stolen from me."

The other man looked at him very hard and somewhat doubtfully. Presently he said, pointing to a bureau in one corner of the room—

"Have you looked in there ? You don't seem to have opened it."

"I'm sure they aren't there," replied Fenwick.

But then, correcting himself, another wonderful thought having occurred to him, he added, eagerly—

"Now I think of it, I'm sure they must be, but it's locked."

"I'll easily break it open with the poker."

"No, no—do not do that. It will spoil it."

The other looked round upon the work of destruction in which Fenwick had been engaged.

ALICE WILLOUGHBY FAINTS ON BEING TURNED AWAY BY MR. WINDER.

"You've grown very careful, all at once," he said.

"No, I am not; only that bureau I prize very much from association's sake. Stop a moment, and I will get you a chisel."

"Where is it?"

"Only in the outer office—I'll be back in an instant."

The other made no opposition to his going, and the old man glided out of the room.

In another instant he had passed through into the passage and double-locked the outer door.

He reached the street, closing the street-door also, and hurried down into the road.

As he came out, the coach in which the other had arrived drove towards him.

He sprang in, and gave the name of a street near to that where he lived. The journey having been rapidly effected, he alighted, and made the best of his way to his own house.

Full of a resolve that he had come to upon the road, he turned the key in the lock, and entered cautiously, and with as little noise as possible.

The men in possession, who were carousing in the dining-room after their wont, for they had it pretty well their own way in this disturbed household, did not hear him enter, and he carefully closed the door behind him.

Then he crept up stairs to his daughter's room.

He knocked before he entered, but receiving no answer turned the handle of the door.

In a low tone of voice he called to her by name, but received no reply.

The fire was burning low and red, filling the room with ruddy light; and as he drew on one side the curtain of the bed, he could see at a glance that she was not there.

He looked around into the empty arm-chairs upon

either side of the fire-place, and strove to pierce the gloomy obscurity of the dressing-room beyond.

The bed had evidently not been lain in. There were no articles of clothing scattered about.

Perhaps she had not retired to rest, and yet it was very late.

As he stood thus pondering, with his hand upon the bed-post, the rustle of a dress behind him caused him to start round.

Much as Ethel Fane and Mrs. Worwold had met before in that room, now did the old man meet his daughter; and the wild terror in the latter's face showed how little she expected to find him there.

"Father!" she ejaculated.

"Ethel! where have you been? What has happened?'

"Great God! what makes you ask me? What do you suppose can have been the purport of my journey at this hour of the night, unless it was to visit his grave?"

The old man staggered back, and his teeth chattered as though with fear.

"What made you go there?" he said. "Isn't it dangerous?"

"How can I remain in uncertainty? If there is danger, I must know it."

"But now that it is done, what is there to be dreaded?"

His daughter clung wildly to his arm, and bent her head close to his, so that she might whisper into his ear.

"Father, the grave has been robbed. The secret of his death is known."

CHAPTER XXXI.

FLIGHT.

THERE was a pause of some moments, during which the father and daughter silently regarded each other with white, scared faces.

Then the old man, pressing his thin hand to his brow with a kind of low, plaintive wail, tottered backwards, and would have fallen had not Ethel eagerly sprung forward to support him.

"Father," she said, presently, in a trembling voice, "why have you been so much away during the last few days? What has happened? Are you in any fear?"

The question reminded him of other dangers; and, covering his face with his hands, he rocked himself to and fro, groaning bitterly.

"There have been so many inquiries about you, father," said his daughter, endeavouring to take the old man's hand coaxingly in hers. "And I have been so unhappy, and so afraid. Do you know what I have been thinking?"

But the old man made no answer. He seemed bewildered and confused, and scarcely capable of comprehending the words addressed to him.

"I have been thinking," she continued "that there is only one course left open to us."

The old man looked about him in a confused sort of way, as though he expected to see it. His daughter went on:—

"Only one way of escape. We must run away, father, before the storm bursts over our heads. There is yet time. We may get far away from danger if we only go at once."

The old man caught the meaning of these last words, and his eyes brightened.

For a moment he sat mumbling to himself.

"Escape—run away—while there is yet time. Yes, yes; that is the only course."

And he rose eagerly to his feet, trembling violently, though with agitation.

"Yes, yes," he said, taking her by the arm, and endeavouring to lead her towards the door. "Let us get away—let us get away."

It was at this moment, for the first time, that Lady Fane perceive the awful change which the events of the last few hours had worked in the appearance of her father.

It appeared as though he had suddenly aged by a score of years—all the elasticity of deportment—all that sprightly juvenility he had been so proud of, and for which he was so noted, had disappeared.

He had lost his brown curly wig, and his scanty locks of silvery hair straggled over his thin, worn face.

His mouth, which had always shown signs of the weakness of his character, now wore an expression which was absolutely silly.

His eyes wandered vaguely from object to object, as incapable of settling for any time upon the same thing for five consecutive minutes as his poor shattered intellect was of grasping an idea and reasoning upon it with any common sense.

Ethel Fane looked at him first with a kind of shrinking terror, as she might have done had she seen him last in ruddy health and found him again in his coffin with the ravages of death visible in his face.

What ailed him? she asked herself. How could this awful change be accounted for?

The sight of the miserable wreck which the old man had become—the old man who, but a short time since, she so well remembered, handsome, witty, and fascinating.

Could this poor, shrunken, withered, witless creature be her father?

She clung to him, yet held him aloof, and gazed with shrinking dread into his face, and strove to fix the eyes that wandered furtively avoiding her gaze, as might have done the eyes of some little child, conscious of wrong doing, and fearing punishment.

A pitiable sight it was, and the dreadful truth that he was childish smote cruelly upon the woman's heart and sorely tried her love.

But not for long.

It was but a brief struggle, and then she had cast aside the unworthy feeling for which next moment she hated and despised herself intensely, and with a burst of passionate and remorseful tears, fell at his feet and clung about him, sobbing.

Threw herself about his neck, and laid his heavy head upon her breast.

Wept bitter tears of sorrow and regret, and poured out all her store of woman's love and tenderness: of the limits of which who shall keep count?

For as she looked upon him in this hour of weakness and fast coming dissolution, the recollection of all his kindness in years gone by came crowding upon her mind and filled her heart to bursting. She remembered as though it had been but yesterday, how, when she was a tiny, golden-haired, little girl, wearing wonderful frocks of spotless muslin, girt in by sashes of broad blue ribbon, and elaborately trimmed by miles, almost, of narrow sarsnet of the same azure hue, she remembered how proudly she toddled by the side of fine papa down the sunny side of the great club-lined streets of the West End; or sometimes how she accompanied him on his stroll in the Park, where so many beautiful ladies admired and caressed her.

He never came home to her in those happy times, when a summer's day was of endless length—but yet far too short for all the happiness to be crowded into it—without bringing her some little present.

He never spoke to her but kindly—lovingly.

All her life through he had fondled, and petted, and spoilt her; and she! what return had she made him?

Ah! there had been one bitter sacrifice which she had made for his sake—he thought, at least: she had married Worwold—the heartless, unprincipled partner, who had got the weak old man into his power and under his thumb.

The old man had supposed that it was altogether upon his account that she had done so, for he was ignorant of that episode of the forged bill of exchange, and of that ugly mystery respecting his daughter's former connexion with Gerard Wilde.

What else did he know of her secrets? What did she know of his?

Though locked now in each other's arms, though mingling together their tears, caresses, and confidences, did not a wide gulf separate them—wide, deep, yawning gulf—a sepulchre which contained the grizzly skeletons of the dead.

Alas! did not the shadow of a dark and unpardonable crime hang heavily upon the souls of one or both, and could there ever more be peace and rest on earth for their guilty consciences?

"Father, we will yet escape: why should we wish to tarry in this place that has been our home, but is so no longer? Not a scrap of furniture that it contains is ours. Why should we linger round the wreck which is fast sinking? Come, dear father. Let us go. I have yet remaining some jewels that we can dispose of, and with their aid procure enough ready money to last us for awhile, and I have talents which surely I can turn to some account. There, dear father, sit still and rest yourself: I will do all that is needful in the way of preparation."

She left the old man seated by the fire-side, watching the dying embers in the grate—striving in vain to gather together his scattered senses—wondering, in a dazed and bewildered fashion, what he ought to do next, and what he ought to try and think about.

Meanwhile his daughter lost no time in making her preparations. Very shortly she returned again to the room, bringing with her a small carpet-bag containing various articles belonging to her father, and also another suit of clothes and a warm great-coat, in which she bade him dress himself as soon as possible.

"But—but—" the old man stammered, "are we in such a hurry?"

"Yes; go at once."

"To-night?"

"This very hour. Do you not say that you have been threatened about those diamonds?"

"Yes, yes; I had forgotten. He will be here directly. He will drag me to prison. Oh, my poor child! what will become of us?"

And the weak old man burst into tears, and rocked himself to and fro again, wringing his hands, the picture of childish terror.

His daughter did her best to soothe his fears; but only with considerable trouble at length induced him to change the rags he wore for another suit of clothes.

During the time that he was so occupied, Ethel Fane had been busily employed, and had made up a packet of those things which she deemed most necessary for the purpose.

She very wisely did not load herself with any cumbersome finery. Her jewellery was very easily packed, and a few articles which she deemed essential, or which she treasured very much—what woman is there who could desert all her household gods without a severe struggle? You may be sure that she shed not a few tears in leaving some of her little treasures behind.

Although she lost very little time in this work, it still occupied several hours, and when at last they were ready to start day was beginning to break.

Ethel looked out upon the staircase and listened.

"All is quiet," she said. "I think we might venture downstairs."

They crept down upon tiptoes, the daughter cautioning the old man to be as careful as possible, and herself supporting him, for he trembled so violently that he could hardly stand.

They went only a few inches at a time, pausing at every step, until they reached the last flight of stairs leading to the hall.

But there they came to a sudden standstill at the sight of the obstacle lying in their path.

The man in possession, who some time since had concluded his carouse, was lying stretched out on his usual bed in the hall, made up with cloaks and greatcoats, and the cushions from the sofas.

To get out at the street-door it was necessary that they should pass over his body.

The old man hung back.

"I—I can't do it," he said. "I shall stumble, and waken him. He will ask what we have got. He will not let us pass. Oh, dear! oh, dear! We had better turn back, and give it up for a bad job."

But to this proposition it was not very probable that her ladyship would agree.

No. She had calculated chances, and she had made up her mind that, if they must escape, now only was the time and this the way that it must be done.

She had passed over the body of one of the sleeping bailiffs ere this, as the reader may recollect. Not very successfully, by-the-by; but still she had managed it, and flattered herself now that she could contrive very easily to get past without awakening him.

At any rate, she was willing to try, and would try.

There was one drawback, however.

The obstacle to success lay in the old man.

Would he be able to pass the difficulty? Not as easily as his daughter, certainly. Not at all, perhaps.

She trembled for him when she looked again at his uncertain gait—his tottering footsteps.

He seemed barely capable of maintaining an upright posture.

He appeared to be every moment upon the point of falling down.

Beneath every footstep the old staircase creaked ominously with his weight.

He clung to the balustrade to support him, and ever and anon caught at the wall to save himself from falling.

But she had thought that he could easily enough have made the journey from her room to the door, in spite of his weakness.

But now, the man lying there at the bottom step seemed to form an impassable barrier to all further progress.

What was to be done?

But while they were yet hesitating upon the course proper to be pursued, an incident occurred which gave them another cause for alarm.

While Lady Fane was in the very act of raising her foot to step across the bailiff's prostrate form, there came a loud knocking at the street-door, and a great ringing at the bell.

She drew back, instinctively clutching at her father's arm.

The summons was, after a moment's pause, repeated even louder than before.

Then the man in possession, half stupified by drink, as was his wont, began to open his eyes and roll his head, and presently called out gruffly—

"Who's there?"

No answer being vouchsafed to this query, and the knocking and ringing coming for the third time—even louder than before—he struggled into an upright posture, and for the first time seemed to thoroughly comprehend from whence came the sound which had disturbed him.

Her ladyship supposed now that detection was inevitable.

The daylight was creeping in faintly through the stained glass window upon the stairs, and her figure and that of her father were plainly visible, had the man looked in that direction.

He did not do so, however; but, rising to his feet, reeled and staggered towards the door.

"Ethel," said the old man, trembling like a leaf, "we are lost."

"No, no, father; let us hope for the best."

"But—but who is he that has come."

"He! Whom, father, do you mean?"

"The man about those jewels. He has come to give me into custody."

"Be brave, dear father," the daughter whispered. "He cannot harm you, and I have yet a sure means of escape——"

"Escape! What! Where! Quick, quick; tell me."

"Can you be very careful?"

"Yes, yes."

"Can you walk on tiptoe?"

"Yes, yes."

"Come, then, father, and for both our sakes be careful."

"Don't fear."

"Come, then. Quick, for we have not a moment to spare."

This conversation had scarcely occupied a moment.

They had spoken in low, hurried whispers.

While they had been doing so, the bailiff had only been shaking himself together after a rough fashion, and very much as a Newfoundland dog shakes himself upon emerging from the water. But he had not yet approached the door.

Indeed, he seemed to be rather uncertain in his own mind whether or not he should do so, as after all this might only be an impudent run-away knock and ring.

But they came again in another moment, louder than ever.

"Hollo, Ikey!" a voice, and from the dining-room; "are you a giving a evening party out there?"

"There's some one at the door."

"So I should think by the row they're making."

"Shall I open it?"

"Might as well, perhaps. They may want to come in, for all you know."

The man in the passage growled and grumbled to himself about the nuisance it was; he could not be allowed to get a quiet night's rest; and went blundering forward to the door.

He had not yet by any means slept off the effects of the liquor of which he had partaken at an earlier period in the evening; and the movements of his hands were as uncertain as those of his feet.

He therefore made a great noise with the bolts, and let down the chain which secured the door with a jangling crash.

While he was thus occupied, Ethel Fane and her father chose this opportunity of attempting their escape.

They crept down the stairs, and round the corner into the lower passage, which was yet enveloped in a grim obscurity, as the weakly struggling daylight had not hitherto penetrated as far.

There was situated the door that Lady Fane, upon a previous occasion, as the reader may remember, let herself in at when she had escaped from Jack Chinnery.

She took hold of her father's wrist, and led him gently, but resolutely, forward.

As she went along she felt in her pocket for the key.

She applied it to the lock, turned it gently—drew back the door with a faint creak.

Very faint it was—not loud enough to be audible to the man at the other door, had not the sudden flood of light betrayed the whereabouts of the fugitives.

He had his hand at the moment upon the door-handle, and happen to turn his head.

He uttered an exclamation of astonishment, and at the same time pulled open the street-door.

It was, as had been supposed by the old man, the person to whom the jewels belonged which had been feloniously appropriated by Balfour Fenwick.

The old man saw this at a glance, and so great was his terror that he almost fell to the ground.

His limbs trembled as though he had the ague. His feet were heavy as lead, and he had not the power to draw them along.

But at this critical juncture his daughter came to his rescue.

She well knew that there was no time to be lost.

She caught him by the arm, and pulled him towards the door.

In another moment they had passed through, and Lady Fane dragged the door to after them.

Then, for a moment, she felt safe, for the means of egress of which she and her father had availed themselves was effectually barred against those inside.

The door opened only with a key, and she had the key in her hand.

But still they might, with but a slight delay, make their exit by another door upon the lower story.

There was no time to be lost.

The old man still was weak and trembling, and totally incapable of saving himself. Again his daughter was compelled to take his arm and pull him along.

At the same time, with prayers and tears, she entreated him to bear up a little while longer, and they might yet be free.

They crossed the deserted garden, and easily enough effected their escape by the gate at the end.

The mews was as gloomy and forsaken as ever. No one was there to bar their passage.

But yet they must not pause.

Placing her arm within that of her father's, she led him along, in spite of his evident inclination to dawdle; for the poor childish old man seemed not to be able to comprehend the full force of the situation in which they were placed.

But there was no time for any explanation. They must get away from the place.

She urged him onward, never pausing; and they were very soon out at the end of the mews.

They hurried along only for a short distance, and then plunged across the road and down a narrow turning.

Proceeding only then about half the length of the street, they turned into another, and hurried on again.

In this way they proceeded for almost half an hour, but not until they had gone more than a mile from the home did Ethel deem it prudent to slacken her pace.

She would not have done so then had not her father shown evident signs of fatigue.

The old man's face was deadly pale, and great drops of perspiration stood upon his brow.

He had been tottering weakly forward for some time past.

Now he suddenly paused, and had he not clung to a door-post, he would certainly have fallen to the ground.

Ethel held out her arms to save him. Then she gently supported him a few paces further on, and seated him in a door-way.

The old man gasped out a few words, and closed his eyes as though he were about to faint away.

Indeed, nothing more ghastly could well be imagined than the old man's countenance at the moment presented.

It was very certain that some severe attack of illness was impending. He must be taken to some place of security at once.

But where?

Ethel gazed around her in despair.

She could see no inviting refuge. The neighbourhood into which they had penetrated and lost themselves was a vile, disreputable place. Around them were squalid courts, looking unutterably wretched, dirty and desolate in the faint light of breaking day.

In such a neighbourhood as this, she thought to herself, surely any one could seek and obtain a hiding-place, however great were the inquiries instituted respecting them.

The hour was one favourable for the purpose—not a soul was to be seen in any direction.

If by any chance she could have found some asylum where they could have hidden themselves away until she had had time to procure some clothes more suitable than those they wore for the life which was in store for them.

When this notion had once entered her head, her ladyship could think of no other plan so likely to prove successful.

Up to now she had had no time to collect her thoughts and settle to her own satisfaction what should be their course of conduct.

A few minutes ago she had had some vague idea that it would be a good plan to seek some respectable lodgings in a quiet suburb.

But could they hope to find anything that would suit them without finding many obstacles placed in their path. Many inquiries would be made. Perhaps they might be asked for references, in which case what could they do ?

But here in the lodging-houses, inns, or coffee-houses, which they might find in this quarter, it was not very likely that any questions would be asked. They might hide here in perfect safety.

She knelt down by the old man's side, and loosened his cravat. Presently he began to show faint signs of recovery.

He gasped and groaned, opened his eyes, and at last asked where he was.

" Don't you know me, dear father ?" Ethel replied. " Try and rouse yourself, we have only to go a little farther."

" Where are we going ?" he asked.

" Not far—not far," she replied, evasively.

Then, having induced her poor father to lean upon her arm for support, she gently guided him onward.

They had but to turn the corner, however, before they found themselves before exactly the sort of home that Ethel Fane had been thinking would suit her.

It had not a very prepossessing exterior, and yet it did not look at all dirty or squalid.

Still, somehow there was something in the dark red blinds closely drawn before the lower windows which Ethel did not like.

But there was very little choice left to her. She could see no other house about. The door of this one stood ajar. It was probably an early house, and they could go in and ask for lodgings without attracting any particular notice or exciting the proprietor's suspicions.

Her ladyship hesitated for a few moments, and then decided that she would venture.

She therefore pushed open the door, and entered the house, which within was dark and silent as a grave.

CHAPTER XXXII.

AFTER THE DUEL.

WE left the hapless Frank Harley, after the duel with the fierce Major Beele, stretched lifeless on his back in Hornsey-fields, wounded nigh unto death. Indeed, his adversary had, as we have said, quitted the ground under the impression that the artist was killed outright.

Gerard Wilde hastened to render such assistance as lay in his power to the unfortunate duellist.

Judge, then, his horror when he could not detect the slightest movement at the wounded man's heart, nor the faintest pulsation at the wrist.

His horror gave way to consternation when he reflected upon the embarrassing position in which it placed him.

Alone at that place with the dead. At such an hour, and the only witnesses fled. Witnesses, too, who would

doubtless have kept silent on the subject at any risk, on account of the part the major had played in the duel.

These thoughts rapidly flashed through his brain, and suggested the possibility—owing to the remarkable combination of circumstances against him—of his being in danger of an accusation of the murder of the artist, should any witnesses arrive upon the spot before he could make good his retreat.

He quite overlooked the infinity of things which he could bring forward to attest his innocence and disprove any accusation at once, if affairs should reach this disagreeable pitch.

In this state of mind he was about to seek safety in flight, when the faintest movement of the insensible artist arrested his steps.

He stopped short, and gazing upon the body, listened intently for the slightest sounds which would indicate the presence of life.

The wounded man breathed a faint sigh.

Gerard Wilde, immensely relieved, dropped on one knee beside the inanimate body of the artist, and eagerly bent his head to the wounded man's chest.

An almost imperceptible beating of the heart announced that life was not wholly extinct, and Gerard Wilde sprang to his feet again with the intention of seeking immediate assistance.

He gazed around him in despair. Although within a short distance of the busy metropolis, the spot had been so appropriately chosen for the combat, that it seemed as far removed from the confines of civilization as the centre of the desert of Sahara.

Not a house was to be seen anywhere near, and all idea of assistance seemed utterly hopeless.

"Ah ! of course," he exclaimed, an idea suddenly occurring to him, "the coachman—I should have thought of that at once."

Saying which, he hastily made his way across the field to the spot where they had left their hackney-coach to await their return.

"I was afraid, your honour," said the jarvey, "that you wasn't coming back no more."

"I want your assistance, my man."

"How, your honour ?"

"To carry a wounded gentleman."

"Wounded ?"

"Yes ; a duel has taken place, and one of the gentlemen is severely wounded. Indeed, I cannot tell how severely. I almost thought that he was dead."

"Dead !"

"I say I thought so ; but he's not. So as there is no prospect of getting a surgeon here, the only thing is to put him in the coach and take him home at once."

"Very good, sir."

And without more ado, the coachman and Gerard Wilde returned to the spot where the latter had left his friend.

The artist groaned with the pain of his hurt as they raised him from the ground, and in spite of the utmost care they evinced as they bore him to the coach, he appeared to be suffering a great deal of agony.

At length, after a considerable difficulty, the poor artist was placed inside the vehicle, and they proceeded leisurely to his lodgings. It took a long weary time to accomplish the journey, because the jolting of the coach, when attempting anything like speed, caused the wounded man excruciating tortures.

At length this was accomplished, and the sufferer placed in his bed, and a surgeon was brought.

"I'm afraid," said the doctor, with a very long face ; "I'm afraid that he is very seriously wounded."

"Dangerously ?" demanded Wilde.

"Scarcely that, if we can keep the patient quiet, as the sword has not reached any vital part. But the wound is so very large, and the blood is so very trifling for such a wound, that it is to be feared that he bleeds internally. You know what that means."

"Good heavens! I feared it. I endeavoured to examine the wound on the ground, but I was so much agitated that my hand shook like an aspen leaf."

"But you took no medical assistance with you to the field?"

"I am a doctor myself by profession, although I haven't a very extensive practice."

"Indeed, then what led you to call me in?"

"I was too agitated to see to him myself. He's game to the backbone, and I was—am greatly grieved to see him in this state."

"At present, then, I think he only needs quiet. We can dress the wound, and then I shall leave him in your care for the present."

The doctor did what was necessary for the patient and left, mentally wondering at Gerard Wilde's want of nerve.

"A pretty surgeon, forsooth!" muttered the man of science, "if the sight of blood unmans him."

Wilde had not told his brother doctor that he had been drinking deeply at the masquerade, and that although he was considerably sobered by the serious events which had since taken place, it was alcohol more than lack of nerve that rendered him incapable of attending his friend.

Having assured himself that the artist slept. Gerard Wilde drew an arm-chair to the side of the bed, and, wrapping himself in a blanket, was soon in a deep slumber.

The next morning—or rather a few hours later on the same morning—Gerard Wilde was awakened by a news-boy in the street, crying his papers immediately beneath the window.

Wilde glanced anxiously at the patient to see if the noise had disturbed him, and, with a mental exclamation, the reverse of a blessing on the news-boy, he ran to the window to motion him off.

The boy without, however, anticipating a customer, on seeing Gerard Wilde appear at the window, held up the paper, at the same time calling out the principal news of the day.

"Full account of the great duel in Hornsey-fields, by an eye witness."

"What?" breathed Gerard, in the utmost amazement.

"The duel in Hornsey-fields—took place last night— one of the duellist killed on the spot, and mysterious disappearance of the body."

Wilde almost doubted the evidence of his ears. Hastily throwing one of the artist's coats over his diabolical masquerading costume, which he still wore, he let himself gently out of the room.

"Here, boy," said Wilde, as he arrived at the street-door, "What paper is that in?"

"Account of the great duel, sir?"

"Yes."

"Times, sir;—fivepence."

Gerard purchased a copy, and quickly regained the sick chamber, where he eagerly sought out the following paragraph:—

"MIDNIGHT DUEL IN HORNSEY FIELDS.

"It is our painful duty to record one of those happily rare occurrences which are blots in the annals of our civilization. A duel has been fought at midnight in the immediate vicinity of the metropolis; the principals being two of the visitors to last night's fashionable masquerade. The quarrel was merely the result of some masquerading frolic, in which one of the combatants was endeavouring to pierce a lady's incognito, and using a great show of violence in trying to remove her mask.

"The maskers were looking on with some interest, when a gentleman—the other duellist—passing the spot, unfortunately mistook the whole affair, and fancying that the lady was being insulted, he rescued her from the hands of her fancied persecutor. Having used an unnecessary amount of violence towards the latter gen-

tleman, a challenge and the midnight duel in Hornsey-fields were the consequences.

"They fought with swords, and after a fierce encounter, the unhappy gentleman, who, in his mistaken zeal and gallantry had interfered in the frolic, fell pierced through the heart.

"The body had been removed from the scene of the duel when assistance arrived on the spot; the blood-stained turf and a handkerchief left behind by one of the duellists, being the only evidences of the fatal encounter.

"No names have as yet transpired, but we believe we could make a shrewd guess as to the name of the successful combatant. He is, if we mistake not, an officer of high rank in the army, and well known in the fashionable circles of society."

Wilde read the above through in the greatest astonishment.

He was well aware of the many and various resources of that mighty power, the public press; but he was equally unable to comprehend how they had managed to get wind of the duel.

They had gone alone to the ground. The major and his second being the only witnesses of the fight beyond himself and the unfortunate Frank Harley.

And then the whole affair was not given out as a rumour merely, but with a positive certainty. And besides which, so many of the details were given, and with much exactness, although some of the facts had been slightly distorted.

For instance, Gerard Wilde had no doubt that the fierce opponent of his friend Harley was in the wrong, and that he had indeed rescued the lady alluded to from his violence.

This led him to think that Major Beele (or, as he thought of him, "the Brigand"—for Gerard, be it remembered, was ignorant of his name) was the author of this account of the duel.

But then he reflected that the gentleman in question would not be likely to put the affair into print, as he had left the ground under the impression that his adversary was killed on the spot, and that he consequently was liable to prosecution for manslaughter should the affair become known to the authorities.

Gerard Wilde was undoubtedly puzzled.

Suddenly he remembered that the news-boy had called it out as being related by an eye-witness, and he thought that he must have overlooked some portion of the account.

On referring again to the paper, he found the following foot-note:—

"Our readers may rely upon the veracity and correctness of the statement of the above unhappy event, as we have it from an eye-witness, who happened to be on the spot under peculiar circumstances. The said gentleman being a writer for the press of some literary distinction."

"Some infernal penny-a-liner!" muttered Gerard Wilde, between his teeth. "But who the deuce could it be? He must have been hidden in one of the hedges. But how came he there at that unearthly hour? Gad, it's a puzzle!"

He glanced up at a timepiece which stood upon the mantelshelf, and was more astonished than ever to find that only a few hours had elapsed since the encounter had taken place. And yet it was already in print.

Wilde thought it over, and puzzled his brain in vain. He could arrive at no satisfactory conclusion.

The artist was still sleeping soundly and peacefully, and Gerard thought that he might now venture upon going to seek some other assistance.

He noiselessly made a hasty toilet, substituting some of the artist's clothes for his late masquerading attire, and sallied forth in search of a nurse.

As he passed by the porter's lodge, he begged the man's temporary aid for his friend, and soon after he sent in a regular nurse.

Shortly after noon of the day in which the events just recorded had taken place, Lady Amatoria Crutchingford was reclining on a couch in her elegantly appointed boudoir, leisurely sipping her coffee, and endeavouring to fix her attention upon the little bits of current scandal which her maid was reading to her from the columns of the *Morning Post*.

But it was very evident that her ladyship's thoughts were far from the subjects touched upon by that fashionable journal.

The mere superficial observer might have seen, by the vacancy in her eye and the palor of her cheek, that affairs of more moment were occupying her mind just then.

"You may put down the paper, Patterson; I'm weary of it."

"Shall I read this first, my lady?"

"No, I cannot attend to it just now; my thoughts are elsewhere."

"Ah! you are not looking very well this morning, my lady."

"No, I've a headache."

"Can I get you anything, my lady?"

"No, thank you, Patterson."

"Here is a capital thing here, my lady."

"Don't I tell you, Patterson, that I am weary of the paper?"

"I merely thought, my lady——"

"You can leave the room, said Lady Amatoria, pettishly."

The girl, with an obstinacy peculiar to the weaker sex, would have the last word. As she laid down the paper, preparatory to quitting the apartment, she read over, half aloud, the heading of the passage in the journal to which she had already called her ladyship's attention.

"DUEL EXTRAORDINARY IN HIGH LIFE."

"What did you say!" exclaimed Lady Amatoria, starting up, and overturning her coffee.

"I was merely reading the heading of an article in the *Post*, my lady."

"What was it?"

"DUEL EXTRAORDINARY IN HIGH LIFE."

"You can stay and read that to me, Patterson."

"Ah! I thought that you would be interested in that, my lady."

"I do not wish to know your thoughts," exclaimed her ladyship, tartly. "I told you to read that."

"Very well, my lady. I'm sure——"

"Do you mean to talk all day?"

The maid coughed down the affront, and then read aloud the account of the duel.

We shall not trouble our readers with a copy of the report; suffice it to say, that it was very nearly the same as the account which appeared in the *Times*, and which we have given elsewhere.

Her ladyship's interest grew greater and greater as her waiting-maid proceeded. At the passage in which the artist was blamed as the aggressor, her cheek flushed with indignation. And when the girl arrived at the supposed death of the gallant Frank Harley, a stifled exclamation on the part of her mistress caused her to stop short, and turn to ascertain the cause of it.

Lady Amatoria had sunk back, half fainting, upon the couch.

At this moment there came a knock at the door.

"See who it is, Patterson," said her ladyship, with an effort. "If it is his lordship, say that I am indisposed, and cannot see him just now."

"No, my lady—a visitor," said Patterson, handing Lady Amatoria a card.

"Mr. Felbridge Winder.—Not down yet."

"Yes, my lady."

The servant who brought the card had no sooner departed with this message, than it occurred to her ladyship that she should prefer to see the gentleman announced.

"Run and see, Patterson," she said; "I wish to speak with Mr. Winder. Show him into the drawing-room, and say I'll join him immediately."

Her ladyship then made some hasty additions to her toilet, and descended to the drawing-room, where she found the gallant Winder anxiously awaiting her arrival.

"My dear Amatoria!"

"Ah! Mr. Winder."

"How delighted I am to see you. After the unpleasant occurrence of last night——"

"It is of that that I wished to speak with you," interrupted Lady Amatoria.

"What of that?" demanded Winder.

"Have you seen the papers yet?"

"No. I was so anxious to see you that I came out as soon as I was up."

"Then you do not know that a duel has taken place between that odious Major Beele and my preserver."

"No—I knew that they were going to fight."

"They have fought."

"Ah! and what is the result?"

"The gentleman—the noble fellow who saved me from the ruffian Beele—has—has—fallen."

"Good Heavens! You don't say so—wounded?"

"No—killed—dead!"

And Lady Amatoria burst into tears.

"Poor Frank Harley!" exclaimed Winder, in about the same tone as he would have used in lamenting the death of a favourite dog.

"I shall never have another peaceful moment," sobbed Lady Amatoria.

"Why so, Amatoria?"

"Why so!" exclaimed the lady. "Have I not been the cause of this brave fellow's death?"

"Why, I don't see that exactly. Poor Frank Harley—I'm dem'd sorry for him, though."

"Who?" exclaimed Lady Amatoria.

"Frank Harley."

"Then you knew him?"

"Yes.—That is, I wasn't very intimate with him. He was only a poor devil of an artist, you know."

The lady was inexpressibly shocked at Winder's levity at such a moment, and she was resolved to end the interview as quickly as possible.

"Do you think it is certain that he is killed?" she asked.

"Why, didn't you say so?"

"I merely told you what I read in the paper you know what mistakes they make."

"Oh! I've no doubt of it, though. What interest would they have in saying he was killed if he wasn't?"

"But could you not go to his lodgings and see?"

"I don't know where he lives."

The lady looked at Mr. Winder with something like disgust. At length she resumed the conversation.

"Harley—Frank Harley. I don't know that name. Was he an artist of any celebrity?"

"Well, I can't say—I don't know much about pictures. But if you're dying to see some of his work, there is a specimen at Dawber's, in Bond-street. I recollect that he told me Dawber was one of his dealers."

Her ladyship rose, and turned to leave.

"You must excuse me, Mr. Winder—I am rather indisposed this morning."

And, with a formal bow, she left the astonished Winder to wonder at the cause of her abrupt departure.

CHAPTER XXXIII.

THE LOVES OF FELBRIDGE WINDER.

WINDER, after waiting the return of Lady Crutchingford for some time, left the house in great disgust.

"Can't make her out, dem me," he muttered.

"Does she fancy perhaps that I didn't much care to look after her last night. Well, but she told me——"

But here, in spite of his endeavours to convince himself that he had simply followed out her instructions, he could not help feeling that he had not conducted himself as a man of honour should, in leaving it to another arm than his to protect the lady he had escorted to the masquerade.

He had thought that her affection for him was too deep to allow such a trifling breach in his good conduct—if indeed such she could consider it—to estrange them.

But as the last straw had broken the camel's back, so had Mr. Winder's last coarseness and selfish speech touching the supposed death of the gallant Frank Harley more effectually destroyed any attachment which Lady Crutchingford had felt for him than could the many solecisms of which he was so frequently guilty.

Consequently, as we have said, he left in high dudgeon.

He walked moodily along Piccadilly, looking neither to the right nor to the left, and did not notice that he had been watched from the house which he had just quitted, and his steps dogged.

It was a girl who was thus following him. She had been walking up and down outside the residence of the Lady Amatoria Crutchingford until he came out, and then had walked on some few paces in his rear.

Presently Winder quickened his step, and gradually increased it, so that his pursuer had almost to run to keep up with him.

There was a strange mixture of weariness and energy in her gait as she proceeded, which would seem to say that she was struggling against nature in continuing the pursuit.

Winder turned briskly down St. James's-street, and the girl paused for a moment, as if for breath, at the corner, and supporting herself by grasping the iron railings with one hand, she pressed the other to her side.

Her momentary pause had greatly increased the distance between her and Winder, and she was forced to run to make up for the lost time.

He turned down Pall-mall, and here the girl walked sharply towards him, apparently with the intention of speaking to him. But then, as if unable to summon up sufficient courage, she stopped short within a pace of him, and followed on as before.

Twice she repeated this, and each time her courage seemed to fail her as she approached him.

He stopped before one of the clubs, and after giving a careless glance about him, prepared to mount the steps.

His foot was upon the second step when the girl bounded up to him.

"Felbridge!" exclaimed a soft plaintive voice, broken with emotion.

"Alice! Phew!"

It was indeed the devoted girl Alice Willoughby who had been following up the worthless object of her love.

She was extremely pale, and her eyes were red, as if she had been keeping a long and weary vigil; and there was a mournful expression in her face which told how sadly and how deeply she felt Winder's cruel desertion of her.

"Felbridge."

"What do you want with me, Alice?"

"I wished to speak with you—only for a moment, Felbridge."

Her voice faltered, her lips quivered with suppressed grief, and her eyes were cast down.

"Another time."

"Felbridge—I——"

"I've an appointment, Alice, and I cannot wait—I'll call upon you."

"Then you will not speak to me?"

"Don't I tell you that I've an appointment."

"Just one word—I implore you—I conjure you."

"It's no use you getting up a scene here, Alice."

"Heaven knows that is far from my wish. But I want to say a few words to you."

"Then, I'll call upon you."

"No, no—I know you will not."

"I say I will."

"Now, now."

One or two friends had saluted Winder as they passed, glancing curiously at Alice; and the hall-porter of the club had taken up his position at the window from whence he was reconnoitring, much to Winder's discomfiture; and he was therefore forced, in spite of himself, to grant the interview she asked.

He walked into St. James's-square, without offering Alice his arm, or even looking to see if she followed him.

"Now, what is it?" he demanded, brutally.

"Oh, Felbridge, why do you speak thus to me?"

"Is that all you've got to say? If so, good-bye."

He turned to leave, but Alice caught him by the arm.

"Stay. What has taken your heart from me, Felbridge? what has occasioned this sudden change? You never found any difference in me—you never——"

"I have already told you."

"You have pretended to be jealous, but that was not real."

"Indeed!"

"No. I know too well. It was merely assumed as an excuse to break with me."

"Oh, you think so?"

"I know so."

"Then what are you keeping me here for?"

"I wish to hear from your lips some cause for your estrangement. Your marriage I know did not take place."

"How do you know that?"

"I was there. Besides, it is in everybody's mouth now."

"Indeed. But what has this to do with you?"

"Everything. I know that your marriage could not have drawn you from me. I know, also, that you were away with that woman—that Lady Crutchingford."

"Well, I was; and what then? Of course I know it all, without giving you the trouble of telling me."

"This woman does not love you, Felbridge."

"How do you know that?"

He spoke rather fiercely, for Alice had touched upon what happened just then to be a particularly sore point.

"I know she cannot love you as I do."

"Bah?"

"She is a notorious flirt."

"Pshaw!"

"And a scandal."

"Do you know that you are wasting my time?"

"What has caused this change in you, Winder?"

"Haven't I already told you over and over again?"

"No, you have not told me the truth."

With an exclamation of impatience Winder turned on his heel.

"Stay—let me but hear once more—say again you no longer love me."

"Why you seem to like to hear it as much as I do saying it." And he laughed a coarse brutal laugh.

"And what has caused your sudden change—your marriage?"

"No."

"This woman—this Lady Crutchingford?"

"No."

"What then?"

"Would you like to know? Well, then, I've got thoroughly tired of you—sick—sated."

He hissed this savagely at her, and the unhappy girl staggered up against the railings of the square as if she would have fallen.

LADY FANE EXCHANGES HER DRESS IN THE SHOP OF THE FAT JEWESS.

Without attempting to assist her, Winder walked briskly back to the club. Before he had gained the top of the steps, Alice had again overtaken him, and once more begged him to return.

"Go away," he muttered, in an under tone. "Don't you see that you are making me look dem'd small before my friends."

"Felbridge—I implore you—another word!"

She clutched him by the wrist as she spoke, and there was an earnestness in her voice and manner which must have excited, at the least' the pity of anyone less brutal than Winder.

He, however, merely bent his head down to hers, and said in a threatening manner—

"You'd better not annoy me any more."

"Annoy you, Felbridge?"

"Yes—demnibly! Remember that there is such a place as the station-house."

With this atrocity he dragged himself from her grasp and entered the club-house.

The poor broken-hearted Alice, inexpressibly shocked and horror-stricken at Winder's conduct, slowly and mournfully retraced her steps homewards.

Just as she turned into Piccadilly, the carriage of Lady Crutchingford drove past, and Alice caught a glimpse of the Lady Amatoria seated inside.

"Might she not take compassion upon me?" thought Alice. "One lover more or less can make but very little difference to her; and I'm sure that she cannot love Winder as I do."

The carriage turned up Bond-street. Alice hastened to see if she could still obtain a view of it, and saw that it had pulled up a few houses along, before the shop of Dawber, the celebrated picture-dealer.

Her ladyship stepped out and into the shop before Alice could reach the spot.

By the reader's permission, we propose entering the picture-dealer's shop with Lady Crutchingford, leaving Alice Willoughby outside, awaiting her ladyship's return.

"Is Mr. Dawber in the way?" demanded the Lady Amatoria.

Mr. Dawber bustled up, and obsequiously inquired the Lady Crutchingford's commands. Mr. Dawber was aristocratic—prided himself upon knowing every member of the "upper ten" of anything like importance, by sight—and, consequently, was acquainted with his customer's name and rank.

If Mr. Dawber had seen the slight expression of annoyance that flitted across her ladyship's countenance as he mentioned her name, he would have understood that, for once, his knowledge led him into an unintentional blunder.

Lady Crutchingford, it would seem, although in her carriage, and proceeding without the least tinge of mystery in her manner, had wished to preserve her incognito as far as she could.

"Your ladyship's pleasure?"

"You had some very bright sketches the last time I was here, Mr. Dawber, by a certain Harvey or Harley, if I mistake not?"

"Yes, my lady; Harley—Frank Harley. Rising man, my lady."

Her ladyship shuddered.

"Could you show me some of them?"

"Most decidedly," my lady."

Some sketches in oil were produced.

"I have a work by the same artist, capitally finished —'The Carnival'—an elaborate, effective scene. Just bring it, Ramsay."

The shopman brought the picture alluded to. It proved to be a scene in Rome, during their great festival. One of the most prominent figures in the scene was a ferocious-looking brigand with a black mask.

The Lady Amatoria felt the blood rush to her face, as it reminded her so forcibly of the great danger she had been in on the previous night at the hands of the ruffianly Major Beele—the assassin (she thought) of the gallant young artist.

"What is the price of this, Mr. Dawber?"

"Forty guineas, your ladyship."

"Forty guineas only; which includes your profit. And this must have taken him certainly not less than two months to paint."

"Yes, my lady, quite that."

"Then at that rate he must be very poor."

"He's an artist," said Mr. Dawber, with a bland smile.

Her ladyship paused thoughtfully for several moments.

"You may send it to my house, Mr. Dawber. By-the-bye, do you know the artist's address?"

The dealer looked blank. It seemed rather like doing him out of his commission.

"His lordship is a great patron of the fine arts, you know, and just now he seems to have almost a mania for this artist's pictures."

"Oh! my lady, I've no doubt that I could undertake any——"

"It is not that," interrupted Lady Amatoria; "but his lordship has a fancy for dealing direct with Mr. Harley."

"Yes, my lady, then I will *endeavour* to find his address."

"Of course your commission will be ensured the same as if he bought through you."

"You are too good, my lady."

"Not at all. Can you give me the address?"

"I will ascertain it, and send round to your ladyship."

"Thank you. Good morning."

"Good morning, my lady."

Lady Crutchingford was stepping into her carriage, when she was accosted by Alice Willoughby.

"Lady Crutchingford," said Alice, with trepidation.

"Yes; that is my name," said her ladyship.

"Could—could I speak with you for a moment—but for an instant?"

"Certainly; I am going home now, and shall be within all the afternoon."

"I know you will excuse me; but I am so very wretched."

There was no doubt of the truth of this. The unhappy Alice's misery was figured in her face; and there was a sadness in her voice which touched the Lady Amatoria's sympathy.

"But what can I do for you?"

"Everything. You can restore Winder to me."

"Winder! What do you mean?"

Lady Amatoria was startled with the abruptness of the address, and the way in which she glanced askance at Alice showed that she, for the moment, entertained some slight doubts as to the poor girl's sanity. Alice half interpreted the look, it would seem, by her reply.

"I have been abrupt—I seem strange, I know; but it is only because I am so agitated."

"Will you come home with me now? We can talk in safety there; at present we are attracting attention."

Alice needed no second invitation, but sprang into the carriage as Lady Crutchingford spoke, and in a few minutes they were closeted together in that lady's boudoir, secured against interruption.

"Now, my dear," said Lady Crutchingford, "take a seat, and tell me what you desire of me."

"I scarcely know how to begin. My name is Alice Willoughby; you may have heard Felbridge mention it."

"Mr. Winder has never spoken of you in my hearing, Miss Willoughby," said her ladyship, coldly.

"You must not be offended with what I shall say, Lady Crutchingford. I can see that you have a kind heart, and you could not have known the wretchedness you were causing when you took him from me."

"Took who from you?"

"Winder."

"But, Miss Willoughby, you surely cannot mean that I——"

"I mean, Lady Crutchingford, that, whether you had any intention or not, you have robbed me of Winder's love."

"I?"

"Yes. At first I thought that he had simply broken with me on account of his marriage; but——"

"His marriage! Is Mr. Winder then married?"

"No. He was to have been—yesterday morning. But when he should have been at the church, I saw him in your carriage in Bond-street."

"Good Heavens! Do you mean really that the bride was there——"

"Yes. I confess it gave me some consolation to find that he did not love her—love is so selfish; but I found that I was equally bad off since that he only loves you. Every particle of the affection he once cherished for me seems to have left him. Indeed, the sight of me appears to disgust him."

"I am very sorry, Miss Willoughby. As a woman I can sympathise with you; but I fear I can be of no assistance."

"You can refuse to see him any more."

"I can and will do so, if you believe that that will bring him back to you."

"You will? How can I sufficiently thank you?"

"I need no thanks, Miss Willoughby. More especially as the proceeding which you propose exactly jumps with my humour at present."

"What—you have no regret in giving him up?"

"Miss Willoughby," said Lady Crutchingford, with frigid dignity, "you use strange expressions. As a friend of Lord Crutchingford, Mr. Winder has paid me some little attentions—mere common-place gallantries. I am sorry that you should imagine his visits here had taken his affection from you, and I shall prove my sympathy by refusing to see him, so that he may gradually drop his visits here. But I must beg you to be a little more guarded in your speech when a lady's honour is concerned. Were half you have said repeated in any gossiping circle, my reputation would suffer considerably."

"Forgive me, Lady Crutchingford. But is it possible you did not love—that you bore Winder no attachment?"

Alice gazed into Lady Amatoria's face as she put the question, half incredulously, as if she could not comprehend how any one could refrain from adoring her lover, that her ladyship could not help smiling in spite of herself.

"Not in the least," said the latter, taking Alice's hand affectionately; "and that is the plain candid truth. It amused me to have him dodging after me; but his selfishness and coarse nature have wearied me. Believe me, my dear Miss Willoughby, that the man is unworthy of a love like yours."

"I know that Felbridge is not exactly disinterested or generous. Neither is he a Solon of wisdom; but love is not guided by reason."

"Truly, my modern Titania, it is not."

"Good-bye, Lady Crutchingford. You have made me so happy."

"Good-bye, Miss Willoughby; and pray call again, for I shall long to learn your progress with the truant lover."

And again reiterating her thanks, Alice Willoughby left; her heart much lighter than when she had entered the mansion of the good-natured Lady Crutchingford.

CHAPTER XXXIV.

THE ADVENTURES OF LADY ETHEL.

WE parted company with Lady Ethel Fane and her father, in the gloomy-looking coffee-house in which the former had sought a temporary asylum, until the sudden indisposition of Mr. Balfour Fenwick had passed.

The shop inside seemed so dismal and sombre, that a sensation of dread passed through Lady Ethel's mind as they entered, and the old man shuddered at the darkness.

"I hope that is not an evil omen," said Lady Ethel to herself. "No—no; he is ill, that is the cause of it."

There seemed to be no one about to attend to their wants, and the lady stamped her foot loudly in great impatience. At length an old woman appeared.

"Can you let me a room for a short time?" said Lady Fane. "This gentleman, my father, has been taken ill in the street."

"Yes, mum," replied the old woman. "Certainly; this way, mum."

She led the way towards a parlour at the back of the shop, but stopped short at the door. It was a glass-door, with the windows whitewashed all over, with the exception of a little square of about four inches in one of the top panes, which was left clean and transparent.

The old woman applied her eye to this spot, and tapped at the door at the same time. Then a scuffling was heard within, a rattling sound, and the old woman pushed open the door and led the way through the room out of a door on the left into the passage.

Lady Ethel gave a rapid glance around the parlour as they passed through. It was a moderate-sized room, decently furnished, and the brilliant lighting of the place from a chandelier suspended from the ceiling, afforded a pleasant contrast with the gloomy shop adjoining.

In the centre of the room was a green-baize table, round which was seated some eight or ten men—all with flushed faces, and all with a more or less dissipated appearance.

Lady Fane did not at all like the look of these men, and she remarked with astonishment, that they were all seated in precisely the same attitude, with their hands under the table. However, she was too much occupied with her own embarrassments to suffer her thoughts to remain long upon any subject which was not immediately connected with her interests.

The old woman led the way up-stairs to the first floor. Here she ushered them into a room at the back of the house, which, in its gloomy, dull appearance, bore a striking resemblance to the shop.

"This will do very well," said Lady Fane, "for the short time we shall remain."

"Can I be of any assistance, mum?" demanded the woman.

"No, thank you." Then it suddenly occurring to her that she ought to give some explanation to the woman, she added—"The gentleman was taken ill——"

"Yes, mum; can I get him anything?"

"Ah! I told you no, thank you; he will be better immediately, if he can rest awhile."

"Has mounseer met with an accident?"

"She takes us for foreigners," thought Lady Fane. "Very good." Then she added aloud — "No, we have just returned from Germany—only yesterday, and we have been robbed."

"Robbed!"

"Yes—of everything we possessed."

"Indeed, mum—very sad thing! How did it happen?"

"We had left our luggage at a booking-office yesterday upon our arrival, and when we went to claim it to-day, they told us that some one had already been and taken it away, demanding it in our name."

"But you didn't, surely, believe all they told you, mum?"

"No; but what could we do? They showed receipts in their books for the goods, and there was an end of it."

"Dreadful, mum. It's my opinion that they are no better than they should be at that booking-office, mum."

"Ethel! Ethel!" groaned Mr. Fenwick, who was rolling about on the bed upon which he had lain down when they entered the room.

"What is it, father?"

"Oh! Ethel—I'm so ill! I think I'm dying!"

"What can I do for you? Shall I send for a doctor?"

"No, no; I—oh!"

"Hadn't we better have a doctor to the gentleman, mum?"

Lady Fane was extremely nervous of having any more witnesses of Mr. Fenwick's infirmities than was actually necessary, and she was secretly rejoiced to hear that he refused to have any medical assistance. Her father was seldom in the enjoyment of good health, and she therefore felt that she could treat him with perfect safety, being accustomed to his maladies.

"No; I don't think it necessary at all," she said, in reply to the old woman. "He never wants any assistance. A little rest and quiet will bring him round."

"Ethel!—Oh!" groaned Mr. Fenwick.

"Yes, father. Will you have anything?"

"Water—water!" gasped the old man.

They soon procured him some water, and he was relieved for the moment. However, he seemed still far from being perfectly recovered, and Lady Fane saw that it would be impossible to remove him that day, at any rate.

"I fear that he will not be able to proceed any farther for the present," she said. "Can you accommodate me with a room for to-night?"

"Yes, mum. There's the next room you can have, if you please. You will be near your father, mum. This door opens into it."

"Ah! that will do for me, then, if there is only a little daylight admitted into the room."

"Daylight," repeated the old woman, as if she did not comprehend the allusion.

"Yes; you seem to shut out daylight in every direction here."

"Yes, mum. You see we are in rather a dark quarter."

"True; but that must be very injurious to your business. Your gloomy-looking shop cannot attract many customers, I should think."

The old woman seemed somewhat disconcerted at this remark.

"Why, no. That is, I don't complain. We don't do much in chance custom. Ours is a subscription house."

"Subscription house—a kind of club?"

"Yes, mum—that's it. We've a number of gents—you may have noticed them in the parlour, mum—who come regularly every day."

"Yes; I did notice them. But they seemed to be taking nothing."

"No, no. I—that is, they were waiting to be attended to."

"They were sitting round a card-table, I believe, were they not?"

"Yes, mum. You see they play at dominoes sometimes, for cups of coffee. Quite innocent amusements, mum; nothing, like."

Here the old woman got rather confused, and floundered about a bit, winding up in something perfectly meaningless.

Lady Fane was too much occupied with her own thoughts to heed her much; and was, therefore, very well pleased when the old woman proposed to show her the room she was to have for the night.

There was nothing remarkable about the apartment, excepting that it was well in character with the adjoining chamber and the shop—gloomy and sombre, and almost innocent of daylight. It had a window in it—a very dirty one, by-the-bye—decorated with some still dirtier chintz hangings, which seemed at a first glance to open flush on to a brick wall. However, upon a closer scrutiny, Lady Fane saw that it looked into a narrow passage, and that the brick wall was some six feet off.

After making some arrangements as to payment, and so forth, Lady Fane dismissed the old woman.

"Is she gone, Ethel?" asked Mr. Fenwick, from the next room.

"Yes. How do you feel now, father?"

"Better; but I'm miserably bad still. Ah! I'm an unhappy old man."

"Hush! We are perfectly safe here, with a little prudence."

"It's a miserable hole! It's like some catacomb above ground."

"It's not very cheerful, true; but so much the better. No one would think of seeking us in this God-forsaken place. But I cannot understand this house at all. There seems something very strange about it. I hope that we are safe."

"Safe!" repeated Mr. Fenwick, seemingly alarmed at the word. "Safe! why shouldn't we be? They can know nothing here."

"Hush! Speak lower, father. I mean safe from molestation; that's all. Of course, they know nothing."

"How do you mean molestation?" repeated the old man, peevishly.

"I mean that, from what I saw of those men down stairs, I have my doubts—very grave doubts—of their honesty."

"Why, what makes you imagine such a thing as that?"

"The brutal expression of their faces. And, seeing us of so much better appearance than the usual run of visitors, their cupidity might be excited. It was partly to provide against any disagreeables of that kind that I told the old woman that we had been robbed. However, we may as well assume as low a position in life as possible while we are here. It can't do us any harm."

"Very well; only don't plague me any more about it. Oh! Ethel!" here he gazed sadly into her large, dreamy, violet eyes—"it's a fearful thing to have upon one's consc——"

"Hush! For heaven's sake be prudent, father, or you will ruin us."

"Dreadful—very dreadful?" mumbled Mr. Fenwick.

"I must see for some money," said Lady Fane. "I have but a mere trifle left."

"What! are you going out?" demanded Mr. Fenwick, peevishly.

"Yes; I have to go. I must endeavour to dispose of something—some of my jewellery."

"Ah! you are going to desert me."

"No, no, father. Why should you think that?"

"Ah! I know very well. I'm a poor, miserable old man."

"Hush! Not so loud, father. I entreat you to be more careful. I am only going to be absent for a short time."

Mr. Fenwick turned over fretfully upon the pillow without replying, and Lady Fane thought this a good opportunity to leave the room.

She made her way downstairs, and pushed open the parlour door, without even knocking. There was a great deal of scrambling, and she distinctly saw one of the men gather up a set of dice from the table as she entered. They all rose to their feet, and began some very coarse language, and oaths anything but mild, at the interruption.

"Hallo!" exclaimed one of the men. "What the h— do you want spying about here?"

"You'll come to grief, young woman," said a second, "if you come here foxing about!"

"What did that old thief, Flanders, mean by letting her in?" added a third.

But, without heeding their oaths or their menaces, Lady Fane crossed the room, and, opening the door, passed through the shop into the street. She was greatly alarmed at their rough manners, and began to half regret that she had chosen such a dangerous asylum for her father. However, it was now too late to retreat, and the safest course was to meet her equivocal position as boldly as possible.

She noted the name of the street, looked about for landmarks, and started off on her errand.

The richness of her apparel excited the attention of many very suspicious-looking persons; and more than once she was followed by men through several streets with evident felonious intent; and she only got rid of them by turning short and facing them, when they slunk away.

As she progressed, the quarter grew a shade more respectable, and the people she met no longer appeared to have that hang-dog look which seemed to distinguish almost every individual she had encountered in the immediate vicinity of her temporary abode.

A short walk brought her across a dirty-looking shop, filled with female clothing of every description. Gaudy muslin dresses and light-coloured silks, all more or less dirty, hung round the window, and a board at the door announced the name and trade of the proprietor.

"Mrs. Israel gives the highest prices for ladies' left-off clothes of every kind. N.B. Age no matter. N.B. Weekly payments taken."

As Lady Fane stood reading this announcement, a fat, greasy-looking Jewess, with a proportion of nose unusual even among the twelve tribes, lolled to the door, and addressed her ladyship in shrill Jewish tones—

"Anything in my way, mum? Can't beat us in the neighbourhood. Buy anything—at a price, from a tenpenny nail upwards."

"I wanted to know if you would buy——"

"Any mortal thing, my dear. Show us."

"If you will allow me to go into the shop. I don't care to transact business in the street."

"Certainly; this way."

They entered the shop.

"Now, mum, what can we do for you?"

"Can you buy this dress—the one I have on?"

"Buy it? Yes; of course—at a price. What do you expect to get for it?"

"That I leave to you. Say what you can give."

This did not evidently suit the wary Mrs. Israel. Afraid of naming a price higher than her customer expected, or would be inclined to accept, she was nervous of giving an absurdly low valuation, lest she should send her in disgust away. Lady Fane, misunderstanding the reason for her hesitation, turned to leave the shop.

"Oh! if it is not worth your while——"

"Stop—stop a bit, my dear—there's no hurry; what do you say to eight shillins?"

The dress had cost, some few days before, rather over ten pounds.

"Look 'ere; say ten shillings. Eh?"

"I wish to make an exchange."

"Exchange!" exclaimed the Jewess eagerly. "What for? Dresses—boots?"

"I want something of a poorer dress than the one I wear."

"I've just thé harticle; see here, my dear."

With this the Jewess produced some eight or ten dresses of every description, from which Lady Fane selected one. Mrs. Israel seldom made so good a bargain as the present one, notwithstanding her growls of discontent all the time, that she was giving her things away, and, consequently, taking the bread out of her own children's mouths, &c., &c.

"That's about it, mum; giving it away; and if I hadn't agreed to take it, nothing under a sovereign, as I'm a woman——"

"If you're not satisfied, that will end the business!" exclaimed Lady Fane haughtily.

"Satisfied! why I give my word——"

"Enough; I can go further——"

Lady Fane made a few steps towards the door, but the Jewess called her back almost frantically. Mrs. Israel was almost too good at her trade.

"I say, mum—stop, mum; a bargin's a bargin. I'm very glad to do the business—it turns the stock over."

Lady Fane paused as requested. She was very loth to quit without effecting the exchange, for, being unacquainted with the locality, she had very little hopes of finding a similar shop within a long distance.

"Can I change my dress here?" she asked.

"Certainly, mum. Step into my little back parlour; here, this way, mum."

Lady Fane went into the little back parlour, and the change was soon effected.

Being in such a disreputable quarter, she had taken the precaution of securing all her money and valuables about her person, and as several things were in the pocket of the dress which she had bartered with the Jewess, these had to be transferred to the new dress.

Mrs. Israel rendered great assistance in this, and used her fat fingers with such dexterity that Lady Fane had not left the wardrobe shop a minute when she discovered that she had lost a small leather case containing a pair of gold ear-rings.

She quickly retraced her steps, and, upon entering the shop, saw Mrs. Israel examining the missing treasure at the little back-parlour door.

"That's just what I've come back for," said Lady Fane.

The casket had disappeared in a trice.

"What say, my dear?"

"I have returned for that case of ear-rings."

"What case?"

"That one which you have put in your pocket."

"Nonsense, my dear; you are mistaken."

"What! would you rob me?"

"Now, don't get abusive. I say, I aint seen no case. There!"

"Why, you have just put it in your pocket. I distinctly saw it in your hand."

"Look here: don't you come taking away a respectable person's character. You just get out, or else I'll have the police on to you in no time."

Lady Fane was not quite the woman to submit tamely to this sort of thing. She seized hold of the Jewess's hand which was in her pocket, and dragged it out with a jerk, jewels and all. She as suddenly regained her property, and turned to quit the shop.

"Oh! that's it, is it, my fine woman? Stop; we'll see to that. We'll have in a policeman and learn where you got all these fine things from. Here—Police, police!"

The enraged Jewess darted to the door before Lady Fane could escape, and barred the exit, at the same time shouting at the top of her voice for the police.

Lady Fane's position was now awkward in the extreme. Another minute and she would be ruined, for an exposure was undoubtedly ruin!

CHAPTER XXXV.

A LADY IN LOVE.

Two days passed, and still the wounded Frank Harley lay hovering on the verge of the grave.

The duel was now talked about everywhere; and it was perfectly well known in all the clubs that Major Beel was the successful combatant. This may be readily comprehended from the strain of the account of the duel in the newspapers the morning after it took place.

The universal conversation was the death of the unknown duellist, and the mysterious removal of the body; and dark hints were thrown out which threatened great damage to the reputation—perhaps even the personal safety—of Major Beel.

Some enterprising man had published "A full account of the great duel in Hornsey Fields," on the title page of which was a portrait of "the murderer." This, however, was an accident which is easily explained. The cut had been hitherto used as a portrait of every man who had been hung at the Old Bailey for the last ten years, at the head of those spicy bits of literature, "The last dying speech and confessions." The printer had transferred the title with the cut.

However, it got about, and the brutal Major was in no little alarm when it reached him.

Meanwhile, as we have said, the artist lay in mortal danger.

Gerard Wilde had regularly attended his wounded friend, and was awaiting with great anxiety the result of the crisis which both the medical men pronounced to be rapidly approaching.

They had engaged a professional nurse, who understood her business very well, but was one of the "Gamp" school, and rather addicted to drops.

This little weakness made itself manifest on the second day of the good lady's engagement. Gerald's coadjutor had directed her to give the patient a draught which stood upon a little round table by the bedside, and the old woman, in reaching across for the bottle, contrived to upset the table, making the room a sea of medicine, saturating a roll of lint, mixing up balms and balsams with powders, and spoiling everything.

The irascible doctor vehemently insisted upon her immediate departure, threatening her with all sorts of horrible punishments—hanging, amongst others—for the murder of the patient.

The old woman whimpered, but the doctor was firm, and, consequently, she had to beat a retreat.

The nurse changed her supplications to threats as she ran down stairs, and even began to abuse a woman who stood at the street-door reading the names of the different owners of chambers in the house, and who did not jump away quick enough to suit her present humour.

"You had better block up the doorway altogether, young woman."

"Excuse me," said the young woman; "can you tell me if this is where a gentleman named Harley resided?"

"Yes, I can. This is where he lives."

"Where he lived."

"I didn't say lived. I said lives, and I mean lives. Do you think I don't know what I'm saying of, young woman?"

"Lives! But do you mean that he is alive?"

"Alive, of course."

"You mean to tell me that Mr. Frank Harley, the artist, was not killed?"

"Killed! Look here, young woman, I've had quite enough of their impedence upstairs. That doctor fellow have been saying of that without you going on at me. If I did upset the table, it was quite by incident. But I do believe that a poor woman—leastways, a poor monthly—has nothing to do with this mortal world but to get abused, and for nothink at all."

The person to whom all this was addressed was quite staggered with the volley; but seeing the old woman had begun whimpering, she hastened to comfort her with a small present of money. Then followed an explanation of the nurse's wrongs.

"And you say Mr. Harley is not dead?"

"No, bless you, mum. He's as good as three dead 'uns yet. He's very bad; had an ugly dig in the side; been fighting a jewel, the doctor says."

"Is he dangerously hurt?"

"No, mum; I don't think there's no danger. On'y wants peace and quiet."

"Then, now he has no nurse?"

"None; and that doctor fellow's to blame if the young gent respires. But I wash my hands of the matter. There!"

Saying this, the nurse toddled off, and the "young woman" went up to the artist's chamber.

She paused a few moments before the door, as if hesitating how to proceed, and then, as if collecting herself, she gave a gentle, timid tap. She had knocked so lightly as to be inaudible even in the passage, and, finding no answer to her summons, she was obliged to repeat it, and this time rather louder.

The door was opened quietly, and Gerard Wilde appeared.

"What is it?" he asked, in a low voice.

"Mr. Harley lives here, I believe?"

She trembled from head to foot.

"He does, ma'am; but he is ill—dangerously ill. Will not be able to attend to business for months yet, if he ever recovers."

"I do not come upon business; I merely——"

"Then, you will excuse me, ma'am; but he can see no one. Should he see any one he knew—any one—the effect might be fatal."

"You misunderstand me, sir; you have discharged your nurse——"

"We have."

"And must need some one to attend the patient."

"We do, indeed; and unless we can find some one immediately we shall be extremely embarrassed; but——"

"I have come to offer my services."

Gerard Wilde looked at her anxiously. There was something in her conversation and address which seemed to remove her so far above the old woman they had just discharged, that he could not help fancying she was not a professional nurse.

The woman perceived his glance, and turned her eyes uneasily away.

"I do assure you, sir," she said, looking up, "indeed, sir, as I should do my dooty by the young man."

"Mistaken," mentally murmured Wilde. "She is the real thing, no doubt."

"I should not mind coming a day or two on trial, if you wished, sir," said the woman.

"No, no; I've no doubt that you will suit us very well. When can you come?"

"I can stop now, if you wish it, sir."

"Capital; the very thing."

He opened the door and admitted her into the studio, and then bidding her await him for a moment, he went into the inner room—the sick chamber—and fetched his brother doctor.

"This is the young woman," said Wilde, by way of introduction.

The doctor nodded his head, and the new nurse bowed gracefully.

"Where the deuce did she get that from?" muttered Wilde in an undertone to his confrère.

The woman coloured as the remark reached her, and she hastily said—

"I have served in the best of families, I do assure you, gentlemen."

"No doubt, no doubt," replied the doctor; "but the present is a case in which quiet and regularity is more required than any skill on the part of the nurse."

"Yes," said Wilde; "the only thing is, we must be assured of your steadiness. I know that nurses, as a rule, are given to—to stimulants."

"Gentlemen, I assure you——"

"Of course—yes—so did the other," said the doctor. "We do not wish to threaten you; but mark! the first suspicion of liquor of any description——"

"Enough, gentlemen," interrupted the woman, with what Gerard Wilde thought to be rather a majestic wave of the hand. "If I am a nurse I am still a woman, and I hope you will engage me without any further disagreeable speeches."

There was something in her manner which effectually silenced the two doctors upon the score of the new nurse's presumed infirmities, and, with a few brief arrangements as to payment and so forth, she was regularly installed.

She took her seat quietly by the bedside, and without even breathing except in reply to a question addressed her by either of the doctors.

At length they both departed, giving her strict injunctions not to disturb the patient upon any pretence whatsoever.

Wilde told her that he should return and see his friend once more in the evening, and that the other doctor would probably come with him.

As soon as they were fairly gone, the new nurse rose from her seat and gazed long and earnestly into the sleeping artist's face.

An expression of pain was on the sick man's countenance as she rose; and every now and then a nervous twitching of the features and a biting of the nether lip indicated that the fitful slumber was rather the effects of pain and weakness than a wholesome rest.

At length his lips parted, and a smothered cry of agony burst from him, but his eyes remained closed.

Two big tears rolled down the new nurse's cheeks.

About an hour passed in this way, and then the wounded man opened his eyes and called faintly for drink.

The doctors had provided for this, and she administered the draught as they had directed.

Temporarily relieved, the artist closed his eyes once more, and the untiring nurse resumed her lonely vigil.

Shortly after dusk, the two doctors returned, and

asked for the latest intelligence of the patient. She reported, and the two doctors consulted in whispers in the adjoining apartment.

Wilde came to the room-door, and beckoned her out.

"The patient, I must tell you, nurse," began Gerard's colleague, "is dangerously bad——"

"Dangerously!" repeated the nurse, in faltering accents.

"Very dangerously. And unless you think you have the nerve to bear the sight of suffering"——

"But I have. Don't fear me, I beg," exclaimed the nurse, eagerly.

"I do not for a moment question your will," said the doctor; "but Mr. Wilde has—and, indeed, I myself have also—remarked that you have not altogether the appearance of a veteran nurse——"

"No matter," said the nurse, "so that I fulfil all the duties required of me."

"True. But Mr. Wilde observing that you were rather a different person to the ordinary run of nurses, has taken an idea into his head, that you are some friend of the patient's, and that your presenting yourself thus as a nurse is simply an act of devotion—heroic devotion, I may say—if he is correct; but likely to do no good to the patient. The least display of feeling on your part—should Mr. Wilde's suggestion be correct—would be most injurious to our cause."

The nurse coloured deeply as the doctor spoke; but, as they were standing in the dark, this was not observed.

"You may rest assured upon that score, doctor," she said. "I should not have offered myself, if I had not felt myself fully capable of fulfilling the duties required of me."

"But that is scarcely a direct answer to me. If the patient, at any critical moment, should recognise your face, the effects might be most disastrous."

"But the patient does not know me."

"Indeed!"

"Yes, sir, indeed; and I see his face to-day for the first time."

"May we rely upon you?"

"You may, indeed, gentlemen."

"We do, then. We place implicit trust in you; but remember, once for all, that the least ebullition of feeling on your part may prove fatal to the patient."

"And we rely upon the truth of your assertion, that Mr. Harley does not know you," added Wilde, somewhat doubtfully. "Satisfied that you are convinced of the necessity of keeping him perfectly quiet. His life depends upon this."

The nurse trembled slightly at these words; but she replied with earnest firmness in confirmation of her statement that she was totally unacquainted with Frank Harley as he was with her.

"I have only one request to make," she said, "before regularly taking up my position here."

"What is that?"

"I should like to return home to make some little preparations. I should not be gone more than an hour. You see, gentlemen, I left home quite unprepared."

They readily gave their consent to this, and the nurse departed.

"I can't make her out," said Wilde, as she left.

"Can't make out what?"

"I'm sure she is no nurse."

"Nonsense—you're mistaken. What reason could she have, if she were not?"

"That I can't tell, unless it's some love affair."

"But she said that she has never seen Harley before."

"True."

"And that he has never seen her."

"True, again; but——"

"No, no. I believe the young woman spoke the truth."

"And I, too; but still there is a ladylike manner about her, and a certain style that assures me she is not what she would wish to appear."

"She is younger and prettier than that horrible old woman—that's all."

"Don't speak of her in the same breath, I beg."

"I wont, as you wish it. Let us hope, however, that the patient may be well attended, and I don't care a fig who she may be."

"Nor I. I greatly fear that he will not need her assistance long."

"Indeed, he will not; unless we can keep the fever down."

They then returned to the bedchamber, and busied themselves in preparing the various drugs and medicines for the patient.

At the expiration of an hour, the nurse returned, and quietly resumed her seat by the bedside.

Wilde remarked that she had made a change in her dress, which was of a poorer description than that which she had previously worn. Now, too, he observed that she wore a cap, which almost hid her features, and gave her a much older appearance.

She had brought back with her a small lady's reticule, from which she took a book, and began to read by the faint light of a small table-lamp.

Wilde mentally settled that this also was a strange proceeding, and at variance with her character of nurse. Professional nurses never read.

At length, with some more instructions as to the care and treatment of the patient, the two doctors retired.

With their departure, the nurse laid down her book, and, rising noiselessly from her seat, she stood by the bedside, gazing long and wistfully at the slumbering artist, as she had done before.

"To what a state have I reduced him," she murmured, in anguish, as she stood. "And in what an equivocal position have I placed myself. But I do not complain—I must not murmur. It is only thus that I can hope to atone, in part, for the fearful injury I have caused him. Poor fellow! brave heart!"

Her breast heaved up, and she sobbed in silent bitterness.

The singular nurse scarcely slept the whole night. The patient was restless, and his demands upon her care were unceasing, until it was nearly morning.

The nurse eagerly attended his lightest breath, and showed that her whole soul was in her duties. At length, towards morning, the artist slept, and the watchful nurse—overcome with fatigue—slumbered in her chair beside him.

She was aroused by a summons at the outer door. It was Wilde.

"What sort of a night has he passed, nurse?"

"Restless—very restless, doctor."

"Ha! a change has taken place, I see."

"He is out of danger?"

"No."

"At least the change is for the better?"

"No."

"Good Heavens! doctor——"

"Hush! I fear the worst—he may be—but what is the matter with you?"

The nurse was taking a phial from the table; but her hand shook so violently, that it rattled against another bottle with a loud noise.

"Are you unwell?"

"No, no, doctor."

"Tired, perhaps?"

"Yes—no; well, I may be a little."

Wilde was alarmed at the deathly pallor of her countenance. She was doing her utmost to disguise her emotion from him. Her teeth were firmly set, and her unemployed hand was clenched convulsively, until her nails dug into her palm and caused the blood to come.

"Sit down awhile—you will recover shortly."

She obeyed him ; but was barely seated when a knock at the outer door announced the arrival of the other doctor, and she went to admit him.

Her look told him that things were not progressing favourably, and he hastened to the sick chamber at once, leaving her in the studio—listening in fearful anticipation of the worst.

"How is he, this morning ?"

"Look for yourself," replied Wilde, in a low voice, full of dreadful meaning.

"Good God ! He's a dead man !—Poor fellow !"

"What's that ?"

"Nurse !"

"Nurse ?"

There was no reply.

Surprised at receiving no answer, Wilde went to the door, and looked into the studio.

Stretched upon the floor, in a death-like swoon, lay the singular nurse.

CHAPTER XXXVI.

THE TRAP.

LADY ETHEL FANE was something more than alarmed when the enraged Jewish wardrobe woman proceeded to open hostilities in revenge for the determined manner in which the former had claimed and re-possessed herself of the stolen jewel-case.

"Police !" shouted Mrs. Israel, at the door.

"I must avoid an exposure, at all hazards," thought Lady Fane. "Better even to sacrifice the ear-rings—and yet, thus to give up our only resource. No."

"Police !" again called the irate Jewess. "I'll just teach you what's what, young woman."

"Stop !"

"Not if I know it. Pol——"

"Silence !"

There was a haughty tone of command in Lady Fane's voice, which evidently astonished the Jewess, for she stopped short, and regarded her customer over her shoulder with apparent curiosity.

"Silence !" continued Lady Fane. "Do you imagine, woman, that I am to be intimidated with all this bluster ? Content yourself that I do not prosecute you for attempting to rob me—that it does not suit my convenience to do so."

Lady Fane moved towards the door ; but the Jewess once more barred her exit.

"No, you don't—not quite like that. Police ! Hi !"

"Stand aside !" exclaimed Lady Fane, with rising passion. "Attempt to detain me an instant, and beware."

"Hi ! Police !"

"Away !" exclaimed Lady Fane, goaded on to desperation at her critical position.

Hitherto the Jewess had only called in a low tone, more to intimidate her customer into bribing her with the stolen ear-rings, than with any idea of summoning assistance. However, as she felt Lady Fane attempting to push past her out of the shop, her calls grew louder, and the attention of the passers-by was quickly attracted.

Lady Ethel felt a sensation in her blood akin to murder. She seized the Jewess by the throat with both hands, and dragging her back with a jerk, swung her round, and dashed her against the counter, where, being released from Lady Fane's clutch, she rolled on the floor, bruised and breathless, while her attempted victim made good her retreat.

Passing hurriedly out of the shop, Lady Fane ran along in the direction she had come, without heeding the cries of the people who had been attracted by the Jewess's noisy summons. Presently, however, the attention of the excitement-loving street boys and public generally, grew so embarrassing, that Lady Ethel made

the unfortunate mistake of quickening her walk into a run or trot ; and now it began to look remarkably like a chase.

"Hi ! stop that woman !"

"She's murdered the woman in the clothes' shop."

Lady Ethel's pride once more came to her assistance ; and before she proceeded many steps, the thought of her disgraceful position—flying before a mob—coming across her, she stopped short, and faced them. Then, as usual, the excitement being destroyed, most of the mob slunk off—some few only remaining to inspect, at a respectful distance, the woman who was charged with murdering the Jewess.

She paused for a moment ; but the idea of addressing remonstrance or explanation to six or seven street boys, was decidedly *infra dig.*, and therefore she continued her way towards the house in which she had left her father ; but now at a pace that did not bear the remotest resemblance to flight. The urchins followed her to the end of the street, and then dropped off with a parting "halloo !"

No one coming forward to follow up the bold charge of murder, which one of the mob had bawled out, Lady Fane walked off unmolested, and highly pleased at the harmless termination of the broil which threatened, at first, to be most disastrous to herself and Mr. Fenwick—as leading to an exposure.

The first idea which crossed Lady Fane upon finding herself out of danger, was the necessity—now more than ever—of converting her jewels and trinkets into ready cash. She saw the danger which was to be apprehended from keeping them about her person, and to leave them in her very suspicious lodging was out of the question.

She accordingly began looking about her for a jeweller's or pawnbroker's.

As she neared her destination, the neighbourhood grew worse, the shops (which, *par parenthèse,* seemed almost without exception to be kept by Israelites) were the lowest and vilest to be easily found in the metropolis.

Silk handkerchiefs hung at nearly every doorpost, and were touted by dirty-faced barkers, at surprisingly low prices. Shelves were built out in front of the shop-windows, on which were ranged in mixed collections of merchandizes, comprising wearing apparel of every description, jewellery, books, pictures, and a variety of articles impossible to enumerate.

At length Lady Ethel came to a dingy-looking shop, which seemed to be devoted entirely to the gold, silver, and jewellery trade. The window was filled with plate, jewels, gold lace, and old coins, all of which seemed of rare value when compared with the poor appearance of the shop. The window was carefully guarded by a stout grating of iron wire, and the strong appearance of the shop generally showed that they looked more to might than to right for protection from their lawless neighbours.

Lady Fane felt naturally anxious about entering the shop, after her late brush with the wardrobe woman. She looked about her in every direction, and then peeped into the shop. She could see no one there. Then she placed one foot upon the doorstep and again peered in.

"Now, then, what's your game ? It's no use, whatever it is. So drop it !"

Lady Fane drew back, somewhat startled at this volley of abuse, the more so that she had not been able to see whence the voice proceeded.

Although she was ignorant of the meaning of the expressions used, she understood them to imply a doubt as to the purity of her intentions in thus hovering about the shop ; and she, therefore, boldly entered, and walked up to the counter.

There was a clattering of feet above, followed by the sound of some one running or shuffling down stairs, and a dwarfish red-haired Jew entered the shop, with a bound—

"What do you want, eh ?"

THE JEW-DWARF IS CAUGHT IN HIS OWN TRAP.

"Do you buy jewellery?" demanded Lady Fane.

"Of course we do; have you got any to sell?"

"I have a pair of earrings."

She produced the casket which had caused her such a disagreeable skirmish with Mrs. Israel, and laid it on the counter. The dwarf immediately snatched it up, and, before she could offer any objection, began scrutinizing a monogramic inscription upon the lid.

"E. F. F." read the Jew. Then looking up in Lady Fane's face, as he held the case further from the reach of her outstretched hand, he continued—

"This don't look like business, you know—the very wuss game out. Many a good man's come to grief for less than that."

Lady Fane was fairly puzzled.

"I am not aware of the meaning of what you are saying," said Lady Fane; "and whatever it is, it must be foreign to my business here. I want to know if you can buy those earrings? and if so, what you can give me for them. An answer, one way or another, will settle the affair at once."

"Softly, softly! there's no need to get your dander up. I was only giving you a little friendly advice."

"Give me an answer—do you wish to purchase my jewels?"

"Ah, that's business. Well, look here——"

At this he turned the earrings over in his claw-like hand, examining them with the air of a perfect connoisseur—

"Well, I should say about twelve shillings is the MARKET value. I don't mind twelve—eh?"

Lady Fane was dumb-foundered. The earrings had cost her about seventeen guineas at Stors and Mortimer's a twelvemonth before.

"Do you mean absolutely twelve shillings?" she asked, scarcely able to credit the evidence of her ears.

"Yes, twelve shillings : it's more than it's worth, but——"

"Give it back to me. I would sooner destroy it than accept such a sum."

"That's our price. I might have said another shilling or two if I hadn't seen these unfortunate initials. They're such tell-tale things."

"Give me the case instantly," reiterated Lady Fane.

But without making the least show of returning the jewels, the dwarf continued—

"Of course you understand that twelve is my price without asking any questions. You understand, perfectly, mum ?"

But Lady Fane would most certainly have not understood if he had not accompanied his last speech with a smack upon his half-opened lips, full of meaning and noise.

"Return me my case," exclaimed Lady Ethel, with mingled rage and fear, at the tantalizing speeches of the unsightly Jew mannikin. "How dare you presume to retain it !"

"Then you wont accept my terms ?"

"I tell you I would rather destroy them, with every jewel I possess than——"

"Every jewel you possess—about you?" exclaimed the Jew, his eyes sparkling with cunning. "You don't mean to say that you've got any more of 'em about you ?"

Lady Fane began to tremble for her personal safety. She saw that she had been hasty and incautious, and immediately resolved to make a final attempt to regain the case of earrings, and depart at once.

"Unless you instantly return me my earrings," she exclaimed, "I warn you that I shall take proceedings elsewhere for their recovery, which you may find inconvenient."

"Gently, gently," said the dwarf, ironically. "Don't get frightening us so. We know our customers too well to heed their threats. If an exposure will suit you— try it on, that's all. We don't mind a show up, all the better for business."

Lady Fane moved towards the door. She had no intention of going yet, but she imagined that an appearance of determination might alarm the Jew into returning her property.

"Stop—stop a bit ; if you've anything you would care to throw in with it, I might say a better price."

"But I have nothing else."

Her voice trembled as she spoke, and gave the lie to her words. The Jew dwarf paused for a moment as if considering about returning the jewels ; and a cunning smile played about his lips, which would have given Lady Ethel an idea of treachery could she have seen it.

"Very well, then," he said, rubbing his hands and *stamping his feet* loudly on the floor ; "take your precious jewels since you want a fortune for them. You wouldn't have caught me freezing myself in this cold shop, though, if I had only known the deuce of a bother you was going to give me."

Here he stamped louder than ever.

Lady Fane observed this, but thought it was simply the mannikin's way of expressing his rage and mortification at not finding her so easy a dupe as he could have wished.

She advanced to the counter to take the case which he now half held out to her. He was about to place it in her hand—stamping his feet as he did so— when a voice, calling out from below, caused him to draw back to listen.

"What do you want ?"

"What do you think ?" roared the mannikin, impatiently. "What should you fancy I was stamping my feet for—eh ?"

The voice from beneath gave a half-suppressed ejaculation of intelligence and died away.

Then there was a sharp clicking sound heard, followed by a noise resembling the straining of wood-work, or the creaking of the wooden-screw of a book-binder's press.

"Then do you mean to give me my property ?" demanded Lady Ethel, turning away.

"Yes, yes, yes—here you are, take it," exclaimed the dwarf, eagerly.

Lady Fane turned towards him once more, and held out her hand to receive it. The Jew placed one corner of it tantalizingly in her fingers, but would not quit his hold of it until he had given her a little parting advice.

"Take it, then, since you don't know your own interests. But be careful in the next place you go to *that you don't get robbed !*"

There was a dreadful significance in the hideous pigmy's tone, which made Lady Fane shudder notwithstanding that she was quite unprepared for the fiendish piece of treachery which was being prepared for her.

"I say, mind you don't get robbed !"

With this he relinquished his grasp of the case of jewels.

The creaking of the woodwork was repeated. This time it was the boards under Lady Ethel's feet.

She felt an agonizing sensation of fear—undefinable, unaccountable horror !

The floor was giving way beneath her !

CHAPTER XXXVII.

THE LOW GAMBLING-HOUSE.

QUICK as thought, Lady Ethel Fane had realized the full horror of her situation.

They had set a trap beneath her feet !

Happily she had not lost her presence of mind for an instant. No sooner had she felt the floor move, than she threw herself forward full length upon the ground.

Thus her body was fairly above ground, one of her feet only being over the trap. She had barely touched the floor when she rose on to her knees, and—— here she felt her foot grasped by a hand from below.

She had no purchase, and it was with the utmost exertion that she could keep herself from being dragged down the treacherous pit from which she had so providentially escaped.

That is, escaped for the moment, for she felt that her danger was not yet over.

"Help ! murder ! help !" she shrieked.

She kicked out with the foot that was clutched by the invisible person beneath the trap, and felt it come in contact with a face.

There was a cry, a scramble, and some fearful oaths and menaces, and the foot was released.

But now, when she had gained her feet, she found a new enemy in the Jew-dwarf, who clambered over the counter, and clutched her by the dress as she was retreating.

"Not yet—not yet, my little beauty," said the dwarf, dragging her towards the pit.

"Help !—help !" again shrieked Lady Fane. But none came ; the inhabitants of the district seemed remarkably heedless of anything like sensation scenes.

The strength of the dwarf was prodigious. Lady Ethel was by no means deficient of physical power, and yet, in spite of her utmost exertions—of her frantic struggles, she felt that she was being dragged nearer and nearer to the pit—perhaps her doom !

In another instant she would be lost.

As a final resource, she feinted to yield, and then, on the edge of the trap, she darted aside, and with a sudden and quite unlooked-for push, the dwarf had taken his would-be victim's place.

There was a wild cry, and the dull thud of a falling body, and victory was once more with Lady Fane.

Without pausing a moment to see the result of her late enemy's disaster, she rushed from the den of treachery, and fled precipitately towards her present abode.

And it was well she did so, for her foot was barely off the doorstep ere there was a fresh arrival on the scene in the form of a thick-set, brawny-looking fellow, with a ferocious and brutal expression of countenance.

This gentleman looked as if he had already been having a little skirmish by the disordered state of his dress, and an unmistakably English black eye, freshly inflicted. This was probably the ruffian from below, and the bruise had been, doubtless, inflicted by the tiny model of a foot of Lady Fane.

However, he was, as we have already said, too late; and great was his chagrin at finding their victim slipped through their fingers, the only souvenirs of her visit being his black eye and the dwarf's broken bones.

Meanwhile, Lady Fane, inwardly rejoicing at her providential escape, pursued her way, and was not long in reaching her gloomy lodgings. Gloomy and sombre they undoubtedly were; but after the stirring excitement which she had undergone in the past few hours, the usual reaction had begun to take place, and any asylum which she could call home was now doubly welcome to her.

It was therefore with almost a feeling of pleasure that she entered that dark deserted shop, which seemed as if no single ray of sunshine had ever penetrated its gloomy shadows.

She took the precaution of tapping at the door before entering the parlour. Then there occurred the scrambling and scuffling which she had before observed, and the door was opened cautiously by the old woman.

"Oh, it's you, mum. Mounseer's been calling after you over an' over again."

The men were still in the parlour, the only difference being that Lady Fane saw one or two strange faces. Now, in spite of her haughty temper, there was something in the look of these men which led her to conciliate them, and she therefore gracefully apologized for intruding upon them as she passed through the room upstairs.

Mr. Balfour Fenwick was groaning in his loneliness as his daughter entered the room.

"Oh, I'm a miserable old man! Ethel, Ethel, why did you bring me here to desert me?"

"Here I am, father," said Lady Fane.

"What—Ethel come back! Oh, I thought I'd lost you for ever."

"I've only been to buy some different clothes, and to dispose of some of my jewellery."

"Jewels!" exclaimed the old man. "What jewels —not——"

"Speak lower, for heaven's sake!"

"No; let me speak as I please," exclaimed the old man, pettishly.

"Father, you will ruin us both—you——"

"Hush! Don't say that, Ethel. I wouldn't ruin you for anything. I would—I would—" and he began to weep in a childish, helpless manner.

"I feared greatly, father, that you had lost me for ever."

"What do you mean, Ethel?"

"I have been in great danger—I know not how great; and I have escaped by a miracle."

Here she related all that had passed in connection with the pair of earrings, and the old man was duly alarmed and shocked, although the events were of too startling a nature for his simple comprehension to grapple easily. And thus ended the first day of the fugitives' pilgrimage.

The next morning Lady Fane was early by her father's bed. She had some most alarming doubts as to the strict integrity of their host or hostess, whichever it might be (for she did not believe the old woman, with which she had made all the arrangements, to be the mistress of the house), and she consequently felt anxious to depart as soon as her father's health would permit.

Mr. Fenwick was, happily, much better; but he peevishly scouted all ideas of quitting their present abode for a few weeks at least; giving one or two causes for it that really sounded like reason.

"You know we are secure here. Who would ever dream of seeking for us in such an out-of-the-way place as this is?"

"True," replied Lady Fane; "but my mind misgives me as to the honesty of the people about. What should we do if we were robbed of our jewels—all we possess?"

"Yes, yes. But we must guard them well. The people don't know that we have any property at all, and so we are safe. They wont insult us, because we must make it worth their while to be civil."

The end of it was that Lady Fane gave way, partly convinced by the old man's reasoning, and partly to avoid any further discussion on the matter. So it was settled that they should stay in their present residence for a few weeks.

Two or three days passed without anything particular occurring. Lady Fane each day disposed of some of her jewels, but now choosing the dealers with great circumspection, until, before a week was over, she had nothing left but a bracelet—an odd one, by-the-bye—with very handsome and curiously mounted stones in it. The reader will please remember that bracelets were only worn in pairs at the period of our tale, and it was therefore rather remarkable to see a lady wearing an odd one, as Lady Fane very imprudently did. True it was concealed beneath her sleeve, but an accident might reveal it, and who can say what might result from an exhibition of anything approaching riches.

Although her store of money, obtained by the sale of her jewels, was not yet gone, Lady Fane calculated by the inroads already made into it that a few months must see them beggared. And now their position began to look serious. In vain did she economize, practise all kinds of self-denial, stint herself in every way—everything cost money.

She speedily came to the resolution that she must seek for some employment. The idea of this was particularly galling to her pride at first, but the necessity for action presented itself more forcibly before her startled imagination as each day rolled by, and found her purse sensibly diminished in bulk.

With this resolution she took a half-an-hour's walk every day into a more respectable locality, and wound up her promenade at a quiet, jog-trot, sort of pastrycook's. Here, provided with some pastry and lemonade (Lady Fane's economy!), she eagerly devoured the advertisement columns of the *Times*.

But here a new difficulty presented itself—an obstacle which she had not even remotely dreamed of. Her manners, appearance, and address gained her the preference over many competitors in her applications for the various appointments she applied for, until came the alarming demand for references.

She passed a weary time, and nothing but her persevering unflagging energies could have kept her in heart after the repeated failures she met with.

At length, as if her embarrassments were not sufficient to keep her employed, the semi-imbecility of her father got them into a dangerous strait, from which they escaped by a mere chance.

Mr. Balfour Fenwick gradually recovered his health, and naturally grew weary of being cooped up in the gloomy four walls—his bed-room. At length his fear of being discovered in the streets gave way to ennui, and he commenced taking a "five or ten minutes constitutional round the houses," as he called it. Thus passing continually through the parlour, which was, as on the day of their arrival, invariably full of men—

generally the same faces—he got into a little chat with them; and one day when Lady Fane returned home tired and dispirited with want of success, she found him fraternising, pewter in hand, with the whole room.

Her fears were naturally excited, for she dreaded that the old man's childish garrulity would ruin them. Like a child caught pilfering, Mr. Fenwick followed his daughter up stairs to their own apartments.

"Oh! father, father, you will ruin us," she exclaimed, as she carefully closed and locked the door to guard against intrusion.

"I'm a poor, miserable, old man," groaned Mr. Fenwick.

"Tell me, father, have you said anything to those men which could in any way compromise us?"

"No—no—that I haven't; trust me for that." Here he looked inexpressibly cunning.

"How long have you been down there?"

"Oh! no time—that I haven't; not ten minutes."

"And what did you converse about?"

"Nothing."

"Nothing! Surely you were not down there ten minutes without saying a word?"

"Oh! we only spoke commonplaces—how d'ye do—fine day—and such like."

And this was all she could get out of him, so she was forced to rest content, although she was far from easy in her mind on the subject.

The next day Lady Fane had to keep an appointment with the principal of a ladies' college, with whom she was in negotiation for an appointment as musical governess. Dreading to leave Mr. Fenwick alone, for she could place no reliance in his assurance that he would not repeat the offence of visiting the parlour customers again, she put off her departure until it was too late, and she had the annoyance of hearing after a long and fatiguing walk that her want of punctuality in keeping the appointment had alarmed the lady principal of the college, who had a few minutes before concluded an engagement with somebody else.

Tired, weary, and dispirited, Lady Ethel walked back, and it was night before she arrived home. She entered the gloomy shop, and, as usual, walked up to the parlour-door to tap, preparatory to passing through to the passage, when a voice within seemed to strike familiarly upon her ear.

She applied her eye to the transparent square in the white-washed window, and there saw a sight which rather startled her. She now understood why the men in the parlour had always flushed faces, and why there was always a deal of scrambling and confusion when she passed through the room.

There, seated round the green-baize table, were the same men she had observed on the day of their arrival at the house, and in the midst of them sat Mr. Fenwick, holding a clay-pipe in one hand while the other grasped a pot of beer, which he held to his mouth. Before him, on the table, lay a hand of greasy, well-thummed playing cards, which a villanous-looking fellow, who sat next him, was conning with great curiosity, and apparently telling their value as well from their backs as he could from their faces.

Lady Fane did not even wait for the usual ceremony of knocking to announce her presence, but burst into the room in great fright.

Mr. Fenwick, although flushed with liquor, was not able to resist his daughter's indignant glance, and so he pretended that he did not observe her, but at once entered into a meaningless, but very animated conversation with his neighbour.

"Father," said Lady Ethel.

"Yes, my dear; is that you?" said Mr. Fenwick, looking round in very simply assured surprise.

"Yes; I want you to come upstairs with me."

"Oh, you may as well leave the old gent with us a bit, miss," said Mr. Fenwick's neighbour; "he's amusing himself."

"Did you hear me, father?"

"Lor'! yes, I'm a poor miserable old man, and I haven't a will of my own," groaned Mr. Fenwick.

"Are you coming up then, father?"

"Ah, bless me, yes. Don't bother me; don't you see I am engaged with these gentlemen? I'll come up presently."

"You had much better come now—come."

The old man mumbled some remonstrances just to keep up his dignity before the low gamblers, but was unable to resist the tone of command in which his daughter had spoken the last words. He rose to depart, but before leaving the room he interchanged some masonic-looking signs, intimating that he would return when his daughter was asleep, with the fellow who sat next him. Lady Fane's heart sank within her as she saw this, and she hurried upstairs, grasping Mr. Fenwick by the hand.

"I must not sleep to-night," she murmured, to herself as she quitted Mr. Fenwick at his bedroom door; "and to-morrow we must leave this place."

With this resolution she threw herself upon her bed to rest, and listened intently for any movement in the next room. After listening thus for nearly an hour, nothing transpired, and the fatigues of the day began to tell upon her. She sunk into a light dose, from which, in the course of a short time, she awoke with a start—

"Ah!" she exclaimed, "I've fallen asleep—Father!" All was silent.

"Father, father!"

But still there was no answer. Alarmed at the silence, she quietly entered Mr. Fenwick's room.

It was empty!

She flew lightly down the stairs, and was upon the point of bursting open the parlour door, when something which she overheard caused her to pause and listen in the utmost consternation.

"Go on, gentlemen," hiccupped Mr. Fenwick, "I'll have one more hand."

"What do you mean?" said the voice of the man who had been seated next Mr. Fenwick when Lady Fane entered the parlour so abruptly; "you haven't got another stiver—you're cleaned out—so you'd better go to bed."

"You be hanged!" retorted Mr. Fenwick, in maudlin indignation; "I've got as much money as anyone here."

"You have—you have?" chorussed the room.

"Cert'ly—or my daughter has; only, she's so deuced careful with it—that's the bother."

"But do you think that you could get any more?"

"Cert'ly; knows I could, and I'll just take my revenge."

"I suppose that you have no end of it?" demanded one of the men, with assumed indifference.

"More than you could carry, or win of me."

"Ah! but you don't know where she keeps it?"

"Don't I? Haven't I seen her take it from under her pillow many a time?"

Poor Lady Fane!

"Then, don't you think you could get some?"

"I'll be off and try; you wait a little."

Lady Fane had not time to retreat unseen, so she darted aside, and Mr. Fenwick staggered out and scrambled upstairs in woful plight.

She was in no hurry to follow him, as she had all her money about her, so she listened as to what might be the result of her father's fatal admission to the lawless company.

"We shan't see the old boy again to-night," said one.

"I know that," rejoined a second. "He's as unsteady as he can be. He'll wake the gal up, and she'll bully him and put him to bed."

"So say I," added a third. "There's something

about that young pusson's figurehead which tells me she's a bit of a Tartar."

Here broke in the voice of the scowling fellow who had been seated next her father, and who, of all the room, seemed to inspire Lady Fane with the greatest dread—

"He'll spile the concern, no doubt. But I daresay we could manage the trick. We're more light-fingered."

There was a silence for some moments, as if the proposal was being considered, and the last speaker resumed—

"I'd do it myself, if need be."

"No, no, no," said the room.

"Oh! fair and square," remonstrated the man, in a tone of injured purity ; "share and share alike."

"Stay," said he, whom we have designated as the second speaker above ; "that gal will resist for a dead certainty."

"What then ?"

"There'll be the deuce of a shine."

"Bah ! I'll undertake to quiet her."

"No, no—no violence."

"Look here, gents : now, she's just the gal to blow the gaff if we let her off."

Here there was a buzz of dissenting murmurs. Lady Fane felt riveted to the spot.

"Do you mean to have the chink?" demanded the ruffian, doggedly.

"Ay, ay—yes, yes," responded the room, with one voice.

"Then there's only one way ; leave it to me. What do you think that that old well in the yard was made for, eh ! if it aint for our convenience ?"

More dead than alive, Lady Fane burst the spell which seemed to chain her to the spot, and regained her own apartment.

There, by the side of her bed, lay Mr. Fenwick, where he had fallen in a drunken slumber, when in the act of robbing his daughter.

"Father, father!" she exclaimed, in a loud whisper.

But the potation which Mr. Fenwick had imbibed had too strongly chained his faculties to admit of his shaking off their effects at once. He simply murmured some maudlin phrase, and sunk again into the same hopeless slumber.

"Wake—wake, father!" she exclaimed, shaking him roughly.

"Whast matter ?" muttered her father.

"Murder is the matter !" breathed Lady Fane in his ear.

"Wh-what ?" gasped the old man.

"Arouse yourself, father, or we're lost."

"What is it, Ethel ?"

"There is a plot on foot to rob and murder us. Do you hear—MURDER us."

This had the effect of thoroughly arousing Mr. Fenwick, who sat up on the floor and looked about him in hopeless, helpless dismay.

"Get up, or we shall be butchered before we can help ourselves. Quick, father !"

Saying which, she dragged Mr. Fenwick to his feet.

"I'm a poor, miserable old man——"

"Hush ! No nonsense now, father. Endeavour to think of some means of getting us out of this strait which your chattering has brought us to."

Mr. Fenwick began to weep.

"Hah ! I have it !" exclaimed Lady Fane. "If we can only gain the passage unmolested we are saved. You passed me by without observing me—so may they ; and they're sure to come upstairs—all of them—lest they should be cheated of their share of the spoil."

"I don't understand——" began Mr. Fenwick.

"We shall lock the doors, to gain time before they discover our flight, then descend into the passage and secrete ourselves in the shade until they have passed up ; then we dart through the shop. True," she added, with a sigh, "it is a risk, but it is our only chance."

The old man, who had not understood one word of all she had said, but who placed implicit reliance in his daughter's skill, simply comprehended that they were in great personal danger, and prepared to quit the room with her.

Lady Fane was about to open the door, when footsteps were heard upon the stairs.

"Too late !—too late !" she exclaimed in terror. "Oh ! father, father, you have ruined us !"

CHAPTER XXXVIII.

A STRUGGLE FOR LIFE.

WE resume our chronicle of the proceedings of Lady Ethel Fane and Mr. Balfour Fenwick, whom the reader will remember we quitted in a most critical position at the gambling-house where they had been lodging since their flight from their late home.

After overhearing the wretches plot her death and even the disposal of her body, Lady Fane had rushed upstairs and awakened her father, scarcely liking to leave him to the tender mercies of the gamblers, although it was his garrulity which had brought them to the present strait.

Her heart beat quickly with terror as she hastily turned the lock upon the cheated assassin.

Cheated for the moment it was true. But could she hope single-handed—for her father was perfectly helpless—to contend against a horde of ruffians who sought her life ?

The door was gently pushed. It made a slight noise, and then followed a short pause. Evidently thinking that their intended victim slept, the assassin was proceeding cautiously, in order not to arouse her.

"They will use force when they discover that the door is locked," thought Lady Fane.

The door handle was gently turned.

"Father ! father !" whispered Lady Fane, "help me to barricade the door with the bedstead."

"We're poor miserable things," moaned Mr. Fenwick, rather over a whisper.

"Hush ! hush !"

The door was pushed, and the lock creaked loudly, as if threatening to yield.

"Good Heavens ! They must know that that would arouse me if I were asleep," murmured Lady Ethel. "In another moment they will use force."

"I'm a poor miserable old man," groaned Mr. Fenwick.

"Cease your babbling, father, unless you would destroy us—murder us !"

"Lor, Ethel, my dear——"

The door was pressed again, and seemed upon the point of giving way.

"Quick ! quick ! Help me with this, father. Take the bedstead there—there—that's it."

"But——"

"Silence—lift that side off the ground, or you will betray all, and we shall be slaughtered—slaughtered—do you hear ?"

The old man was so alarmed at the earnest tone of Lady Ethel Fane, who hissed the words in his ear that he hastened to obey her at once with too much zeal. Consequently, he stumbled and fell sprawling upon the ground with a loud noise, roaring out an exclamation of pain.

They were now worse off than ever. For in addition to their helpless condition, the assassin, doubtless, assured by the noise that the inmates of the room were about, would dispense with stealth and caution, and boldly break in to complete his mission of blood.

In vain she looked eagerly around for some means of barricading the door. Nothing presented itself.

Mr. Fenwick scrambled to his feet, and once more caught hold of the bed, as his daughter had directed him.

A rush was made at the door from without, and the old man again let go his hold of the bedstead in the greatest terror.

The siege had now commenced in real serious earnest. A second blow at the door shook it so violently that Lady Ethel saw in consternation that it could not withstand the assassins for five minutes longer.

Five minutes! she had calculated then even over the mark.

A third kick administered from without caused some portion of the fastening to give way with an ominous snap.

Lady Ethel gave a final despairing glance at her father, who was shivering with fear near the chimney-piece, and then making a rush at the bedstead she exerted her utmost force in pushing it towards the door.

Happily it was possessed of two castors, and with some immense exertion she succeeded in pushing it to the door as another assault had carried the lock by storm.

As the door opened into the room she was safe, or at least it was a temporary respite.

Almost overcome with the violence of her exertion, she sank exhausted upon the bed, thus adding her own weight to the barricade, which she had succeeded in placing there in so opportune a moment.

In vain did the ruffians hammer and push the door; their utmost force failed to make the least impression.

Recovering herself, Lady Fane hastily rose, and eagerly collected every weighty article of furniture she could find, and gave additional strength to the barricade.

The attacking party from without had evidently been reinforced, for a tremendous rush at the door shivered it, cracked the panels in every direction, and made the bedstead crack and give way slightly, notwithstanding its ponderous burthen.

Mr. Fenwick, now somewhat recovered from his fright by the immediate danger being over, contributed his assistance, and the damage was immediately repaired.

There was a short pause whilst Lady Fane and her father repaired their defences. The attacking party were holding a council of war.

Lady Ethel judged this from the hum of voices, and her fears were evidently correct, for in less than three minutes after some formidable instrument was burst against the door as a battering-ram with terrific violence.

The panels of the door were now almost splintered; but still the barricade held bravely out.

A second blow at the door had forced in the barricade some few inches.

However, during the pause which occurred from the recoil of the invaders after their vigorous attack, Lady Ethel had, with a well-timed effort, replaced the defences in their former position.

Convinced that they were safe for the moment—that the fortress was impregnable at least for a time, Lady Fane turned her attention to some means of escape.

Their defences were all very well as a temporary respite, but at a last extremity the ruffians might reduce them by famine.

All the faculties of her vigorous mind were called into full play at the fearful emergency, and she proved herself fully equal to the task.

The noisy attack had so alarmed Mr. Balfour Fenwick that he had once more relapsed into that hopeless imbecility which rendered him worse than helpless.

Without, therefore, wasting a second thought upon the old man, his daughter gave her whole attention to the window.

She shuddered as she looked down into the gloomy depth beneath. The utmost exertion of her vision failed to pierce the black shadowy space.

She could not even distinguish the wall of the house beyond eight or nine feet below.

A deep despairing sigh burst from her lips as she turned from the window.

"Better remain and take my chance with these wretches than cast myself forth into that chaos—into almost certain death. At the least I should be maimed for life."

Shivering with terror, occasioned by the frightful picture which her excited imagination had conjured up, she turned once more to the door.

At this instant a vigorous blow upon the upper panel of the door was followed by the appearance of a murderous knife in the aperture.

The natural instinct of self-preservation immediately changed the current of Lady Ethel's gloomy thoughts from despair, and yielding to continuing the defence.

Whipping up a fire brick from the grate, she dashed at the weapon and snapped it off short, leaving nothing in the possession of the individual who had dealt the threatening stab at the door but the handle of the the knife.

A volley of oaths and execrations announced that the assassin had discovered the prompt and effectual resistance with which Lady Ethel had opposed the first step in the carrying out of their new plan for reducing the stronghold—namely, by literally cutting their way through.

Then followed another pause in the attack, which was even more alarming to the helpless Lady Fane than the attack itself. She knew then that they were considering and devising fresh schemes for the attack, and she shudderingly acknowledged to herself how simple it would be for eight or ten determined men to break their way through her comparatively frail defences if they but allowed themselves time for considering or organizing any plans.

Fortunately, however, instead of rendering her powerless, as it might have done—as it most probably would have done some women—it only turned her thoughts once more to the previously abandoned mode of escape.

The hideous weapon which she had been so fortunate as to break off, gave her some idea of the mercy she might expect from the gamblers, now frenzied at her obstinate defence, should she fall into their clutches.

She gazed once more into the misty night.

"It's fearful," she murmured. "Almost certain death. But nothing remains—I have no choice; and had I not better end thus my struggles and sorrows, than fall beneath the knives of these fiends. Fall, perhaps, by a hideous, torturing death! Ay, perhaps, even breathe my last sigh—my last cry for mercy, in that hideous well. Great God! how fearful! Yes I'll do it!"

The attack upon the door had not yet recommenced, and so she had still time to consider some plan of proceeding.

The first thing she did was to seize the bed-clothes, and with all possible speed she succeeded in fastening the two sheets together.

Quick as she had been in her movements, she had barely concluded when the ruffians returned to the attack and heavy blows, evidently dealt with ponderous hammers, on every part of the door, made the whole room rattle again.

The whole efforts of the besiegers turned of a sudden to the top of the door, and after a momentary pause, the instrument which they had used as a ram in the earlier part of the attack, was dashed against the upper panels with a terrific force which burst them through, and sent the splinters flying about the room in every direction.

A shout of triumph resounded through the house.

Encouraged with the success, they followed up the attack with a vigorous onslaught upon the framework of the top part of the door, which was speedily burst through.

And now there was an aperture sufficiently large to admit the body of a man.

This was quickly seen, and the man who had all throughout been the prime mover in the would-be bloody business—he who had instigated the attempted robbery and murder, was the first to take advantage of it.

At his own request, given in the vilest oaths and the most abusive incitations, he was speedily hoisted upon his companions' shoulders, and his villanous physiognomy distorted, and rendered more repulsively hideous by the thirst for the unhappy Ethel's blood, appeared at the aperture.

An oath and a shriek of pain burst from him as he supported himself upon the broken panels of the door. Some of the splintered wood had peirced his hands through and through.

But even at this fearful moment Lady Ethel's presence of mind did not forsake her.

The knife-blade which she had so opportunely broken off from the handle lay where it had fallen—upon the bed. To possess herself of this and bind it in her grasp with her handkerchief, was the work of an instant.

She then clambered on to the bed boldly to face her foes, determined to do them battle to the last.

The ruffian was bending forward, now speechless with the pain of his self-inflicted wounds, and presented his whole back to the woman's avenging knife.

She did not hesitate to strike. No feminine qualms withheld her hand.

Raising the weapon high aloft, she brought it down with her whole force and murderous precision into the ruffian's neck, almost severing the head from the body.

The blood founted up as she withdrew the weapon, and sprinkled the ruffian's companions below.

A fearful groan of horror announced that they comprehended the deadly vengeance which their would-be victim had taken upon their instigator to the deed of blood that they were there to accomplish.

Some two or three even shouted with terror when the blood bespattered their faces, and they hastily stumbled down the stairs to fly from the fearful scene.

Some others, on the contrary, remained—now more than ever bent upon the slaughter of Lady Fane, their companion's fall giving an additional impetus to their bloody intent.

All that was animal in these ruffians now came out. Blood made them thirst for blood ; and, shouting out vengeance upon their " pal's " destroyer, they once more returned to the attack.

The lifeless carrion of he who had been sent with such sudden and awful violence to his last, long account beyond this life hung over the splintered door, and thus fortunately for Lady Ethel, blocked up the aperture.

This occasioned a considerable delay, during which Lady Ethel was enabled to carry out her arrangements for the descent from the window.

" A ladder—a ladder !" cried several voices in the passage.

Then followed a rushing down stairs and a scrambling about, which told Lady Fane that every instant was now more important than ever.

She tried the sheets—pulled them with all her force—succeeded in making her father take one end while she tugged at the other, and the trial proved satisfactory.

However, when this was done she had another fearful difficulty to encounter. How should she fasten it securely ?

This she shortly got over. She raised the window only sufficiently high to allow her body to pass through. Then, taking up the fire-irons from the hearth, she quickly fastened the end of the sheet round them.

This done, she cast the sheets forth from the window, and placed the fire-irons perpendicularly against the window.

She had no time to make the support fast, and was therefore obliged to trust to the weight of their bodies to keep it from slipping.

" Come, father—come !" she said, turning to the old man, who was gazing on her preparations with curiosity and alarm.

" What do you want with me !"

" Come quickly—come. You will ruin us."

" Ethel, you will murder me, I know."

" Good heavens ! you will be too late !"

" I'm a poor, miserable old man."

" Come—it s quite safe ; I will hold it."

As she said this, she attempted to drag him to the window, but he resisted and shrieked so violently that she was in despair.

Suddenly it occurred to her that she might frighten him into acquiescence. She seized the knife which had done her such good service, and held it, all reeking with the dead man's blood, and held it over her father's head.

" I'll murder you as I murdered him !" she exclaimed, with fearful earnestness.

She had succeeded in her aim. Mr. Fenwick flew to obey her with alacrity.

Clutching the sheets with a trembling grasp, he rapidly descended.

Lady Ethel gazed after him until he disappeared in the darkness, and then suddenly the sheet slacked.

She had heard no fall. Then he must have reached the ground.

With as much caution as possible she passed through the window, and began her perilous descent.

Barely had she proceeded a yard upon her journey when the room door, barricades and all, were carried with a tremendous crash.

CHAPTER XXXIX.

" NOT DEAD YET."

LADY ETHEL FANE'S position was now critical in the extreme.

Hanging from the window of that terrible gambling house—suspended many (ah ! how many ?) feet from the ground—her very life depending upon the security of the shifting fastenings above.

And, to put a terrible climax to this fearful combination of horrors, her enemies—the ruffians who sought her blood—were above ; had burst through the barricaded door, and in another instant she must inevitably be lost.

She dared not quicken her movements lest she should shift the frail support upon which her safe descent depended, and hurl her headlong down into the gloom beneath—into the valley of the shadow of death !

These thoughts of terror passed through her mind with lightning speed, but did not impede her movements. She continued the same steady progress as if she had no further cause for alarm than at the commencement of her perilous journey.

A few brief moments more. A hurried trampling above, and the crashing of the furniture about the apartment, betrayed the rage and mortification of the would-be assassins at her presumed escape, for in the blindness of their maledictions upon the head of their companion's destroyer, they imagined her to be already beyond their reach.

But, alas! for Lady Ethel, the perils of that night of horrors were not near their termination yet.

The attention of the ruffians was naturally attracted very shortly to the half-opened window, and then the discovery of the means by which she had contrived to elude them quickly followed.

They dashed at the window, but, thanks to the pitchy darkness without, they were unable to catch even a glimpse of the retreating form of their prey.

At the same instant Lady Ethel, who had only descended some twelve or fourteen feet from the window—

for the whole had, of course, occurred in far less time than we have taken to relate it—thinking that she was lost, began to quicken her movements, and the supports slipped with a jerk that nearly caused her to relinquish her hold.

Here, however, the blind goddess once more favoured her. One of the men, thinking to impede her progress, in the confusion, seized hold of the rope and held it with a firm hand.

Another minute, and the rope had slackened in his grasp. The fugitive had reached the ground in safety.

Thus had the ruffians by accident contributed most importantly to her escape, or, at least, to one of her grand steps to that end.

Great was the Lady Ethel's surprise—joyful surprise—at coming so quickly to terra firma. Having been unable to discern anything at all definite in the thick fog, she had at once concluded that she was a fearful height from the ground. However, a moment's reflection dissipated the illusion and changed her wonderment to chagrin at having forgotten that, after all, her apartments were on the first-floor, and, consequently, the distance from the ground could be nothing.

What a time—what precious moments had she wasted in her foolish fears to trust herself to the mercy of those sheets, and simply because she had been unable to see the ground on which she stood !

However, her presence of mind returned at once, and she immediately turned her attention to the passage in which she now found herself.

Here there was another great difficulty. Right and left was a thick impenetrable mist. A brick wall was upon either side of the passage, about five or six feet apart.

Right or left led, doubtless, to the open streets and to freedom—but which ?

As this perplexing query stayed her progress for an instant, the men's voices above in an animated discussion of her escape, with various suggestions for her recapture, did not tend to allay her excitement.

"After her !—after her !" shouted several voices.

"Hi ! stop !" said one. "Give a hand here ; I'll go after the b—— down her own blasted stairs."

Ethel trembled with fear. A moment, however, and she was reassured. Pale as death, with her teeth firmly set, she stood at the foot of the sheet listening eagerly as the ruffian passed through the window above, her whole demeanour looking, could she have been seen in those grim shadows, determination and mischief.

The ruffian glided swiftly down the sheet, but before he had reached the ground by six or seven feet, he felt himself grasped by the ankles from below.

Then, ere he had time to think even of struggling, he was dragged by a sudden and vigorous pull to the ground, and, with a smothered cry, he swooned.

The man had fallen with a fearful violence upon his head, which had the lucky effect of silencing the cry which rose to his lips and left the ruffians above in doubt.

Lady Fane darted upon the man as he fell, but immediately discovered that the fall had done him mischief enough without giving herself any further trouble in the matter.

She therefore possessed herself of a knife which had fallen from his person on to the ground with a clatter, and quickly rose to her feet.

"Williams," cried a voice from the window ; "Williams, what's up ?"

This was addressed to the insensible ruffian at Lady Ethel's feet.

"Answer, Williams, that she-devil hasn't nailed you, has she ?"

But still no reply.

"By G—— she's finished him off, too ; down after her. We'll skin the b—— alive !"

"You go down into Paradise-place," shouted another ; "I'll get to the other end. Off you go !"

There was a scrambling and a rush of feet above.

"Great heavens !" murmured Lady Ethel, "when will these horrors end ? They've gone to block up each end of the passage ! Too late !—too late !"

Gathering up her skirts, she darted off to the left, resolved to make a last attempt at flight, or, at the worst, to oppose the ruffians until she fell lifeless.

A man turned the corner as she gained the end of the passage.

She struck at him wildly with the knife, but had not calculated her stroke, and missed him entirely.

The next instant he had grasped her round the neck with a pair of powerful arms.

This, however, left her arms partially free, and she was not slow to take the advantage of such an opening.

With her arm flung round his body she drew back her hand as far as possible, and buried the knife almost to the hilt in his back.

A spasmodic shudder passed through his body from head to foot, simultaneously with the blow.

His grasp of her neck relaxed, and she dragged herself from his clutch.

But in instant he had seized her again, but this time his grasp lacked force. She easily pushed him from her, and rushed past him.

The ruffian fell to the ground, clutching the edge of her skirt—fell to the ground—a corpse !

Glancing over her shoulder she saw the man fall, and with a cry of horror, she rushed from the passage into the street.

Here her foes rose up a legion. Three men darted from the house by the shop-door, and confronted her.

However she simply swerved in her course a few feet, and flew past them—her dress almost sweeping their outstretched hands.

Shrieking, she fled, pursued by the three ruffians, who were now rendered reckless of all danger in thus hunting down a woman in the open streets, by the fierce desire of avenging their companion's fall.

Now, however, in spite of their knowledge of the locality, their greater convenience of dress, and the sincerity of the revenge which urged them to the chase of the unhappy Lady Fane, the fears of the latter lent her wings, and she speedily distanced them.

Still on—on she ran, long after their voices and the echo of their footsteps on the deserted pavement had died away in the distance.

On she ran, with undiminished speed, nothing but her great energy keeping her up, until she had left the thieves' quarter far behind her.

Then, without the slightest warning, her strength left her on a sudden, and she sank prostrated with her tremendous exertions upon a doorstep.

As she sat, the faintest break in the clouds above gave the grim night adieu, and announced the early approach of the new-born day.

With a feeling of intense satisfaction she saw the night departing. It tended more to reassure her than any amount of rest she could take after her great exertions ; and she breathed a silent thanksgiving for her safe delivery from the perils of that dreadful night.

She was so earnest and absorbed in her thoughts that she did not notice the heavy tread of a policeman who passed the spot on his beat. Immediately that he perceived the exhausted fugitive upon the doorstep, he turned the glare of his bull's-eye lantern full upon her, and bade her, in harsh rough tones, to "move on."

"I was only resting awhile——" began Lady Fane, meekly.

"Move on ! d'ye hear ? Off ye go."

It immediately struck her that she might get into an awkward mess if she hesitated, and therefore rose to obey him at once.

As she turned from the spot, as if to tell her that the troubles of the night were not yet over, the policeman caught sight of the blood-stains upon her hands and dress.

THE PIEMAN PUNISHES MR. QUIRK.

"Hi! stop a bit, young woman. What the dickens is this?"

"What?"

"This blood."

Lady Fane stammered, and knew not what to say. She dared not give him any explanation of the doings at the gambling-house, as it must undoubtedly have led to a question upon his part as to the cause of her presence in such a den. In which case a refusal to say anything of that portion of her tale would most probably have aroused the policeman's suspicions, made him question the truth of her statement, and probably finish the matter by securing her person in the name of the law.

Truly it was most perplexing.

"Don't ye hear me," iterated the policeman, "What's this ere?"

"I—I—I have been taken ill, policeman; my nose has bled severely—and—and——"

"Gammon!" interrupted the civic functionary, with considerable emphasis.

"I assure you——"

"It's no go, young woman. "You'd better assure Mr. Wilkins o' that."

"Who?" said Lady Fane, innocently.

"Mr. Wilkins."

"Who is Mr. Wilkins?"

"Who?" reiterated the constable, disgusted at her ignorance. "Who? why the inspector who takes in the night charges, to be sure."

"But why explain to him?"

"Why—'cause I'm going to take you with me."

"Oh! pray don't; you are mistaken."

"Come on. You can easily explain that to them as

is paid to listen to it, and settle all these little things. My dooty is only to take you to the station-house, and I'm a going to do my dooty, I can tell you, young woman."

"But——"

"Now it's no use humbugging about it. You'll have to come, and you may as well come quietly."

"But I've done nothing—I've committed no offence, I swear."

"I don't say you have. Only it looks awkward, and it's my dooty to take you before the inspector. It's no distance from here, and you might just as well walk there with me as sit upon that doorstep. A few words will do the business one way or another."

"I cannot—cannot go."

"But you must."

"I cannot, indeed. I'll give you money—anything you like; but I cannot say anything."

"This begins to look very queer indeed; and now I'm more determined than ever to take you. So come on."

He took her by the arm, and as gently as he could he dragged her on a few paces.

"I'll give you a sovereign if you let me go, policeman," said Lady Ethel, now thoroughly alarmed.

"Not if I know it."

"Stay one moment."

"Not half a moment."

"But if I can give you a good reason for these strange appearances?"

"I must do my dooty."

"You shall—you shall," she said eagerly. "I can give you such explanations in a few words that you will accept my present without the least scruples, and allow me to depart."

The policeman began to waver a little. He still remonstrated—insisted upon taking her to the station, but no longer in the same authoritative tone.

"No, I must do my dooty."

"Will you listen to my explanation here? You can but proceed to extremities afterwards, if you do not find it satisfactory."

"Well, there's no harm in hearing what you have to say—but——"

"Do you not see by my manners and appearance that I am not what you would take me for?"

"I do, mum. And it's that as rather corpsed me."

"Well, then, policeman, I may tell you that some time since I left my home to avoid the persecution of my relations, and sought refuge from them in a dreadful quarter, being the last place in which they would seek me. I took lodgings in a house which afterwards I found to be a gambling-house, infested with the vilest characters. By some means they found out that I had money about me, and last night I overheard some of those wretches plotting my robbery and murder!"

"Good heavens!" ejaculated the policeman. "You must give me the address, mum."

"That I can't do."

"Why?"

"Because it would avail nothing without my testimony, which I cannot give as I wish to keep my whereabouts a secret from my relations."

"We'll look 'em up, then, without troubling you, perhaps, mum."

"If you can do so, of course I shall have no objection."

"But how do you account for this?" demanded the policeman, pointing to the blood stains.

"That," said Lady Ethel, with a shudder, which was unmistakably natural—"that is a most horrible tale. I escaped by a miracle—perhaps at the sacrifice of life."

She then entered into a little more detail, giving him a rapid outline of her battle with the gamblers.

"Well, mum," said the policeman, as his hand closed upon a sovereign with which she purchased his forbearance, "it certainly looks rather wild-like—but I believe you, indeed I do; this wouldn't buy me if I didn't—nor

nothing neither. Besides which, the house you mention is well known to us."

"Well known! Why it looks a most out of the way——"

"Looks—ah! of course. We've been after 'em there for five year, mum, but can't catch 'em napping."

"Five years—good gracious, do you mean it?"

"Lor' bless you, mum, that's nothing! There's one drum—a fence we've had a hi on for one-and-twenty year, and they're not be had at any price."

Thus ended a particularly embarrassing finale to Lady Fane's adventurous night.

The policeman, who was a very civil fellow, when he had received the explanation, escorted her to the limit of his beat in the direction of a more respectable part of the town, in which he had recommended her to some apartments.

Lady Fane thanked him again and again for his kindness, and assured him of a substantial acknowledgment of it when her present embarrassments had passed.

She proceeded to the part to which he had directed her, and as early as possible in the morning she engaged some apartments.

We take our leave of Lady Fane, therefore, for the present, in a quiet lodging-house in Norfolk-street, Strand, while we again briefly glance at some of the other personages in our drama.

CHAPTER XL.

ENEAS QUIRK, THE CAT SCRAGGER.

IT was a pouring wet night.

All day long the rain had been descending steadily enough, with but few intervals of fair weather, which those whom business compelled to be abroad made the best possible use of. But now night had set in, the elements seemed to be in league to do their worst.

The leading thoroughfares which upon other evenings at this time—nine o'clock—were crowded by pedestrians, were fairly deserted now, and the rain poured down like water-spouts upon the drenched pavement.

Where there was any shelter to be had up doorways, the shelter had been eagerly appropriated, and ancient females of mouldy flavour and dilapidated aspect congregated and conversed.

Or houseless beggars crouched and cringed in the least cold corners they could find.

Or thinly-clad gay women shivered in their summer clothes, and tried to be merry with burst boots and aching hearts.

The policemen, who were well protected against the weather, plodded moodily by, keeping a sharp look-out for small beggar boys—their legitimate prey, pouncing down upon them from time to time, and cuffing and kicking them according to their wont, with as little mercy as justice.

The cabs were doing a good trade.

The public-houses were crowded with wet and dry customers.

"It's a coming down," said the potman, at the Great Mogul, to the gentleman who sells trotters to the aristocracy of the lane.

"Like blazes," replied the purveyor, after trying in vain for a better simile.

"Good night for trade," remarked the potman.

"Average," responded the purveyor.

"Take care you don't get your stock in trade washed away, though," said the potman.

"I'm not afraid of that," responded the other, not without anxiety. "But I have to keep rayther a sharp eye on the pepper; but after all, trotters would never go off as they do if it was not for the condiments."

Farther down the lane Mrs. Stiggins meeting Mrs. Higgins, and they together running against Mrs. Wiggins in a way which was, so to speak, "permiscous," they all agreed that it was dreadful weather.

"It's an awful night," Mrs. Stiggins said.

Mrs. Higgins suggested "a soaker;" and Mrs. Wiggins, upon reflection, thought that "squelcher" was perhaps more appropriate.

"It's a dreary night," said Mrs. Stiggins, "and gives one the shivers."

"It's just the sort of night that one could take a little drop of something warm," said Mrs. Higgins.

"The only night I should ever think of touching such a thing," said Mrs. Wiggins.

"And then only the least taste in the world," said Mrs. Higgins.

But if it was a dreary night down Drury-lane what must it have been out in the suburbs.

There the rain poured down in torrents upon the long deserted roads which looked, if possible, more desolate than usual.

Here and there a faint light burning within the small villa residences made the wretched pedestrian, who chanced to be abroad, more miserable than ever when he thought how warm and snug it was within, and how wet and cold without.

The great rambling newly-built public-houses standing at the beginning of what, when they were finished, were to be new streets leading to populous neighbourhoods, yet in the bricklayers' hands, were grim and ghastly, and their great roomy bars looked like vaults, and echoed awfully with the sound of the solitary customer's voice who wandered in and gave his humble order.

It was indeed a horrible night to be out in, and one that you would have supposed nobody could possibly have selected for an out-door excursion.

Yet it was, nevertheless, the case that two persons lingered intentionally out in the rain in one of the most melancholy suburbs of London, and appeared to be in no particular hurry to get out of it.

It is true that one of them carried an umbrella, by which it might be implied that he wanted to escape as much water as possible.

At least, it might have been so supposed until you had taken a good look at the umbrella in question.

But it would then have been found to be such a dilapidated machine, so full of such huge rents and tears, that the idea of shelter was preposterous.

The person who carried it was very warmly wrapped up as far as his neck was concerned.

But here, again, his motive was open to question.

Did he intend to wrap himself up to keep himself warm, or was it to conceal the lower part of his face?

When you came to get a better view of this individual, it was questionable whether you would not have been of opinion that had he concealed all his face there would have been no complainable loss to society.

Perhaps such a horrible countenance was very rarely ever seen.

It was, to begin with, covered by dreadful blotches of a purple tint.

The nose had, at some time or other, been smashed and split.

The eyes had great, red, inflamed lids.

The mouth was an unsightly gash, without lips.

It was, in short, the face of our friend Lazarus, the gaoler, from the nunnery.

His companion was by no means so ugly, but still he was not a very inviting person.

He was a young man of perhaps four or five and twenty.

His countenance was very sallow, and he had bushy black eyebrows.

He was very thin, and his cheeks were sunken.

He had enormous front teeth, which, when he grinned, he exhibited like an ape.

He was poorly dressed, and his clothes were by no means suited to the inclemency of the season.

What he wore though had once been black, and there was some small pretence of gentility about him which, though very small indeed, was just perceivable.

This person rejoiced in the name of Eneas Quirk, and he was the assistant of a medical man residing in Blackman-street, Southwark Bridge-road, with whom the reader is already acquainted.

This doctor's name was Caul, and he was extensively known—as, I believe, I have previously mentioned—to the various procurers of subjects whose habit it was to ransack the metropolitan churchyards.

Mr. Quirk was also most zealous in the pursuit of scientific knowledge.

He threatened in time to be almost as clever as Dr. Caul.

Already he had made a little name round the neighbourhood where he resided.

It was said that he had made a good deal of money, too, for all he looked so shabby.

The doctor, his master, contracted with the parish to usher young paupers into existence at half-a-crown per head, which is surely not an unreasonable charge, under the most advantageous circumstances.

Mr. Quirk practised a little in this way himself.

But there were ugly whispers afloat.

There had just been the faintest shadow of suspicion that he had helped to decrease the population, instead of to increase it.

He was learned in drugs.

It was said, though whether with truth or not I cannot tell, that certain medicines were more easily obtainable of Mr. Quirk than at an ordinary chemist's shop.

Only, however, at a high price, and under vows of solemn secrecy.

Let this be as it might, it is very certain that this worthy young practitioner had, by some means or other, obtained a small reputation in Blackman-street, Southwark Bridge-road, and that he was well if not personally known to most of the footmen and frail but cautious beauties of the neighbourhood.

But what was the errand upon which he and Lazarus had come out this evening in the pouring rain?

They carried with them a couple of black bags.

Neither of these bags were large enough to contain ordinary-sized subjects.

Had they been so, it is not likely that Mr. Quirk and his friend would have carried dead bodies through the streets upon their backs, or between them by their head and heels.

The bags were just large enough to have held babies.

But babies were not the mercantile commodity with which it was intended to fill them.

What then?

The reader would probably have been rather astonished had he or she peeped at the contents of one of the bags when full.

Then they contained——

But we anticipate.

Mr. Quirk plodded along through the mud, sometimes stumbling over the rough stones, sometimes floundering in the gutter.

Lazarus shambled along by his side, smoking a short pipe, which occasionally, when he took a stronger draw than usual, brightly illuminated his hideous face, and imparted to it a demoniacal hue.

They journeyed thus for a long time in silence.

Now and again, though, they halted and looked around.

This was always before one of the villa residences by which they were passing.

When they stopped thus, Mr. Quirk made a mewing sound with his mouth, and waited and listened.

Then, after a while, they plodded on again.

At length Lazarus broke the silence.

"Curse the cats," said he.

"We've no luck to-night," observed Mr. Quirk.

"I didn't suppose we should have."

"I did, though."

"You did?"

"Yes."

"Why?"

"Because I think wet nights are the best."

"But cats don't like water."

"But they always come out, nevertheless."

"Have you caught any before?"

"Of course I have."

"But it wasn't round this humbugging neighbourhood?"

"No; it was round about where I live."

"They're not looked after there as they are here."

"We might as well go on as we've come so far."

"We might as well look for mushrooms; we should find as many."

"I don't like going home without any, though."

"You must find them round about your quarter."

"I can't do that."

"Why?"

"There's been a row about it as it is. Some old woman has offered a reward, and the police are looking out for us."

"You mustn't get caught, then, that's certain, or you will get tortures worse than the cats."

"Everybody sets their face against the spread of science in this idiotic country," grumbled Mr. Quirk.

They then plodded along again in silence, splashing through the mud.

Neither of them was in the best of tempers.

Indeed, how could they be?

Quirk by this time was completely drenched to the skin. The rain was pouring from his coat-tails. The brim of his hat had long ago reached a pulpy state, and the rain continued to ooze forth from it, dripping down the miserable young doctor's face, which he strove in vain to wipe dry with a wringing wet coat-cuff.

As he walked along, his soaking boots emitted extraordinary squealing sounds, which caused his companion more than once to turn sharply round and stop and listen.

"What's that?" he asked, upon one occasion.

"What's what?"

"That row."

"I didn't hear any."

"I did."

"I didn't."

"Come on, then."

A little while afterwards Lazarus came to a pause again.

"Do you mean to say you didn't hear that?"

"Hear what, in the name of goodness?"

"That squealing."

"No."

"Why, there it goes again."

"There what goes?"

"You'd better take care."

"What do you say?"

"Don't do it any more; that's all."

"I wasn't doing anything."

"Don't you try to make a fool of me, if you please."

"I tell you I aint doing anything."

"And I tell you, you are."

"What am I doing, then?"

"Squealing."

"Why, it's my boots."

"Oh, very well," said Lazarus, in a warning tone; "have it as you like; only, drop it. Do you hear? just take my advice, and drop it!"

There was something so very threatening about the expression of Mr. Lazarus's hideous face, that it was perhaps as well for Mr. Quirk's bones that at that moment the former caught sight of one of the feline species, the first they had come across during their long, wet walk.

They were at the time in the front of a small, detached villa, standing in a large garden, and surrounded by a brick wall about six feet high.

Upon the top of this wall was a cat.

A splendid black Tom it was, picking his way very gingerly along among the fragments of broken glass.

"Hush!" cried Lazarus suddenly, as Mr. Quirk was about to make some remark with reference to his boots; "Look there!"

"What a beauty!"

"If we can only bag him!"

"Have you the bait?"

"Yes; here it is."

"Give it me!"

Mr. Quirk took a piece of fish from his companion, and, advancing gently, called, as he went—

"Puss! Puss! Pretty puss!"

Pretty puss, though, did not feel too certain of the gentle stranger's kind intentions.

Perhaps he was not very hungry. Perhaps he did not approve of fraternizing with chance acquaintances.

He hung back, and his tail expanded.

"Puss! Puss!" cried Quirk.

But Tommy would not be persuaded.

"Puss! Puss!"

No; he had no confidence in the sparse gentleman's good intentions.

Did he "mean honourable?" That was the question which Thomas asked himself. Perhaps not without reason.

There are deceitful times decidedly, and there are many smooth-tongued evil-doers for ever going about upon the look-out for the verdant and confiding—many hungry wolves seeking whom they can devour.

The youngest maidens and the most innocent young ladies—if there are any innocent young ladies now-a-days —can tell you as much.

Thomas was the property of a spinster who had had in her time her trials and temptations, and perhaps he had been warned against the deceits of men creatures.

He looked askance at Mr. Quirk.

Mr. Quirk peeped up at him, and made chirping sounds with his thin lips.

Poor Thomas thought the fish which the wily medical man produced was loud smelling, and most seductive.

Thomas sniffed it from afar, and thought it was delicious.

At first he had made up his mind to have nothing to do with the persuasive stranger, but, unfortunately, he took another sniff.

To sniff was to hesitate—to hesitate was to be lost.

Upon consideration, he thought he would come a little nearer.

Rash feline! he was approaching his doom.

He came slowly.

Quirk waited and watched.

He made ready for a pounce.

The other villain got the bag prepared, glaring the while like an ogre.

Thomas, meanwhile, came a little nearer.

A step at a time. Very daintily he picked his way over the broken glass. The nearer he got to the fish the better, I suppose, he thought it smelt.

It had somewhat the same effect upon this unhappy catawauler that the rattlesnake's eye is said to have upon the small birds which venture within reach of its influence.

Perhaps he thought he was acting unwisely. Perhaps he thought he had much better go back.

It is very certain that, if he thought upon the subject, he must have known that Miss Tabitha Buckram, his spinster mistress, would never have approved of such conduct.

He ought to have gone back then, but he did not.

No, rashly he advanced. He came at last within Mr. Quirk's reach.

The young medical man clutched at him.

Then Thomas saw how he had been deceived. He would escape. Was there time? He would try.

He was a fine strong cat, and he fought and struggled terrifically.

Mr. Quirk, though accustomed to this sort of business, found some considerable difficulty in keeping his hold upon him.

Thomas dragged with all his might and main.

Quirk had only got a very uncertain hold of his tail.

Thomas's body hung over the other side of the wall, and with his claws set in the bricks, he seemed to be trying either to pull Quirk over the wall, or pull his own tail off.

"Curse the cat," cried Quirk at last, after he had struggled for some time in silence.

"Pull him up," said Lazarus.

"Pull him up yourself," retorted the younger man. "He's pretty well sawing my wrist off."

Indeed the pain that the cruel wretch was suffering was almost sufficient to make him loosen his hold, much as he desired to secure the prize he was so near obtaining.

If it had not been for Lazarus's grinning horribly at his uncouth antics, he certainly would have done so.

The cat was a great weight, and was very strong. It had got into such a position that it could exert its strength with effect.

It was pulling furiously at Quirk's hand, and grinding his wrist to and fro upon the sharp, jagged edge of a bottle.

Quirk was suffering horribly.

He gnashed and ground his teeth.

His curses were low and deep.

O! if he managed to capture this unhappy feline how he would torture it.

But how to capture the ferocious Tom?

There was only one way to do so that he could think of.

"Give us a leg up," he said to his companion.

Lazarus was only too happy.

He took hold of Mr. Quirk's leg and hoisted him high —rather suddenly.

At the same moment the Tom cat gave a vigorous pull.

Mr. Quirk flew up like a ginger-beer cork, then came down like a rocket.

He gave a wild cry of alarm, but he still contrived to retain his hold upon the cat's tail. The result was that he fell upon the top of poor Thomas, and though he narrowly escaped breaking his own neck, which would not have been of the slightest consequence, he contrived to kill the cat, which was a deplorable accident.

If he was not killed, though, he was very much bruised and not a little dirty, when he picked himself up out of a newly-dug-up flower-bed that the violent rain had made so much mud of.

He picked himself up and wiped his nose, which was bleeding profusely, and clawed the sticky mud out of his left eye, which was effectually bunged up with this unpleasant clammy substance.

Then he revenged himself upon the cat by kicking its dead body, and upon Lazarus by flinging the dead body over the wall into his face.

After which he picked up his hat, smashed out of all shape, and groaning with pain climbed back over the wall, cutting his hands by the way.

"We've one at any rate," said Lazarus.

"It's all we'll have to-night, though," said the other.

"Can't we catch any more?"

"No."

"Not after coming all this way?"

"No."

"As you like."

"Come on."

The two ruffians turned their faces homewards, and plodded along in silence. Lazarus, though at times he thought fit to adopt a somewhat familiar tone, was nevertheless in the other's pay, and upon occasions found it to his interest to be respectful. He thought that perhaps he had gone far enough now, and, therefore, held his tongue.

On they plodded, and soon leaving the suburb where they had been so unfortunate, came by Kennington home.

Some distance from where they lived, however, Mr. Quirk, attracted by the brilliant exterior of a public-house, suggested a glass of something hot.

Mr. Lazarus willingly assented, but when they had partaken of the liquor together and they were out in the street again, he mildly intimated that he was hungry.

It was growing late, and there were very few shops open. The rain had in a great measure subsided. An energetic potato-man or two had ventured out, but Lazarus did not approve of this food.

"Trotters?" suggested Mr. Quirk.

But Lazarus did not like the notion.

"There's nothing else, then, unless——ah! pies!"

A fine establishment was before them. A wonderful place, with a large quantity of looking-glass and some very showy landscapes, impossibly blue and green, but extremely effective.

In the window were many pies, with inviting brown and crisp crusts, which looked light and puffy. There were also vases of artificial flowers, and a couple of salad bowls containing the luscious fruit from which some of the pies were supposed to be made.

A beautiful damsel, highly perfumed and pomatumed, with a necklace round her neck accurately indicating how far down she washed it, sat behind the counter, and did needle-work at intervals between the serving out of the pies.

There was also a fierce-looking man of a rubicund countenance who attended to the business at intervals, but managed between whiles to keep a very sharp eye upon the beautiful damsel, between whom and himself there might or might not have existed tender relations.

The shop contained a good many persons, but yet the business did not appear to be of a very flourishing character.

There appeared to be a tendency upon the part of the customers to hang a long while over a small outlay in refreshments, as you may have observed to be the case in cheap Italian ice-shops and those wonderful repositories of filling confectionery where everything looks so stale, flabby, and repulsive, which have of late years sprung up all over the metropolis, mostly bearing over their shop fronts some eccentric variation of the name of "Alexander."

Here in this pie-shop the customers seemed to be rollicking and revelling, but not eating too much for all that.

One penny bottle of ginger-beer entertained a whole tableful, and two or three had a twopenny pie between them, and took a box to eat it in.

The ruddy-faced proprietor didn't seem very much to approve of this behaviour upon the part of his customers, and he approved less of the conduct of one or two in particular, who ate their pies at the counter and winked with their mouths full at the fascinating damsel in the necklace.

There was a curious mixture of classes in the company assembled. There were some very ragged and wretched who gorged themselves with pie as though they never in their lives before had tasted anything half so delicious. There were some very young girls, very haggard though and highly painted, who were partaking of some horrible mess called "cherry brandy," by the proprietor. There were some smart young shop-boys, and there were a couple of drunken swells.

These two last excited the ruddy-faced one's wrath more than any other. They lolled with their arms upon the counter, and puffed their cigars between each mouthful of pie. They had treated the young ladies just mentioned to the cherry brandy.

They had made sundry advances to the lady with the pearls. They had been extremely insulting to the ruddy-faced.

When Mr. Quirk and Lazarus entered the shop all the assembled thieves and prostitutes were listening with no small amusement to a dispute which was at the time going on between the proprietor and one of the swells, and which grew warmer and warmer as it progressed.

"I don't want any more of your pies, my good man," the swell was saying; "I've had enough of them, I assure you. As many as I can safely take with life."

"It wouldn't have hurted you if you'd never been brought up on nothing less wholesome," said the proprietor.

"I should never have reached maturity if I had," said the young swell.

"Reached what?" asked the other with sarcasm. "You've never got as far as that, have you?"

"Let's have another pie," said the swell without replying.

"What sort?" asked the proprietor, eagerly.

"Cats," answered the swell, and everybody roared, while the red-faced man grew more red-faced still with rage and mortification at having left himself open to the insulting rejoinder.

The wit was not very brilliant, but it was perhaps good enough for the time and place, only the proprietor did not seem inclined to contest any longer for the champion's belt.

Upon the contrary, he became suddenly loud and angry.

"Shant serve you."

"Shant what?"

"You shan't have no more in my shop."

"Are you afraid I can't pay?"

"It's all you can do if you're able."

"Let me have half a dozen."

"I don't want your custom."

"Rubbish. Pies round."

While the proprietor was indignantly protesting that he would not execute the order, the young lady with the necklace had produced the pies and placed them before the swell.

"Thank you, my dear," said he; "I must apologize to you for the old man's bad manners."

And as he spoke he felt in his pocket for his purse.

But much to his apparent surprise he could not find it there. He rummaged in his other pockets. Then exclaimed—

"I've been robbed."

Nothing was more probable, seeing what sort of company surrounded him, but the pieman did not choose to believe it, because he was only too anxious for a good cause of quarrel.

"You're a couple of infernal cheats," he roared; "but you wont do me that way."

And almost before the words had quitted his lips he had vaulted over the counter.

The next moment he had clutched the young gentleman by the collar.

The latter struggled to free himself.

"You blackguard what do you mean?"

"I'll show you what I mean!"

"What do you take me for?"

"For a couple of swell mobsmen."

"Leave go of me, will you?"

"Not till the police come."

"You wont?"

"No."

"Take that then."

As the young man spoke he dealt the pieman a tremendous blow under the chin, which fairly lifted him off his legs.

He staggered back, and fell with a crash upon one of the small tables, from which the other customers ran shrieking.

But when he was about to rush back upon his antagonist the pieman was brought to a stand-still by the occurrence of a somewhat unexpected incident.

The young swell's friend feeling in his pockets for his purse, with the intention of paying for himself and companion, found that he also had been robbed.

By whom? He glared round him fiercely. At that moment Quirk was standing close behind him.

When the young gentleman turned he found that he was in rather a suspicious attitude. He held in his hand a bag.

What was in it?

The young gentleman insisted upon seeing. Mr. Quirk was quite as determined that he should not.

They began to struggle.

The general public took the part of the young gentleman, and the real thieves were the most zealous in their endeavours to expose the imaginary culprit.

Lazarus meanwhile seeing that the day was going against his friend, like a coward as he was, turned tail and fled.

Then Quirk, overcome by numbers, had the bag wrenched from him.

Some of the thieves held him by the throat while some others inspected the contents of the bag.

They did not find the purse though, if they had expected so to do.

One of the thieves plunging in his arm seized hold of what he supposed at first to be a part of a lady's victorine, instead, though, it was Thomas's tail by which he hauled the dead cat forth amidst general consternation.

Nobody now thought any more about the robbery.

General indignation set in against the pieman.

Nobody would believe that Mr. Quirk was not connected with the establishment, and he and the unhappy proprietor were cuffed and buffeted within an inch of their lives.

A general riot then set in at the instigation of the young swells, and everything, except the young lady with the necklace, was more or less damaged during the general confusion.

She saved herself by flight, and was heard screaming with all the strength of her lungs in the little room at the back of the shop.

But the thieves were only too delighted to have a chance of mischief. The pies were scattered upon the ground and trampled out of shape.

The looking-glasses were broken. All the strings of the ginger-beer bottles were cut.

A large quantity of ham, cooked veal, and mutton forced down the proprietor's throat, and his head rubbed over with congealed gravy.

At last there was an alarm of police, and the blackguards decamped.

The proprietor, more dead than alive, scrambled on to his feet and following them, barred the door.

Then leaning his back against it he glared round savagely upon the scene of desolation.

His eyes in so doing fell upon the wobegone face of the unhappy Quirk, who was hiding his diminished and broken head beneath one of the tables.

"Come out of that," roared the proprietor.

"Don't be violent," pleaded the victim.

"Come out of it, I say."

"You wont hit me if I do?"

"I'll kick you if you don't."

"I haven't spoilt your things."

"I don't care what you've done. Come out of that."

If Mr. Quirk had only come out at once without further explanation he would have more easily escaped.

But instead he unwisely remained under the table, and continued to plead his cause.

"It wasn't my fault that they saw the dead cat in my bag," said he.

But he could get no further. The pieman boiled over with rage.

"You was the scoundrel who brought the cat here, was you?" he roared.

He had not before recognised Mr. Quirk.

When he did so his only thought was vengeance.

He dived under the table and tried to get hold of the young medical man by the collar. Quirk flung himself upon his back and kicked violently.

But the proprietor got hold of him by the leg and dragged him forth neck and crop.

Then, if ever in all his life Mr. Quirk came in for a drubbing, he did on this memorable occasion.

For every damaged pie he had a thump, and many or more kicks as there had been bottles of ginger-beer wasted.

Luckily the pieman was somewhat weak from the thrashing he had had himself, or else he would certainly have been the death of his unhappy victim.

As it was, he cuffed and kicked at him as long as he could see him. Then he rolled over him and fell upon him.

Then together they wallowed in smashed pies till they were a sight horrible to behold.

At last when the proprietor was thoroughly worn out, he dragged Mr. Quirk, or rather I should say, what remained of him, and kicked him out into space.

How he managed to crawl home, all bumps and bruises, it is almost impossible to say, but at last he did reach Doctor Caul's door.

He felt in his pocket for his latch-key, but he had been so shaken up in the pie-shop that this and his other property had been shaken out of his possession.

He did not want to ring the bell, because the housekeeper went to bed early and he did not wish the doctor to see the state he was in.

Indeed the atrocities the ruffian committed upon the wretched cats were unknown to Dr. Caul, as were also the particulars of the little reputation he had made in the neighbourhood.

Quirk, on his side, was not admitted to any confidence by his master. He knew that Caul dealt largely with body-snatchers, but what was the nature of the experiments performed upon the corpses he could not say.

The assistant had some suspicions of his master, and he was in the habit of watching him when he got the chance, which, however, was very seldom.

A singularly good opportunity presented itself to-night though, of which he eagerly took advantage.

Mr. Quirk being desirous of getting into the house quietly, without having to enter into any explanations respecting his late "cat scragging" expedition, as he termed it, thought he would try and get in at the back of the house.

There was a wall which he could climb up easily. He had done it before; and a window he could let himself in at without much trouble.

He was not long in putting his plan into execution.

He soon scrambled up the wall and raised the window sash.

Then crept into the house, congratulating himself on his success, and little dreaming what a horrible discovery he was upon the eve of making.

CHAPTER XLI.

THE NEW GOVERNESS.

WE parted company with Lady Ethel Fane in her new abode, a lodging-house, in Norfolk-street.

She passed several days in her quiet apartments without attempting to follow up her search for employment.

The great reaction which always takes place after such exciting scenes—such a terribly exciting scene as had occurred in the gambling-house from which Lady Ethel had barely escaped with life, had taken due effect upon her and the first days in her new residence found her utterly prostrated.

She recovered by slow degrees, and then her whole thoughts were directed to her father.

Had he succeeded in effecting his escape?

He had disappeared so silently from the passage into which he had been lowered by Lady Ethel's assistance, that he must have got clear off; must have got clear off unless—then came a terrible idea—unless his progress had been stopped as she had stayed the movements of the ruffian who had ventured to pursue her by her own mode of escape.

He might have been stunned by a sudden and sharp fall, carried noiselessly and unresisting to the well, the destined receptacle for her own body; and never heard of more.

These, and similar thoughts, did not tend to make Lady Ethel very cheerful.

The consequence was that her gloomy forebodings for her father—of his possible—even probable untimely end, rendered her more reserved than ever in her demeanour towards a particularly loquacious landlady, and a pert servant-of-all-work, both of whom regarded their lodger as an object of mystery.

From this the servant, with characteristic boldness, even ventured to surmise that there was something amiss.

Indeed, when the landlady one day in the course of a gossiping dissertation upon her lodger's reserve and strange bearing generally, had charitably given it as her opinion that Lady Ethel had made a *faux pas*, and was grieving at her desertion by some faithless and unmarriageable swain, the maid shook her head in significant denial, and threw out some dark hints about the disappearance of a suspected culprit in a sensation poisoning case of the period.

Several days passed when an incident occurred which served to rouse Lady Fane from the lethargy which had possessed her of late.

Beginning to feel the ill effects of keeping so long within doors, she began taking short promenades in the evening, and once as she was passing along the passage on the way to take her constitutional, she overheard the pert maid-of-all-work having a confidential chat with—to use the lodging-house slang—the back parlour.

As she caught the name of Mrs. Morley (Lady Fane's present appellation), she paused to listen.

The pert maid-of-all-work was not particularly nice in her expressions, and that Mrs. Morley was "no better than she should be," was the mildest opinion expressed by the young lady.

Lady Ethel then began to see that she had been wrong to keep herself so aloof from everyone about, and to fear that the gossiping might prove very embarrassing to her.

To avoid this therefore she determined to make another move, and that very night she made a contract with an adjacent newsvendor to supply her with the *Times* every morning, by which means she was enabled to continue her search for employment in answering advertisements of every description.

A wearisome labour she had found this before, and wearisome she still found it; but she persevered, and at length her efforts were crowned with success when she scarcely expected it.

She received the following letter from a certain X.Y.Z. who had advertised for an English governess for young ladies, and whose advertisement Lady Ethel had answered, almost without hope, but upon principle:—

"Mrs. Stibbington is in receipt of Mrs. Morley's application for the vacancy now occurring in the establishment of the former, and shall be able to speak further upon the subject with Mrs. Morley any morning before twelve o'clock at 'The Chesnuts,' near Quincey-crescent, Hendon."

The next morning found Lady Fane, *alias* Mrs. Morley, at Hendon.

She was considerably surprised, and at the same time rather disappointed, to find Mrs. Stibbington's establishment a small detached cottage, very dilapidated, and dirty, instead of the important semi-collegiate building which her imagination had pictured it in consequence of its high-sounding appellation.

"However," thought Lady Ethel, "I mustn't be discontented until I am assured that I have a chance of being accepted."

With this she rang the bell. Her summons was answered by a pale-faced, interesting-looking little girl of about ten years of age, dressed almost in rags, and looking thin and emaciated, as if actually wanting for food.

The child gazed into Lady Ethel's face with a pair of big lustrous hazel eyes full of expression of timid inquiry.

"Is Mrs. Stibbington in the way, my dear?" asked Lady Ethel.

Without replying to the question the child still gazed into the visitor's face as if she had not caught the import of Lady Fane's speech.

"Is Mrs. Stibbington in?"

"Yes—oh! yes, ma'am. Shall I go and say you want her?"

"Hadn't I better come in—Mrs. Stibbington expects me?"

"If you like, ma'am."

The child then closed the street-door, and ushered Lady Fane into an apartment to await Mrs. Stibbington, whom she ran to acquaint of the visitor's arrival. It was a dull, spiritless-looking room, meagrely furnished, and bearing an indescribable air of discomfort.

Altogether Lady Fane's impressions were not of the most agreeable description.

In the course of a few minutes Mrs. Stibbington entered the room with an easy sort of nod and an ill-bred stare at her visitor.

"Mrs. Stibbington, I presume?" said Lady Fane, by way of a beginning.

"To be sure," said the lady, with another nod. "Mrs. Stibbington is my name, of course; but what's yours?"

Somewhat staggered at this, Lady Ethel did not reply very briskly, and the question was repeated with some asperity of tone.

"My name is Morley," said Lady Fane.

"Morley—Morley! Let me see—oh! I recollect. A young person I wrote to about the assistant governess I advertised for?"

"Yes, ma'am, it is I."

"Then, young lady, you are too late."

"Too late? Why you told me in your letter to call any day before twelve o'clock, and here I come on the first morning and it is now barely eleven."

"I'm quite aware of what I wrote you, without wanting any rude allusions."

"Do you mean to say, madam, that you have found some one to fill up the place?"

"Yes, to be sure. I've made an arrangement with a young party who's to come to-morrow."

Poor Lady Ethel was speechless with chagrin at this new disappointment, and she rose to depart.

"Good morning, ma'am," she said, after a while.

"Stay a moment," said Mrs. Stibbington. "We might possibly come to terms, now even."

"How so?" demanded Lady Fane, with a faint hope.

"She is to have sixteen pounds a year."

"What then?"

"If you like to make it twelve, I think I could put her off."

Lady Ethel heard this monstrosity proposed in the utmost astonishment. She was not much acquainted with the rate of reimbursement for such accomplishments as she offered, but the sum appeared to her so insignificant that she could scarcely believe that the woman was in earnest.

A glance at the cold, expressionless face of Mrs. Stibbington assured her that she was serious, and she therefore began to consider the possibility of accepting such an offer.

"Really, madam," she said, "the sum is so trifling that I have some doubts as to the possibility of living upon it."

"Living!" exclaimed Mrs. Stibbington. "I provide everything. You would simply have to find yourself in clothes and washing out of it. However, you know your business best. That's my offer. Accept or reject it as you please, only decide at once, for my time is money."

"Must I give up this chance, poor as it is?" mused Lady Fane. "No! I can but make a trial of it, and even then I shall be no worse off than before. Besides which, with this woman I shall avoid all embarrassing questions." Then she added aloud—"I accept your offer, Mrs. Stibbington."

"Very good."

"And when shall I come?"

"At once."

"Not to-day?"

"Why not?"

"I was merely asking the question, madam."

"And I'm merely answering it. To-day, and at once."

"Very well, madam."

With this Lady Fane departed, not over pleased at the prospect of taking up her abode with such a very unpleasant person as Mrs. Stibbington.

The little girl who had admitted her saw her to the door, and as she was going asked her in a tremulous undertone if she was to be the new governess.

"Yes, my child. Why do you ask?"

"Nothing, only——"

Her speech was cut short by the shrill voice of Mrs. Stibbington.

"Phillis!"

"Yes, ma'am."

And in a state of fright she ran off, leaving Lady Ethel to close the door after her.

That day Lady Fane closed her account with her landlady in Norfolk-street, and the evening found her regularly installed in her future residence and her new duties.

"There, Mrs. Morley," said Mrs. Stibbington, "that's your room. You sleep there, and——"

"What haven't I a room to myself?"

"No, Phillis, that girl you saw to-day, will sleep in the room with you. In your bed or on the floor, as you like. However, here she sleeps, and that's all about it."

Lady Fane simply bowed her head in acquiescence with Mrs. Stibbington's decree.

"We rise at seven here, Mrs. Morley—that is, you rise at seven, and I too, of course; but I have other duties which will keep me from the school-room until nine or half-past."

Lady Ethel bowed.

And Mrs. Stibbington continued—

"To-morrow all the children come back from the holidays. My course of instruction I will explain to you while we take our supper. But perhaps you have already supped?"

Lady Fane had not supped; as she had arrived there somewhat before six o'clock in the evening, this was not very singular.

However, Mrs. Stibbington seemed rather annoyed when Lady Ethel accepted her particularly indirect invitation.

Mrs. Stibbington marshalled her new governess off to the school-room.

THE SPY IS ALARMED AT THE SIGHT OF THE SKELETON.

"There, Mrs. Morley, that's your desk; this one is mine. You keep your desk—I keep mine, and we shall get on all right, I dare say."

Lady Ethel did not doubt it.

"Now, Mrs. Morley," said Mrs. Stibbington, "suppose we go and take this snack? At the same time, let me recommend you to be sparing with this meal; nothing is so promotive of indigestion and all kinds of ills as heavy suppers."

"Good gracious, madam!" exclaimed Lady Ethel, out of all patience; "do you take me for some gluttonous child? We shall get on all the better if you will allow me to think of such things for myself."

"Hoity! Toity! Bless me! I'm sure, young woman, that you're——"

The remainder of Mrs. Stibbington's speech was drowned in the noise she made as she bustled downstairs.

She led the way into the parlour, followed by Lady Ethel.

This room, like the others, seemed to share the cheerless, unhomely aspect indicative of the presence of the lady of the house.

Mrs. Stibbington rang a small hand-bell, at the same time stamping her feet on the floor, apparently to signal some one below.

In a short time the pale-faced little girl entered the room.

"Phillis," said Mrs. Stibbington sternly, "did you hear me ring?"

"Yes, ma'am," replied the child, timidly.

"Then why did you not come immediately?"

"I came as soon as possible, ma'am."

"What do you mean by 'as soon as possible?' It is possible to come at once."

The child made no reply, but stood there trembling visibly.

Lady Ethel's sympathy was aroused for the girl, but her slight knowledge of Mrs. Stibbington's character told her that she had better not interfere.

"What does the girl shake about?" shouted Mrs. Stibbington.

But the poor child, as a natural consequence, only shook all the more, until Mrs. Stibbington administered her a steadier, in the form of a smart slap on the shoulder.

Lady Fane was about to make some indignant remonstrance, when Mrs. Stibbington interrupted her by following up the chastisement with instructions to the trembling child about the supper.

The girl left the room, and speedily reappeared with a tray bearing bread and cheese, glasses, &c.—a far too weighty load for her slender arms to bear.

She struggled into the room with her unwieldy burthen; but not managing to steer quite clear of the doorway, she jerked, stumbled, and fell sprawling upon the ground, breaking to atoms platters, glasses and all.

With her mouth full of opprobrious epithets, Mrs. Stibbington darted upon the unhappy child, and beat her about in a most unmerciful manner.

Unable to witness this cruelty, Lady Fane interposed between the irate schoolmistress and her victim.

Then the whole violence of Mrs. Stibbington's passion was turned from the child to her protector. Never before had Lady Ethel heard such a volley of expletives come from one mouth, and that mouth a woman's.

The end was that the child beat a hasty retreat to bed, and was speedily followed by the new governess, who left her employer almost foaming with rage.

Thus ended Lady Fane's first day at "The Chesnuts."

CHAPTER XLII.

THE SUFFERINGS OF A POOR LITTLE GIRL.

It was with a strange mixture of sensation that Lady Ethel Fane arose upon the second day of her arrival at the establishment of Mrs. Stibbington to assume her new duties.

She had not, of course, been sufficiently long with Mrs. Stibbington to get much knowledge of that lady's character beyond the little display of hastiness of temper which had led to the trifling rupture on the previous night; and she was, therefore, rather curious to know what notice Mrs. Stibbington would take of the affair.

She felt sure that it would undoubtedly have resulted in instant dismissal had she awaited on the spot the further ebullition of Mrs. Stibbington's temper.

However, she hoped that, having calmed down, Mrs. Stibbington would reflect upon the unusually low remuneration that the new governess was to receive, and let that consideration act as a balm to her wounded vanity.

The little girl, Phillis, was already stirring when Lady Fane awoke, and was hastily dressing herself to descend and open the domestic drudgery of the day.

There was something so superior in the child's manner, in spite of the rags in which she was clothed, that Lady Ethel's curiosity was aroused, and she questioned the child as to her parentage.

"What is your name, my dear, besides Phillis?" asked Lady Ethel.

"Phillis——." Then she paused and thought awhile, as if she had forgotten her name; and then, a smile of intelligence lighting up her face, she said: "Oh! Phillis Ebury—I remember."

"Remember!" repeated Lady Ethel, in astonishment; "surely you hadn't forgotten it?"

"Why, almost—it's so long since I heard it, you see."

"Good heavens!" exclaimed the new governess, "forget your own name?"

The girl looked up into Lady Ethel's face, and then it suddenly seemed to strike her that there was something rather strange in the circumstance of a person forgetting their own name, for she blushed as she continued apologetically, in explanation,

"Why, ma'am, you see, I don't think that it has been asked me twice for—oh, ever so long—ever since I was brought here."

"Brought here?"

"Yes; by my uncle Zachary."

"Then, what were you brought here for?"

"To learn—the same as the other girls."

"And how long is it that you have been here?"

"I don't know; but it must be long, very long."

"Years?"

"Oh, yes; many years."

"And is Mrs. Stibbington always meek—always good to you?"

The girl stared into Lady Ethel's face, as if to comprehend the drift of the question—whether it had been put merely to ensnare her into some unguarded speech about her tyrant, Mrs. Stibbington, or in bonâ fide earnest.

"Did you not hear what I said?" asked Lady Fane.

"Yes, ma'am; but did you mean it?"

"Of course."

"But you know she is never good to me."

"Never?"

"Never. She is always as you saw her last night—sometimes even more unkind."

"But why so?"

"I don't know."

"Surely there must be some reason. Do you never complain to your uncle when you see him?"

"But I never see him. I have never seen him since he brought me here."

"Have you no father or mother?"

"None that I know of."

"Nor relations of any kind?"

"I know of none."

"But don't you recollect your mother?"

"No. My only recollections, before I came here, are of a stern, cross old man, with a long white beard, who lived in a dark, gloomy old house, near some water. The only person who lived in this house, besides the old man and myself, was an old woman, who used to attend to me."

"Was not she your mother, perhaps?" demanded Lady Ethel.

"No, no. I never called her mother. I was always very sad there. The old nurse, whom I used to call Martha, never smiled even, and Uncle Zachary was very petulant and touchy; and until he brought me here I never knew what it was to be the least bit happy. I had no playmates, no playthings, no gay clothes, and no kind words. The first time I learned what was the meaning of the word pleasure was when Uncle Zachary said he must bring me to school. I didn't know what it was, but I knew it was a change; and although I had never longed for a change, because I had never thought of it, when the change came I was I can't say how glad. I remember the day so well. Uncle Zachary was taken suddenly ill one day, and the doctor was called in. Well, it was through that doctor that I was sent here. He saw me one day there, and I heard him speak of me to Uncle Zachary, and tell him that I was wasting away—dying by slow degrees—from being cooped up in the house. Then there was a great deal more talk, and Uncle Zachary promised the doctor to send me to school. As soon as he got better, he brought me here one day, and I never saw him again."

"Do you know if he still pays for you?"

"No; I never thought of that. I only know that I left that cold, cheerless home without regret—without even bidding Martha or Uncle Zachary good-bye. I came here and found a number of friends. All the children pitied my forlorn and friendless state, and their sympathy was the first delight I ever felt. It is true that, though I had never had any pleasures at Uncle Zachary's, I had never had any pains. My life then was one long unchanging night—dull, and always the same. But at school I soon learnt to sigh for things that I had never dreamed of before. Then, as the holidays came round, how unhappy I felt to see all the children—all my companions go home to their parents, leaving me to pass my holidays alone."

"But, my dear," said Lady Ethel, "was Mrs. Stibbington always so unkind with you?"

"No—that is, she did not beat me at first. She was always more strict with me than with my schoolfellows; but that was rather good for me than otherwise. I was so afraid of the punishments which she gave me for the slightest thing, that I learnt everything better than any of the school. Then I soon got to be the head of all. As soon as I found myself getting on so well, I began to take an interest in the lessons for the sake of learning. I improved myself greatly, until I began to be of some assistance to Mrs. Stibbington in the school."

"How is it, then, that Mrs. Stibbington makes you a mere drudge, my dear, if you are of any service to her in the school?"

"I have to be in the school as well, ma'am, when the pupils come back."

"That is to-day, then."

"To-day? Oh! I am so glad—so glad."

"Why glad?"

"Mrs. Stibbington is always less unkind with me when they are here. She is never very cross with me before them. I think it is because she is afraid that they might speak of it to their friends."

"Why do you not leave here, if Mrs. Stibbington is so unkind to you?"

"Where should I go to, ma'am?"

"To your uncle."

"It is now more than a year ago that Mrs. Stibbington told me that my uncle Zachary was dead."

"Dead?"

"Yes. I did not feel his death much, on account of his cold, unkindly ways. But I cried a great deal, more from a feeling of loneliness at having lost my only relation, than anything else."

"If your uncle Zachary is dead, you are now dependent upon Mrs. Stibbington for support?"

"Yes, ma'am."

"Then that partly accounts for her harsh treatment of you."

"Yes. She seemed to change altogether from the very day after she told me of Uncle Zachary's death."

"How change? In what way?"

"For something I had made some fault in—something trifling, that I had done many times before, she scolded me and called me many bitter names—a pauper among the rest—and ordered me from the house. It was then that I felt how very dreadful was my position; and I begged her, in tears, to let me remain."

"Then, after all, she was not altogether unfeeling."

"Well, ma'am, I scarcely know. A week after that she discharged the servant, and I have done the whole work of the house ever since. You see, Mrs. Morley, it is a profit to Mrs. Stibbington. I am not so well fed as the servant was, and I get no wages at all."

Lady Fane was astonished at the acute observations of so young a girl. Her admiration of her naturally begot sympathy, and she was now more than ever determined to befriend her, if possible.

"Do you know how old you are, Phillis?"

"No, ma'am; I've no idea."

"I should say from your appearance that you are not more than twelve."

"No, ma'am, I should think not."

Just then a bell was rung loudly.

"Mrs. Stibbington's bell!" exclaimed Phillis, the colour forsaking her cheek.

"What does she want at this time in the morning?" asked Lady Ethel.

"Her breakfast."

"Breakfast? But——"

"Oh, I have to take it up to her in bed."

And off she ran in the greatest fear.

Lady Ethel dressed herself and quickly descended the stairs. At the bottom she encountered Phillis bearing a tray containing Mrs. Stibbington's breakfast.

"Make haste, Phillis," said Lady Fane. "I wish to speak with you for an instant when you return."

Phillis nodded her reply, and sprang off to obey her tyrant's summons.

Lady Ethel stood at the foot of the stairs listening for the result of the girl's entrance into the presence of the passionate Mrs. Stibbington.

At first she caught the sound of Mrs. Stibbington's voice in great wrath. Then there was a pause of several moments, which was followed by Mrs. Stibbington's angry tones louder than before.

Then another pause, and Lady Ethel began to hope that she had heard the end of it. But then a scrambling sound above, followed by the falling of some weighty body, which might have been caused by Mrs. Stibbington springing off the bed, warned her that she was about to witness a recurrence of the painful scene of the previous night.

She had already become interested in the unfortunate child, and she could not endure the thoughts of her ill-usage at the hands of the inhuman schoolmistress.

The sounds now grew alarming.

A subdued buzz of voices had burst into something more formidable, and the sound of a blow, administered doubtless to the shrinking Phillis, told Lady Fane that she must proceed at once to the scene of the conflict, if she intended to interfere upon the girl's behalf at all.

Another pause in the sounds above, again led Lady Ethel to hope that this disgusting scene was terminated.

Suddenly Mrs. Stibbington rattled out in a loud tone of abuse. This was followed by the sound of the girl's voice in supplication, but her appeals were only rewarded by the brutal woman with a quick succession of violent blows which caused the unhappy girl to shriek with pain.

Lady Ethel could bear it no longer.

She sprang up the stairs with the intention of putting a summary termination to the brutality of the vicious-minded Mrs. Stibbington.

With this purpose, she had just gained the top stair, when the sound of a third—and, to Lady Ethel, a strange—voice in Mrs. Stibbington's apartment, caused her to stop short.

"My dear Stella," said the voice of an old man, "don't be so violent—don't be——"

"Don't make a fool of yourself!" interrupted Mrs. Stibbington, brutally.

And then, as if to show how little she heeded the remonstrances, she delivered the shrinking Phillis a slap between the shoulders which would have made short work of an asthmatic subject.

"Consider, Stella, my dear," again urged the old man in trembling, querulous tones, "consider the——"

"Get away, you old idiot!" shrieked Mrs. Stibbington.

"But, my dear——"

"Stand away!" screamed the schoolmistress.

"Go, go—Phillis, go," said the old man, in alarm.

There was a scramble.

A tussle.

A blow!

A blow was struck upon some one which had brought them to the ground with a dull, deathly thud!

"Oh!" shrieked Phillis in accents of terror, "you have killed him!"

Lady Fane rushed forward, and dashed open the door.

The sight that she saw there caused the blood to curdle in her veins.

Stretched upon the floor, apparently dead, lay an old man bathed in blood, flowing from a fearful gash in his forehead.

His silvery hair was bedabbled with the gore, and the effect produced was ghastly in the extreme.

A long dressing-gown had fallen open, and the white shirt beneath was spotted with blood; and, altogether, this, the prominent figure in so terrible a picture, presented a most alarming appearance.

Phillis was kneeling by the side of the body, endeavouring to stanch the blood, which flowed in a copious stream from the wound.

Mrs. Stibbington stood leaning against the bed, staring vacantly in the direction of the wounded old man.

Her arms hung helplessly by her sides, and upon the floor, immediately beneath her right hand, lay a stone water-bottle, with which, doubtless, the fearful blow had been dealt.

CHAPTER XLIII.

THE MURDERER.

AN awful, death-like stillness reigned in the doctor's house, when his assistant, having raised the sash of the window, peeped cautiously in, and listened.

" I wonder whether he's gone to bed yet ?" the assistant muttered to himself.

He sat upon the window-sill as he thus reflected; and, feeling very curious upon the subject, for some reason or other best known to himself, he thought he would make sure of the fact before proceeding further.

With this end in view he left the window, and, sliding down to the ground, again retraced his steps for a short distance.

He came then to a spot from which he could obtain a view of the doctor's window—the window of the room where the mysterious medical man passed so many hours in the pursuit of his studies.

There was a faint light burning, and he recollected now that he had noticed it before; but the events of the night had so agitated and upset him, that it was with extreme difficulty he contrived to remember, from minute to minute, what had happened a minute before.

Yes, there burnt a light, but it was very faint indeed.

" It's only the fire, I think," said the assistant, doubtfully; " or he has hung something up across the blind."

He remained for several moments pondering upon this question, but unable to solve it.

" If he has gone to bed," he said, at last, "and the door's open——"

A gleam of pleasure lit up the young man's small, cunning eyes as he spoke.

After a while he added, though with much less confidence—

" The door's certain to be fastened. 'Catch a weazel napping.' "

He gave up the idea he had originally entertained—whatever that might have been—and again approached the window.

He climbed up as before, and, with the greatest caution, let himself into the house.

It was a curious, old-fashioned residence, and had, probably, once been in the possession of persons of consideration. Now it was half unfurnished; for the house was much too large for its present occupants. There were two staircases. One, however, was very rarely used; and it communicated with a dark and narrow, ill-paved alley at the back of the house by a heavily-ironed door, which, since the assistant recollected it, had always been kept locked and bolted, its rusty fastening festooned over by dusty cobwebs.

Through a window, leading into this staircase, the night-prowler had now admitted himself; and he meant to regain his own side of the house by a somewhat circuitous route, and by opening a door of communication, with the lock of which he had trifled upon a previous occasion.

On his way, however, he was obliged to pass by the door of Mr. Caul's laboratory; and the greatest caution was, therefore, necessary.

Although, as we have seen, this assistant had gained a certain small reputation in the neighbourhood, in consequence of his medical knowledge of drugs, he was, nevertheless, not yet in a position to be able to quarrel with that portion of his bread and butter which came from the doctor's table.

Although he contrived to make a nice little sum of money by his nefarious practices, he was reduced to great straits at the present moment for a little ready money.

The fact was, that he was a great profligate, and indulged in a variety of expensive and vicious pursuits, which effectually drained his purse.

He must, then, when the night's debauchery was over, eat large quantities of humble pie at the doctor's hands, and bide his time.

Ah! but his time would come.

He never doubted that he would have wealth before he died!

The only difficulty was to decide in what direction he should turn his eyes to look for it.

If he could only manage to get Caul into his power!

Ah! that would be a great triumph indeed! Then he could dictate terms.

Caul would make him a partner—open his purse-strings to him; for the young villain shared with the rest of the world—at least that portion of the world which interested itself in the doctor's affairs—the idea that Caul was a miser, and very rich.

The assistant, therefore, said to himself, if he could only find something out to his master's discredit, he might be able to hold a threat over him.

And he was determined that he would find something out. He would not rest until he had done so.

Although as yet he had decided nothing.

He had not, in spite of constant watchings, pryings, and spyings, been able to ascertain for a certainty that Caul bought bodies from the body-snatchers.

If he had done so, here would have been the commencement of the rascal's triumph; for such an act was at the time not only illegal, but extremely unpopular in consequence of the wholesale desecration of the grave-yards, which, for some time past, had been committed in the metropolis.

The assistant suspected his master, although he could prove nothing.

He was very anxious, too, to ascertain what was the nature of the doctor's nocturnal studies.

He was in his study to-night, and how employed?

Could this be a proper time for discovering his secrets?

The spy determined that he would make a venture, at any rate.

He very carefully took off his muddy boots, which were so wet and sticky that it was only with the greatest difficulty that the operation could be accomplished.

Then carrying the boots in one hand, he stole onwards upon tip-toe.

As he reached the door of the laboratory, however, a sharp exclamation, uttered in a loud shrill tone, close at hand, almost scared him out of his senses.

He tightly clutched his boots and staggered back.

" Wh—w—what was that ?" he asked himself.

He fancied somebody had called him by name.

He was on the point of answering "Yes." Luckily, though, he stopped himself just in time.

The voice was inside the laboratory.

Upon the other side of the door close to which he now stood there was a low murmur.

The terrified assistant's first idea was to save himself at once by flight.

But then came the reflection—something mysterious was going on in the doctor's room.

Now was the time to discover the secret.

Now or never.

The thought had no sooner passed through the spy's mind than there followed the determination of finding out the secret if it lay in his power.

He crept forward, therefore, and stooped before the door.

He brought his ear in close juxtaposition to the keyhole, and listened.

There were two voices within. One belonged to his master, Doctor Caul, the other to a stranger.

It was with some difficulty that at first he contrived to distinguish what each said.

After a while, however, the words more plainly reached his ears, for the speakers had grown somewhat excited—at least one of them—the stranger.

The doctor was tolerably calm, though his voice as he spoke showed that he was struggling with his rising wrath.

"Look here, Worwold," the spy heard him say, "what do you complain of?"

"What do I complain of?" the other repeated, surlily.

"Yes," said the doctor. "You seem to me to be trying to find something to object to; though what you suppose you will find is more than I can understand."

"It does not seem to me," grumbled the other, "that there is anything very unreasonable in my feeling dissatisfied."

"Why not?"

"Why not? Look at what I have had to suffer?"

"Suffer?"

"Yes, do you not call this suffering? See what a weary life I have led this fortnight past."

"Well?"

"Has it not been enough to drive me out of my senses being in this frightful place?"

"Why?"

"Why? Why need you ask? Do you suppose I am accustomed to the charnel-house company you delight in? Why, man, I have at times been well nigh scared out of my wits at the horrors of this horrible dissecting-room."

The doctor laughed contemptuously as he stirred the fire.

The other, seemingly talking to himself more than to his companion, continued without heeding the interruption.

"There have been times when the loneliness has been so awful that I thought I should have gone mad. When the silence has seemed to gather round about me, and crushed me with its weight. When the air has grown suffocatingly thick, and I have fancied that I have felt the hot breath of unseen demons upon my face—unseen, did I say? Great God! the blackest darkness has been made noonday ere now by the hellish glitter of their eyes."

The doctor remained silent for a moment or two, listening to the other's wild and excited talk.

Then answered with a sneer—

"Have the company of two or three dirty old skeletons and half-a-dozen bottles of preparations frightened you out of your wits? I thought you were a different sort of person, Worwold, upon my soul I did."

"I don't know exactly about being frightened," retorted the other man; "I am weary of playing at hide-and-seek here, I tell you."

"Weary?"

"Yes."

"And what do you propose doing?"

"I can do nothing, you know that well enough."

"Oh, ah! You can do nothing, can't you? I thought you were going to take the matter into your own hands."

"I did not say so."

"I thought you were going to propose a stroll out in the open streets. What a sensation you would create if you met any of your old creditors; they'd take you for your own ghost."

"I don't wish to go out before the proper time," said Worwold, savagely. "I wish you to hurry your movements, that's all."

"Perhaps you think that I am wasting time purposely?"

"I don't know what you're doing."

"Perhaps you think you could have got some one else to do the business much better?"

"I don't know that I couldn't."

"Suppose you do, then?"

There was a pause, in which the spy heard the poker rattling against the bars, and heard the fall of the ashes.

He could not see the faces of either speaker from the keyhole, but he could easily imagine that both were distorted by the rage and hate which smouldered in their breasts like pent-up flames waiting for a loophole to burst forth with forked tongues.

"I don't wish to find any one else, but I wish the matter to be brought to an end," said Worwold, at last breaking a long silence. "I should have thought it might have been done by now. I cannot understand how it is that there should have been such a delay in receiving the money. The insurance office does not generally take so long a time to transact its business."

"I have already told you there have been delays and procrastinations."

"But I understood you to say that they have admitted the policy effected upon my life to be perfectly correct, and the other documents all regular."

"They did at first, and afterwards disputed them. I have told you that, also, I believe?"

"I don't know, I am sure," grumbled Worwold; "you have it all your own way, at any rate. I am nothing but a tool in your hands."

"You are right," cried the doctor, suddenly, in a loud, fierce voice; "you are in my power, and if you wish me to act fairly by you, don't provoke me, or you shall never touch a halfpenny of the money."

"What! you threaten me?"

"I do."

"You villain! I believe you are cheating me now. But do not fancy that you will do it with impunity. No, curse you! If I hang for it myself, you shall hang with me, and——"

"Silence, you idiot! or you'll not live long enough to take your trial. All the world thinks you to be dead, as it is, and why should I not——"

"What, wretch! you—you would take my life?"

"Why not? Why should I parley terms with you? The money will then all be mine. Why should I preserve your life, only to keep living an accomplice for whom I have no longer any use? No! by——"

There was the sound of some heavy piece of furniture overthrown.

Then a stifled cry for help.

Then a heavy fall upon the ground.

The spy could see nothing of what passed within the room, but as he strained his ears eagerly, he could hear that a fierce and deadly struggle was going on.

A wrestle for life or death, in which the two combatants strove their utmost for the mastery.

He heard their panting breath.

He heard low, savage exclamations from time to time hissed forth betwixt their clenched teeth.

Then the sounds of distress. One was tightly held in the other's grasp, and was struggling in vain to free himself from the deadly grip set upon his throat.

Then there was a wailing cry for mercy.

A cry unheeded by the murderer.

Then the sound of a heavy thud.

A sickening, smashing, cracking sound which must have been caused by a death-dealing blow upon the skull of one of the two combatants.

Again and again it was repeated, each time seeming to grow, to the terrified listener, more and more horrible.

And then there followed a death-like silence.

The spy stood rooted to the spot.

He could not, to have saved his life, have dragged himself away, although he feared every moment that the survivor, from the fearful struggle that had taken place, would burst forth upon him.

The silence, however, in another moment was broken by a faint, rustling sound. Then by a long-drawn breath.

The spy, still listening, heard a sound as though a heavy body was being dragged along the floor, and then there was a chopping noise which the assistant could not comprehend the meaning of.

But he feared to remain longer. He fancied that he heard footsteps approaching the door, and he fled precipitately.

He went upstairs with great strides. He slipped his foot, and stumbled.

Then, scrambling to his feet again, stood with bated breath listening in terror for the murderer's approach.

Yes; he fancied that he could hear a creaking upon the stairs behind him.

He rushed wildly on now, never pausing to look back or to listen.

He reached his own room, sprang in, and double-locked the door.

Then, clutching a poker from the fireplace, stood panting in expectation of an attack.

But no one came.

After a long and awful pause, in which he seemed to live an age, he determined upon lighting his candle and undressing himself to go to bed.

He found a match, and with some difficulty ignited it, for his hands trembled violently.

Then pausing to listen every moment, he very slowly divested himself of his apparel.

It was a weary process, so drenched were his clothes, and so difficult to unbutton in the state to which the rain had reduced them.

But at last he had finished, and having put on some dry linen, crept into bed.

He, however, placed the poker upon a chair by the bedside, and left the candle burning, to provide against accidents.

He sat up in bed and listened for awhile. All was perfectly still.

He had not been heard, and he thought he would go to sleep.

Go to sleep! Why, the idea was absurd. How could he possibly hope to sleep after what he had heard?

How could he lie there in the house where this horrible murder had been committed without taking any steps in the matter?

Besides, he did not even know which of the two was the successful combatant.

How could he rest in this uncertainty? It was not to be endured.

He rose again, and dressed himself in another suit of clothes.

Then, grasping the poker, he stole out upon the landing.

All was perfectly still.

He hesitated whether or not he should take the candle, and after a brief hesitation, determined that he would do so.

But, then, he thought it would be best to allow some time to elapse before he set out upon a voyage of discovery. He came back, therefore, to his bedroom, and sat down and waited.

He passed more than an hour thus, thinking that day would soon break, for he was ignorant of the time.

There seemed to be no hope of this, however; and when he set forth the night was still pitchy dark, and the rain, as heretofore, descending heavily and rattling against the window-panes with what seemed to him a ghostly music.

This time he decided not to carry the poker, but a large clasp-knife, which he put loosely into his pocket; so that it might be ready for use when the occasion offered.

He set out, then, upon his voyage of discovery, proceeding with great care and caution.

He bent his steps towards his master's bed-room, and listened at the door.

There was a light burning within.

The spy tried the door-handle very cautiously. The door was locked.

He listened; and, after a time, he fancied he heard the sound of regular breathing.

He was not a little astonished at this. Was it possible that he had gone to sleep?

At any rate, the spy thought he could with safety venture down into the laboratory, for he had once before opened the door, though he had been frightened at the time, and had then been compelled to beat a retreat before he had crossed the threshold.

Upon this occasion he was more fortunate.

The door was not locked he discovered, much to his astonishment; and he was not, therefore, obliged to force back the bolt, as he had intended to do, by inserting the blade of the knife he carried.

He entered now very stealthily.

He trembled violently—his heart beat fast—and he pierced the inner darkness with eager eyes.

After a moment's pause, he crept in, and closed the door, looking around him in silent terror.

Close to his feet there was a dark stain upon the ground. He held down the light.

It was blood!

He advanced a few steps further on, gazing round him, but without being able to see anything of that which he expected to find—the body of the victim!

He held the candle on high, so that he could see into all the corners.

In one there was a bundle. The spy crept towards it, and gently raised the cloth.

But the body was not there.

Where was it?

He opened one of the cupboard doors, and started back with a half-suppressed scream, at the sight of a skeleton's white, glistening bones!

But he rapidly recovered himself, and continued his tour of inspection.

Two more cupboards did he open, but they neither of them contained the object of his search. He looked about upon the floor, expecting to find some blood spots which might guide him towards the spot where the victim's corpse had been concealed.

But, although there was blood in several places, no discovery followed.

There was a smaller inner room, however, before the entrance of which hung a curtain.

It must be here!

He raised the curtain, and peered in.

Some object which he could not distinguish in the partial darkness lay upon a sink.

He trembled like a leaf as he approached, raising the candle high in the air.

But at that moment he heard the door of the outer room open and shut.

Then a heavy foot fell upon the floor.

The spy threw a despairing glance around, searching for some place of concealment.

Then hastily extinguished the light.

Then clutched his knife.

CHAPTER XLIV.

MR. JAGGERS' MYSTERIOUS LODGER.

MR. JAGGERS had a lodger.

Mr. Jaggers's neighbourhood was unlike the generality

of neighbourhoods in one respect. That being, nobody paid any particular attention to anybody else's business.

Everybody, in fact, was rather shy of being noticed down in Mr. Jaggers's neighbourhood. They had strange hours of business. They went out and came in with large and unaccountable bundles, and they did not wish to be objects of public attention.

Mr. Jaggers had his peculiarities like the rest, and did strange things, but nobody took any particular notice of his actions.

He had a lodger, about whom there was a good deal of mystery; but nobody endeavoured to unravel it. We, however, with the reader's kind permission, will endeavour to find out of what the mystery consisted.

This lodger, then, came at dead of night in a hackney coach, and was helped into the house by Mr. Jaggers.

He was evidently suffering, and when once safe indoors he was put to-bed; a bed had been prepared for him, so he was evidently expected.

Here for a whole fortnight he lay supine, hovering 'twixt life and death. The tender cares of Mrs. Jaggers alone saving his life, for the supply of medical attendance was of such an extremely irregular character that it would not be said to do him much good, if any.

He lay here in a wretched little attic, damp and close, which Jaggers spoke of as the "upstairs room," and tossed wearily upon his bed of sickness.

He was so ill at one time that he required constant watching, and as Mr. Jaggers had something else to do, and Mrs. Jaggers had her household duties to attend to, Mr. Jaggers's impish son was elected nurse, and fulfilled the duties assigned to him in a fashion which, if satisfactory to himself, afforded the unfortunate patient a very small amount of gratification.

The young gentleman being of a somewhat restless turn, naturally enough found the time spent in the sick chamber to hang somewhat heavily upon his hands.

He had a natural taste for music, and practised upon a penny whistle in a way which was perfectly agonizing to the unfortunate sufferer, who tried in vain to sleep through the noise.

It was rather cold and cheerless the young gentleman soon found out, and so, to keep himself warm, he borrowed one of the patient's blankets, in which he wrapped his own legs.

Seeming to think that the patient might feel rather dull, the youthful nurse proposed to read up to him, and read passages from the "Newgate Calendar" in a loud tone of voice, and he occasionally volunteered a little harmony.

Being, though young in years, an adept in the vices of his elders, the Imp smoked and drank enormously.

He selected from choice the very strongest and rankest shag tobacco, and the vilest quality of gin.

This being his taste, there was no occasion for him to purchase spirits and tobacco himself, as his fond parent's stock was exactly of the desired quality.

The Imp was of an ingenious turn, and had found the time and opportunity to take an impression in wax of the keyhole of the cupboard where his papa kept the articles in question.

Having done this, it was easy enough for the Imp to procure a key, which, with a little filing, would fit the lock; and he helped himself pretty freely whenever he wanted anything that was locked up.

Now, Mr. Jaggers, senior, had no notion that his hopeful child possessed a duplicate key. His idea was that Mrs. Jaggers was partial to strong drink, and had a weakness for a quiet pipe.

Therefore, when he missed his spirits, he straightway accused Mrs. J. of being drunk.

Mrs. J. had at all times an uncertain and wandering gait. She had fits of giddiness which arose from weakness, and she staggered as she walked, and sometimes clutched at what came in her way to save herself from falling.

"Drunk again," was a favourite observation of Mr. Jaggers.

"I'll sober you in half a crack," he used to say. And the way he managed it was to take off his hob-nailed boots and fling them at the lady's head.

"And there's nothing like it," said Mr. Jaggers, "for taking the bounce out of her."

The Imp then indulged freely in strong drinks, and smoked to such an extent that the unhappy patient was well-nigh suffocated.

Sometimes he woke up with a violent fit of coughing which seemed to tear him to pieces. The Imp said this was affectation.

Sometimes he gasped for breath, and in a weak, wailing tone, begged for a drink of water.

"Try some gin," suggested Master Jaggers.

"Water—water!" moaned the invalid.

"Ain't got none," said the Imp, lighting a fresh pipe.

"Water. For God's sake, water!"

"Oh, Rabbidge, what do you want with water?"

The patient moaned pitifully, and Master Jaggers lit another pipe.

"Water indeed," said he. "Pack of humbug! What's the good of water, I should like to know? I never have anything to say to it myself—leastways not neat."

And, indeed, to look at the Imp's grinning face it was not difficult to believe this to be the case.

But the unhappy patient was of a different opinion.

He moaned and groaned and feebly licked his dry parched lips, murmuring as before.

"Water, water! For God's sake, water!"

"Oh, be blowed!" growled the Imp, getting out of patience. But as the invalid persisted, Master Jaggers administered a small quantity of the desired fluid, which he found in an almost stagnant state, in an apology for a washhand-basin standing in one corner of the room.

Refreshed by this horrible mixture of dust and tadpoles, the invalid was quiet for a time.

Not for long, though. Soon again he was wearily tossing to and fro.

Throughout the livelong night he lay thus suffering a martyrdom, while the Imp smoked his horrible rank pipes until he fell asleep, when he snored like thunder.

A truly miserable time of it did this poor sufferer have in Mr. Jaggers's establishment.

Surely, if he had known what was in store for him, he would never have sought shelter beneath such an inhospitable roof.

Perhaps, though, he was glad of any resting-place; for Mr. Jaggers said that he was a soft-hearted fool for having taken the invalid in; but then was it possible that Mr. Jaggers could be soft-hearted if he made nothing by it?

It is a difficult matter to settle, and time alone will show us.

One night Mr. Jaggers sat smoking his pipe in the kitchen. The Imp was not attending to the patient, who, wonderful to relate, had not died during his nursing; but was growing gradually better. The Imp was seated in the chimney-corner. Mrs. Jaggers had her usual place, the most uncomfortable one in the room—a corner where there was a strong draught.

Mr. Jaggers was dull and thoughtful. Mrs. Jaggers was nodding. The Imp relieved the silence by whistling shrilly, and beating time with the heels of his boots.

"Drop it!" cried Mr. J., in a warning voice.

The Imp whistled louder.

"Drop it, I tell you!"

"Eh?"

"Drop it!"

"Drop what?"

"You'll find out what, if I have any humbug with you, my fine fellow," said the fond father, picking up the poker.

"I aint a harming you, am I?" asked the Imp.

"Yes, you are," replied Mr. Jaggers. "Hold your infernal din."

"Yah! you aint got no more notion of music nor a pig."

"I'll get better music than that out of you, my cricket, if you don't hold your jaw. Here's a tuning-key that 'll bring out the harmony, I'll bet a penny."

Mr. Jaggers shook the poker at his infant as he spoke; and, though the Imp laughed derisively, he nevertheless deemed it advisable to be quiet.

He left off whistling, therefore, and drummed his heels against the door of the oven, upon which he was seated.

Mr. Jaggers fretted for a time.

"Drop it!" he roared, presently.

The Imp was quiet, and Mr. Jaggers went on with his pipe.

A minute or two afterwards the devil's tattoo again commenced.

Mr. Jaggers raised his hand, and took an aim at his child's head.

The child, however, was rather too sharp for him. As he saw the blow coming, he suddenly ducked, as Shallabalah does when Punch hits at him with his stick.

Mr. Jaggers, therefore, instead of hitting his son, hit his own fingers a very smart rap against the wall.

The pain threw him into a passion. He aimed again, and again missed.

The second time the Imp bobbed, and his papa hit the wall.

Then Jaggers senior was furious.

He caught up the poker, and gave chase.

Jaggers junior dodged his parent round the table. Jaggers senior hit wildly in the air, pretty well jerking his arm out of the socket by so doing.

Round and round they went, the father growing more and more wrathful as his wind grew shorter. At last he thrust the table up against the wall, and obliged his hopeful son to come forth.

But now the Imp kept his father off with a chair, and, watching his opportunity, flung it, with all his force, at his parent's head.

Then ran for the door.

The blow knocked Mr. Jaggers backwards upon the top of poor Mrs. J., who always, upon all occasions, came in for some ill-usage, and to whom Mr. Jaggers now administered a kick, asking, "why the deuce she couldn't get out of the way."

After which he rushed out in pursuit of his son.

But this young gentleman, who had fled in the direction of the back-yard, contrived to place an unexpected barrier in the way.

This was a wooden form, which usually stood outside the back door. The Imp, as he went out, stopped and pulled it across the doorway.

Then Jaggers senior, rushing pell-mell forth from the light into the darkness, never saw the obstacle, but, coming full crash against it, went sprawling out upon the stones.

He picked himself up again, swearing horribly, and rubbing his bones, half of which, at the first shock, he thought he had broken.

As, however, he was not seriously injured, he set out in pursuit of the Imp, vowing deadly vengeance.

To vow vengeance, however, was an easier matter than to accomplish it.

The first difficulty was to catch the wrong-doer.

"First catch your hare," as Mrs. Glass says.

Mr. Jaggers rushed into the middle of the yard, but then he came to a stand-still, and listened.

He could hear nothing of his hopeful progeny.

It was pitch dark, and impossible to see him.

What was Mr. Jaggers to do, then? Decidedly he did not like the idea of giving up the chase so early.

"Where are you?" he roared.

But he did not get any answer, even if he expected one.

"I'll half-flay you if you don't give yourself up at once."

But there was no reply.

"It's no use thinking you're going to get off, you young warmint, 'cause, sooner or later, I shall cop you, and when I do——"

"Cock-a-doodle-do!" sounded shrilly from a remote corner.

Mr. Jaggers glared savagely into the darkness.

He very strongly suspected that it was his hopeful child who thus derided him, but still, as he kept poultry in a shed over upon that side of the yard, he could not be quite certain.

He, however, made a rush in the direction from which the sound emanated, with no other result than the extremely unsatisfactory one of knocking his head against the wall.

Then again he was compelled to come to a stand-still, and listen.

The Imp was not slow in discovering what were his parent's tactics.

He, therefore, picked up a piece of slate which lay at his feet, and sent it scudding across the yard.

Mr. Jaggers thought this noise was caused by his son's endeavouring to escape in that direction.

He made another rush, and found no one.

Again and again did the Imp so deceive him, varying the amusement by flinging stones in the direction where he heard his parent's voice.

For full an hour did this game continue, but at length, finding that the pursuit was quite hopeless, he went, cursing, indoors, vowing, however, that as soon as he laid his hand upon his son again, he would more than half-murder him.

He was in anything but an amiable temper, as may be supposed, when he again took his place by the fire-side and resumed his pipe.

He had not caught the Imp, and he had had all his trouble for nothing. He had hurt nobody but himself.

This sort of thing would not do at any price. He must have his revenge upon something or somebody.

He kicked a stool to the other side of the room.

He savagely stirred the fire.

He flung a lump of coal at his dog.

None of these acts, however, satisfied his craving for vengeance, and he was at a loss what to do next, when suddenly he thought of Mrs. Jaggers.

He turned towards the corner where he had left her sitting, but she was there no longer.

"What had become of her?" Mr. Jaggers asked himself.

Then he paused to reflect and to listen.

"It can't be," he said.

He listened again.

"She'd never have the cheek."

Once more he listened.

"She has!" he cried, suddenly. "By Gosh! I'll warm her, though."

For the third time, however, he listened, so as to make quite certain this time, though there could be no mistake, he thought.

"I hope I may be scragged," said Mr. Jaggers, "if that woman hasn't had the cheek to go to bed."

Now, although, as a general rule, the unfortunate female in question dare scarcely say her head was her own, she was not in the habit of asking permission to go to bed.

This was quite a new idea. Indeed, generally, Mr. Jaggers professed himself to be only too glad to get rid of her.

This time, though, as we have seen, he wanted to vent his spite upon some one.

A PRIEST'S CONFESSION.

Mrs. Jaggers was generally the scapegoat in these cases, and it did not signify much whether or not she had done anything to deserve ill-usage.

If anything went wrong, it was Mr. Jaggers's custom to give her a kick.

He did not care a —— (button, shall we say?) whether or not she had done anything wrong.

"Curse her, she will do if she hasn't," was his remark, as he raised his highlow in the air with savage intent.

"Hallo, you there !" he called up the stairs upon this occasion.

Mrs. Jaggers heard him, and trembled.

"Don't you hear ?" roared Jaggers.

"Do you want me?" she asked.

"Who the blazes should I want ?" he responded. Then roared like thunder, "Come down, will you ?"

"I'm in bed, John."

"I don't care where you are, come down—or I'll come and fetch you."

Poor Mrs. J. !

She got out of bed shivering, and crept downstairs.

"What is it, John ?"

"What is it ? Curse you, how long do you suppose I'm to be kept waiting ?"

"I am very sorry."

"It's a lie !"

"A—what ?"

"It's a lie, I say ; are you deaf ?"

"I am sure it isn't a lie, John."

"Don't contradict me, or I'll knock your teeth out."

"I beg your pardon, John."

"Don't jaw, now."

"What am I to do for you ?"

"Go out and get some gin."

"I am afraid the public-house is shut."

"Go and see."

"It—it is past one."

"Go and see, or I'll make you."

The unhappy victim peeped out into the bleak night without.

It had begun to rain heavily.

She knew very well that there was not the least good in going, and that she would be drenched to the skin, and yet she was obliged to go, or the ruffian would well nigh have murdered her.

Mr. Jaggers sat down to his pipe and waited. After a lapse of time, which he filled up with curses, his wife returned.

"What's made you so long?"

"I have been knocking at the door."

"What door?"

"The public-house door."

"Why, you fool?"

"I was trying to get in."

"Were they shut, then?"

"Yes."

"Well, where's the gin?"

"I didn't get it."

"Didn't get it, you fool?"

"They wouldn't open the door."

"And yet you were all this cursed time?"

"I—I—tried all I could."

"Curse you, take that, and try and be wise for the future!"

And Mr. Jaggers administered one of his gentle reproofs in the shape of a cuff on the side of the head, which made the victim see half-a-dozen candles in the place of the solitary one burning on the chimney-piece, stuck into a black bottle.

"You'll have another if you don't hold your jaw," said Mr. Jaggers, as his wife rubbed her head and groaned; "so look out."

She thought it advisable to be quiet, and consequently rubbed her head without groaning for the future.

Mr. Jaggers went on with his pipe, and about a quarter of an hour passed thus.

Then Mrs. Jaggers asked in a very humble tone whether he would allow her to go to bed.

"No!" roared Jaggers, and went on smoking.

Mrs. Jaggers sat down meekly in her usual place—the corner where the strong draught was, and resigned herself to her fate.

Mr. Jaggers smoked his pipe and enjoyed himself. It did not very much matter to him whether or not anybody else was uncomfortable.

He had a half-bottle of brandy in the house, which he had kept for medicinal purposes, and he determined upon drinking this, as he could get no other.

He therefore ordered his wife to fetch it.

"And stir your stumps," said he.

She did as desired.

"Anything else?" she asked.

"Not at present. P'raps I may want something presently."

"Yes, John."

"You can wait," said he; "you've nothing else to do."

It was in vain to complain, and so Mrs. Jaggers waited.

After a long time though, she was quite worn out, and fell asleep.

Then she snorted, and caught herself in the act of falling.

Mr. Jaggers swore horribly, and threw some coals at her.

"Don't do that," said he.

"No, John."

Another hour passed. Mrs. Jaggers struggled desperately to keep her eyes open.

"Are you going to set up much longer, John?" she asked.

"Yes," said he, "I'm going out at four, and it aint worth while going to bed before that."

The unhappy woman groaned.

"If you don't want me any more, John, I should very much like to go to bed."

"I do want you; stop where you are."

"Yes, John."

Presently Mr. Jaggers broke the silence, by saying—

"There's a newspaper in the next room; just get it, will you?"

Mrs. Jaggers obeyed.

"Read it up," said he.

"Read it?"

"Don't repeat every word I say, you idiot!" roared Jaggers; "but do as you're bid."

"My eyes are so bad, John."

"I don't care for your eyes; do your best, or I'll warm you."

There was no help for it, so Mrs. Jaggers resolved to do her best, and opened the paper.

"What shall I read?"

"Something interesting. Is there any police?"

"Yes, John; here's a pickpocket case."

"Oh, blow that. What else is there?"

"A murder."

"Ah! that's the sort."

"Murder of a wife."

"Oh, is that all? I don't care about hearing that."

"I don't know what to read," said Mrs. Jaggers, after a pause. "There isn't anything that I can see except——"

"Well!"

"Except—oh!—"

"What's the matter now, stupid?"

But Mrs. Jaggers made no reply.

For some reason or other she became very much confused.

Mr. Jaggers eyed her savagely. What did she mean? It was quite sufficient for him that she refused to speak to make him determined that she should.

"D'ye want your head knocked off?" he asked, kindly.

"What shall I read to you?" inquired Mrs. Jaggers, without replying to his question.

"Read what it was made you bawl out."

"It was nothing."

"Eh?"

"It was nothing, Jaggers."

"Oh, it was nothing, wasn't it?" growled the ruffian. "Come here, will you?"

But the woman at first did not move.

"Come here!" he roared.

The woman silently rose and slowly approached him.

Then Jaggers grasped her by the wrist.

"Will you tell me what it was?" he asked.

"It was nothing."

"Will you tell me?"

"It was nothing."

"It's a lie!"

"Jaggers!"

"It's a lie, I say!"

He clenched his fist as he spoke, and placed it close to the shrinking woman's face.

She trembled slightly, but said nothing.

"Don't you play the fool with me, now, woman," he cried, "or by God you'll repent it. What are you dodging me for? What was it in the paper? What was it, I ask you? Will you tell me?"

His rage was terrific. The veins swelled up black and strong upon his forehead; his eyes gleamed like those of a savage beast.

"Will you tell me?"

"No," she answered.

"You wont?"

"No."

She was white as death, but yet calm.

Her eyes were fixed upon the villain's face, and there was in them something of helpless defiance such as a little child's face might have expressed in the presence of it's torturer, which, in the case of one less brutish, would have surely moved the heart to pity.

There was no pity, though, in the composition of this scoundrel.

He drew back his fist, and took a steady aim at her.

"Will you tell me?" he asked again.

"No."

"You wont?"

"No."

"Take that, then, curse you! You've only got yourself to thank for it."

As he spoke, he struck her a fearful blow in the face, which in a moment covered it with blood.

The unhappy woman uttered a faint groan.

Then reeled a step or two and fell senseless upon the floor.

Jaggers stood by scowling at her with his fist still clenched.

Then roared out,—

"Get up, will you, or you'll get worse?"

But as the poor creature did not respond to this kind invitation, Mr. Jaggers roared louder,—

"Damn you! none of your shamming."

Shamming or not, she seemed to lie very motionless and still.

Mr. Jaggers thought so presently, and grew a little bit alarmed.

"I didn't mean to kill the idiot," he said. "If I had I should have done it in two or three turns."

He stooped down over his prostrate wife, and laid his hand upon her heart.

Perhaps you may think that a pang of remorse disturbed him—that he was sorry for what he had done.

You wrong him. No such notion entered his head. He was only a little frightened.

Therefore, when he found out that her heart did beat, he got up and gave her a kick.

"She's always giving me some trouble, that woman is," said Mr. Jaggers. "If I wasn't a tender-hearted fool I should have knocked her head off long ago, but kindness is thrown away upon some people."

He had no idea of being jocular when he spoke, and he probably thought that he behaved quite well enough, as a rule, to this unhappy woman.

He paid no further attention to her, however, at present, because he had other—and, to his idea, more important—matters to think about.

What was this she had seen in the newspaper?

Something there must have been, or she would never have been so agitated. Jaggers was burning with curiosity. He would have given a good deal to have found out, but there was a difficulty in the way.

Perhaps the reader will not very easily guess. This was simply that Mr. Jaggers could not read.

He picked up the newspaper and turned it over and over.

He held it sideways and upside-down. He looked at it, in fact, from all points of the compass, but, for the life of him, could not make out where lay the mystery.

The longer he puzzled at it the more savage he grew.

Once or twice he cast a despairing glance towards the insensible form of his wife.

He had half a mind to try and restore her to consciousness, and again endeavour to wrest the truth from her.

But he had little hopes of making her obey him.

"She's as obstinate as a pig," he muttered. "There's no wringing anything out of her when she makes her mind up. Curse her!"

As a rule, Mrs. Jaggers was passive and docile enough, in all conscience. But, as Mr. Jaggers observed, there were times when she appeared to pluck up a spirit.

Then, when an idea got into her head, nothing would turn her.

She would have suffered the tortures of the rack—you might have burnt her at the stake—but yet she would have been resolute in her determination.

The ruffian, therefore, concluded that, by arousing her, he would gain nothing.

"Infernal fools," said he, turning over the newspaper, "I wonder what they must go inventing such humbugging stuff as this for, that nobody can make head or tail of."

He was in a dreadful fix, for he did not know whom to appeal to. He did not like to go to any of his pals in the neighbourhood who might have enlightened him, because he did not know what could be the nature of the announcement.

Perhaps he might point out to them something that they would take advantage of at his expense.

"It can't be a reward for me, I should think," he said, after some reflection; "because she'd have told me that. What the deuce can it be?"

Presently he recollected the Imp, who had had a few pennyworth's of education at a parish school, and had also learnt a thing or two when temporarily incarcerated for some small felonies.

Jaggers, therefore, determined to make another effort to find his hopeful son.

He first of all went up into the Imp's bedroom, and into the lodger's room, to look for him, but without success; and then, lighting a lantern, sallied out into the yard to bring him in.

As he could see him nowhere, he began to roar out his name; but there was no response.

"He's gone to sleep," thought Jaggers.

And he roared louder.

But there was no reply.

"He's afraid I shall hide him, I suppose," thought Jaggers; and he then called out, in a coaxing tone—

"I want you to do something for me, and I shall give you a shilling, if you look sharp."

The only reply to this offer was, however, an ironical laugh.

"Oh, you are awake, are you?" roared Jaggers.

"Rayther," replied his offspring, derisively.

Jaggers looked round and listened. He could not for the life of him make out where the Imp was hidden.

He ground his teeth with rage, but deemed it wise to put on a friendly aspect, until his object was gained.

"Come on, now," he said, in as soothing a tone as he could. "Don't give me no more trouble, I shant hurt you."

"He! he! he!"

"Don't be a fool, I say. Haven't I gave you my promise?"

"Ho! ho! ho!"

"If I wanted to thrash you, you young duffer, I could easy enough do it another time."

"Ha! ha! ha!"

"You wont come, then, wont you?"

"Not if I knows it."

"By heavens, I'll pretty near skin you when you do turn up, though."

"When you ketches me, you mean!"

"Ketch you. Curse you, you spawn of the old 'un, I'll ketch you soon enough."

The Imp made no reply to this threat, and Jaggers, who had worked himself up into a state of demoniacal rage, seized up a heavy piece of wood, garnished with rusty nails, and went in search of him, vowing deadly vengeance.

"I'll have your life this time, you young hell-pup!" he muttered between his clenched teeth, and then the hunt began.

All round the yard, behind the sheds, up and down, round and round.

The Imp always contrived to evade his would-be captor's grasp.

Jaggers rushed after him, swearing fearful oaths.

More than once he had heavy falls, and as he picked himself up again, and rubbed his aching bones, he could hear the Imp laughing hysterically.

Bruised and sore, and awfully savage, the ruffian still pursued him, howling out his vows of vengeance.

In his tumbles he somehow contrived to preserve the lantern he carried from injury; but this was no particular advantage to him, for two reasons.

The first reason was, that it did not aid him very much in his search, as it only illuminated a very narrow space around him, and threw no light upon the hiding-places of the fugitive. In the second, it afforded the unnatural son an opportunity of taking aim at his parent with pieces of slate and quarter brickbats, which every now and then came rattling about Mr. Jaggers's ears, giving that gentleman some most unpleasant knocks.

The chase continued for more than an hour, and grew more and more exciting; but at last Mr. Jaggers's wind would hold out no longer, and he was compelled to give up.

Then, bruised and bleeding, he limped back into the house, swearing horrible oaths; while the Imp sent a jeering laugh and a brickbat after him—wishing him better luck next time.

Meanwhile, within the house a strange scene had been occurring.

CHAPTER XLV.

MRS. JAGGERS TO THE RESCUE.

NOT long after Jaggers had left the room in search of the Imp, his unhappy wife heaved a sigh and opened her eyes.

Then slowly and painfully she raised herself from the floor.

She rose to her feet, but was giddy and weak from loss of blood, and staggering like a drunken person, would have fallen to the ground had she not clutched to the wall for support.

Wiping away the blood which disfigured her face, she went in search of some cold water, and taking a few sips, felt somewhat revived.

But when she came to look at herself in the glass, she burst into a violent fit of sobbing.

How cruelly he had beaten her.

Her face was cut and swollen. Beneath one of her eyes was a deep purple stain.

As she stood there, looking with a kind of shrinking terror at her own distorted image, the recollection of a life of cruelty and ill-usage rushed back upon her mind.

How often had this cowardly ruffian beaten and ill-treated her?

From the very first, when brutal and mercenary parents had forced her into the hateful marriage, she had done nought else but suffer.

Was there no release—no hope?

As she reflected thus, wild thoughts of revenge flitted through her disordered mind, mingled with incoherent schemes of flight—utterly impracticable.

But suddenly the recollection of a duty which she had to perform flashed upon her.

She passed her hand across her forehead, as though by the action she strove to collect her scattered thoughts, and at the same time her heavy eyes rolled slowly round, taking in the particulars of the apartment.

She glanced at a peg behind the door where Jaggers was in the habit of hanging up the hat and coat which he usually wore when he went out. The coat and hat still hung there.

"Where has he gone?" she asked herself. "He can't be far off. Where is the newspaper? It is gone also. Has he got it? Ah! I see it all. He has gone to ask some of his associates to read it to him. They will find the advertisement, and all will be lost."

All these thoughts passed rapidly through her brain, as she stood gazing round the room. She was by no means too quick either of motion or thought, but upon this occasion her faculties seemed to be brighter than usual.

She remained for a short time pondering upon the course of action which it would be best for her to pursue.

Then, suddenly deciding, she took a candle in her hand, and rapidly ascended the stairs towards the room occupied by the mysterious lodger.

CHAPTER XLVI.

THE FIGHT IN THE DARK.

IN a miserable attic, from the slanting roof of which in some places the plaster had fallen in great patches, leaving bare the unsightly laths, beneath which a fanciful person might have likened to the ribs of a decomposing corpse stripped of its blackened flesh, lay a man upon a truckle bed. He was decidedly handsome, although his face was deadly pale, and his hair and beard ragged and neglected.

He had had a severe and dangerous illness, and was now slowly recovering. In a few more days he might have been able to go out again; but hitherto he had, at most, managed to crawl downstairs, and sun himself in an apology for an easy-chair upon the doorstep.

As the woman held high the light and looked down at the face of the sleeper, she muttered softly to herself—

"Poor fellow! I hardly think he's well enough to move yet. But it must be done."

In fact, there was not only a pressing necessity for him to be moved, but that as little delay as possible should take place before steps were taken.

She stooped down over the sleeper then, and laying her hand upon his shoulder, shook him gently.

He was not, however, very easily to be aroused.

"Jack! Jack!" she said, in a loud whisper. "Wake up, Jack Chinnery! Wake up!"

Our old friend of the nunnery—for such it was—opened his eyes with alarm, and made as though he would have sprung into a sitting posture.

At the same time he opened his mouth, as though he would have uttered some exclamation.

She, however, laid her hand upon his lips, and motioned to him eagerly to be silent.

"Make no noise," she said. "Your life depends upon your silence."

"What has happened?" he asked, in a whisper.

"Nothing, as yet; but there is great danger. I was upon the very eve of betraying you, but, thank God, I stopped myself in time—just in time."

The sick man looked at her in wonder. He could not understand the meaning of the words she uttered, and he felt half-inclined to believe that her mind was wandering.

"Are you strong enough to get up and walk?" she asked, eagerly.

"I hardly know," he said.

"But you must try. Your life depends upon it."

"How so?"

"Oh, do not ask me. Tell me, are you strong enough to walk?"

"I think I am," said the sick man, doubtfully, "but not very far."

"Oh dear, oh dear, but you must get right away. You must not remain in the neighbourhood, or my husband—hush! don't you hear him below?"

"I hear some one."

"It is he! He has come back!"

They listened silently for some moments, and could hear heavy footsteps crossing the floor, then ascending the creaking stairs.

And now a new terror seized upon the unfortunate woman.

"God help me if he finds me here!" she cried. "What can I do? Where can I hide?"

There was a closet in one corner of the room, and she sprang towards it.

Then followed a moment of intense anxiety and terror lest she should not be able to open the door, for it was sometimes kept locked.

Upon this occasion it at first stuck fast, but after a violent, though brief struggle, she dragged it open.

Then she blew out the light, and crept into her hiding-place.

Scarcely had she done so when Jaggers entered.

Chinnery, meanwhile, lay back passively in his bed, wondering what on earth was the meaning of all this excitement and mystery upon Mrs. Jaggers's part.

The Resurrection man opened wide the door, and shading his eyes threw the reflection of the light he carried upon the sick man's face.

"You are awake then?" said Jaggers.

"Yes," replied the other. "Why?"

"I didn't want to disturb you if you hadn't been, that's all. But I want you to do us a turn if you will."

"What is that?"

"To read me something in the newspaper."

"What! at this time of night?"

"I've a particular reason for it."

"Oh, very well. Let me look at the paper. What do you want read?"

Jaggers handed him the newspaper, and took a seat himself by the bedside.

"What do you want me to read?" asked Chinnery again.

But Mr. Jaggers hesitated, for he hardly knew what to say.

"Run your eye down it," said he, after a little consideration, "and call out what its all about."

"That'll be rather slow work, I'm afraid?"

"No, no; just say what the things are called, I'll soon tell you when you come to anything."

Chinnery, in consequence of what the woman had said, felt no small curiosity himself upon the matter, or he would probably have refused to comply with this rather unreasonable request, for it certainly was unreasonable, as you must allow, when you reflect that it was made between the hours of one and two in the morning, to an invalid just awakened from a sound slumber.

Chinnery, however, after rubbing his eyes, and yawning, applied himself to his task, and read aloud the headings of the articles as he came to them, while Jaggers, seated by his side, watched him eagerly, and to the best of his ability endeavoured to see that his companion skipped nothing in the paper.

"Money Market," read Jack, "Mining Market, Stock Exchange, Closing Prices of Stocks and Shares. Is that your sort?"

"No, blow that," responded Jaggers. "There can't be nothing in that part about me."

"Not much, I should think. Here's an account of a charity sermon, would you like me to read it to you?"

"Not if I know it."

"Here's Police Intelligence, that's your sort, I should say."

"I don't know. Just run it down. I think it's a little further on."

Chinnery mumbled through a portion of each case, then turned over that side of the paper.

In like way he went through the contents of the journal, but could find nothing which appeared to be of any interest to the Resurrection man, who growled forth exclamations of disgust and disappointment as he proceeded.

At length the last page was reached, and yet nothing had been discovered.

"There seems to be nothing that will suit you," said Chinnery. "Here are some advertisements, and that is all. Do you want to buy a horse, or a house? Here's a public-house for sale, and—ah!"

"What's that?" cried Jaggers, suddenly. "Read it up."

"Read what up?" asked the other.

"What you were reading."

"What, about the public-house?"

"The public be hanged. Wasn't there something else?"

"No." What should there be?"

Jaggers glared at him savagely, and the sick man fixedly returned his gaze.

The Resurrection man, though, felt convinced that he was being cheated. He felt certain that the other had seen something.

He could not help noticing a momentary flash upon Chinnery's cheek.

He was evidently agitated. And what was the cause of it?

One thing was very sure, Jaggers thought, and that was, that what Chinnery had read in the paper must have related to himself, or he would not have been so moved by it. What was it, then?"

"Look here, Chinnery," said Jaggers, after a brief pause. "Don't let us play at cross purposes. There's something there that you want to keep dark; and, by heavens, I know what it is.

"What is it, then?" retorted Chinnery.

"Both you and my wife were taken aback when first you saw it. I can't read myself; but do you suppose I am altogether a fool on that account? Any one with half a grain of sense in their head would see the whole business as plain as a pikestaff, without waiting for a lot of these scribbling fools to explain it to him."

"I don't understand you," replied Chinnery, coldly.

"I'll tell you what it is, then, by God!" roared the ruffian, with a sudden fury. "There's something between you and my idiot of a wife, and they've put it in the paper."

For a moment Jack Chinnery stared at the man in blank astonishment.

His first impulse was to burst out laughing, for the idea of there being, as Jaggers had expressed it, something between him and that poor attenuated fragment of humanity, Mr. J.'s good lady—by which he of course meant passages of a tender nature—was rather too ridiculous.

Indeed, if the reader will kindly turn to Mr. Browne's picture, upon page 41, he will probably allow that Mrs. Jaggers, in her best moments, could scarcely be the sort of person to inspire any one with notions of intrigue.

She was extremely angular, and rather ancient; Mr. Chinnery, too, had in his time been highly successful in his love affairs. It was, if anything, rather insulting to attribute such a mean conquest to him, even if there was the ghost of a shadow of a reason for so doing, which, however, there was not.

Chinnery, then, I say, was at first inclined to laugh, but then came rather an unpleasant reflection.

For a moment he had forgotten a little circumstance which now flashed upon his mind with unpleasant distinctness.

This was that Mrs. Jaggers was at that moment concealed in the room.

If the ruffianly husband were to discover her, what then?

"You talk like a fool," Jack Chinnery retorted, angrily. "I don't know what you would be driving at."

"Oh, you don't, don't you?" sneered Jaggers.

"No."

"Look here, now; don't you fancy that you can play with me as if I was no better than a puppet. Let's try and talk reasonable."

"I wish you would."

"Well, then, there's something in that paper that you don't want me to see. There's something it's your interest to keep dark."

"What makes you think so?"

"I'm certain of it. I saw it in your face at the first glance."

"Indeed."

"Yes. Don't try to deny it. By heavens, I tell you I know it."

"Well?"

"Well, in that case I ask you to read it to me."

"I shall do nothing of the sort."

"You wont."

"Certainly not."

"What end do you suppose you gain by refusing? I can get some one else to read it."

"Well?"

"If I do that, it will be letting some one else into the secret."

"Suppose that is to your disadvantage, how then?"

"Do you mean to say that what's in the paper will injure me as well, if others know it?"

"I said nothing of the kind. I told you I should give you no information."

Jaggers ground his teeth with rage.

"Curse you!" he cried, savagely. "I'll make you suffer for this, or I'll know why."

Jack Chinnery made no reply, however, and allowed the Resurrectionist to fret and fume without paying the least attention to him.

Presently the latter sprang to his feet.

"We shall see," he cried. "I wont rest to-night, until I have found out what this infernal mystery is."

He moved to the door as he spoke, and paused upon the threshold to look round at the sick man; but Chinnery made no sign, and left the room.

Chinnery listened to him as he cursed his way downstairs, rustling the newspaper which he had taken with him as he went.

Mr. Jaggers was certainly in a quandary, and the obstacles which everybody seemed resolved to throw in his way exasperated him well-nigh beyond endurance.

"Curse that vagabond!" he said, grinding his teeth. "I only hope I ever get the chance of hanging him. Curse that woman, I wish I'd killed her! Curse that whelp! as soon as ever I do manage to get hold of him, I'll twist his ugly young head off, I will by —— ! I wonder whether I could coax him in somehow to read this newspaper."

He had half a mind to go and make another trial, but the recollection of his previous failures had such a dispiriting effect when he came to reflect upon them, that he thought he must give the matter up as a bad job.

What Chinnery had said about the newspaper paragraph being likely to affect him personally, made the Resurrection man rather cautious about taking any steps towards making it public.

Nothing, therefore, remained but to be as patient as possible until next day, when, probably, by fair means or foul, he would be able to persuade one of his amiable family to read the newspaper for him.

He had determined not to go to bed, because he had a job on at a very early hour, and had no fancy for early rising. He therefore curled himself up upon a sofa in his best parlour, and, covering himself over with a couple of great-coats, thought he would take a little nap.

Now, as Mrs. Jaggers was usually kept in total ignorance of her husband's doings, she was not aware that he had any work upon hand, and had supposed, when he determined upon sitting up all night, that it was only one of his many amiable weaknesses, most of which resulted in her especial discomfiture.

She, therefore, when Jaggers had gone downstairs, crept forth from her place of concealment, and in a terrified whisper besought Chinnery to save himself.

"You must lose no time," she said.

"It wont be safe to stir yet, will it?"

"It is not safe to remain."

"But he is downstairs."

"He is most likely going to sleep. Sometimes he sleeps before the fire, or, perhaps he has gone out. I don't hear him."

"Perhaps he has gone to get some one to read the paper for him."

"Ah! If he only asks the boy, you are lost. Did you read it yourself?"

"Yes. I read an advertisement offering a reward for my apprehension."

"Offering a hundred pounds."

"A large sum, is it not? I thought when I read it——"

"Yes; you thought that Jaggers could not resist it."

"I hardly liked to trust him."

"Nor I. That was why we had a quarrel to-night. I knew if I told him that he would be eager to get hold of the blood-money."

"I don't doubt him. He would never have given me shelter at all, if it had not been that he thought that he could make something out of me; he would never have allowed me to lie here at his expense as long as he has."

"No; he is revengeful and treacherous, as you know full well. And I think, now that, perhaps, ——"

"That, perhaps, what?"

"Oh, dear! oh, dear! that, perhaps, it was my fault in crying out, when I saw the advertisement. But, oh! indeed, it came upon me so suddenly, I could not possibly help it."

"You are no more to blame than I am, I am sure," said Chinnery. "If I hadn't been a fool I should never have let him see by my face that I was interested. But about my escape——"

"Yes, we are wasting valuable time, I am afraid."

"Will you see, then, if the coast is clear, and I will get dressed?"

"Yes; be as quiet as you can, though. I will steal out on to the stairs and listen."

She was absent for some short time, and presently returned.

"Well?" he whispered.

"Hush! for the world make no noise."

"Where is he?"

"He has come upstairs, and gone to bed."

"Gone to bed?"

"Yes."

"He must have come very quietly."

"He is there, though; I hear him snoring."

"What? asleep already?"

"Yes; and he has locked the door."

"Now, then, is the time for action."

"Yes. Are you dressed?"

"I am all dressed, except my boots; but I can't find them!"

"Oh, I forgot that! What shall we do?"

"What is the matter now?"

"Your boots are downstairs in the parlour. Shall I go down and fetch them?"

"No, no; it will only lose time. I can get them easily myself while you keep watch; but stay——"

"What is the matter?"

"What a selfish wretch you must think me!"

"Why so?"

"Do you suppose that I will consent to leave you here?"

"Why not?"

"What, to be murdered by that villain?"

"What else is to become of me? Where else could I go for a home?"

Chinnery, as she spoke, felt a pang of remorse.

Here was a woman who had done all in her power to help him—who was risking her life for him; and awhile ago he had been thinking of her with ridicule and contempt.

He ought, and he did, feel ashamed of himself.

She was certainly a poor fragment—a bony, skinny, ill-shapen creature; but the most beautiful heroine in the world could not have behaved more nobly than she had done.

"Come away with me," he said, "and I will endeavour to find you a home in some quiet place, where you will no longer be molested by the villain who has made your life a misery ever since you knew him. Come—what do you say?"

But when she had pondered for a few moments over this proposition, she replied, with a sigh—

"No; I cannot go. I have chosen my life. I must remain here to the end.

"What! remain to be murdered?"

"Yes; if that is to be my fate. I must stay here; but you must go."

"No, no; not without you."

"But I will not leave the house."

"I will stay, then, also."

They argued the matter for some little time. But Chinnery, finding at last that it was quite hopeless to try and persuade this poor creature to escape, thought that he himself had better no longer delay, or else he also might lose the opportunity which had been afforded him.

The plan of action was soon arranged.

The wife was to keep watch on the stairs by the door of Jaggers's bedroom.

Chinnery was to creep down, and having had full instructions respecting the place where he would find his boots, it was not supposed that he would have much difficulty in obtaining them.

Then to let himself out by the house door was not a very arduous task, for there was nothing very elaborate in the way of fastenings, and the door was only secured by a single bolt at the bottom.

Having once more vainly striven to induce Jaggers's wife to make her escape with him, Jack began his descent of the stairs, guiding himself with one hand against the wall.

Arrived in the kitchen below, into which the stairs led, his first care was to find the house door, that he might draw the bolt and have everything prepared in case of accident.

Having done this, his next care was to get his boots.

He was pretty well acquainted with the position of the parlour door, and it was lucky that he was so, because the kitchen was pitch dark, and he had to grope his way blindly towards it.

He turned the handle very gently, and opened the door; then crept in and felt for the sofa, underneath which his boots had been placed.

Unfortunately for the success of the scheme of escape, Mrs. Jaggers had made a great mistake.

It was not Jaggers whom she had heard snoring in the bedroom upstairs, but Jaggers's hopeful son.

The fact was, that the Imp had climbed in at the bedroom window, knowing that his father was not going to bed; but had nevertheless taken the precaution of locking the door, for fear that his father might, by some unlucky chance, take it into his head to come upstairs and surprise him.

When Chinnery entered the parlour, he heard no snoring; for although when asleep Mr. Jaggers snored horribly, at this present time he was not asleep, and was purposely breathing as lightly as possible.

The fact was, he had heard some movement in the kitchen without, in spite of the caution that Jack had used to avoid making any noise.

The idea at once occurred to him that it was the Imp who had entered the house.

Then Jaggers sat up and listened.

"He'll go to bed directly, perhaps," thought he, "then I'll creep up after him and wring his young neck."

But while he was thus reflecting with a fiendish chuckle, he heard a slight noise at the handle of the door.

Then the door slowly opened, and Jack Chinnery crept into the room.

It was pitch dark.

Mr. Jaggers in vain strained his eyes, but could not perceive the faintest outline of the intruder's form.

However, he felt convinced that it was the Imp.

"I wonder what he wants."

The figure crept nearer to him in the dark, and Jaggers made ready for a spring.

With a grim smile he clenched his fist.

"When he comes a little nearer," thought the ruffian to himself, "I'll send his head on one side."

Poor Jack, meanwhile, all unconscious of what was in store for him, went down upon his hands and knees, and groped about the floor.

He very soon found the sofa, and, feeling under it as directed, got out his boots.

They were a good way under, and he leant his hand upon the sofa to steady himself while he felt for them.

In doing so, he placed his hand upon Jaggers's breast.

The bodysnatcher no sooner felt his touch, though, than he sprang into an upright posture, and let out a terrific blow, which, had Jack's head been in the way, would certainly have materially damaged it.

Such, however, was not the case; for Jack's head was, at the moment, under the sofa.

The Resurrectionist, therefore, having hit with such strength, in consequence lost his balance, and came heavily to the ground, rolling Chinnery over as he went.

Chinnery then disengaging himself as rapidly as he could, and clutching his boots, made for the door.

On the threshold Jaggers seized him, and a terrific struggle ensued.

It did not, of course, require long for the Resurrection man to discover that he had been mistaken in the person with whom he had to deal; and as quickly did he determine how to act.

Chinnery he was resolved should not escape.

He, therefore, clutched him by the collar, and exerting all his strength dragged him towards the stairs.

But weak as he was from the effects of his recent illness, Jack yet contrived to defeat his object.

In vain the ruffian tugged and hauled.

In vain he strove with violent jerks to loosen his hold of the side of the door.

Jack still held his ground.

And then the robber lost all patience, and gave way to the most diabolical rage.

"Curse you!" he roared, savagely; "you shall go one way or the other."

Then suddenly ceasing to pull, he easily enough contrived to drive Jack before him downwards.

In this way he forced his antagonist to the door of a cellar opening from the kitchen.

There was a steep flight of stone steps leading from this door down into the depths below.

"If you wont come up, you shall go down," said the ruffian; and Chinnery easily understood what was to be his destination.

He, however, determined to do all in his power to avoid it.

He made no resistance, though, until he reached the door, for he had another plan.

He allowed himself to be dragged along.

He then remained passively in the Resurrection man's hands; the latter undid the door.

But then, of a sudden, he exerted all the strength that he possessed, and wrenched himself from the ruffian's grasp.

At the same moment he sank down upon the ground, and grasped Jaggers's knees.

He was an adept in wrestling, and, weak as he was, had not yet entirely lost all the science.

In an instant Jaggers was raised in the air.

In the next, before he had time to make an effort to save himself, he was flying, head first, down the steps into the dark cellar beyond.

He came down with a tremendous crash.

Then lay perfectly motionless.

Jack Chinnery stood for a moment, panting for breath.

Then listened anxiously for some sound from below.

But all was still.

"He's either stunned, or he's broken his neck," thought Chinnery.

He did not, to tell truth, care very much which it was; but making for the outer door, flung it open so as to admit a little light.

The darkness without was less than that within, and so he contrived to obtain a faint notion of the state of things.

He bolted the door of the cellar, to provide against the evil results which might accrue from Jaggers's accidental recovery; then looked for his boots, which had been flung down in the late struggle.

Having found them with a little trouble, he put them on and left the house.

He walked rapidly away from the door, across the garden, and along the road, and was soon a hundred yards or more from the scene of his encounter with the Resurrection man.

But having gone thus far, the artificial strength which had hitherto supported him began to depart.

He was seized suddenly with a faintness and sickness, which compelled him to pause and lean against some palings for support.

He recovered himself, however, after a time, and crept on again.

But again a faintness seized upon him.

He reeled on a few steps further.

Then sank down in a swoon.

How long he lay thus, he had no means of judging. Yet he fancied it could not have been a long time, for when he opened his eyes, it was still dark.

He made an effort to raise himself, thinking he was still lying upon the cold ground; but, to his astonishment, he found that he was in bed.

Where was he, then?

He lay passively for a few moments endeavouring to collect his scattered thoughts.

Ah, he thought he had been recaptured and taken back to Jaggers's attic.

He spread out his hands in the dark to feel the sides of the bed.

But the objects that met his touch filled him with astonishment.

Instead of the rough woodwork that he was accustomed to, there was smooth, polished wood.

Instead of the coarse and dirty coverlet with which his bed had hitherto been covered, he felt soft quilted satin.

While he was yet wondering what could be the meaning of this astonishing change in his circumstances, the door opened, and a beautiful woman, bearing in her hand a small lamp, and clad in a dishabille which displayed the matchless symmetry of her lovely form, entered his bed-chamber.

CHAPTER XLVII.
THE UNDERGROUND MYSTERY.

CHINNERY'S first impulse was to raise himself upon his elbow and contemplate this beautiful and unlooked-for vision.

But another thought occurred to him.

It would be better to feign sleep, for he heard other footsteps approaching, and doubtless if he remained quiet he might hear something that would explain how matters stood.

In this he was right.

He closed his eyes, therefore, after casting one glance towards the door, and seeing that the other persons who had entered were two more women dressed very much like the first, and enjoying an equal share of personal attractions.

The last of Chinnery's mysterious visitors having carefully closed the door, they all three approached his couch upon tiptoe.

And then a whispered conversation commenced, every word of which Jack listened to with greedy ears.

"What do you think of him?" one asked.

"He is certainly not bad looking."

"Bad looking, indeed," said the third; "he is far from that."

"Why not acknowledge at once that he is extremely handsome?"

"I will acknowledge it if it is any gratification to you."

"It must to a certain extent be a gratification to all of us, I suppose."

"Most decidedly so."

"Of course it is. We would not have had a common-looking wretch."

"And will you allow," asked the first speaker, "that some credit is due to me for my selection?"

"Most decidedly."

"Not, however, that I can take all the credit to myself, either."

"How so?"

"Because, as I told you, it was in a great measure owing to my wonderful good fortune that I found him."

"You have told us that already; but now tell us, if you please, how it all happened."

"To be sure I will. But first of all, it was necessary that you should see the bird himself before you heard how he was caught."

"Most decidedly. There would not have been any merit in the affair if it had been an ugly bird, of course."

"I knew you would think so, and that was why I would not tell you first."

"You were quite right; and now I am dying with impatience to hear the story."

"And I also," cried the third speaker.

Jack Chinnery felt inclined to say "And I also, too," but he did not deem such a course of conduct very judicious.

Hitherto, all that had been said was of such a mysterious character he could make neither head nor tail of the conversation.

He listened eagerly, therefore, for an explanation of the riddle, and was not a little afraid lest the ladies should leave the room without enlightening him.

But such was not the case.

"Last night, then," said the first speaker, "or rather early this morning, when I was coming home, I was walking along in a dreamy state, for I was unable to get a cab, and somehow I missed my way. I got into a dreadfully wild part of the town, evidently inhabited by the most dreadful people, and I was not a little afraid, from the few specimens I from time to time encountered perambulating the streets, that I should presently be eased of my watch and purse. For a very long while I did not meet any one of whom I should have liked to have asked any questions, and therefore the further I went the more I kept losing my way. At last, I found myself in a most dreary spot, and well-nigh dead with fatigue."

A SCENE AT THE NUNNERY.

"Well?" said one of the other ladies, seeing that her companion paused, "it is beginning to grow more interesting."

"You would have found it not only interesting, but rather exciting, if you had been in my place," retorted the first speaker. "Nevertheless, I was so dead beat that I could not, for the life of me, contrive to keep my eyes open."

"You went to sleep in the street?"

"Well, I did not exactly go to sleep, but I walked along with my eyes shut, and I believe that I dozed a little by the way."

"It is a wonder you did not run against a wall," said the others, laughing; "or run into the arms of one of the natives."

"I did neither, though," replied the first speaker. "On the contrary, I ran right on to the top of the handsome stranger whom you see before you."

"Well?"

"Well?"

"He lay upon his back on the pathway, and at first I supposed him to be intoxicated."

"So should I have done."

"My first notion, therefore, was to give him a pretty wide berth, and if, when I came towards him at first, I had had my eyes open, I certainly should have done so."

"Now, however, you did not do so."

"No, no. I came so close to him before I was aware of his presence that I was able to see his face. The first thing I saw was that he was handsome."

"I suppose that is the first thing any woman would have seen."

"To be sure it was. I then saw that he looked very ill."

"And interesting?"

"And interesting, certainly. It struck me, too, that there was a certain air of superiority about him. I said to myself, therefore, 'This is either a poor and unfortunate man or a vagabond; if he is a vagabond, I wonder whether he is a poor one.' By the appearance of his face I came to the conclusion that he must recently have suffered great privations. You can see for yourself how careworn and haggard he looks."

"He does look as if he had not lately had many good dinners."

"This is the sort of person we are in want of, I thought; but, then, I wanted some particulars respecting him."

"To be sure. To pick up an insensible man in the street, who is unable to answer any questions as to who he is, and where he comes from, and to bring him away for the purpose of placing in his hands a secret which would be the ruin of all of us, does seem rather a hazardous proceeding."

"And one which I do not think I am quite capable of," replied the first speaker, rather angrily.

"No, no," said the third of the ladies, interposing. "It is very unjust of you to talk in that way; but you are only jealous because your own efforts to obtain some one suited for our purpose have failed so signally."

"I am not jealous at all!" the lady who at first had interrupted here eagerly exclaimed; "and I am very sorry, I am sure, to offend you."

"We must not quarrel about the matter, in any case."

"No, no;" it is to all our interests that our secrets are kept. Let us all work happily together, if we can."

"I see no earthly reason why we should not do so."

"To continue your story, then."

"Very well, as I was saying, I wanted some particulars respecting this man whom I had found lying insensible in the street."

"What did you do?"

"I thought, of course, that I could not apply to a better quarter for the information I desired than the man's pockets."

"The best place of all."

"I searched them, and found——"

"What?"

"In the first place, that he had not got a single farthing of money about him. In the second place, I found his name."

"His card?"

"Well, not exactly."

"What was it, then?"

"What do you suppose was the next likely place to find it?"

"On a letter?"

"No."

"On his pocket-handkerchief?"

"No."

"Inside his hat?"

"No."

"A cigar-case, perhaps?"

"No; nothing half as common as that."

"I found in his pocket an official document of a very important nature."

"An official document?"

"Yes."

"What on earth was it?"

"A ticket of leave."

"A ticket of leave!" echoed the two others.

"Yes," replied the first speaker; "nothing more nor less. Not a sailor's ticket of leave, mind, nor a soldier's. I found that our friend here was a returned convict."

"And therefore the very person suited to our purpose."

"Not a bad one in this case, at any rate, for he is evidently not the ordinary kind of ruffian."

"No; that is easily to be seen."

"Besides, I will tell you what I thought."

"What was that?"

"That he had been, in all probability, trying hard to get work to do, and had failed. You know what difficulty there is for one of these men to obtain honest employment."

"Nobody will believe in their repentance."

"No one will give them any work if they know it; and if the police find that by any chance they have contrived to creep into a situation, even if they are going on well, and striving to their utmost to redeem the past, it is the officer's invariable practice to seek out their master and put him on his guard respecting the character of the person in his employ."

"It is certainly a hard fate, and yet those people who pretend to have the most sympathy for the convict would be the last persons to employ him themselves."

"That's always the way with all your philanthropists. But about our friend."

"I found that his name was John Chinnery."

"John Chinnery! It is not a very pretty name."

"It may be a false one, for what we know. In any case, it matters little to us whether he has a name at all; and for the work upon which he is to be employed——"

The speaker suddenly paused, for a movement from one of her companions caused her to glance towards the bed.

"Is he awake?"

"I thought he moved."

"Hush!"

It was true that Chinnery had half-opened his eyes. The conversation was of such an extremely personal nature that it was with considerable difficulty that he contrived to keep his countenance.

Cautioned, however, that his movement had been perceived, he lay perfectly motionless, hoping that they would continue the conversation.

In this, however, he was doomed to disappointment, for the three ladies left the room after a few more words.

"He is waking up," one said.

"We had better go, then."

"If he is well enough to-morrow we will explain the matter to him."

"Then, whether he agrees or not—" began one of the speakers. But she concluded the sentence in so low a tone that Chinnery could not possibly catch the words she uttered.

"That is very certain," replied one of the others, also speaking in a whisper, but with an angry emphasis, which made her words distinctly audible. "In either case, he dies when we have no further use for him."

The door closed upon their retreating forms almost the next moment after these words were uttered, leaving Chinnery to digest their meaning at his leisure.

His sensations, when he repeated them over to himself, can be readily imagined to have been anything but of a satisfactory character.

"I thought at first," he said to himself, "that I had dropped in for rather a good thing; but now I'm by no means so sure of it."

Indeed, the prospect looked anything but inviting.

To die in either case! A pretty prospect, surely; and what might either of the cases be.

"And what on earth do they want me for?" Jack said to himself. "If it's to make love to them, I shant so much mind; but otherwise, what the deuce can it be? And even if it's the love-making, hang me, if ever I heard of such sanguinary-minded young ladies. They tell tales about some Roman Empress, who used to make very short work of her lovers as soon as she was tired of them; and I've heard of an African Queen, too, who used to eat 'em after they had made love to her; but to think of these young ladies in London carrying on such extraordinary tricks, I could not have believed it to be possible."

It was a very puzzling affair, certainly, and though he racked his brain for a long while, hoping to find a solution to the mystery, he could not possibly do so.

The only way to hope to learn anything of the company into which he had fallen was by hearing them talk among themselves, and of this there appeared to be very little chance just at present.

As he lay pondering, he began to feel rather thirsty, and also a little peckish.

"I wonder whether they are going to starve me," he thought; and as the time slowly rolled away and nobody came to help him, he began to grow very impatient.

At last his thirst became so great that he could no longer endure it,

He crawled out of bed, therefore, and went in search of a water-bottle, supposing it probable that there was such an article in the room.

When the mysterious ladies had first entered the apartment, he had had his eyes open so short a time, that he had not been able to take any observation of its inner arrangement.

His first proceeding now was to try the room door. He found it locked.

He then felt his way about, and was not long before he discovered the water-bottle of which he was in search.

He took a refreshing draught from it, and went back to bed again.

Then, with the best grace he could, he made up his mind to wait and see what would happen next.

He waited a very long while, though, and found the darkness and silence which enveloped him extremely fatiguing.

At length, worn out, he fell asleep, and slumbered long and deeply.

When he again awoke, he found himself very much refreshed, and feeling much stronger than he had done before.

He found this time a lamp burning in the room, and raising his head found one of the ladies whom he had previously seen sitting by the bedside.

Hearing him move, she drew back the curtains to look at him.

"Are you better now?" she asked.

"Yes," he replied; "much better. But to whom do I owe all this kindness?"

"Do not speak of that," she replied. "Make yourself easy; you are among friends."

"I must be among very good friends," said Chinnery, "for them to treat me so well—so much better than I deserve, or than I could ever have hoped to be treated by strangers."

"You're not entirely a stranger to us, John Chinnery," replied the lady, in a way which the robber supposed was intended to convince him that he was to a certain extent in the power of his fair hostess.

As he did not wish to show them that he already knew something more about them than they supposed, he thought it best to display surprise at the extent of her knowledge.

"What! do you know my name?" he said.

"I know that, and that you are a returned convict; but there are other matters upon which I desire to question you. Do you think you are strong enough to talk for a short time?"

"I am quite strong enough, and shall be happy to give you any information about myself that it may be worth your while to desire to be acquainted with."

The lady made no immediate reply to these professions of Mr. Jack Chinnery, which, perhaps, might not have struck her as being quite as sincere as she could have desired. They were, however, sufficiently so to cause her to continue, after a brief pause, with an assurance that if he for his part only acted fairly, he would have little or nothing to complain of in the treatment he received at their hands.

"In the first place," she said, "I want to inquire what you have been doing since you returned from transportation."

Chinnery hesitated; something convinced him that it would be best not to affect too great a show of virtue, as he rather fancied that such would not be much of a recommendation in his new place.

After a little hesitation, therefore, he said—"What do you suppose a man could do who has come back from such a place, and without a character to recommend him? Nobody would be particularly anxious for my services, as you may suppose. There is not much chance for a returned convict in a civilized country."

"I am aware of all that," interrupted his companion, somewhat curtly. "I asked you what you had been doing."

"I have been doing nothing."

"How have you lived?"

"With some of my old companions."

"You have been thieving, I suppose?"

"No, I have not; but I should have done if I had had the chance, I dare say.",

"Have you tried to get any honest work?"

"No, I shouldn't be able to get it if I did."

"Then you would enter again upon a life which could not fail to lead you to destruction?"

"What else could I do? I have no choice."

"Perhaps I can offer you one, if you would like to accept of it."

"I should be happy to accept of anything in my present circumstances," said Chinnery; "and I am sure that the conditions of your offer will not be very hard ones."

"I don't know how you can be sure of anything of the kind."

"I only judge by your kindness hitherto."

"This, however, is a world in which few people do any kindness without a selfish motive," said the lady, somewhat mockingly.

She was certainly very beautiful; but her expression at this moment Mr. Chinnery did not admire.

The sentiment which she expressed was anything but an agreeable one under the circumstances.

And Jack Chinnery felt pretty certain that he had fallen into the power of some one who could, if she chose, be as cruel as was ever Roman Empress or African Queen.

"Will you name the conditions?"

"I can do so in a few words," she said.

Then after a brief pause continued—

"For the performance of certain work you will have everything that you desire in the way of board and lodging. The most sumptuous apartments, the most dainty food, and most costly wines."

"So far I am agreeable," said Jack Chinnery, with a smile.

"The work that you will have to do is by no means laborious, and there is not sufficient to occupy many hours during the day."

"That's not bad either," said Chinnery.

"No, I do not think that when you hear more about it you will consider this to be a very bad place."

"As far as you have gone I cannot help thinking it a very good one.

"But," said he, "I should very much like to know what is the disagreeable part."

"Do you mean to say that you want to know what the work is?"

"Yes."

"You must be employed, then, in coining money."

Chinnery opened his eyes rather widely at the first surprise, but yet he was not as astonished as he might have been; he did not suppose that it was any lawful calling which was to occupy him.

If it had been, what occasion was there for all the mystery that had been employed in the matter?

He remained so long silent, however, that the lady appeared to think that he was dissatisfied. She therefore questioned him.

"What is the matter?" she asked. "Do you decline the offer?"

"Not I," said Chinnery; "but I cannot understand why you should require my services, because you might so easily coin yourselves, and then your secret would be your own."

"Our secret will still be our own."

"What after having told it me?"

"Have we been wrong in placing reliance in you—in telling you our secret?"

"It is safe enough with me," replied Chinnery; "but yet you might have made a bad choice in a confidant."

"We considered the matter well before I spoke to you. Before entering upon your work, too, you must swear to keep our secret."

"I will, most willingly."

"And you think you are not likely to grow soon weary of your employment?"

"I don't think it likely."

"It is surely better to be thus provided for than to live from hand to mouth, and to be sent from gaol to gaol as you are retaken after each fresh offence, until in the end you perish miserably upon the gallows. Here you will, at least, lead a safe and easy life."

"Why safe?"

"Because there is not the faintest possible chance of detection. The base coin can never by any possible accident be traced from the persons employed in uttering it to you who will be employed in its manufacture."

"However, I can stand the risk. I like the sound of the place, and I am willing to try."

"You are willing to join us?"

"Most certainly."

"When?"

"As soon as ever you like. The sooner the better, as far as I am concerned."

"You are hardly well enough yet to leave your bed, but to-morrow I do not see why you should not begin work."

"I should like to do so," said Chinnery.

And here the lady rose, with the intention of leaving the room. At the door, however, Chinnery called to her—

"I beg your pardon, madam," he said.

"What is it?"

"I hope you wont think me rude if I make an inquiry."

"What do you want to know?"

"I only wished to ask, what was done—what became —that is, who had my place before me?"

"The person who had it has it still."

"Oh!" said Chinnery; and here the conversation ended.

The lady then left the room, and left Mr. Jack to his reflections.

He certainly was rather puzzled when he tried to make out what was the nature of the establishment of which he had become an inmate. He ventured out of bed again, and tried the door, which, as before, he found to be locked.

The lamp had been left this time, which was a decided improvement, and enabled him to have a good look at his surroundings.

He found, then, that the room was very beautifully furnished, and that the paintings upon the walls were of the highest style of art. A soft carpet covered the floor, and the sofas and chairs were covered by purple velvet, with trimmings of gold.

The whole appointments were luxurious in the extreme, and must have belonged to some house of great pretensions; but still there was a close and choking air about the place, which, at first, he found a difficulty in accounting for.

All at once it struck him, though, that there could be no ventilation.

When this thought came into his head, he naturally enough looked after the window.

Where was it?

He turned from side to side in amazement; there were no signs of a casement.

In one corner of the room there was a heavy damask curtain, but this could not cover a window.

As, however, he felt some curiosity to know what it did cover, he approached it, and drew it on one side. Then there was disclosed to his view a narrow door, iron clad, which, however, was destitute of lock or bolt.

He thought, perhaps, that it might have been left open; but when he tried, he found it fast.

Continuing his examination of the apartment, he presently found in the place of the somewhat ragged suit of clothes which he had worn when, at last, he recollected to have worn any at all, a handsome velvet coat, and other garments to match, all of the best quality, and evidently the work of a first-rate tailor.

"They are meant for me, I suppose," said Chinnery; "and, by Jove!" he continued, as he proceeded to try them on, "they couldn't have fitted much better if I had sat to Poole for them myself."

When he had put on the clothes, he admired himself for some time in a pier-glass; and, at last, he sat down, and burst out laughing.

"I don't know who the deuce it is whose hands I've fallen into," said Mr. Jack; "but they certainly mean to do the thing handsome while they are about it."

Presently, however, rather an unpleasant thought occurred to him.

"There must be something deuced unpleasant about the affair, when I come to know it," he said, "though, as yet everything seems the colour of the rose; but presently I expect I shall know what's what."

He felt as if he had had enough bed for one time, and so determined to sit up for awhile.

There was plenty to amuse him in the volumes that he found upon the well-filled book-shelf, and when he made another tour of inspection, he found that there were some very choice cigars in a cupboard, and that in fact nothing was wanting to make him comfortable.

There was, nevertheless, an uncertainty about the life in store for him, which made him rather uncomfortable in spite of his efforts to be at his ease.

"Hang it all," he said, after he had been thinking some time in silence, "they never be going to murder me. I can hardly believe that they could be guilty of such atrocities; nevertheless, it is very evident that they do pretty well what they like. Upon my soul, I half wish I was out of it, and if I only saw my way clear to a bolt."

This he did not do, though, and he was, therefore, compelled to make his mind easy, and wait until such information as he desired was afforded him by those in whose power it was to give it.

What bothered him more than anything else was to know what time it was.

As it was pitch dark there were no means of judging.

"It certainly does not feel like the middle of the night," said he; "but I have had such a precious lot of bed lately, it seems to me that I could sit up for ever."

While he was thinking thus, the door was opened and a tray thrust in—then shut-to again, before he could ascertain who brought it.

When he went to examine the contents of the tray, he, however, had no cause to grumble about being neglected.

The most beautiful little spring chicken, a small decanter of astonishingly fine sherry, and some trifle in the way of pastry, which was extremely delicate.

Mr. Chinnery disposed of these viands without much difficulty, and again congratulated himself upon his good fortune; he passed away the remainder of the day (for such he supposed it to be) very comfortably, and nobody coming to see him, retired to bed, when he had tired himself out, though not before he had once more congratulated himself upon the fine quarters he had dropped into.

In the morning some one knocked at the door and inquired if he was ready for breakfast. Then as Mr. Chinnery professed himself ready for anything, another tray was pushed in through the door. Jack got up without further waste of time, and found such an astonishing repast in the chocolate and coffee, Yorkshire pie, and other matters of that sort, that Mr. Jack's admiration burst all bounds.

"One oughtn't to grumble at being murdered after a good bout of this sort of thing," said he; "it's worth ten years of anybody's life to spend a month with such prog as this."

He passed the day very much as he had done the preceding one, for he had an enormous appetite after his illness, and as long as he got plenty to eat he could do with very little other amusement.

Towards the evening one of the mysterious ladies called upon him, and asked whether he was ready to go to work. He was smoking a cigar at the time; he put it down, and expressed himself willing.

"Come with me, then," she said.

As she spoke, she drew on one side the curtain, and knocked once upon the door. Jack for the moment felt a little uncomfortable, but he was not very easily daunted, and followed her without hesitation. The lady led the way through the aperture to a place which was only dimly lighted beyond, and Chinnery followed. When they had proceeded, however, for a few yards, his leader motioned to him to go first, and he did so, although he had half a suspicion that he would presently go head over heels down some pit-hole such as he had fallen into at the convent.

Such was not, however, going to be his fate. When they had walked on up a gloomy passage, they came to a door similar to that through which they had previously passed.

Chinnery walked on for a yard or two, and then, not hearing his companion's footsteps behind him, he stopped and turned.

Bang went the door.

Jack Chinnery was alone, and in the dark.

"What a fool I was," he muttered, "to be let into a trap like this."

He stood silently listening. Not a sound could he hear, nor could he imagine what on earth had become of his fair companion.

"What the deuce do they want to do with me?" he thought. "I'm hanged if I don't think they are cannibals."

While he was thinking thus, he suddenly found himself enveloped in a blaze of light.

A lamp in the ceiling had been lit, and the wonders of his prison-house were at once disclosed to him.

He found himself in a spacious apartment, with a vaulted roof.

In one corner there was a bed. There was a large table in the middle of the room. There were a couple of chairs, a furnace, and a scrap of carpet. There was none of the luxury of which the beautiful lady had spoken of.

"What a fool I have been," said he. "I might have known it was all lies."

He found on one side of the room a small well similar to that used by pawnbrokers.

In this machine he found some food, but it was by no means of the same class as that which he had been hitherto enjoying.

He had brought an end of cigar with him, with which he endeavoured to console himself by sitting down and smoking.

But he could not console himself much in this way.

"How the deuce am I to make my supper of beastly-

boiled beef and drink filthy beer. I daresay the chap before me had worse, though they'll bring me down by degrees, I suppose. They'll have me down to bread-and-water at last.

He could not smoke. He let out his cigar, and made a tour of the apartment.

"I wonder what the last chap had to eat," said he.

Then came another reflection, and rather a disagreeable one, too.

"I wonder what became of him."

Jack Chinnery was by no means too sure now about the fate of his predecessor.

That he had been murdered he felt pretty certain, and with this fate before his eyes he could not feel over-comfortable.

"There's no chance of escape, either," said he. "They say there's no fear of the beaks. Damn it! it's lucky there isn't; for if they were to come, I should be nicely nobbled down in this hole."

He looked all round the room, but could see nothing which afforded any clue respecting the fate of the last victim.

There were all the necessary implements for coining, and some written instructions; but of these latter he had no need, for he was not fresh at the work.

He thought it would divert his mind a little to have a spell at the metal; but he could not give it any attention, and soon left it to wander about the room.

There were a few books, but nothing he cared about. At last he determined to lie down on the bed, and try to go to sleep.

He found that this was a difficult matter, and he rolled from side to side, awakening with a start whenever he closed his eyes for a short time, expecting to find the assassin's knife at his throat.

Next morning—or rather what he supposed was next morning—he arose unrefreshed, and lolled about in front of the furnace, which was still burning. He put some coke on and then washed himself.

Then began to wonder when breakfast was ready.

After he had been waiting about an hour, a noise at the well aroused him.

He ran to it and found some tea and bread-and-butter, and some bacon, coming down for him.

A voice called down at the same moment—

"Send up your dirty plates."

Jack Chinnery did as he was desired, then in his turn called out—

"I say!"

"Well," said a voice which he knew to belong to the lady who had talked to him on the previous day.

"How long am I to stop down here?"

"Why?"

"Because it is not what you promised me."

"What is there to complain of?"

"Why everything. The victuals in particular."

"But you must be content."

"For how long?"

"As long as we think fit to keep you."

"But how long is that?"

No answer was returned to this question, and the trap at the top of the well was closed down again.

Jack Chinnery got a book, and seating himself before the furnace, read and enjoyed himself as well as he could for an hour or two. Then he fell asleep, and did not wake until he heard the trap moving.

The lady's voice called down to him—

"Have you any coin ready?"

"No, not yet."

"You must get some at once. Do you understand how?"

"Yes."

"Get some made, then, before dinner."

"What?"

"Make twenty pieces and then you shall have your dinner."

"I'll see you hanged first," retorted Chinnery. "I wont do a stroke."

He sat down sullenly by the side of the furnace and asked himself what he ought to do next."

"If I could only get up the well," he thought.

But its formation rendered such an attempt an impossibility.

The idea of sitting down and suffering in silence he could not entertain.

No, an effort must be made. But what?

The worst part of the business seemed to him to be, that he had no notion when the inmates of the extraordinary household of which he formed a part went to bed.

Therefore he could make no attempt at escape without a fear of being overheard.

When he came to reflect about what had passed, he recollected, though, that the mysterious ladies when they were talking together they had spoken about his good looks, and congratulated themselves upon having found some one so handsome.

In that case it would appear that he would at some time be brought into contact with them.

In that case he was not doomed everlastingly to be locked up in this horrible place.

What should he do, then?

Should he submit to his fate with a good grace apparently, and await his opportunity.

These thoughts occupied him all day, and when he heard the well again he had not done any work.

The lady's voice called to him—

"Have you any coins ready?"

"I've had an accident with them."

"Send me up what you have done."

"I have not finished any yet."

"Send them up as they are."

"Oh, there! Hang it all. I haven't done any."

"I thought not. There is no dinner for you, however, until you do."

"What do you say?" roared Jack, in a fury.

But the trap was banged to, and no answer given.

Jack then returned to his seat by the side of the furnace, and began furiously to probe at it with the poker.

He was for a long time much too angry to think of doing any work, but after an hour or so had slipped away he began to feel very peckish.

"Curse 'em! I must knock under, I suppose," said he.

Then he read up the instructions, pulled off his coat, and went to work. In a very short time he had produced a few good specimens of sovereigns, had filed their edges, and polished them on washleather.

While he was putting the finishing strokes the door opened at the top of the well, and the lady's voice said—

"Well?"

"Done some," replied Jack, glumly.

"Send them up."

Jack obeyed, and the door shut again after his gaoler had taken away the coins.

Presently down the well came some food, a little better this time, and half-a-pint of wine. Jack bawled out to know whether he could not have a cigar, but no answer was given to him.

Some time afterwards, though, a cigar was sent down, which Jack solaced himself by smoking.

He did not suppose he would be called upon for any more work that night, and so he thought he would enjoy himself as well as circumstances admitted of.

"Not that I can stand this sort of thing very much longer," said he. "I'll be hanged if I can."

When he was dozing before the fire, he was interrupted by the sound of the well.

The lady's voice called down to him—

"I have sent you down a real sovereign to copy from.

Try and do better to-morrow. What you have done is no good."

Jack Chinnery made no reply to this pleasing intelligence. He took the coin in his hand, and tossed it high in the air; caught it again, and sat down to examine it closely.

"I wish I could make real ones," he said, with a sigh.

After he had pondered over the matter for a short time, though, he took off his coat again, and fell to work. In about an hour he had turned out a coin which was to his liking. He compared the two together—the real and the sham—and came to the conclusion that though his might be of less value, it looked much the best.

Again he sat down by the side of the furnace, and not having anything of much interest to read in the little library at his disposal, fell a-thinking.

He thought, whatever could have become of the last tenant of this strange subterranean abode?

Had he been murdered?

If so, was his body hidden in some part of the place?

The idea was a horrible one, and when once it came into his head, he could not, for the life of him, dismiss the subject from his mind. If he shut his eyes for a moment, he awoke with a start, fancying he heard a groan. Then an irresistible impulse caused him to go and peep under the bed. Nothing, however, was there.

All at once, though, his attention was drawn to the floor. Something curious at his feet aroused his suspicions.

He made a close examination of the edges of the stone upon which the furnace stood.

Then he came to a conclusion.

No, he could not be mistaken. The furnace stood upon a trap.

He rose eagerly to his feet, and then exerting all his strength, contrived to drag the cumbersome crucible and ironwork on one side.

There, upon the spot which had been covered up was a trapdoor, as Jack had suspected.

With some difficulty he contrived to raise it, and saw before him a flight of steep steps.

For a moment he stood undecided, fearing that some unknown danger lay lurking below.

But he did not long hesitate. If this were a chance of escape he must profit by it.

He had noticed lying about a small end of tallow candle. This he lit, and without any further consideration, commenced the descent.

The air struck very cold and damp as he proceeded, and he several times thought of his adventure in the convent, and glanced anxiously about him, dreading that some unseen pit-hole might be there awaiting him.

At the bottom of the steps he found a heavy door, which he could only drag open after a violent struggle.

Having done so, however, he passed into a great vault, the gloom of which the flickering candle he carried was not sufficient to illuminate.

He was, however, doomed to follow out his researches under more disadvantageous circumstances still, for the door slammed-to suddenly behind him, and blew out his light.

He strove to open the portal again, but in vain.

All around him was pitch dark, and silent as death.

CHAPTER XLVIII.

A STRANGE SCENE IN A LADY OF TITLE'S BED-CHAMBER.

BUT Jack Chinnery did not feel inclined to abandon himself to despair at this early period in his adventures. He kept his hand upon the wall, and feeling his way with caution, made a half-tour of the cellar.

Arrived half-way, though, he found a hole in the wall. Through this he crept without a moment's hesitation, and commenced the same proceeding in the next cellar, keeping his hand on the wall as before.

He then came to a door, which he contrived to open, and found himself in a passage, where there was a faint light.

Slipping off his boots, he kept upon his way, and presently came to a kitchen door standing ajar. Peeping in, he saw a fat cook at needlework, and leaving her thus employed, he crept on up some stairs, and found himself, to his great joy, in a spacious hall, from which opened the street door.

"Now for liberty," said he to himself, making towards the means of egress.

But at this moment he heard a door opening between him and the outer portal. His only chance of escape was to go forward upstairs, unless he retraced his steps, and this latter course he did not approve of.

Upstairs, therefore, he ran nimbly and lightly, pausing on the first-floor landing to listen.

But, rather to his disgust, he heard steps approaching.

The person, whoever it was, was coming upstairs.

Jack ran up another flight, supposing that the person was going into the drawing-room.

This, however, was not the case.

On the contrary, the steps came up and up.

"I must hide somewhere," thought Jack.

Where was it to be, though? He tried the handle of a door.

It yielded to his touch, and he entered the room. A bed-chamber it proved to be, containing a handsome bed with a valance, and Jack, not knowing where to hide himself, or where he would be safest, darted under the bed and lay still.

But scarcely had he there secreted himself, when to his amazement the door was opened, and the person who had ascended the stairs behind him entered the apartment.

"It's lucky I got under in good time," thought Jack, with an inward chuckle. "I hope they wont be long,"

He had not yet had time to think whether his pursuer was male or female.

A rustling of silk, however, now apprised him that she was of the softer sex.

When he had made this discovery, he was not very long before he made another, and this was rather a startling one.

The lady who had entered the room locked the door. She therefore intended to stop.

This was her bed-room, then, and she was probably going to bed.

"I'm in for a nice thing, I must say," said Jack to himself.

But whether or not he spoke derisively it was rather hard to decide. In fact, perhaps he would have had some difficulty in saying himself.

He lay in the position into which he had thrown himself when first he crept under the bed, and in this attitude he was unable to see anything that took place in the room.

As, however, he was anxious to get a glimpse of the lady whose entrance into the bed-chamber had placed him in so awkward a position, he began very slowly to twist himself over on to his breast.

There was a loud rustling of silk which seemed to indicate that its wearer was undressing herself.

"She's a lady, I should say," thought Chinnery. "I wonder whether she is old or young—plain or beautiful."

The best way was surely to look.

He therefore persevered in his twisting; but, somehow, he managed to make a slight noise with one of the boots which he had carried in his hand.

In an instant the rustling of the silk ceased, and Jack knew instinctively that she was listening.

He therefore lay as still as a mouse until he heard the rustling begin again.

But then he was frightened for his life to move much, lest she might hear him again ; for if she once suspected where the noise came from, what would be more likely than that she should pull up the valance of the bed and discover his hiding-place.

Luckily in the position which he now occupied he could peep out.

The lady stood before the looking-glass with her side face towards him, and the light of some wax tapers shone upon a head and form which the robber thought, at the moment, were the most beautiful he had ever seen.

She had by this time assumed a graceful robe of a softer and almost transparent nature, which displayed to the utmost the symmetry of her lovely person ; and her hair, which she had loosed from its bonds, fell in rich luxuriance over her plump, white shoulders.

"I wonder who she is," thought Chinnery to himself. "She's beautiful enough for a goddess, and—my eyes ! what jewels she has got."

Upon the polished throat and the fair, rounded arms of the beautiful woman glittered some magnificent diamonds, which sparkled in a most tempting fashion before the robber's greedy eyes.

"If I only got hold of that lot," said he to himself, "I should be set up till the end of time. I wonder whether there's any chance of it."

There were great hopes he thought. If he waited until the lady retired to rest, he would probably be able to effect the robbery and make his escape.

"I wonder whether she's a sound sleeper," he thought.

Then he began again wondering who the lady could be, and to wonder whether she was maid, wife, or widow ; and to think how very beautiful she was, and what a fine thing it must be to be a swell, and the proprietor of anything half as beautiful.

But after a time he began to think that she was a very long while in getting ready to go to bed, and to exclaim against the absurdity of her brushing her hair so much.

"She's got very stunning hair, certainly," said he ; "but I wonder how it is she don't have a lady's-maid. I begin, after all, not to be quite so sure about her being a swell. And yet, if she were not some rich lady of title, how does she come to have those splendid diamonds? I can't make it out."

Perhaps this lady had some particular fancy for her own society. At any rate, she did not appear to be at all afraid of being alone.

She presently took a seat by a fire which was fast expiring, but yet flickered faintly in the grate, and seemed plunged in deep thought, as she sat there with her head resting upon her hand.

So very long, indeed, did she remain in the same position that Jack Chinnery at last came to the conclusion that she had gone to sleep.

"Why the deuce don't she go to bed like a Christian," thought Jack. "If I were to crawl out now I should be popped on to a certainty. How long will she be, I wonder?"

There could be no doubt but that she had gone to sleep now, for her head had fallen a little on one side, and she still remained silent and motionless.

Chinnery's patience was sorely tried.

"What was he to do?" he asked himself. "Perhaps she'll sleep in that chair all night. But as yet I don't know that she is asleep. If I were only certain I—ah !"

This whispered exclamation was caused by a slight noise in the room, which attracted his attention.

It was a noise at one of the windows—the sound of some one raising the sash.

At first he thought he must have been mistaken, but

he was not long in doubt. The blind was drawn on one side, and a hand crept in between it and the shutters.

Then a head appeared, and after a brief pause a man let himself gently down into the room, and stood silently upon the spot where he had alighted.

The intruder had a somewhat peculiar appearance.

His costume puzzled Chinnery not a little, until he came to the conclusion that it was a dress of a Roman Catholic priest.

His face might not by some have been considered to be altogether displeasing, yet there was a certain sly look about it hardly to be admired.

He stood for a moment or two looking round, and when, at length, his eyes alighted upon the sleeping form of the lady, a smile flitted across his cadaverous countenance.

He advanced on tiptoe towards her, and gently laid his hand upon her arm.

Then, as though she had been stung by a viper, she awoke with a start, and, rising to her feet, met him with a look which was full of defiance.

"You did not expect me, my lady," said he.

"No," she answered, "nor did I want you. How did you come?"

"Your doors were locked against me, I know," said the priest, "but when one is anxious—I knew you would forgive me."

She looked at him scornfully and made no reply; then turned away her head.

The priest smiled, and seated himself very coolly by the side of the fire.

Then a silence of some moments' duration ensued, and then the lady spoke.

"What do you want here?" she asked. "What has brought you?"

"I know that you forbade my coming into your presence again, but I had some information which will be of service to you, and which I was determined you should have from my lips alone."

"What is the information?" asked the lady. "What new pretence is this?"

Again the priest smiled, as though he said to himself, "Let her do her worst, my turn will come presently, and then she shall suffer."

"When you despised the love you had grown weary of, perhaps you thought that I did understand the motive which prompted you to cast me off as though I had been one of your ladyship's old gloves?"

She returned no answer, and he continued—

"Do you suppose, though you kept it so secret, that I should not hear of your proposed marriage? But I did hear it, and yet made no interference."

"Made no interference?" the lady repeated, with a sneer.

"Why not?" he answered, blandly. "If I had choosed, what a pretty story I could have told about a great lady's amours and intrigues; and what would her future husband have given me to remain silent?"

"You would not—you dare not—have been so base."

"Why not? Ought I to have remained silent out of gratitude, because your ladyship is always so considerate of me?"

She made no reply, however, and the priest went on.

"I knew, of course, that your ladyship had a rival—younger, and, if possible, more beautiful."

The woman started slightly, but quickly recovered her self-possession.

"Of course, your ladyship would like that rival removed?"

"I would," she answered. "Can you do it?"

"With the greatest ease."

"What are your terms?"

Again the priest smiled in the sly way that he had done, and glanced out of the corners of his eyes at the beautiful lady's averted face. Not that at this moment it wore a very inviting expression, for the lips were tightly compressed, and the brows contracted with anger.

Yet did she still look very beautiful. It was not the beauty of a loving woman, but rather that of an avenging angel—grand and awful.

The priest appeared to hesitate for a time, as though he were afraid of saying what was uppermost in his mind. Yet as she was waiting for his reply, he must speak, and he presently answered, in a low tone of voice, which had something supplicating in it and something cringing, yet still an under-current of defiance, which threatened every moment to blaze out into open violence.

"I know very well, my lady, that you despise me," he said. "I hardly dare to think that I am of sufficient consequence to be hated; but I am sure that I am despised. So despicable a creature, then, cannot be expected to be actuated by any noble sentiments. I own I never was, and yet I think that if I had not been despised I might have done better things than I have. I am only a poor priest, then, living, or rather starving, on a pitiful stipend. If I can be of any great service to your ladyship, I am sure that your ladyship will do all——"

"Yes, yes," replied the other, in a somewhat weary tone. "I will give you what you like—name a sum."

The priest rubbed his hand over his chin and reflected.

"Your ladyship is so generous I am sure I would do best to leave it to you."

"Very well, I will pay you liberally; but first say how you have got rid of—of this girl, and where she is."

"At present she is at home. To-morrow morning, though, if your ladyship wishes it, she will be safely locked within the walls of a nunnery."

"A nunnery!"

"Yes, my lady. She sees the folly of human ambition, and is tired of the gaieties and pleasures of this world. She seeks that rest."

"What nonsense is this that you are talking?"

"Only the truth, my lady, which is stranger than fiction."

"But in a month's time she was to have been married. Has she quarrelled with the Earl?"

"Her father confessor has done something, my lady, towards bringing about a rupture—but from the best and purest motives as you may conceive."

"And are you sure that she will remain in the nunnery when she is there?"

"Quite sure of it, my lady, if I wish her to do so."

"But suppose she gets tired of the confinement?"

"I am afraid that that will avail her nothing."

"Why, would you keep her against her will?"

"When once she has passed the threshold and renounced the vanities of this world, it would be in vain for her to try to escape."

"What, cannot she leave again when she chooses?"

"When once the gates close upon one of these nuns they close for ever."

The lady thoughtfully regarded the fire for some moments, and a deep unbroken silence reigned in the apartment.

She appeared to be pondering upon the meaning of the words which her companion had just uttered.

Presently, however, she said—

"Do you mean to say that if the police authorities were to interfere they could not immediately obtain the release of a nun immersed in a convent?"

"Of course they could, my lady; but why should they do so?"

"Why should they interfere?"

"Yes."

"If a nun is ill-treated——"

"But when are nuns ill-treated? Whoever hears of it? Who is there to tell tales out of school?"

THE MYSTERIES OF A CONVENT LIFE.

"There are no spies among you, then?"

"None."

"But if the nuns really are ill-used, as of course they are, how is it that they do not all join together and break out from their prison-house?"

"Ah, your ladyship has no notion what a beautiful system ours is, and to what a state of subjection our sisters are reduced. There is nothing like rebellion to be dreaded. Each is afraid of the other, and one might easily be tortured to death without the slightest fear of the rest interfering."

"And in the first instance each nun enters with her own consent?"

"Most certainly. We never take a nun without her full consent, unless it is in the case of young girls who are confided to us for certain reasons by their relatives. Sometimes, then, they are too young to know their own minds, and as of course their relations know best what will be good for them, we take the elders' opinion."

"In the case of Marion Leicester, however, she has entered of her own accord?"

"She has."

"And she will remain?"

"As long as your ladyship chooses."

"Let her remain there until her death——"

"Which might occur very soon, my lady."

"I care not when it occurs, so long as she does not cross my path."

"She shall not, if your ladyship will but trust in me."

"I will trust in you."

The priest glanced eagerly at her face, then sideling nearer to her, said, in a low but earnest tone—

"How happy it makes me to think that you can trust me still. I was afraid that you despised me too much for that, and yet I have served you faithfully. Yet I have always had your interest at heart—yet I have worked for you——"

"And I have rewarded you," said the lady.

"Yes," replied the priest, though in a tone of hesitation.

"Are you not content?" she asked.

The man looked at her fixedly, and she turned her face towards him, so that their eyes met.

Then suddenly catching at her hand, he said, in trembling tones of concentrated passion—

"Eleanor, why have you cast me off? What have I done to displease you? I would, as you know, willingly work the flesh off my bones to serve you. Have I not, as it is, perilled my soul in your cause? Oh, Eleanor! how can you be so hard-hearted? How can you treat me so harshly—I who love you so devotedly?"

He fell upon his knees, and, stretching out his arms, strove to clasp her waist, but she twisted from his grasp and waived him off with an angry gesture.

"Are you mad?" she cried.

"I am," he said, desperately. "How can I otherwise account for my idiotic infatuation for a hard-hearted, passionless idol such as you are? Mad enough, heaven knows, or I would never have done what I have."

The lady laughed mockingly, as she turned away.

The priest, meanwhile, covering his face with his hands, seemed to shiver with violent emotion—

"Oh, why did God make you so beautiful, Eleanor, and yet so cold and false? How many victims are to die at your shrine? How many careers to be blighted and souls plunged into crime on your account? And yet you can go to church and pray with seeming piety—yet you can seek your luxurious couch, and smile, as placidly as ever baby did, in your tranquil slumbers—undisturbed by one remorseful dream. How is it that such things can be? And yet fools say that there is a divine justice above."

It would have been impossible, Chinnery thought, to imagine anything more beautiful than the priest's companion looked at this moment, as she stood with the ruddy firelight shining upon her angelic face; a smile of pity parting her red, pouting lips.

The soft, half-transparent fabric of which her dress was composed, clung about, but scarcely concealed the magnificent contour of her voluptuous figure.

Her snow-white bosom was revealed, and upon it, in the soft, thick masses, hung her rich tresses in graceful waves.

Her dark eyes were full of bewitching beauty, and her red lips slightly parted, revealed a row of teeth of dazzling pearl-like nature.

To possess the love of such a divine creature as this was surely enough to have tempted most men to destruction.

The seductive influence of her treacherous smile seemed all-powerful in the case of this priest, who, now at her feet, besought her in passionate tones to listen to the love prayer which in wild eloquence he poured out.

But she was like a marble statue, and stood looking down upon him, half in pity, half in contempt.

At length she said, impatiently—

"I can bear no more of this. I am willing to reward you with money, if that is what you want, for the service you have done me, but I can never love you more. The past must remain the past; therefore, leave me at once."

But the priest, maddened by his passions, ground his teeth as he exclaimed—

"Why should I for ever be a puppet in your hands? Why should I play the suppliant, when you are in my power. No, by heavens! you must and shall be mine!"

Then springing to his feet, he seized her in his arms, in spite of fierce struggles to release herself from his embrace.

At this moment, however, Mr. Jack Chinnery was interrupted in his contemplation of the strange love scene enacted before him by a still stranger occurrence, of a most unexpected nature.

This was no other than a sharp blow on the back. Mr. Jack started as though he had been shot.

He was too much surprised and knocked out of time to think about any of the ordinary rules of caution.

Luckily, the two actors in the exciting drama of which he had been a witness, were too interested to be easily disturbed, or else he would most certainly have been discovered.

He twisted over sharply to see what had happened.

Then came a surprise, the like of which he never recollected to have experienced during the whole course of his previous career.

It was such a tremendous surprise, indeed, that it took away his breath—it deprived him of the power of speech.

It absolutely dumbfounded him.

For there, within six inches of his nose end, was the nose end of another individual under the bed.

Yes, there lay another man looking at him fixedly.

Jack Chinnery stared at him with all his eyes. The other man stared at Jack.

"What the devil is he doing there?" thought Mr. Chinnery.

The other party, perhaps, asked himself the same question with regard to Jack.

"How long has he been there?" thought Chinnery. "He must have been here when I came."

That was certainly the case, extraordinary as it might seem.

Jack had run upstairs and plunged under the bed without pausing to see whether that place of concealment was already occupied.

Perhaps this was a burglar, who had there ensconced himself, and thought that his hiding-place was quite safe.

Somehow or other, just now, in his anxiety to see what was going on, this party must have given Mr. Chinnery a nudge, and this had led to the result I have described.

And thus it was that Mr. Jack Chinnery lay staring at the stranger, and the stranger lay staring at him, while the lady, quite unconscious that her bed-chamber was so well filled, struggled silently, but resolutely, with the priest.

CHAPTER XLIX.

THE LIFE AND SUFFERINGS OF A NUN.

A YOUNG lady possessed of considerable wealth, twenty-one years of age, was one day in the year, when this history opens, admitted into the convent of Saint Theresa, in —— Street, London.

She entered of her own free will, and was accompanied to the religious establishment in question by two female relations and a male friend.

Their attendance had been requested by the young postulant* and by the Sisters, who were anxious that it should be clearly understood by the lady's connexions that she entered the convent by her own wish and without the slightest coercion.

That this was the case there was not the least doubt, and the matter was never disputed, although in the end the horrible fate of this poor young creature led to certain investigations, with which this story will have to deal.

At present, however, it is a narrative of her dreadful sufferings that we have to record, in the course of which will be revealed some almost incredible details connected with convent life, of so shameful and revolting a character that nothing but the great cause of truth could induce the writer to enter upon so bold and, under other circumstances, unjustifiable a disclosure.

* Candidate for recluse.

The parlour of the convent—as the room was designated into which the visitors were shown—was a cold and gloomy-looking apartment, with strongly barred windows and bare naked walls and floor, looking uninviting enough.

Nor were some rules, which, written in a crabbed hand, and enclosed in a black frame, hung in one corner of the apartment of a very enticing character.

These rules—called "Rules by the Reverend Mother" —hung also in the "Community" and the "Refectory," and in the cells of all the nuns, and it was the duty of every novice to read them through at least once a week.

They ran as follows :—

1. To rise on the appearance of a superior.

2. When reprimanded to kneel at once, and humbly kiss the floor until the signal be given to rise.

8. When speaking of the Superior to say "our mother," when speaking to her and the professed Choir Religeuse, "Ma mére." To say "Sister" when speaking to the novices: of them "Miss," and of the professed choir "Mrs." To say "our" or "ours," instead of "my" or "mine."

4. To say *Ave Maria* every time we enter the community.

5. Before entering any room to give three knocks at the door, accompanied by some religious ejaculation, and wait until they are answered by three from within.

6. Not to lift our eyes when walking in the passage ways.

7. Never to touch each others hands.

8. To stand while spoken to by the Father or Superior, and kneel while speaking to them. To speak in a particular tone.

9. If necessary to speak to the Superior during the time of silence, approach her kneeling and speak in whispers.

10. Never to leave a room without permission, giving at the same time a reason.

11. To rise and say the "Hour"* every time the clock strikes, except when the Father is present, who, if he wishes, makes the signal.

The following are the rules and penances for our holy Father St. Emanuel, together with those of Saint Theresa :—

1. To kneel in the presence of the Father until his signal to rise.

2. Never to gratify our appetites except with his holiness the Father's or the Father Confessor s permission.

3. Never to approach or look out of the window of the monastery.

4. To sprinkle our couches every night with holy water.

5. Not to make any noise, or movement, when in our cells of a night.

6. To wear sandals and hair-cloth, to inflict punishment upon ourselves with our girdles, in imitation of a saint.

7. To sleep on a hard mattress, or couch, with one coverlet.

8. To walk with pebbles in our shoes, or walk kneeling until a wound is produced.

9. Never to touch *anything* without permission.

10. Never to gratify our curiosity, or exercise our thoughts on any subject without our spiritual director's knowledge and advice.

11. Never to desire food or water between portions.

12. Every time on leaving the community to take holy water from the altar of the Blessed Virgin, and make the sign of the cross.

18. If a religieuse persist in disobeying a Superior,

she is to be brought before the Father, and punished as he may think proper.

14. Never to smile except at recreation, and even then not contrary to religious decorum.

15. Should the Honoured Mother, the Superior, detect a religieuse whose mind is occupied by worldly thoughts, or who is negligent in observing the rules of the Monastery, which are requisite and necessary to a perseverance and perfection in a religious life, she shall immediately cause her to retire to her cell, where she shall enter into a retreat.

16. Full confession of the innermost thoughts to be made to the Father Confessor once every week, at which, shall any sin, however trivial, be withheld and afterwards discovered, the culprit shall be put through a course of extra penance and self-humiliation—shall be compelled to lick the floor of her cell, to sleep upon the bare stones, and to lacerate her flesh with a whip provided for the purpose, until such time as she shall receive the Superior's permission to cease from this punishment.

The male friend of this young lady, whose name was Marion Leicester, read these rules and regulations with astonishment and indignation, and called the attention of the novice to their extreme severity.

But the young lady replied, that she thought they were but reasonable and just.

While they were discussing the question somewhat warmly, the Lady Superior entered, and warmly greeted the new comer.

Then, after a few brief words of conversation, and some perfectly useless endeavours upon the part of Miss Leicester's male friend to dissuade her from the rash step she was about to take, the young lady signified her desire to enter the convent.

Her friends then said, "Good-by," and retired slowly and sadly from the presence of this poor misguided girl, who coldly watched them depart, little thinking what a life of misery was in store for her.

She had bidden adieu to all the pomps and vanities of the outer world, she had chosen for herself a life of prayerful seclusion in preference to living in the turmoil and bustle of the world.

She had voluntarily retired from the glaring daylight of fashionable life, she had forsaken the world of sin and sorrow for the calm and quiet of the convent. There she hoped to live, hearing but seldom of the doings of the world she had left, till at last, at the appointed time, her soul should wing its flight to other regions where pain and sorrow are unknown.

These were the thoughts which filled the mind of Marion as she followed the Lady Superior from the room after taking what she believed to be an eternal farewell of those friends whose persuasions had been insufficient to turn her from the course she had resolved upon adopting.

"My sister," said her guide, opening the door of a room, "this is to be henceforth your home. Here you will live, and in prayer and holy books endeavour to forget all connected with the sinful world you have quittted."

Marion looked around the apartment. It was small, and meagrely furnished. A plain table and chair, a pallet bed, and a large wooden crucifix, constituted all the furniture.

There was a damp, chilly air about the room, and the novice could not refrain from shuddering at having thus suddenly brought before her the knowledge of the place in which she had decided upon passing the whole of her iife.

"I will send the Sister Margaret to you," continued the Lady Superior. "She will instruct you in the various forms and ceremonies which it is requisite you should observe."

Marion bowed her head in silent acquiescence, and the Lady Superior withdrew.

* The *Hour* is a prayer. There are twenty-four hours in the day, for each of which is a different prayer. Every time the clock strikes, one is repeated by the nun whose turn it is to do so.

No sooner was she left alone in the room she was to occupy than a thousand recollections thronged into her brain.

Despite prayer and tearful entreaty she had remained firm in her resolve. She had obtained her wish, and now—and now—

Did she regret the step she had taken?

The question came unbidden.

"No, no," she exclaimed, energetically. "I do not regret. What is the world to me that I should bestow a single sigh at quitting it? What attractions have the sham, hollow tinsel charms of society for me? None—none. I have left them for ever. Here, before this crucifix, I register my vow—never, never to return to the cruel world of sin and shame."

"It is a good resolve," said a voice by her side.

She turned quickly round to the spot from whence the voice came.

There, standing by her, was a tall woman, clad in the garb of a nun.

How had she entered?

Marion's eyes had been towards the door (for near it was the crucifix placed) ever since she had been in the room; and since the departure of the Lady Superior, she was positive it had not been opened.

A feeling of alarm, which she strove in vain to repress, took possession of her; neither did the appearance of the nun tend in any degree to allay it.

Instinctively she felt an aversion to the tall, gaunt woman who stood upright before her, her brows contracted as she bent her gaze full upon the novice, as if to take the measure of her intellect.

There was certainly a repulsive expression upon the face of the nun.

There was a look of cunning in the small, restless eyes, while the lips and the lower part of the face were coarse and sensual looking; her voice, too, was harsh and grating, and though she evidently did her best to moderate it in addressing Marion, she could not make it either pleasant or musical.

"I am Sister Margaret," said she, after a long pause, during which Marion had been vainly endeavouring to recover her composure sufficiently to address her visitor.

The novice bowed her head.

"The Lady Superior has sent me hither to instruct you in our customs."

"I am glad to learn."

"It is well, sister. Your reply shows a becoming meekness, without which your life would necessarily be a blank."

The novice took in the sound more than the words, and again bowed her head, while the Sister Margaret continued.

"The Lady Superior has informed me of the circumstances which led you to become one of us, and I can only agree with her in welcoming you, and applauding your desire of being received into the bosom of our Mother the Church."

If these words were intended to be what they professed—a cordial welcome—the cold, chilling tones of the speaker completely marred the effect they were intended to produce.

Again Marion shuddered, as, lifting her eyes, she found those of the Sister Margaret fixed earnestly on her face.

"I shall be glad to learn something of the duties I shall have to perform," said the novice.

"The duties?"

"Yes."

"Is that the proper term to apply to them?"

"Why not?"

"Should you not rather call them pleasures?"

"Excuse me if my phraseology offends you."

"My child," said the Sister Margaret, endeavouring to assume a maternal tone, and failing miserably—"my child, you have much to learn; but in time, I trust,

you may become a creditable member of our holy society."

"Such is my desire."

"Remember, you have nothing to fear. Gentleness and kindness hold dominion here. The evil passions of the world are subdued, and a meek, loving spirit reigns supreme. All is kindness and——"

As if to give the lie to her words, a piercing shriek rang through the house.

Marion started violently.

The Sister Margaret turned almost paler than usual.

With a great effort to appear calm, she resumed.

"Kindness and a loving spirit govern all our hearts, and——'

Again a scream of pain.

Another, and another.

They followed each other in rapid succession.

They were cries as of a woman in the intensity of suffering.

It was no longer possible for the Sister Margaret to feign deafness to the heartrending cries.

"What is that? What does it mean?" cried the novice, eagerly, clutching the nun's arm.

She remained silent.

"There is some poor creature in distress," continued Marion. "Where do the sounds come from? Let us fly to help her."

The nun neither spoke nor moved.

"Is this your gentleness?" cried the novice, angrily. "Where is the gentle, loving spirit, you told me of? Nay, if you will not accompany me, I will go alone to her rescue."

She ran towards the door as she spoke.

"Stay!"

It was the Sister Margaret who spoke, and her tone was one of stern command.

She stretched forth her long, muscular arm, as she uttered the word, and held the novice back.

Frightened, and totally unable to explain the mystery, she looked to the nun for explanation.

Again the screams echoed through the room, more piercing, if possible, than before.

"I will not stay here while a fellow-creature is in torture," cried Marion, struggling to escape the nun's grasp.

"Remember one of the first duties you must learn is that of obedience," said Sister Margaret, sternly. "The cries you hear proceed from one whose forgetfulness of that duty has brought upon her well-merited punishment.

The novice said not a word, but her thoughts recurred to the sentences respecting kindness and gentleness she had just heard.

She could not reconcile those precepts with the practice which called forth the heartrending cries which still echoed through the chamber.

"They will rouse the whole neighbourhood," muttered the nun, between her teeth. "Fools! Could they not have managed better."

As she spoke these words to herself her face assumed an almost diabolical expression.

The worldly passions had certainly not been altogether conquered in her.

Marion had buried her face in her hands.

For some moments she remained lost in reflection.

Was it possible that after all she had been deceived in believing the convent a happy home—where all was quiet and contentment?

It was soon for her dream to be dispelled. Yet she could not disbelieve the evidence of her senses.

Of the crime of which the poor sufferer had been guilty she was ignorant, still she could not reconcile to her mind that punishment which could call forth such cries of anguish was agreeable to the doctrine of love and charity which they taught, whatever might be the fault which called for correction.

Marion turned to address a remark to that effect to Sister Margaret.

She was gone.

Just then the screams again resounded through her chamber.

She was unable any longer to withstand the woman's inclination which prompted her to fly to the succour of one of her own sex in distress.

She ran to the door of the room and essayed to open it.

It was locked.

She shook it with all her feeble strength, but the fastenings were secure.

Her endeavours were of no avail.

She was a prisoner.

At this fresh confirmation of her suspicions that the outside and the inside of a convent were very different places, she could hardly refrain from tears, but the shrieks she still heard nerved her afresh.

She remembered that Sister Margaret had gained access to her room without passing through the door.

It was evident that there was some other entrance.

But where was it?

Eagerly she set to work to examine the wall in the hope of finding some secret door.

Her search was rewarded.

There was a secret door, but so carefully was it constructed that but by chance she might have searched the whole day through without discovering it.

Sister Margaret in leaving the chamber had omitted in her haste to close the door properly, and Marion's quick eye soon detected a narrow black crack extending from the floor up the wall to a height of about four feet.

This, without doubt, she thought, was the door for which she was seeking.

She was right.

After some little trouble she succeeded in opening it.

It disclosed a steep flight of stone steps which led downwards.

Without a moment's hesitation she descended.

Arrived at the bottom she found herself in a narrow vaulted passage, so low as to prevent her from walking in an erect posture.

She was in total darkness.

The cries had ceased.

She had no means of ascertaining in what direction the passage led.

She hesitated.

Should she proceed or return to her room?

While she yet deliberated a loud shriek wailed dismally along the vaulted passage. It sounded much nearer than when in her chamber.

This decided her.

Come what might she determined to use every endeavour to solve the mystery.

Accordingly, with much caution, feeling her way along the wall, she proceeded through the passage. Her heart beat violently with an undefined sensation. She longed, yet dreaded, to pierce the mysteries of the convent, yet shuddered at the thought of what her fate might be were she discovered in doing so.

On, still on she went.

The passage seemed interminable.

At last, some distance before her, she saw bright rays of light, which told her her journey was approaching its end.

Hastily she pushed forward.

Her haste nearly proved her undoing, for she tripped over some obstacle in her path, and it was with great difficulty she recovered herself.

For some moments she remained motionless, to make sure the noise her stumbling occasioned had not revealed her presence.

Reassured at the silence which reigned around, she proceeded.

The rays of light she found shone through a crevice caused by a door left partially open. Eagerly she peeped through, but though by the hum of voices she was aware that there were people on the other side, she was unable to see them.

All she could observe through the crevice, however, convinced her that the vaulted passage in which she stood led into a chapel.

Portions of architecture and a variety of decorations revealed this much to her; but her view was so circumscribed that she could ascertain nothing more.

Should she endeavour to ascertain more and run the risk of discovery, or should she return again to her room and wait for a more fitting opportunity to resume her researches?

That was the question which agitated her mind.

The same shrill cry of anguish she had already heard so many times sounded again, and this time quite close to her.

It decided her.

At all hazards she determined to learn the cause of the cry, and from whom it proceeded.

Gradually, and with the greatest caution, she slowly pushed the door open, thus widening the aperture through which she made her observations.

The dread of discovery allowed her only to remove it the least bit at a time, but at last she had the satisfaction of widening the opening sufficiently to permit of her seeing the whole of the interior of the chapel.

A strange sight it was which presented itself to her astonished gaze.

A sight which sent a cold thrill of horror and disgust throughout her frame.

A sight so revolting that she absolutely sickened at it.

Could it be possible, she asked herself, that women could be such barbarians, and those women, too, of a class who professed the greatest regard for religion, who preached gentleness and philanthropy?

Oh, it was a sad, sad mockery. It was a delusion, a hollow deceit, an empty pretension!

To join them she had forsaken the world on account of its wickedness and hollowness, and had taken refuge with the disciples of deceit, hypocrisy and pretence.

The chapel was small and low.

The vaulted roof was supported by massive stone columns which formed narrow aisles upon each side of the nave.

Round the walls were hung pictures representing the tortures of the various martyrs of the church painted in all their ghastly solemnness. The capitals of the columns were decorated with hideous grinning skulls.

All this Marion perceived in a momentary glance around, but when her eyes reached the altar the spectacle she saw there arrested her attention, and almost obliterated the recollection of the painted horrors on the walls.

Kneeling on the cold stones before the altar was a young and beautiful girl. The majority of her clothes, which appeared to be those of a nun, had been rudely torn from her.

Over her stood a hideous old woman, who, whip in hand, had evidently been bestowing severe punishment upon the poor unfortunate whose cries had reached the sympathizing ears of the novice, who now, with straining eyeballs, was gazing at the scene before her.

Round the altar stood several of the nuns looking upon the revolting spectacle.

While Marion still watched, the whip was raised again.

The blow fell with force upon the shuddering form of the half-naked girl, who was still forced to retain her kneeling position before the altar.

Again the irrepressible cry of anguish escaped her lips as the cruel lash cut into her quivering flesh.

Again and again was the blow repeated.

Again and again the cry of pain announced the force of the blow.

The novice felt herself powerless.

She was unable by herself to befriend the poor sufferer, though her anger and indignation almost overcame her prudence.

She restrained herself by a great effort from breaking into the midst of the circle, and dragging the unfortunate girl away before another blow could descend.

By-and-bye, though the lash still fell with the same force, the cries became fainter and fainter, till at last only a low moan, and a convulsive shudder of her whole frame, told that the poor sufferer had sufficient consciousness left to feel the pain.

At last nature gave way.

The pain, and consequent exhaustion, overcame the poor girl, and she sank into a mass of bleeding, bruised humanity upon the cold pavement before the altar, upon which stood the emblem of mercy.

It was indeed a pitiful mockery.

Two of the nuns stooped to examine the condition of the girl who, in religion's name had suffered so much. Then they spoke a few words to the hag who, whip in hand, still waited to ascertain if the victim could bear more torture.

The result was, that the whole party left the chapel by a door opposite to that at which Marion watched, leaving the unfortunate girl lying bruised and senseless on the ground.

No sooner had the last of the nuns disappeared than the novice sprang forward and hastened to the side of the victim of superstition and cruelty.

At first she believed her dead.

She placed her hand upon her heart, and found however, by the slow, feeble pulsations, that life was not yet extinct.

By the altar stood a vessel, containing holy water. With this Marion plentifully besprinkled the brow of the senseless girl, and, after a while, had the pleasure of seeing her slowly return to consciousness.

No sooner did she open her eyes and perceive where she was, than a convulsive shudder passed through her frame, and a low gasping sound, between a sob and a moan, escaped her lips.

"Do not fear," said the novice. "They are gone. I will not hurt you."

Her gentle tone served to reassure the suffering girl.

"Who are you? How came you here?" she asked, in a feeble voice.

"I am a novice. I found myself here by chance."

"Fly—fly. Return at once. If you are discovered your fate will be worse than mine."

"I cannot leave you while you are in this state."

"Do not mind me—think of yourself."

"Tell me, how came they to punish you so fearfully? What had you done?"

"What you have. Discovered more than they wished me to know."

"What was it? Tell me, I beseech you."

"Not now. If we both live, we shall meet again, and I will tell you all; but Heaven grant, for both our sakes, that death may release us soon."

"But——"

"Fly for your life. I hear footsteps approaching."

Alarmed and afraid, Marion hastened to the entrance to the vaulted passage.

Following the wall as before, she speedily reached the stone steps, and thus her own room, without discovery.

Carefully closing the secret door, she threw herself upon her bed, and reflected upon the dreadful scene she had just witnessed.

From a species of stupor she was aroused by the clanging of a deep-toned bell.

Though she heard the sound and wondered what it portended, a strange lassitude, produced by the late ex-

citement, seemed to weigh upon her, and prevent her rising.

Her limbs were too weak to sustain her, and when she attempted to rise, she fell back prostrate on the bed.

Though her eyes were closed, she soon became conscious that she was no longer alone in the chamber.

Partially opening her eyes, she saw with horror several faces peering in at her from the half-open door.

Among these faces she recognised, with feelings that can be more easily imagined than described, the repulsive features of the hideous beldame who had played the executioner's part in the dreadful tragedy of which she had just been a witness.

But she was not alone.

Several priests, with malicious grins upon their far from prepossessing countenances, were watching her as well as the old woman.

She closed her eyes with a shudder to shut out the sight of the faces.

What did it mean?

What could it portend?

Had it been discovered that from a hiding-place she had been witness of the horrible tortures inflicted upon the poor girl in the chapel?

CHAPTER L.

FOLLOWS THE FORTUNES OF LADY ETHEL.

It is now high time that we took a brief glance at Lady Ethel Fane.

We left her at Mrs. Stibbington's scholastic establishment.

Here she had, upon the second day of her residence with her very unpleasant employer, made a discovery which had given her a most severe shock.

Phillis, the little girl who seemed to act as maid-of-all-work to the house, had gone upstairs to Mrs. Stibbington's dressing-room in answer to that lady's summons.

Having been gone some time, Lady Fane had grown a little uneasy on the child's account.

Mrs. Stibbington was as brutal as she was coarse and vulgar.

Lady Fane had on the previous evening been made a witness to a disgusting ebullition of temper and spite upon her part.

She began to fear now, therefore, that the child might be again suffering from the violence of her tyrant.

After awhile she heard a cry proceeding from the direction of Mrs. Stibbington's bed-room.

Accordingly, she resolved to acquaint herself with its cause.

With this purpose, she ran upstairs, and was considerably startled to overhear the querulous tones of an old man in feeble remonstrance with the irate Mrs. Stibbington.

This was singular. She had seen no man in the house as yet.

But she had little time to reflect upon this.

There was a scuffle taking place overhead which attracted her whole attention.

This was rendered still more alarming by the shrieks of the unhappy little girl Phillis.

Lady Fane darted on.

Before she had reached the door, however, affairs had reached a climax.

The continued thuds and slaps stopped of a sudden.

A scuffle was taking place.

High words on the part of Mrs. Stibbington, and remonstrances on the part of the old man, told Lady Ethel that Phillis was for the moment respited.

The wrath of the schoolmistress was turned against the child's protector.

There was a blow.

A groan.

A fall.

Then Lady Fane gained the door of Mrs. Stibbington's bedroom.

A fearful picture met her view. A picture full of horror and blood.

An old man lay upon the floor bathed in his blood.

A fearful gash in his forehead was bleeding copiously and defying all the efforts of the startled Phillis to stanch it.

The infuriated woman, now considerably calmed down, stood by gazing vacantly upon her bloody work.

It was at this period we quitted Lady Ethel Fane and her fortunes.

And here we resume.

Lady Ethel rushed forward into the room with a cry of horror.

"Oh, Mrs. Morley," cried Phillis, "come and help me. He's dead, I fear."

Lady Ethel was known as Mrs. Morley, be it remembered.

She needed no second bidding, but at once lent her assistance to endeavour to restore the old man to consciousness.

Mrs. Stibbington never moved or spoke.

She seemed perfectly unconscious of Lady Fane's entrance.

"Get some water," said Lady Ethel to the child.

"Yes."

The water was brought in an instant.

"Now give me something to bathe the wound with."

"What shall I get?"

"Anything—be quick."

"But there is nothing here."

Lady Ethel looked up at Mrs. Stibbington for assistance.

But a glance told Lady Fane that she could expect no assistance from her.

The author of this bloody business stood still, gazing vacantly upon the old man.

Apparently as unconscious of all that was passing around her as the object of her violence himself.

Lady Fane turned from her in extreme disgust.

She began to look about for some linen.

Her pocket-handkerchief was soaked through and through.

Besides which, she wanted something larger wherewith to bind up the wounded man's head.

"Phillis."

"Yes."

"Tear up one of the sheets of the bed into strips."

The child looked frightened.

She glanced from Lady Ethel to her tyrant.

But never offered to stir.

"Foolish girl," exclaimed Lady Ethel, angrily, "do you hesitate when it is a matter of life and death."

But the child did hesitate.

Her spirit was broken with the long chapter of tortures she had undergone.

"Here, Phillis, hold the handkerchief to his head," said Lady Ethel.

"Yes, ma'am."

And she obeyed with alacrity.

Lady Fane then dragged off one of the sheets from the bed, and with a little difficulty contrived to tear it up.

With one of these slips she fashioned out a bandage.

"Can you fetch me some brandy, Phillis?" she asked.

"I don't know."

"Have you none in the house?"

"I think that there was some, Mrs. Morley."

And she glanced up timidly at Mrs. Stibbington.

"Mrs. Stibbington," said Lady Ethel.

But there was no reply.

"Mrs. Stibbington, will you say where there is any brandy?"

Mrs. Stibbington was still silent, and there was every chance of her remaining in her present semi-somnoletic condition for some time to come.

"Then you prefer to see the victim of your brutality die?"

These words operated upon the schoolmistress like magic.

She started from her reverie and began to look about her.

Her whole bearing was that of one just recovered from a fainting fit.

She drew a key from her pocket and tossed it to the child.

"Phillis."

"Yes, ma'am."

"In the parlour cupboard you will find some brandy."

"Yes, ma'am."

And she ran off.

The old man was laying remarkably still.

Lady Ethel observed this with the greatest alarm.

She bent her head to his lips, but could not catch the faintest breath.

Could not hear the faintest pulsation.

The heart was still.

That is, it seemed so to her unpractised touch.

Mrs. Stibbington stood by looking on in horror.

"What is the matter?" she demanded, hoarsely.

Lady Ethel looked up into her face.

She was pale as death.

"The worst?"

"Do you mean that he is——"

"Yes."

The schoolmistress shivered visibly from head to foot.

Then sank against the bed.

"I fear the worst has come, Mrs. Stibbington; and——"

"Silence! for God's sake spare me!"

"It is all over!"

Lady Ethel spoke these fearful words with such an assurance that Mrs. Stibbington did not dream of questioning their correctness.

She shut her eyes.

Then came a host of the most terrifying thoughts.

If he were dead!

If—why, that it amounted to murder!

And she was a murderess!

And what was the murderer's fate?

What, indeed, but death!

Death of ignominy and shame!

Death upon the scaffold!

Death at the hands of the hangman!

And her horror at this was great, as may be readily conceived.

Then how to avoid it.

She must shift the blame from herself to another.

But who?

This was difficult.

There had been no one but Phillis present when the fatal blow was struck.

This was a poor excuse.

And an excuse not at all likely to be accepted.

But her only one.

And so resolved, she immediately set to work.

To work to deceive Lady Fane, and this in the presence of her victim.

"It is a fearful thing, Mrs. Morley," she began.

Lady Fane looked up surprised.

"A fearful thing," she repeated.

"Yes, it is, indeed."

"And perhaps the more so under the existing circumstances."

Lady Fane did not understand.

Mrs. Stibbington interpreted her look, and began to explain.

"I say, under the circumstances, Mrs. Morley."

"I don't understand you," was the cold reply.

"I mean to say that it is a fearful thing."

Lady Ethel was too much shocked at the coldness of this speech to pay her any attention.

She turned towards the old man with a gesture of impatience.

Mrs. Stibbington continued—

"What I meant to say was this, that it is a fearful thing for one so young to have been guilty of, although quite unintentionally."

Lady Fane looked up with a puzzled air.

"I don't understand you."

"Not understand me?"

"No."

"I say that it is all the more fearful from having been perpetrated by a child, Mrs. Morley."

"A child?"

"Yes."

"You don't surely mean——"

"I mean that it was Phillis who did it."

"Impossible!"

"I scarcely wonder at your saying that, Mrs. Morley."

Lady Ethel was upon her guard.

She was convinced that Mrs. Stibbington was attempting to deceive her, notwithstanding her show of candour.

Mrs. Stibbington's face looked truth itself.

"I must be upon my guard with this woman," thought Lady Fane. "She's dangerous, I find. She would no doubt sacrifice me to save herself, did the occasion present itself."

Mrs. Stibbington saw that she was scarcely convinced.

But she did not give up her idea with this.

"You see, Mrs. Morley," she said, "no one would believe that child to possess the fearful temper that she does."

"Indeed!"

"I assure you——"

"I should not have thought so from what I have seen of her."

She turned to the old man.

He was still motionless.

The blood had ceased to flow from the wound in his forehead, which was now bandaged up with the strips of the sheet she had torn.

"Poor old man! Poor murdered victim to this vile woman's wrath!" said Lady Ethel, sadly.

"What, Mrs. Morley?" said the schoolmistress.

"Mrs. Stibbington," said Lady Fane, sternly. "Can you look upon this and swear it is not your work?"

Mrs. Stibbington trembled violently.

"Certainly."

"You can swear that this blow was dealt by Phillis?"

"Yes."

"Then—ha she's here."

Phillis entered the room with a decanter of brandy.

"Give me the brandy, Phillis."

The child did as she was bid.

Lady Ethel poured some of the brandy into a glass, and wetted the old man's lips with it.

But without effect.

He was still apparently without life.

"Can he be really dead?" murmured Lady Fane.

"Oh, no," said Mrs. Stibbington; "that's impossible."

"It looks extremely like it."

"Why?"

"Had he only swooned, the blood he has lost must have restored him to consciousness."

"Dead!" exclaimed Phillis; "oh, don't say so."

"I fear it is too true."

"Shall I go for a doctor?"

"Yes."

"Stay!" said Mrs. Stibbington.

"Fetch a surgeon at once, Phillis," said Lady Ethel.

But the child did not offer to stir.

"Mrs. Stibbington, is it possible that you carry your brutality to this extreme? Are you not satisfied with what you have already done?"

"What do you mean?"

"This. That if this man is dead, I shall denounce you."

"For what?"

"His murder!"

"Mrs. Morley!"

"I am serious."

"Beware what you say."

"Pshaw! you cannot frighten me with your big words."

"I tell you, that if he's dead, she alone is to blame."

"This child?"

"Yes."

"Phillis, do you hear what Mrs. Stibbington says?"

"No, ma'am."

"She says it was you who struck this blow. Is that true?"

"Me?—oh, no, no."

"Phillis?" exclaimed the schoolmistress; "do you dare to deny it?"

The little girl was trembling with fear at the sound of Mrs. Stibbington's voice.

"Answer, Phillis."

The child was silent.

Again Lady Ethel begged her to speak; but without avail.

Mrs. Stibbington had caught her eye.

Her glance seemed to fascinate the poor girl.

"Phillis," said Lady Fane, "you must speak the truth now. You must not fear Mrs. Stibbington. I will protect you from her."

"No, no; I did not——"

The schoolmistress would not let her conclude.

She turned upon Lady Ethel a perfect fury.

"So, madam," she exclaimed passionately, "you wish to teach the girl to exculpate herself and criminate me by a falsehood."

"I wish her to speak the truth."

"And I too."

"And she shall."

"She will."

The schoolmistress was speaking with her rattlesnake eyes fixed all the while upon the trembling victim of her fury.

Poor Phillis dared not to speak until she had received her cue.

"Phillis," said Lady Ethel, "look this way—look at me."

The girl was very well pleased to obey.

"Now answer me truly—who struck this blow?"

"Phillis——"

"Pay her no attention. Answer me truly, I charge you."

"Beware, Phillis."

"Who was it?"

The child trembled from head to foot.

"It was Mrs. Stibbington," she faltered out.

"You are sure?"

"Yes."

"You shall suffer for this, Phillis."

"Fear nothing, Phillis, I will protect you from her."

Phillis drew nearer to Lady Ethel as she spoke.

All this time Lady Fane had been unceasing in her attentions to the wounded man.

And at length her efforts were rewarded.

The wounded man breathed a sigh.

Faint and almost inaudible to all but the eager ear of the little girl.

"He lives!" she ejaculated.

THE CONVENT CHAPEL ON FIRE.

"Lives!"

"Yes."

"How did you tell?"

"I heard him breathe."

Lady Ethel leant forward.

She felt a faint breath upon her cheek.

"You are right, Phillis. He lives, and all is saved."

The child took the old man's hand between hers, and called upon him by name.

A name which considerably startled Lady Fane.

"Speak to me, speak to me, Mr. Stibbington," she said.

"Mr. Stibbington?" repeated Lady Ethel.

"Yes."

"Is that Mr. Stibbington, then?"

"Yes."

"Certainly it is, Mrs. Morley," said the schoolmistress.

"Your husband?"

"Who else do you suppose in my chamber?"

Lady Ethel was dumbfounded.

It was something beyond her comprehension.

The coolness which Mrs. Stibbington had displayed was decidedly unfeminine.

More, it was unnatural.

But when the person so concerned proved to be her own husband, it was something more than either.

And still she could scarcely believe the schoolmistress.

It was not very likely that she should have been there so long without discovering the presence of Mr. Stibbington in the house had he been there all the time.

She determined to question Phillis about it afterwards.

Mr. Stibbington was now almost recovered.

His eyes opened, and his glance rested upon his wife.

He turned his head away with a shudder.

"My head! Oh, my head! How it aches?" he groaned.

"What can we do for you, Mr. Stibbington?"

The old man looked up at the speaker in surprise.

"Who are you?"

"Mrs. Morley," was Lady Fane's reply.

"The new governess?"

"Yes."

"You are very good to a poor old man," he said.

Lady Ethel started.

It was almost the voice, and certainly the tone, of the plaintive lamentations of Mr. Balfour Fenwick.

"How do you feel now?"

"Ill—very ill."

"Shall we fetch a doctor for you, Mr. Stibbington?"

"No, no."

"What do you want, then?"

"Rest."

"Assist me," said Lady Ethel to Mrs. Stibbington. She pointed to the bed.

Mrs. Stibbington advanced to aid Lady Fane in placing her husband.

But as she placed her hand upon him he shrank from her touch as from a serpent.

"Murderess!" he said. "Stand back! Stand off!"

"Stibbington, don't be ridiculous, I pray, my dear."

Her voice was thick and husky.

Her colour, which had gradually returned to her cheeks, now left it upon a sudden.

It was easy to perceive that her husband's horror of her affected the schoolmistress not a little.

Again she advanced to assist in placing him upon the bed.

But the old man grew so violent that she was forced to desist.

"Keep her from me!" he cried, "keep her from me!"

"Stibbington," said his wife, "you don't know what you say."

"Don't let her touch me, Mrs. Morley, will you?"

"Very well."

"Thank you. There's blood upon her hands—blood on her soul!"

"You rave, Stibbington. Beware what you say!"

"Stand back!"

Mrs. Stibbington withdrew, and her husband grew quiet.

"Phillis," said Lady Fane, "Come and assist me."

The child obeyed her, and together they succeeded in placing Mr. Stibbington upon the bed.

The old man took the little girl's hand in his, and looked into her fair face sorrowfully.

"So fair,—so young and innocent," he murmured.

And a big tear rolled down the old man's cheek.

"Don't cry Mr. Stibbington," said Phillis, nestling her head down to his.

At the same time she deluged his pillow with her tears.

Mr. Stibbington stroked her golden hair and looked upon her with touching tenderness.

There was a mixture of sadness and sympathy in his glance which Lady Ethel could not comprehend.

The only sensation that Mrs. Stibbington experienced was rage and disgust at Phillis.

"Phillis!" she exclaimed, ferociously.

The child started, and would have quitted the old man's side but he withheld her.

"Stay with me, Phillis," he whispered. "Don't go to her."

"No, no."

"Phillis, come away this minute, I command you."

The child trembled and changed colour.

"Stay, stay—don't go to her!" whispered the old man.

"I must, Mr. Stibbington," and Phillis struggled to get away.

"Keep from her, Phillis! keep from her! or you'll rue it."

"What are you telling the child?" cried his wife, angrily.

But Mr. Stibbington only reiterated his entreaties.

"I tell you to come to me, Phillis," said the schoolmistress.

"Let her alone," cried the old man.

"I shall not touch her."

"No, you shall not, in my presence at least," said Lady Ethel.

"You forget yourself."

"Not at all, it is you who forget yourself."

"How dare you insult me?"

"I don't insult you. I speak but the truth."

"What do you mean?"

"That you forget yourself. Here is the best proof of it."

Lady Fane pointed to her husband's wound as she spoke.

"Enough of this, remember that I am mistress here."

"I shall not forget it, Mrs. Stibbington, never fear."

"You have."

"Indeed!"

"And do."

"Woman, woman!" cried Mr. Stibbington, "is not that devil within you yet appeased?"

"You rave."

"No matter. I conjure you, Mrs. Morley, to heed me."

"I will."

"Let not the child go from your sight, as you would.——"

He paused.

Much as he had said, he appeared to think twice before speaking the words which now trembled on his lips.

Lady Fane urged him to continue.

She was anxious to learn the full extent of his fears.

"As I would what, Mr. Stibbington?" she said.

"As you would preserve an innocent life!"

There was a general start.

"Life?"

"Yes."

"What do you mean?"

"Mrs. Morley don't you see that he wanders in his mind?"

Mrs. Stibbington seemed strangely agitated at his words; but Lady Ethel was all anxiety to learn the worst; for she felt assured that there was some hidden meaning in the old man's warnings—something concerning the former life of the schoolmistress.

"You are unwell, Mr. Stibbington," she said.

"No, no."

"You must rest and compose yourself. To-morrow—"

"Will be too late!"

"For what?"

"Mrs. Morley!" said the schoolmistress, indignantly.

But Lady Ethel persisted in her questions.

"For what, Mr. Stibbington?"

"Too late to preserve the child from that fury."

"I am sure that Mrs. Stibbington will not harm her."

This was of course spoken by the governess herself.

Mrs. Stibbington preserved a cold, sullen silence.

"She will, she will!"

"Nonsense, Stibbington, your hurt has affected you."

But he was not to be talked down thus.

"Beware of her, I say. The warning that I have cannot be meant in vain."

"What warning?"

"A sad presentiment. Evil will come, I'm sure."

"Be more yourself, man," cried his wife, enraged.

"Woman be less yourself and you may avoid——"

"What?"

"The gallows!"

CHAPTER LI.

CRUELTY.

LADY ETHEL was strangely impressed with Mr. Stibbington's words.

More so than she cared to acknowledge even to herself.

But she endeavoured to combat the feeling and to change the subject.

A summons at the street door aided her in her project at this juncture.

"Phillis," said Mrs. Stibbington, motioning to the door.

The child quitted the room.

"Poor doomed little one," murmured the old man.

"Cease this nonsense, Stibbington—learn to be a little more yourself."

"Make some allowance for your husband now, at least," said Lady Ethel thoroughly disgusted.

"Allowance, Mrs. Morley — what do you mean by that?"

"You are hurt, sir; and——"

"And you think that I am as my wife says, eh?"

"No, no, but——"

"That I am mad?"

"Consider the severity of the blow that you received."

"Tut, tut. Believe if you will that I am an idiot."

"Oh, sir."

"But do not neglect my caution."

"I will not."

"Keep the child out of her reach, as you would preserve her."

And Mr. Stibbington closed his eyes to rest.

"Mrs. Morley—the children are arriving."

This was meant as a hint to quit the room.

However, Mrs. Morley declined to perceive it.

The street door was opened.

Then followed a hum of voices.

The congratulations and welcomes that Phillis was offering to some of the returned pupils.

"Who can that be, I wonder," muttered Mrs. Stibbington to herself.

And then, to satisfy her curiosity too, went into the passage to listen.

The old man opened his eyes.

Then, seeing that his wife had quitted the apartment, he beckoned Lady Ethel to draw nearer to him.

"Don't slight my warning, Mrs. Morley," he said, earnestly.

"I will not."

"Don't think of it as of the babblings of second childhood."

"No, no—I——"

"It is earnest—fearful, downright earnest."

"You think that your wife would again venture to harm her?"

"Yes."

"After what has occurred?"

"Do you think that that has affected her in the least?"

"Why, surely."

"Pshaw! I know her. There's blood in her glance to-day."

"Mr. Stibbington, you are harsh! Consider, she is your wife."

"Alas! I do. It is thus she looked when——"

"What is the meaning of this?" exclaimed the schoolmistress.

She had silently re-entered the room for the purpose of listening to the entreaties of her husband upon the little girl's behalf.

"Mrs. Morley, if you have any decency, you will at once leave the room."

Lady Ethel reddened up to the roots of her hair.

She feared that the insulting tongue of the schoolmistress would lead her into some fresh indignity if she remained, and so she at once quitted the room.

As she left, the old man called after in a loud impressive voice—

"Remember!"

Lady Ethel descended the stairs in a whirl of excitement.

The events of the morning had terribly shaken her.

The sight of that poor old man lying weltering in his gore was a startling thing in itself.

Yet strange as it may appear she felt considerable more alarm at the vague indefinite warning which he had so earnestly endeavoured to impress upon her.

She feared she knew not what.

Anticipated horrors—horrors whose nature she could not explain to herself.

Indeed she would have been puzzled to render an explanation of any of her terrifying forebodings.

She entered the schoolroom.

Phillis was there surrounded by some eight or ten children of all ages.

All were talking together, and the noise was deafening.

Phillis herself was laughing and clapping her hands in joy.

Phillis who a few minutes before had been mingling her tears with the poor wounded old man upstairs.

The girl with true childish volubility had totally forgotten Mr. Stibbington and his wounds.

As Lady Fane entered, the hum of voices hushed at once.

The schoolmaster or governess is, and always has been, a being to inspire awe, and the girls simultaneously tortured themselves into silence, position, and the academical curtsey.

"The new governess!" was buzzed about from one to the other.

And they all stole furtive glances at Lady Ethel, mentally making up their minds that she was a Tartar.

The new governess on her part had behaved rather in a way calculated to promote this belief.

On entering the schoolroom she had simply acknowledged the curtsies of the pupils by an inclination of the head somewhat slight and formal.

She was far too pre-occupied by her thoughts to give much heed to the children.

"Why did she interrupt us, then," said Lady Ethel to herself, "just at the moment when he was about to speak? I feel assured that he was about to make some revelation which would have been unpleasant at the very least to Mrs. Stibbington. I must see him again. Whatever is this singular feeling which possesses me? I feel as if I were upon the eve of some fearful catastrophe—some dire calamity—whether to myself or not, I scarce can think. But this is ridiculous. I am affected, and no wonder, by the fearful events of this morning. What would my late friends and associates say if they knew that I was affected by such fancies? My strange life, and the scenes of horror I have witnessed of late, have filled me with strange fancies. I must shake them off. But at the same time I must heed the old man's caution."

She looked up at Phillis.

The child was standing with a group of her companions.

All of them were laughing and chatting; but now in an undertone, on account of the presence of the new governess.

All looked the picture of mirth and happiness, even including Phillis and herself.

"Phillis!" said the new governess.

"Yes, ma'am."

"Come here!"

The girl ran up to her.

"Yes, ma'am."

"How did that occur this morning?"

"What?"

"That—upstairs."

The colour left the child's cheek.

The whole affair had been forgotten in the joy of welcoming her companions back again.

Lady Ethel saw it, and almost regretted having broached the subject.

Phillis looked around carefully before venturing to reply.

Her eye rested upon the door.

This action spoke volumes for the brutality of Mrs. Stibbington.

Then, when she did speak, it was in a very low whisper.

So low, indeed, as to be almost inaudible.

"Speak up, Phillis!"

"I dare not."

"And why?"

"She—she would kill me."

"No, no—fear nothing."

"She told me that if I dared to tell you a word she——"

"But I tell you she shall not harm you in my presence."

"But out of it."

Lady Ethel looked upon the little girl in astonishment.

The fear she manifested at the thought of Mrs. Stibbington's displeasure was something extraordinary.

And yet she could forget it entirely in an instant.

Forget it and be as happy as you could wish to see a child.

"Phillis, tell me why Mrs. Stibbington was so out of temper this morning—how it happened?"

"Mrs. Stibbington is always very cross with me, you know."

"Yes."

"And Mr. Stibbington always takes my part."

"Yes, and this morning?"

"She wanted to strike me."

"For what?"

"She said that I hadn't come quick enough when she rang."

"And did she touch you?"

"Yes."

"Were you hurt?"

"She hurt my arm very much."

And she pushed up her sleeve to show the marks of her tyrant's brutality.

The fleshy part of her right arm was all discoloured.

Lady Fane could scarcely repress a cry of indignation.

She mentally resolved to make a scene in the schoolroom upon the first occasion of a repetition of this conduct, that should cause Mrs. Stibbington to tremble for her reputation.

She judged that from the woman's vulgar mind this would be the most effectual stop upon it she could devise.

Nothing, she thought, would be so likely to affect her as anything that could endanger her personal interests.

Much as she had seen in her brief stay at the school, Lady Fane did not yet know the extent of this vile woman's malice.

Truly has it been said, that the wicked hate those whom they have injured.

Lady Ethel was anxious to hear the whole of the particulars of the violent scene of the early morning.

So she cut short her meditation, and pressed the child to conclude her account of it.

"How was this done?"

"With the water-bottle."

"She struck you with the water-bottle, Phillis?"

"Yes."

"And then?"

"Then Mr. Stibbington interfered."

"And how did he receive that dreadful blow?"

"Why, he stepped between us, and then she dragged him away, and struck at me. But he had darted back again too quickly, and so it struck him instead of me."

"Then she really meant to strike you again with it?"

"Yes."

"Great heavens! I see now how needful was his caution."

A footstep was heard without.

Phillis heard it first.

She, of all, was the first to recognise it as the step of the schoolmistress.

She sprang back to her companions, and seated herself at a desk.

Here she endeavoured to look as occupied as possible with a book that chanced to be lying open upon it.

The poor child had early learnt the necessity of deceit.

Mrs. Stibbington entered with a very stately curtsey.

Lady Fane was surprised.

To have seen the grace thrown into this action, none would have conceived it possible that Mrs. Stibbington was capable of the atrocities of which Lady Ethel had been a witness.

"Good morning, ladies, all," said Mrs. Stibbington, kindly—"good morning, and welcome back to 'The Chesnuts.'—I hope you have all spent your holidays pleasantly.—Miss Forsyth you're not looking well I'm afraid. Too much dancing I fear?"

"No, ma'am, not too much."

"Of course not. And is your mamma quite well?"

"Thank you, ma'am, quite well."

"That's right."

"And she desired her best respects, ma'am."

"Thank you : she is a charming lady."

All the pupils looked in envy upon the favoured Miss Forsyth.

Such an honour to be publicly addressed by Mrs. Stibbington.

What would they not have given for such a mamma?

Mrs. Stibbington made herself particularly affable.

She gave every one in turn some pleasant speech.

And the new term began under the most pleasant auspices.

"Now, young ladies, a word, if you please," said the schoolmistress.

She rapped the desk with a ruler, and all was silence.

"I have to introduce to you Mrs. Morley, who will henceforth assist me in the duties of the schoolroom. A most amiable lady, Mrs. Morley; and I have no doubt but that you will do your best to deserve her affection and respect."

Wonder upon wonder!

Mrs. Morley herself could scarcely look her acknowledgments for her astonishment at Mrs. Stibbington's amiability.

A moment's reflection, however, explained it all.

This was a portion of Mrs. Stibbington's programme.

As a portion of her establishment it was to Mrs. Stibbington's interest to praise her up as much as possible.

She doubtless thought, too, that all she said upon this point was repeated to the parents of the pupils at the first opportunity.

And then the scholastic duties regularly commenced.

It is not our intention to dwell very minutely upon all the details of this episode in Lady Fane's career.

We shall merely say that she gave every possible satisfaction in her new vocation, and that the whole burden of the school rested upon her.

And now she found it much harder work than she had anticipated.

True, the hours were not very long.

But while she was at it she found it a terrible job.

The constant hum of voices, and the noise, that it was utterly impossible to restrain, was deafening.

And for the first few days she suffered severely from headache.

However, custom is everything.

A day or two's apprenticeship, and she surmounted this difficulty.

Every day found her more and more attached to the little girl, Phillis.

The intelligence of the child made her wonderfully useful.

Although, by no means, the eldest girl of the school, she was, by far, in advance of any in her studies.

This enabled her to attend almost unaided to the younger girls.

She had not received anything of a classical education.

She had received her whole education in Mrs. Stibbington's establishment.

Mrs. Stibbington was decidedly illiterate, so that this is scarcely to be wondered at.

However, this had not been without its benefits for Phillis.

She had got so thoroughly well-grounded in the first steps to knowledge.

After a short time Mrs. Stibbington made the discovery that her new governess was a musician; and so she made the best use of this accomplishment forthwith.

She very speedily issued a new circular for the special purpose of advertising this new branch of instruction.

Although it added materially to her labours, Lady Fane had no objection to instruct in this.

It was some amusement for her at the same time.

In this, as in all the studies, Phillis took the lead.

Seeing which, Lady Ethel greatly exerted herself to push her forward.

The child had a melodious and very powerful voice.

This, Lady Ethel did her utmost to cultivate.

She had a special purpose here.

She could see that at some future day the girl would have to seek her livelihood away from the violence of Mrs. Stibbington; and she doubted not that she might find an opening here.

Some few weeks passed without any particular event.

Mr. Stibbington was gradually recovering from the effects of his wound.

His progress was not very marked, but still it was a progress.

Lady Fane asked regularly after him every morning.

And every morning she received the same reply from Mrs. Stibbington.

A quiet acknowledgment of the politeness, and an equally quiet assurance that he was much better, thank you.

This was the exact state of affairs.

But Lady Fane contrived to get somewhat nearer to the truth through Phillis.

She saw Mr. Stibbington every day, and brought messages backwards and forwards.

Lady Ethel had not seen Mr. Stibbington herself since that memorable morning.

Things were going on with such quiet regularity, that Lady Ethel began to hope she had over-estimated the ill effects which were likely to accrue from Mrs. Stibbington's violent temper.

Indeed, the whole bearing of the schoolmistress seemed to have undergone a total change.

From being coarse and uncivil she had become scrupulously polite and courteous to her new governess.

The little girl, too, seemed to be faring much better of late.

One night, when they were retiring to rest, Phillis even assured Mrs. Morley that Mrs. Stibbington had not so much as slapped her the whole day !

From this Lady Ethel concluded that the terrible scene in which Mr. Stibbington had been so maimed had had a salutary effect upon his wife.

At length, however, Lady Fane was so struck with Mrs. Stibbington's affability, that she could not but imagine the descriptions of her ill-temper, which she had heard from Phillis, were somewhat over-stated.

Strangely enough, Lady Ethel had scarcely been seized with this idea when Mrs. Stibbington discovered the girl had made some trifling mistake which she seemed to construe into a wilful falsehood.

The facts were distorted and highly-coloured, and then retailed out to the whole school in order that the hapless Phillis might experience the full extent of her humiliation.

In vain did the child protest through her tears of her innocence.

Mrs. Stibbington sneered away every protestation she offered.

And thus poor Phillis was publicly disgraced.

Irritated in some measure at this, the girl imprudently ventured upon a retort to one of the schoolmistress's sneers.

The words were no sooner pronounced than the schoolmistress pounced upon her and administered her two smart slaps upon either cheek in rapid succession.

Then she was bustled out of the schoolroom.

Mrs. Stibbington followed her from the room, and Lady Ethel doubted not that she had taken every advantage of the luckless child's imprudence to indulge her own vicious passion on her.

However, it appeared that Phillis had really committed a fault, and so Lady Ethel could not interfere.

Still she felt uneasy.

Mrs. Stibbington was absent from the schoolroom some minutes.

At length she returned looking as composed as possible.

Nothing even seemed to disturb the tranquillity of her expression.

Phillis did not reappear all day !

Lady Ethel glanced continually towards the door.

As the time went on she grew more and more uneasy.

She could not help recurring to the reiterated caution of Mr. Stibbington.

Three weeks had not elapsed since she had heard and been so affected by his cautions, and yet she had neglected them when it was most necessary to observe them.

The day was over and no Phillis.

A long weary day it was, too, after the unpleasant affair in which her *protégée* had once more suffered from the cruel persecution of Mrs. Stibbington.

As soon as school was over for the day, Lady Fane repaired to her room.

She half hoped to find the child there; sobbing, as she had often seen her, as if her little heart would break.

But no Phillis.

She then made such alteration in her dress as was usual, and as hastily as possible, and descended.

But no Phillis !

Then came the tea.

But still the child was missing.

Lady Fane could now with difficulty restrain her uneasiness.

Still she dared not put any question about her to Mrs. Stibbington.

She was afraid that this would incense the vile woman still more against the poor little innocent.

The tea was no sooner over than Lady Ethel made her way into the garden.

Here she searched every corner, but could find no Phillis.

The girl had disappeared.

Then Lady Ethel made a tour of such portions of the house as she could in anthing like decency venture upon.

But with the like result.

And now she began to grow extremely uneasy.

It began to assume the appearance of a mystery.

At length bed-time arrived.

But still Phillis was missing.

Lady Ethel could stand it no longer.

She must at any risk ask an explanation of Mrs. Stibbington.

"Mrs. Stibbington, where is Phillis?"

"What?"

"What has become of Phillis?"

"Eh?"

Lady Ethel repeated her question, greatly annoyed.

She perfectly understood Mrs. Stibbington's interrogations.

She had at once comprehended the question addressed to her.

The queries were then evidently to gain time.

Lady Ethel prepared to hear some atrocious falsehood. In this she was not disappointed, as we shall see.

"Where have I put Phillis to, Mrs. Morley?"

"Yes."

"What a strange question!"

"Why strange?"

"To ask where we have put the child to."

"Not at all. The girl disappears—disappears without a word."

"Of course—there's nothing very startling about that, is there."

"Perhaps not. I only wish to know where she is."

"And so you shall if you wish to."

"Then I most decidedly do wish to—where is she?"

"I've sent her to——"

She paused.

"Yes—where?"

"Up to bed."

"To bed?"

"Yes."

"When?"

"This morning."

"That is false."

"Mrs. Morley, you are forgetting yourself—beware how you speak."

"I say again that it is false."

"How do you know, pray?"

"I was up in my bedroom just before tea."

"And what then?"

"She was not there then."

"And what does that prove?"

"Everything—she was not sent to bed."

"She was, and is there at this very moment, probably."

"You speak in riddles, Mrs. Stibbington."

"Not at all. I say she went to bed. I don't say your bed, you'll understand."

"She is no longer in my bedroom?"

"No."

"And where is she now?"

"Tut, tut, Mrs. Morley—less questions, if you please."

Lady Ethel saw plainly that she could do no good by urging the child's cause.

However, she spent her first night of solitude since her arrival at The Chesnuts full of gloomy presentments.

"Poor child," she murmured; "what can have become of her?—why did I neglect Mr. Stibbington's caution. To-morrow I'll see it to the end."

CHAPTER LII.

STRANGE BEHAVIOUR OF THE PRETTY NURSE.

WE parted company with the wounded artist, Frank Harley, a long time since.

We dread to think how long we have neglected this rather important personage in our history.

At the conclusion of the thirty-fifth chapter we shall find that he was given over by the two doctors who were attending upon him.

The wound he had received in his encounter with the ferocious Major Beele was of a very serious nature.

But the doctors had somewhat overrated the gravity of the case.

Frank Harley was still as good as ten dead men.

He did not die.

The singular nurse who had proffered her assistance just in the nick of time was greatly affected by the decision of the doctors, that Frank Harley was a lost man.

Gerard Wilde had overheard some strange noise in the studio adjoining the bedroom like the falling of a heavy body.

The nurse was there.

He called her.

Receiving no reply, he went to the door and looked into the studio.

The nurse lay upon the floor in a fainting fit.

Restoratives were speedily applied, but she was a long time recovering her senses.

As she returned to consciousness a word or two that escaped her were overheard by Gerard Wilde, and served to confirm a notion of his that she was no ordinary nurse, but some victim to the tender passion, who was proving her sincerity in this substantial, albeit somewhat romantic, fashion.

"Harley—Harley," she murmured, "poor fellow—no, no."

"As I thought," said Gerard Wilde to himself, "she is no nurse."

"Frank—speak! It is I, I, who——"

She opened her eyes.

"Where am I?"

"You are better now?"

"Better. Oh! I remember."

"Yes. How came you to be taken ill?"

"I don't know."

Gerard Wilde looked stedfastly at her.

She blushed and grew confused beneath his scrutiny.

And this more than ever convinced him that she was no nurse.

"You have deceived me."

"How so?" demanded the nurse.

"You told me that you did not know Mr. Harley."

"What then?"

"You seem to be well acquainted with him."

"I?"

"Yes, so it seems."

"But I tell you that I had scarcely ever seen him—that I had never seen him—I mean before yesterday."

"Are you sure of that?"

"Yes."

"Then how came you to be so affected at his condition?"

"I—I suppose——"

She stammered and knew not what to say.

Gerard Wilde charitably came to her assistance.

"Will you take my advice—the advice of a friend."

"Yes."

"Then you will give up your idea."

"What idea?"

"Of attending to Mr. Harley."

"Oh, no, no."

"And why not?"

"You have engaged me, and—and——"

"And what?"

"I hope that I have given satisfaction. Have I not?"

"Yes."

"Then why should you wish me to quit, sir?"

"I speak merely for your own sake."

"Mine?"

"Yes."

"I don't understand you, sir."

But her tremulous tone gave the lie to her assertion.

"I will tell you plainly, then, what I mean," said Wilde. "I am of opinion that the presence of a person like yourself——"

"How do you mean?"

"I mean interested as you are in the recovery——"

"I, sir?"

"Decidedly."

"You mistake me."

"Not at all. It is plain enough to the least discerning."

"Indeed, sir, you are in error."

Gerard smiled at her vehemence.

"If I am mistaken," he said, "how do you account for the susceptibility you have shown upon his account?"

"I was startled, and——"

"Then if you are so easily startled, you are scarcely qualified for a nurse."

This was a startling way of putting it.

However, the nurse persevered in her purpose.

She would not give up her point without a struggle.

"Give me a chance, at least, sir."

"I would willingly; but——"

"Consider, sir. It would be ruin to me to be discharged upon so short a trial."

"And so, because it might prevent your engagement at another time, I must sacrifice the patient—kill the stoutest heart that was ever known?"

"Kill, sir?"

"Yes."

"Then you think that there is still a chance of his recovery?"

"Of course."

"But you pronounced him beyond all hope but now."

"True. But while there's life there's hope, the saying goes; and in my professional career I have frequently tested its worth."

"Do you really, then, think that he still stands a chance of recovering?"

He shook his head.

"Slight."

"But still a chance?"

"Slight—very slight."

"Thank heaven!"

Gerard Wilde was struck with the fervour of her tone.

"But, as I said before, everything depends upon the patient being kept perfectly quiet."

"You may rely upon me for that, I assure you, sir."

"No, no—you must——"

But he had not got the heart to finish the cruel words.

The nurse was looking into his face with an expression of such earnest entreaty that at once yielded the point.

"After all," he mused, "poor Harley is a gone 'coon now, and the girl may as well stay if it amuses her."

Then he continued some concluding admonitions aloud.

"Then you would prefer to remain here, nurse, eh?"

"If you please."

"Very good. I need scarcely say anything more upon the treatment of the patient."

"Certainly; I have quite understood you, you will find."

"I hope so. The treatment of the patient means no treatment at all. Rest and quiet will do him more good than all the doctors' stuff in the United Kingdom. See that he has this, and you may consider that you have saved the patient's life."

The look of unutterable gratitude with which the nurse repaid this speech was such as to cause the heart of the young doctor to leap to his mouth.

The other doctor was at the bedside with the patient.

Gerard Wilde re-entered the sick-chamber and beckoned him away.

"What was it, Mr. Wilde?" demanded the other.

"The nurse had fainted."

"Fainted!"

"Yes."

"From what?"

"She was frightened."

The other regarded him doubtfully for a minute.

"Sure?"

"Yes," said Wilde.

"She isn't drunk?"

"No, no, no."

Wilde was shocked at the idea.

And why?

He had not been shocked at her predecessor's weakness for stimulants.

But then the present nurse was many years younger than she.

She had altogether such a thoroughly *distingué* appearance that Gerard Wilde could not imagine such a thing possible for a moment.

"It's rather a rum go, Mr. Wilde," said his brother doctor. "I don't like to hear of a nurse being frightened, especially when they fall down insensible."

"Oh, no; you are mistaken here," said Wilde.

"How do you know?"

"Her appearance."

"Tut, sir; appearance goes for nothing."

"Besides, did you not see her weep?"

"Oh! she wept—did she?"

"Yes."

"That's another proof, then."

"Of what?"

"That I am correct."

"Correct in believing that the nurse was drunk?"

"Yes; that's the way it goes—that is, with most persons who are accustomed to strong waters. The first stage they are as serious as Methodist parsons; the second stage they shed a few maudlin tears; the third stage their speech grows thick, and the fourth they generally find their level in a most uncomfortable manner. This woman's not likely to be an exception to the rule."

"But she is."

The doctor smiled.

"You are quite enthusiastic in her cause, Mr. Wilde."

"Not enthusiastic: but I am quite sure that she is no nurse. However, nurse or no nurse, do you think she had better stay after what has transpired?"

"No."

"That's awkward."

"Why?"

"I've more than half promised her already."

"Then that being the case, Mr. Wilde, why ask my opinion?"

"Oh, my decision is of course subject to your approval."

"Not at all."

"Oh! but it is."

"Then by all means let her stay."

"Very good."

"After giving her one or two words of a sort upon her late conduct."

"Certainly."

But although he spoke so positively upon the subject, nothing was further from his thoughts.

There was something about the nurse which inspired respect in spite of himself.

And not alone respect; indeed he felt rather frightened while addressing her.

"How long do you think he may last like this?" asked Wilde.

"It depends."

"On what?"

"If your pet nurse amuses herself by—fainting away—I think you call it, eh?"

"Most decidedly—if you will allow me to be competent to judge."

"Eh? Oh! my dear sir—don't pray be offended."

"Not at all, but——"

"Not for worlds, I assure you. 'Gad, but that would look like impeaching your professional reputation."

"Scarcely that."

"Well, well, the nurse was fainting, then. Only she had best not faint again—unless we happen to be present, and she can perform—eh? oh—I mean unless she can faint in the next room, and without any noise."

"I'll answer for her."

The other smiled. Gerard Wilde was annoyed at his colleague's scepticism; but as he could not carry on the discussion for fear of disturbing the patient, it was very prudently dropped.

Harley was doomed.

On this point both were agreed.

Neither of the Æsculapian marvels, however, could fix the date precisely of the doomed artist's dissolution.

It was certain, however, that he could not last over two days.

Both gave this as their opinions with a positive certainty that must have carried conviction to the hearts of all hearers had there been any.

But there were none.

They took care to pronounce all their decisions when entirely alone.

The nurse would fain have remained to listen.

But Wilde requested her to remain in the studio.

And now they were careful, at Gerard Wilde's request, to speak in such a low tone that they could not possibly be overheard by the nurse.

After some time the two doctors took their leave.

To the nurse they reiterated the strictest injunction respecting the keeping of the patient.

The nurse was profuse in her promises.

Her replies were given with the greatest appearance of calmness.

This rather astonished Gerard Wilde after what had taken place.

He was convinced now that his first surmise was correct.

The swooning had quite confirmed him in this belief, if indeed confirmation were wanting.

However, he only augured well from the present appearance of calmness.

He reasoned, and with apparent truth, that if she could so command her feelings now there was every reason to suppose that she could suppress her emotion sufficiently to attend upon the patient.

The great shock was over.

She had learnt the worst.

To this she must grow resigned after awhile.

However, the two doctors had no sooner departed than the nurse gave way to her grief, and solaced herself with a flood of bitter tears.

"Harley, Harley!" she exclaimed, in a voice none the less full of agony that it was subdued. "You are lost, and I—I alone am to blame. Oh! shall I ever pass one happy hour again?"

She walked upon tip-toe to the sick chamber door.

The patient slept—a fitful restless slumber, which bore testimony to the artist's sufferings even in sleep.

"And this is my work!" said the nurse, half aloud.

The wounded man was moving about in his sleep.

At length, as if stifling, he threw back the bed-clothes which were almost touching his face.

The blood had oozed through the bandages and stained the bed-linen.

The nurse, as if unable any longer to bear the sight of this, turned from the door and strode into the studio, weeping and wringing her hands piteously.

She put the case before her already excited imagination in its most harrowing form, and almost tortured herself into madness with the visions thus conjured up.

Her fears having reached a climax, naturally enough took a turn.

At length she proceeded so far in the opposite direction that she even began to think that the medical men might have been mistaken in their judgment.

She recollected a dozen instances in which the doctors had been similarly mistaken.

"Why not?" she mused. "Doctor Gilks was wrong about Herbert's disease—and was not my father given over in his youth—and—oh! they must be mistaken. At any rate I'll not believe that the worst has come yet. He has everything in his favour. He's young and healthy—and—what's that?"

She fancied that she had heard a knock at the outer door.

She waited awhile.

Then the knock was repeated.

"Can it be the doctor returned? I must see."

The new comer, evidently growing impatient at the delay, repeated his summons, and now so loudly that there was some danger that the patient might be disturbed.

The nurse ran to the door.

Before she could open it, however, the visitor spoke.

There was something in the tone of his voice which caused her to start back and change colour.

It was evidently familiar to her.

"Great heavens!" she exclaimed. "What can he want here?"

"Is Mr. Harley in the way?" demanded the visitor without.

"I must be careful."

The nurse pulled her cap over her eyes carefully.

Then as carefully opened the door.

Who should then appear but our friend Felbridge Winder!

The lady-killing Felbridge Winder, as large as life.

"Is Mr. Harley in?"

"Yes—that is—no—no, he's not."

The nurse was all confusion.

She stammered and blushed in a way that must have set an observant person thinking.

Mr. Felbridge Winder, however, was not an observant person.

Of this the reader must be by the present time pretty well aware.

"Look here, I say," said Mr. Winder; "what do you mean by this—He is—he isn't—he is? Is he in or out? Just answer that."

"He's out."

"Hallo, there! Why, what the dooce——"

Here Mr. Winder stared at the nurse in astonishment.

He dodged about in every direction to get a look at her features.

But in vain.

The cap with its dreadful frill which she wore effectually concealed them from his gaze.

Indeed, so well was her face hidden by the cap, that it almost seemed to have been assumed for that purpose.

Here we would point attention to another remarkable circumstance.

The first words which the nurse had addressed to Mr. Winder were in an assumed voice.

Her soliloquy had been delivered in a tone which was music itself.

But when speaking to the visitor her voice appeared gruff and harsh.

In short, the most inexperienced might have detected the assumption.

But Mr. Winder had not.

His remark was occasioned by observing a most noticeable and singular change in her voice.

She had forgotten herself.

Her last words were given in her natural voice.

And this Mr. Winder appeared to recognise at once.

That is to say, he recognised in it the voice of some familiar friend; but for the life of him he could not say who.

Hence his desire to get a look at her face.

LADY ETHEL DISCOVERS PHILLIS CONFINED IN THE VAULT.

"By Jove!" he muttered, half aloud; "I've heard that voice before."

The nurse trembled.

"I say, young woman."

"Yes, sir."

The nurse's gruff voice had returned as if by magic."

"Where the deuce have I seen you before?"

"Me, sir?"

"Yes; you."

"You're mistaken, sir. I never saw you before, I am sure."

"You are sure?"

"Quite."

"Deuced strange, though. Well, I s'pose she's right. But I want to know how is Mr. Frank Harley?"

"As bad as he can be, sir."

"Oh, indeed! you don't say so? I'm sorry to hear it, I'm sure."

Mr. Felbridge would have been somewhat surprised had he seen the look of indignation with which the nurse greeted this cold, heartless commonplace.

However, the cap-frill kept even her indignation from him.

"But, I say; can't I see him—don't you know, young woman?"

"No."

"By Jove! I must, though."

"You cannot."

"And why?"

"He is dying."

"By Jove!—he isn't?"

"And the doctors say that the least disturbance mightprove fatal to him on the instant."

"By Jove! that's awkward. I can't go without (this was *sotto voce*). Amatoria wont see me, I know, unless this freak of hers is satisfied."

The nurse bit her lip until the blood came.

She made a movement as if she would close the door.

"But, I say—don't you know?—I must see him, though."

"You cannot——"

Winder attempted to push half-a-sovereign into her hand.

But she withdrew her hand, and resolutely barred the entrance.

"Sir," she said, coldly, "I have told you that it would be death to the patient to allow any visitor to come into the room. If you attempt to enter I must call for assistance."

"Oh, oh!—by Jove! No, we don't want any row, you know. I'm off."

And Mr. Winder vanished.

The nurse closed the door, and walked across the studio, muttering to herself.

These were her words—

"The cold-blooded idiot!"

CHAPTER LIII.

THE CEREMONY IN THE CHAPEL.

"IT could not have been she."

"Hush!"

"Do you not see she is asleep?"

"It may be pretence."

"That we can easily ascertain."

"If it is——"

"Well?"

"It had been better for her that she had never entered the walls of this convent."

"Why?"

"Why? Do you suppose we should ever give a chance to those who discover our secrets to blab of them?"

"No; but——"

"But what?"

"She is a novice. We might gammon her with some tale."

"It will not do. If she knows anything, she dies."

This was the whispered conversation which Marion Leicester heard as she lay upon her bed.

That it referred to her she had no doubt.

It was evident it had been discovered that some stranger had obtained entrance to the chapel.

Suspicion had fallen upon her, but proof was wanting. Were that proof obtained, she knew she had no mercy to expect; but fate had forewarned her, and she simulated sleep as the old woman, accompanied by the priests, advanced towards her bed.

The beldame bent over her till Marion felt her breath upon her cheek.

"No; this is not feigned sleep," said she.

It is impossible to describe the joyful emotion with which Marion heard these words.

"Be not too sure of that," said a priest, who had hitherto remained silent.

"Do you doubt it?"

"I do not say so."

"What then?"

"I say you have not tested the matter fairly. Remember the importance of the matter."

"What do you propose?"

"Stand on one side; I have an infallible test."

Marion heard these words with alarm. She dreaded discovery, for she felt it would be impossible for her to retain her composure for any length of time.

In an instant an idea flashed through her brain.

She resolved upon the course she would pursue.

As the priest advanced towards the bed on which she lay, she languidly opened her eyes with well-acted amazement.

For a moment she stared round her as if lost in astonishment.

"Where am I?" she asked, at length.

No one answered her.

"What does this mean?" she asked, after a pause, with indignation, which was not wholly feigned. "What does this unwarrantable intrusion mean?"

Her sudden awakening was a contingency for which the priest was totally unprepared.

He stepped back a few paces and stammered forth—

"Call it not intrusion, my daughter; we were only anxious for your welfare."

"Was it anxiety for my welfare which brought you all hither?" asked Marion. "Am I to be allowed no peace—no privacy?"

"Certainly, my daughter; but——"

"But what, sir?"

The priest commenced two or three sentences to excuse himself and his companions, but broke down lamentably in them all.

Marion had risen from the bed, and with flashing eyes faced the assembled priests, who shrank back from her gaze.

At last, after a few muttered apologies, they left the room, satisfied that whoever had been the intruder in the chapel, Marion Leicester was not the person.

So well had she acted her part, that all suspicion was completely allayed. They were thrown off the scent, and turned to look in another direction for the discovery of the intruder in the chapel.

Marion's relief when she found herself once more alone may be easily imagined. Every moment while they were present she dreaded that some chance word or action of hers might reveal the fact of her knowledge of the secret passage.

It was difficult, too, for her to answer calmly the wretches who had instigated the cruel torture of the unfortunate girl in the chapel.

How should she be able to live amongst them!

That was the question she asked herself ever and over again.

They would never suffer her to escape. Of that she was certain. Her friends could not assist her, for she had thrown off her allegiance to them. How bitterly she now regretted that she had not listened to their counsel and entreaties.

But it was too late!

The past was irrevocable.

All through the night her mind was haunted by the pale, pinched, yet beautiful face of the girl who had been so cruelly scourged.

She fancied she again saw before her that bruised and bleeding form.

The morrow brought with it calmer and more sober reflections.

Regrets were useless.

Escape seemed impossible.

She would be allowed no communication with the outer world.

She determined to wait with what patience she could muster, and watch for the first opportunity to escape from the thraldom of the convent.

It came sooner than she expected, and in a way no one could have foreseen.

It was the fourth day of her abode in the convent.

She had as yet mixed with none of the nuns. She had seen only two or three of them, and had spent the whole of the time in the seclusion of her own chamber.

But this was not to continue.

On the fourth day the door of her cell was unfastened, and the lady superior, whom she had not seen since her arrival, entered, and closed the door behind her.

"Marion Leicester," said she; "it was your desire to become numbered of us."

"It was."

"Your praiseworthy wish shall now be fulfilled. To-night you will be received amongst us."

"To-night?"

"Yes; it is the anniversary of the founding of this convent, which it is our custom to celebrate with a grand religious festival. What more fitting occasion could there be for welcoming to us a new sister?"

"That is true."

"Sister Margaret will wait upon you shortly and array you for the festival, and from henceforth remember Marion Leicester is dead, but lives in the name of Sister Catherine."

Marion silently bowed her head, and the lady superior quitted the room.

Every fresh step which Marion took to bind herself to the convent caused her more grief and pain than can well be imagined.

Every ceremony, every action, every word, seemed to lessen her chance of escape, and she well knew that after once entering solemnly into the sisterhood, all attempts at forsaking it would be looked upon and dealt with as a most flagrant crime.

Still she was powerless.

What could she do?

Any attempt to draw back would only lead to suspicion. She would be closely watched, and escape rendered impossible.

No; the only chance for her was to feign what four days previously she had really felt, and thus disarm suspicion.

It was not long before Sister Margaret made her appearance, bearing in her arms the vesture which Marion was to don.

Over a simple nun's dress was placed a long, white, flowing robe.

Upon her head was placed a wreath of white roses, which contrasted well with her luxuriant dark hair, which rippled over her shoulders.

Thus attired, Marion looked more beautiful than ever.

The simplicity of the dress became her; and even the harsh, stern Sister Margaret was betrayed into an expression of admiration at the appearance of the novice.

She immediately checked herself, however, and gave utterance to a few sour phrases condemning the pomps and vanities of the world, and denouncing beauty as a delusion and a snare.

Poor thing! It must have been a great comfort to her to know her personal appearance could never have deluded or ensnared the unwary.

The ceremony was not to take place till midnight, and as yet it wanted nearly an hour to the time; so once more was Marion left to her own sad reflections, while she sat and waited for the summons to the chapel.

She saw matters now in a totally different light to what she had done four days previously.

Everything was changed.

The sight which she had already witnessed in the chapel rose before her eyes, and seemed to mock the religious ceremony in which she was about to take a part, and it was with a weary sign that she heard the bell commence to toll solemnly for the service.

To her it sounded like a death-knell.

It was not that she regretted the world she was about to leave, for to that she was quite reconciled; but it was the knowledge of the inhuman nature of those to whom she would be linked for the remainder of her life.

She shuddered as she thought it might, ere long, be her turn to take the place of the wretched girl before the altar; but better that, she thought, than be compelled to stand by and see the torture inflicted.

The bell ceased, the door of her chamber was thrown wide open, and at the threshold stood four nuns, who, without speaking, beckoned Marion with their hands.

She obeyed the signal.

Accompanied by them she traversed long passages, ascended and descended steps, till, at last, they entered a long, gloomy passage, illumined by a solitary lamp which made the surrounding darkness appear the blacker.

Along this passage they proceeded till further progress was stayed by a massive door, studded thickly with large nails.

At this, one of the nuns knocked in a peculiar manner.

There was a pause.

A dead silence.

Marion heard her own heart beat, as it palpitated violently.

The silence became oppressive.

What did it portend?

The suspense was hardly bearable.

Suddenly the door was thrown open.

A flood of bright light poured upon Marion, completely dazzling and bewildering her.

The sound of many voices, and the rich, swelling tones of a magnificent organ joining in a splendid anthem, struck upon her ear.

So sudden was the transition from darkness to brilliant light, from perfect silence to a burst of harmony, that Marion remained standing, partially paralysed by the unexpected change.

After all, it was but a theatrical effect; but the end of the priests was gained.

In the same way that, in the days of old, the advertisement of a thousand additional lamps at Vauxhall proved a great attraction, so the priests, when they wished to produce a "sensation," spent a few pounds in wax tapers and colza oil.

The chapel was literally a blaze of light.

Round the pillars which supported the roof twined lines of light, before the picture powerful lamps were hung; but the altar was the most dazzling of all.

Candles in profusion decorated it.

Their light was reflected back a hundredfold from the magnificent gold ornaments which adorned it, while immediately above it a cross, which appeared to be composed literally of light alone, sparkled, quivered, and glittered in dazzling brilliancy.

No wonder that Marion stood amazed.

No wonder that for the moment she was bereft of her self-possession.

She shaded her eyes with her hands for a few moments, and then, at a signal from her conductors, stepped forward into the interior of the chapel.

A hundred voices rose and fell in measured cadence, the organ swelled forth its finest tones as she advanced towards the altar, and where at the order of her guides she stayed her course, with the full blaze of light from the cross resting upon her, the voices burst forth in a joyous, exultant strain, which almost seemed to shake the roof as they vibrated along the aisle.

The effect was almost magical.

It would have had an overpowering effect upon Marion, but for one circumstance.

But for that all that the priests desired from their display would have been accomplished.

But Marion, as she looked and listened, remembered how she had seen the chapel on a former occasion.

How it had looked dark and dreary, how in place of the blaze of light before the altar there had been a poor helpless girl quivering beneath the lash, how in place of the swelling anthem her cries of distress rang through the vaulted aisles.

All this she remembered, and the pageant lost its solemnity.

All, all was a mockery.

She had quitted the world on account of its sin and deceit, only to find it in a different form in the retreat she had chosen.

The nuns completely filled the chapel, with the exception of the small space in front of the altar reserved for Marion and her conductors.

The crowd of pale, thin faces, surmounted by the nun's hood, had a strange effect to one unaccustomed to it ; but, after the first surprise was over, and Marion had recovered her self-possession, she was able to look around her, and view all that was taking place calmly and quietly.

In the front rank of the nuns, and close by the spot where the novice stood, was one whose face she instantly recognised.

It was the poor girl whose torture she had witnessed, and whom she had succoured when deserted by the others.

She could not refrain from giving a slight start at thus coming face to face with her again so near the spot where they had first met ; but she resolutely refrained from glancing towards her again, from fear of betraying herself.

The anthem came to an end, and the ceremony in which Marion was to play so prominent a part commenced.

Again a dead silence reigned in the chapel, which was only broken by the voice of a venerable white-haired priest, who in sonorous tones, read a long Latin prayer.

At its conclusion the organ again peeled forth.

The four nuns who had never quitted Marion took the wreath of roses from her head and supplied its place by the ordinary head garniture of their sect.

Her white dress was removed, leaving her standing in the plain garb of the sisterhood.

The dress and the wreath were cast on the ground before the altar as an emblem that Marion had renounced the pomps and vanities of the world.

Then again the solemn tones of the priest's voice reverberated through the chapel, but ere the prayer was concluded, a wild shriek from the nuns interrupted the religious service.

"Fire! Fire!"

It was too true.

A lamp insecurely fastened had given way.

It had been fed with naptha.

The spirit caught fire, and poured in a blazing stream upon the floor, igniting everything with which it came in contact.

The pictures, the wreaths, the decorations were all shortly a blaze of fire.

The nuns' dresses caught.

The smoke and stench became almost insufferable.

Hither and thither ran the poor women, in vain endeavouring to find some other exit than the narrow door which was now so blocked by those vainly endeavouring to make their way through it that egress was impossible.

The door opened inwards.

The crowding was so great that it was impossible to open it.

The priests caught the infection and fled for their lives.

A door behind the altar gave them comparatively easy means of escape, but it was barred against the nuns.

In vain were the agonizing entreaties of the suffering women.

The priests having deserted their charge, and saved an armful of tawdry tinsel-covered images, locked the door and left the nuns to their fate.

Incredible as it may appear, this was the literal fact.

The door behind the altar led to the room where the machinery of their clumsy juggles, which they offered to the world as miracles, was kept.

Were the nuns to see it their power would be lost.

They preferred to leave them to a painful death.

No words can describe the shrieks of agony which filled the chapel.

The devouring element made irresistible progress.

Everything inflammable fell victim to its insatiable appetite.

Smoke in thick volumes rolled along the aisles, causing many to fall senseless on the ground.

The tongues of flame licked up all within their reach.

The heat was terrific ; the smoke suffocating.

Heaps of dead and dying encumbered the ground.

Happy was the fate of those whom the smoke rendered insensible before the flames reached them.

No one now thought of Marion.

It was everyone for herself, and the poor novice had but little chance.

One corner of the chapel alone seemed free from fire, and thither Marion ran.

All the other nuns were vainly struggling to escape through the narrow doorway by which the novice had entered the chapel.

They strove and fought, but all in vain.

Senseless and dead bodies extended on the pavement prevented the door from being opened.

Madly they struggled till the thick vapour rolling towards them laid them senseless and helpless beside their companions.

It was a fearful scene.

A scene in which hundreds of human beings vainly struggled for life.

A scene where heartrending shrieks for help and despairing groans of anguish rent the air.

And all the while the flames came steadily on, hastening to complete their work of destruction.

There it was true characters appeared.

Some fell upon their knees and invoked the aid of their patron saints ; others blasphemed and cursed in their anguish.

But all alike perished.

Marion had, as aforesaid, made her way to a niche which the flames seemed to have spared.

There was a slight current of fresh air there which blew both flame and smoke in a contrary direction, still it was scarcely possible to bear the heat.

For the first few moments Marion believed herself to be alone in this niche, but a low moan attracted her attention.

A figure, habited in a nun's garb, lay stretched upon the stones.

A closer examination revealed, much to Marion's surprise, that it was no other than the unfortunate girl whose flagellation before the altar she had witnessed a few days previously.

She raised her in her arms and drew her further back into the niche.

More away from the fury of the flames.

Nearer to the fresh air which found its way in.

Where did that fresh air come from ?

Marion asked herself this question, and in answer a joyous thought flitted through her brain.

Was it possible that by good chance the niche in which she had taken refuge was that which contained the secret door ?

She passed her hand along the wall to discover the exact spot from whence the fresh air proceeded.

It came from behind a small image.

Eagerly she caught it in her grasp with the intention of pulling it down, in order to discover if her surmise were correct.

There was no occasion to do so.

No sooner did she touch the statue than the apparently solid wall gave way, revealing a dark passage, which Marion had no difficulty in recognising as the one she had traversed on the occasion when she had witnessed the horrible scene of punishment in the chapel.

A cry of joy escaped her lips.

"Saved—saved !" she cried.

Then raising the thin, wasted form of the nun in her arms, she unhesitatingly plunged into the gloomy passage, which she knew would ultimately lead her to the room she occupied.

Still bearing the senseless form of her companion in her arms, she reached the stone steps which led upwards to her cell.

Notwithstanding her burden, she mounted them rapidly; but only to meet with disappointment.

The door which led into her chamber was fastened, and she was unacquainted with the spring by which it was opened.

Placing the still unconscious nun upon the steps, she beat against the massive door with her small delicate hands.

She cried aloud, but met with no response.

She hammered with her white hands against the obstacle till her knuckles were bruised and bleeding.

The smoke from the chapel was already curling along towards her.

Hope, which had revived at the discovery of the secret passage, became again well-nigh extinct.

She had escaped burning in the chapel, but to be suffocated in the vaulted passage.

Just as she was about giving up her attempt at escape in despair, her hand encountered a metal knob.

She pressed it.

Silently the door revolved upon its hinges, and in another moment she stood within her own cell.

To drag the senseless nun in, to lay her on the bed, and again close the secret door, was but the work of a few moments.

Then obeying an involuntary impulse, she fell upon her knees and returned fervent thanks to Heaven for her miraculous escape.

The nun whom she had rescued shortly showed symptoms of returning consciousness, which Marion promoted by all the means in her power.

CHAPTER LIV.

MRS. GOLIGHTLY'S FIRST FLOOR.

"WHERE am I? What has happened?" asked the nun whom Marion had rescued.

"You are in my room—safe for the present. There has been an accident——"

"Stay—I remember. There were flames. I recollect all now," and she shuddered as the hideous events which she had witnessed thronged into her mind.

For a few minutes there was a complete silence; then suddenly the nun started to her feet.

"What are we doing here? Why do we linger? Now is the time to escape. During this confusion we shall pass out unnoticed. Come—come."

She spoke rapidly, and ere she had finished had already led Marion in the direction of the door.

It was a chance not to be lost.

Marion felt this, and eagerly agreed to her companion's plan.

The priests, in making their escape, had unlocked all the doors; but their hurry had been too great to allow them time to reclose them.

The passages were all deserted, and the two girls pursued their way without hindrance, till at last they breathed the fresh, cold night air in the courtyard of the convent.

Lying on the stones were two large cloaks, dropped apparently by some one in their hurried flight.

The idea of hiding their nun's garb beneath them occurred to both the fugitives, and they hastily donned them.

They descended to their feet, and hid the dress which would have betrayed them directly they were in the streets.

The key was in the lock of the large door which formed the exit from the nunnery.

Marion turned it, and in another moment found herself with her companion outside the convent walls.

Without speaking, they walked rapidly side by side through the deserted streets till they had put a considerable distance between them and their late home.

"What are we to do?" asked Marion.

"Walk about till morning, and then seek some hiding-place."

"Hiding-place! What do you mean?"

"Some unpretending lodgings in a quiet street, where we shall be safe until we can communicate with our friends."

"Who are your friends? I do not even know your name."

"Call me Lucy," replied the nun, evading the question.

The two paced the streets together undisturbed.

Occasionally some roysterer came staggering past, howling the refrain of some Bacchanalian ditty; but they shrunk back into some dark archway or narrow court whenever they heard any one approaching, and took good care not to emerge from their hiding-place till the sound of footsteps died away in the distance.

By-and-bye a pale grey light stole over the sky, then the clouds became tinged with a roseate hue, the gas-lamps paled before the coming day. Market-waggons from the country rolled heavily along, labourers appeared in the streets on their way to work, and all around signs that another day had commenced.

Suddenly Marion stopped, and pointed to a shop-window from which the shutters had just been removed.

It was a small, unpretending kind of shop, doing a mixed trade in tobacco, groceries, and cheap periodicals.

Pasted in the window in a conspicuous position was a piece of paper, upon which was inscribed in legible characters the word "Apartments."

"Shall we go in?" asked Lucy.

"Yes. I can no longer walk the streets; my strength is well-nigh exhausted."

"No wonder; it is six hours since we left the convent, and——"

"Hush! Not a word of that dreadful place."

"But how shall we account for our dress?"

"Leave that to me."

The two girls entered the shop together.

A wretched, cracked bell tingled as they opened the door, and summoned the proprietress of the shop from a little back-parlour about eight feet square.

She came forth smiling, bringing with her a baby and a strong smell of red herrings and onions.

She stared hard at her customers; for it must be remembered that, although their dress was hidden by the long cloaks they wore, their heads were only covered by the ordinary nun's hood.

"What can I do for you, ladies?" asked Mrs. Golightly (for such was her name), in a merry, cheerful tone.

"We see by the notice in the window that you let apartments."

"Yes I do—but—but——"

It was evident from her hesitation that the old lady was unable to comprehend the dress and unprotected appearance of the girls.

"You mean you require some reference, I suppose?"

"Well, not that exactly, Miss, neither; but you see I'm a lone woman; a husband in Australia not counting as such, but though poor, I'm respectable, and two young ladies with black and white things on their heads a-coming without luggage at eight o'clock in the morning, and asking for lodgings, do look queer."

"We have only just arrived from a journey. We have been travelling all night," said Marion.

"May I make bold to ask, Miss, if that's your travelling dress?" said Mrs. Golightly, indicating the hood.

"It is for us. We belong to a religious community, and always wear it."

The old lady seemed to be by no means convinced.

Just then, Lucy, who had borne up bravely hitherto, turned suddenly pale, and grasped the counter for support.

"A glass of water, for mercy's sake!" cried Marion, as she saw with alarm the condition of her companion.

"Dear—dear, she do look bad, sure-ly!" said the old lady, as she bustled to get the required restorative.

Still, however, Lucy showed no signs of recovery.

Her frame had been enfeebled by the torture she had so recently undergone, and though the excitement of the escape had kept her up throughout the night, the reaction had now come.

All colour faded from her cheeks, and she would have fallen but that Marion perceived her condition, and ran to support her.

"Dear heart alive!" exclaimed the good-natured Mrs. Golightly, "to think of this, now! Come in, there's a dear."

So saying, she opened the door which led into the tiny back-parlour, and with some difficulty wedged the two fugitives into the room.

After some little time Lucy showed signs of returning to consciousness, but she was still so weak as to be unable to stand without assistance.

Mrs. Golightly, who was by nature very tender-hearted, had in the meantime been talked by Marion into agreeing to allow them to rent two rooms on the second floor for a week.

Marion paid the money in advance, and thus eased her landlady's mind from pecuniary doubts, and Lucy, as soon as she was sufficiently recovered, was removed to a small, but clean bed, upstairs.

In a couple of days, Mrs. Golightly's mind was completely set at rest.

She saw that her lodgers were quiet and respectable. That much known, their being pretty and helpless was sufficient passport to her good graces.

"Poor thing! she's a lady born and bred, I'll warrant," said the landlady, gently smoothing the hair of the sleeping Lucy. "Never mind, dear, I don't want to know your story if you'd rather not tell it," she added, turning to Marion.

She was a kind, good-tempered, quaint old creature, was Mrs. Golightly.

She was short in stature, large in circumference, rotund in form, and ruddy in countenance.

A few straggling wisps of yellow hair surmounted her jolly-looking face, and in these, apparently, she took much pride, always keeping them wrapped up in leaves from the back numbers of such of the publications as had little sale.

But for Sundays she had a wonderful head-dress.

Then it was she donned a black front, which was always slipping on one side, in spite of the huge cap she wore, for the express purpose of keeping it in its place.

Then it was she wore a flowered chintz dress, alarming in its profusion of colour; but in spite of all her eccentricities in attire and grammar, Mrs. Golightly had a kinder, warmer heart beating beneath her flowered chintz than many a fine lady beneath her silk and lace.

"You see, my dear," she once explained to Marion, "you see, my dear, trade is doubtful; groceries may sell, but if they don't, they go bad; and as for penny numbers, no one can tell whether they'll go off or not."

"Then that is the reason you took to letting lodgings?"

"Precisely so, my dear. I have a first floor that comfortable I can't imagine how anybody could leave it. The last gent as had it, he says to me, says he, 'Mrs. G., that room of yours is a little Paradise,' but yet he left it—left it, owing three weeks' rent, and taking with him a pair of sugar-tongs, plated that natural he took 'em for silver."

"Then your first floor is vacant now, Mrs. Golightly?"

"It is, indeed, my dear; and unless I get a lodger soon, goodness knows where my quarter's rent's to come from."

In listening to the old landlady's conversation, and in attending upon Lucy, who, from the exertion and excitement she had gone through, had sunk into a species of low fever, Marion's days passed.

She had not yet acquainted her friends of her whereabouts; indeed, they were ignorant that she had quitted the convent.

A species of foolish pride prevented her from at once confessing to them that it would have been better for her had she listened to their advice and persuasions.

She knew it must come out at last; but she shrunk from informing them herself.

Not that she acknowledged this to be the reason.

She endeavoured to persuade herself it was her duty to watch by her sick companion, ignoring the truth that she would be much better taken care of if surrendered into their hands.

By fragments she learned from Lucy an outline of her history.

It was a sad story, but an old one.

She had set her heart upon a young man of good ability, but slender means.

She had bestowed upon him all her affections.

The passion was mutual, but her parents would not hear of the alliance.

They had far more ambitious views for their only daughter.

She had been betrothed, when in her cradle, to the son of her father's most intimate friend—a man of rank, wealth, and position.

The marriage was most repugnant to her.

She could not force her father to give his consent to the union she wished; but, in her turn, she could and did refuse to wed the man her parents desired.

It is an old story. There were prayers and entreaties, tears, harshness, and commands; but all were equally ineffectual.

Then came the dread alternative.

She must marry the man she hated, or pass the remainder of her life in a nunnery.

She chose the convent.

Her lover, however, discovered her whereabouts. He managed to get a letter conveyed to her secretly.

By means of bribery they managed to carry on a correspondence.

More than this. There was a window in the convent, closely barred and grated, it is true, still looking into the courtyard, and thither she would often steal, when all besides were hushed in sleep, to hold converse with him for whose sake she had immured herself within the convent walls.

It was while proceeding to one of these stolen interviews that she became unintentionally the witness to a terrible scene.

No questions on Marion's part could induce her to disclose what it was she had witnessed. She declared it was too horrible for narration.

Whether it was an orgie, such as the worshippers of Bacchus in the olden times might have held,—whether it was a scene of pain and torture,—whether it was the punishment of a nun who had broken her vows—she could not be induced to disclose.

She never referred to it without a shudder; and Marion, seeing the pain it gave, forbore to question her.

While watching this dreadful scene, half paralysed with terror, accident revealed her presence.

She was dragged before the altar and made to swear a solemn oath of secrecy.

The punishment which Marion witnessed had resulted from the same cause.

It is needless to say Marion did not learn all this sad story at one time. Piece by piece Lucy related it to her when her strength was sufficient for conversation.

One afternoon, when the two fugitives had occupied Mrs. Golightly's second floor for nearly a week, Marion was sitting by the bedside of her friend and companion in flight, when a knock sounded at the door, and the landlady entered in an apologistic manner.

"Begging your pardon, my dears, for intruding," said she, "but looking upon you as one of the family, though perhaps I should say, too, I took the liberty of coming in to inform you that I've got a lodger for the first floor."

"I'm glad to hear it," said Marion, smiling at the delight which beamed over Mrs. Golightly's face. "I'm glad to hear it. I hope he wont run off with the sugar-tongs."

"Oh no, my dear; he's quite the gentleman, I assure you, though I'm nigh upon certain he wears a wig. He agreed at once to all my terms, but asked a number of questions about you, my dears."

"About us?"

"Yes. He said he was very particular about his fellow-lodgers, so I just told him you was two quiet and well-disposed young ladies, and then he smiled and said he was quite satisfied."

"Is it possible he can be—what was he like, Mrs. Golightly?"

"Well, he's tall and dark; he's got a——"

"I beg your pardon, ladies," said a voice from the door, with a slightly foreign accent; "I have mistaken my room."

"That's the man himself," cried Mrs. Golightly, triumphantly, as the door closed upon him. "Bless my heart, I wonder if he wants anything! Perhaps I'd better go and see."

Whereupon the old landlady bustled out of the room and lumbered downstairs to see that everything was properly arranged for her new lodger.

When Marion turned to address some trivial observation to Lucy, she was startled at the extraordinary change in her countenance.

A ghastly pallor had spread itself over her face.

Her eyes were fixed upon the door where the new lodger had momentarily appeared, and her whole frame betrayed excessive agitation.

"What is it, Lucy?" cried Marion, alarmed. "What makes you look in that way?"

"Did you see that man?" she asked, clutching her companion's arm with nervous force.

"Yes."

"Do you not know him?"

"No. Why do you ask?"

"Have you never seen him before?"

"Never."

"Yet it must be. I cannot be deceived."

"Do you know him, Lucy?"

"Yes."

She shuddered as she spoke, and an expression of loathing flitted across her face.

"Who is he?"

"Father Anselmo."

"Father Anselmo? I never heard the name."

"He is the real chief of the convent from which we have made our escape!"

CHAPTER LV.

HOW LADY ETHEL PLAYS THE SPY.

ANOTHER day passed at "The Chesnuts," and the little girl Phillis had not reappeared.

Inquiries were whispered about the school-room amongst the children; but no answers were forthcoming.

Affable and pleasant in the school-room as on the preceding day, Mrs. Stibbington did not venture the slightest explanation of the child's absence.

There was something in the bearing of the school-mistress which prevented the pupils from demanding the cause of the child's absence.

Something stern and forbidding, in spite of her kindliness of manner.

And yet the sensation it created in the school-room was very marked.

From the youngest to the oldest of the pupils there was an appearance of restraint all over the school.

All seemed to feel uncomfortable in Mrs. Stibbington's presence.

And why?

The reason was obvious enough.

They had seen the unnecessary severity with which Phillis's fault had been treated, and feared that their turn might come next.

But they need not have feared.

Mrs. Stibbington's violent temper did not stand in her way at all.

It would not have paid her to be cruel to her ordinary pupils.

After talking about the missing Phillis all the day, one of the pupils, immediately that Mrs. Stibbington left the room for a few moments, ran up to Lady Ethel's desk, and in a hurried, whispered tone, asked her if Phillis would be permitted to return to the school-room that day.

"I don't know," replied Lady Ethel. "Mrs. Stibbington has said nothing to me about her."

"But Mrs. Stibbington was very harsh with her," said the girl.

Lady Ethel said nothing.

She did not care to touch upon the actions of the schoolmistress during her absence.

The little girl seeing that Lady Fane was not, at least, displeased with her thus far, ventured to put the question to her point blank.

"Don't you think, Mrs. Morley, that Mrs. Stibbington has been very harsh with Phillis?"

"I fear we are treading upon delicate ground, my dear."

"Well, that's what all the young ladies have been saying."

"Indeed!"

"Oh, yes; and they want you to ask Mrs. Stibbington——"

"Nothing."

"You will not, Mrs. Morley?"

"No."

"But why, ma'am?"

"Because Mrs. Stibbington might think my remark out of place."

"Oh, she couldn't."

"Indeed, but she would."

"Then you cannot ask?"

"No, my dear."

"Good gracious me! Then poor Phillis must. Oh! shan't we see her again, Mrs. Morley?"

"Not see her again?"

"Yes."

"What makes you think that?"

"Well—I mean not for a long time."

"Oh, yes, you will. Why not speak to Mrs. Stibbington yourself?"

"I don't like to."

"Then somebody else."

"There's nobody dares."

"Dares!"

"No; nobody at all."

"But why?"

"I don't know. Indeed, nobody but me would speak to you about her."

"Why, they're surely not afraid of me, my dear?"

"No, not exactly afraid; but——"

"But what?"

"I scarcely know what. However, none of them would do it."

"Has Mrs. Stibbington ever ill-treated—I mean—that is—has Phillis ever misbehaved so before?"

"Once before."

"And then——"

"She did not come into the school-room for more than two weeks."

"What became of her?"

"I don't know."

"Didn't she say where she had been to when she came back?"

"No."

"Did no one ask her?"

"Oh, yes; every one did; but she wouldn't say."

"Did she complain at all?"

"No; but they all said that it was because she feared to."

"Feared?"

"Yes."

"Feared what?"

"Feared Mrs. Stibbington. Haven't you noticed how she fears her?"

"No; that is, not exactly."

"Oh, she is dreadfully afraid of her. And Mrs. Stibbington hates Phillis."

In spite of her caution, it would seem that the schoolmistress had not succeeded in keeping this from the pupils.

Children are great observers in their way.

The girl's remarks, however, tended considerably to restore Lady Ethel's peace of mind upon the unhappy Phillis's account.

She did not so much fear that Mrs. Stibbington's malice would do the poor child any severe bodily injury, since it occurred so publicly.

Her personal interest would not permit it.

This was the conclusion which Lady Ethel at last arrived at.

And it was only then that she acknowledged to herself the extent of her fears.

And so another day passed, and no Phillis.

The next day brought a crisis to affairs.

The pupils could no longer restrain their impatience.

Accordingly, Mrs. Stibbington had barely taken her seat at her desk to commence the morning's duties, when she was waited upon by a deputation, consisting of six girls, headed by Miss Forsyth, to intercede for Phillis.

"Well, young ladies, what do you want of me?" demanded Mrs. Stibbington, with unusual sternness.

Miss Forsyth tremblingly rejoined, that she had come to beg that Phillis might be forgiven her fault, and allowed to return to the school.

Mrs. Stibbington scowled viciously as they mentioned the name of her innocent victim.

However, the girls, although greatly frightened, continued their petition to the conclusion.

When they had finished, Mrs. Stibbington addressed them in a deep voice, with which the children were duly impressed.

"Well, Miss Forsyth, have you said all you intend to say?"

"Yes, ma'am."

"You have gone through it all very well, and do great credit to your teacher."

Here she glanced spitefully at the assistant-governess.

"Mrs. Stibbington," exclaimed Lady Ethel, "I must beg you will not allude to me in this matter."

"Oh, indeed!"

"I have had nothing whatever to do with it."

"No, indeed, Mrs. Stibbington."

"Miss Forsyth."

"Yes, ma'am."

"You are growing very bold."

"Oh, no, ma'am; only——"

"Sit down."

"But——"

"Take your seats. Good Heavens! How many times am I to speak? Have we got up a rebellion in the school?"

One of the girls alone returned to her seat.

The remainder resolutely continued their supplications.

Mrs. Stibbington turned from them greatly enraged.

"Mrs. Morley," she exclaimed, turning furiously upon Lady Ethel, "you have well performed your duties here."

"Madame!"

"Tut, tut! Don't madame me."

"Mrs. Stibbington, you are disgracing yourself."

"Mrs. Morley, immediately quit the school-room."

"Such is my intention."

"And also quit my house."

"You may rely upon that, too, Mrs. Stibbington."

The girls here had all collected in a corner of the room, greatly alarmed at the outburst.

Some of the more courageous began to murmur aloud at the injustice of the schoolmistress.

At length, when Mrs. Morley, the assistant-governess, rose from her seat to quit the room, their murmurs burst out into open remonstrances.

But Mrs. Stibbington was now blinded with passion, and could not see the danger of her present conduct.

"Mrs. Morley, leave the room—do you hear me?—this instant!"

"I shall do so."

She moved towards the door.

"No, no."

"Don't go, Mrs. Morley."

"Where's Phillis?"

"Bring up Phillis."

All was confusion.

The girls all spoke at once.

Each demanded the return of Phillis, and each in different words.

"Silence!" said Lady Ethel. "Silence! Listen to me."

The voices were hushed on the instant.

"Mrs. Stibbington has thought fit——" began Lady Fane.

"Am I or am I not mistress here?" demanded Mrs. Stibbington, in a voice of thunder.

"Mrs. Stibbington has thought fit to behave in a manner to me that must preclude all possibility of——"

"Miss Morley—or Mrs. Morley, whatever you may choose to call yourself—you are determined that I must have you forcibly ejected, I see."

Lady Ethel in vain endeavoured to conclude her address to the scholars.

The schoolmistress interrupted her each time.

Finding this impossible, Lady Ethel addressed a few words to Mrs. Stibbington herself.

These were of rather a striking nature.

"Very well, Mrs. Stibbington, since you will not allow me to speak——"

"Begone!"

"I go."

"No, no;" and "Stay, stay, Mrs. Morley," from the pupils.

"And I go to take immediate steps about the child Phillis Ebury."

"Ebury!"

The schoolmistress changed colour at the name.

All the pupils looked surprised.

Many of them had been at "The Chesnuts" over two years, and had never heard the girl addressed by any other name than Phillis.

Few of them had ever thought of the girl's surname.

"Who do you mean by Phillis Ebury, pray?"

"Who should I mean but the child you have so cruelly maltreated, Mrs. Stibbington?"

"THEY HAVE KILLED ME, MRS. MORLEY!" CRIED PHILLIS.

The consternation exhibited by Mrs. Stibbington as Lady Ethel had mentioned the name of Ebury, convinced her ladyship that there was some fresh mystery attending the girl of which she had not yet dreamt.

"So, so," she thought. "I can make a point of that, perhaps, with this cruel woman. I must endeavour to work upon her fears. She evidently fears now that I am acquainted with something which may endanger her interests—else why her alarm? I must follow this up."

Then she continued, aloud—

"I say, Mrs. Stibbington, that I go at once to the nearest magistrate."

"For what?"

Mrs. Stibbington was already less noisy in her demand.

"To lay the facts of the case before him, and see if the law cannot protect the helpless child."

"What can you do by that, do you think?"

"Much."

"Indeed!"

"Much that you might find unpleasant."

"What do you mean?"

"That certain discoveries——"

"What?"

"Which might be made would look ugly in print."

"What—what discoveries do you mean, Mrs. Morley?"

The voice of the schoolmistress faltered.

She sank into a seat, quailing beneath the gaze of the assistant governess.

A lucky hit had placed the winning cards in Lady Fane's hands.

"I have touched upon some chord there," said Lady Fane to herself, overjoyed at the change in Mrs. Stibbington's manner.

The schoolmistress, however, as if anxious to learn the worst, reiterated her demand for an explanation.

Lady Ethel gave none.

One of her principal reasons for this was that she had none to give.

So, like a prudent general, she did not venture into open combat again.

She preserved an ominous and terrifying silence.

With her eyes still fixed upon the schoolmistress, Lady Ethel walked to the door.

Before she could cross the threshold, however, Mrs. Stibbington called her back.

"Mrs. Morley."

"Madam."

"You are going?"

"Yes."

"Stay."

"What do you want of me, Mrs. Stibbington?"

"One word."

"When I wished to speak you would not hear me,"

"I was out of temper then."

"And so think yourself privileged to insult me?"

"Indeed you must excuse me."

"I cannot."

"I yield to your wishes."

"What wishes?"

"Your desires—whatever they may be.   You'll understand."

She looked at her subordinate significantly.

"I am supposed to know something curious here," mused Lady Ethel. "Very good. I wont undeceive her. It may benefit both Phillis and myself."

She simply bowed gravely to the schoolmistress.

This could not damage her interest in any way.

"And Phillis shall return to the schoolroom, Mrs. Stibbington?"

"Yes."

"At once?"

"Yes—that is, no——"

"No. Not return?"

"Not at once."

"When, then?"

"I don't know—but——"

"Is this what you call acceding to my wishes?"

"Mrs. Morley, she shall come back to-morrow."

"*Come back?*"

"Yes."

"Is she not in the house, then, Mrs. Stibbington?"

"No matter. I say she shall come back to-morrow."

And with this they were forced to be contented.

Lady Fane could press the point no further.

Order was once more restored, and the scholastic duties proceeded with.

But now Lady Ethel remarked that the pupils were all very careful to avoid the schoolmistress.

Not one of them ventured near her.

The lessons which Mrs. Stibbington was in the habit of hearing were now all heard by the assistant governess.

Fortunately Mrs. Stibbington seemed too preoccupied with her thoughts to notice this.

And so was another day concluded.

After the children retired for the night, Mrs. Stibbington and Lady Ethel were in the habit of taking supper together in the parlour.

On this occasion, however, Lady Ethel chose to avoid her employer.

She had gained an advantage over the other's fears by some knowledge she was supposed to possess of some of the schoolmistress's secrets.

Of this Lady Fane was assured.

And she did not wish for a *tête-à-tête* with Mrs. Stibbington.

Some explanation might have been demanded of the words which had fallen from her lips in the school-room.

As Lady Ethel knew of nothing beyond the scene she had witnessed in Mrs. Stibbington's bedchamber the morning after the arrival at "The Chesnuts," and the harsh treatment of Phillis, she did not wish to risk losing her command over the schoolmistress.

While Mrs. Stibbington was in doubt all was well.

Her civil treatment was assured.

Moreover, it must ameliorate the sad condition of poor Phillis.

Once let her suspect that her fears were groundless, and all was over.

Therefore Lady Ethel, without a word to Mrs. Stibbington, donned her walking-dress, and strolled out.

It was a beautiful evening, and so she thought that she could well stroll about until bed-time.

She walked across a field adjoining the house, heedless of the falling dew, and gained a narrow lane which led to the back of the house.

At the bottom of the garden of "The Chesnuts" was a door which opened into this lane.

This door was never locked.

Lady Ethel well knew this, and thought that she could enter the house that way upon her return, and gain her chamber unmolested by the schoolmistress.

Lady Fane walked slowly down this lane, passed the garden-door, and—

"What was that?"

She had barely passed the door when she fancied that she heard a rustling in the hedge behind her.

She turned sharply round.

But not the slightest sign of mortal man met her view.

"I must have been deceived," she said.

And strolled on.

It was a glorious sunset, and the sky was one vast canopy of a bright blood-red, tinted with gold.

There was not a breath of wind stirring.

The leaves were motionless.

It was one of the tropical epochs of this eccentric climate of ours.

Lady Ethel, although as we have seen rather worldly-minded, was duly impressed by the grandeur of the scene.

It was such a night as poets love to dream about.

But such a night as is more frequently met with in poetry than elsewhere.

Lady Ethel, however, for once in her life, felt the influence of the sunset in all its poetizing power.

Let not the reader misunderstand us, however.

We do not for a moment wish to imply that Lady Ethel felt in a mood to pen a sonnet.

With all her faults and foibles Lady Fane had never been guilty of this sort of thing.

Her ideas, her pleasures, her pastimes, were always more material.

However, the sunset and its glow did affect her in another way.

It set her thinking.

The extreme quietude of the scene was favourable for thought.

And Lady Ethel Fane rambled onwards, musing over the many and mundane influences upon her fate.

Of the strange change chain of events which had brought her into her present position.

And of the strange position itself.

Of the strange Mrs. Stibbington and the helpless Phillis.

And she came to the conclusion that this was by no means the least singular passage in her chequered career.

Of this and many other things she thought as she strolled on.

But there was one circumstance which she was quite overlooking.

It was growing late.

And it is probable that she would not have observed this for a considerable lapse of time, had she not received a warning that it was high time to retrace her steps homewards.

Mr. Sol had dropped down behind the eastern horizon like the flickering wick of a used-up dip.

And all was dark.

With its tropical temperature Hendon had almost adopted the tropical and unpleasant knack of dispensing with twilight.

And now that the wanderer began to be recalled back to herself, it struck her she had rambled a considerable distance.

And the ground had to be got over again.

This was no joke.

Although very pleasant at sunset, it was a highly disagreeable road to traverse in the dark.

And the moon would not be up for some hours yet.

There was one branch of her education in which Lady Fane had improved since she had taken up her residence at "The Chesnuts."

She had grown somewhat rustic and weatherwise.

Her knowledge in this instance did not add to her comfort.

However, she did not waste an instant in idle regrets.

Putting a bold face on the matter, and her best foot foremost, she began her journey home.

"Home," she called it.

Home it was, too, for the moment.

But only for the moment.

Fate seemed desirous of converting her ladyship into a kind of Wandering Jewess.

She was destined to make another move very shortly.

But we are rambling, too.

To return to Hendon and to Lady Ethel Fane.

A sharp walk brought her to the lane in which was situated the garden-door.

The windows all up, the house was dark.

The inmates had evidently all retired for the night.

"That's fortunate," said Lady Ethel, as she crossed the grass-plat, which was known at "The Chesnuts" as the LAWN.

Half-way across her foot kicked something, which clattered over the narrow gravel-walk and on to the grass again on the opposite side.

"What was that?"

She stooped to search for it.

Her ear had caught the direction it had taken, and she was not long in dropping upon the spot.

She thrust her hand in the long grass which grew at the edge of the path, and drew out a short staff.

It was very weighty for the size, and the handle was ornamented with a binding of cord.

At this moment Miss Lunar behaved as abruptly as Mr. Sol had done.

She had allowed the wanderer to struggle all this way home in the dark, and now shot out as brilliant as the noonday sun.

This enabled Lady Fane to scrutinize her treasure-trove.

It was one of those short, sconce-breaking clubs known as a life-preserver.

"Great heavens!" murmured Lady Ethel. "A life-preserver! How came it here? There's not such a thing in the house, I know."

She had now arrived at the door opening into the house.

To her right was a flight of stone steps leading to the kitchen.

This being below, the level of the garden was hidden from the view at a few paces distance.

She was therefore not a little surprised to see when she arrived here that there was still a light burning in the kitchen.

Who could it be?

Mrs. Stibbington usually retired very early.

As she paused there, wondering who it could be, it suddenly struck her that she heard voices below.

She listened intently.

Yes, there were two persons below.

Of this she was assured.

It remained only to ascertain who these two persons were.

For this she was determined to do as soon as she made the discovery of their strange, untimely presence there.

She knelt down and peered into the room.

As she had conjectured, there were two individuals.

One of these was the schoolmistress herself.

The other was a man.

A rather tall, broad-shouldered man of gentlemanly appearance.

The candle upon the table unfortunately seemed to trouble his eyes, and he was shading them from its glare with his right hand.

Thus his features were hidden.

Lady Fane could simply see that he had a light brown beard.

They were seated at a table, upon which they were resting their elbows.

Both were leaning forward, and carrying on an animated but whispered conversation.

Mrs. Stibbington was talking in a deferential manner to her visitor, which convinced Lady Fane that he must be some person of note.

But she was not satisfied with this knowledge.

She was all impatience to know the whole truth.

The meaning of his presence there at that strange hour.

In short, to hear their conversation.

But how?

If she could have descended the kitchen-steps unobserved she might have attained her object.

But this was impossible.

Then there was but one other way.

And this was to enter the house, descend the stairs, and try the acoustic properties of the kitchen-door keyhole.

But this had to be accomplished without the slightest noise.

A task of no little difficulty.

She tried the door gently, and it yielded to her touch.

Yielded with a little, ever-so-little, noise.

Then it was as noiselessly closed.

Shivering with excitement, she descended the stairs.

But, oh! did ever stairs creak as did that kitchen-flight upon the present occasion!

Every step she made was sufficient to awaken the whole house.

At length this was accomplished.

And in safety.

At least, so she judged, as there was no evidence of her entrance having been discovered.

She crept close up to the kitchen-door.

Applied her ear to the keyhole, and——

Could hear nothing.

She could hear them conversing within, but their conversation was carried on in an undertone.

Every now and then she caught a word, but it was invariably some commonplace expression which did not give her the slightest clue to the subject they discussed.

After awhile, however, her ear grew accustomed to the "buzz buzz," and she managed to make out a few sentences.

These even rewarded her for the trouble she had taken.

"You see, sir," said Mrs. Stibbington, "I have done everthing in my power to serve you."

The stranger returned some answer, which the listener failed to catch.

She judged, however, that it was a doubt of Mrs. Stibbington's sincerity by the tenor of her reply.

"Indeed you cannot say that."

"Indeed I can."

"But I tell you that the danger I have run, and do run, is of a very grave nature."

"Pshaw! You are full of these nonsensical ideas, woman."

"Not at all——"

"You are. Had you not have been, I should not now be here—pestered with your nonsense. But hark you, I shall leave her here."

"No, you cannot."

"Not leave her here?"

"No."

"Why not?"

"Because I can promise nothing further about her."

"You cannot promise?"

"No."

"You cannot promise me the fulfilment of the contract?"

"No."

"And what may be the meaning of this new freak of yours?"

"The meaning is that I cannot endanger my neck for you."

"Soho! You forget that it is already endangered, eh?"

"I do not. And I don't forget the use you have made of your knowledge, either."

"Indeed! But it began to look like it, excessively."

"I tell you once more that this woman is as cunning as a fox."

"What woman?"

"My new hand."

"What, Mrs. Morley?"

"Ah, Morley she calls herself."

"What do you mean by that, pray?"

"That is an assumed name."

"Then your remedy is at hand if you will but use it."

"How so?"

"You're losing your wit as you increase in years."

"But how?"

"It lies in a nutshell. You have simply to find out her secret to secure her forbearance."

"Her secret?"

"Yes."

"But has she one?"

"Of course. What does she want with an assumed name?"

Pleasant for Lady Ethel.

She could scarcely restrain her emotion at this.

"What's that?"

"What?"

"Somebody at the door, I think."

"You are mistaken."

Fortunately they did not come to see.

Lady Fane felt that she could not have stirred to save her life.

"To come to the end at once," said the stranger, "what have you brought me here for to-night?"

"To take her elsewhere?"

"When?"

"Now."

"What, to-night?"

"Certainly. Don't I tell you that a few days perhaps may see the worst else? This woman—would that she had been at the bottom of the sea before I had come across her."

"Amen!"

"—— already suspects something."

"Suspects what?"

"I haven't got it all out of her yet. She had gone up to-bed with the girls to-night, or I should have managed it at supper."

Lady Fane could scarcely refrain from chuckling aloud.

How capitally had she frustrated Mrs. Stibbington's schemes!

But she put off her delight for a more convenient opportunity.

Mrs. Stibbington had resumed her explanation.

"But from certain words that she let fall to-day in the schoolroom, I am certain that I don't fear her without good cause."

"What was this most terrifying observation, pray?"

"In the first place, she demanded that Phillis Ebury should return to the schoolroom."

"Phillis Ebury?"

"Yes."

"Are you sure as to the Ebury?"

"Yes."

"Where could she have learnt that from, do you imagine?"

"From Phillis herself."

"The girl has forgotten that name long since, I should say."

"Oh, no; her memory is wonderful."

"Curse her! she's like her mother in that, at any rate."

"Is she indeed, sir?"

"Silence; I did not address that remark to you."

And the schoolmistress was silent at once.

"He should be the Great Mogul himself," thought Lady Ethel.

It was indeed remarkable.

The schoolmistress, usually so haughty and imperious, was cowed into submission on the instant.

Lady Fane, too, recollected the sudden change which her manner had undergone in the schoolroom that morning.

And all through a few words which had escaped her.

Words to which she had attached no importance whatever.

So far from this, she could not remember now what her words were.

The stranger was speaking again.

"And supposing that I cannot take her with me to-night?"

"Then the risk be yours."

"What risk?"

"This: to-morrow, at all hazards, I must bring the girl back to the schoolroom."

"What of that?"

"Her appearance will occasion some unpleasant remarks."

"Don't she look healthy?"

"No."

This was a short dry "No," that carried great significance with it.

Had the listener been able to see their looks she might have been considerably astonished.

They sat there looking things into each other's eyes which they dared not whisper.

Things which they would not have dared to whisper even in solitude.

However, their words told the listener sufficient.

"Has she fallen sick, then?" asked the stranger, in a whisper.

"Rather."

"Changed colour at all?"

"Yes."

The questions and answers were delivered in low, hoarse whispers.

A tone of voice that sounded like murder itself.

Lady Ethel shuddered.

Bitterly did she now regret that her fugitive position would not allow her to bring these fiends to justice.

But it was useless to think of such a thing.

To attempt it was to sacrifice her father.

Perhaps herself.

She doubted not, still, that Mr. Balfour Fenwick had been guilty of the death of Jabez Worwold.

And then, might not she, as being so nearly concerned

in it, be implicated, in the event of the old man's conviction?

However, these were but passing thoughts.

Her whole attention was again engrossed in the fate of Phillis Ebury.

"Something she has taken has not agreed with her?"

The stranger's voice now sounded hideous.

Mrs. Stibbington returned a whispered affirmative, which, however, Lady Ethel failed to catch.

"Then I must take the girl with me to-night, you say?"

"Yes."

"Positively?"

"Positively."

"If I must, I must, and that's all about it."

"True."

"Though, hang me, if I know what the deuce I'm to be up to."

"I think I might offer a suggestion."

"Let's have it, then."

"How do you go back to town?"

"The way I came."

"And that is——"

"On foot."

"And you passed by the ponds?"

"You mean upon the Heath?"

"Yes."

"I did."

Then followed a long silence.

Lady Fane could scarcely repress a chattering of her teeth, which would probably have speedily betrayed her.

"Speak up, woman. What do you mean? Out with it."

"If you pass the ponds——"

"Yes——"

"And the girl——"

"And the brat was to find her way to the bottom of one of them, with a stone round her neck?"

Lady Ethel listened in vain for the reply.

The schoolmistress simply bowed her head to this atrocity.

"Well, I'll tell you what. It strikes me that it is a devil of a way to get her to."

"It is all I can think of."

"Very well, then; since it must be so. Where is she?"

"In the beer-vault."

"Oho! Then we shall probably find the young lady mops?"

"You must be careful with her. If she should scream?"

"I can stop her mouth with—eh? Hallo? I've lost my life-preserver. I thought I had it. I could have sworn I had it when I came in."

"Never mind—take this."

"Ha! this'll do; but the other thing is so handy."

"Come on—gently!"

They were coming towards the kitchen-door.

As quickly and as noiselessly as possible Lady Fane reascended the stairs.

She had gained the top of the basement flight, when the kitchen-door was opened.

Here was a perplexing situation!

What was to be done now?

How could she venture to interfere?

She doubted not that she would pay for her temerity with her existence.

And yet she could not stand tamely by, and see murder done.

No: that was out of the question.

The stranger and Mrs. Stibbington were crossing the passage below.

Not a moment was to be lost, if she would save the child.

Invention would not aid her.

She could think of nothing.

And yet the child must not be sacrificed, without an effort upon her part to save her.

As a last resource, she was upon the point of rushing down to the rescue, at all risk of personal danger, when a happy thought occurred to her.

Happy, indeed!

It was, undoubtedly, the saving of two human lives.

She was standing upon the landing, outside the bedroom-doors of some of the pupils.

She had but to awaken them, and all was safe.

Quick as thought, she threw open the doors upon each side of the landing.

Then, without waiting to arouse the girls, she called out over the stairs—

"Who's there?"

And then—

"Thieves! Burglars!"

"Damnation!" exclaimed the stranger. "It's all up for to-night."

"Thieves! Burglars! Help! help!"

"Hang your throat!" muttered the stranger. "Here, Mother Stibbington, let me out. Curse you!"

CHAPTER LVI.

THE NIGHT-WANDERER.

LADY ETHEL FANE had triumphed.

Murder was defeated.

Mrs. Stibbington's strange visitor beat a hasty retreat, leaving the assistant-governess in possession of the field.

Lady Ethel continued her shouts until the whole house was aroused.

The pupils all huddled together in their night-dresses upon the landing.

However, as soon as her object was attained, the assistant-governess ran upstairs, gained her own apartment, and speedily disrobed herself.

That is, sufficiently to appear as if she had only just quitted her bed.

Then she returned to the scene of excitement below.

No one had seen the assistant-governess at all.

Some of the pupils had run out when she was in the passage.

But as it had all occurred in the dark no one had been able to distinguish her form.

Every one was half-asleep.

Consequently Lady Fane's voice was not recognised.

"What is the matter?"

"Who was it that called out?"

These questions were being asked by every one.

And by every one in a different form.

The scene, in consequence, was confusion itself.

In an instant after Lady Fane's return from her bed-chamber, the schoolmistress arrived on the spot.

Mrs. Stibbington bore a candle in her hand, and she held it aloft as she reached the spot to gain a better view of the whole.

She had not yet learned the meaning of the alarm.

Her sensations were, in consequence, not of the most agreeable nature.

"Oh, Mrs. Stibbington, whatever is the matter?" demanded one of the elder pupils.

"What is it?"

"Have you had an attempt to break in, Mrs. Stibbington?"

This last query was addressed by the assistant-governess.

Mrs. Stibbington looked upon the group in amazement.

Although she had not detected Lady Ethel's voice, she had shrewdly suspected that the alarm had proceeded from her.

However, the latter's expression of astonishment appeared to be so genuine, that the suspicions of the schoolmistress were at once disarmed.

"Young ladies," she said, "what is all this disturbance, pray?"

"What does it all mean?" added the assistant-governess.

No one could answer this.

Miss Phipps had been awakened by Miss Pennyfather.

And Miss Pennyfather had been awakened by Miss Forsyth, who in turn had been aroused by a loud noise, and shouts of "Burglars! Thieves!" &c. &c.

But who had given these cries?

This no one could answer.

Mrs. Stibbington appealed to the pupils each individually.

But each declared that they were not even the innocent cause of the tumult.

Each averred that they had been awakened by an alarm of thieves.

But no one could throw the least light upon the originator of the tumult.

"Mrs. Morley," said the schoolmistress, at length, "can you say nothing whatever upon the subject?"

"Nothing."

"How did the cries arise?"

"I don't know. I only reached the spot at the same moment as yourself."

"Strange!"

"It is. And I was really alarmed at first."

"About what?"

"I was afraid that I had heard some strange noise below."

Mrs. Stibbington started.

"Strange noise?" she said, eyeing Lady Ethel sharply.

"Yes."

"What was it like?"

"I heard voices and footsteps below."

"That is strange."

"So I thought."

"I have just left the kitchen, and there was no one there."

"It must have been my imagination, then."

"I suppose so."

"But would it not be advisable to assure ourselves of this, Mrs. Stibbington?"

"In what way?"

"The only one."

"And that is?"

"To search down there ourselves."

"No, no; I'm sure that it is all right."

"But——"

"No, no; I say. It is not necessary, and that's all about it."

"Very well, Mrs. Stibbington; my suggestion was merely to ensure the safety of the house—nothing more."

"Of course not."

"But hadn't the young ladies better retire?"

"Yes, of course. Get to-bed again at once. Don't stand shivering there. We'll talk this affair over to-morrow morning; and I only hope that I may find the originator of all this disturbance."

The pupils scrambled back to their respective beds.

"Mrs. Morley."

"Madam."

"Don't you think that you might give a shrewd guess at the person's name?"

"What person?"

"The person who has created this untimely noise."

"I, Mrs. Stibbington?"

"Yes, you. It strikes me, you might if you pleased, Mrs. Morley."

The schoolmistress eyed Lady Fane as if she would read her inmost thoughts.

But she had to deal with no novice in the art of deception.

Lady Fane was an adept.

"Mrs. Stibbington," she replied, calmly, "what can lead you to suppose such a thing? Has anything occurred to-night which——"

"Eh? Oh, no, no."

"Then what should lead you to suppose that I had anything to do with the cause of all this disturbance?"

"Nothing; but——"

She stared rudely into Lady Ethel's face, but not the faintest expression betrayed that she knew more of the affair than she avowed.

After vainly attempting to stare Lady Ethel out of countenance, the schoolmistress broke out suddenly with—

"Well, it's high time to get to-bed again, I should think."

"Yes; though I fear," was Lady Ethel's reply, "I fear that my rest is spoilt for to-night."

"How so?"

"The alarm of thieves has quite shattered my nerves."

"No doubt. I'd give something to ascertain who started the cry."

"Yes. It is singular."

"Yes. But let us get to-bed—to-bed. We must be approaching midnight."

Lady Ethel was alarmed at the haste which the schoolmistress displayed for her to retire.

The danger was not over yet.

Mrs. Stibbington, no doubt, thought that she could yet carry out her hellish designs.

The stranger was perhaps awaiting her close by.

All these surmises threw the assistant-governess into the utmost consternation.

At all risks, Phillis must be guarded from evil for this night.

The next day she would seek the poor child in her prison, and set her free.

"Good night, Mrs. Stibbington," said Lady Fane.

"Good night."

"And you can retire to bed in security. I shall keep watch."

"Keep watch, Mrs. Morley?"

"Yes."

"For what?"

"Thieves."

"But you don't suppose that there is any danger?"

"I hope not; but——"

"Nonsense, nonsense. You get to-bed with all possible speed, Mrs. Morley, and fear nothing."

"I cannot sleep—I'm sure I cannot."

"Ridiculous!"

"Never mind. I shall sit down and read till daybreak."

The schoolmistress bit her lip in silent vexation.

The slightest word on her part, she thought, must have made the assistant-governess suspect that all was not right.

So concealing her chagrin as best she could, she bade her a surly good night; and they retired to their several apartments.

Lady Ethel, as she had told the schoolmistress, sat for awhile to read.

This was a futile attempt to tranquillize her excited nerves, so terribly shaken by the atrocities which she had heard down below, and which, as we have seen, she had been the means of frustrating for the moment.

She held her book open in her hand merely as a blind, lest the schoolmistress should come to her apartment upon any pretext.

This was, perhaps, a stretch of caution.

But the desperate crisis which affairs had now reached demanded that she should not omit the least precaution.

She sat for more than an hour, straining her sense of hearing to the utmost.

But she was most agreeably disappointed.

The schoolmistress, it would seem, had instinctively divined the danger which threatened her nefarious projects and had not ventured out of her chamber.

Thus was the hapless Phillis spared for one night.

Lady Ethel intended to remove her forthwith from the clutches of the vile, unscrupulous schoolmistress.

But how ?

Of this she had not as yet formed any definite plan.

The first step was to seek out the prisoner while there was yet time.

The apartment of the schoolmistress was upon the same landing as that of Lady Ethel Fane.

Unfortunately for her present movements it was only a few feet distant.

But she was not to be daunted by an obstacle comparatively so trifling.

She commenced operations by placing her lamp in a corner of her bed-chamber where its rays would not be reflected into the passage through the open door.

Then she stepped lightly forth.

The door of the next apartment was closed, but as she approached she could hear a light footfall within, and rustling of the grey silk dress which adorned Mrs. Stibbington's person.

Lady Ethel turned back affrightedly to her bed-chamber.

But before she had crossed the threshold she had once more changed her mind.

"Mrs. Stibbington will probably not retire to-night. Now is the time or never ; every moment lessens the chance—renders the poor child's hope of escape from these assassins less and less. I should never forgive myself if any serious harm came to her. At all hazards she must be free to-night."

Carefully concealing her lamp in the folds of her dress, she once more ventured forth.

Now all was still in Mrs. Stibbington's apartment.

Treading as lightly as possible, she crossed the passage and descended the stairs.

So far all was well.

Mrs. Stibbington had apparently not overheard her movements.

But now came a discovery which considerably startled the adventurous Lady Fane.

In crossing the ground-floor to the basement stairs she chanced to glance casually at the door leading into the garden—the one by which she had entered on returning from her ramble.

It was wide open.

At "The Chesnuts" they had the particularly usual habit of making no use of their locks, bolts, or bars to preserve them from lawless intrusion.

But at the same time the doors were always closed.

The door being open upon the present occasion was sufficient to alarm Lady Fane at this critical moment.

She saw in it danger to her project.

The stranger had either returned to the house or was to return.

"Or was to return." She repeated these words to herself again and again.

Had he ever quitted the house ?

True, she had heard his exclamation of rage when she had given the alarm, and his hurried and by no means courteous farewell to the schoolmistress.

Still it was not sure that he had left.

Mrs. Stibbington might have concealed him below until the excitement above stairs was over.

And after all it was their intention to carry out their hellish plan that night.

This thought was terrifying to Lady Fane.

Fears of personal violence were now added to her anxiety for the preservation of the child.

For she doubted not that if she had chanced to encounter the stranger, he, rendered desperate by danger, would hesitate at nothing to secure his safety.

The conversation which she had overheard convinced her that she had little to hope from this man's scruples if affairs reached the worst.

And now, sincere as was her sympathy with poor Phillis Ebury, Lady Fane was more than half-inclined to leave her to her fate.

This idea, however, was abandoned almost as soon as thought of.

She could not thus resign the child to the fiends who sought her life.

Descending one or two of the kitchen-stairs, she listened eagerly for some evidence of the stranger's presence.

All was silent.

Growing bolder by degrees, she crept as gently as possible the rest of the way.

Not the faintest sound denoted the presence of any living soul but herself.

Still she proceeded with caution.

As silently as she could she made for the vault in which she had heard the schoolmistress say her victim was confined.

Lady Fane was tolerably well acquainted with the geography of "The Chesnuts," so she had speedily arrived at the spot.

At this instant a sob—a sob of bitter grief reached her.

Lady Ethel flew to the cellar-door.

But here, alas ! a sad obstacle presented itself.

The door was fastened with a padlock, of which Mrs. Stibbington kept the key.

What was to be done ?

Before Lady Ethel had time to give this the slightest consideration, a cry from within announced that her presence was known to the hapless prisoner.

We had better say a presence, for it was evident that the suffering child had not dreamt that the visit was a friendly one.

She gave a cry, in which Lady Ethel shudderingly distinguished a mixture of terror and pain.

A cry that told its own sad tale !

"Phillis, Phillis !" said Lady Ethel, rapping gently on the door with her knuckles ; "It is I—Mrs. Morley."

"What is it ?"

"It is I—Mrs. Morley ; I have come to free you !"

A wild cry of joy greeted this announcement.

"Mrs. Morley, oh ! Mrs. Morley, I am dying !"

"Patience ; a little patience, Phillis, and I shall be with you !"

"Come at once, I pray, or——"

"Where is the key of the cellar ?"

"Have you not got it ?"

"No."

"And you cannot come to me ?—cannot set me free ?"

"Not until I get the key."

"Then that you can never do ! Mrs. Stibbington has it in her pocket, I know. Can't you wrench off the padlock ?"

"Ha ! I must see !"

The staples to which the padlock was fixed were old and rusty, and could have offered but a feeble resistance to a person possessed of the least physical power.

To Mr. John Chinnery or Jaggers it would have been the work of an instant, and the meanest child's play.

Breaking off padlocks, however, was a branch of Lady Fane's education which had been woefully neglected.

It is not surprising, therefore, that her efforts were not crowned with immediate success.

She tugged, and tugged at the stubborn fastenings, grazing her delicate fingers in vain.

She began almost to despair of succeeding in her object at last.

"I'm afraid, Phillis, that I can't——"

Before she could conclude, the unhappy child had interrupted her speech with a wild cry—

"Oh! don't say so, Mrs. Morley! Don't—don't, for the love of Heaven! I am dying!"

Animated by the poor girl's cries, Lady Fane tugged at the padlock with renewed vigour.

It yielded.

Then gave way with a jerk that made Lady Fane stagger back several paces.

The padlock and staple fell to the ground with an alarming clatter.

But without pausing a moment to consider the consequences of this, Lady Fane tore open the door, and rushed into the vault.

Upon raising her lantern aloft to get a better view of the maltreated child, a sad spectacle met her gaze.

Phillis was upon her knees at some few feet only from the door.

She had evidently been overcome with exhaustion in struggling to get at it.

She was truly in a most deplorable condition.

Her hands were held up imploringly almost in an attitude of prayer.

As the door was thrown open, she called out faintly some few inarticulate words, and fell forward breathless upon her face.

Lady Ethel darted forward and raised her from the ground.

She had fainted.

Resting the lifeless form for an instant against the cellar-door, Lady Ethel ran back into the kitchen and procured some water.

With this she sprinkled her face and moistened her parched lips.

Slowly—very slowly—she began to revive.

She lay upon the ground, resting her head in the lap of Lady Fane, who was kneeling, bathing her pale, emaciated face with the water.

The few days had wrought a fearful change in her.

Her eyes had entirely lost their lustre, and there was an expression in them as she looked sadly into Lady Ethel's face which caused her ladyship to shudder instinctively.

It was not until long afterwards that Lady Fane had fully interpreted to herself her sensations at this moment.

"How good you are, Mrs. Morley!" said the little girl, faintly.

"Tell me, Phillis," said Lady Fane; "tell me what they have done to you."

"They have killed me!"

Conviction accompanied these words so pronounced, that Lady Ethel at once apprehended the worst.

There was no fear of death in the child's tone.

She shook her head sadly and earnestly, and with an expression which Lady Ethel saw conveyed far more sorrow for her assassin's crime, than resentment for the death they had given her.

And now Lady Fane perceived for the first time the fearful change her complexion had undergone.

Her ordinarily fair skin was now a ghastly yellow.

She had no sooner perceived this, than she reflected upon the remarks which she had overheard from Mrs. Stibbington's late visitor.

"Great Heavens!" ejaculated the assistant-governess. "She has poisoned her!"

"Poisoned me!" demanded Phillis.

"Yes, my poor, slaughtered innocent."

"I thought so."

"What have you taken?"

"Bread and water."

"Nothing else?"

"Yes. Yesterday morning—I think it was yesterday morning, but it is all morning, noon, and night here—all one long, long night."

"What was it she gave you?"

"Some soup. It was very bitter—I could scarcely swallow it."

"Then why did you take it?"

"I was very hungry, and I was afraid of offending Mrs. Stibbington."

"How so?"

"She left it some time before I had taken it, and when she came back only a little time afterwards she was very cross indeed with me for not having drunk it."

"And so you drank it?"

"Not all."

"Where is the rest of it!"

"I threw it up in that corner, that she might not see it."

"There?"

"Yes. There was a lot of sediment to it."

"Hah!"

"And it was all so bitter."

"Were you sick after it?"

"Oh! very, very."

"And—but, come; we must not stay here any longer. Do you think you could walk a little way? I shall help you along, and a doctor——"

"Cannot save me, Mrs. Morley; I am sure of that."

"Poor child! But try."

The girl shook her head.

"I cannot."

"There. Take my hand—now."

But the poor child sank back, half insensible.

"My limbs are so stiff and sore, I cannot move."

"Has Mrs. Stibbington, then, beaten you again?"

"Fearfully."

"How dreadful!"

"And all for nothing."

"And have you really given her no provocation?"

"None."

"Nothing but what occurred in the schoolroom?"

"Nothing. She struck me so fearfully about the head, that I asked her if she intended to murder me?"

"And what did she do?"

"Nothing. I told her that I was dying fast, and that she would be answerable for my death."

"It was wrong, Phillis, to incense her further against you."

"It did not incense her against me. Neither did I intend it to. I merely spoke to her as quietly and seriously as I am speaking now."

"But did she say nothing in reply to this?"

"No. It led her to think it over seriously, too."

"But it did not serve to ameliorate your condition."

"No, Mrs. Morley; but it has made me also think over Mrs. Stibbington's brutality."

"To think it over?"

"Yes."

"And what conclusion have you come to, Phillis?"

The child's remarks were so full of thought and wisdom, that Lady Ethel almost forgot her extreme youth in addressing her.

Phillis replied to the last question with the gravity of a woman of forty.

Had it not been for the nature of the case, and the fearfully prominent position which Phillis Ebury took in her own narration, Lady Ethel would have felt amused.

As it was, she noticed nothing strange in it.

Nothing but the startling proximity which she arrived at in her guess, for that is all it could have been.

"I am sure, Mrs. Morley," said the girl, "that she is killing me for some purpose which I don't understand—some money or something which she has robbed me of, or is to rob me—or——"

Here she broke off short, and resting her head in her hand, she sat still in meditation for several minutes.

"NOW THEN, MRS. MORLEY, WE MUST COME TO TERMS," CRIED THE STRANGER.

"But how can that be possible, Phillis?" said Lady Ethel. "Had you any money?"

"I don't know."

"Then how can it be?"

"—Not for certain. But it is very possible, if Uncle Zachary is dead. You know that I told you so."

"Yes; it may be so. But now we must be going before it is too late."

"We?"

"Yes."

"And you, Mrs. Morley, would go with me?"

"Certainly, my poor child. What else would you do?"

"Oh, how kind and good you are! How very good!"

"Come, come—we are losing time."

"I cannot."

"You cannot walk?"

"No; it is too late!"

"But make an effort, at least; try once more."

"In vain; I—I—my head swims; my eyes grow dim—hah!—I—oh!"

The unhappy child slipped from Lady Ethel's grasp. Fell heavily—a dull, leaden weight—upon the ground —a corpse!

"Dead!" shrieked Lady Ethel. "Dead—murdered! Great God! how fearful!"

She could scarcely realize it.

But a moment before she had spoken; and now——

"Oh! impossible, impossible!"

She again had recourse to the former remedy—the water she had brought when the child had fainted.

Too late!

The earthly part of Phillis Ebury alone remained.

Almost convinced—battling, we might say, with conviction—did Lady Ethel Fane exert every art she knew to restore the—she fondly hoped—fainting sufferer to consciousness.

And it was only when the dreadful truth was too apparent to be doubted more that she gave up her task.

Then, overcome with mingled sensations of grief and regret at the untimely end of the hapless victim—horror and indignation against the assassins—she knelt over the corpse before her and wept aloud.

"Poor murdered innocent! poor slaughtered child! victim to this bloody-minded woman's treachery and craft. But, by the heavens above, you shall be avenged! Fully avenged! I swear it!"

She raised her lamp and surveyed the vault.

It was a damp, noisome cellar. The plaster on the walls on either side hung loosely about in soft, pasty patches.

Although it was dignified at "The Chesnuts" by the appellation of the beer-cellar, there was no appearance of any of the beverage from which it derived its title.

Indeed, it seemed well fitted for a subterranean prison of some old castle of the chivalric era.

Although Lady Fane raised the lamp high above her head, she could not pierce its gloomy depth.

At some eighteen or twenty paces from her she lost the outline of the vault in the sombre shadows.

"What a fearful den is this!" exclaimed the assistant-governess, with a shudder. "The very place for the perpetration of this heinous crime. What is beyond there, I wonder?"

Curiosity prevailing over every other feeling in Lady Ethel's mind, even at this fearful moment, she rose to her feet and walked across the vault.

"Great Heavens!" she exclaimed; "what can this immense space have been used for? Such a cellar seems strangely out of character with the rest of the house. I've not yet learned all the mysteries of "The Chesnuts."

Arrived at the extremity of the vault, which was at least twenty feet deeper than she had at first taken it to be, Lady Ethel was considerably surprised to see some small heaps of ashes here and there.

Some odd pieces of furniture, all more or less damaged, were scattered about the place.

It had apparently served as a receptacle for the lumber of "The Chesnuts."

Stepping across a portion of a broken chair, one of the legs caught in her dress, dragging the chair some few feet along, and slightly damaging the robe.

She stooped to extricate it, when her hand came in contact with some hard substance, which slightly grazed her knuckles.

A glance at this was sufficient to acquaint her that the vault had not served as a prison to Phillis Ebury alone.

Some human bones lay at her feet!

Lady Ethel turned in horror from this sickening spectacle.

"Oh! what a den of infamy have I fallen upon here. This vile woman thrives upon wholesale murder. It shall be the purpose of my life to reward her as she deserves."

In an instant Lady Fane had regained the side of the murdered child.

The hands were already assuming the coldness of death.

The face seemed already to have undergone a slight change.

The expression, so full of pain at the moment of dissolution so few minutes before, was now placid and calm, as if the unhappy girl had been in a sweet slumber.

And now, for the first time, Lady Ethel began to feel a sensation of dread stealing over her.

That vague, indefinable fear which we all more or less experience in the grim avenger's presence.

All was silent.

The awful stillness of the vault, unbroken by the faintest echo, was too much for the unstrung nerves of our adventurous heroine.

She glanced nervously around her.

Half-rose from her kneeling posture with the intention of retreating from the cellar.

But a glance at the inanimate corpse before her recalled her to herself.

Was it thus that she was to follow up her vow of vengeance upon Phillis Ebury's destroyer—her vow so lately uttered?

No. Be her sensations what they might be, she was resolved not to quit the cellar until she had such proofs of Mrs. Stibbington's guilt as would satisfactorily bring her crime home to her to the minds of a British jury.

Her first idea was to seek some traces of the poison which had been administered to her.

But these had been carefully removed by the schoolmistress.

In despair at this, Lady Ethel began to wonder if she should not be able to find some of the traces she sought about the girl's garments.

Beside her on the ground lay a pocket-handkerchief, with which Lady Ethel had seen the poor child wipe away a white, frothy foam which oozed from between her lips.

The very thing!

Here was all the evidence she sought, and in the smallest possible compass.

She quickly transferred this to her pocket.

Then, with a farewell, lingering look, she was turning once more from the dead girl's side, when——

What was that:

She heard a faint noise at her side.

The next instant she felt a cold iron ring applied to her cheek.

"Hah! who's——"

She turned her head round.

Found herself face to face with Mrs. Stibbington's visitor, the stranger, who was holding a pistol at her head!

"The faintest cry—a breath—and I plaster that wall with your brains!"

CHAPTER LVII.

BOUND AND GAGGED.

WE leave our readers to judge what were the sensations of Lady Ethel Fane upon making the discovery we described upon quitting her.

The stranger—the man Lady Ethel had seen in the kitchen with Mrs. Stibbington, and whom she had overheard plotting the destruction of the slaughtered Phillis Ebury with the schoolmistress—this man, we say, was standing over her, with a pistol presented at her temple.

The conversation which she heard in the kitchen was sufficient to prove him a desperate man.

Unscrupulous to a degree.

Blood-thirsty and desperate, and one who would, doubtless, hesitate at no crime to secure his personal safety.

Under these circumstances, it is little to be wondered at that the assistant-governess was, at the least, startled.

She endeavoured to scream.

Fear, however, had chained her tongue, and she could not articulate.

The stranger was the first to break the silence.

"Now then, Mrs. Morley, we must come to terms."

Lady Ethel was silent.

"Mrs. Morley," continued the stranger, "if you are prudent—which you are not, or you wouldn't be here—but suppose we say, if you have learnt wisdom by this lesson, you will keep silent as to this night's work."

The spell was in part broken, and Lady Fane began to move.

She endeavoured to rise to her feet.

The stranger, however, pushed her back with a grasp of iron into her old position.

Then, with the cold iron ring of the pistol on her brow, he once more addressed her, in terrifying remonstrance.

"Foolish woman! Would you slay yourself?"

"Slay?" faltered Lady Ethel.

"Ay. Slay."

"You would not murder me?"

"No, I would not, unless I find it convenient."

"Beware, man."

"Pah! It isn't convenient, and that's all about it. So I would much prefer coming to terms. So just keep quiet."

"Never."

"You'll change your mind."

Lady Ethel turned her head with a shudder from the cold touch of the pistol.

Her eye rested at this moment upon the lifeless Phillis Ebury.

"Never, never. By heavens! I swear it!" she ejaculated.

There was so much fervour and energy in her tone, that it quite took the stranger by surprise.

"Well, Mrs. Morley. I could admire you for your spirit; but my safety says that you must—mark me—must knuckle under."

"I'll denounce you, as I live."

"As you live? If you live; but you will not."

"Assassin! does not this night's work satisfy you?"

"It does; I'm sated with it; and therefore would save you."

"Save me? From what?"

"Death. For you will assuredly die, unless you will take an oath that I shall prescribe."

"Never, never."

"Your life is in your own hands, remember."

"I can but repeat, that I shall denounce you, if I live."

"You will not take the oath, then?"

"Murderer! keep from me. You reduce me to your own level by even offering me conditions."

"Pshaw! All this is very absurd, you know, Mrs. Morley."

Lady Ethel turned from him loathingly.

"You had much better come to terms. Just think it over."

"It is not necessary. Now, or an hour hence, I shall think the same."

"I'm sure you wont."

"Ruffian! keep from me."

"I'm an easy-going man, Mrs. Morley; but your obstinacy may aggravate me to do something disagreeable."

"Do your worst."

"Oh, oh! You defy me, then, do you?"

"Defy and abhor you."

"Come, come; draw it mild, young lady. What can you do for the girl, now, if you did denounce us, as you say? Though as for myself, I'm sure, I am indifferent upon the point. But, supposing you still persist in refusing to take the oath I require, I shall put you out of the way, and put it out of your power to harm us."

Lady Ethel said nothing.

The stranger augured favourably from her silence.

"You have thought better of it, Mrs. Morley?" he continued.

"Of what?"

"Of my proposals."

"Ruffian!" exclaimed the assistant-governess, turning upon him furiously. "Would you reduce me to your own degraded level?"

"Forbear, madam, forbear," exclaimed the stranger.

But heedless of his menaces, Lady Fane continued—

"Make a compact with a murderer?"

"Silence!"

"'Twould be to share your crime."

"Then you refuse my proposals, madam?"

"Ay."

"You refuse?"

"I do—with the scorn and indignation they merit."

"You'll repent of this."

"Never, by heaven!"

"You will, or I'm a Dutchman."

"Stand from my path, assassin! ruffian! Begone."

"This wont do, you know."

"Release me."

"Upon one condition."

"Conditions with such as you?"

"Ay, madam, with me."

"I tell you, murderer, if there is law, justice, and a gallows in England for the homicide, that fate shall be yours. I go from here——"

"Do you?"

"To denounce you."

"You rave, woman. In the first place, you will not go from here."

"Would you dare?"

"Anything to save unpleasant consequences."

"I can believe that."

"Oh, pray reserve your witticisms; I don't understand them. I admire your pluck."

"Wretch! your admiration is loathsome to me."

"Now, that's unkind."

"More disgusting to me than words can express."

"You are really not complimentary, Mrs. Morley, and upon a first acquaintance, too."

"Dare to impede my departure another moment, and I alarm the whole house. The children would bear witness against you, and you would find it hard to remove them all from your path. Though, doubtless, the task would be agreeable to you."

"I can bear all that; but let me advise you not to attempt it. If you so much as breathed in a way that I thought to be unpleasant, I should take immediate steps to secure your silence."

"I defy——"

"Now don't do that. I am of an excessively nervous temperament, and if you agitate me with more menaces——"

"Stand back."

"Foolish woman. Your bearing plainly shows that you haven't the remotest idea of the dangerous contrivance known as a hair-trigger. Now, the pistol I hold has a hair-trigger. The slightest excitement upon my part would most surely cause my hand to tremble. The finger, which is on the trigger, might twitch nervously, and you'd be a dead woman that moment."

Lady Ethel drew back affrightedly.

But the pistol covered her wherever she moved.

"Come, come," continued the stranger, soothingly; "I don't want to terrify you by a host of senseless threats. Let us come to an understanding."

"I can have no understanding with a murderer."

"But I am none."

"Or with a would-be murderer; or even as defender of such a deed of blood."

"Tut, tut, woman. Listen to me. You are in possession of certain facts, which it would be, say unpleasant, to have made public."

"But which will be."

"A moment, if you please. Now see. I offer you these conditions: I will let you pass—get off scot free, to do as you please. Quit the house, with all your bag and baggage, or remain in your present position in this house."

"Remain—oh!"

"Ah? and not as you were before. For now you would be assured of Mrs. Stibbington's consideration."

"Silence! Think you that I could rest beneath this roof?"

"As you please. It might be better for all parties, perhaps, that you should leave. In this case, you would have the best of testimonials to enable you to obtain a speedy re-engagement; and as we might consider that your departure would be in some sort due to Mrs. Stibbington, I should recommend her to pay you six months' salary."

"Salary!" repeated Lady Ethel, aghast.

However, the stranger took her exclamation in a very opposite sense to that which was intended.

He rather fancied that she was complaining of the insignificance of the sum proposed.

"Or if you think that not quite just," he continued, "she would doubtless make it a twelvemonth's salary."

"Assassin! would you dare attempt to bribe me into silence?"

"Bribe—that's a strange word."

"Think you that because I am poor I would sell my soul for a few paltry pounds!"

"Oh! I see; you don't object to selling your soul—it's merely a question of price. By gad, madam, you're a treat!"

Lady Ethel sprang to her feet, and brushed past the stranger before he could intercept her.

In an instant, however, he had overtaken her.

"This is fooling; you cannot escape. Before you should quit this house alive, and without having taken the oath I tell you of, I would risk alarming the house by putting a bullet through you! Once more, do you accept my——"

"Bribe?"

"As you please—my bribe?"

"No!"

"You reject?"

"All. The twelvemonth's salary—much as the sum would doubtless be to sacrifice out of the spoil——"

The stranger winced.

"Out of the plunder of this murdered child."

The stranger's expression at this moment was anything but pleasing.

Had Lady Fane observed it, she would probably have repented her somewhat rash taunts.

She had made a chance shot, which had told.

"So, so, madam!" said the stranger; "you know too much. Now, your decision cannot affect your fate."

"Fate!" faltered her ladyship.

"Ay, madam; you die!"

He placed the pistol in his breast, and then drew from his pocket a hideous huge clasp-knife.

"Now, then, I give you five minutes to prepare yourself—to make any prayers you desire—for necessary as your death is to me, I would not sacrifice you unprepared."

Lady Ethel's astonishment was so great at this extraordinary speech, that it completely mastered her fear for the moment.

A murderer speak thus to his victim!

How could one about to take a fellow-creature's life have any respect for HIM, or a thought of a hereafter?

"You're astonished," said the stranger, who had observed her look of amazement. "Do you think that because I must do murder that I have lost all thoughts of that? In slaying you I but submit to my fate. It is doomed that you should die at this hour. I am selected as the instrument for this work, and I obey my fate."

"A fatalist," said Lady Ethel; "I thought so. How many men persuade themselves to this as an excuse, however slight, for their bloody deeds."

"Well, I can spend the five minutes in arguing that, if you please so. The ordinary murderer is no fatalist, believe me."

"No; he has less excuse than the ordinary murderer. The latter is usually a victim to circumstances. A quarrel—a blow, and the evil's done. The fatalist goes deliberately to work, and has not even the excuse of passion to urge."

"Ah! it's plain that the world is not of your opinion."

"Because the man who does murder deliberately is brought in insane. A certificate—two doctor's signatures. But these are exceptions, after all."

"Really, there is something in your argument; and I would spare you if it were possible."

It must not be supposed that Lady Ethel was by any means at her ease.

In spite of her arguments and her calm defiance, her cheeks were blanched with fear.

Her thoughts were far from the subject she discussed so coolly.

She was calculating with terrible earnestness her chances of escape.

It was, therefore, with considerable satisfaction that she saw her self-appointed executioner put by the pistol with which he had hitherto menaced her.

It is true that he had produced an ugly weapon in the form of the clasp-knife that, after all, there was a chance with this, she thought.

It reduced it to a struggle.

From this she began to hope for the best.

Had she not already overcome difficulties as great?

Had she not resisted and defeated a whole host of foes at the gambling-house?

And should she, in face of these facts, give up all hope in the present strait?

"Well, Mrs. Morley," said the stranger, who had been silently watching the expression of her countenance as these thoughts flitted through her mind; "I suppose you're resolved to take the oath by this time?"

He paused for her answer.

"An answer one way or the other, as quickly as possible."

"My answer is now as it was at first."

"You decline——"

"Having any compact with a felon and an assassin!"

"Fool! take the reward of your pig-headed obstinacy, then!"

He rushed upon her with the uplifted knife.

He seized her by the wrist and pressed her back with a sudden jerk that sent her scrambling upon the ground.

This action, however, gave her a brief respite.

He had only intended to bring her to her knees.

Consequently as he struck at her the blow fell short.

Before he could recover his balance, Lady Fane had regained her feet, and possessed herself of a piece of broken chair which lay at a corner of the cellar.

Then, quick as lightning, she dashed at the man.

Notwithstanding the slight weight of the weapon, it did Lady Ethel good service.

A blow in the face with it staggered him as he advanced.

She was not slow to follow up this advantage.

A second and a third blow followed in rapid succession, and her foe was beaten to the ground.

Throwing the weapon from her, Lady Fane rushed to the door.

But alas! only to find herself face to face with Mrs. Stibbington.

"Ha!" shrieked the schoolmistress, grabbing at her.

Lady Ethel had almost rushed into her arms, so that there was no retreating.

A vigorous thrust pushed aside the schoolmistress, leaving the exit free.

Fortune, however, at this junction deserted her.

As Mrs. Stibbington staggered against the cellar-door, her foot slipped, and she fell sprawling upon the ground.

Thus she was enabled to reach the edge of Lady Ethel's dress as she fled past.

It being a stout material the skirt withstood the shock.

The schoolmistress had got a firm grasp too, and although the fugitive governess hugged and tugged to release herself her struggles were in vain.

She only succeeded in dragging Mrs. Stibbington on to her knees.

Then the schoolmistress suddenly released her grasp, and poor Lady Ethel was precipitated some paces forward by the jerk.

And now the day went against her altogether.

Mrs. Stibbington beat her to the ground in an instant.

Almost at the same instant up came the stranger.

And now the unhappy Lady Ethel was in extreme peril.

Enraged at her determined resistance, the stranger would have made short work of it had not the schoolmistress have interposed.

"Wait," she exclaimed, catching his arm as it descended.

"For what?"

"It cannot take place here."

"Not take place?"

"No."

"And wherefore?"

"What, would you fill the place with her tell-tale blood?—place a halter round your neck?"

"What do you mean to do then?"

"Remove her from here."

"And place a halter round your neck thus?"

"No—the pond."

"Ah! true. Singular that that never crossed me."

"Help! help! murder!" shrieked Lady Fane.

"Smother her!" roared the stranger.

"Help! help——"

Her cries were speedily stifled.

The next minute she was gagged and bound, helpless as their mercy.

"Now then," said the stranger, "how the deuce are we to get her all the way?"

"Carry her."

"I?"

"Yes."

"That sort of thing is more practicable on the stage and in novels than elsewhere."

"You cannot?"

"No."

"Then—stay—why not put the pony to the chaise and run down?"

"No—that wont do—it would be overheard."

"At this hour?"

"Or at the least it would most certainly leave some traces which would be indisputable."

"You are growing fearsome, Mr. ——"

"Silence—no names."

"What can it signify?"

"I don't care to hear my name buzzed about."

"Not even in the presence of two dead bodies?"

The schoolmistress was refined in her tortures.

And in her tortures alone.

The "two dead bodies" was meant to inspire the unhappy Lady Fane with terror, and she pretty well succeeded in this if indeed her fears had not already reached the highest possible pitch.

"Look alive, then, Mother Stibbington," said the stranger, impatiently. "As much expedition and silence as possible."

Thus admonished, the schoolmistress quitted the vault.

The stranger paced up and down impatiently until she returned.

"Confound her!" he muttered, between his teeth. "What a time she is. Does she imagine that this is a pleasant business? Bloody-minded old hag!"

Presently he paused beside the body of Phillis Ebury.

After gazing upon it in silence for some seconds, he knelt beside it and scrutinized the features.

Lady Ethel, who was eagerly following every gesture he made, was horrified at the coolness with which he surveyed his work.

"Poor little devil," he muttered. "What made you cross my path? It had been much better for all parties had you never seen the light."

There was not the remotest traces of remorse in this strange being's face.

Not the slightest quiver of a muscle denoted that he regretted the dark deed.

"I believe that I may trace my whole chapter of wrongs from your birth, unhappy child. A chain of circumstances which have rendered your removal an imperative necessity. I would have spared you the pain of the death which you have suffered, but it was impossible. I could not choose my means. Ha! here's Mother Stibbington."

The schoolmistress re-entered the cellar.

"All is prepared."

"You've got the trap ready?"

"Yes."

"Did you think to muffle the pony's hoofs?"

"No."

"We must do it."

"Shall we take her up first?"

The schoolmistress indicated their living victim by an inclination of her head.

The stranger then took Lady Ethel's shoulders, the schoolmistress took the feet, and in this unceremonious manner they bundled her upstairs and into the little chaise which stood by the street-door.

This done, they descended for the body of the child.

They had no sooner disappeared than Lady Ethel heard a footstep in the road.

She could see no one.

Was powerless to stir or to utter a cry.

CHAPTER LVIII.

MORE ABOUT THE PRETTY NURSE.

A WEEK has elapsed, and in spite of drugs and doctors, physics and predictions, Frank Harley still breathes.

As day succeeded day, the sapient leeches have given it to each other in the most serious earnest that the artist cannot last the day out.

The nurse day by day watches eagerly the expression of the two doctors' countenances.

This is the only means she has of arriving at their opinions; for since the day she swooned upon overhearing their fatal decision, they have been careful not to utter a word in her presence.

But, however, from the anxiety she displays, the constant worry and torment, it is apparent that their "faces are books wherein men read strange tales."

Had not words been invented, according to the witty Frenchman, to conceal men's thoughts, the two doctors must have altered their cruel opinions for some time since.

In their hearts of hearts they must have known that the patient was now just at a dangerous crisis.

That he was in fact out of danger.

We must acknowledge also that they are not the ornaments to the medical profession that we believe them to be.

The truth is, that they do not care to acknowledge to themselves even that they have been so egregiously mistaken as to the state of the patient.

That loss of blood and fever together have so reduced the patient that they were misled by appearances.

So Gerard Wilde and his coadjutor repeat day by day their fatal decision.

Upon the ninth day, however, the change for the better in the wounded man is so marked that they are forced to begin a compromise with themselves.

Their opinions gradually veer round.

They for the last time gave out their sad sentence. But now in a less certain tone.

Gerard Wilde ventures upon a convenient "if" in concluding his daily opinion.

The other doctor eagerly catches at the compromise.

"Of course, Mr. Wilde, unless, &c."

From this their way is easy enough.

"A most remarkable instance, Mr. Wilde," said the doctor.

"Of what?"

"I was alluding to the patient's strange improvement."

"Ah! yes."

"Perhaps it is about the only case on record in which a man with——"

"One leg in the grave——" suggested Gerard Wilde.

"Exactly. A man with one leg in the grave recovered."

"And so greatly recovered, too, in this short time."

"Yes."

"By-the-bye, there's no need of carrying on our conversation in a whisper for the future."

"Of course not."

"Suppose we call the nurse and let her into it?"

"Very good."

"Nurse."

"Yes, sir," replied the nurse, who was engaged in needlework by the artist's bedside.

"Come here for a moment."

The nurse obeyed.

"We have some agreeable news to communicate."

"Regarding the patient, doctor?" she asked, eagerly.

"Yes."

"You think that he is better?"

"Much."

"Out of danger?"

"Almost."

The worthy doctor did not care to give an opinion even to the nurse which was in such flat contradiction to his late assertion.

"Oh! how glad I am to hear it, doctor."

And Gerard Wilde could not help remarking the unmistakable happiness which was now depicted upon the nurse's countenance.

She seemed as if just relieved from a load of guilt which had weighed her down.

"Yes, nurse," continued the doctor, with great emphasis, "it is my opinion, and what's more, my friend Mr. Wilde's, that another week of quiet attention will see the patient another man—eh, Mr. Wilde?"

"Quite so."

"And I think you can manage that, nurse?"

"What, sir?"

"The quiet."

"Ah! indeed I can, sir," was her earnest reply.

"You appear to me, nurse, to be remarkably interested in the patient's recovery," observed the doctor.

Gerard Wilde here thought that he saw the nurse's colour heighten beneath her cap frill.

"Interested? I, sir?" she repeated, somewhat confusedly.

"Yes. Mr. Wilde has noticed it to me also. And I think——"

"No, no," said Wilde; "I——"

"And I think so too now," continued the remorseless doctor. "In fact, it was Mr. Wilde who first pointed it out to me; else I shouldn't have noticed it at all. I do not consider myself much of an observer of things in general."

"My interest in the patient's recovery is nothing strange."

"No, nurse. An interest—but your interest is——"

"What do you mean to imply by that, doctor?"

"Simply, that nurses ordinarily do not evince much sympathy with their customers."

"No sympathy?"

"Not much."

"Are they not fellow-creatures, although customers?"

"Sure; but——"

"You think that because a woman is a nurse, she loses all natural feelings, doctor?"

"Almost."

"Heaven keep me from being a nurse, then."

"Oh!"

"I mean a nurse of that description, doctor."

"Oh! But you see, the women of your class grow callous on account of it being their business."

"As with the doctors."

"Oh, oh! you see that's different altogether."

"I do not exactly perceive the difference, doctor."

"Oh, but it is. Eh, Wilde?"

"Yes, yes; decidedly a difference, doctor, I should say."

"But, whether or no such is the case, may there not be some exceptions to the run of nurses?"

"Decidedly."

"There may be," said Wilde. "But still we have noticed——"

The nurse did not allow him to conclude his speech.

"And what, then, is there out of the way—that is, sufficiently so, to be remarkable in my desire for the well-being of the patient?"

"Nothing; you're right. But I shouldn't think that you were brought up for a nurse, were you?"

The nurse made no reply to this.

"I thought not," said Wilde.

"And what led you to think so?" asked the nurse.

"Your address is not exactly that of a nurse."

"How so?"

"Well, nurses are not usually the most educated community in this country, at least."

"But what of all this? What would you infer?"

"That you have some secret object in being here."

"You think so?"

"I am sure so."

"And yet, knowing that to be the case, you would wish to discover my secret, eh, doctor?"

"No, no."

"It seems like it. And, believe me, it is not the way to secure anybody's esteem."

"Egad! Wilde, she has you there," said his colleague.

And he chuckled again at Gerard's discomfiture.

"She has, indeed," said Wilde, with a show of exaggerated vexation (which, however, was half joke, whole earnest).

"Retire. You're beaten, Wilde."

"I will. Very well, madam. I prefer our old relation to each other. Instead of a mysterious lady, and——"

"A curious gentleman."

"Granted—a curious gentleman. We will be simply doctor and nurse."

"Very well, doctor." You will not find me wanting in this respect."

"I do not doubt that."

"Good day, nurse."

"Good day, Mr. Wilde."

"Good night, madame—that is, I mean nurse; and look well after the patient."

"We do. Good night, nurse."

"Good bye, Dr. Cupper."

The two doctors with this left the house.

Gerard Wilde did not long keep by his resolution of standing upon his dignity with the nurse.

As he passed across the threshold, he made the nurse an elegant bow, which the nurse returned in a fashion equally inelegant.

She bobbed down with a jerk, nodding her head comically at the same time.

This was evidently her notion of a salutation à la Gamp. . . . .

Several days passed, and Frank Harley continued to improve.

His progress towards convalescence was slow, but marked.

The two doctors every day spoke more favourably of his condition ; and great was the nurse's joy.

Gerard Wilde could not repress his curiosity about this singular and devoted woman.

And, moreover, he could not hide it from the nurse herself.

But she was untroubled by it.

That is, it did not affect her at first. But, however, after a few days she began to grow apprehensive of the ill effects of the young surgeon's curiosity from another cause.

Frank Harley had now sufficiently recovered to be able to talk with the doctors and nurse.

And when alone together, the artist and his nurse held long and interesting conversations together upon every possible subject.

Nothing seemed to come amiss to the nurse.

She discussed literature and the fine arts, and particularly charmed poor Harley by her enthusiastic admiration of his profession.

She was perfectly at home, too, upon all subjects of the amusements of the day.

Music and the drama served as an inexhaustible theme for them.

She was a bit of a linguist also.

The artist was not a little astonished to find that she could gabble French and Italian ; had some knowledge of German, and a smattering of Spanish.

She also proved herself a clever amateur artist. And her talent in some branches of the art quite took the artist by surprise.

Notwithstanding all this, he continued to address his fair attendant as nurse.

As for the nurse herself, she quite lost all prudence in chatting with the artist.

At first, she made some futile attempt to keep up her character ; but the effort was too much for her.

She struggled on with her irksome task bravely enough for the first two days.

Then gave it up in disgust, and opened all the stores of a richly-cultivated mind for the benefit of both patient and nurse.

Singular as it may appear, Frank Harley seemed scarcely to be surprised at the refinement and education which his nurse displayed.

Notwithstanding that their daily conversations were of the most intellectual, he never appeared to consider the brilliant wit of his attendant at all out of place.

The reader has doubtless perceived, with Gerard Wilde, that the nurse was there incog.

With this difference only, that the former has probably made a shrewd guess as to the nurse's identity, whilst the young doctor can simply resolve that she is by no means what she would appear.

Since the open avowal of Gerard Wilde, and the consequent small brush which took place between him and the nurse, she had thrown off all appearance of disguise in her manner, and now shone out a thorough-bred lady.

But she still kept her features veiled from curious eyes by the large frill, before alluded to, which ornamented her cap.

Many a weary hour did she beguile by her ready wit, and cheerful spirits.

The artist, as his wound mended, and he grew better,

became so thoroughly impatient at being forced to keep his bed, that he would most certainly have broken through all restraint, at any risks to himself, had it not been for the soothing influence of his nurse's remonstrances.

"Nurse," said he, one afternoon, as he turned over heavily upon his sides, "it strikes me that you're a wonderful woman."

"Indeed !" said the nurse, laughing. "In what way ?"

"Every way. Now, I should say, that you must be always engaged ?"

"Engaged ?"

"Yes ; I suppose you are nearly always in employment ?"

"Oh ! yes."

A quiet smile was hidden by the convenient cap-frill.

"And have always engagements which pay you well ?"

"Pretty well." ·

"Of course."

This set him thinking.

He was an artist, and as a natural consequence, miserably poor.

He was, therefore, troubled in his mind about an adequate reimbursement for services such as hers.

He could not afford to pay her as he could wish.

And his dread of doing anything which would not be the right thing was very great.

He determined upon consulting Wilde at the earliest opportunity.

"And yet," he thought, "that would be little use. Wilde is a selfish, worldly-minded fellow, and would not look at it in the same light as I do. He would, no doubt, consider the merest trifle sufficient to repay her services. However, I'll speak with him about it."

The next day the nurse and her patient got into rather a delicate discussion, in the course of one of their chats.

Their subject was their native poets.

This led to an animated argument upon affairs of the heart.

The artist took a very worldly-minded view of it, as is natural to most men.

The nurse took a feminine and romantic view of the subject.

"Ah ! nurse," observed Harley, "you haven't my experience."

"Has it, then, been so very great, Mr. Harley ?"

"Very."

Here he gave a deep-drawn sigh, which caused the nurse to smile.

"And you think, then, Mr. Harley, that all love is——"

"Bosh ! and I don't think about it, nurse."

"That is the remark of a man who has been trifled with."

"It is the remark of a man of experience, nurse."

"Perhaps ; but still of one who has been jilted. Confess, Mr. Harley, that the grapes are sour."

"Not at all."

"I know that it is common amongst men to talk in this strain."

"And common amongst women to talk romance and stuff."

"A truly manly speech !"

"A truly rational one."

"I know that men shift all the ridicule of these matters on to us."

"Oh ! they do ?"

"Yes, while they share the profit."

"That sounds rather commercial, by-the-bye, nurse."

"But it expresses my meaning."

"Love is an idea, after all, nurse, and nothing more."

"A mere idea?"

"Yes."

"Why, Mr. Harley is surely not such an old man that he should get such very strong ideas upon this point?"

"Old—no; do none but old men get these ideas?"

"Unless, as I said before, men who have been jilted."

"Ah! but I can prove my words by a very simple reasoning."

"Very simple, no doubt!"

"And sage, at the same time."

"Then let us hear your simple sage reasons, Mr. Harley."

"What is the object, aim, end of love?"

"Now for something terrifically cynical," said the nurse, shutting her eyes, and looking very serious.

"Ah! you think to cheat me out of the argument by saying smart things at my expense, nurse."

"Not I, Mr. Harley."

"Well, then, à nos moutons. What is the end of all love, nurse?"

"I wait for your reply, Mr. Harley."

"My reply is—matrimony."

"And a very sensible reply it is, too—for a man."

"And is not that a most horrible thing to look forward to, nurse? Come, what do you say?"

"Really, I'm not competent to give an opinion."

"Not competent, nurse?"

"Not I."

"Then how dare you attempt to defend the gentle passion?"

"I made no defence of matrimony—I only said——"

"One moment. From that I should infer that you are married, nurse?"

The nurse stammered out something which the patient failed to catch.

"What did you say, nurse?" demanded Harley.

"I said that young men generally delight in talking cynically upon this theme until they are caught."

"And then?"

"Oh! then they go into all sorts of extravagancies in the opposite directions."

"Worthy, indeed."

"Yes; and the more extravagantly they talk, the more follies they commit when once they are ensnared."

"You speak learnedly upon the subject, nurse."

"Or I should not venture a discussion with such a cynic."

"As you please, nurse. Don't spare me, I beg."

"I will not."

"But you did not answer my question——"

"Then I must presume," broke in the nurse, abruptly, "that you have never yet been caught?"

"Indeed I have, though."

"And while the fit was on you, did you argue thus, pray?"

"While the fit was on me I—well, perhaps not!"

"I thought so."

"But the fit was soon off."

"Inconstant man!"

"It all goes to prove the veracity of my assertion."

"Which?"

"That love is, after all, a mere idea."

"I do not exactly see the argument, myself."

"Well, I consider myself to be rather susceptible."

"Indeed."

"I may say very susceptible to weaknesses of the heart."

"A general lover?"

"Yes."

"The acknowledgment does you infinite credit."

"But I am a man of scruples—a man of honour."

"I should be sorry to doubt it."

"You are very cruel, nurse. But you will believe in my sincerity, at least, when I tell you that the smallest accident has, before now, changed my warmest admira-tion—nay, even a stronger feeling, for a woman—to indifference—to disgust!"

"Indeed; you are rather a changeable lover, Mr. Harley."

"Not at all. But I flatter myself there is a degree of finish in my feelings which is not universal."

"Happily. But what may these accidents have been?"

"Various. The discovery of little deceits which your sex practise."

"You are kind."

"I am candid."

"Well, you are at least that, Mr. Harley."

"Thank you."

"Il n'y a pas de quoi."

"By Jove!" muttered Harley to himself, "these nurses are decidedly smart; and I am so full of conventionalities that I always thought them to be old women—ugly, gin-drinking, and dirty. Now, this one must be young, and I'll wager not ill-looking if I could only see beneath that cap; I must look out for an opportunity."

"Well, Mr. Harley, you are silent. Are you thinking of something severe and witty for me?"

"Gad! nurse, you've already thought of something."

"And what other objections may you have to our sex?"

"Good heavens! I have not any objections to the sex."

"It sounded like it."

"No—no—I spoke of individual examples."

"Well, then, to individuals?"

"Many trivial things."

"Of course they are trivial."

"I said so, nurse. In one instance I remember to have been suddenly cured of an ardent, but early passion, on discovering that my fair inamorata's hands were rather red out of gloves."

"Ha! ha! ha! Now, really, Mr. Harley. Then possibly you will continue a life of single-blessedness to the end of your days."

"I fear so."

"You fear?"

"Eh!—oh!—no—I hope so!"

"I fancied you sighed as you said fear."

"That's right, nurse; you may have fancied, that was all."

"I fear you are losing your candour, Mr. Harley."

The wounded man coloured deeply.

The nurse had not been mistaken; Harley was thinking of Alice Willoughby as he had spoken.

He therefore endeavoured to change the conversation.

Unfortunately, he returned to a subject which the nurse had betrayed some anxiety to drop.

"By-the-bye, nurse, you haven't answered my question."

"What question?"

"Are you married?"

"Oh—ah—it is getting late, Mr. Harley. You will exhaust yourself; and we are not carrying out the doctor's orders, I fear."

Harley was an obedient patient, so he at once addressed himself to sleep.

"She is a most agreeable woman," thought the artist.

"He's decidedly a pleasant fellow," murmured the nurse.

"So brilliant and witty; such a musical voice, and—oh! I must question Wilde about her."

"He's so unsuspecting," thought the nurse; "and I think my task is nearly over. I must beg Mr. Wilde, however, not to communicate his suspicions to his friend."

THE RESCUE BY JACK CHINNERY.

CHAPTER LIX.

THE ABDUCTION.

BOUND hand and foot Lady Ethel Fane lay in the pony-chaise at "The Chesnuts."

In broad daylight it was such a solitary road at the period of which we write, that she would have had little hope of coming across a living creature on the journey to her fate.

And at the hour of the night that these dark deeds were being committed she had positively not a hope.

Her end was so nigh that it confused every faculty.

She could not even think to prepare herself for the dread hereafter.

Prayer was driven from her thoughts by the terrors of the violent end that awaited her.

For a moment hope was restored to her by overhearing a footstep in the road.

It seemed to be close to her.

However, bound and gagged as she was, it was impossible to make the slightest attempt at attracting the attention of the stray traveller—for such she concluded it to be.

Her agony at this moment was greater than ever.

To have assistance within reach, and yet be unable to call it to her.

She tugged and pulled at the thongs which held her captive, until they cut into her flesh.

But in vain.

The schoolmistress had bound her too securely to allow of her liberating herself by any exertions, however violent.

The effort she made, however, had one good effect.

The desperate position in which she found herself placed, together with the exhaustion consequent upon her struggles, quite overcame her, and she lost all consciousness.

When she recovered her senses, the chaise was rumbling along an uneven road at a smart pace.

The stranger ran at the pony's head, clutching the bridle.

It was a bright moonlight night, and the heavens were dotted with clusters of diamond-like stars.

As the chaise jolted onwards, the creaking of its rusty springs rang out a mournful death-knell, which gave Lady Ethel a sensation of horror that she never forgot.

She had passed through many an escapade—all full of imminent danger; but never had the possibility of escaping her cruel fate seemed further than at that moment.

And she could not resign herself to her doom.

Every instant added a fresh terror to her position, and bitter were the tears she shed in her despair.

The jolting of the chaise over some deep ruts in the road shifted her some few inches, and caused her to come in contact with the body of the child.

A shudder thrilled through her frame, but she was forced by her helplessness to bear the contact with death.

"Poor child!" thought Lady Ethel; "poor girl!—how horrible it is to think that I should so feel to touch her now—and how willingly would I have borne her in my arms but a few hours since."

The forehead of the body was resting against Lady Ethel's forehead, and much as the contact with it caused her to shudder, she could not move from it.

After a while, however, she had somewhat conquered the aversion she had at first experienced.

She still felt all the awe of death, but without the disgust with which it had inspired her in the first place.

She forgot her peril for a moment, and fell into a deep reverie from which she recovered with a start.

The flesh of the body which rested against her cheek seemed to have lost its deathly coldness.

Could it be real?

Was it possible that after all—but no.

There was no doubt that the unhappy child was dead.

The imprisonment in the damp vault alone was sufficient to guarantee this.

Then the poison which Mrs. Stibbington had administered to her would have doubtless finished the fiendish work had the child been in robust health before this last incident in the long chapter of tortures which she had endured under the tyranny of the schoolmistress.

And yet it was singular.

The face of the corpse now seemed no colder than one might reasonably expect the face of a living creature to be, uncovered in the bleak night-air.

Lady Ethel's attention was so engrossed by this idea that she almost lost sight of her own terrible position for the moment.

Suddenly she felt a tug at the cords which bound her ankles together.

They were pulled again and again, as it seemed to her, as if some one was endeavouring to drag her from the chaise.

Then, with a jerk, the cords were severed.

Her lower members were free.

At this moment she fancied she heard the suppressed breathing of some one close at hand.

In another instant she saw a hand, grasping a knife, pushed over the side of the chaise.

Her alarm was now very great.

As her feet were free, she made the best use of them in struggling out of the reach of the threatening knife.

Although she did not make the least progress, it had the effect of attracting the attention of the stranger.

"Hallo, there!" he exclaimed, in a subdued tone; "what's that noise?—By Jupiter! you've managed to get those feet free. You must have struggled for that, I know. We'll soon set matters straight again."

And Lady Ethel began to repent her late conduct.

Her feet were free, and might not that have been a step towards her liberation?

Bitterly did she now regret having let her fears get the better of her discretion thus.

Better, far better, have risked destruction from the blow of the knife held by an unseen hand, than have made her immolation a certainty in the still waters of the pond her destroyer had spoken of.

The stranger, as he spoke, ran to the back of the chaise; and, in spite of Lady Fane's most frantic struggles, succeeded in refixing the cords more securely than before.

But what had become of the mysterious knife?

Whither had the owner of the hand which grasped it so singularly disappeared?

These were unanswerable questions.

Not the faintest noise—not the slightest echo of a footfall had betrayed the presence of a witness to the assassination which the stranger was on his way to perpetrate.

These questions gave the captive food for thought.

The more she pondered over it, the more apparent was it to her that the mysterious presence could but bode good to her.

It was some secret assistance lurking at hand.

Assistance, too, perhaps, that she—Lady Ethel—had rendered futile by her indiscretion.

It was evident that the owner of the hand and knife was afraid of giving his—or her—assistance openly.

Then was it not probable that, alarmed by Lady Ethel's struggles and the disturbance she had made, the individual had sought safety in flight?

Giving up all hope of aiding her in an attempt to escape.

And once more poor Lady Ethel's sensations were unmixed chagrin at what she unjustly deemed her own folly.

"A chance, at any rate, within my grasp, and I have thrown it away," she thought, while tears of vexation coursed down her cheek.

Then she added, with what would have been a noisy burst of passion, had her utterance been free to her.

"A chance—by Heaven! freedom itself and life! Idiot, fool! Now to myself alone I owe my death. The suicide's death with the suicide's tomb be mine. Oh!—rare pass of idiocy to have reached a worldly-minded criminal woman like myself, clinging to life and its pleasures, though God knows few of its pleasures have been mine of late—too guilty—too full of sin to die—dreading the grave as—oh! I could not bear the bitterest, heaviest of earthly torments. And yet to give myself up when freedom was at hand, I could out of my very chagrin hasten to the end I so much dread—dash myself to pieces were my limbs at liberty this moment."

Silently cursing herself and her captor by turns, the unhappy woman soon exhausted herself by the strength and intensity of the feelings which agitated her.

A dull moody despair succeeded this fit.

And still the chaise continued its fatal journey.

At length they began the descent—a steep incline.

Some trees at this spot served as landmarks for Lady Ethel.

They were approaching a piece of water!

The beginning of the end!

Lady Fane had now literally banished all hope.

The immediate approach to the lake which they were nearing was too steep to allow of the chaise going nearer to the water than some fifteen or twenty feet.

Accordingly, the stranger tied the pony by the bridle to a short stumpy bush close at hand.

Then, silently as the death which he was about to give to his unhappy victim, he raised the body of the Phillis Ebury in his arms.

Lady Ethel was so situated now that she could see him the whole time.

He cautiously picked his way over the uneven stones, and had speedily arrived at the water's edge.

"Farewell!" murmured Lady Ethel to herself. "Farewell, poor child—murdered innocent! It is something to share a grave even with such a guileless martyred creature."

Poor consolation this, however, to a woman of Lady Ethel's temperament.

The stranger was by the water's side.

One last look more.

Another instant and all that remained of the slaughtered Phillis Ebury would be hidden from mortal sight in the stagnant waters of the lake.

The stranger raised the body in his arms preparatory to hurling it from him, and——

But here Lady Ethel's attention was diverted from the stranger and his victim.

A movement of the shrubs close at hand announced the presence of a witness of the dark deeds which were now being perpetrated.

Before she had even a second to speculate upon this, the thongs which bound her ankles were tugged as they had been before.

Her heart leaped to her mouth.

In an instant the cords were once more severed.

An arm was thrust over the side of the cart.

But now she did not let any foolish fears betray her.

A moment after her arms were free.

Then, without waiting an instant, she sprang from the cart.

There was not a soul in sight.

Her preserver had disappeared!

Gone without leaving the slightest trace of his presence.

And she had not so much as seen the face of the being to whom she thus owed her preservation.

However much she might have regretted this, she did not pause to waste a moment, so precious as the moments were to her now upon useless regrets.

Choosing the road which took her the farthest from the pond and the stranger, Lady Ethel ran off at great speed.

Some short distance along the road curved round to such an extent as to be almost a right angle with her starting-point.

A little way on brought her to a narrow lane between hedges running right and left.

Here she paused for breath.

It then struck her that her safety from pursuit would be more ensured by making as many turnings as possible.

For, she reasoned, if the stranger should happen to hit upon the road she had taken, very little exertion upon his part would doubtless suffice to overtake her.

Therefore, after a moment's indecision, she chose the right-hand turning.

She felt that she was by no means out of danger yet, and continued her flight at a swinging pace.

Suddenly the hedges upon either side ceased, and she found herself in an open country.

A bound brought her in sight of the pond again.

She had arrived at the other side of the water by the circuitous route she had taken.

This, naturally enough, was alarming to her at first.

Then after a while she began to consider that she was tolerably safe, as it was probably the very last place in which her persecutor would think of seeking her.

She could see very clearly across the lake.

The stranger's big form was standing out in bold relief in the moonlight.

He had just scrambled up the bank, and had gained the side of the cart.

Had he discovered his would-be victim's flight?

But it is necessary that we should cross the lake to watch the movements of this man more minutely.

At the moment Lady Ethel felt her bonds cut asunder, the stranger raised the inanimate body of the girl in his arms, and was about to cast it forth into dark waters, when some of the flesh coming in his clutch he could not help remarking, as Lady Ethel had done, that the corpse was not yet cold.

This startled him considerably.

"Can it be possible," he muttered, half aloud, "that she yet lives—that after all I am about to slaughter her? I had thought that this was done for me—that I was spared the crime of slaying his child. I do not feel half the compunction—I may say none at all about the job which remains."

He alluded to the drowning of Lady Ethel, whom he thought to be at that moment tied hand and foot in the chaise.

"But it must be—perhaps it has rested against that woman Morley and so, but I always understood that a corpse could never regain heat, or even warmth, under any circumstances. Pshaw! It must be so—she has been dead hours."

Again he raised his arms to cast the body into the water.

And again they sank down by his side as if he were powerless to commit what he almost felt, in spite of himself, to be another crime.

A third time he raised the body.

Then as he held it high in the air above his head his manner underwent a sudden change.

It was the manner of one in an excess of fear.

His legs trembled beneath him, and his knees almost knocked together.

For a moment he paused thus as if spellbound.

His breast heaved convulsively, showing the sincerity of his emotion.

Then recovering himself, with a mighty effort, he cast the inanimate form from him.

He greeted the dull heavy splash of the falling body with a wild unearthly cry.

Then bounded up the bank, shouting in a frenzied manner.

"She lived! she breathed!" he cried.

A stride seemed to bring him to the side of the cart.

A glance acquainted him with his victim's escape.

His sensations upon making this discovery were of a mixed description.

In an instant he had mentally assigned a dozen different causes for it.

He was evidently a strong-minded man, taking the phrase in its ordinarily received acceptation.

And yet the thought which most possessed him was that some supernatural agency had been at work.

If allowances were necessary, some might be made for this when we think of the nature of his business and the unearthly hour—the wild district and the deed just committed.

And the strong man cowered in an agony of fright.

Lady Ethel, who was watching his movements from the further side of the pond, lost all discretion in her curiosity, stood out in the moonlight herself, quitting the shadow of some trees which had previously hidden her.

The stranger caught sight of her.

Instantly his supernatural fears left him.

He was once more the being of clay, full of all the evil passions of man—he had to cope with a living, breathing foe, and he was himself again.

Drawing his pistol from his breast-pocket he levelled it, took a deliberate aim at the imprudent Lady Ethel, and fired.

He was evidently a splendid shot, and nothing but the great distance would probably have made him miss the mark.

But fortunately he did miss it.

Lady Ethel heard the bullet whistle past her, and snap some twigs upon a bush at her side.

At the moment Lady Ethel heard the shot she turned and fled from the spot.

Simultaneously with the report of the pistol a large

stone was hurled by an unseen hand at the stranger, and with deadly precision.

It struck him upon the head.

With a hollow groan he sank, all of a heap, upon the cold clay soil insensible.

Then came an explanation of this.

A figure darted out from some stunted shrubs and bushes close at hand.

It came along with a bound, and paused a moment by the stranger, as if with the intention of ascertaining his condition.

Apparently satisfied upon this point, the figure sprang down the declivity leading to the water's edge.

All this had taken place in very considerably less time than we have taken in describing it.

A minute had, perhaps, elapsed since the stranger had hurled the body of Phillis Ebury into the silent waters.

The figure had flitted along so quickly that there had been scarcely time to detect its exit.

A moment's pause upon the brink of the pond, however, satisfied this point.

With a hurried movement he (for it was a man) threw off his coat.

Then sprang forward, and bounded head foremost into the pond.

CHAPTER LX.

THE SOLUTION OF THE MYSTERY RESPECTING THE PRETTY NURSE.

MR. FELBRIDGE WINDER has been for over a week in the utmost despair.

For Lady Amatoria Crutchingford has been from town for over a week.

Every day has Mr. Winder called at the Crutchingford Mansion in May Fair.

Every day had Mr. Winder been disappointed.

Every day he receives the same answer to his eternal demand for the beauteous Lady Amatoria.

She has gone out of town and no one knows when she is likely to return.

No one knows either whither she has gone.

When we say no one, of course we don't include the lady's husband.

He doubtless knows what direction his wife has taken.

But Mr. Felbridge Winder cannot, in common decency, ask a man about his own wife's whereabouts, when it is the fashionable scandal of the time that one is carrying on a flirtation with the lady, however platonic it may be.

Mr. Felbridge Winder was not, however, withheld from this step by any compunctions, any thoughts or feelings of common decency.

For, in good sooth, he was possessed of none.

He only came to a standstill here because he had some doubts as to how the husband of his cruel inamorata would listen to any questions he should have wished to put to him.

There is always an assumption of virtue and honour —hollow mockeries, as they are tacitly understood to be in the *beau monde*—which will not allow a man to receive direct overtures to his own wife.

These little things may take place under his own eyes —may become the topic of conversation with all the scandal-mongers—he may almost hear himself become an object of pity in the fashionable world, and can wink at it.

But with all this, singular as it may appear, the easiest-going husbands have a limit to their forbearance.

They must, at least, appear to be ignorant of all.

It is, of course, understood amongst the insinuating dowagers and *blasé* spinsters that this even is a mere sham, but still it is custom and can be got over thus.

Hence Mr. Felbridge Winder is sorely perplexed.

He has pumped and fee'd every individual member of the Crutchingford household.

But without avail.

He has even invented a few weak plots to arrive at the cause of her ladyship's sudden departure from town, and her protracted stay in the agricultural districts.

For it is given out that Lady Amatoria has gone to some remote and rural spot, although no one can give him the slightest idea in which direction it is situated.

The shadow of the volatile Winder hovers eternally about May Fair and its vicinity.

And his steps are eternally dogged by the cast-off mistress of his affections.

Alice Willoughby still remains faithful to the shallow-pated rascal who has so cruelly deserted her.

Again and again he had insulted her in the street, growing more violent and abusive at each successive interview, but without producing the desired result.

Like some poor cur, the unhappy Alice Willoughby seems to grow only more affectionate and fond at each rebuff, returning to lick the hand that spurns her.

At first the gallant Winder only seemed to experience a fatigue of her society—satiety of the affection which the loving girl lavished upon him so prodigally.

This feeling, however, as is invariably the case, ripened into disgust, and, finally, dislike and hatred, as poor Alice perseveringly followed up her Adonis.

Mr. Winder, it is almost superfluous to observe, was no great light.

What he wanted in wit, however, he endeavoured to make up in cunning.

It was this cunning, therefore, which told him that he had offended Lady Amatoria Crutchingford by his coldness with regard to the fall of Frank Harley.

The man who had rescued her from the perils of an exposure at the masquerade, and thus preserved her honour.

Accordingly, he began to ponder over some means of making the necessary reparation for his fault.

The result of these cogitations was the visit of Mr. Felbridge Winder to the wounded artist at his chambers.

This we have already described in a previous chapter.

Mr. Winder, however, was not to be thrown over by the obstinacy of the singular nurse in refusing him admission to the artist's presence.

For a while he had been somewhat cast down at the signal failure of his mission.

But he speedily resolved to turn it to account.

He repaired to his lodgings, and there in the solitude of his chamber penned one of those flowery epistles for which he rather fancied himself famous.

It contained a long tissue of the grossest lies which the inventive genius of Mr. Winder could imagine.

Here he was almost at home.

He gave a full account of Frank Harley's death, spicing it up with some little touches of pathos, which were really not bad.

This he carefully copied upon some highly-scented pink note-paper, and left it at May Fair with the strictest injunctions (and a sovereign) that it was to be delivered to her ladyship immediately upon her return.

But this produced no result.

So it became evident to him that Lady Crutchingford had not received his letter, as he felt sure that she could not have resisted sending him an answer.

He was still very well pleased with his personal appearance.

And feeling sure that his charmer was likewise enamoured of his person, he thought that he had but to make the reparation he had made in visiting the sick artist to show his contrition, and to ensure his re-establishment into favour.

But he was perfectly mistaken in this.

Lady Amatoria had thrown him off without the smallest tittle of regret.

His senseless movements had frequently disgusted her, but his latest brutality previous to her departure from May Fair ripened this feeling into something approaching resentment.

And now, to add to Mr. Winder's woe, he began to be troubled from another quarter.

The infuriated relatives of the happy girl whom he was to have made his wife threatened him with an action for breach of promise.

Substantial John Bull makes even affairs of the heart associate with his three national graces, £ s. d.!

A good round sum in damages compensates for love, honour, and everything; healing broken hearts and blighted hopes.

The girl that Felbridge Winder was to have made wretched for the rest of her (or his) days happened to be possessed of some feelings of decorum, and refused in toto to have anything to do whatever with the settlement of her woes in the court of Cupid in a court of law.

The parents and relations, generally, were obstinate in the matter, and for some time it was undecided as to how the affair would end.

Winder was a capital bird to pluck.

Immensely rich, and a most egregious ass.

Finally, the firmness, or, as the grasping relatives styled it, the obstinacy of the girl, settled the matter.

They were forced to relinquish all idea of the breach of promise action.

But their wrath was not yet appeased.

One of the more inventive and less scrupulous of his foes entered into a not over-creditable convention with the relatives of the soft-headed Winder, who shortly found himself the subject of the most embarrassing attentions upon the part of the Commissioners in Lunacy.

At first he treated this lightly enough; but he was speedily convinced that there was really no joke in the affair.

He only began to look very seriously upon it when he discovered that the prime mover in the affair was his next of kin and heir.

Then he set himself boldly to work to defend his reason and his liberty.

But both were in great peril.

He found his relatives and dear friends were the most implacable foes he could have.

Every tittle of evidence which could tend to attain their end was raked up against him by the prosecution.

This is the literal if not the legal styling of the author of the scandalous action.

Every trifling fault or caprice of his past life which were of the most trivial description in a family history, but which appeared almost as crimes in print, tortured and twisted about by his relatives, were brought before the public.

Everybody voted Winder a fool and his relations rogues.

But although the flagrant injustice of the inquiry was the universal theme of conversation, it went on to the end.

The fabulous sum which the action cost was the first terrible drain upon the purse of Felbridge Winder, which gave warning of the ruin which was about to follow.

In the end he triumphed over his enemies, to the satisfaction of the public and such acquaintances as he had.

But his very success in this instance worked his ruin in another way.

In revenge upon his perfidious relatives, he squandered away his princely fortune, so that they might reap no benefit from it at his decease.

He sold off every bit of land which was not entailed, and, in the space of a few years became comparatively beggared.

This, however, amply revenged his relatives upon himself at the same time.

For with the destruction of the magnificent property he lost caste at once.

He was shunned by every individual who had previously courted his society; and now many of the scheming mammas who, for several seasons had angled for him for their marriageable daughters, gave him the dead cut in public, and gave it as their opinion that it was a sad pity the friends of poor Winder had not succeeded in putting him under restraint.

From the epoch of the lunacy inquiry, Mr. Winder's passion for Lady Amatoria gradually diminished, and after a while died a natural death.

Love could not endure for ever in any case, and in turn Alice Willoughby grew less fond of her adored Winder.

The chief cause of this was the fast increasing respect and esteem which she felt for the absent artist. Absence made her heart grow fonder every day, and at length she began to look forward to his return to the world—to Half Moon-street and to her feet, with the utmost impatience.

But in the meantime, other hearts were changing in their allegiance, like her own.

The long illness poor Harley had suffered had worked as wonderful a change in him. The attraction which the society of the nurse had for him at length astonished himself.

He only made the discovery of the true state of his feelings upon one occasion when the nurse alluded to the improvement in his condition, and suggested that her services would, doubtless, be shortly dispensed with.

Then the invalid grew frantic. He made the nurse some very violent avowals of affection—love at first sight, and other absurdities, which very speedily brought about the end which had caused his excitement.

One morning, when he awoke, he found himself alone.

The nurse had disappeared without the slightest warning.

Upon a chair by the bedside he found a letter directed to himself from the nurse.

This informed him that the writer had been forced, by domestic matters, to take her departure thus abruptly, and that she hoped at no distant day to meet with her patient again, and have the pleasure of congratulating him upon his restoration to robust health. There was no signature to it, and Harley reflected, for the first time, upon the singular circumstance of having passed several weeks in the same house—almost the same room, with a person of whose name he was in ignorance.

Nurse had been her only title that he thought of.

The shock was severe to the sensitive artist, and somewhat retarded his convalescence.

A long explanation ensued between him and Gerard Wilde upon the subject, and the latter greatly reassured him by the statement of his conviction that the nurse was desperately enamoured of her patient, and would certainly reappear at some time or other—probably in a very brief period.

The shock of the first disappointment over, Harley mended apace.

He grew stronger every day, and welcomed the first hour of work as if it had been a jubilee.

His protracted illness had reduced his finances to a very low ebb, and nothing but the closest application to his labours, and the strictest economy could possibly save him from a state of bankruptcy.

So to work he went boldly.

But it was long enough before he was able to realize sufficient to cover the pressing demands of landlord, butcher, and baker.

Still he went on manfully.

Some months after he had been restored to health, he received an unexpected aid from a private amateur of pictures—an old nobleman, who was reported to have a magnificent collection which had been principally got up by his wife, a lady of letters, and a great patron of the fine arts.

His lordship had bought a small historical painting of Dawber, the dealer in Bond-street, and came to Frank Harley with a commission of some considerable magnitude.

Some weeks of close labour, and the works were completed.

Harley, himself, took them home to May Fair, to Lord Crutchingford's mansion, and there was gratified with an introduction to her ladyship.

"Gad!" murmured the artist to himself, as he made a deep reverence to the brilliant Lady Crutchingford, "I'm growing fearfully susceptible to female charms; I feel half gone here already."

Then when her ladyship addressed him a most cordial welcome, there was a winning grace in her voice and manner which took him by storm.

There was something in Lady Amatoria which seemed familiar to him. Not, perhaps, to strike him at once, but come upon him by degrees as they conversed.

The old lord invited him frequently, and they became very great friends.

On one occasion, shortly after his introduction, Harley had a five-minutes' chat with Lady Crutchingford upon the subject of her resemblance to an individual in whom he was greatly interested, which seemed to cause her ladyship some trifling embarrassment.

"Pardon me, my lady," said he, abruptly, "have you a sister?"

"What a singular question, Mr. Harley. But I have none. Why do you ask?"

"Strange; I once knew a lady whose voice and manner so resembled yours, that one might almost mistake you for the same."

"Indeed," observed her ladyship, drily.

Harley fancied that her tone was somewhat cold, and wisely forbore to pursue the subject.

A few months rolled on, and Harley was almost a daily visitor at the May Fair mansion.

The tender artist had forgotten Alice and the nurse in the enslaving presence of the beauteous Lady Amatoria.

But being a noble-hearted fellow, he stifled his passion as best he could out of respect to his generous patron, her husband.

The regard which Lord Crutchingford evinced towards him completely won his heart.

One day, when Frank was smoking a cigar with his lordship (and wishing himself in Lady Amatoria's presence), he was considerably startled by a request that his patron made him.

"My dear Harley," said Lord Crutchingford, calmly, "I have a favour to ask of you. I am in a difficulty, and I want you to assist me."

"Command me, my lord."

"I will do so. I have an affair of honour with a most dishonourable scoundrel, and you must act for me."

"Good heavens! my lord; you don't surely mean——"

"That my honour is assailed, and I have to defend it."

"Explain!"

"Well, I must tell you that my wife has been annoyed by the persecutions of a man I imagined to be a bosom friend—one Major Beele. I will enter into details another time. This has become the subject of public conversation, and yet her ladyship, out of consideration for me, has foreborne to mention it. And even now she does not know that I have taken any step to protect her from molestation. Now to the point—will you act for me?"

"With all my heart. But I am not exactly *au fait* at this sort of thing. I have never been engaged but once in a similar affair, and then it was as a principal."

"Indeed; you never told me of this."

"Oh, I wasn't the successful party, else you would have known it."

"There you scandalize yourself. But I have put matters off to the last; to-morrow morning, at six, we meet."

"So soon. Consider, my dear lord, before you go rashly into this. You are not a young man."

"Bah! all the more reason that I should look zealously after my family reputation now. Besides which, at the worst, I only give up a year or two of life; men of my age do not generally look forward to a long life. I'm turned seventy, sir."

The old nobleman was obstinate, and the next morning, at five o'clock, they started off upon their murderous errand.

They were the first upon the ground, but were speedily joined by the enemy.

At a glance, Harley recognised in Major Beele his old antagonist, the Brigand of the masquerade.

This recognition, however, was not mutual. This is scarcely to be wondered at, when we reflect that the major believed the artist to be dead.

Preliminaries were very shortly arranged between the two seconds, and it was arranged that Harley should give the word to fire.

"If I should fall," whispered the old lord, as he squeezed his second's hand; "and should that villain escape, you will not desert my wife. Protect her, Harley, as I would, and God bless you! I have left all prepared at home. See they're ready. Give me the pistol."

The artist felt a rising sensation about the throat, which prevented his replying; so with a silent return of his lordship's pressure, he presented him with a pistol, and proceeded to give the word.

Directly he spoke, Major Beele removed his glance from Lord Crutchingford, on whom it had been fixed with the steadfastness of hate, and stared at the artist in dismay.

"One! Two! Three! FIRE!"

There were two distinct reports, and Harley saw that his lordship's left arm hung helplessly by his side.

He darted up to his side, and eagerly demanded the extent of his injuries.

"Nothing, Harley; I've got this arm rather damaged. But see, Beele is unhurt."

The major was standing motionless as his lordship spoke, but the next instant he tottered and fell forward upon his face; never to rise again.

His lordship suffered from his wound for several weeks, and then gave up the ghost.

It was far more severe than was at first supposed, and the unskilfulness of his surgeon, together with his advanced age, were too much for him.

The handsome way in which he provided for the penniless artist was a source of great surprise to him.

Almost at his last moments he called his wife and Harley together at his bedside, and then put some painfully embarrassing questions to them.

It was his lordship's request that if ever his lady took a second husband that that one might be their mutual friend Frank Harley.

As the dying man was obstinate in his request they assented, sprinkling his couch with their tears.

For fifteen months after his noble friend's decease Frank Harley travelled upon the Continent, and at the expiration of that period returned to the land of his birth.

It is scarcely necessary to say that his first visit was to May Fair.

Lady Amatoria, looking more lovely than ever in her mourning, welcomed the traveller home with a warmth which gave him the wildest hopes.

The brightest dreams he had ever indulged in were realized, and the day of his return he was formally engaged to Lady Amatoria.

At Harley's urgent request their union was fixed for an early date by the young widow.

One word more before we take our leave of them.

Two days before the wedding was to take place the artist was seated with his beloved looking over an album, when he chanced to come across two sketches which caused him no little amazement.

One of these was a scene at a masquerade, in which Harley himself, the brigand, and a maroon domino were going through a well-remembered struggle.

The other was a bed-chamber, a wounded man, a nurse with large frilled cap!

"Good heavens!" exclaimed the artist. "Where did you get this from?"

"It is no use, Frank," said Amatoria, laughingly. "I know all about it. The fierce love you made to the nurse——"

"I—oh—I?"

"Hush! I've got her here in the house."

Before he could reply she ran out of the room, leaving him in amazement.

In another minute the door was reopened, and who should enter the apartment but his old nurse, sober dress cap, frill, and all.

"Nurse," faltered Harley.

"Yes, Mr. Harley. When we parted you made me an avowal——"

"Oh, I was mad—I——"

"Then you repent of what you said to me upon that occasion?"

"Decidedly—I——"

"Enough, sir. Then all is at an end between us."

She pushed back her cap as she said this, disclosing the smiling face of Lady Crutchingford.

"Amatoria—nurse—you Amatoria!" ejaculated Harley."

"Yes, sir, and the maroon domino as well."

"Bliss upon bliss—I have all my loves in one!"

CHAPTER LXI.
CONCLUSION.

WE left Jack Chinnery, as the reader may remember, in a very strange situation.

Escaping from the coiners' cellar, he had found his way into the next door house, and had sought shelter under a lady's bed.

Scarcely was he there when the lady had come into the room; to her then came a priest, who began to make fierce love.

Jack had got very interested, and to get a better view was twisting round in his place of concealment, when he found himself face to face with some other person who had also taken shelter under the bed.

His first idea was that this person was a burglar, and a glance was sufficient to show him that the stranger could not be there for any but a felonious motive.

Meanwhile, the lady's struggles in the arms of her lover became fainter and fainter, though she yet defended her honour with all her remaining strength. In the course of the fight for the mastery, however, the dressing-table was overturned, and came with a loud crash to the ground, extinguishing the lights.

Jack did not want to see whether or not the scoundrel priest would succeed in his lawless design, but profiting by the noise and darkness, crept from his hiding-place.

His object was, of course, to make his escape.

That also was the object of the other party under the bed, who in a few hasty words explained that he was there to rob the house, and suggested that they should make good their escape by the stairs and out at the street-door.

He then made a rush in that direction, but Jack did not follow; and it was lucky that he did not, for scarcely had the man reached the bottom of the first flight of stairs than he found himself in the arms of the servants, coming up to see what was the cause of the noise. Jack hearing their cries, hastily fastened the door, seized the lady's jewels from the table, thrust them into his breast, and rushed towards the window through which the priest had come. He very easily managed to let himself down on to a balcony, from which he clambered on to a wall, and with but very little difficulty reached the ground.

He stayed now only to cast a hurried glance around, so that he might know the house again, read the name of the street at the corner, and beat a hasty retreat, for he could hear loud cries for help coming from the window he had climbed out of.

As he had not got a halfpenny in his possession, and as he was very anxious to discover what was the real value of the diamonds he possessed, he set off at once for the den of a certain old Fence of his acquaintance.

This person lived down a narrow court at the back of Blackman-street, Southwark Bridge-road, and to reach his residence Chinnery was obliged to pass by the house of Doctor Caul.

As he did so, glancing up at one of the windows, his attention was attracted by the sight of a man climbing in through a window.

For a moment the moon shone upon his face, and Chinnery recognised an old companion of his early days of profligacy, a treacherous villain, who had been instrumental in bringing about his transportation.

This man was Eneas Quirk, the doctor's assistant.

Although Chinnery must surely have gone through sufficient adventures this evening to satisfy any reasonable appetite, yet he eagerly played into another. He owed Quirk a grudge, and thought that he here saw a way of revenging himself. Without any hesitation, then, he climbed over the wall and followed the cat-scragger into the doctor's house.

* * * * * * * * * *

We left Quirk when he had found the murdered man's body on the sink in the closet listening to the sound of an approaching footstep.

When the door opened he found himself face to face with—not the murderer, as he supposed—but Jack Chinnery.

For a moment the two men regarded each other silently, then Chinnery, catching sight of the body, clutched his companion by the throat.

"Tell me, wretch," he cried, who is this victim you have murdered?"

"Mercy, mercy," cried the other, "I am innocent. It is Doctor Caul who has done it."

"Doctor Caul, I know him, and whose is this corpse?"

"His name was Worwold."

"Worwold—Jabez Worwold! But that cannot be, for he was dead and murdered by his wife!"

Such was the story which Mrs. Jaggers had told to Chinnery when he was lying ill at the body-snatcher's dwelling, but in a moment the whole truth flashed upon his mind.

Always having his wits about him, the robber saw here a way of getting money much more easily than by burglary or pocket-picking.

He, therefore, took his companion into his confidence, and together they resolved upon planning the spy upon the doctor's actions for the next two or three days, and making the best market of what they already knew of his horrible secrets.

By so doing they soon learnt more of his villanies—black and terrible as that with which they were already acquainted.

Dogging him to the home of Mrs. Stibbington at Hendon—for he was the mysterious stranger who had connived with the unnatural schoolmistress in murdering poor Phillis, he watched him convey his victim's body to Hampstead, and came in time to save the life both of the poor little girl and the beautiful Ethel Fane.

At the first sight of her deliverer, however, our heroine would have fled in terror, had he not stopped her, for his face brought back to her recollection the crime which she supposed her father to have committed, and likewise had been the cause of her flying from home. But there was no need of future hiding, for Caul, the murderer, was quickly bound and handed over, with the assistance of the cat-scragger, to the care of the local police.

* * * * * * * *

A long explanation ensued, but it was not for some time afterwards that Chinnery obtained the clue to many mysteries which now strangely puzzled him.

In the first place he required an explanation of the reason why Lady Fane had sought him out at the thieves' public-house, which the reader may recollect she did in the second chapter of this story.

Her motive she would not, however, explain, and it was not for a long while that he came to the conclusion that to save her father, whose life she supposed to be in the hands of Gerard Wilde, she had at that time meditated Wilde's murder, and it must have been to assist in his assassination that she had required Chinnery's help.

But there was no need now of such a horrible crime, for the profligate old man, for whose sake she would have even stained her hands with blood, was dead.

He was found stabbed to death in the street, in the neighbourhood of a low gambling-house, but there was no evidence to connect his murder with the haunt of wickedness in question.

As to Caul's reason for wishing for the death of the little girl, Phillis, was soon explained.

She had been intrusted to his care, and he had made away with the poor child's fortune.

The dark cloud of guilt removed from Lady Fane's life, she was now able to face the world again without fear or shame. But she disappeared shortly afterwards, and was supposed to have gone into some religious house to end her days in peace and prayer.

You may be sure that Jack Chinnery was not slow in turning to account what he knew of the lady of title and her lover the priest, Father Anselmo.

Both the lady and the priest were only too glad to pay a heavy sum for hush-money, and by the influence which he had obtained over the latter, he also hoped to have been able to effect the deliverance of the unhappy nun whose tortures he had witnessed.

But, alas! in this hope he was doomed to disappointment.

The nunnery was broken up, it is true, but only to be established in another part of London.

Lucy and Marian were again recaptured, though with the horrible details connected with their fate this history does not deal.

As yet only a faint picture of the brutalities practised in a London nunnery has been given.

It has been the writer's painful task to expose in all their revolting horrors the licentious orgies of priests and nuns.

THE END.